WARS OF THE NEW HUMANITY
COLLECTION ONE

By Michael J. Brooks

Contents

This collection comprises books one and two of the
Wars of the New Humanity series.
(2025 edition)

Republic Falling: Advent of a New Dawn
(book #1)

and

Republic Under Siege: Threat from Within
(book #2)

Paperback ISBN: 9781737929369
Ebook ISBN: 9781737929376

Library of Congress Control Number: 2023914177

Printed in the United States of America

Michael J. Brooks
Mount Rainier, Maryland 20712
www.authormbrooks.com

2025 edition

Praise from
The Book Commentary

"This collection of two books is a gorgeous offering . . . It provides strong and resonant themes, a reflection of some of the ills of contemporary society where the majority must work hard to support the lifestyles of the few. The richly textured writing, the captivating world-building, and the intrigue kept me moving from page to page. It will have you invested from start to finish and left wanting more."

—*The Book Commentary*

REPUBLIC FALLING

Advent of a New Dawn

By Michael J. Brooks

Wars of the New Humanity
Book One

About This Book

Content Warning

Republic Falling: Advent of a New Dawn is an action-filled science fiction book that contains violence, strong language, and detailed scenes of lovers making love.

Content Meter

2025 Edition

You are reading the 2025 edition of
Republic Falling: Advent of a New Dawn.

2025 edition

Praise for
Republic Falling
Advent of a New Dawn

The BookLife Prize

"A satisfying sci-fi thriller, the plot is evenly paced and the conflict is engaging."

"Action scenes are exciting and enjoyable."

"The fictional universe . . . features plenty of supporting details and technologies that flesh out the world."

"The characters are . . . presented with a sufficient complexity and internal conflict to help propel the plot and action satisfactorily."

Rabia Tanveer for *Readers' Favorite*

"While the topic of the fight between the upper class and the lower, less privileged is a common topic, very few authors have the skill to tackle it with grace and clarity. Kudos!"

Honorable Mention from the 2022 Hollywood Book Festival

Acknowledgments

I would like to thank my cover designer, Ida Jansson. She is truly a creative visionary. I would also like to thank every single person who chose to read this book. All of you have my utmost gratitude.

Glossary
(nonalphabetic order)

Earth Era: the era of humanity before intergalactic migration from Earth

Commonwealth: humanity's star nation consisting of four planets —Eden and satellites One, Two, and Three

Eden: humanity's utopian motherworld inhabited by three-fifths of the human population

Satellite One: humanity's dystopian secondary world inhabited by two-fifths of the human population

Satellites Two and Three: vacant worlds belonging to the Commonwealth, used for military training exercises and mineral excavation

Edenite/Eden citizen (synonymous terms): human beings living on Eden, whether born on the planet or during Earth Era

Highborn: a moniker referring specifically to human beings born on Eden

Colonist/colony citizen (synonymous terms): human beings living in the colonies of Satellite One, whether born on the planet or during Earth Era

Commonwealth Defense Force (CDF)/Defense Force
(synonymous terms): the Commonwealth's military force

Guardian: a soldier in the Commonwealth Defense Force

Cadet: a Guardian in training

Commonwealth Government/central government (synonymous terms): the governing body of the entire Commonwealth, which includes the Parliament and the Office of the Chief Executive

Republic of Unified Colonies (RUC): the republic formed by colonies One, Four, and Six after they declared sovereignty from the Commonwealth

The Three-Week War: the war initiated and won by the Commonwealth Government to reclaim colonies One, Four, and Six after they declared sovereignty from the Commonwealth

The Coalition of Rebel Factions/the Coalition (synonymous terms): a coalition of rebel factions formed by the remnant fighters of the RUC to continue combating the Commonwealth Government

The Interplanetary Union: the intergalactic alliance consisting of the Commonwealth and planets Ghanrax, Dhalgratt, Varsh'Ru, Zirkran, Rumanoah, and Taramassia

CHAPTER ONE

Armed dissidence: *avoidable armed retaliation resulting from long-term solvable friction between two or more disharmonious, uncooperative, or unaccommodating parties, for which the weaker party, feeling imperiled, is usually the retaliator*
—Earth Era lexicon—

Excited chatter echoed through the Academy's auditorium as the military graduates awaited their commencement ceremony. They stood tall and proud in their dress uniforms—earned at the expense of blood, pain, and sleepless nights. For the men, the uniform sported creased pants and oxfords. The women's uniform featured skirts, stockings, and heels. Affixed to both uniforms' jackets was a waist-length white cape symbolizing righteousness, the very ideal a Guardian embodied.

Momentarily, these young cadets would be officially inducted into the Commonwealth Defense Force (CDF). They were about to become the newest defenders of humanity's intergalactic republic, a republic fraught with homicidal war.

Twenty-two-year-old Cadet Randal Scott isolated himself in a lonesome corner, completely uninterested in joining the pre-ceremonial gabfest. Arms crossed, eyes shut, and chin tilted down, he was preoccupied with thoughts of getting payback.

He had sworn to exact revenge on the traitor responsible for his mother's death and the besmirching of his family's legacy. His father, a decorated serviceman he had once admired, was now a disgrace. In Randy's eyes, his sins could never be atoned for.

Being Linked *(cerebrally connected)* with his mother as she was atomized out of existence, Randy suffered both mentally and emotionally. Psychologists claimed that if a loved one's death was inhumane and brutal, being Linked during their demise could cause long-lasting psychic trauma, especially if psychological treatment was delayed.

The sharing of thoughts, emotions, and memories—courtesy of a nanochip beyond human ingenuity—was a scientific breakthrough credited solely to the Commonwealth's Union-approved trading partner, the Quilgarians.

A Link with another human being—upon mutually granted access—elevated empathy, rapport-building, and emotional intelligence. Such mental communion had been attempted but never achieved during humanity's bygone Earth Era.

Randy's psych evaluation for CDF admission had been conducted before the murder. Only he, his aunt, and his girlfriend, Cadet Stacie Spencer, knew he was Linked with his mother when she was obliterated. A new evaluation and some therapy would benefit him, but he couldn't risk a mental-health discharge, not until he made the bastard pay.

The skin between Randy's brows wrinkled as fond memories of his treacherous father tormented his mind. *Why?* he wondered. As he thought about his mother's funeral, the repulsion on his face worsened twofold.

He had once held the utmost respect for his father, Captain Arson Scott. The man had been a common laborer, toiling in the quarries of Colony Four on mankind's secondary world, a ringed planet designated Satellite One.

Arson later met the woman who would become his wife, a visiting Edenite named Kathleen Warner. Following in the footsteps of his father and grandfather, he left behind the drudgery of the quarry pits and answered a higher calling, enlisting in the military to assuage his yearning to serve humanity and provide for his wife and son.

Forging an esteemed career in the CDF, Arson fought in the Phazharian and Bhalkran wars, ultimately earning the Commonwealth Meritorious Service Medal, the highest commendation awarded.

Randy's admiration for his father inspired him to enlist in the Defense Force. The revered war hero had made his family and compatriots proud. Then, roughly six months ago, Arson mysteriously went AWOL, deserting his command post. His disappearance from the CDF had crushed Kathleen, inducing worry, sorrow, and recurring depression, some of which Randy experienced firsthand as a result of their Link.

At times, Kathleen would raise her firewalls to spare Randy's mind from being immersed in her personal distress.

Soon, rumors and allegations spread across Eden and Satellite One, claiming that Arson Scott had joined the terrorist insurgency opposing the Commonwealth Government. Randy later witnessed Arson take part in Kathleen's murder.

Vengeance became Randy's new motivation for enlisting. It fueled his drive to overcome the crucibles of Basic Combat

Training (BCT). During the intense mental and physical rigors he endured, his yen to see Arson pay gnawed at him constantly.

Determined to excel, he graduated from BCT as Warrior Extraordinaire, a recognition of outstanding achievement earned by performing at an exemplary level. Now he stood ready to take the Guardian's Oath and quell the outrage burning in his soul. He'd put an end to Arson Scott, whether it be by death or capture. Preferably the former.

A cherubic voice waded into his mind, saying, *Randy, it's me, honey.* Soft and soothing, the voice unmistakably belonged to . . .

Randy's eyes shot open. A luminescent, ghostly illusion of his mother shimmered before him. She wore a simple blue dress decorated with floral patterns. It was a favorite of hers, Randy recalled.

Leave the past in the past, Randy, Kathleen pled. *This vendetta of yours is decaying your soul. Move on.*

Randy shut his eyes. *Go away. You're just an apparition conjured from the pain and trauma recycled by my cerebral implant. Just a metaphysical figment of my subconscious spawned by alien tech that got overloaded with an influx of horror. You're the part of me wondering what my mother would say about me hunting down Dad. You're the boy in me crying for her to still be here, even if as some untouchable guardian angel. You are . . . my personal damnation.*

Kathleen said, *Randy, please—*

Go the fuck away! he demanded. Kathleen's voice disappeared.

Randy realized that these recurring manifestations of pain and longing in the image of his mother might be signs that fractures were forming in his mind. Maybe his unconquerable rage and thirst to eradicate his father were red alerts too. Still, he decided he'd gladly risk a lifetime of psychological damage if killing his father would bring serenity to his tortured soul.

A white-gloved hand clasped Randy's padded shoulder from behind. His eyes flicked open. On reflex, he spun, jerking his shoulder loose.

Standing smack-dab in his face was a striking blond woman. She had sun-kissed skin, cobalt-blue eyes, and a lovely red smile. She was Stacie Spencer—his peer, confidant, and significant other. And she was the only other class member to earn the mantle of Warrior Extraordinaire. *<Hey, you okay, Randy?>* the spirited young woman asked in a cheery voice through their Link.

Unrelated persons permitting access to each other's cerebral implants was one of the foremost acts of intimacy among the New Humanity. It topped or rivaled a touch, a kiss, or even intercourse. Access to a cerebral implant provided entry into the mind, a bridge to a wondrous symbiotic experience yielding unparalleled interconnectedness.

Proper-consent classes taught people to grant such a privilege judiciously. Even so, the granter could choose to safeguard specific feelings or memories, lowering their boundaries at their own pace.

Stacie's brows quirked in confusion. "Why the heck are you over here brooding?" she asked Randy aloud. "This is what we busted our asses for. Put some pride on that handsome face of yours." She playfully bumped her knuckles against his chest.

Though still perturbed, Randy dismissed her concern in a neutral tone. "I'm fine, Cadet Spencer." At the moment, there was no exorcising the anger plaguing his mind. Not here. Not in the same auditorium where, as a young boy, he had watched his father swear to uphold the very oath he was now about to take.

"Did you just call me 'Cadet Spencer'?" Stacie said in a feigned satirical tone, as if Randy had committed some heinous atrocity. It was a force of habit while in uniform, one he was still trying to shake. She placed a hand on her hip and wagged a finger at him.

"You and I are an item now, *remember?*" Her lips stretched tighter, and her tone shifted to something more perky. "So it's just 'Stacie' from now on, *even* in uniform. Got it?" She gave her boyfriend another energetic fist bump to the chest.

The past refusing to relinquish its stranglehold on Randy's peace of mind, he replied with a dull, curt, "Yeah, I got it." He didn't even crack a smile in return. Not even Stacie's vibrancy could liven him up, as it normally did.

Stacie folded her arms. Her smile deflated into a counterfeit frown. "Don't let me have to remind you again, *buster*," she teased, her humor meant to brighten Randy's serious disposition.

Randy's expression remained rigid. "I won't. But hey, we'd better get back over there." He jerked a thumb over his shoulder at their fellow cadets. "The Master of Ceremony should be here anytime now." The Master of Ceremony was running late due to unforeseen circumstances but was said to be arriving within the hour. And the hour had just about expired.

The automatic sliding doors hissed open. Heads swiveled. Lively chatter faded to a murmur, then died completely.

In stepped a tall, thin colonel with a weathered face and a ring of shaggy gray hair crowning his balding scalp—the Master of Ceremony. He wore a green dress uniform, which had a long tailcoat. The ribbons, medals, and campaign badges pinned to his chest were proof of his work ethic, leadership, and dedication to duty.

"Oh, shit," Stacie said. "Let's move."

She and Randy hurried to rejoin their cohort.

With gravitas, the colonel strode down the aisle, wearing the sternest of expressions. There was no apology for his tardiness, only a silent, stringent expectation that the cadets fall in line at his mere presence. Excited, they formed a formation on both sides of the aisle, precisely as rehearsed. Then they composed themselves, straightening their uniforms.

As Warrior Extraordinaires, Randy and Stacie assumed their rightful place at the forefront of the class, their status signified by the patch on their left shoulders. The patch had a gold border shaped like an inverted triangle. On each line, black lettering spelled out "Extraordinaire." In the middle of the patch was a gold fist; a pair of gold thunderbolts intersected behind it.

Upon the colonel's approach, Randy and Stacie pivoted to face each other, making way for him. Once he passed, they spun back toward the stage, fell into position side by side, and steeled their posture—shoulders squared, heads high, eyes locked on the Master of Ceremony.

The colonel ascended a short set of wooden stairs to the top of the stage and stood behind a lectern. At his back hung a red tapestry that draped the entire wall. In its center, embroidery depicted the Commonwealth's emblem: Eden encircled by three smaller planets—satellites One, Two, and Three. Satellite One comprised the colonies inhabited by the remaining two-fifths of humanity. Satellites Two and Three were vacant worlds used for military training exercises and mineral excavation.

The Commonwealth was a member of the Interplanetary Union, an alliance of worlds. The seven races of the Union— Ghanrax, Dhalgratt, Varsh'Ru, Zirkran, Rumanoahan, Taramassian, and human—had united to pool resources and support one another. And all Union members were bound by the Union Charter, a system of rules, laws, and regulations.

Ready to induct the Defense Force's newest Guardians, the colonel cleared his throat and spoke into the mic. "I applaud each one of you for choosing to bear the burden of protecting the New Humanity," he said, loudspeakers amplifying his strong, raspy voice.

The tableau of cadets stood in silence, locked in the position of attention. Unable to contain their emotions, some cadets had tears in their eyes. They had made it to commencement, unlike those who had quit—or had become training casualties.

The pitch of the colonel's voice climbed. "You survived the infernal, insufferable temperatures of Satellite Two." Higher still. "You *valiantly* trudged through the arctic wasteland of Satellite Three."

Stacie winced and squeezed Randy's hand. He glanced at her from the corner of his eye.

A fleeting flashback of her nearly perishing from hypothermia stole her focus. She remembered being medevacked to the infirmary that day, and Randy had stayed by her side the entire flight. Later, she endured a severe viral infection, and Randy had visited her sickbed daily as she convalesced. A flurry of bonding moments reeled in her mind. During every grueling step of BCT, Randy had provided unwavering support and encouragement.

An "ahem" from Randy jolted her back to the here and now.

Realizing she'd broken ceremonial posture, she swallowed past the thickening lump in her throat, let go of Randy's hand, and snapped back to the position of attention. Then she simply said to him, cerebrally, < *Thank you.* >

"Everything was done to test your mettle," the colonel said. His histrionic gesticulations swept the air as he spoke. "Everything was done to break you, but you *did not* break!" Excitement suffused his veins as his fist hammered the lectern's surface. Some initiates flinched at the resounding *whack* that reverberated across the auditorium.

"Now you join the *mightiest* military force of the Interplanetary Union," the colonel continued, his fiery oration making chests swell with pride. "I welcome you to the family known as the

Commonwealth Defense Force, a force that repulsed the nefarious Phazharians and defeated the Bhalkrans.

"The enemy we *now* face, however, comes from within our own republic. They will tell you we are the tyrants. They will try to convince you that their actions are justified. Do not be swayed by their insidious lies, as some have."

Randy scowled, thinking about his father.

Arson's betrayal made no sense to him. Arson's own father had been denied Eden citizenship, even after devoting twenty years to U.S. military service. It didn't seem right to Arson. But by becoming a venerable war hero in the CDF, he had brought his father's—and his family's—years of selfless service during Earth Era into the public eye. Randy wondered why Arson had chosen to tarnish the Scott family's legacy. Why? Well, now it was up to him, Randal Scott, to uphold his family's honor.

The colonel lifted a hand. "Repeat after me." A sea of white-gloved hands rose in perfect unison. "I—"

A plethora of emotions flooded Randy's thoughts. "I, Randal Eugene Scott—"

Stacie's moist eyes shimmered. "I, Stacie Lyn Spencer—"

The colonel continued, voice steady and solemn. "—take this oath with no reservations." His words were echoed back in one powerful voice. "And I promise to protect the Commonwealth and its allies from all enemies, foreign and domestic." Again, word for word was repeated verbatim. "Till my final breath or till such time my commitment expires." Every voice rose high, saying the last of the Oath.

The colonel clapped a palm against his heart and then thrust his fist outward. The motion was mirrored with precision and crispness. "Congratulations," he said, "you have now officially transitioned from cadets to full-fledged Guardians of the

Commonwealth Defense Force. Welcome to the fight."

Class Alpha 9-5 became the eleventh class of this cycle to graduate. Since their specialization was Land Combatant, they'd be deploying straight to the war zones of Satellite One.

Cheers and hurrahs erupted, pounding eardrums. The noise level was so loud it practically vibrated the auditorium.

After the colonel exited, everyone began to mingle.

One male Guardian laughed and said to his comrade, "Do you remember that big-ass hairy monster on Satellite Three that attacked our camp? Looked like a four-armed man-ape or some shit."

The other Guardian smirked. "Yeah, I heard it ripped apart seven Echo Company cadets. I'm glad we survived the big ugly motherfucker."

Emotional from all the trials and tribulations she had triumphed over, Stacie sniffled, and her lashes fluttered. Unshed tears of joy surfaced. Today was a defining moment for her.

Randy brushed a few errant strands of ashy-blond hair from her face and pressed a kiss to her forehead. "I'm gonna go say hello to my aunt. It's been three months. I know she'd kill me if I left the Academy today without dropping by. So I'll see you tonight at the banquet, okay?" The appreciation on his face was a silent confession of how much Stacie meant to him.

For a moment, Stacie lost herself in Randy's caring, intelligent brown eyes, realizing just how fortunate she was to have him in her life. She returned his tenderness, cementing a kiss to his cheek. Still collecting herself, she felt her voice lose some of its strength. "Later then, handsome." She wiped away a tear.

Randy pivoted and made his way toward the exit.

Stacie watched him quietly maneuver through clusters of celebrants, avoiding the post-ceremony gabfest. After his mother's murder, he had become a solemn man who built walls around himself, allowing only a select few into his personal space. And though he excelled at everything he put his mind to—academics, sports, soldiering—he never let success go to his head. He remained humble.

The kudos and accolades that came with being exceptional meant little to him. They were a byproduct of hard work, not the motivator. For Randy, excellence wasn't about recognition; it was simply his personal standard, a way of life.

Stacie thought she and Randy seemed like a total mismatch, polar opposites. As an alpha woman, she loved the limelight. She craved recognition. And usually, she gravitated toward flashy men, men similar to her. It was a pattern that consistently yielded disappointment. Those kinds of men always ended up being jerks, especially the guy who preceded Randy.

Randy was a refreshing change, and she liked him. His high standards of conduct showed in every aspect of his life, especially in how he treated women. Sometimes, though, he needed to loosen up more. But she could help with that, just like the night during BCT when she finally cajoled him into a risky sexual escapade. They were lucky they didn't get caught in the act.

He was the yin to her yang, and vice versa. She was the remedy for his reclusiveness, and he was the remedy for her moral laxity and dissoluteness. They complemented each other's strengths and counteracted each other's flaws. And when it came to sex, they more than satisfied each other's needs.

Stacie felt she'd hit the jackpot. Tall, fit, and handsome, Randy stood out. He came from good genes. Even looking his worst after a day of BCT—golden-brown hair disheveled and uniform begrimed—didn't detract from his sex appeal. Naked, he was even more marvelous, her wet dream.

A brown-skinned Guardian swaggered up to Randy and stuck out his hand. He was Jarius Ford, aka "Mr. Larger Than Life," a nickname given to him by his peers. "Congrats, Randy," the young black man said exuberantly.

Randy clasped Jarius' hand and shook it firmly. "Congrats to you too." Though Randy remained straight-faced, he was glad to see Jarius.

"I saw the placement chart. You, I, and Stacie are gonna be stationed at Colony Four with Charlie Battalion's Lima Company." Jarius sounded pumped, his enthusiasm sky-high. "I guess it's no surprise. The training cadre said most of our class would probably end up at Four, since shit's so outta control there."

Randy responded with a slight nod and a terse, "Uh-huh."

He had connections within the CDF and knew many of the higher-ups, who had great respect for his family's generations of military and law-enforcement service. These high-ranking allies sympathized with his loss. They vowed to support him in any way they could as he sought to restore honor to his family name and eliminate his father—a man who had betrayed them, too, and embarrassed the CDF.

Because Randy had such a wide sphere of influence, he didn't have to leave any aspirations to happenstance or formal request. Colony Four, his father's home colony, was where his father was operating his resistance faction. Forgoing his personal values for the sake of vengeance, Randy pulled the necessary strings to get himself and Stacie stationed at Colony Four in the same company.

Arson had commanded Charlie Battalion's Lima Company Headquarters, and Randy thought the personnel there could answer the questions nagging him.

Jarius' eyes shifted to Stacie. She and two female Guardians were giggling together.

Jarius' downcast gaze climbed Stacie's well-developed calves up to her pert backside. "A *fine-ass* woman," he said, radiating high-octane energy. "*Whoo-wee*, you sure know how to pick 'em." He whistled licentiously, ogling the blond bombshell. "I heard she's a little on the wild n' dangerous side, though. But I can't understand why a wealthy heiress would join the CDF." Baffled, he cocked a brow. "She's a goddamn modern-day princess."

Stacie's family was one of the Eight, nicknamed the Eight Elite. They were a clandestine conglomerate of aristocratic families whose reach extended to top government officials, and their enterprises were the first private ventures to expand into intergalactic markets during Earth Era.

"Let's just say she has her reasons," Randy said. Not being in a social mood, he made short work of the chitchat, excusing himself. "I've gotta go. I've got something to take care of."

Jarius slapped Randy's back cheerfully. "Yeah, sure. I'll see you tonight at the banquet. And lighten the fuck up, will ya?"

Randy went on his way, giving off loner vibes. He enjoyed Jarius' brotherhood and was sure he'd go far in his military career. His charisma and magnetic personality drew many people to him. And he came just a few metrics short of Warrior Extraordinaire qualification. Randy figured Jarius would make a fine officer someday. With his type of dynamism, Jarius might've even been better suited for the Ambassador Corps. Anyhow, the Land Combatant Corps, the backbone of the CDF, was lucky to have him.

Randy walked into the corridor. To his left and right were white walls that had glass partitions. Behind them, students sat at desks in high-tech paperless learning environments.

The Academy was where onboarding and Phase One of BCT took place, which consisted of two weeks of basic-knowledge classes such as CDF history, weapon mechanics, drill and ceremonies, and customs and courtesies.

After completion of Phase One, cadets were shipped offworld for Phase Two—boot camp. The Academy was also where some of the more technical MOS schooling took place: Maintenance, Analysis, Intelligence, Administration.

In a classroom of fifty cadets, an instructor stood beside a holo projector generating a revolving 3-D representation of the CDF's mechanized combatwear. "This is what we call a Shell," she said to her students.

Model M-X02 was a dangerous wearable armament composed of smart fibers and gunmetal Kryoplaste armor. It had the aura of a cutting-edge superhero battle suit, engineered with sleek design aesthetics. The M-X02 was leaps and bounds beyond its predecessor, the clunkier unisex M-X01 exoskeleton—which resembled Earth Era war machines. The cadets were viewing the M-X02's male variant.

The instructor said, "Shells are thought-operated mechsuits that take commands via cerebral interface with your nanoimplant. They're fully weaponized—" Her voice faded from earshot as Randy walked further down the corridor, his footfalls clacking against the floor.

In another roomful of cadets, an instructor could be heard giving a history lesson. He explained that during the most recent war between the Falgoah and Chalderat clans of the Noshkanu province—a Commonwealth protectorate on planet Zelaforia—the Noshkanu High Council had requested CDF intervention to stop the genocide.

Because the Falgoah were the aggressors, the CDF sided with the Chalderat. After the Falgoah's surrender, the Parliament and Chief Executive invoked the Commonwealth's authority over its protectorate and exiled them. The instructor stressed that this decision had not only preserved countless lives but also prevented the Commonwealth's incorporated status—Union status—from being jeopardized. The Union didn't tolerate genocide on member planets or within their territorial holdings, such as protectorates.

Randy passed a purple-haired female and dark-haired male cadet exiting a lab. Technicians had just reformatted their implants for Shell-interface capability. Cringing in discomfort, the male cadet said, "I hope this fucking headache goes away soon."

Randy remembered how that felt.

He made a left into Corridor C, where the scent of chemical disinfectant permeated the air. A little dome-shaped scrubber golem crisscrossed the floor, its rotary buffer burnishing the tiles to a sheen. The bot chirped and paused to let Randy pass.

After entering classroom C-12, Randy lounged against the back wall to watch a batch of new military hopefuls receive an informative orientation. Their instructor was his aunt, Merriam Wells, whose knowledge and experience in military affairs were extensive.

Merriam noticed him as she took position behind the classroom lectern. She was a rather slim woman with neck-length silver hair. Milestones in genetic enhancement, due to the technology of other species, stretched the human lifespan and slowed aging, so she actually looked to be in her early forties instead of her mid-fifties, and she felt just as spry.

Her white instructor uniform had a black cape attached to her gold epaulets, symbolizing her status as a Master Instructor.

She acknowledged Randy, nodding once. Then she faced her class and put on a serious expression. "Good morning," she said into the mic. Static crackled from the loudspeakers. "I am Master Instructor Merriam Wells, and I'll be giving you a thirty-minute lesson on the history and inner workings of the terrorist organization that threatens the peace and stability of the Commonwealth, the Coalition of Rebel Factions."

Merriam laid a computer tablet on the lectern's surface, powered it on, and pressed a red icon onscreen. The video-wall behind her flashed to life, mirroring the display on her tablet—a star grid of humanity's sphere of planets, the Commonwealth.

"As you know, it was ten months ago that three of Satellite One's six colonies started the Independent Movement and unconstitutionally declared sovereignty from the Commonwealth, forming the Republic of Unified Colonies (RUC)." Merriam touched each settlement on her tablet's screen as she said their designations. "Colonies One, Four, and Six." Red circles flagged the trio of rogue settlements on the video-wall.

"Eden's Chief Executive and the Parliament launched a three-week military campaign that recovered the renegade colonies. Those colonies were then placed under martial law to eliminate the rebel remnants and prevent further rebellion."

Every cadet sat ramrod straight, ears tuned in, eyeballs unmoving. Failure to pay attention could lead to immediate discharge.

Merriam kept an eye out for anyone slouching or dozing off while she spoke. "The rebel remnants who fought for their colonies' liberation in the Three-Week War call themselves the Coalition of Rebel Factions. They believe they're some last bastion of hope for freedom from the external ordinance of the central government, which they allege to be cruel and autocratic.

"These underground factions mainly operate inside the occupied colonies. They carry out guerrilla warfare on government facilities and Defense Force bases. They try to spread their Independent Movement propaganda and Arman Reza's liberation philosophy to manipulate the gullible into joining their forlorn insurrection."

Merriam swiped a finger across her tablet's screen. On the video-wall, a news article replaced the graphic of the Commonwealth. The headline read: UNAFFILIATED TERRORIST-BOMBERS DETONATE EXPLOSIVES OUTSIDE CDF BASE IN COLONY SIX. A slideshow of articles with similar stories cycled.

Animosity weighted Merriam's voice. "Many citizens of the occupied colonies have become radicalized and secretly support the Coalition. They act as suppliers, financial backers, and even lone-wolf operators. These people *think* they're freedom fighters, but what they are is traitors. They've been transformed into radical dissidents, minds hijacked by Reza's liberation philosophy and this . . . Independent Movement nonsense.

"Reza's dogma has even now tainted minds here on Eden, breeding a small vocal minority of Independent Movement sympathizers. They argue the central government should've condoned treason and granted the RUC its independence. These *anarchists* have incited riots and formed armed extremist groups."

As Randy watched, memories of his own orientation session surfaced. He had sat where these cadets were now, listening to Merriam. Her patriotism, strict adherence to the Constitution, and the pride she took in being a Master Instructor were qualities that had made an impression on him.

"This Independent Movement *contagion* is spreading, and we are the cure." Merriam's tone grew uglier. "You will hear the anarchists say the central government was wrong for its aggression. That it should've attempted reconciliation first. That it should've tried *diplomacy*. These delusional halfwits act as if colonies One, Four, and Six were a sovereign entity to be negotiated with.

"Following the RUC's declaration of independence, the Chief Executive generously allowed them five days to cease and desist their treasonous actions. Those actions, unbeknownst to the central government, involved the illicit establishment of planetary partnerships to procure arms for their paramilitaries. *All* external commerce transactions *must be* authorized by the Union."

Worlds outside the Union underwent extensive vetting before the Commonwealth, or any Union member, conducted business with them. That way, the Union didn't end up funding governments with nefarious activities.

Merriam said, "By Commonwealth law, the central government is the only entity in our republic that can transact with external vetted partners. The RUC broke law after law. That cease and desist was their opportunity to set things right and avert war. Instead, they persisted in separating from the Commonwealth."

She suspected some cadets still believed that military action against the colonies had been excessive. She intended to shatter that illusion. "Declaring sovereignty is *treason*, as outlined in our Constitution," she said in a harsh tone. "So the five-day cease and desist was an act of benignity. Tell that to the simpletons who contest the government's civility."

Randy nodded in agreement, puzzled by why Arson started fraternizing with the enemy. Something volatile rose inside him, screaming for answers, screaming for retribution for his mother.

Merriam held up a finger, as if to stave off any forthcoming criticism. "And mobilization of troops to dismantle the RUC *did not* violate Article II of the Union Charter."

A cadet worked up the courage to raise his hand, challenging Merriam. "Excuse me, Ma'am. If the Commonwealth didn't violate Article II, as you say, then why was a proper-conduct investigation launched by the Union's planetary leaders?"

A coldness settled in Merriam's eyes, and the corners of her mouth turned downward.

Pressure built up in the cadet's chest, but he didn't back down. "They've had major doubts about the validity of our actions. For weeks, they've been reviewing our justification for use of force.

"When the emergency summit happens next week, they're going to present their deliberations. Some people believe those deliberations aren't going to be in our favor. We're basically going to be on trial. We might get exiled from the Union." He mentally patted himself on the back for speaking up.

A muscle twitched in Merriam's jaw, and she slammed her hands down on the lectern.

Color drained from frozen faces.

"Oh, shit," a female cadet whispered.

Merriam's voice tore through the air. "First of all, when a planetary leader enacts Article II's Exception to Force Clause without consulting the others—to stop an abrupt uprising—those leaders have the right to launch a proper-conduct investigation. It's standard procedure.

"Secondly, no matter what the critics say, we acted within the boundaries of the Exception to Force Clause. You should believe that beyond a shadow of a doubt," she added threateningly. The cadet spared himself expulsion, not challenging the Master Instructor any further. "The Commonwealth is always righteous. Now, does anyone else have anything to interject?"

A green-haired woman in her twenties, wearing square spectacles, raised her hand.

Merriam's eyes spotted the brave soul and glanced at her name tag. "Speak, Cadet Wilmington."

The lanky cadet took a bold stance and spoke her mind. "I lived in Colony One, my birth-colony, before the lottery granted me

Eden citizenship two years ago. Unfortunately, my parents weren't so lucky." She lowered her chin, concerned for her parents' well-being. A thought of them passed, and she lifted her gaze, meeting Merriam's cold grimace. "Like the other five colonies, the conditions there are dire." Despair bathed her features. "Temporary housing units are falling apart, filtration systems are malfunctioning, and—"

Merriam rolled her eyes and cut off Wilmington, who was grating on her nerves. "And your point is what?"

Wilmington asserted herself, saying, "My point is rebellion happened because the central government naysaid the colonies' plight. They failed to respond to people's grievances, galvanizing the citizens of colonies One, Four, and Six. Armed dissidence was bound to occur. So don't you think the government bears some responsibility for being remiss—?"

Merriam, about to blow her top, interrupted. "Cadet Wilmington, as Master Instructor, I pronounce you ill-suited for military service. You are hereby expelled from the Academy. Now remove yourself from my classroom."

Wilmington's face blanched. "But—"

"Leave," Merriam demanded in a livid tone, making a sweeping gesture with her hand.

Tears welled up in Wilmington's eyes and poured down her cheeks. She rose from her seat, head bowed, and stomped toward the doorway, muttering.

Randy, impassive to the outlier's predicament, silently watched her pout.

"*Bitch*," she mumbled, exiting the room.

Merriam tapped a sequence of icons on her tablet's screen, marking Wilmington's profile as "disloyal" and alerting Academy Enforcement. To question her about her subversive leanings, they would pinpoint the signal from her tracer beacon and intercept her before she could leave the building.

"That's what we get for letting immigrant nadir into the prestige of the Defense Force," a snooty female voice whispered from one of the rearmost seats.

"As you can see, anti-government sentiments *will not* be tolerated, and anyone caught listening to Arman Reza's rhetoric will be culled from our ranks as well," Merriam said ferociously. "Independent Movement sympathizers like Cadet Wilmington become defectors. That's what we don't want. Better to nip a problem in the bud now before it grows into a bigger one."

Merriam recovered from the distraction and resumed her lecture, adjusting her voice and posture. "You have been selected not only to defend the Commonwealth from foreign threats and protect our allies, but also to help maintain law and order in the colonies of our great republic. You should feel proud." She pressed a purple icon on her tablet's screen. "But the CDF's mission reaches far beyond the Commonwealth and the Union. Observe."

The lights in the room dimmed, and overhead, a wire-frame holographic projection of planets, moons, and stars spread out. It displayed a conflict grid marking the Commonwealth's Mission Worlds, which were located across multiple quadrants of the galaxy. These were all Tier 1 civilizations, fragile worlds where individual governments had become protectorates in exchange for military assistance or essential resources.

The terms of these agreements varied from one government to another. Some required surrendering a portion of trade profits to the Commonwealth, while others involved arms deals or long-term financial compensation that sometimes had negative effects on a protectorate's economy.

Agreements remained in effect until their expiration date,

which ranged from months to years. Then it could be renewed, renegotiated, or terminated.

The populations of some protectorates viewed the Commonwealth's intervention as benevolent service, while the populations of others saw it as imperial expansion driven by economic and political interests. Sometimes unrest and upheaval within protectorates resulted in opposition movements that sought to overturn existing governments using various means, including force, to cancel the Commonwealth's agreements.

There were Union leaders who had now grown concerned about the Commonwealth's lucrative planetary-impact missions. They feared these missions could infringe on sovereignty, disrupt people's well-being, or lead governments to become dependent on the Commonwealth. And there was a possibility that opponents of these missions might harbor animosity toward the entire Union.

Merriam deactivated the projection, and the room's lights brightened. She double-tapped a thumbnail on her home screen, and a picture of Arson Scott—the man once held in high esteem—enlarged on the video-wall. "This is one of the most-wanted terrorist leaders of the Coalition." In the image, Arson's dark hair was cropped short, and he had a deadly expression creasing the brow of his rugged face.

Randy glared at his father, his scathing countenance a mirror of his vengeful heart.

Merriam brought up the war criminal's prior CDF service sketch. On the video-wall, black text materialized against a blank backdrop. "As you can see, this *convert* isn't someone to take lightly," she said in a severe tone.

The text denoted Arson's military exploits, exploits that demanded respect and would even amaze some of the most seasoned warfighters. After giving the cadets a minute to internalize just how dangerous her brother-in-law could be, Merriam minimized the info and double-tapped another thumbnail.

Picture number two took over the video-wall: Arson, outfitted in CDF battle garb, tracking targets through the scope of a high-powered rifle. The black-and-gray camo-pattern uniform included a protective vest and a tactical belt carrying dual handguns.

"Arson Scott is one of the toughest sons of bitches this galaxy's ever seen," Merriam warned. "After the Three-Week War concluded and martial law in the renegade colonies commenced, he became influenced by the Coalition's doctrine. He defected, divulging CDF secrets, fighting against his own, and becoming one of the chief terrorist leaders of the Coalition." *And he ceased being a dedicated father to Randy and a loving husband to my younger sister,* she added silently.

Randy's heated glare stayed fixed on the picture of his father. His pulse quickened. The room seemed to shrink, suffocating him, and his mind took him back to the harrowing night the Coalition murdered his mother . . .

Randy guided his red sports cruiser across the night sky, enjoying the wind rushing through the open top. He landed the fancy flyer between two yellow lines, parking outside a three-story facility surrounded by forest.

The facility was A-1 Defense Solutions, a major defense contractor where his mother worked as a senior tech engineer. To celebrate her promotion to Chief Tech Engineer tomorrow, he was going to treat her to a meal.

He flipped a switch on the dash, and the engine purred off. He got out, smoothed back his windswept hair, and approached the building. It was after hours, and it was extremely rare for anyone to be at work at this time, especially since today was Commonwealth Observance Day, a holiday commemorating the inception of humanity's intergalactic republic.

Randy was nervous. Defense contractors had faced attacks from the Coalition. His mother's might be on their list.

Randy tapped the centerpiece of his wrist computer (wristcom). The electronic band beeped, ringing his mother's.

<Hey, honey, up here,> came Kathleen's voice from inside his mind. He looked up and saw her waving at him from one of the tall third-floor windows. Realizing she was within range of their Link, he canceled the call. *<Be down in fifteen minutes,>* she said.

"Wait, someone's still in there!" an outraged voice shouted from somewhere. "Intel said the building would be vacant tonight!"

Startled, Randy twisted left and right, sneakers scraping against the pavement. His eyes methodically combed the darkness.

<Randy, what's going on out there?> Kathleen asked, voice teeming with worry.

<Not sure,> Randy replied, swiveling his head. His panicking heart thumped frantically.

Suddenly . . . *FWOOSH!* The third floor erupted in a thunderous burst of flames. The second and first floors soon followed, explosions shattering windows into fragments.

The cruelest of pains burrowed into Randy's mind and razed every atom in his body, shivering his entire being.

He gripped his head, releasing a gut-wrenching, shrill scream that could wake the dead. The mental torment clawed at his psyche until it was in shambles. Speechless and disoriented, his face as pallid as a corpse, he died without dying. Then color returned to his face, and he heaved in ragged drags.

Lightheaded, tears upwelling, he sank to his knees.

24

Ash drifted, and wild undulating flames licked the air.

Randy stared at the inferno, shuddering, ears ringing. Intermittent throbs stung his mind. Words couldn't articulate the agony he had experienced.

A racket of gunshots stole his attention. Still on his knees, his vision blurred by tears, he canted his head to the left. His jaw dropped. Security personnel were discharging small-arms fire at three Coalition rebels geared up in modular vests and tactical equipment. One of them was Arson Scott.

One of the two men with Arson unslung his rifle and fired warning shots at the security guards. "Let's move!" His rifle's muzzle flashed, and expended shell casings pinged across the pavement.

All three rebels retreated into the trees.

"Where'd they go?" a guard said. He swept the darkness with the beam of his wrist light.

The rumble of an engine shook the forest. Birds cawed and chirped among rustling leaves. Twigs snapped. A heavily armored flyer emerged from a thicket of trees and climbed into the sky. As it zoomed away, its taillights disappeared into the night.

Randy stood up, whimpering. There was now a black hole in his heart that would never seal. His mother had been snatched away from him in an instant. The worst part was that his own father was involved in robbing him of his mother and mentally scarring him. Now, the war had become personal.

A guard ran up to Randy. "Hey, are you okay?"

Brows knitted in anger, the now-motherless son said nothing.

Emergency vehicles screeched onto the scene. Doors clicked open. Muffled chatter blared over radios.

Concerned, the guard asked Randy again, "Are you okay?"

Firemen hosed the conflagration using wheeled water cannons.

Randy remained silent, smoldering debris and the pungent scent of smoke wafting in the howling wind . . .

Randy's memory broke. The suffocating feeling lifted, and his muscles relaxed. He pulled himself together.

"I'm going to break here for ten minutes," Merriam said to her students. "You may stay or leave the classroom." At a brisk pace, she went toward her nephew, heels clicking the floor. Eyes followed her as she and Randy stepped outside.

Some students got up to leave; others explored the learning modules in their desks' info terminals.

Merriam grasped Randy's shoulders. "Dress Blues suit you." She brushed his shoulders and tugged on his uniform, straightening wrinkles. As she absorbed his appearance, the Warrior Extraordinaire patch registered. Her brows leapt. "And you graduated top-tier of your class. Fantastic. Your mother would've been *so* proud of you." She swung open her arms, and Randy embraced her.

A faint smile touched the corners of Randy's mouth, a pained one. He wanted his mother to see him graduate today.

Chatting as they left the canteen, two faculty members sauntered by, holding mugs of steaming brew.

Randy hugged Merriam tighter. "I wanted to let you know I received approval for my request," he said softly. They released each other. "I'm going to be stationed at Colony Four."

"Where your father is?" Merriam asked to confirm. Randy nodded, his expression tense. "I know, betrayal hurts. It stings. And rage burns inside you, as it does me." Her voice hardened. "But remember: duty first and foremost." She jabbed a finger against her nephew's chest. "You got that, Randal Scott?"

"Yes, Ma'am." He headed down the corridor. "I've got to get going. I'll call before I depart for my duty station."

"Anything you need, you let me know, Randy."

"I will," he replied, walking away.

• • •

Stacie moved down a corridor identical to all the others, on her way to leave the Academy. The loud and proud-sounding click-clack of her heels echoed. Her stride exuded confidence, and rightfully so. Not because she was ultrarich or because she had a body that turned heads—all of which inflated her ego. It was because she had transcended the expectations of naysayers and uncuffed herself from the prescribed lifestyle of the Eight by joining the CDF.

Thrilled about her first military deployment, she beamed.

Near the glass partition of the security office, three male cadets and one female lollygagged. Stacie slowed her stride and came up behind them, wondering what had their attention.

Wearing a black sleeveless spandex half-top and shorts, Cadet Wilmington sat in a chair with her hands bound behind her back.

Uniformed in dark blue, a tall, broad-shouldered Academy enforcement officer loomed over her. Hellbent on getting a confession, he pressed a shock baton to her chest.

Electricity buzzed and crackled.

Wilmington screamed.

"Are you a Coalition plant, Telisha Wilmington?" the officer demanded.

Tears pooled in Wilmington's large green eyes. "No! I already told you that!"

The officer clamped a hand around her jaw. "Are you a member of some other anti-government group?" he asked, while the female officer at the worktable behind him inspected Wilmington's uniform for nanosurveillance devices.

Wilmington's breath hitched. A cold film of sweat slickened her skin. "I'm not a member of *any* anti-government group," she replied, voice quavering.

"You sure?" The officer's shock baton discharged another jolt of electricity.

Wilmington winced, muscles coiled tight as she weathered the pain. "Yes, I'm sure!" Her face paled from the wave of fear that almost made her piss herself. "Now please stop! Please!"

Without a hint of compassion, the officer gestured for her to stand. "Get up so we can transfer you to detainment." Pure hatred strained his features.

Wilmington stood, her knobby knees trembling.

Stacie "tsked," shaking her head. *When will these sympathizers learn?* She walked away as the four onlookers pointed and giggled.

Stacie exited the Academy, stepping out onto the front portico.

Young cadets in battledress passed by her, going and coming.

A blue-haired male was in awe of her Warrior Extraordinaire patch. "Wow!" he exclaimed. "That's what I wanna be, Warrior Extraordinaire!"

The gawker's words pandered to Stacie's ego. She loved the recognition such an accomplishment brought her.

Under the lavish gazebos of the campus's sprawling courtyard, cadets sat on benches, engaged in free-ranging discussions.

A female Guardian, her back pressed against the Academy's wall, was making out with a male Guardian. Both were recent graduates. The woman's partner shoved his hand under the back of her skirt, nearly ready to have celebration sex right then and there.

Though strict during military exercises, assignments, and operations, the CDF was a far more relaxed fighting force than the militaries of Earth Era. Public displays of affection in uniform were permitted, aligning with Eden's permissive culture and the belief that excessive austerity for active-duty Guardians was unhealthy. Hair-color and tattoo regulations were also lenient, a stark contrast to the rigid codes of Earth Era's militaries.

A male cadet made a pass at a female, pinging her cerebral implant. Access was denied. Salty, he "humphed," and his face pulled into a pompous scowl.

Commotion broke out near the schoolhouse to Stacie's left. She turned. Two Academy enforcement officers wrestled an eighteen-year-old cadet to the ground.

"Get off!" the cadet yelled. His mop of teal hair brushed his forehead as he struggled to free himself. "I was just . . . trying to understand the enemy better, that's all!"

"Bullshit!" one officer blurted. "Now your ass is gonna be out-processed!"

The cadet's tablet lay beside him. He'd been viewing one of Arman Reza's incendiary orations on the net, a cyberspace nexus for information and communication, which was accessible to both Eden and Satellite One. Anytime cyber authorities took down one of Reza's vidcasts, it would resurface days later, and the location of the upload remained untraceable. No digital footprint. Nothing.

Using the net as his pulpit, over time Reza fathered the Independent Movement with his vehement declamations of colony equality.

No one had any idea who this dangerous inciter was, as he always wore a cowl and metal mask to conceal his identity. He also spoke through a vocoder, further ensuring he remained unidentifiable.

From the tablet, Reza's modified voice said, "The Commonwealth Government is undeniably wrong for our—"

One of the officers stomped the tablet repeatedly until it broke, silencing the harangue.

Stacie shook her head at the youngster. *Fucking idiot.*

Cadets milled around on the well-tended green spaces, chattering about what had just transpired.

Stacie spoke into her wristcom. "Options for transportation services." Following an electronic warping sound, a hololist materialized in midair. Stacie dragged a finger down the list, browsing various options. She touched the transport service she wanted, debiting her wayfare. Within three minutes of her transportation request, a driverless capsule-shaped flyer descended.

The overhead flip-up canopy snapped open. "Thank you for riding with Air Escort, the best in air-cab transportation," said a crisp artificial voice.

Stacie settled into the exotic leather interior, enjoying the luxury of massage seating. She recognized the flyer as having been manufactured by one of her family's acquisitions.

The canopy clicked shut.

"Destination, please," the computerized chauffeur requested.

Stacie buckled up and provided an address.

The nav-panel hummed to life, buttons blinking and go-lights flashing. Electronics chirped, navigation programs charting coordinates toward Stacie's given address.

"Destination logged," the computer reported as the flyer steadily ascended. "Now proceeding. Please sit back and enjoy the ride." The flyer cruised into an air lane.

Below was a magnificent panoramic view of Eden's capital, Cornerstone City. It was the epicenter of business, entertainment, politics, and commerce on the planet. The Academy, Parliament Building, Supreme Judiciary, and Chief Executive's Manor formed the Quad and were located in the center of the booming metropolis.

Maglev trains inside sky tunnels dipped and climbed at high velocities. Flyers whisked everywhere. A mass of ground transportation crawled to a gridlocked halt on the congested solar-paneled streets. Pissed-off motorists yelled obscenities and honked their vehicles' horns.

Men and women in lavish attire ambled along avenues of multifarious restaurants and storefronts. Behind clothing-store windows, holographic skins of mannequins cycled between the latest couture. Giant video banners across the city displayed colorful advertisements and infographics. In the major shopping district were large multiplex retail centers up to twelve stories. In the residential district, swanky high-rise apartment buildings loomed over the streets.

Many people were unaware that the Eight Elite's handprint was all over the city's construction.

Stacie's flyer soared by a business complex ten floors high. An employee in his office issued a voice command, causing the windows to become opaque for privacy.

Further out from Cornerstone, quiet rural suburbs provided relief from the hustle and bustle for those who liked life slower. To the east were colorful glades that were home to popular hot-spring resorts.

Though Eden was the utopia of the Commonwealth, a good deal of its citizens had resorted to illegal methods for generating wealth during humanity's turbulent transition period. So beneath Eden's glitz and glamour, a sinister underworld thrived. Evil and sin seemed to be the imperfections humanity couldn't extinguish, even in its new enlightened, evolved state.

Stacie said to her wristcom, "Call Mom." Rhythmic electronic chirps sounded. For the third time today, her mother refused to answer, letting her end go to voicemail. Stacie canceled the call, pressing a finger to her wristcom. Her face grimaced. *Three months and you don't want to talk to me?* "Figures." She expelled a heavy sigh. She needed a distraction. "News," she told the cab in an irritated tone. A holoscreen wobbled into view.

A stylish pod-shaped flyer whisked past hers, traveling in the opposite direction.

"Please designate a station," the cab's computer said.

"Any, as long as it's news." A blip on the holoscreen signaled the start of the autosearch. Seconds later, the system presented the first newscast it detected. With her fingers, Stacie stretched the screen to her preferred size. "Perfect."

A green-eyed, orange-haired reporter was onscreen. She said, "Lottery beneficiaries here on Eden have family living in the occupied colonies. Their loved ones have told them the CDF maintains law and order with extreme prejudice, raiding homes without warrants. They even say mandatory curfews are sometimes enforced with death. And eyewitness accounts are circulating about arbitrary arrests and forced confessions by means of intimidation and coercion."

Stacie heard the Master of Ceremony's words in her mind: *"They will tell you we are the tyrants. They will try to convince you that their actions are justified. Do not be swayed by their insidious lies—"*

Coalition propaganda, Stacie thought.

It wasn't beyond comprehension that some unjust acts were being perpetrated by Guardians. There were corrupt people in all professions and walks of life. But Stacie, like most Independent Movement antagonists, believed that the Coalition and their supporters were overexaggerating these rare occurrences—and completely fabricating some, to fool the masses.

"With me is one of the protesters who participated in an Independent Movement rally, here on Eden, just an hour ago," the reporter said.

A heavyset, fully bearded man spoke into the camera. "My daughter lives in Colony Six. She tells me all the time about how Guardians and military vehicles are always roaming the streets."

Stacie wanted to yell at the screen, *Yes, counterinsurgency operations are always ongoing, to catch the terrorists and defend the Commonwealth.*

"My daughter says Guardians have unfairly stopped, questioned, and frisked her and other law-abiding citizens," the man said. "Before the war, people in Colony Six received shitty treatment. Now they're being treated even shittier. And because of net restrictions, colonists can't expose what's happening and prove how lousy their living conditions are. The central government's got everything under lock n' key, to keep us on Eden oblivious to all the fuckery going on."

Stacie scoffed. *Stupid kook.* She had heard enough. "Another station."

On this newscast, a male anchorman in a blue suit sat at a sleek table. To his left sat a menacing, aged man with an aquiline nose, wearing a plethora of ribbons on his uniform. To his right sat a dark brown woman of African heritage in her middle years. Waist-length locs, decorated with colorful beads, framed her prominent facial features. Her attire for this interview consisted of a headdress and a purple robe bearing abstract patterns.

The anchorman, facing the camera, announced, "Joining me to discuss the Commonwealth's unrest are two members of the Parliament. First, we have Chairman Cornelius Gould." The camera panned to the man. His pallid face remained stoic. "In addition to his role as a chairman, he occupies the third highest government position, serving as Secretary of Defense *(Deputy Chief was the second highest government position)*." He also had a well-deserved reputation for being a master of manipulation, intimidation, and torture tactics. "He opposes the Independent Movement and favors the use of military force to suppress it."

The camera panned from the stern-faced combat guru to the colorfully dressed brown woman, a woman who had survived many hardships, a woman who had labored in the agricultural fields of Colony Two.

"Next, we have Chairwoman Oviereya Amaechi," the anchorman said. Oviereya's presence stood out on so many levels. "Just like Chairman Gould, she holds dual positions. She is also Chancellor of the Supreme Judiciary, the fourth highest position in the government.

"She doesn't approve of colony autonomy, yet she acknowledges the perspectives of colonists who desire independence. And she believes the Independent Movement was justified due to what she considers government negligence."

Election year was ahead. There were rumors that Oviereya and Cornelius might be vying for the Chief Executive seat. The people on Eden and Satellite One watching this interview considered it a preview of future debates between the two.

"Increase audio," Stacie said. The sound system's volume rose.

Oviereya had been the midwife for Stacie's mother, and she became a dear friend to Stacie. Though Stacie didn't always agree with her politics, she was glad that someone who had morals and a generous spirit had been elected to Parliament.

Oviereya, in a voice of assertion, spoke. "Inadequate housing, minimal access to health systems, unequal resource distribution, economic deterioration, rising poverty levels, and a lack of industrial development are what incited the civil unrest that sparked the Independent Movement. And who is to blame? The Chief Executive and the Parliament.

"The governors of the seceding colonies sat at the parliamentary meetings every cycle. Time after time they aired their people's grievances, with little ability to do anything else. All they could do was advocate for their colonies' welfare and submit proposals to the Chief Executive and Parliament regarding possible solutions, and those proposals were ignored. Two-fifths of humanity is living in today's Dark Ages."

Cornelius countered in a snide tone. "A new genesis for humanity isn't easy to accomplish. That is common sense. There were bound to be setbacks to intergalactic migration. Yes, the colonies' people need aid, but to say they're living in today's 'Dark Ages' is ridiculous." He let out an unsympathetic chuckle.

Oviereya's dark brows dipped. "No, quite the contrary."

To give her critics context behind her perspective, she decided to recount the events that had led to the rebellion, and perhaps she also intended to persuade voters for the upcoming election. Since most Edenites had never visited a colony, it was important that she offer an accurate portrayal of the colonies' dilemma—one that only a former colonist like herself, a lottery beneficiary, could provide.

Her shoulders tensed. Her throat turned dry. It was crucial that she get her message right. "This stratification of humanity began when we had to abandon Earth, a world that had fallen to pieces, to migrate to a new planetary habitat."

Humanity's venture into intergalactic arms procurement during Earth Era ignited an unprecedented arms race. Alien weapons of mass destruction fell into the hands of warlords, despots, and tyrannical regimes, plunging the world into an apocalypse.

Oviereya settled into the moment, anxiety draining from her body. Addressing such a large live audience was far from the hardest thing she had ever done. She told herself she had this under control. "With assistance from the Union Worlds and other intergalactic governments, we established the Commonwealth. But Eden, the Commonwealth's motherworld, has only a single continental landmass; it simply wasn't big enough to accommodate all of humanity. So a two-world solution was necessary.

"To avoid human bias in conceptualizing humanity's future, AEGIS (Advanced Exascale Global Information-collection System) was invented. It was supposed to formulate the best strategy for survival using logical calculations and unbiased reasoning. By analyzing census data from all nations, it decided who would inhabit Eden and who would inhabit the abject, substandard habitats of Satellite One, primarily consisting of manufactured housing units (MHUs)."

A tempest raged in Oviereya's eyes at the unjust classification labels assigned to colony selectees, determined by supposed value coefficients. She gazed straight into the camera, as though the people watching this interview were standing in front of her. "The AI stratified humanity into upper and lower-level classes. Those identified as being the most capable of pioneering the New Humanity were selected to inhabit Eden, as if they were the crème de la crème of the human race." About to erupt, she paused to gather herself.

Cornelius quietly growled at her "colony sympathizing."

Proceeding to pour out her soul, she said, "AEGIS categorized colony selectees as *inferior*, based on socioeconomic status, IQ, preexisting medical conditions, genetic predisposition, and other prejudices. They were determined to be the most expendable. They were told they were best suited to serve humanity as resource harvesters, merely *serfs* for the Commonwealth Government and Eden's megacorporations that—"

Cornelius spoke over her. "Typical progressionist blather, using manipulative, sympathy-inducing terms such as 'expendable' to further your agendas. Neither I nor any other government leader has described colonists, our own brethren, as 'expendable.'"

The chairwoman raised a hand. "No talking out of turn."

Cornelius grunted, eyes flaring.

The anchorman felt the tension between them escalating.

Oviereya collected her thoughts and continued her appeal to win over hearts and minds. "To pick up where I left off: AEGIS sent the lower-level classes to work as resource harvesters on Satellite One, where living conditions are harsh. The majority of time and assets were relegated to developing Eden's utopias, to give the upper-level classes—the chosen pioneers of the New Humanity—the best chance at persevering.

"Some people questioned the fairness of AEGIS's socioeconomic design, but not enough. Many were simply glad to have the chance to escape Earth and get a shot at survival. During that time of strife, most opponents of AEGIS didn't have the willpower or wherewithal to oppose Earth's highest orders. So they became compliant with the exodus directives designating them the lesser of humanity.

"But they remained hopeful; the low-grade living conditions were to be only temporary, a stepping stone. Their world was to become a paradise too, once or *if* the Eden migrants successfully completed their transition. Maybe that was the intention at first, but this promise got thrown by the wayside."

The anchorman appeared captivated by how soulfully Oviereya spoke. He had no doubt there were colonists watching who were in tears.

Oviereya said, "Over time, the migrants of Eden gave birth to the next generation of Homo sapiens. Their children underwent genetic editing, and they received genetic enhancement *(for gains in immunity, healing, pain tolerance, reflexes, physical strength, and other attributes).* No such human-performance augmentation was administered to the people of the colonies."

She became riled, remembering friends who had perished in her birth-colony, Colony Two, waiting for inoculations against diseases that Edenites were immune to contracting.

Her eyes narrowed. "It seemed Eden's people were being molded to be a sort of neohuman. The disparities between Eden and Satellite One grew as infrastructural development and life quality accelerated here but slowed in the colonies."

Nor did it need to accelerate in the colonies, Cornelius thought.

Passion infused Oviereya's words. "The years of colony progression that did happen appeased people at the time. Individual governments and an economy were established. The net was set up. Infrastructural growth was happening. But when the progression suddenly plateaued, people were no longer appeased.

"Colonists seemed to become a subclass of the New Humanity. They were being excluded from mankind's evolution technologically, genetically, and industrially. It was the people of Eden, AEGIS's chosen ones, who were prospering and becoming the new leaders of mankind."

Cornelius glowered at Oviereya. *As we were meant to be.*

Oviereya didn't miss a beat, maximizing every second she had to speak. "Humanity became divided into a privileged class and a sort of servant class. As more time went by without the central government resuming colony development, Eden-born became referred to as 'Highborn' by their colony brethren.

"Eventually, colony governors organized protests and conducted surveys to gauge their citizens' views on breaking away from the Commonwealth. These 'illegal' exodus polls were intended as a wake-up call to the central government. They revealed overwhelming support for secession in colonies One, Four, and Six, with eighty-four percent of their population voting 'yes.'

"The central government slapped the governors with fines and reduced their colonies' resources to punish them. After so many years, Eden's progression was still the top priority. The government's evolving development plan for the Commonwealth continued to discriminate against the colonies."

Cornelius listened on, his entire demeanor radiating pure apathy. Oviereya's words didn't move him or evoke any emotion.

Oviereya said, "Colonists felt like they were being dismissed. They felt like AEGIS's blueprint for humanity was being exploited to maintain a socioeconomic hierarchy that kept them at the bottom of the totem pole. Their anger grew.

"Sure, the colonies were given governors and even an annual lottery that allows several people to become registered Eden citizens each year, but that was only a *minuscule* step in the right direction. Don't get me wrong, though: I'm truly grateful the immigration lottery exists. I was a beneficiary of it."

Oviereya became an icon to the colony peoples. She was the first and only of them to be elected to Parliament. She was their homeworld heroine.

"However, colonists have started to believe their governors and the lottery are just ploys meant to keep them content. They were originally told their governors would give them a voice within the central government, but that wasn't the case. The status quo is being deliberately maintained because an AI has determined that colonists' value lies in hard labor."

Cornelius' fingers drummed the tabletop idly. Oviereya's opinionated historical recap bored him. "Thank you for your overblown, overly grim narrative the progressionists within the Parliament usually employ for political gain."

Oviereya's jaw tightened, and she shook her head. "My tale of events is no exaggeration. Chief Executives and the Parliament assured the colonies of change time after time, yet nothing happened. *Zilch.*

"Denialists within the central government claim we're an inclusive society and that the colonies have not been forgotten. At the moment, we *are not* an inclusive society. Colonists can't even enlist in the CDF unless they become lottery beneficiaries." Her inflection turned spiteful. "That doesn't sound fair to me."

Cornelius twisted his hands together beneath the table, fighting to repress the wave of disgust sprouting through him.

Oviereya said, "There were hopes that Chief Executive Jared Kerner would be different, but he's done little to alter the course set forth by his predecessors, which include his father.

"For too many years, it's been 'Eden first.' After the colonies had been neglected for so long, it's no surprise the governments of One, Four, and Six grew seditious and sought autonomy.

"They wanted to become self-governing entities and apply for Union membership independent of the Commonwealth. That way, they could engage in commerce transactions directly with other Union planets and external partners, no longer having to wait for hand-me-down resources from the central government.

"Chief Executive Kerner was never going to allow that. His failings, along with those of his predecessors, fueled colonists' dissatisfaction. Frustrated, the governors of colonies One, Four, and Six declared independence, an action most of their constituents supported, as the 'illegal' exodus polls indicated."

Cornelius' patience wore thin, every word from Oviereya chipping away at his composure. He rested his elbow on the table, cradling his forehead in his hand, while his eyes wandered to anything but her. He couldn't wait until it was his time to speak.

Oviereya was pleased to be irritating Cornelius. The two of

them getting along was impossible. Eager to share more of her thoughts, she persisted. "Discontent with the central government is rising among the other three colonies' populations. Rumors say Colony Five's governess, Samantha Hayley, is secretly supporting the Coalition. After all, her daughter lived in Colony Four and died fighting for its independence in the Three-Week War.

"Governor Rich of Colony Two has been suspected of forming backdoor alliances with outer worlds to boost economic growth and achieve self-sufficiency. He's finally become fed up with the central government's inertia. It may be only a matter of time before the unoccupied colonies push for independence."

Cornelius didn't care if the other three colonies rebelled. He'd just send in troops to restore order.

"If we don't end martial law, reinstate the imprisoned governors, and undertake drastic revitalization initiatives in the colonies, more rebellion will follow," Oviereya guaranteed. "Then what? We deploy more Guardians to engage in more homicide? We're already in jeopardy of violating Article II. This mercurial mess could easily implode if the government doesn't develop an action plan to address the colonies' poor state."

Cornelius seethed internally. He saw the chairwoman's words as a pitiful confession of weakness.

Oviereya kept delivering her message, her zeal matching that of someone campaigning for the Chief Executiveship. "Remember, the entire Interplanetary Union is watching us more closely than ever. When the Union leaders meet for the emergency summit next week, including our Chief Executive, the Commonwealth can be penalized or, worse, ousted by vote, if it is in violation of Article II *(which governed the use of force against a Union member's own people)* or even Article VI *(which mandated sound ethics)*."

We've outgrown our need for the Union, Cornelius thought.

Unlike him, Oviereya felt the Union was an indispensable ally. "To maintain incorporated status, we must comply with the Union Charter's articles. They're the criteria and guidelines that must be followed, or *else*. If we're expelled from the Union, times will get difficult. The Union Worlds are vital to our economy and defense.

"Without them, we'd be vulnerable in this vast galaxy, at the mercy of many technologically advanced foreign powers, like the Inkriex. The only reason hostile forces hesitate to attack the Commonwealth is because of our Union affiliation. If expelled, no one is coming to the Commonwealth's aid if it is attacked."

The anchorman signaled to Oviereya that her time was up. He had let her speak long enough and needed to be fair.

Cornelius grinned. His words were chambered like bullets, and he was ready to fire.

Her voice sharper than a knife, Oviereya gave her last statement. "While we've advanced technologically, economically, and militarily, it's still not enough to sever ties with the Union. Even if we could stand on our own, we're stronger together than apart."

"Mr. Gould, your thoughts?" the anchorman asked, now that the minority leader was done with her lengthy history analysis.

Cornelius spoke, his directness unadorned. "Rebuilding our *entire* civilization in this new galaxy takes time. It's important to remember that it's only been a few years since the Bhalkran and Phazharian conflicts. Those wars diminished resources and stalled progress on both Eden and Satellite One. Plus, the Commonwealth has an *astronomical* amount of debt to pay back to the intergalactic governments that helped establish our republic. That includes the Union Worlds."

He leaned forward slightly. "And yes, it's true that more funds are allocated to Eden than Satellite One, but there's a reason for that: Eden is the heart of humanity's intergalactic republic, and without the heart, all else dies. I'm not denying that more can be done to upgrade the colonies, but it's unrealistic for the government to undertake 'drastic revitalization initiatives' at this point."

Oviereya thought, *It's not unrealistic. You're just a coldhearted son of a bitch.*

Cornelius said, "I'm a man who gives people the reality of a situation, not what simply sounds good, unlike the chairwoman here." Oviereya grunted. Cornelius finished, saying, "An aid package would be sufficient to stabilize things."

Outrage engulfed Oviereya. "An aid package? That's like putting a bandage on a gunshot wound and hoping the bleeding stops. Again, a proposition that does zero to actually resolve the problem. We're spending billions of G-credits on military proliferation. I say we redirect funds from defense and use them to revitalize the colonies. And once the colonies' people experience progress, this internecine war will cease." She stared daggers at Cornelius, a look that could kill.

Cornelius shook his head. "Weakening the CDF's mission-essential functions would be detrimental to both the Commonwealth and the Union's safety. I believe we are fundamental to the Union's defense capability. That's why, even if I thought we had violated Article II, I wouldn't buy into the hysteria about us getting exiled. Without the Commonwealth, the Union would have fallen to the Phazharians, the Bhalkrans, or some other fiend."

Cornelius believed the Commonwealth had progressed enough to survive without the Union, and he saw the Charter's strict mandates on military force as a nuisance hindering the central government from delimiting the CDF. He also felt that the central government should have sole authority over planetary-partner approval, rather than waiting for the Union's consent, which he viewed as needless red tape.

In its infancy, the Commonwealth needed the Union, but much like a child that no longer needs a mother after reaching adulthood, Cornelius believed the Commonwealth had outgrown its dependency on the Union. The prior Chief, Jared Kerner's father, Thom Kerner, concurred.

Thom and Cornelius were military colleagues at one time and saw eye to eye on many affairs. Together, they set in motion a covert plan for the Commonwealth to achieve self-sufficiency. Military proliferation was a critical part of that plan, which was why Cornelius was hellbent on continuing to funnel G-credits into the defense-industrial complex instead of the colonies.

Leaving the Union to extricate the Commonwealth from the Charter was also part of the plan. Thom and Cornelius envisioned the Commonwealth evolving into an intergalactic superpower—essentially its own union of worlds—since other governments were becoming quasi-members as protectorates.

Therefore, for Cornelius, having the Commonwealth's incorporated status revoked would be a positive thing. But many of Cornelius' colleagues in Parliament, the people of the Commonwealth, and Chief Executive Jared Kerner opposed leaving the Union, so he catered to popular opinion to save face.

Cornelius added with cold aggression, "Right now, we cannot make grand promises to the colonies that we cannot keep, which is why I say an aid package must do for now."

To Oviereya, Cornelius was merely regurgitating the same dogma she had heard all her life, one designed to keep the colonies suppressed even longer.

Cornelius intended to drive his point home. "If we make

promises and fail to deliver, we'll face another wave of colonist transgression to combat, which could trigger yet another worrisome Union investigation.

"To end this internal conflict and keep the Union off our backs, we must intensify our efforts to wipe out the Coalition and other rebel groups, rather than give in to their demands. That's *another* reason to continue increasing military funding.

"Crushing these terrorists is the surest way to end the tiresome bid for independence from colonies One, Four, and Six—and to deter rebellion in the others."

Oviereya didn't like what she was hearing, and her face showed it. "So you believe more force is the only way to end the insurrection? There are no nonmilitary solutions?"

"Correct," Cornelius affirmed. "I also believe that to ensure the other colonies don't follow suit, additional . . . preventive measures are needed."

"Such as?" Oviereya asked calmly, camouflaging her disdain under a guise of professionalism.

"Routine inspections and audits of Two, Three, and Five's government operations. Permit mass surveillance of those *entire* colonies if necessary. In this State of Emergency, the Chief Executive has the power to do that. We need to keep tabs on *everything*. If we suspect any of the governments or citizens of those colonies are providing assistance to the Coalition or other rebel groups, then we launch investigations."

"More military-power expansion? Spoken like a power-hungry overlord," Oviereya said, tone tempered yet powerful.

A vein pulsed in Cornelius' temple. "No, spoken like someone who cares about his military and government too much to allow terrorists and their backers to beat them into passivity."

Time restraints forced the anchorman to end the debate and

ask his final question. "Election year is coming. The Chief Executive and Parliament seats are all up for grabs, and the political climate is very tense. Some people want a more aggressive solution to the war, such as Chairman Gould's; some want a peaceful one. But all are tired of it. People are seeking a new direction, a new vision. Rumors suggest both of you might run for the Chief Executive seat." He craned his head left, then right. "Any truth to that?"

"I have no comment at this time," Oviereya said.

Cornelius crossed his arms tightly over his chest. "Neither do I."

"Off," Stacie said. The holoscreen dematerialized into pixels and dissolved. "Maximum shade, please." The windows polarized, masking the sun's rays. "Set alarm for three minutes till landing."

"Alarm time logged," the flyer's computer said.

Stacie closed her eyes and dozed off.

• • •

Cornelius strode into the vestibule of the news station, shoved past a turnstile, and pushed his way out one of the four revolving doors. Outside, an armored black limo waited, flanked by an escort vehicle in front and another behind.

As he approached, one of the limo's doors clicked and hissed open. He ducked inside, settling beside a woman in a black pantsuit, her honey-blond pixie cut precise and professional. She was his executive assistant and apprentice, Gillian Bass.

"You did well, Sir," Gillian said.

Cornelius scoffed. Compliments meant nothing to him.

The lead escort vehicle slowly accelerated onto the four-lane street. At the proper interval, Cornelius' driver pulled behind it, and the rear escort vehicle followed in tandem.

A divider separated the front and passenger compartments,

allowing Cornelius to discuss confidential matters. "Any new developments from our intelligence on Orqron?" he asked Gillian.

She unlatched the attaché case on her lap, revealing a portable, high-efficiency information terminal.

She skimmed the report in front of her. "With the help of Orqron's Ministry of Defense, General Conlan's intelligence team has confirmed that—among the various tribes the Orqron Government is feuding with over land—the Nagamasulli Tribe was responsible for shooting down Zenith Combat Technologies' (ZCT) delivery transport.

"Perhaps if ZCT hadn't relied so heavily on the Orqron Government for protection and had bolstered its own security, this disaster could've been avoided."

"Perhaps," Cornelius replied. "But the Orqron Government is a Union-approved trading partner. Any interference with our arms industries' distribution services warrants a severe response. If it were up to me, I'd deploy a retaliation force to Orqron to obliterate the Nagamasulli Tribe. That would send a message to every tribe on the planet that the Commonwealth has zero tolerance for anyone attacking its people or disrupting its business practices.

"We need to instill fear in them. And though deploying a retaliation force to Orqron wouldn't violate the Union Charter, since the Nagamasulli drew first blood, Chief Executive Kerner believes engaging in active combat on Orqron isn't in the Commonwealth's best interest. He's too concerned about being perceived as a warmonger. We need a leader who prioritizes doing the right thing over their image, someone who isn't afraid to make tough calls, regardless of public scrutiny."

"Such as yourself, Sir?" Gillian asked, though she already knew the answer.

Cornelius didn't waste words. "Indeed. Now what of the

Falgoah Clan? Recently, I've become quite wary of them." Gillian fell silent as a growing sense of unease took hold. "Something bothering you?"

"It's just that . . . the central government casting an entire race of Zelaforians off their homeworld and turning them into refugees seems cruel," Gillian said ruefully. "The Falgoah and Chalderat are the only ones who should resolve their age-old feud."

There wasn't a detectable trace of compunction on Cornelius' face. "The Falgoah themselves are responsible for jeopardizing their existence," he replied frigidly. "The Ambassador Corps warned both the Falgoah and Chalderat about the consequences of violating the negotiated ceasefire. Instead of complying with it, the Falgoah made inroads into Chalderat territory and started another war.

"Disobedience and betrayal must have severe consequences. The Falgoah's belligerence could not be tolerated in the Commonwealth, just like the Coalition's belligerence cannot be tolerated. Now proceed with the report."

Gillian tapped a series of keys. A holovid ballooned from her info terminal. "Our surveillance drone recorded this footage. It shows a Falgoah clansman meeting with a man." She touched the holovid to enlarge the man's face. "Facial-recognition programs confirmed he is Drake Vikander, leader of the Vikander Faction."

Cornelius curled a finger around his chin, deep in thought. "So the Coalition has formed an alliance with the Falgoah."

"But why would the Falgoah ally with the Coalition? What do they stand to gain by the central government ceding to the Coalition's demands for independence or equality?"

"What they want is to return to their homeworld and reclaim their land from the Chalderat." The wheels in Cornelius' brain turned. "Perhaps the Coalition has grown exhausted with the government's refusal to compromise and is now planning a complete takeover of the government, which would allow them to invite the Falgoah back to Zelaforia."

Gillian powered off the info terminal. "That's a reasonable deduction."

"We should retaliate against the Nagamasulli Tribe. We should attack the Falgoah immediately; however, that video lacks sufficient proof that the Falgoah are working with our enemy. None of the Union leaders would authorize deploying Guardians to exterminate the Falgoah on the planet where they currently reside."

Gillian said, "Yes, and besides, the Union says the Falgoah have already paid their penalty with the Commonwealth's decision to exile them, ensuring they won't disrupt the peace in Noshkanu anymore. The Union claims there's no need either to attack or to monitor them. That means the video footage is illegal. So it can't be used to incriminate the Falgoah. In fact, it'd incriminate you."

"Not necessarily." Cornelius projected an air of certainty. "There are loopholes in every rule, regulation, and policy, loopholes a smart Chief Executive would exploit to keep an eye on a potential threat. We're surrounded by enemies seeking to tear apart our republic, and many of my confrères and the Chief Executive do *nothing*. Apparently, they'd rather be reactive than proactive, and inaction has negative consequences, as you know."

A memory of horrors beyond description seized Gillian's mind. She wrestled it away, then said, "Well, starting fights with our enemies before they've even tried to attack us might actually have negative consequences itself. If we do that, we could come off as the scourge of the universe, enabling our enemies to garner more support to overtake us."

Cornelius replied, "We'd simply crush their 'support' as well." Silent for a moment, he reflected. "I watched lands and oceans become mass graves because Earth's politicians hesitated to take preemptive action that could have prevented widespread Armageddon. I had to watch *billions* of people die.

"Those politicians wanted to be as *punctilious* as possible. They were frightened of being labeled as *belligerent*. Yet, their overly cautious approach to defense was the very thing that cost lives. I'll be damned if I let history repeat itself."

He gazed out the window. Uniquely shaped flyers soared high above. Richly dressed citizens, citizens he had sworn to protect, rode the slideways, which were moving conveyor-like sidewalks. Infographic pop-up holos appeared as the slideways transported the citizens past shops.

Cleaner golems sucked up trash and swept, keeping solar-paneled streets perfectly pristine. Far out, more buildings were being erected, their scaffolding and ironwork reaching a thousand feet heavenward. Construction flyers hovered.

Cornelius said, "Peacemongers like Chairwoman Amaechi want to divert funds from the defense budget to appease the colonists and cater to their emotional mandates. But our military might is why foreign hostiles have not overrun the Commonwealth and the Union. Debilitating our military, our greatest asset, would be disadvantageous.

"The chairwoman's compassion for the indigent is admirable, but right now, when we have enemies seeking to harm us, the indigent cannot be prioritized. If a few succumb to death in the meantime, so be it.

"The chairwoman's naiveté is further demonstrated by her willingness to placate the Coalition's demands. Giving in would make the central government appear weak."

Cornelius' motorcade swerved right, onto another street. A mix of Eden citizens and intergalactic tourists sauntered past storefronts and open-air cafés. Tourists from the Union Worlds and the Commonwealth's trading partners often flocked to Cornerstone City. It was a magnet for intergalactic tourism.

"The chairwoman also rebukes the social structure that AEGIS created." Cornelius' disdain for Oviereya seeped into his tone. "The system defined the proper function for everyone, ensuring we don't waste time, education, or resources preparing people for roles they aren't fit for. Some are simply better positioned for success in life as resource harvesters. The function AEGIS assigned to colonists aligns with the value they bring to society."

A grim mask settled on his face. "The integration of divisive immigrants into the CDF, such as the female cadet detained at the Academy today, proves that when AEGIS's social structure is deviated from, even slightly, the perfection of that structure is corrupted. The lottery experiment should be abolished."

Indignation rattled every fiber of his being. "Instead of worrying about colonists' frivolous woes, we need to expand our military's capability to hunt down the intergalactic sex traffickers, marauders, and other scourges terrorizing our great republic. Destroying this scum is the responsibility of the CDF.

"If I had the final say, I'd triple the number of expedition parties scouring the galaxies these fiends' operations span. They need to be annihilated completely, to rid the universe of them, so they will no longer harm us or any race of beings."

Cornelius had no limits when it came to doing what he thought was right to protect his people. When he was a U.S. soldier on Earth, his superiors reprimanded him for using unlawful interrogation tactics on POWs. As a general in the CDF during the Bhalkran War, he ordered bombs dropped on innocent Bhalkran villages to eradicate the Commonwealth's enemies hiding among them. He concluded that if a few must die to save the many, so be it, especially when the "many" were his own people. Such actions made him a controversial figure in the Commonwealth.

"We must have the strongest military possible," Cornelius declared. "We need to be feared. Neither Chairwoman Amaechi nor our feeble-minded Chief Executive is fit to lead the New Humanity. We must become the superpower we have the potential to be.

"No one knows what threats exist in the universe. It may be only a matter of time before something terrible comes to our doorstep. We must be ready."

Cornelius had tried to continue his and Thom's agenda to expand the military and its reach, an agenda hampered by filibuster and other bureaucratic red tape. It also didn't help that Jared was nowhere near the militant his father was, being more of a centrist.

"Truth is I'm hoping our incorporated status gets revoked, to unchain us from the Charter's constraints," Cornelius said. "Then we wouldn't have to play politics to fully utilize our military. Even if I were in the Chief Executive seat, it'd be next to impossible to convince two-thirds of the Parliament to rescind our incorporated status—because too many of my fellow conservatives have reservations about detaching from the Union. Maybe this civil war will be a blessing in disguise."

"So when *do* you plan to announce your intention to run?" Gillian asked.

"Next year's election is too far away. We need to steer the Commonwealth in a new direction as soon as possible. So I have decided to proceed with Operation New Wave."

"Kerner's assassination?"

"Yes. Not my favorite course of action but a necessary one, one to the liking of my . . . special benefactors." Benefactors who remained a mystery to Gillian. "Jared is nowhere near the Chief Executive his father was, a man I was proud to serve under. By decree, I'd be next in line to assume the Office of the Chief Executive once Kerner and Deputy Chief Norton are dead."

"What's your plan to eliminate them?"

"When Kerner—" In front of the limo, a burst of flames and smoke shot skyward, a ferocious boom assaulting the ears of every citizen outside. "What the hell?" The explosion flipped the lead escort vehicle onto its roof, glass and metal crunching.

The driver of the limo swerved around the ruined vehicle, tires squealing, then accelerated.

Both security personnel inside the mangled, flipped-over vehicle were dead.

Shouting, screaming pedestrians chaotically scrambled across the slideways.

Another explosion tossed the rear escort vehicle into a rollover. A third whipped the limo into an uncontrollable tailspin until it careered into a commercial van.

Breathing heavily, Gillian said to Cornelius, "Sir, you okay?"

Cornelius cringed. "Fine," he blurted. He reached a hand behind his neck, massaging the ache caused by whiplash.

Assassination attempts while traveling were the reason he preferred ground-based transportation. If he had been blown out of the sky in a flyer, he'd be dead.

What was left of the dashboard flashed colors and rang noisily. The driver's seat destroyed, Cornelius' chauffeur was dead.

Gillian stiffly reached for the sidepiece stowed in her harness, shoulder hurting. "Sir, stay inside." She pulled the door handle. A click sounded, yet the warped door remained stubbornly shut. "Damn it!"

She pulled the handle again and threw her throbbing shoulder into the door, prying it ajar. She rammed her shoulder into the door one more time, exacerbating the pain. It shrieked open, and she stepped out, heels clicking the pavement.

With a shaky two-handed grip, she extended her firearm and raked the air from left to right, searching for hostiles. Her heart thudded as her memory reunited her with the mayhem of urban warfare: people screaming all around her, staccato pops of gunfire, noisy sirens. It was a killing hell she didn't want to relive.

Her nervous eyes scanned the devastated street. A bead of sweat snaked down the bridge of her nose.

She spotted dead Union World citizens, two Rumanoahans and one Varsh'Ru. Nearby lay a dead Orsodonian from the Commonwealth's trading partner Orsodonia.

This was the first time foreigners had died on Eden soil. The incident was bound to cause political chaos. Gillian stood within history in the making.

She dragged a lungful of smoke-scented oxygen into her nostrils, exhaled, and stabilized her posture. It had been years since she was in a high-stress combat scenario.

She said into her government-issued wristcom, "Mayday." It was the call sign for Cornelius' emergency evac flyer.

A droning sound neared.

Alarmed, she spun to her right as a hoverbike whooshed to a stop in front of her. A helmeted man in dark clothing reached for the pistol holstered on his thigh.

Gillian's heart hammered her chest. "Fuck!" Military reflexes kicking in, she yanked the door closer and quickly sank down into a crouch.

Shots rang out. Sparks flew as a barrage of bullets ricocheted off the armored door. The mystery assassin emptied a full magazine and thumbed the release.

The sound of the magazine clattering to the ground was Gillian's cue. Her adrenaline spiked, and she rose, killer instinct in her gray eyes.

The assassin slapped a new magazine into his pistol, but it was too late. Gillian raised her gun and double-tapped the trigger. The weapon kicked in her hands as it discharged two shots.

The bullets slammed into the assassin's vest. He recoiled from the impact, and his pistol slipped from his grasp.

With deadly neohuman precision, Gillian locked him in her gun's sights and fired the fatal round. The bullet shattered the glass visor of his helmet, piercing his skull between the eyes.

A mist of red liquid spritzed the air as he fell to the ground.

Hands trembling, Gillian remained on high alert. Her eyes scanned the area for more assassins. "Stay inside, Sir!" she ordered Cornelius. "Your evac team is on the way!"

"I'm well aware of security protocol, Ms. Bass!" Cornelius snapped, a high level of agitation in his voice.

As the man responsible for implementing martial law, Cornelius had become a primary target for violent anti-government radicals and fringe groups. The mere rumor of him possibly running for Chief Executive only emboldened them further.

Gillian stood in front of the limo, maintaining her aplomb.

Sirens wailed, growing louder as they got closer. The roar of an incoming aircraft drew Gillian's attention skyward. Cornelius' evac flyer approached.

• • •

Stacie's air-cab closed in on a palatial mansion nestled in the lowlands on the outskirts of Cornerstone City, gliding above green pastures that extended as far as the eye could see.

The flyer's alarm chimed three minutes before touchdown, as programmed. Stacie stirred and rubbed her eyes.

"We have reached our destination," the computer informed her, lifting the windows' tinting to reveal the picturesque blue sky. The flyer slowly descended. A low pulsing hum was followed by a quiet clunk as it came to a stop. "Thank you for choosing Air Escort." A red flashing warning-notification told Stacie to yield movement. "Please ride with us again." The canopy opened, and all warning lights dimmed to black.

Stacie's seat belt unbuckled automatically. A chirp signaled it was safe to exit. She swung one stocking-covered leg out, then the other, and stood, stepping into the heat. She arched her back, stretching her stiff joints.

The cab received its next passenger's location and zoomed away.

Stacie approached the wrought-iron fence, her high heels making a soft clacking sound against the pavement. She pressed her palm to the electronic gate's biometric scanner. Once her identity was confirmed, the gate screeched open along its guiding rail, granting her entry into the immense, well-manicured yard.

She walked down a winding flagstone path framed by trimmed hedges. Above, birds chirped in green-leafed trees bearing brightly colored berries. All around the estate, colorful flowers bloomed. In the distance, greenhouses stood. They were where the Spencers' farmers cultivated crops for them.

The path looped around a sculpted fountain of an angel clothed in a tunic, her wings outstretched. It then continued onward.

Stacie reached the mansion, an incredible feat of modern architecture that had more windows than one could count. She walked up the five steps to the colonnaded veranda. The overhead shelter provided much-needed relief from the sun's simmering heat.

She wiped sweat from her glistening brow. Before she could scan her biometrics again, one of the large ornamental doors creaked open. An elderly bald man stood in the doorway. He had a bushy gray mustache and wore an elaborate purple tux.

"Greetings, Madam Spencer," the butler said. Security sensors had informed him of Stacie's arrival.

"Clifton, good to see you."

Clifton bowed from the waist. "You as well, Madam Spencer."

"I take it Mother and Father are furious."

"Indeed. You joined the Defense Force without their blessing."

Stacie scoffed. "I don't need their blessing." She turned her nose up and folded her arms, leaning her hip against the veranda's balustrade. "I'm a grown-ass woman, not a *fucking* child. I told them I was enlisting and that nothing they said could stop me."

Clifton had hoped the CDF had changed her, but it hadn't. He was still staring into blue eyes full of vanity, arrogance, and stubbornness. That, however, was her mother's fault.

Stacie took a long, slow breath, calming down from her rant, but a rant not without merit. She unsnapped the red fasteners on her service jacket. "So, where are Mom and Dad, at some *high-profile* meeting?" she asked, her tone rightfully snappish.

"Your mother awaits you in the common room. The baron is away on business."

Stacie wrestled off her jacket. Patches of sweat wet her white dress shirt.

After neatly folding the jacket and wrapping the cape around it, she passed the garment off to Clifton. Her voice carried a trace of worry as she asked, "How is Father, by the way?"

"His health has not been the best, but he is managing."

Stacie undid the first three buttons of her shirt and tugged on the collar for air. "Good." That news relieved her worry.

"Shall I escort?"

Stacie replied, "No, I'm a big girl. I can escort myself." She was direct and independent as usual, Clifton thought. Some of her better traits, though. "Take that uniform piece to my room for me."

"Yes, Madam."

"Thank you."

Stacie crossed a broad, lengthy hall, passing housekeeping golems tending to the mansion's upkeep. The skylights set into the ceiling spilled sunlight onto the expensive red carpet. She braced herself for confrontation, her features steeled by courage.

The hall widened into a grand oval foyer where a semicircle of family portraits hung. Stacie stilled and tilted her chin upward, staring thoughtfully at the hard-copy photos of the cute little girl with a long, plaited ponytail. The girl's adorable smile stretched from ear to ear, puffing out her cheeks. But that radiant smile was all show for the camera, a masquerade. Her small, innocent eyes were devoid of happiness.

Stacie's perfectionist mother had tolerated nothing short of excellence from her in academia and every single avocation she pursued. That constant pressure marred Stacie's childhood.

She thought back to the one-year horror of the Eight Elite's preparatory school, where they sent their seventeen-year-olds to prepare them for post-high school education. She dreaded the days spent learning how to "walk like a lady" or performing absurd exercises, such as balancing pewter dishes atop her palms or head to master balance and coordination.

It was no wonder that after enrolling at Cadwell Institute of Higher Learning for her undergraduate studies, she went totally wild. Her first two years revolved around alcohol, parties, recreational drugs, and sex binges. By year three, however, she longed for a life beyond frivolous decadence and the expectation of someday running the family business. So, after graduation, she enlisted in the CDF.

Stacie walked through the archway in the middle of the foyer and entered a richly decorated, well-furnished common room.

Dark rugs spanned the floor. Landscape paintings adorned the walls. Windows framed by lavish curtains let in sunshine.

Her daunting mother, Darlene Spencer, sat in a high-backed armchair fit for a queen, an unlit fireplace behind her. She wore a black dress with ruffled sleeves and an ankle-length ruffled hem. On her finger was a gold ring bearing the family crest—a man wearing a crown and holding a sword atop a horse standing on its hind legs. Glaring at Stacie intensely, she genteelly and silently sipped from a ceramic cup of hot tea.

Stacie went up to her. "Mother," she spat in a fiery tone, anticipating an earful of chastising.

The cup tinked the glass coffee table as Darlene set it down. Her expression spoke volumes about her feelings toward her daughter's new military career. Brows knitted, she heaved herself to her feet and then swung her hand, smacking Stacie's cheek.

Darlene was proud of the financial empire she and her husband had built. Stacie was the heir to it all, and to Darlene, it was time she started acting like it. "You insolent little degenerate. I thought we raised you better than this."

Stacie rubbed her stinging flesh. The slap that was all too familiar put a frown on her face. "Selfish? I—"

"Quiet," Darlene thundered, cutting her off. "Your father is ill, and you go off to play Guardian? You sully our estate with this . . . uniform?"

Stacie shot back, a hard edge in her voice. "This uniform is a symbol of prestige, Mother." Maybe to "regular" Edenites, but not the alpha, the Eight Elite. "And Father—"

Darlene interrupted Stacie again. "You have an obligation to your family. Your grooming to be our successor was to begin. You were supposed to attend the quarterly assemblies of the eight family heads. You were to familiarize yourself with our organizational structure. What the hell were you thinking?" She threw her arms up.

"I'll take up the torch after you guys croak," Stacie said, causing Darlene to freeze in shock. "Right now I need to—" Stacie searched for the right words. "I need to prove I'm more than . . . more than *this*." She whipped her arms out wide.

Darlene wrinkled her nose. "More than *what*?"

Stacie sighed. Her tone softened. "More than just some . . . some blue-blooded, silver-spoon nepo baby." Her eyes pled for a semblance of understanding. "Is that so hard for you to comprehend, Mother?"

Darlene shook her head in disappointment and huffed. "Your father could pass any year, any month, any day now. You are to succeed us. Instead, you risk getting yourself killed? Such fucking stupidity." Her tone became even frostier. "You need to live up to the responsibilities that come with being a Spencer."

Stacie rolled her eyes. "Forget it." She whirled around to leave, footsteps landing hard.

"Stacie Lynette Spencer, where do you think you're going?" Darlene demanded of her wayward daughter.

"To my room. I've got a graduation banquet to rest up for. Tomorrow, I leave for my duty station. Don't expect me to come to you in the morning to say bye."

Darlene pinged Stacie's implant. Stacie rejected her Link request, a sign of total disobedience for a daughter of the Eight.

Get lost, Mom, Stacie thought.

Darlene muttered under her breath. She figured maybe she should've slapped Stacie harder.

Stacie ascended the carpeted staircase to her room. She couldn't wait to arrive at her duty station, an escape from the stringent expectations that came with being a daughter of the Eight. Her parents expected her to take over the family business, leaving her no say in her own destiny. She was to always conduct herself in a moral, ethical, and honorable manner and never act in a way that would disgrace or humiliate the family.

She recalled the night she got her first DUI and totaled her car, which she probably should've put on autodrive. After explaining the incident to her parents, they subjected her to the archaic, draconian disciplinary measures outlined in the Eight Elite's rule book. Even the slightest infraction was unacceptable.

As the female head of household, Stacie's mother decided the punishment: ten belt lashes to her back. Just like when she was a child. Foolishness, in her eyes.

She opened the door to her room and toed off her heels. Next, she shrugged out of her shirt and slid off her stockings. Then she pushed her skirt down to her ankles and stepped out of it.

Clad in white cotton lingerie, she plopped onto her bed as the cool air conditioning soothed her skin. Beside her was her uniform's service jacket, placed there by Clifton.

Golden light poured in from the window, bathing her in its warmth. The stunning view of green meadows and rolling hills outside had always given her a sense of tranquility, even during the harshest moments of her childhood.

She glanced at the stark white walls surrounding her and flattened her lips together. After butting heads with her mother, she needed a more soothing color to clear her mind. "Change wall color to pink," she instructed the mansion's virtual assistant. A soft pink hue washed over the walls. Easily her favorite color. "Better."

She unscrewed the locking lid of the humidor on her nightstand, extracted a cigarette, and flicked a lighter to life. Tucking the cigarette between her lips, she inhaled deeply, letting the nicotine scour her mind of her and Darlene's past quarrels—memories dredged up by their argument downstairs. She was on the verge of ditching the habit, thanks to Randy—Mr. Righteousness, Health, and Fitness. But today would have to be a cheat day.

Her wristcom rang.

She ground out the cigarette in the ashtray and tapped her wristcom to accept the call.

Oviereya's voice flowed from the micro-speaker. "I just wanted to congratulate you on your graduation. I'm proud of you."

"At least someone is."

"Sounds like your parents aren't too thrilled?"

"Of course they aren't. You know them."

"Well, I commend you for making such a life-altering decision and redirecting your future down a path you desire. However, you still have family responsibilities. Don't forget about them."

"Yeah, yeah." Stacie changed the subject. "I saw you on a newscast earlier. Are you gonna run for Chief Executive?"

"I'm . . . considering it."

"I think you should totally do it."

"I have to go. Parliament has an emergency meeting in an hour. Again, congratulations." The call disconnected.

Stacie closed her drowsy eyes.

Her life was on the brink of transformation. Until now, every credit in her bank account had belonged to her parents, and they could take them all away on a whim. They owned her life, but not anymore. She was her own woman now. No more being caged.

She had postponed the burden of preparing to inherit Spencer Enterprises until she decided she was ready. She was *free*. And soon, she'd be on Satellite One, helping to end the insurrection. After that, maybe the CDF would send her unit to a Mission

World. And Randy would be with her. She envisioned a life of just helping people and making love to her boyfriend.

A calmness settled over her as she drifted off to sleep.

• • •

Randy, wearing a tailored black suit, escorted Stacie into a banquet hall filled with circular tables, his arm anchored around hers.

The sparkly red dress that clung to Stacie's frame made her a sight to behold. Although civilian attire was permitted for the evening, the thigh-high slit and the plunging neckline flaunting her breasts violated the dress code. Stacie's audacity knew no bounds. She had a splendid physique and wasn't bashful about showcasing it, always eager to be the center of attention.

Servers in white aprons set up buffets. A female chef, wearing a hairnet, wheeled in a rack of exquisite dishes from the kitchen. Until dinner was served, hundreds of sharply dressed graduates from multiple classes mingled.

Randy and Stacie strolled about, taking in the convivial atmosphere of the evening.

Jarius walked past them in a snazzy black tux and red bow tie, laughing merrily with his date, a well-endowed light brown woman sporting a silver halterneck dress and stilettos. "Lookin' good, Randy," he commented, his natural charm shining bright. He sipped his highball.

As Jarius and his cute n' curvy companion went to a table, she whispered something into his ear and pressed her glossy red lips to his cheek. He laughed out loud and rested his free hand on the small of her bare back. The evening seemed to be off to a good start for him.

"So how'd you and Specialist Ford become so buddy-buddy?" Stacie asked Randy.

"We met and became tight during our senior year at

Commonwealth University."

"I see."

Randy and Stacie navigated throngs of Guardians dressed in immaculate suits, tuxedos, gowns, and dresses. Some women eyed Stacie contemptuously, as her refusal to conform to clothing guidelines—to unapologetically show off—suggested she thought herself special. Men, though, welcomed the sight of her exposed flesh. After all, she was quite the physical specimen.

"Randal Scott!" came a powerful, jovial voice.

A man approached Randy and Stacie, his burgundy suit barely hiding his hefty physique. He had a neatly trimmed goatee, and a cybernetic prosthetic replaced his left hand.

Randy smiled upon seeing him. "General Conlan."

General Michael Conlan was the Chief of Defense Force Intelligence. His towering height, muscular physique, and booming voice could be intimidating when first encountered, but once you got to know him, you'd find him exceedingly affable.

He treated his subordinates as if he'd known them a lifetime, making them feel comfortable confiding in him about anything— family, relationships, career, and so on. Even during his time as a platoon leader, he'd fellowship with his men as if he were their friend. This informal attitude earned him tremendous respect.

However, those familiar with him knew that his kindness didn't equate to weakness. If you got on his bad side, disobeyed directives, or neglected responsibility and duty, you'd incur his wrath, receiving the harshest of reprimands.

"Randal, it's been a while," Conlan said. "I haven't seen you in —"—he curled a finger around his chin—"two years?"

"Sounds about right, Sir."

Awe lit Stacie's gaze as it lingered on her lover. "You know General Conlan?"

"He's a family friend," Randy replied.

Conlan shifted his friendly topaz eyes toward Stacie. Strong cheekbones; a thin, pretty nose; piercing blue eyes; and an attractive figure. Randy had snagged himself a treasure, Conlan thought. She reminded him of his late wife when she was her age. "And who might this *tantalizing* young woman be?" he asked.

Stacie replied, "Stacie Lyn Spencer, Sir."

Conlan's brows jumped. "Ah, daughter of Patrick and Darlene Spencer." He leaned his massive frame inward and politely kissed Stacie's hand. "A pleasure to meet you, dear."

Randy delicately coiled an arm around Stacie's waist. "Sweetheart, could the general and I have a moment?"

Stacie planted a kiss on his lips. "Ten minutes, babe, then I come hunting." She twirled and, with the elegance of a runway model, strutted past a male caterer balancing hors d'oeuvres atop a tray. He did a double take to be sure his eyes weren't exaggerating her beauty.

"Quite the catch," Conlan commented. "A member of the Scott and Spencer families getting together is a dynasty waiting to be born. She'll bear you excellent children."

"Let's not get ahead of ourselves. There are no wedding bells planned anytime soon. We're . . . still testing the waters."

"Well, everything happens in stages," Conlan provided.

Randy conspiratorially glanced left and right to ensure no one was within earshot and changed the subject, lowering his voice. "General, I'd like to thank you for making sure I got stationed at Lima Company. You have my deepest gratitude. Now I can see that my father pays for Mom's death."

Exercising forethought, Conlan gestured toward the balcony with a tilt of his head. He wanted to have a private conversation. "Let's step outside."

Randy looked bemused. What was this about? "Sure." He tucked his hands into his pants' pockets and followed the general.

Conlan pushed open the glass double doors leading out onto the curved balcony. He and Randy stepped into the warm night air.

The doors shut behind them, muting all the joyous merrymaking of the newly initiated Guardians.

Conlan relaxed his arms over the balcony's safety wall and sighed apprehensively, staring at the glowing city lights that went on forever in all directions.

A variety of flyers streaked here and there under the night sky's sparkling constellation.

Hands still in his pockets, Randy stood in silence, waiting for Conlan to speak.

Conlan contemplated his words carefully. "Randy—" He paused, reconsidering his decision. Putting aside his qualms, he continued. "—sometimes war isn't . . . black and white. There are . . . gray areas."

Randy cocked a brow. "What are you saying?"

Conlan said, "There are two sides to this war." No shit, Randy thought. "We . . . we choose the side we believe has the moral high ground. The side embodying our values the most."

Randy's brows came together. "Wait a minute. Are you trying to rationalize that bastard's betrayal?" The memory of A-1 Defense Solutions erupting in flames haunted his mind.

Conlan turned around. He pushed forward an open palm, halting the specialist from jumping to conclusions. "Listen, I'm just saying—"

Randy pointed a finger at Conlan and cut him off before he could form another word. "No, *you* listen. I wanted to fight the Coalition under my father's command. Imagine hearing, just two months before BCT, that your father, the man you wanted to emulate, had been confirmed to have gone rogue and joined the enemy.

"I thought it was some mistake. Maybe he was undercover or something. I came up with every excuse I could imagine. Then, three weeks before my departure date, the Coalition starts attacking the CDF's defense contractors here on Eden. A-1 Defense Solutions was hit, and my mother was killed. And who took part in that terrorist attack? My father. I was even Linked with Mom when that explosion stole her life."

Conlan lowered his chin in sympathy, chewing on Randy's words.

Randy said, "A week later, I attended my mother's funeral, but there was nothing left of her to lay to rest." Grief throbbed in his heart. "I will make my father pay."

"It's not like Arson premeditated her death. It was an accident, Randy. Arson didn't mean to—"

"It doesn't matter if it was an accident or not," Randy countered. He wondered how Conlan would feel if his dad had accidentally killed his mom. He wanted . . . No, he needed Arson to pay. Arson was the bane of his existence.

"He regretted what happened that night," Conlan insisted, his conviction absolute. "He never meant to cause Kathleen any hardship by leaving to—"

A questioning gleam entered Randy's eyes. "You sound as if you have firsthand knowledge of his thoughts and feelings. Did you have contact with him? Do you have contact with him now? Has there been any collusion between you two?" Stonewalling, the general said nothing. Randy's volume rose. "Conlan!" he pushed, in pursuit of answers.

The doors to the balcony squealed open, ending the standoff.

A tipsy Stacie strode forward, a wineglass of something strong in hand. She concentrated hard to maintain her balance. The alcohol had definitely taken hold. "Ten minutes are up, babe." She hooked her arm around Randy's. "C'mon, let's go," she said, voice unnecessarily loud and words slightly slurred.

Randy's feet stumbled as Stacie wrested him from the general. "Stacie, I—"

Conlan raked his fingers through the air, shooing Randy away. "We're done here, Specialist Scott. Go enjoy yourself."

As Stacie dragged Randy away, he peered over his shoulder at Conlan. Ire creased his brow. *This isn't over yet, General.* The balcony doors shut.

Conlan glared at his cybernetic prosthetic. *Thanks to you, Arson, I lost only a hand. I'm sorry you chose the other side, my friend.*

In Stacie's company, Randy forgot about his fallout with Conlan and engaged in dancing, dining, drinking, and conversation for the rest of the evening.

CHAPTER TWO

Arson Scott, his face black and blue, sat slumped against a dingy wall. Randy stood over him, grimacing, and leveled a pistol at his forehead. Hesitantly, he began squeezing the trigger. Then he suddenly froze. After three tense seconds, he fired. Arson's brains splattered over the wall and . . .

"Attention, we are nearing atmospheric entry," the shuttle pilot said over the intercom, taking Randy out of the dream.

He groaned awake as the hull shuddered.

The shuttle exited Hyperspace Leap, and the rainbow of colors outside the windows dissolved to reveal the black of normal space. Ahead, Satellite One was in view.

The fifty new Guardians assigned to Charlie Battalion's Lima Company sat in their BDUs, awaiting planetfall.

Randy ran a hand down his face. He stared through a porthole into the dark void, his expression unreadable. *Father.* Even in his sleep, the traitor bedeviled his mind.

Stacie awoke, too, rubbing her groggy eyes. She had slept off the hangover from all the drinking she did at last night's banquet.

"Hey, you okay, babe?" she asked, then yawned.

Randy's response came in the form of a quiet, unconvincing, "Yeah." He gripped his armrests tightly, banishing Arson from his thoughts for the time being.

Stacie didn't have to access their Link to know what was weighing on him. She knew he was thinking about his father. Wearing concern on her face, she placed a comforting hand over his. There was much chaos within him. She was happy to be a source of relief. After all, no one should have to hurt alone.

Jarius sat two rows up from them. Like all the Eden-born Guardians aboard, he had never actually visited a colony and seen the grim conditions the downtrodden complained about. He'd heard stories about newly trained Guardians, upon their first deployment to a colony, becoming so shaken by what they saw that they empathized with the locals and even defected. The unknown had him twiddling his thumbs. But he wasn't alone; everyone aboard was a little on edge.

As the shuttle penetrated Satellite One's atmosphere, the hull's metallic rattling grew louder. After planetfall, the shuttle descended into a sky of gray clouds, bumping against turbulence.

Once over Colony Four, the pilot routed a trajectory toward Annex 13, a small CDF outpost occupied by Charlie Battalion's Lima Company. Their mission was to keep the peace in Zone 03 of Sector 05. Zone 03 encompassed the towns of Halfin, Stanlow, Guthram, and Holbeck *(one urban district)*, along with a scattering of interim settlements. Captain Arnold Seymour led the company. He was Arson's XO and friend. He assumed command after Arson's desertion.

Three platoons currently made up the entire company. Because of the upcoming summit and the possibility of being expelled from the Union, Chief Executive Jared Kerner had mandated a troop surge to bolster the CDF's manpower. Now fifty of the recent Academy graduates were being sent to Lima Company to form a fourth platoon.

A platoon of callow Guardians with zero combat experience wasn't ideal, but desperate times called for desperate measures. Platoons of novices were being organized across the occupied colonies to dismantle the insurrection. The central government needed to convince the Union leaders that the revolt was under control.

Below stretched a patchwork of barren red earth and industrial towns. Infertile land made ninety percent of Colony Four unfarmable, but the colony was rich in valuable rocks and minerals. As a result, refineries, mines, and manufacturing plants served as the primary sources of income generation for its citizens. Colony Four also played a vital role in defense, as its citizens mined and refined sixty-seven percent of Satellite One's dimatanium, a metal element used to produce an armor alloy for the CDF's war machines.

With insurgent groups growing in number, anonymous hit-and-run attacks on Guardians becoming more frequent, and public displays of civil unrest escalating into violent clashes, Colony Four was becoming a powder keg.

Randy took in the magnificent, desolate mountains; valleys; and plateaus passing by below. *So this is your home colony, Father.* In Colony Four resided all of Arson's family, flesh and blood Randy hadn't met. Though he was born here, this would be his first time setting foot on its soil. Arson had told him a lot about the colony, but seeing it now made everything feel more real.

"This is Air Transit Control. Incoming aircraft, identify yourself," said a voice from the shuttle's comms, audio choppy.

"This is passenger shuttle niner-six-niner," the pilot replied.

"Requesting permission to land."

A burst of static followed before a response came through. "Permission granted."

The shuttle soared above a landing port crowded with aerodynes. As it slowed into a controlled vertical descent, its braking jets flared. After the landing struts deployed, it touched down between two boxy air freighters. Then the engines powered down with a hiss, followed by the creak of cooling metal.

The starboard hatch slid open, and a set of stairs extended to the tarmac.

Restraints clicked as the Guardians unbuckled themselves. Some stood from the fold-up seats and stretched, their stiff joints cricking.

Heavy, purposeful footfalls thudded up the stair-ramp. A six-foot-tall sergeant first class marched into the fuselage, sporting a white-blond crew cut. His unfriendly visage and the dangerous glint in his eyes made it clear he was all business.

Crossing his arms over his chest, he took care of the formalities. "I'm Sergeant First Class Lars Freeman. I'll be your platoon sergeant." He paced up and down the gangway, hands clasped behind his back.

There was an air of intimidation in the way Lars spoke and carried himself. He was clearly a no-nonsense person, a total hard case. "All of you survived hellacious warrior trials to wear that uniform. That means you have the heart of a warrior. But you're green. You've never been downrange, and trust me, it's a whole different beast in theater compared to BCT. So don't go thinking you're some sorta stud just because you aced some tac-sims and know how to operate a Shell."

Grouses, disgruntled muttering, and hard expressions came from Guardians who just got their pride hurt.

"Don't worry, you're in good hands," Lars said. "Your squad and team leaders are all adept combat professionals. I'm certainly no stranger to combat." The scar bisecting his brow and left cheek was a memento from one of his many missions, and his service sketch included the Phazharian and Bhalkran wars. "I can't promise all of you will live, but I can promise I'll do my damnedest to give you the best shot possible at staying alive.

"Some might say I'm a hard-ass, but if you follow my orders and are where you're supposed to be on time, then we're good. Do the opposite and *piss* me the fuck off, then . . . Well, let's just say you don't wanna cross that line. Am I clear, Fourth Platoon?"

Everyone shouted, "Yes, Sergeant!" Formalities taken care of.

"Good. Tomorrow, it's game on, because we have a mission. Mission brief starts at oh-seven-hundred hours. Leave your gear on board for now. You can off-load the shit after I give you the tour. Let's head out."

The Guardians filed out of the shuttle, down the stair-ramp, into the cool weather of the overcast day.

Annex 13 sat on the seaward edge of Halfin, providing a splendid, unobstructed view of the West Ocean. Off the coastline were scenic island landmasses lined with mountains.

While crossing the tarmac, Stacie heard a woman close behind her say, "Hey, princess, don't think you're gonna get special treatment. Your high n' mighty status doesn't mean squat here. Nobody's gonna hand you anything, especially not rank. And nobody's gonna coddle you or kiss your li'l privileged ass."

Stacie recognized the Russian-sounding voice and looked over her shoulder. A pale-skinned woman with an upturned nose and indigo eyes walked closely behind her. The woman's hot-pink highlights stood out boldly against the black tresses of her bobcut, and a conspicuous mole sat to the right of her mouth.

She was Private Emilia Rhineheart. Her adversarial relationship with Stacie had started during BCT. Emilia, a beneficiary of the lottery, was one of the few colony-born cadets in the class of Alpha 9-5. She formed a clique with the others, and Stacie, not only a Highborn but also a child of one of the Eight Elite—the uppermost echelon of the wealthy—became a prime target for their ire. Together, they bullied her and attempted to sabotage her success on more than one occasion.

I didn't know her ass was aboard, Stacie thought. "I'm not here for handouts," she snapped. "I work for my achievements, so can it, Private."

"The loudmouths yapping their goddamn traps need to shut the hell up," Lars said from the front of the platoon.

Stacie grunted. She had heard childish gibes like Emilia's too many times. That was part of why she'd nearly driven her body into the ground to earn the title of Warrior Extraordinaire, an accolade earned through blood, sweat, and grit.

Emilia knew Stacie was seething beneath her controlled facade. Determined to needle her, she lowered her voice so Lars wouldn't overhear. She couldn't help herself. "Pissed off, aren't you, princess?" She chuckled. *Your sensitivity meter's always been easy to push.*

Stacie smirked and whispered back. "All bases have a sparring suite, right? Meet me there at twenty-three-hundred hours so this princess can shut that big mouth of yours."

Emilia gave a smirk of her own. "Deal."

Randy fell into step beside Lars. "Can you tell us anything about the mission tomorrow?"

Eager to learn. I like that. Maybe he has leadership potential, Lars thought. Loudly, he said, "Listen up, everyone! Citizens for Change (CFC) is a nonviolent activist group here in Colony Four. They organize peaceful demonstrations and protests. They're staging several rallies in Halfin tomorrow. The problem is you never know what fanatics might join these rallies and turn them into anarchy.

"Lima Company has been tasked with keeping the peace and ensuring things don't get out of hand. It's basic crowd control. But don't let that dull your situational awareness. There are malcontents out there who know there'll be a CDF presence and can't wait to take potshots at us."

Lars showed his new Guardians the motor pool and outdoor track, then went indoors and showed them the mess hall, physical training center, infirmary, and the platoon's assembly room.

The group strode down a corridor. Two sergeants in civvies approached them from the open lounge area at an easy pace.

"These the newbies, Sergeant Freeman?" the blond one asked, then took a sip of the energy drink in his hand.

"Fourth Platoon, meet Staff Sergeant Jason Mansford, leader of First Squad." Lars' chummy smile conveyed Jason was a Guardian he held in high regard. "Depending on how the roster shapes up, he'll be the squad leader for some of you. And though he can be a cocky son of a bitch, he's one of L-Company's best. Check out his service sketch and you'll probably agree." He gestured to Jason's dark-haired buddy. "This is Sergeant Nico Fleming, leader of Second Squad." He put his business face back on and proceeded. "Now c'mon, we gotta finish up."

As Stacie walked by, her beauty caught Jason's eye. Eager to make contact, he pinged her implant.

A slight look of annoyance swept over Stacie's face as she rejected Jason's Link request. *Yeah, right, jerk. Like I'd ever Link with someone I don't know.*

Jason pulled his eyes away and moved on.

Nico jovially elbowed Jason's shoulder as they parted from the new arrivals. "Easy there. I know what's on your mind. You can't go sleeping with all the ladies now. Practice some self-restraint."

Stacie heard them, faintly. *Womanizers.*

Lars took the platoon into the armory through two automatic sliding doors. The room hummed with electrical current. Encased in glass-pod alcoves were rows of Shells plugged into power receptacles. Above the alcoves were digital displays of Guardians' names.

"This new model of Shell is a huge upgrade compared to the old M-X01 chassis you operated in BCT," Lars said. "More advanced weapons. A lighter, closer-fitting design to cut down on the bulk and reduce mobility lag." He patted one of the glass casings. "I think you'll like these babies a hell of a lot more. They even have a more advanced CPU incorporated and an AI Combat Assistant called Oracle."

"AI Combat Assistant?" a male Guardian whispered inquisitively.

Lars said, "As you know, a Guardian and their Shell are kinda yoked via cerebral interface. You and your Shell's CPU and the new AI assistant operate in concert as a single fighting entity.

"Your implant constantly feeds your suit's CPU data about your combat coefficients, such as ease of movement, aim, speed, reflexes, trigger squeeze, the works. Using that data as feedback, the CPU makes performance evaluations and calibrates your suit for optimal combat effectiveness. Your Oracle reads that same data, along with the CPU's evaluations, to learn more about you and better assist you."

Jarius chimed in. "So, there's like a running conversation going on between our cerebral implant, the CPU, and the Oracle. We transmit thought-commands and . . . brain data or something; then the Shell's tech receives and responds to what we transmit to help us out."

"Sounds about right, Specialist Ford," Lars said. "It's like a constant feedback loop."

"And this AI Combat Assistant, just how sentient can it get?"

"The bounds of the AI, and even the chip in our noggins, are still unknown to us and even the Quilgarians, who made it all." Lars went to a wall panel and keyed a three-digit code. The dials lit up, and a section of the wall shifted aside—one of two entries into the adjoining room beyond.

Fourth Platoon entered an octagonal space of computer workstations displaying complex nomenclature and mind-boggling reams of data. Seams along the walls and floor gleamed blue, and the room resounded with electronic chirping, humming, and buzzing.

"This is the Nerve Center," Lars said.

Gray-uniformed analysts sitting at the glowing panels and monitors spoke technical lingo.

A wall-mounted screen displayed a newscast. The anchorman said, "An hour ago, reporter Milan Jung caught up with Secretary Gould. Here's the exchange."

The replay showed Cornelius standing on the landing above the steps of the Parliament Building. The reporter and her cameraman hurriedly approached him from behind.

"Secretary Gould, a word?" Milan asked.

Cornelius turned. "Of course," he said. He wasn't in the mood for the press.

"What do you say to critics who call your execution of martial law in the colonies a mess?"

"I've said it before: The CDF had never handled this kind of operation. The early phase was bound to be rough. That phase is over. We've got everything under control now."

"Some people think your viceroys *(in charge of martial law)* have given the CDF too much leeway, transforming the colonies into a nightmare? Are your viceroys exempt from your supervision?"

"My viceroys give the CDF room to do their job, just like I give them room to do theirs," Cornelius said, his tone firm. "They don't need micromanaging. Neither do their forces."

"These viceroys are all former military colleagues appointed by you. Some call it an old-fashioned good-ole-boy network, and—"

The replay kept rolling as Fourth Platoon huddled around Lars.

Lars pointed to a row of analysts sitting at computer stations. "That's the Spec Ops team. Their telemetric systems capture everything that happens inside your Shell. Every thought you transmit to the CPU. Every movement. Your emotional state. Everything you can imagine.

"The team can pull that data and tell me whatever I need to know, like whether firefights are scaring you shitless or if you're reluctant to kill. That helps me identify who isn't measuring up." He zeroed in on one of the analysts. Her fingers danced over keyboards, eyes flitting from one screen to another. "Nijah, front and center."

The young analyst of Middle Eastern descent paused her busy fingers, took off her headset, and scooted her rolling chair back from the sophisticated console. She stood and walked over to Fourth Platoon.

"Nijah here will be Fourth Platoon's Overwatch," Lars said. "Her call sign is Overwatch 04."

Every platoon had an Overwatch assigned. Overwatches controlled platoons' Sentinels, aerial drones that transmitted a top-down view of the battlefield. Acting as Guardians' eyes in the sky, Overwatches provided intel and warned them of emerging threats.

Lars continued. "If they skipped this part in BCT, let me make it clear: You can't just tap into Sentinel 04 with your Shells. Nijah has to authorize access. Too many of you trying to sync with the drone would overload its circuits."

A smile traced Nijah's thin lips. "Good to meet you all. I've got your backs out there."

"Thanks, Nijah. You can return to your duties now," Lars said. She headed back to her workspace. "Alright, everyone, the tour's over. You're dismissed for today, and don't be a second late to my briefing tomorrow."

The Guardians filed out of the room to get settled in their quarters and get some R&R.

While leaving, Stacie and Emilia exchanged glares.

"Tonight, don't forget," Stacie said.

Emilia flashed a shark-like grin. "Wouldn't dream of it."

Stacie exited into the corridor. She thought back to the day during BCT when two female cadets had lured her outside. They told her a drill sergeant wanted to see her. As soon as she stepped onto the empty drill yard, Emilia and her clique ambushed her. They forced her to the ground, piled on top of her, and began hitting her repeatedly while hurling insults.

Stacie left that verbal and physical hazing bruised, bloody, humiliated, and wearing bedraggled, torn battledress. She wouldn't be able to make the rest of those miscreants pay, but she could at least teach Emilia a lesson, a painful one. She couldn't stand people of Emilia's ilk, and she was eager to humble her.

• • •

At 2300, the door to the sparring suite retracted. In came Stacie. Her hair was styled in a bun, and she wore a sports bra, spandex shorts, elbow and knee pads, and grappling gloves. She carried her headgear in her hand.

Her attire showed she was in peak physical condition.

Emilia was already there, dressed similarly, her outfit revealing the intricate tattoos on her arms, torso, and left leg. She punched the air, shadowboxing to warm up. *Now to teach this Highborn upstart a thing or two.*

Stacie appeared to have the advantage in height, standing a solid five-nine. Emilia was six inches shorter, though stoutly built.

"I wasn't sure you were gonna show, princess." Emilia cut the air with a blur of punches as she bounced on the balls of her feet.

Challenge in her eyes, Stacie slipped on her headgear and fastened the chin strap. "Wouldn't miss this chance for the world." She powered on the data-input kiosk to program the bout. "A hundred points to win?" she asked.

Emilia folded her arms confidently. "Whatever you want."

Stacie entered their surnames, the impact points needed to win, and pressed START.

A disembodied artificial voice said, "Combatants are Spencer and Rhineheart. Impact points needed for victory: one hundred."

Stacie warmed up, stretching her limbs. A thrill electrified her veins. In a sparring match, she could get some payback without earning a write-up in her service sketch. "You should've left your envy back at BCT. Hope you're ready to get your ass kicked, Private."

Narcissistic snob, I don't envy you. I don't wanna be anything like you, bitch. Adrenaline raging through her bloodstream, Emilia bumped her knuckles together. "Cut the banter, princess. Let's fight."

Stacie rolled her shoulders.

The two adversaries stepped onto the blue padded mat and shifted into the combat stance their training had instilled in them.

"Combatants are ready," said the computerized ref. "You may begin sparring."

Without preamble, Emilia lunged at Stacie like a rampaging

bull, taking her down with a vicious tackle.

They tumbled across the mat—wrestling, grappling, and trading choke holds. Emilia ended up on top of Stacie. Just as she raised her fist to nail Stacie in the face, Stacie twisted and tossed her aside.

"Impact points: thirty for Rhineheart, fifteen for Spencer," said the ref. A holographic scorecard flashed in the air: 30 POINTS–RHINEHEART / 15 POINTS–SPENCER.

Stacie rose. *Little twerp hits hard.*

Emilia stood up from the floor. "Too slow, princess. Why don't you request your release now and go back home to play with Mommy and Daddy's G-credit accounts? Go back to getting banged and shitfaced. Probably what you're actually good at."

"Your stupid wisecracks don't faze me. I've heard similar rubbish far too many times. Stuff like"—Stacie modulated her voice in mockery—"'you're just a rich tart who gets everything handed to her.'" Shifting her voice back to normal, she added, "But I graduated *Warrior Extraordinaire*. I proved I'm not just some . . . entitled brat.

"I don't have to ride my parents' coattails. I can achieve success on my own." Stacie beamed proudly. "I proved I'm willing to get my hands dirty and step away from the affluent lifestyle and predecided destiny that come with being the offspring of a baron and baroness. I'm the first child of an Eight to do this."

Emilia offered false applause, clapping her hands. "Bravo, nice speech." She cackled. "So you enlisting in the CDF was just about self-validation? You needed to do something unorthodox to show up Mommy and Daddy, is that it? Being a Guardian isn't something you do just so you can pat yourself on the back and say, '*There, I showed everyone.*' You're so sensitive and insecure I could vomit. Totally pathetic.

"Compared to the humiliation I've had to face, the teasers that get your fucking panties in a bunch all the time are nothing. I've been called slurs like 'nadir' by rich twits like you, and even fellow BCT cadets.

"And when I became a registered Eden citizen, I was supposed to receive my genetic upgrade, but apparently, we 'immigrants' aren't very high priority. It took me joining the CDF to get my upgrade, because it's absolutely required for enlistment."

Emilia's eyes blazed as she continued. "Isn't it funny how the government refers to us lottery beneficiaries as 'immigrants,' even though we're supposed to be equal citizens of humanity's intergalactic republic? If anyone should have a chip on their shoulder, it's me. You were birthed into privilege. You don't *really* have anything to be pissed about, princess."

Tired of being called princess and told she should be grateful for her perceived "fantastic" upbringing, Stacie channeled her unvoiced rage into a savage right hook, aimed as if she were trying to decapitate Emilia.

Emilia zagged to avoid the punch, Stacie's knuckles coming within a hair's reach of brushing her nose. Emilia immediately countered, kneeing Stacie in the kidney.

Stacie doubled over.

"Impact points: five for Rhineheart," the computerized ref announced. 5 POINTS flashed in midair.

"Just what I thought, princess: all mouth and no show," Emilia said, throwing a punch.

Stacie dodged the blow and quickly locked her arms around Emilia's outstretched limb. After applying an aggressive torque, she heard a satisfying *crack* as her pesterer's shoulder dislocated.

The pasty-skinned smart-mouth wheezed, her face twisted in pain.

Stacie derived satisfaction from hurting Emilia. After releasing her, she shoved her hard, throwing her off-balance.

Emilia staggered backward. Then, gritting her teeth, she popped her shoulder back into place.

She had underestimated Stacie's ruthlessness and fighting prowess. Before she could move again, Stacie took her legs out from under her with a sweeping kick, knocking her on her ass.

"Impact points: ten for Spencer," the ref announced. 10 POINTS flashed.

Stacie wore a cocky smile. "You're all mouth and no brains, Private. Probably why I'm a Warrior Extraordinaire and you're not."

Emilia sprang to her feet and charged, but Stacie caught her. Using Emilia's momentum to pivot into a flip toss, Stacie hurled her beyond the mat's boundaries.

Arms and legs flailing the air, Emilia landed back-first on the floor.

The ref declared the victor. "Combatant Rhineheart has left the sparring zone. Winner: Spencer."

A holographic WINNER! hovered over Stacie's head. Virtual confetti of all colors rained down.

Triumph fizzed through Stacie's veins.

Emilia undid her chin strap, gasping for air. She removed her headgear, its interior padding sweat-dampened. "A fluke win, princess. In a real fight, I would've whooped your ass," she muttered grudgingly.

Stacie walked toward the door. It whistled open. "Spoken like a true sore loser." Standing in the doorway, she said, "Oh, and I suggest you refine your stereotypical thinking, Private. Not every Highborn thinks lowly of colony citizens. My mother's midwife was Oviereya Amaechi, after all, and I love that woman as if she were my mother." *Maybe even more than my mother.* "So I'm not some . . . xenophobic, haughty bitch."

The door shut behind her.

As Stacie walked down the corridor, Emilia's words stalked her. So what if enlisting was about proving something to herself and people who doubted or badmouthed her? Not everyone joined the CDF out of some moral inclination to serve humanity. Some joined to build a career; others joined simply for money. Her reason didn't mean she was some insecure self-validation chaser, did it?

Jason Mansford fell in step behind her, following a little too close for comfort. He wore sleeping pants and a shirt. "Up late and in sparring gear. Needed a workout, huh?" He couldn't defeat the urge to give her backside—shown off in detail by her tight-fitting shorts—a once-over.

Stacie glanced over her shoulder. *Oh, go fuck yourself.* "Yeah, something like that," she replied harshly. She wanted to be left alone. *Damn it, do I need "Do not disturb" V-inked on my back?*

Jason strode up beside her, still lusting after her. She checked all his boxes. Abs? Check. Nice ass? Check. High and firm breasts? Check. And she was blond. "I'm just trying to break the ice and get to know you, Specialist, that's all."

Stacie quickened her pace and kept her eyes forward, not granting him any of her attention. *More like trying to bamboozle me into your bed.* "Good night, Sergeant. I have a briefing to rest up for," she said. *Not well-versed in the art of romantic seduction, are you?* She retreated into her quarters, feeling Jason's eyes on her the entire way.

Jason watched the door click shut. He'd been spurned again. *Oh, well.* He returned to his quarters as well.

• • •

Stacie entered Fourth Platoon's assembly room fifteen minutes late. She had overslept.

Lars was midway into his briefing. Everyone else had arrived promptly and was outfitted in their sleeves—black one-piece suits, with support padding at the joints, worn beneath their Shells. The formfitting flex material allowed ease of movement inside the combat machines.

Lars paused his briefing and made eye contact with Stacie. "Specialist Spencer!" he shouted, voice sharp and cutting.

Stacie jerked and froze in place. A wave of embarrassment rushed over her.

Lars nearly stared a hole through her pupils. "I don't know what they let you rich chits do at Cadwell, but *here*,"—he jabbed a finger toward the floor—"we don't just show up whenever the fuck we want. *Capiche?*"

Stacie's reserve wavered, her face flushing as anger took hold. She thought Emilia must be elated.

Her mouth opened for an angry retort, and boy, did she have a mouthful of unkind words for Lars, but she subdued them, clamping her trap shut. It was a no-win argument. She had goofed up and had to own it. Going off on a superior, on top of being late for her first mission brief, would only make her seem even more undisciplined—hardly fit for real soldiering, at least in the eyes of her comrades.

She stiffened her spine, forced the scowl off her face, and maintained military bearing. "Loud and clear, Sergeant."

"Good."

Her wandering eyes found Randy. He patted the aisle seat, which was to his left, letting her know he'd kept it off-limits for her.

She lowered herself beside him and crossed her arms.

"You okay?" Randy asked.

She nodded a yes. The lingering frown on her face and her body language said otherwise.

Lars continued his briefing. "Don't expect any aggression from the Coalition during these rallies. They only strike hard targets.

"This might come as a surprise to some of you, but the Coalition isn't foaming at the mouth to kill us Guardians. They try to avoid confrontation. They want to cripple the CDF and wear us down, with little to no fatalities if possible, all while trying to portray the central government in an unfavorable light and spread their ideals throughout the colonies to gain more supporters.

"They hope a combination of guerrilla warfare and growing support for colony autonomy will lead to one of two results: drastic revitalization efforts or full sovereignty." The latter was the least likely.

"So they're trying to beat us by attrition," a male Guardian said.

"Exactly," Lars confirmed. "However, if it comes down to us or them in a firefight, the Coalition will kill to defend themselves. And let me make something *absolutely* clear: The Coalition having a moral playbook and trying to be nice doesn't mean jack-shit. You hear me, Fourth Platoon?

"They are the enemy, and we always shoot to kill. You got that?" There was silence. "Let me hear a fucking 'Yes, Sergeant!'"

Lars' tone was so harsh that it made shoulders snap back.

Everyone shouted, "Yes, Sergeant!"

"Good. Now, though not nearly as powerful or influential, there are less prudent, more radical insurgent groups operating inside Colony Four who like to make statements whenever they can. Any opportunity to kill a Guardian, they take it. Those are the groups we need to be cognizant of while we're out there today."

Lars powered on his tablet. The wall screen synchronized with it, showing a man's face.

Lars gestured to the screen. "This is Eric Vaughn Ritter. Age twenty-seven. He's charismatic and knows how to appeal to the youth. He's also a maniacal sack of crap.

"He's an ex-Coalition rebel who believed the Coalition's actions weren't extreme enough. So he formed The People's Revolutionary Party of Colony Four. They aren't big in stature or numbers, yet. But they're growing.

"People who think the Coalition is being too soft join Ritter and other extremist groups like his. It's a power struggle for the minds of the rebellious, between the Coalition and these more radical groups.

"Ritter's Revolutionaries are nothing more than thugs who've appropriated some dangerous tech from inside and outside the Union. Be warned: Unlike the Coalition, these guys' mission is to off as many of us as possible. Two weeks ago, an off-duty Guardian was found dead in an alley."

Lars pressed a button on his tablet. The screen cleared and swapped Eric's mug for a macabre crime scene: a man lying next to a dumpster, his jugular lacerated. A grotesque amount of blood saturated the ground.

A female Guardian threw a hand over her eyes, goose bumps prickling her flesh.

Lars' voice toughened. "Sutherland, take your hand off your *fucking* eyes! You're not a little girly girl anymore! You're a goddamn Guardian!"

The young fair-skinned ginger jerked her hand away from her eyes. "Ye-yes, Sergeant." Her heart pumped in her ears.

Lars snorted, his contempt for weakness unmistakable. "This murder has the People's Revolutionary Party written all over it. Former Coalition rebels, and even some Guardians, make up about thirty percent of the group. They're all loony, anti-government ideologues like Ritter. Ten percent are teens off the streets, promised money, housing, and a sense of belonging. The remaining sixty percent are disgruntled adult citizens at odds with the central government."

Lars summarized more anti-government groups for fifteen minutes. Then he shut off the screen. "Alright, the briefing's over. I know some of you softies are already getting cold feet. I suggest you do whatever is necessary to shake off the nerves. Pray to your Almighty, or whatever."

"What do you do? To shake off the nerves, I mean," a male Guardian stuttered, hoping for some professional counsel.

Lars scoffed. "I don't get *nerves* anymore. But way back when I was a newbie like you, I just clung to my training and the gun in my hand. I sure as hell didn't sit around letting cowardly thoughts stew in my head. And since I don't pray, I didn't do that either."

Being a secular man, Lars found solace only in his training and the killing power of his Shell when in combat.

He said, "We leave in thirty mikes. Now get your fannies moving and get shelled so we can meet our hit time." He shot Stacie a withering glare. "Something some of us may not know a lot about." A verbal jab obviously aimed at her.

A smattering of chortles came from different directions.

Stacie's emotional buttons had been pushed, and her professional poise was on the verge of shattering. Randy settled a calming hand on her shoulder.

Everyone began orderly clearing out of the room.

Randy and Stacie got up and proceeded to leave as well.

Right behind Randy, Stacie was just about out the door when Jason Mansford approached her.

"Still ticked off, huh?" he remarked.

Stacie jutted out her chin. "No, I'm fine. I shook it off." By her intonation, that wasn't true in the least.

Jason saw right through her facade. "Don't let what Lars said get to you. I checked your service sketch. You graduated Warrior Extraordinaire, so you gotta be more than just a pretty face with riches, right?"

"Thanks," Stacie said casually, allowing some subtle warmth into her voice.

The room continued to thin out, Guardians chattering as they left.

"Just to let you know, you've been assigned to my squad," Jason informed Stacie. "I've designated you Alpha Team's sub-lead."

Stacie's face lit up. "Me?"

"Yeah, *you*, and don't worry, I didn't designate you sub-leader just to woo you or something. I'm a professional. A lot of thought and discernment goes into every decision I make. I did a deep dive into your service sketch, personality profile, and curriculum vitae. I genuinely think you have what it takes to fill that role." Stacie was a collegiate athlete, a Warrior Extraordinaire, an honors graduate from Cadwell, and a top-scorer on the CDF fitness test. Her credentials had impressed Jason.

Stacie thought, *Maybe I was wrong. Maybe he is more than just some playboy.*

"There'll be time to chat more later. For now, let's get shelled."

Stacie cracked an unexpected smile. "Right."

• • •

Randy stepped into the infrastructure of his Shell. The rear paneling of the powerful combatwear sealed, enclosing him. He drew his helmet from the magnetic catch on his hip and put it on. The featureless faceplate slid down. He said the suit's activation code: name and citizen registration number. "Scott: C-Seven-Three-Six-Seven."

His HUD booted up, populating with colored icons. Data scrolled, diagnostic check in progress. His mind pinged, cerebral implant tethering to the Shell's CPU. INTERFACE COMPLETE streamed across his HUD, and the CPU spoke to him, green-lighting all functions. The merger between mind and machine was complete.

The Shell made the necessary autoadjustments, morphing fibers conforming—snugly—to his height and size, creating the perfect custom fit. The outer chest, arm, and leg panels of Kryoplaste conformed as well, tiles of armor telescoping into place.

A little uncomfortable, he thought. Sensory receptors registered the haptic feedback, and the CPU refitted the suit. *Awesome.* The internal HVAC adjusted to his body temperature.

He tried out the CPU's syncing capabilities, accessing the net and bringing up juxtaposed street-camera feeds, all superimposed over his visuals in multiple windows.

People wondered if cerebral-interface technology would someday allow them to connect to more than just a Shell's CPU—such as personal computers, wristcoms, vehicular navigation systems, and even a home's mainframe.

People imagined what it would be like to access the net or control their homes' functions using only their implant. Cerebral-interface technology could likely evolve to that point, but the central government would never allow it. Such modifications posed serious security risks. Besides, the purpose of cerebral implants was to connect people more intimately, not to cybernize the human mind. The implant was meant to elevate people's humanity, not diminish it.

Randy tested his limbs, his movements flexing the morphing

fibers. The new model indeed had less armor density and far better reaction time. All his movements were quick and fluid.

He brought his Oracle online with a thought.

"Oracle now activated," an androgynous voice said.

"Great." Randy accessed the platoon roster published to the CDF's intranet cloud to learn the names of everyone assigned to First Squad, his designated squad. It read:

SSGT Jason Mansford (Squad Leader)

SGT Jack Holister (Alpha Team Leader)

SPC Stacie Spencer (Alpha Team Sub-Leader)

SPC Randal Scott

SPC Jarius Ford

PVT Emilia Rhineheart

SGT Olivia Slovak (Bravo Team Leader)

SPC Eli Manson (Bravo Team Sub-Leader)

PVT Ryoko Nahara

PVT Seth Youngblood

The roster window blinked away at Randy's mental command. He hoped the squad could find time to get to know each other. Squad bonding would build camaraderie.

Stacie moved her joints, getting acquainted with the M-X02. Actuators groaned. She felt powerful, unstoppable inside the suit— like a superwoman.

She explored the customizable weapons package on her HUD. The standard-issue ballistics carbine was the currently equipped primary weapon, though it could be swapped for others, like the heavy-duty Gatling gun, designed for extreme combat missions. The plasma-energy gun was the secondary. It was small, but every blast packed a hell of a punch.

More weapons were embedded in the Shell, such as extendable shoulder cannons for launching explosive rocket projectiles. Besides a battery of deadly weaponry, the Shells were equipped with stealth-cloak camouflaging technology.

Via cerebral interface, Guardians could also access manuals for weapons and vehicles, all stored in the CPU.

Stacie glanced down at the CDF insignia—a crossed sword and hammer—laser-engraved into the Shell's left shoulder. She was glad to be with Lima Company, representing the CDF, rather than attending some corporate meeting with her parents, where they'd be showing her the ropes.

Lars' voice came through the platoon's secure cerebral-communications (C-comm) channel. <<*Sergeant First Class Freeman, shelled and ready.*>>

The platoon responded with their rank, last name, and "shelled and ready."

Lars said, <<*If something crazy does kick off and you need to go lethal, remember to use plasma-energy weapons sparingly. The energy gun doesn't have many shots, and the energy weapons installed in your Shell sap a lotta power.*>>

Fourth Platoon proceeded to the motor pool to board Battle Utility Stations (BUSs), armored all-terrain lorries that would transport them to their respective rally sites. Lars joined First Squad for this op.

In transit to their rally sites, the new Guardians got culture-shocked by their first glimpse of the deteriorating infrastructure in the colony: dilapidated buildings, shanties, crumbling bridges, and crummy roads. It was a complete contrast to Eden's grandeur. The outdated fashion people wore and the vehicular relics they drove also astounded the Guardians.

Some now understood why colonists were so upset. It was revelations like these that caused Guardians to defect. But as Fourth Platoon arrived at their rally sites, the suffering of the people was pushed from their minds. It was game time.

• • •

Halfin was one of several unfinished towns in Zone 03. As shoddy as it was, it was upscale for Colony Four.

In front of Halfin's town hall, a large gathering of unruly CFP demonstrators waved signs and chanted in unison, "End the occupation! Peace, not war!" Citizens began to congregate and join in.

Viceroy McLaughlin, aware of today's protests, wasn't in his office inside the town hall. He was somewhere safe.

On the landing at the top of the town hall steps stood Lars and Alpha Team of First Squad, rifles at the ready. Bravo Team was stationed at another rally site. Parked beside the building was the BUS First Squad had arrived in. Its multiple gunports, twin pulse cannons, and spiked rims made the spacious, eight-wheeled vehicle a baleful sight.

The team had toggled their rifles' selector switch to NONLETHAL, to subdue the protesters with rubber rounds if they needed to.

As Randy's gaze swept over the area, his CPU fed him data about his immediate surroundings: approximate number of protesters, potential enemy approach routes, hiding spots, distance of passersby—everything. *Awesome,* he thought. The new, advanced CPU was giving him heightened tactical awareness.

"A lot of discontent out there," Jarius commented, noting the contemptuous faces in the crowd.

On a raised platform, a heavyset woman wearing round spectacles, a knee-length dress, and a denim vest took center stage. She spoke into a wireless handheld mic, her voice dripping outrage. "For too long we've seen our people get stopped, frisked, and questioned with no probable cause! We've had our homes barged into and searched, and we've seen people who have absolutely no Coalition ties get interrogated! Well, I say enough!"

The protesters gave the CFP mouthpiece a standing ovation, applauding and pumping their fists.

"You guys think there's any truth to that stuff?" Jarius asked.

Offended that a Guardian would dare entertain the idea that a government objector had a valid point, Lars was about ready to tear Jarius a new one. "Specialist Ford, are you questioning the moral standing of the Commonwealth Government?" he asked, voice gritty. He rested his thumb on his rifle's selector switch, ready to toggle it to LETHAL.

Jarius' brain scrambled to organize an acceptable response. He settled for an evasive, "Uh . . . no, Sergeant."

Lars took his thumb off the selector switch and turned back to the crowd. "Good." *Because I would've blown your ass away on the spot.* Which was completely permitted under CDF regulations if a Guardian exhibited behavioral signs of becoming an insider threat.

Curious to learn more about Colony Four's state of affairs, Jarius accessed open-source info from Satellite One's net. He browsed web articles, articles that couldn't be transmitted to Eden because of the net filters in place.

One article described how relief-aid nonprofits—created by humanitarian tycoons on Eden sympathetic toward the colonies— had built Assistance Living Centers, roads, and buildings and even provided some private-sector employment.

Jarius found pictures of deplorable living conditions and came across reports stating that depression and suicide rates were on the rise.

He thought, *Darn, after years of the government doing business with the Union Worlds and trading partners, you'd think it would've done more to advance the colonies. But then again, I ain't no subject-*

matter expert. This funding stuff's beyond my wheelhouse. Hopefully, plans are in the works to help the people here.

He continued searching the net and discovered some articles that detailed several accounts of Guardians mistreating civilians.

An article describing the miners' strike he had heard about, which took place in Colony Four a while back, caught his attention.

The strike had created a sizable labor shortage.

Cornelius had activated Reserve units to force the miners back to work. He cited their strike as destabilizing the Commonwealth's safety and prosperity, given the essential nature of the minerals being harvested. After being threatened with government charges, the miners had no choice but to return to work without securing their demands for better conditions. Otherwise, they risked jail time, leaving their families to starve.

The article slammed the central government, calling its retaliation against the miners' stand "egregious." It also claimed that Guardians opened fire on several defenseless miners, killing five.

Jarius found another article about the strike and read the headline: OUTRAGED PRIVATE AHMED HAWSAWI ATTACKS SERGEANT OVER SENSELESS KILLINGS.

A throaty male voice coming from his helmet's transceiver scolded him. "Specialist Ford, this is the Nerve Center. Is there a reason you, a dedicated Guardian of the Defense Force, are browsing Satellite One's net mid-mission, evaluating propagandist material defaming the central government?"

"Uh . . . sorry." Jarius quickly closed all articles and images. *Dang, is our every move monitored?*

The team's auditory comlink came alive with Nijah's voice. "This is Overwatch 04. Dubious activity detected at the zone's comms tower. There's a woman kneeling next to it with some sort of bag.

Could be an explosive ordnance."

"Randy, you're with me," Lars ordered. "Shouldn't take long."

"Gotcha," Randy acknowledged. *Finally, some damn action, instead of people watching all day.*

"I'll load Sentinel 04's snapshots of the woman into your suit's hard drive," Nijah said to Lars.

A message appeared on Lars' HUD: UPLOAD COMPLETE. With a mental command, he accessed the pics. In the top left corner of his HUD, pixels coalesced into an image of a scrappy-looking woman in a stylish black jacket, white tank top, and ripped jeans. Wild, dense ruby-red hair spilled from beneath a blue denim bandanna, reaching halfway down her back. Small gold studs adorned her nose and bottom lip.

<<*Randy, I'm sending you pics of our person of interest,*>> Lars relayed over the C-comm. He queued the images for transmission and mentally pressed SEND.

Randy's helmet chimed. DECLINE, in red, and ACCEPT, in green, flashed on his HUD. He instructed his CPU to accept the images. <<*Received,*>> he informed Lars.

They racked their weapons onto their backs. Then they dragged two hoverbikes from the rear of the BUS and mounted them.

Lifters powered up, displays came to life, and intake valves hissed open.

Randy and Lars twisted the hand throttles, and the bikes sailed off. They shot past cluttered markets, run-down shops, and towering stacks of tenements barely holding together.

Lars examined the graphic map superimposed over his visuals. Nijah had merged his Shell's navigation map with Sentinel 04's target tracker, which was keeping tabs on the woman.

Lars said to Randy, "Sentinel 04 shows our suspect leaving the comms tower and heading down Jefer Street on foot. We'll cut her off at the intersection up ahead."

A twist of the throttles gave the bikes a boost of power.

Lars pointed to the woman in the snapshots. "There she is."

The woman noticed Randy and Lars closing in on her at breakneck speed and darted into a grimy alleyway covered in anti-government graffiti.

Lars and Randy braked hard. The bikes sighed to a quick stop, whooshing up dust.

On the decaying balcony of a tenement looming over the streets, a shirtless hairy-chested man bellowed from his outdoor chair, "Damn CDF bastards, leave the lady alone!"

A gang of bystanders on the street backed him up. "Yeah, let her be," one of them said, wringing his fist.

Ignoring them, Lars jumped off his bike and sprinted through the mouth of the alley. "You, halt!" he said to the woman.

A scruffy critter scurried into a sewer grate.

The woman wedged her fingers into the gaps of a wire fence, preparing to climb over.

Lars' rifle clacked. "Don't make another goddamn move! That's a warning!"

Randy came in behind Lars.

The woman let go of the fence. Wire rattled. She froze in place. *Oh, fuck me. Just my damn luck.*

Lars visually inspected her for bombs or weapons.

"Did I do something wrong?" the woman asked, meeting Lars' menacing gaze.

Lars' voice shifted to a low, dangerous pitch. "What sorta mischief are you up to?" His eyes fell on the satchel slung over the woman's shoulder. "And what's in the bag?"

"Nothing," the woman retorted.

"Bullshit. Turn back around, nice n' slow." The woman spun and faced the fence. "Hands up and spread your feet." She dropped the satchel, raised her hands above her head, and spread her feet shoulder-width apart. Lars stepped a pace closer, an empty soda can crunching underfoot. "Where does your loyalty lie, with the Commonwealth Government or the Coalition of Rebel Factions?" he asked. The woman remained tight-lipped. "Are you an Independent Movement sympathizer?" Still no response. Lars pressed the muzzle of his rifle against her spine. "Speak up."

"Fuck off," the woman spat, revolt in her voice.

Lars rammed his rifle's buttstock into her back. She tumbled to the ground. This wasn't the first time her sassy mouth had landed her in trouble with a Guardian, and it probably wouldn't be the last.

Randy cringed, his heart flipping in his chest. He knew the blow hurt, especially for an unenhanced human. "Hey, lighten up, Sarge." He instinctively reached out a hand toward Lars' shoulder, but caught himself. He knew that laying a hand on a superior might get him reprimanded. "She hasn't done anything to warrant —"

"Quiet, rookie," Lars said sharply, ending Randy's protest. "We do things as we see fit."

Randy remembered what a drill sergeant had said to him and a bunch of cadets in formation on the drill yard: *Ruthlessness and fear are two of your greatest assets against your enemy! Soft hearts get you nowhere but the grave! And who is your enemy? Anyone shooting at you! Anyone who badmouths or defames the Defense Force or central government! It could be a civilian! It could even be the Guardian standing next to you! Whoever it may be, show them no mercy and treat them like the excrement they are, man or woman! Is that clear?*

The memory ended, and Randy thought, *We're human beings for goodness' sake. Does the CDF want us to be cold-blooded or something?*

"Get up," Lars said to the woman. She slowly pushed herself up onto her hands and knees. Becoming impatient, Lars raised his voice to a roar. "Hurry up! Stop wasting my fucking time!"

The woman's freckled features twisted into a pissed-off frown. "Kiss my fine ass, ya goddamn prick."

Lars savagely kicked her in the gut.

Unease rippled through Randy.

"You've got a big mouth, you know that, you snarky little bitch?" Lars growled.

"Why, thank you." The woman coughed. "Trash-talking's one of my most endearing traits," she added sarcastically, though her gut throbbed.

Lars snorted. "Enough jabber. Now get the hell up." The woman stood, raising chafed hands high above her head. "Check her, Specialist Scott."

Lars stepped back and continued to hold the facetious woman at gunpoint while Randy conducted the inspection.

"Hold still," Randy told her. He knelt and patted down her pant legs.

"Finest legs you'll ever touch, huh?" she joked.

"Lady, just shut up and let me do my job." Randy stood, checked her rear pockets, and extracted a plastic ID card.

"So who's Ms. Smart-ass here?" Lars asked, the business end of his weapon still aimed at the woman.

Randy dipped his chin, studying the credentials. "She's a courier for Dynamic Relief Provisions." He brought up the organization's webpage on his HUD. "They're the major relief-aid org on the planet. Her name's Kesley Whittaker." The credentials showed she was thirty-one.

A bloodcurdling boom diverted Lars and Randy's eyes from Kesley.

"What the hell?" Lars shouted. Smoke trails billowed from the rally site. "Lars to Overwatch 04, patch me in to Sentinel 04. I need eyes on the rally site." His visor interfaced with the drone, relaying him an overhead view of complete bedlam: fire, stampedes of people running, his Guardians discharging rounds. <<*Mansford, sitrep,*>> he sent over the C-comm.

<<*Multiple hostiles opening fire,*>> Jason responded. <<*They're Ritter's Revolutionaries. We got four civilian fatalities. Sergeant Holister's injured.*>>

The fence creaked. Randy and Lars wheeled around and saw Kesley climbing to the top of it. She swung to the other side with her satchel, gained her footing, and broke into a run, limping slightly from a sprained ankle.

"Forget her," Lars said. "Shit just hit the fan. We've gotta get back to the rally site."

"What about the comms tower?"

"I'll send someone to check for sabotage after the mission. Now let's go."

Randy deposited Kesley's ID in a personal compartment. He and Lars hopped on their hoverbikes. The plasma-charged aft boosters built up thrust, and the bikes soared off, thrumming.

"You struck that woman. That wasn't right, Sergeant," Randy said, a bitter undertone in his voice. "She didn't do anything to provoke that kind of force."

Lars glanced over his shoulder at Randy, who was following behind. "She was obviously hiding something. We needed to know what."

Randy and Lars sped past terribly maintained, half-built structures. They slowed the bikes to a smooth stop as they arrived at the rally site.

They saw battered phyocrete and injured noncombatants.

Jarius had a medpack and was kneeling beside one of the wounded, making good use of his Combat Lifesaver Skills. Jason was administering first aid while shouting commands. Emilia was trying to resuscitate a woman who was already gone, using the defibrillators in the fingertips of her suit. Sergeant Jack Holister, Alpha Team Leader, sat against a wall, the leg of his Shell breached.

Jack groaned. The injury hurt like hell. With him sidelined, Alpha Team's sub-lead, Specialist Stacie Spencer, was now in charge.

The injured civilians and casualties hadn't been intentional targets. They were collateral damage, the result of negligence by the reckless, untrained hostiles now lying dead. There were five of them, all young men no older than eighteen. They wore makeshift body armor slapped together from discolored scrap metals. Red armbands stitched with "RR" identified them as Ritter's Revolutionaries.

Lars shook his head in disgust. *Kids brainwashed into becoming martyrs for Ritter's insane cause. This bloodshed's gotta end.*

Stacie spoke over the C-comm. <<*So what do we—?"*>> A crackling cerulean blast exploded against her torso plating, bursting into a brilliant spray of sparks and propelling her backward like a thrown javelin.

She crashed to the ground back-first and skidded, her armor shrieking against the phyocrete. If not for her Shell's shock inhibitors, she would've felt the full brunt of the blast—and the impact of the landing.

She rose, armor darkly singed.

Everyone was on alert, scanning for the hostile.

Come on, where the hell are you? Stacie thought. Her targeting reticle panned left and right. Suddenly, another blast boomed, streaking past her shoulder. "Shit!"

A third, lower-powered shot clipped her helmet, whipping her neck back. Her helmet's optics damaged, she saw her visuals jump side to side.

Lars activated his helmet's external sound port, which amplified his voice like a bullhorn. "I'M SERGEANT FIRST CLASS LARS FREEMAN OF THE COMMONWEALTH DEFENSE FORCE! CEASE YOUR TRANSGRESSIONS AT ONCE!" Another haphazard shot exploded against the side of a building, raining rubble over his suit. "Fuck!"

"Hostile, three o'clock!" Jarius shouted, smoothing a medical slip over a civilian's leg wound. The slip's adhesive antiseptic membrane sealed the gash and staunched the bleeding.

Stacie turned toward the enemy, her mechanical joints whining.

One of Ritter's Revolutionaries was using a car for cover. A harness secured a heavy-caliber energy cannon to his armored torso. He clutched the outstretched handles and squeezed the discharge levers. The cannon's capacitor crackled as it built up enough energy for another shot. The longer he held the levers, the bigger and more devastating the blast would be. Stacie was lucky the shot that had clipped her was low-powered.

Her impaired vision made an accurate shot nearly impossible. She'd have to neutralize the hostile face-to-face.

As she ran toward him, her mechboots thumped against the ground.

He let go of the levers and recoiled as the cannon thundered, unleashing another energy blast.

Stacie crouched. Then her jumper struts launched her into a powered leap over the incoming shot. She could hardly believe how light she felt in the M-X02.

Behind her came a boom and the crash of shattering glass.

The roof of the car the hostile was using as cover screeched inward as Stacie landed atop it. Lacking time to fire another shot from such a slow-to-discharge weapon, he flinched.

Stacie hopped down. She leveled her rifle at his head. "Enough. It's over. Now remove the cannon, or I'll splatter your brains over the phyocrete, and I fucking mean it. Your call."

The hostile unstrapped the cumbersome armament and dropped it. Then he raised his hands in surrender, heart hammering his rib cage.

Stacie examined the foreign weapon, consulting her index for an ID. ARTIFACT UNRECOGNIZED flashed on her HUD, distorted by static and jagged lines.

The intergalactic innovation was likely illegally obtained from, and the brainchild of, a race outside the Union. It wasn't very advanced, though. All targeting was done via iron sights, and precision aiming was nearly impossible. But then again, this type of hardware wasn't meant for precision. It was meant for mass-scale destruction—the wrong choice of weaponry to take out a few Guardians without putting civilians at risk.

Stupid dipshits, Stacie thought. But Ritter incentivized enemy kills. And sometimes, young, battle-inexperienced men would go off half-cocked, grab some destructive weapon without thinking, and hunt for Guardians to slay.

<<*Good work, Spencer,*>> Lars said. <<*We—*>> A parked car vanished in an eruption of red-orange fire, cutting him off mid-thought. A shower of phyocrete fragments tinkled off his armor. "Damn it! We've got another hostile with one of those goddamn energy cannons!" he shouted. "Overwatch 04, we're taking fire! We need to know where from!" Lars swept the air with his rifle, hunting for the hostile.

"Already working on it," Nijah replied.

Another loud boom, softened by the Shells' noise reducers, rattled the scene. Crumbs of debris hailed down.

"Well, hurry the hell up!" Lars barked.

"Found him," Nijah said. "The hostile is atop the incomplete construction to your left."

"I got him!" Randy yelled, spotting the hostile. He considered his options. Given the hostile's elevation and distance, he couldn't make a manual kill shot, even with high-magnification targeting.

Suddenly, a bomb drone the size of a golf ball deployed from his armguard.

Randy said, "What the hell? I didn't deploy that—"

"Projectile launched," his Oracle said. It was helping to reduce a Guardian's cognitive load, as purposed. "Due to the target's distance and elevation, the optimal weapon is the Predator Bomb. Does the user disagree?"

Randy blinked, still shocked. "Uh . . . No, you're right on," he stammered. The Oracle had quickly formulated the best solution to achieve Randy's intended outcome: the hostile dead. Machine learning at its finest.

The Oracle input the seek-and-destroy prompt. Zigzagging through the air, the self-guided projectile homed in on its target.

On the rooftop, the hostile was screwing a fresh power-cell canister into his cannon. Before he could fire again, he heard a faint buzzing sound in his ear. From the corner of his eye, he caught a glimpse of the silvery sphere. "Oh, fuck!"

The bomb's glowing red iris blinked and beeped. The hostile drew his last breath, and then a sonic boom thundered, followed by a blue flash and a halo of shock waves. There one moment, gone the next, the hostile had been vaporized from existence—along with a chunk of the roof. That was the power of encapsulated plasma energy unleashed.

<<*Target neutralized,*>> Randy said.

The scent of plasma-burned ozone drifted.

"You're going to be put away for a long time for the mess you caused today," Stacie told her captive, who was now cuffed.

A clever grin played across his lips. "What if I could get you guys Arson Scott, in exchange for immunity?"

Randy removed his helmet and racked it on his hip. His brow furrowed. "*What?*" Mood darkening, he stormed up beside Stacie and seized the captive's throat in one hand. "Where is he?" His voice trembled. "If you know where that traitor is, tell me *right now.*"

"Stand down, Specialist Scott," Stacie ordered.

His mother's pain, never to be quieted, ignited a tension headache. Unable to rein in his emotions, he thoughtlessly squeezed the young man's throat, threatening to shut off his airway. He was slipping into a trance of rage.

Gagging, the near-asphyxiated captive wheezed.

"Spencer told you to stand the fuck down!" Lars barked.

Stacie batted Randy's arm away, armor clacking against armor. "That's enough, Specialist Scott," she said firmly.

The captive let out a long exhalation.

Taming the surge of emotion, Randy pulled back, shocked by his loss of control and violation of his own code of conduct.

Stacie stripped off her helmet, cursing the damaged HVAC as she undid her bun and let her sweat-laden hair spill free. Wisps of blond strands fell disheveled over her features. "Hey, Randy, I know you and I are involved," she said, alternating her finger between the two of them, "but out here in the field, I'm still your superior."

"Just got a little carried away, that's all," Randy spat smugly.

Amusement raised Stacie's left brow. She scoffed. "A little?"

Randy crossed his arms stubbornly. "Whatever, Stace."

Stacie's features twitched. *Whatever, Stace?* she thought.

The "Who the fuck do you think you're talking to?" look on her face was priceless—and had Jarius stifling a giggle.

Lars, helmet racked, barged between them, breaking up the squabble. Armor clanged. Stacie stumbled backward. He came nose-to-nose with Randy. "You were out of line, Specialist Scott!" He tapped his finger against Randy's chest plate. *Tink, tink.*

A matching scowl on his face, Randy gave the sergeant his comeuppance. "Just like you were out of line with that woman in the alley?" he snapped.

Lars' visage dared Randy to say one more goddamn word.

Fists clenched, Randy grunted and shouldered Lars aside. He walked away to cool off.

Irritation creased Lars' forehead. "Specialist Ford, Specialist Spencer, get the prisoner ready for transport," he ordered, voice hoarse from all the yelling he'd done today. He stared at Randy with a disapproving glower.

Jarius and Stacie replied simultaneously: "Yes, Sergeant." They went over to the captive, took an arm each, and heaved him to his feet.

Lars put on his helmet and lowered his faceplate. On his HUD, he brought up Randy's psych profile from the intranet, accessible only with the correct authorization code. Nothing adverse was logged, and his BCT dossier described him as smart, studious, and straitlaced. And from what Lars could see, he definitely had a backbone.

The dossier listed no demerits whatsoever. Randy was a promising young Guardian. However, whenever anyone mentioned his father, his temper flared. And he exhibited some antisocial tendencies.

Despite the clean record, Lars still questioned the fragility of

Randy's mental health. *Maybe I was wrong about that leadership potential. This hothead needs eyes kept on him.*

• • •

Randy, shirtless in his boxers, lay on his bed. Unrest churned in his soul. He wondered if the captive had given up Arson's location yet.

<So what the heck was that all about today, with the prisoner?> Stacie said from the glass-enclosed shower in the bathroom, water jets hissing.

<I . . . I just got carried away. I realize sometimes my anger gets the best of me.> Randy's emotions were indeed volatile, to say the least. *<I have to . . . compartmentalize better. It won't happen again.>*

<Maybe you need that psych eval. You've obviously got some PTSD from your mom's death. An official diagnosis might—>

<You know I can't risk a mental-health discharge, Stace.>

<Well, you can't be so damn impulsive. You don't want a write-up for dishonorable conduct in your service sketch. And if you go bonkers again like you did today, Lars is gonna have the behavioral specialists order a psych eval anyway.>

Stacie shut off the jets. Water gurgled down the drain. After the drying cycle, she emerged from the bathroom. Clad in silky pink lingerie, she displayed her sun-darkened, statuesque physique—which had been sculpted by grueling workouts.

Lips curved into a disarming smile, she sat next to Randy on the bed. "So, what are you thinking about now, babe, hmm? I know when you're feeling troubled about something." Her tone sounded chirpy.

Randy, staring glumly at the ceiling, said, "Conlan might've had contact with my dad. I don't know if there's been collusion between them. Both he and my dad have disappointed me, and I don't know if I'm even going to get my hands on my dad to make him pay for his misdeeds. So all the hurt, anger, and uncertainty have . . . just got my headspace all fucked up right now."

You spend too much time in your head, babe. "You need to take your mind off all that, and I think I have the solution," Stacie said in a sultry timbre. Her eyes twinkled.

Randy's attention drifted from the ceiling and settled on Stacie. Damn, she had the prettiest shade of tan he'd ever seen, and her musculature was hella impressive. She was temptation incarnate. Truth be told, he'd always been drawn to blond women with athletic builds.

Stacie crawled onto the bed and rose upright on her knees. The springs squeaked beneath her. She snared Randy's solid midriff between her thighs and peeled off her bra, tossing it aside. Then she leaned in, dangling her breasts over his face.

Randy fixed his eyes on her impeccable nipples. Exhilaration compounded in his groin, lengthening his lower extremity.

He couldn't ask for a better girlfriend: gorgeous, smart, affectionate, hypersexual. His eyes devoured every inch of her. Her figure was curved in all the right places and well-toned where it mattered.

Stacie smashed her lips against his, gifting him a breathtaking, ravenous kiss.

Randy cradled her scantily covered buttocks in his hands, sinking his fingers into her seamless flesh.

His mind revisited the night he and Stacie had snuck into the decommissioned barracks during BCT. He thought they'd just indulge in a little foreplay, but Stacie's bold aggressiveness shattered his commitment to rules and regulations, giving him one hell of a gut check.

Before that memorable night, they'd been limited to mindplay and dreamscape sex through their Link, experiencing external stimulation without physical touch.

Randy remembered the rush of dragging Stacie's underwear down her hips for the first time. In a five-second flash, his implant replayed their entire escapade, every vivid sensation, every breathless thrill . . .

Letting go of all restraint, Randy's high-tempo thrusts rocked the bunk, sating his hunger for Stacie's body. She squirmed and panted, clawing the bedsheets as they used their Link to guide each other in giving pleasure. Back and forth, she experienced his sensations, and he experienced hers.

Both mentally enshrined in a sex-induced delirium of physical and mental euphoria, Randy took Stacie's wrists and sank them into the mattress as he steamrolled more thrusts into her. Sixty seconds nestled between her legs seemed like a godsend, after being cooped up with a bunch of rowdy males for days on end.

Linking heightened bodily stimulation to thresholds unchipped minds couldn't fathom.

Randy nailed Stacie with a thrust that stiffened her nipples and sent her to the brink of unconscious bliss. From the overabundance of stimulation, her eyelids blinked, her pupils dilated, and a wheeze caught in her throat, morphing into a soft groan. Randy slackened up but kept fucking her.

Muscles convulsing, he yearned for a release. Somehow he mustered the will to pull out in time. He could only indulge so far without taking prophylactic measures.

In fear of getting caught, Randy and Stacie dressed and went back to their respective barracks, sleeping off the hangover produced by their cerebral implants' expansion of the human sexual experience . . .

Tonight, Randy and Stacie would have infinite time to test their bedroom stamina. Their orgasmic sensations from their previous night of pleasure had been archived, and Randy and Stacie were ready to explore new depths of bodily gratification.

Randy held Stacie at the waist and rolled her onto her back. Now on top of her, he gazed into her blue fuck-me eyes.

"What are you waiting for, an invitation?" she said.

Randy's starving lips trailed down her neck, each kiss a prelude to the carnality about to unfold. He sucked on one of her delectable nipples, causing it to perk up and harden in response.

The inebriating feel of Stacie's naked skin drove him wild. Every bit of her was perfect.

He slid his hand down her firm abs and into her panties. Then he claimed her with an unhurried, torturous rhythm until her mouth hung agape. She opened her legs wider, inviting him deeper into her. He obliged, pushing his fingers further. An expression of orgasmic pleasure drifted across her face.

Amping things up, Randy wrenched Stacie's panties down her lean, defined legs; tossed them away; and buried his face between her splayed thighs. His warm breath conjured sparks in her belly.

She arched her back, grinding her loins shamelessly against his mouth. As he flicked his tongue, her whimpers entertained his ears.

After orally fucking her nether region, he discarded his boxers and positioned himself above her. His body dying to release all the stress and tension from today, Randy's erection was as straight as a flagpole.

Not sparing another tormenting second, Randy sank into Stacie and thrust to his heart's content. Each collision of their loins soothed his needs and his frustrations.

Satisfaction danced in Stacie's eyes, and she made a raspy noise of approval.

Randy arranged her wrists above her head and burrowed into her with no intent of slowing down, her shallow gasps fueling him. This was going to be a night even more unforgettable than their BCT sex night.

• • •

The door to the Intensive Inquiry Unit slid open. Lars and Jason walked into the dank room. The prisoner sat in a metal interrogation chair bolted to the floor, wrists manacled to the armrests.

"We searched your name in the terrorist database," Jason said. "You're Nelson Weaver. Age twenty-one. Former Guardian with Zulu Battalion's Echo Company. You joined Arson Scott's faction but thought the Coalition was too passive for your tastes, so you joined Ritter."

"Yeah, that's right," Nelson confirmed.

"Alright, asshole, I'm not gonna play verbal ping-pong with you," Lars said. "Now where's Arson Scott?"

"First, I need assurance that I'm going to be off the hook if I give you that information," Nelson demanded. "I want to be free to go, and I want my name erased from the terrorist database."

Lars brutally drove his fist into Nelson's gut, knocking the wind out of him. "You're not in a position to be making demands, you little punk. Now I'm gonna ask you again, Where's Arson?"

Nelson coughed. "No deal, no Arson."

"Is that so?" Lars slugged him in the gut again.

Nelson wheezed in pain. "Physical abuse of POWs is illegal, last time I checked," he stuttered, laboring for breath.

Lars said, "Define physical abuse." He turned Nelson's face into a punching bag, mauling it until it was black and blue. "Where's Arson?" He slung Nelson's blood off his knuckles, and red spots mottled the dingy floor.

Nelson spewed a glob of blood. "*Go to hell.*" He spat out a loose tooth soaked in red.

Lars gripped Nelson's hair and hoicked his head back. "Resilient little bastard, aren't you?" He blew a disgusting spray of spittle into Nelson's wrecked face. "Come on, Sergeant Mansford, let's give this hardhead the night to come to his senses."

"We'll be back tomorrow," Jason said as he and Lars headed toward the door.

A line of blood oozed from Nelson's mouth. "Prisoners are required to have three meals! Where's my dinner?"

The door clanked shut. Locks clicked into place.

CHAPTER THREE

Kesley Whittaker woke to the blare of her alarm clock, squinting against the sunlight bleeding through the window.

Outside her third-story unit, the hum of midday traffic blended with the laughter of children frolicking around derelict structures—the usual sounds of the day.

After completing a late shift last night, she wished she could stay in bed longer, but the relief-aid org she worked for needed her.

Dragging her weary body out of bed, she sat upright and dropped her feet to the floor, eyes still adjusting to the sunlight. *Gotta get to it.*

Standing in the buff, she stretched until her joints cricked, basking in the sun's warmth. Every day she got to feel those rays on her skin was a blessing—lately, too many acquaintances had ended up dead or locked away, accused of supporting the Coalition. Ever since the troop surge, the CDF had been coming down harder, showing no mercy, no restraint.

Beginning her usual wake-up routine, she padded over to her worn-out laptop, voluminous red tresses brushing her back. She tapped the power button repeatedly. *Come on. Work, damn it.* When the outdated machine finally came to life, she opened a vidcast of Arman Reza for some words of aspiration and encouragement.

At the bathroom sink, she turned on the faucet. Recycled water belched out murky brown before clearing. While brushing her teeth, she listened to Reza preach hope, rebellion, and a future for the forgotten. His gospel always lifted her spirits.

After showering, she slipped on a pair of cutoff shorts and a white tee that hugged the buxom curves of her chest. Over the shirt, she wore a black jacket to hide a gun. Firearms were contraband under the current moratorium, but that never stopped her. A blue bandanna came next, then a crucifix necklace.

Done dressing, she gave herself a once-over in the cracked mirror before heading out.

Her feet clattered down the creaky metal stairs. Once she hit the ground floor, she stepped outside into the earthy-smelling air. Unpaved roads and bare rolling slopes stretched in every direction; not a single phyocrete street existed for miles.

Across from the residential complex she lived in was a row of ramshackle shops, their facades scarred and weathered signs barely readable. Built during the first phase of migration, they desperately needed renovation. Clearly, Eden's society was advancing while Satellite One's remained stagnant, lacking luxuries like airborne transportation and modern tech.

Kesley walked up to her flatbed carrier vehicle. Just as she was about to open the cabin door to get in, a voice called her name.

Startled, she spun around, heart racing. Consternation drove her to reach for the prohibited firearm stowed inside her jacket. "And you are?" she asked, eyeing the stranger.

It was Randy. His trained eyes noticed the bulge beneath her jacket. He approached calmly, careful not to escalate the situation.

"My name's Randal Scott. I'm a Guardian."

Kesley shot him a look of admonition, halting him in his tracks. "Hold it right there, soldier boy."

"I'm not here to harm you, ma'am," Randy assured her. He chanced another step forward.

Kesley's muscles tensed, her trembling hand tightening around the grip of her firearm. She held Randy's humble gaze with an incredulous stare. "What the fuck do you want with me?" she asked, distrust lacing her voice.

"I'm the Guardian who patted you down in the alley yesterday. I'm sorry about how my superior treated you. I just wanted—"

Kesley's lips pursed. "I already told you that—"

Randy reached into his pants' pocket and gingerly pulled out her credentials. "I just wanted to return this. That's all, Ms. Whittaker." He extended a sturdy arm, giving the feisty redhead her card.

Kesley cast her eyes on him for a long moment—evaluating, assessing, judging. Trusting her instincts, she made her call. Randy wasn't trying to hoodwink her. He was trustworthy.

Her muscles relaxed, and her heartbeat slowed. "Call me Kess," she said, her demeanor softening. "Sorry for being so uptight, but when strangers come calling my name, I get a little jumpy." She withdrew her hand from her jacket and took back her credentials. "I'm surprised. Guardians rarely do anything this courteous. They usually spend their time harassing civilians."

The irony in her words ticked Randy off. "You act like we're a bunch of dicks."

Kesley shrugged. "Most of you are."

Randy's brow creased. "We're fighting to bring peace and stability back to the Commonwealth."

Kesley fastened her hands on her curvaceous hips. "Depends on your point of view," she said with spunk.

"You're an Independent Movement sympathizer, aren't you?"

"I prefer 'advocate.'"

"All just semantics."

A dented, rusty clunker chugged by, its growling engine momentarily interrupting the squabble.

Once the noise subsided, Randy and Kesley resumed their conversation.

"Look," Kesley said, tone cooling but still edged, "you seem like one of the decent ones. After all, you returned my creds, and you didn't cop a feel when you frisked me, unlike most of your buddies." She yanked open her carrier's cabin door. "Ride with me while I pick up and drop off my delivery. Let me show you why the folks in Colony Four hate the Defense Force and central government so much."

"I've already seen some of Colony Four's infrastructure issues, down by Halfin Town Hall."

Kesley scoffed. "Then you ain't seen shit." She jerked her head toward the passenger side. "Get in."

Randy hesitated for half a beat. The duty rotation had Fourth Platoon off today and tomorrow. What harm could going with Kesley do? "Maybe I'll be the one doing the enlightening," he muttered, circling to the passenger side and hopping in.

The refurbished engine sputtered to life, coughing and rattling.

With the AC shot, the cabin was a sweatbox. Randy and Kesley rolled down their windows, letting in gusts of warm, dusty air.

The carrier lumbered over the dirt road, its exhaust stack spewing dark fumes. On Eden, environmental standards would've had the vehicle scrapped long ago.

Kesley's mobile phone buzzed. She grabbed it from the door cubby and held it to her ear while steering with the other hand. A voice crackled on the line. "Yeah, don't worry, I didn't forget," Kesley said. She hung up and tossed the phone back into the cubby.

"A mobile phone?" Randy said, brows raised and voice dripping with disbelief. Such a device was totally obsolete.

"Welcome to the colonies, Highborn. We don't get your fancy gizmos out here. This primitive tech is the best we've got. No wristcom upgrades for us."

Up ahead, Guardians in battledress were hectoring two seventeen-year-old boys. One of the teens mouthed something profane. A second later, he was eating dirt, shoved to the ground by one of the Guardians.

As the carrier rolled past, Kesley leaned halfway out the window and threw up the middle finger. "Fuck you, assholes!"

"Fuck you, bitch!" one of the Guardians shot back.

Randy grimaced at Kesley. He thought she must have gone crazy. "Are you outta your damn mind?"

"Fuckery begets fuckery, soldier boy. Those assholes treat us like garbage every damn day." The carrier rumbled past some Guardians going into a decrepit building. "Bet they're sniffing around for Coalition rebels again. Rebels like to use these ghost blocks to stage nearby ops. But that doesn't give Guardians the right to treat those boys like accomplices to murder or something. They were just kids minding their own damn business, out playing games and having fun n' shit."

"You don't know that," Randy retorted. "You don't know what that altercation was about. Those kids you claim are *innocent* might've been aiding and abetting rebels. There's not a lot you can discern while speeding by in a damn truck. So calm down."

Kesley snapped her head toward him, eyes full of fire, then refocused on the road. "You see? This is what I'm talking about!"

Her voice rose, sharp and hot. "You guys are like some kind of fucking mafia! You cover each other's asses no matter what!"

Randy checked his anger and adopted a gentler tone. "Listen, I understand that Guardians have committed some terrible acts, but I believe they're the minority. I'm truly sorry if the CDF has treated you or anyone you know unfairly."

Kesley calmed down. Randy's acknowledgment of Guardian misconduct renewed her faith in his rationality. "Well, that's a start. Maybe I shouldn't write you off just yet, soldier boy."

An awkward but defusing silence hung between them. As the carrier crested a hill, a cluster of interim housing units came into view.

"What are those?" Randy asked. Visibly disgusted, he stared at the drab box-like domiciles.

"Culture shock, huh, soldier boy?" Kesley said. "They were supposed to be temporary shelters during migration. But . . . 'temporary' kinda turned into 'indefinite.'"

"So families are stuck living in those abominations until the government decides to build them something better?" Disbelief crossed Randy's face.

Kesley nodded, her expression flat. "Something should've been done by now."

"The government *definitely* needs to do more for these people," Randy said, voice thick with sympathy. Barefoot children played with each other outside the units. A frail elderly woman watched over them. The sight hit Randy in the chest. *This is a humanitarian failure. Our leaders need to wake up.* He could only begin to grasp how deep Colony Four's struggles ran. On Eden, people would riot over conditions half this bad.

The carrier left the settlement and rumbled past a brick building that had the Coalition's motto spray-painted across its side: *Keep the Faith.*

The next stop on Randy's tour was a row of charred, near-collapsing slums. "What happened here?" he asked.

"A big firefight during the Three-Week War," Kesley replied. "The bureaucrats promised Colony Four restoration funds ages ago, but we're still waiting. We lost med clinics, as shabby as they were, and a hell of a lot of markets and shops. Now the people who live around here have to make a damn near two-hour trip just to get basic necessities.

"I don't know why the colonies always get the short end of the stick. With this area still in ruins, it's become a hotspot for black-market dealers." An arms broker, standing inside the skeleton of a bombed-out building, showed two younger men a selection of handguns tucked inside his trench coat. "I used to think all the destruction would've pushed the government to finally rebuild and renovate these buildings.

"They've been here since the first arks arrived. They need fixing. Hell, they were never meant to be permanent anyway." Memories surfacing, Kesley stopped the carrier. The brakes rasped. "A lot of people died here—men, women, children."

The devastation triggered a traumatic, eidetic flashback: streets awash in blood, lifeless bodies scattered everywhere, eerie green sensor scans from aircraft slicing through the night, bullets flying, and a cacophony of chilling screams echoing from all directions.

Amid the chaos, Kesley lost track of her brother. Coming out of an alley, she stumbled onto a grisly scene and found his small corpse lying among other war casualties. Weeping, she took the keepsake from around his neck, the very crucifix necklace she wore today.

Randy saw his own pain mirrored in Kesley's somber eyes. "I'm sorry for your loss."

Kesley snapped back to the present. "Huh, wha-?"

"I can see it in your face. You lost someone. Family?"

"Yeah. My kid brother," she said, grief in her voice. "He was seven. He got caught in some crossfire." Kesley took her foot off the brake and pressed the acceleration pedal. The cabin jerked, and the carrier rolled on. "So, you lose anyone? To the war, I mean."

"My mother. She died when the Coalition destroyed the building where she worked." Randy's expression darkened, the memory of Kathleen's death once again tormenting his mind. "And my father, Arson Scott, played a part in the incident," he added, brows knitting together.

Kesley's eyes widened. "You're the son of Arson Scott!"

Randy's features twitched. "Unfortunately."

"He's one of the most sought-after Coalition rebels."

"No fucking kidding."

CDF aircraft roared overhead, scouring the area for rebels.

Kesley switched on the net radio. A newscaster reported, "The number of fatalities from the terrorist attack that nearly claimed Secretary Gould's life has risen. Authorities have confirmed five additional deaths—three from Zanvetera and two from Nebosaa, both Union-approved trading partners.

"The emergency summit is scheduled for the day after tomorrow, and though the deaths of the visitors have placed the Commonwealth under intense scrutiny, Chief Executive Kerner assures the public that incorporated status will not be lost. Also today, Chairwoman Oviereya Amaechi made this announcement."

On the replay, Oviereya said, "I, Chairwoman Oviereya Amaechi, am announcing my candidacy for Chief Executive. I realize the RUC's declaration of independence was an illegal act that plunged the Commonwealth into war. And I despise war. I denounce it. But I understand the animus that incited the

Independent Movement. I understand why colony citizens feel ignored and oppressed. It's no mystery why they've reached their emotional apex.

"The central government has fostered downtrodden societies within its own republic. Martial law must be lifted, and our political system needs reform. Colony governors should have more autonomy, and all colonies should be allowed to engage directly with Union Worlds and external partners, so they won't have to—"

Kesley turned the volume knob all the way down. "I hope she comes out on top. Gould hasn't announced his intention to run, but you know he's going to, and he won't change a damn thing. I reckon things'll only get worse under his leadership. I hope that control freak keels over and breaks his fucking neck.

"Oviereya, I'm confident, will get the central government back on track. Hell, there've even been rumors the government's planning to fund the construction of artificial mini-islands, not for us poor bastards, of course, but as an attraction for intergalactic tourists. A project that'll take fucking *years*. *Hello?* Can someone please shine the spotlight back on colony development? Shit, has helping us become an afterthought?"

The carrier chugged onward south, passing roadkill.

• • •

After scrutinizing her appearance in her mirror, Stacie, clad in a sleeveless maroon dress that had a nice grip on her form and showed off her legs, left her quarters. She was in a good mood, having had Linked intercourse with her boyfriend last night—and again in the shower this morning. When he returned to base, it'd be time for round three.

She sashayed into the lounge, dress swishing over her thighs. Inside, Guardians in civvies were socializing, playing holo table-games, and scarfing down grub from the mess hall. Her eyes found

Jarius at a small round table.

A female Guardian—with Korean features, short cyan hair, and purple-dyed irises—was seated on his lap. She wore a crop top, blue jean shorts, and calf-high boots. After she and Jarius shared a laugh, she stood.

"Later, Yoon," Jarius said over the guffaws.

"Later, hotshot," she replied, walking away.

Jarius missed the warmth of her tush on his lap already.

Stacie came over. "Specialist Ford, mind if I sit?"

Jarius took a sip of his orange fizzing drink. "Not at all, Sub-Lead." Stacie sat opposite him and crossed her legs. "Look at you, all spruced up."

"Hey, what can I say? I enjoy being fashionable," Stacie remarked. She glanced around the room at everyone enjoying themselves. "Could you imagine being stuck in uniform twenty-four-seven on deployment? And no sex life on top of that?" She made a face. "*Bluh*, that'd suck."

"The old guard says that we new-gen soldiers are pampered way too much. They think we're undisciplined and that lax regulations have made us soft."

Stacie laughed. "Babe, I'm anything but soft."

"I'll give you that. You're a Warrior Extraordinaire, after all." Jarius couldn't deny she was one kick-ass lady.

Stacie activated the table's menu panel. She tapped the image of a blue cup on the order display. A boxy server golem floated from the mess hall to the table and set a frothing blue beverage in front of her, then zipped away.

Jarius took another sip of his drink. "So what made a woman of your stature join the CDF?" he asked conversationally. "You don't need the credits. Your parents set you up for life. Spencer Enterprises is basically a financial empire."

Aversion tightened Stacie's features. "That's my issue." Her voice was rough-edged. "I don't want an entire life built by my parents. I don't want my identity to revolve around being a daughter of the Eight." She quickly changed the subject, steering the conversation away from her parents and the Eight. Too many bad memories were being dredged up. "So what about you? Why'd you join?"

She spat out the question at rapid fire, with a grouchy tone. Jarius figured that he'd brought up a touchy subject. "There were many career tracks I could've taken, but they just seemed . . . unexciting." He gave Stacie a sharp grin. "And bland and boring ain't me."

The two kept chatting, gradually easing into lighter topics. As the tension faded, they discovered they had common interests. Both liked sports, surfing, and going to virtual arcades.

• • •

Kesley pulled the carrier up to a gate. Gravel crunched beneath the tires.

A small, weather-worn sign wired to the gate read: PROPERTY OF DYNAMIC RELIEF PROVISIONS.

A security officer in blue exited his booth.

"Am I going to be a problem?" Randy asked Kesley.

She shook her head. "Nah. As long as you're with me and I've got my creds, we're good."

The officer went up to Kesley's door. "Hey, Kess, how are you?"

"Doing as fine as I can, Steve." She showed him her creds.

He nodded and went into his booth. A few seconds later, the gate rolled aside. Kesley drove through, passing busy repositories.

She entered her usual loading station, a small warehouse packed with cargo containers, and slid the gearshift into PARK. The carrier's brakes scraped, and its engine compartment rattled and hissed.

The faint smell of metal and lubricant lingered.

Big rigs bearing the Dynamic Relief Provisions logo trundled in and out.

A train of freight crates, lined one behind the other, moved from station to station on an assembly line. At the midpoint, the double-pronged arm of a robo-loader set packages inside each crate.

A foreman entered Kesley's plate number into his tablet to access her daily manifest. He then gestured to the crane operator, a man in orange coveralls and a yellow hardhat.

The operator returned to his station and maneuvered the crane's magnetic clamp, suspended from the hoist, over a stack of containers. Once a container was secured, he lowered it onto the carrier's cargo bed. After releasing the magnetic clamp, he raised the hoist and swung it to the right to retrieve the next container.

"So how'd your mom and dad hook up?" Kesley asked Randy, waiting for her bed to be stacked.

"My father lived here and worked in the quarries. My mom, an Edenite, was sent here through her employer's temporary placement program for a voluntary special assignment. They hit it off, she got pregnant near the end of her stay, and after I was born, Dad made the lottery. Then they left to start a life together on Eden, got married, and lived . . . not so happily ever after."

So Randy was born here. He's essentially a Highborn with colony ties, Kesley thought.

Once her bed was loaded, Kesley drove off the premises to make her delivery. After some more get-to-know-you talk and a bit more verbal sparring over moral high grounds, Kesley and Randy arrived at Kesley's destination.

Randy eyed the brick building. "What is this place?"

Kesley rolled her eyes. "Don't you know anything?" Randy frowned in response. "It's an Assistance Living Center, one of three in this district. Dynamic Relief Provisions built all three. Children orphaned by the war and men and women who were displaced stay here. My payload is their food and supplies for the week. The place we left is one of Dynamic Relief Provisions' distribution hubs."

"I see," Randy said, compassion in his eyes. "We . . . on Eden hear about these things, but we don't see them unless we travel to a colony. And we rarely have a reason to."

Two ten-year-old boys zipped past the carrier on a pair of air scooters. Their laughter pealed.

"Time to give Joey and Kimberly their turn," a female service worker said, half stern.

Kesley stepped out of the carrier.

A middle-school-aged Indonesian girl and her two elementary-aged twin brothers rushed across the dirt path, excited to see Kesley. The girl wore a shirt and overalls, and she had inky-black pigtails that reached her shoulders. The twins wore matching yellow shirts and beige pants.

"Did you bring us candy this time?" one of the boys asked, his grin stretching ear to ear.

"Sure did, kiddo," Kesley replied. She mussed up his already-wild hair with her hand.

The girl squinted up at Randy, curiosity in her pearly dark eyes. "Who's he? Your boyfriend?"

Kesley laughed. "He's a friend of mine, from Eden."

The girl's jaw dropped. "You're a Highborn?" She pointed at Randy.

"Uh, yeah, I am," he said.

The girl's eyes lit up. "Are there really big, tall buildings on Eden called skyscrapers?" She spread her arms high and wide to mimic the scale. "And flying cars too?"

Randy bobbed his chin. "Uh-huh. Here, let me show you something." He pressed a button on his wristcom, and a shimmer of digital color morphed into a 3-D image of his sports cruiser.

"Cool, a hologram!" The girl snatched Randy's wrist.

Randy's feet stumbled forward as the girl pulled him closer to get a better look at the holo. "Whoa!" he exclaimed. The girl's adorable, innocent eyes gazed unblinkingly at the gleaming image. *The things that fascinate them are so ordinary for us Edenites. A shame,* Randy thought.

A bearded man—dark brown skin weathered from time and stress, bags under his eyes like he'd been fighting sleep for years—walked up to Kesley. A cigar smoldered between his lips, and he held a metal thermos in one hand. His jeans ragged and checkered flannel shirt wrinkled, he could be mistaken for a drifter.

He took the cigar out of his mouth. A dusting of ash slipped off the tip and scattered. "Who's he?" he asked, voice gravely.

"A Guardian," Kesley answered. She watched Randy play with the boys, drawing their laughter. "One of the good ones." *And a hunky one to boot,* she thought. She'd heard Highborn men, thanks to their genetic upgrades, were unreal in bed. But she'd never met one worth confirming that rumor with. Until now.

"Wasn't sure good ones existed," the smoker said. A sip of water from his thermos wet his dry throat. "I'll go grab the guys. We'll get some power pallets to unload everything." He tucked the cigar between his lips.

The limp in his leg, caused by an unjustified beating from some Guardians, made the short walk to the center feel like a trek.

Daylight waning, shades of orange emblazoned the sky.

As twilight fell, Kesley and Randy made the commute back to her residential complex. They spent most of it comparing their upbringings, which were like night and day. She had discontinued high school to help support her family; he had graduated from Commonwealth University. She had grown up in a small housing unit; he had grown up in a high-end family home. Her family had to be frugal; his didn't.

Kesley parked the carrier in the gravel lot, beside a hatchback that had seen better days. She and Randy got out.

Hyped, Kesley said, "Man, all the wonders of Eden you've been talking about and showing me on that doohickey wristband—I'd love to see them in person someday." Her voice was full of childlike enthusiasm. "I wanna see the skyscrapers and multiplex shopping centers. I wanna ride in a flyer."

Randy rested a hand on her shoulder. "How about we go there one week when I'm on leave?" he offered sincerely. "I'll show you everything. I'll even take you for a ride in my sports cruiser."

Kesley sighed. "It'd probably take forever just to get a two-week travel pass."

"What do you mean?" Randy felt chagrined by his lack of knowledge. "I don't really know how the pass process works. It's not something I've ever had to think about."

"Well," Kesley began, "after you get through security, you've gotta wait hours in a long screening line. First, you hit the ID-check station, where proctors thumb-print you to run a full background check, which now includes making sure you're not flagged in the terrorist database."

With feigned exhaustion, she went on. "*Then* you wait again, till they sit you in front of a computer to answer a long-ass checklist of *stupid* questions. And now it's stuff like, 'Have you ever been approached by anyone asking you to join an anti-government or terrorist organization?' or 'Do you have friends who are members of one?'" Annoyance clouded her face, and Randy looked unsettled. "Third," she continued, "a proctor takes you through a medical exam to make sure you don't have any communicable diseases, and that all your vaccinations are current."

Kesley's shoulders sagged. Just thinking about the process was exhausting. "The process was already a pain in the ass. I imagine now it's gonna be a *double* pain in the ass. And after all that, you still have to wait anywhere from six to twelve months. And there are way too few staff processing all the applications."

"I can see how irritating it is just to get a plastic card to go to Eden," Randy said. "The process needs to be streamlined."

Kesley scoffed. "Funny, isn't it? We're all supposed to be equal citizens of humanity's *great* intergalactic republic, but it's like we're together but separate. And if caught with an expired pass on Eden, you get locked up, so you better make sure your butt doesn't miss the return flight." She shook her head. "Hell, intergalactic tourists and vacationers get quicker access to Eden than us colonists, because they're feeding the economy."

"Total bullshit," Randy said.

"Yeah. And I get that you can't cram all of us colony folks onto Eden. It's only got one continental landmass, which ain't big enough for all of humanity. But still, you shouldn't have to go through a buncha hooey just to visit your fellow human beings."

"I agree," Randy said. "The goal, though, is to have Satellite One eventually become an 'Eden.'"

"Yeah, well, that's not happening anytime soon."

Randy's stomach growled.

Kesley giggled. "Guess you're pretty hungry, huh? Gotta be. We haven't eaten much all day." She started walking toward the complex's front door. "Let me take care of that stomach for you."

"I . . . I don't know. I should probably get back."

"What for? You're off the clock today. No one's searching for you, right? As long as you're back when you're supposed to be, no one really gives a hoot about how long you're offsite."

"Yeah, true," Randy said, still unsure if he should stick around.

Kesley gestured for him to follow. "Then c'mon."

Randy sighed and gave in. "Fine."

They went into the building and entered Kesley's third-story unit. The stale air permeated their nostrils.

Randy's eyes swooped over the cramped square space. The kitchenette, living area, and bathroom were all crammed together, boxed in by flaking white paint. To him, this place felt abysmal.

Without a beat of hesitation, Kesley wrestled her clammy shirt overhead, outright baring her naked flesh.

Randy flinched in surprise. "What are you—?" His heart stopped. Was this an unspoken invitation for . . . ?

"Just changing shirts, soldier boy. It's been a long, sweaty day." Free-spirited, Kesley strode over to her closet, completely unashamed. Her voluptuous breasts waggled with each step. "I'm not shy about showing some skin, if that's what's got you all dumbstruck. *Geesh*," she said. "Honestly, a devout nudist like me would rather be naked all the time."

The shape of Kesley's body was enticing. Randy couldn't help but stare, eyes drawn below her collarbones. She had a rack that was impossible to ignore—one with plenty of bounce.

She slipped a gauzy white tube top over her chest, and Randy's admiring gaze ended. The orange print on the shirt said SCREW THE GOVERNMENT. Randy hoped she wouldn't wear that shirt in public; the controversial words would attract attention.

Done changing, Kesley opened the fridge.

Randy wondered if she had a thing for him, if undressing in

front of him had been a seduction tactic. Maybe her choice of clothing was another—the thin tube top exposed the lower curves of her breasts and the outline of her nipples.

She pulled out two plastic containers of stew, slid them into the microwave heater, and tapped the two-minute timer. "Be ready in a jiffy. Just make yourself at home."

Randy took a seat on one of the two wooden crates at the table, its surface hidden by a white linen cloth.

When the microwave pinged, Kesley retrieved the containers and set them on the table. "Mom's recipe. You'll enjoy it, trust me." She grabbed two spoons from the cupboard and gave one to Randy. "Bon appétit."

Randy scooped a bite of stew into his mouth. The spicy flavor hit instantly, titillating his taste buds. "This is good. Your mom knows her stuff."

"Thanks."

As annoying as Kesley could be sometimes, Randy appreciated her taking him on her delivery run. The trip gave him a new perspective on colony life. "Hey, I want you to know that everything I saw today was a real eye-opener."

"Yeah, that's what I was hoping for. The route we took, so you could see all that, was intentional."

Randy blinked. "What do you mean?"

"That was the scenic route to the distribution hub. I could've gotten us there way faster." Kesley paused, letting that land. All the ruins and low-grade housing were intentional waypoints. "People like you might be able to make a difference, if you're aware of what's really going on here. Because as long as people stay in the dark, this oppression's gonna keep going. But if enough people like you open their eyes, maybe they'll actually do something for their fellow human beings."

"And what do you hope 'people like me' will do?"

"Stop turning a blind eye to pain and suffering. Divvy up some credits and donate to Assistance Living Centers. If you see Guardians messing with people, find your balls and stand up to them. Not too much to ask, right?"

"No, it's not." Randy downed some more stew.

Kesley was unlike most women he'd known. She was scrappy, street-smart, pushy, unrefined, and completely unfiltered. A far cry from the prissy women he'd befriended or dated in his home city, Frenchester Heights, or at Commonwealth University. He found that kind of attitude obnoxious but also . . . attractive.

After a few more spoonfuls of stew, Kesley added, "Who knows, maybe the more that open-minded people like you learn about what's going on here, the more likely it is that Oviereya becomes the next Chief. That's part of my hopes and dreams, anyway."

"Mine too." When Randy finished his meal, he stood. "Thanks for the hospitality, Kess. I should head back now."

Kesley walked him to the door. "It was nice getting to know you, Randy."

"You too. I'll definitely come back and visit." Randy's eyes landed on Kesley's satchel in the corner. "So, what were you doing at the comms tower yesterday?" The Guardian Lars had sent to check out the tower found no tampering.

"Nothing you need to be concerned about," Kesley said coyly. "But I've got a little gift for you to remember me by." A sensual smile tugged at her lips.

"What would that—?"

Kesley's mouth captured Randy's in a delightful, wet n' wild kiss. A kiss that almost knocked him off-balance. As she gradually pulled back, she pinched his lower lip with her teeth, a strand of saliva stretching between their mouths.

Warmth flooded Randy's cheeks. He'd been caught off guard. "I, uh—" His wristcom chirped. Lars had forwarded a message to the platoon. "Excuse me." Randy faced away from Kesley so she wouldn't see the confidential content.

Holowords in a text box said WE'RE GOING TO BE ON DUTY TOMORROW AFTER ALL. SO MAKE SURE YOU REST UP. OUR CAPTIVE JUST GAVE US ARSON SCOTT. WE KNOW WHERE HIS FACTION'S HIDEOUT IS.

Body pumped full of pain analeptics, Nelson had cracked fast. Even a finger poke evoked unspeakable agony thanks to the drugs.

Randy pressed a finger to his wristcom. The text dissolved. He turned back around, a rigid set to his jaw.

The heated look on his face—a look that could melt steel—gave Kesley goose bumps and made her take a step back. "Something up?"

Randy ground his teeth. The agony in his chest stabbed at his heart. A-1 Defense Solutions exploding into a burst of fire and smoke flashed in his mind, the last memory of his mother. "My platoon has a big impromptu mission tomorrow. I've gotta go." He yanked open the door and took off down the stairs.

Kesley closed the door behind him.

Randy made his way back to Lima Company on his hoverbike, speeding through a town. Arson temporarily off his mind, he thought about the bleak living conditions the people of Colony Four had to accept. *People on Eden who never visit the colonies might think their citizens are just bitching and moaning, but they do have a legit gripe.*

Randy heard the tumble of a trash receptacle and the sounds of a scuffle. As he shifted his body to the left, his hoverbike veered toward the commotion.

132

Two Guardians in battledress—one tall and brawny, the other short and stocky—slammed a man against a brick building. The sign in front read: MICKEY'S BAR.

"You a rebel?" the tall Guardian asked.

"I didn't do nothin'! Lemme go!" the man begged.

Randy decelerated, cut off the bike's engine, and dismounted. He bolted onto the scene, passing an inebriated civilian who was lumbering out of the bar and taking a swig from a flask.

Randy flashed his military ID. "What's going on here?"

The shorter Guardian replied, "In the bar, we overheard this bum making disparaging comments about the government. He could be a Coalition rebel."

"Last time I checked, anti-government discourse wasn't a crime," Randy said. "Are you really that paranoid?"

The tall Guardian replied, "We can't take any chances." He gripped the man's shirt and curled his fingers, bunching the fabric in his hand. "This gutter trash might be someone who kills one of our brothers-in-arms, and I sure as hell couldn't live with myself if that happens."

Randy's jaw clenched. "Yeah, but you can't compromise the integrity of the Defense Force—or deface its image—by roughing up every person you're suspicious of."

The short Guardian snorted. "Well, excuse the fuck out of us. The people of this mud-ball colony hate our guts and want us gone. Sounds like we've got a little cause to be concerned."

Randy pointed a finger at them. "You shouldn't have signed up for the job if you're gonna be so easily scared."

The tall Guardian flicked his hand, dismissing Randy. "Forget you. Get outta here."

Randy bristled at the insult. "Maybe you don't know who I am. I'm Randal Scott, and I've got connections to people who can have you mopping floors for the rest of your military careers."

The short Guardian let out a pissed grunt. "C'mon, let's go," he said to his comrade. They both left.

"You okay?" Randy asked the man they'd been hassling.

He tipped his head. "Yeah, I'll be alright."

"Need a ride or anything?"

"Nah, you go on. Thanks, though. Good to know there are Guardians like you who stand up to bullies like that."

"No problem at all."

Randy took off on his hoverbike.

He was fresh out of military training. He hadn't been a witness to the mistreatment of colonists by the CDF until coming to Colony Four. Guardians graduated from training with the belief that the CDF was always in the right, acting with the highest morality. He'd known the CDF had some imperfections, but maybe there were more cracks in the armor than he'd expected.

Guardians were told colonists were wrong for being anti-government, but after what he saw today, Randy understood why they were. That didn't mean he believed rebellion was the answer to their problems. After all, colonies Two, Three, and Five continued to enact change using a nonaggressive approach, rather than start a war.

It seemed the rogue colonies' citizens distrusted the central government because it had neglected them for so long, and they disliked Guardians because they were the government's enforcers, agents of the status quo. On the flip side, Guardians disliked the rogue colonies' citizens, viewing them as military-haters, whiners, and nonconformists. Their training conditioned them to see all government opponents that way. It was a difficult dilemma to fix.

Randy reached Lima Company and slowed to a stop at the checkpoint. After the Guardian on security detail confirmed his identity via retina scan, he drove past the gate and parked in the motor pool, in a row of hoverbikes. Ready to call it a night, he headed toward Annex 13.

For a moment, he thought about Kesley and their journey today, grateful for what it had shown him. Kesley had made an extraordinary impact on his thinking. His heart went out to her for the struggles she had endured and for the loss of her brother.

The memory of her mouth smothering his flashed across his thoughts. He guessed he'd made an impression on her as well, her planting a kiss on a Guardian. To deny she was sexually attractive would be foolish. He knew she'd make some man extremely happy, if he could stand her in-your-face attitude.

His mind refocused on business. Tomorrow, he'd have the opportunity he'd been waiting for. It was the reason he had Conlan get him stationed at Colony Four. Tomorrow, he'd confront his father . . . hopefully.

His implant pulsed like a warning siren—Stacie was near.

She burst through the front door, her face alight with energy. "You missed chow. Everything good?" she said, voice vibrant.

Randy didn't waste a second; he pinned her against the iron door, kissing her. His lips blazed a trail down to her cleavage. "Yeah, everything's good." He claimed her lips again, while reaching underneath her dress to stroke her thigh. Arson was a problem for tomorrow; tonight, more sex with Stacie awaited.

CHAPTER FOUR

Blue-to-red strobe lights flashed throughout Arson's stronghold. An earsplitting claxon-like alert blared. The sound of shoot-outs echoed.

"Hurry!" Arson shouted, racing down a corridor toward the shuttle bay with a slew of rebel troops, all armed. He and nine others wore white humanoid mechsuits, their headgear appearing to have an open-face design.

The reinforced entry door lowered behind them as they rushed into the bay, a cavernous space that resembled a warehouse.

A thunderous wham struck the blast door in front of them.

"They're using a battering ram!" a male rebel yelled.

Everyone fanned out, rifles in hand. They took defensive positions behind crates and containers.

Arson barked exhortations. Voices overlapped, rebels swearing and shouting in hysteria. Everywhere, there was heavy breathing. Terror swirled through minds.

One quivering young woman quietly recited the Coalition's motto. "Keep the faith, keep the faith, keep the faith."

An exhausted man ran up to Arson, fighting for breath. "The enemy has infiltrated every wing, sir," he panted. "We here in the bay are the only ones who have a shot at making it out alive. Everyone else is going to be killed or captured."

"Damn it! How'd they find us?" Arson blurted, wondering what security vulnerability led to this. He spun and gestured to the only pilot in the bay. "What are you waiting for, Richter? Get that shuttle prepped for takeoff! We're abandoning base!"

"Roger, sir!" the pilot replied. "Since the shuttle just came back from a run, it'll take at least fifteen minutes for the power banks to recharge enough for us to get anywhere!"

"Just get it done! And tell the incoming cargo ship that we've been compromised! They are to abort the delivery of the assets and reroute to Bravo Camp!"

The pilot sprinted off.

I can't believe we're it, Arson thought.

A rebel woman in a black tee and olive-green tactical pants came to his side. Her complexion wasn't as brown as her father's, nor as fair as her mother's. She had short dark brunette hair, deep brown eyes, and was in her late thirties. "Don't worry, we'll escape." She kissed Arson's lips.

"Thank you, Sariah." A boom buckled the blast door inward, metal screeching. "They're using a plasma cannon now! Get ready, everyone!" Arson heaved a deep sigh of remorse. *Once again, we're left with no choice but to fight back. It's us or them. Commonwealth Government, if only you'd end this madness. Then we wouldn't have to*

—

Another boom blew an opening in the blast door, twisting, warping, and liquefying metal.

Lars and squads One and Two of Fourth Platoon bum-rushed the bay, footfalls pounding the floor. The rotary barrels of their

Gatling guns—the equipped primary weapon—spat an onslaught of heavy-caliber rounds, cutting unarmored rebels down into a bloody slush of limbs, organs, and body parts.

Rebels returned fire with a mix of bullets and energy blasts.

The backpacks feeding the ammunition belts into the Guardians' Gatling guns radiated heat as rounds tore through everything, shredding crates and containers, punching holes into walls.

The nodes on Arson's headgear illuminated. His rebels' mechsuits were operated by brain-computer interface, like Shells. At his mental command, interlocking plates enclosed his face, but not before Randy caught a glimpse of him.

Father, Randy thought.

Since Randy had last seen him, Arson had grown a thick dark beard, and his face bore a few stress-induced wrinkles.

"Careful, everyone!" Lars shouted. "I count ten with some sort of strange armored combat suit not cataloged in our index!" Including Arson, there were seven men and three women. The rest of the rebels wore plain, ragged clothes. Lars C-commed the leader of his third squad. <<*This is Sergeant First Class Freeman to Sergeant Thornton. Is the motor pool secure?*>>

Thornton's rifle rattled, a burst of bullets mowing down a rebel. Blood sprinkled over the phyocrete. <<*Motor pool is now secure,*>> he said to Lars. A hiss of steam escaped his rifle's barrel.

<<*Roger. Be advised: The enemy has unidentifiable mechsuits at their disposal, and there's no telling—*>> Combat interrupted Lars in mid-thought. <<*Gotta go.*>>

An assault vehicle blew apart in a shattering blast that hurled nearby Guardians into the air.

Shelled bodies, dust, and debris flew past Thornton. "Holy shit!"

The explosion slammed one Guardian against a vehicle's hood, cracking its windshield.

Thornton scanned the area for hostiles and caught a strange armored figure in his sights. *Must be what Lars was talking about.* "Target, left!"

The armored rebel held a sizzling sphere of plasma energy in his hands. With a kinetic push, he jettisoned the energy projectile at the infiltrators.

Guardians scattered, shouting colorful expletives. Another vehicle exploded, reduced to a heap of flaming wreckage.

The rebel balled more plasma energy with his hands. The complex, foreign tracery on his white armor glowed, and the suit emitted ghastly whistling noises.

"Open fire!" Thornton shouted.

Rifles rang as a conflux of bullets pelted the alien mechsuit.

Thornton saw the bullets fragmenting on impact. But how? The armor? Some kinetic output? Just like everyone else, he was awestruck. "Hold fire!" he ordered. *Fucking unbelievable.* "Switch to energy weapons!"

The rebel paused and dissolved the projectile. After a moment of stillness, he gave a nod, receiving a command to retreat.

His vernier jets ignited, launching him into the air.

Damn, these suits are aerial-combat capable too, Thornton thought. "Stand down, everyone!" Shells and weapons clattered. *Where the hell did these rebels get something like that?* he wondered.

"Arson," Sariah said, two pistols recoiling in her hands, "I've got your six!"

Arson was crouched behind a revetment. "Thanks, Sariah." He

stood and fired five shots from his energy rifle.

Jarius' Oracle analyzed the possible moves, tactics, and targets he was considering, then transmitted to him the best course of action. He took the advice, rotated left, and turned his Gatling gun on a rebel aiming at a fellow Guardian. Jarius' bullets riddled the rebel, ending his life.

"Get down!" Stacie shouted at Emilia. With her Gatling gun already depleted and discarded, she easily dove onto her adversary, tackling her to the floor and out of the path of incoming energy blasts.

Emilia, now sitting on her tailbone, stared at the smoking holes in the wall. *Whew, that was a close call.* "Nice save, princess."

Stacie, kneeling and facing her, said, "Yeah, thanks to my hardware." Heightened mental acuity was another perk of the upgraded CPU.

Streaks of energy zipped overhead, startling Stacie and Emilia.

"C'mon, let's get these motherfuckers," Emilia said.

Setting aside their mutual dislike, Stacie and Emilia jumped back into the fight as a team.

Stacie, using arm-mounted weapons, and Emilia, wielding her Gatling gun, concentrated their firepower into a fusillade that plowed down a group of rebels.

Bullets from Randy's Gatling gun spun bodies into bloody pirouettes. Shell casings spewed from the backpack's ejection port, pinging into a growing pile on the floor. Exhaust hissed along the gun's vents; then, suddenly, the trigger only clicked. AMMO DEPLETED flashed on Randy's HUD.

With a thought, he detached the backpack, sending it clanging against the floor. He dropped the heavy Gatling gun, and it thudded. His Oracle initiated the next step before he could give his CPU the command.

His secondary sprang up from a recess on his leg panel. He gripped the handgun, pulled it free from the securing clips, and drew it forward. "Thanks, Oracle."

"User is welcome," the AI replied.

The recess sealed. Randy discharged a deadly pulse of blue energy that exploded the chest of an unarmored rebel. A mess of red splotches and spalled flesh fragments sprayed in all directions. "Father!" He advanced toward Arson.

Arson turned to him, recognizing his son's voice. "Randal."

Randy commanded his faceplate to go away. It slipped up, exposing a seething expression.

It's been a while, Son, Arson thought.

Randy's faceplate resealed. He continued his pursuit of vengeance, firing blasts at anyone who got between him and his father, the betrayer who plagued his mind.

Closing the distance, Randy scored a shot to the abdomen of a plainclothes rebel. Bits of the rebel's body splattered grotesquely against his Shell. Another lethal blast burst a woman's head into a cocktail of blood and brain matter. Shot number three destroyed a man's leg below the kneecap.

A rebel jumped from behind the crates at Randy's six and ambushed him. A rocket launcher rested on the husky man's shoulder.

"No, wait," Arson said. But it was too late. The rebel had squeezed the trigger.

Randy craned his head. *Damn it.* He saw a rocket speeding toward him.

His Oracle made a tactical decision for him, activating his Shell's plasma-energy barrier.

A blue bubble ballooned around Randy. The explosive projectile collided with the energy field and scattered apart, metal shards darting across the bay. The Oracle expanded the barrier further, ensnaring the rebel in its wake. He screamed, the energy field incinerating him into ash.

The barrier deflated and crackled away as the Oracle dissolved it.

"Thanks again, Oracle," Randy said. The AI Combat Assistant was a true partner.

Randy checked his Shell's power cell. The vitality gauge on his readout was at level two, ten being full power. The cell was nearly depleted because of the barrier shield, but had the Oracle not activated it, he might be dead. Drawing from the auxiliary reservoir, he restored four units of power.

Sariah raised her pistol at Randy.

"No, don't get involved. That's an order," Arson said to her.

Bullets and energy blasts crisscrossed the bay in a barrage of destruction.

Randy checked his handgun's power-status indicator and saw the cell was drained. He sealed the weapon in the recharging holster and pressed a button on his armguard. Plasma energy coalesced into a flickering purple blade that extended from his wrist, his close-quarters weapon.

Rebel blood drenching his armor, Randy stared down Arson, an apoplectic look in his eyes. "I want answers, Father!" He swung his plasma saber, cutting the air.

Arson jinked, dodging Randy's swift attack.

A flurry of sizzling swings came at Arson. The blade sliced two gashes into his nanoengineered armor, but they instantly sealed.

Self-repairing tech? Randy thought.

Sariah jerked her pistol up at Randy. "Darling, I can help."

Darling? Randy thought, roiled. Was she his mom's replacement? It was bad enough that Arson had participated in his wife's murder, but now a new woman was in his life?

Enraged, Randy charged at Arson, screaming and brandishing his saber.

Arson kicked him onto his back, armor clanging against armor. Then he reiterated his order to Sariah. "I told you, *don't* get involved."

She lowered her pistol.

Randy leapt to his feet, the death of his mother consuming him.

A metal cable catapulted from a recess under Arson's wrist. The magnetic clamp clung to Randy's Shell.

"What the hell?" Randy said. He gripped the cable with his left hand and lifted the blade of his right. Before the blow could fall, a crippling plasma charge electrified the cable.

SYSTEM OVERLOADING blinked on his HUD, and circuits blew out. A harsh pang killed the cerebral link between his mind and the Shell. As his visuals flatlined, he let out an awful scream, and his legs buckled.

Arson retracted his taser coil and caught Randy's crumpling form in his arms, hauling him easily over his shoulder.

"Arson, Richter has informed me the shuttle is ready for takeoff," Sariah said.

"Everyone, fall back into the shuttle for evac!" Arson shouted.

The other nine armored rebels laid down suppression fire as their comrades withdrew into the craft through its rear-deck door. They took up staggered positions so they wouldn't get picked off easily. One of them generated an energy sphere in his hands, hurled it at a Guardian, and watched him disappear in a bright burst, remains blown all over the bay.

"Man, that's some crazy fucking firepower!" a female Guardian yelled.

A Shell would severely drain its power cell if it launched an energy attack that strong.

Jarius saw Arson heading into the shuttle with Randy. *Darn it,* he thought. *I've known you too long to let these guys take you from us. Hang on, buddy.* He activated his Shell's stealth cloak, which disguised him by replicating his surroundings.

Power consumption for stealth cloaking was on the high end, so Guardians couldn't stay cloaked for long. Jarius would have to move fast. How he and Randy would escape was still unclear, and he didn't have time to figure it out. Brave or stupid? Either way, it was too late to get cold feet now. He and Randy would have to improvise when the time came.

Jarius maneuvered into the shuttle, its rear-deck door slowly lowering. He'd have to be vigilant; stealth cloaks didn't make a Guardian completely unseeable or mute sound.

Lars shouted as the outgunned rebels fled into their escape craft, "Move in and take that shuttle out!"

The Guardians walked their gunfire forward, trying to overtake the retreating rebels.

The rear-deck door clamped shut. All the surviving rebels had made it inside. With them out of the line of fire, the shuttle's exterior gun batteries whined to life.

"Shit!" Lars yelled.

A salvo of hot slugs from the guns ripped into Guardians' Shells. Blood sprayed.

Guardians quickly bubbled themselves inside their barrier shields.

As the shuttle powered up for liftoff, the guns whined to a stop. An opening in the ceiling parted.

Nico lowered his shield. He extended his arm, and from a slot on his armguard, a tracer blasted out and tagged the undercarriage of the craft as it elevated into the sky, making a getaway.

Barrier shields went down, their shimmering auras crackling away. Cooling weapons hissed.

Nico thought, *The dog is injured and on the run. We've got you, Arson Scott.*

Lars said, "Sergeant Mansford and Sergeant Fleming, check your people and give me an ACE Report."

A Guardian removed her helmet and vomited, unable to withstand the sight of all the massacred bodies, CDF and rebel alike.

"Someone, help," a barely alive Guardian drawled through a mouthful of blood. His Shell had been breached and organs damaged.

In the aftermath of the violent skirmish came a din of pain-filled wails, plaintive cries for help, panicked voices, and shouted instructions.

Team leaders got headcounts, logging who hadn't survived.

Stacie, breathless and fatigued, said to Lars, "They got Randy." Dents, fractures, and sooty marks blemished her Shell, and red blotches of blood stained the gunmetal Kryoplaste. Her faceplate slid up. The inflection of her voice soared to a dramatic pitch. "What are we going to do?" In a knee-jerk reaction, she gripped Lars' shoulders with her suited palms.

"Nothing we can do," Lars replied laconically. "And Jarius is missing. A Guardian said he saw him cloak and go after Randy."

"Can't the Nerve Center track Randy's signature?" Despair cast its shadow over Stacie's face. Worry swarmed in her belly.

Lars said, "Already tried. His Shell's gone dark. It's completely off the tracking grid. Must be offline."

Stacie expelled an acquiescing sigh.

Lars hated losing any of his Guardians, whether by death or

capture. "Randy's my soldier, no matter how much of a pain in the ass he is, so I don't like it either." He walked away.

A knot of dread settled in Stacie's chest. She prayed Randy would somehow return safely.

Looking at the carnage sent a chill traveling down her spine. When her eyes landed on a sight too graphic for words, her mouth fell open. Emilia's body had been torn apart. Swimming in her blood was a grotesque mix of entrails, minced flesh, and Shell scraps—all hers. This was the handiwork of a plasma-energy attack from one of those alien mechsuits.

Still acting as First Squad's interim Alpha Team Leader while Holister recovered from injury, Stacie logged Emilia as "killed in action." *Great job, Stacie,* she thought bitterly. *One KIA and two MIA.*

Nausea churned in her stomach. She averted her eyes from the gore and covered her mouth with her hand, shaking in horror.

As Guardians scrambled to help their injured comrades, the blood-soaked floor squelched beneath their mechboots.

"I am detecting elevated levels of psychological stress," said Stacie's Oracle. "Should I administer the SR-21 sedative to help —?"

"No! No psychotropic drugs," Stacie replied. She shut off her Oracle, removed her helmet, and racked it.

Jason Mansford went up to her and placed a hand on her shoulder. "Don't worry, the psychs are on duty tonight if anyone needs them. The chaplain's available too. I know this stuff can really mess with your head." He pulled out a cigarette from his chest plate's personal compartment, holding it out to her. "Want one? It helps."

Stacie eyed the offering and took it from him. "Oh, what the hell," she said. "Thanks."

Jason produced a lighter and lit the cigarette.

Stacie said, "I've been trying to quit, but under the circumstances—" Her voice was ragged. She shuddered at all the destroyed human bodies. "*Ugh*, gross." She felt herself getting queasy. "You always keep these on hand?"

"We have to use personal compartments for something."

Stacie drew smoke into her lungs, nicotine alleviating her nausea. She exhaled a mist. "They got Randy. Hope they don't harm him." Her voice quavered, and her thoughts were a tangled mess of worst-case scenarios.

"Well, Arson is his old man, so I don't think his life is in any danger."

"I hope not." At the mercy of the unknown, Stacie closed her eyes and kept smoking.

Subjected to combat stress for the first time, young Guardians —who had never fought in an actual battle or taken lives—sat on containers to decompress.

A Guardian studied the bay. "So what was this place?" he asked Lars.

"It was originally an alloy-processing facility for Mining Absolute, a top mining corp on Eden, owned by some entrepreneurial bigwig named Kenneth Lords. Apparently, the Scott Faction repurposed it as a base. Since Arson was a quarry worker, he naturally had industry connections, and private property off-limits to the CDF without proper justification made for the perfect hideout.

"Whether Lords is a Coalition supporter and was aware one of his decommissioned facilities was being used as the Scott Faction's base remains to be seen. Could be one of his quarry managers was helping Arson under his nose. He's being taken into custody for questioning."

Stacie pondered how Randy was doing as the glowing tip of her cigarette smoldered.

<<*Spencer,*>> she heard over the C-comm. It was Lars. <<*You can calm down a little. Sergeant Fleming has just informed me he tagged the shuttle with a tracer. We might be getting Randy back soon.*>>

Stacie's spirits lifted, and a subtle smile of relief livened her face.

Lars transitioned to audio. "Listen up, everyone. Sergeant Fleming tagged the shuttle. I've gotten permission from higher to dispatch a squad to follow it, while the rest of us stay behind to secure the facility and harvest any beneficial data. I'm guessing most of it's been scrubbed.

"Mansford, you and your squad will pursue the shuttle. Wherever it lands, you are to stand by for backup and observe. Under no circumstances should you engage. That clear?"

"Understood," Jason replied. He C-commed his remaining squad members: SPC Stacie Spencer, SGT Olivia Slovak, SPC Eli Manson, PVT Ryoko Nahara, and PVT Seth Youngblood. <<*Alright, no recess for us, people. Get your asses in gear, and let's get into a BUS and tail that craft.*>>

They all C-commed back "Roger."

•••

Randy came to. Through his slitted lids, the bright overhead light stung his eyes. He winced and rubbed them with his forearm. He was lying face-up on a metal bench in his sleeve, his head throbbing. The whirring of turbines reached his ears. Obviously, he was still aboard Arson's evac shuttle.

Randy brought himself to a sitting position and took in his surroundings. Metal walls boxed him into a constricted square space that had a barred window. He was in a detention cell.

He got to his feet. His back ached from lying on the hard metal surface.

The thunderhead outside crackled and flashed, promising a violent storm.

He moved to the cell door and peered through its small rectangular grille. Two rebels were guarding him. One had almond-colored skin, a thick build, and a close-cropped dark beard streaked with gray. The other was of Vietnamese descent, had a medium build, and appeared to be in his mid-twenties. He wore his dark hair in a neck-length ponytail, and scruff covered his jaw. They were watching a newscast on the tablet the bearded rebel held.

An anchorwoman onscreen said, "The emergency summit happens tomorrow. People are on edge. We now know the assassin who tried to kill Chairman Gould was a lone wolf inspired by Arman Reza's anti-government rhetoric—"

Randy rapped the cell door with his knuckles. "Hey."

"You're awake," said the bearded rebel.

The ponytailed rebel contacted Arson using a palm-sized comm-set. "Sir, your son is awake."

The comm-set squawked. "Bring him," Arson replied.

"Yes, sir." The comm-set beeped and went silent.

The bearded rebel punched a code into a wall module. Locks clacked. The cell door screeched open. "Come on, we're taking you to your father, and don't cause a commotion like your comrade did." He kept his weapon trained on Randy.

"What comrade?" Randy asked, his voice a low rumble.

"Guy's name is Jarius. He stupidly sneaked aboard to play hero." Jarius' heroics had simply ushered him straight into enemy hands.

"Was he harmed?"

"He's fine. Just locked up."

"Well, you don't have to worry about me trying to escape,"

Randy assured the two rebels. Venom in his voice, he added, "I'm actually looking forward to this."

Randy's escorts led him down the shuttle's central corridor.

A downpour pummeled the craft's hull.

With his patience fraying and emotions high, the short walk felt like an eternity to Randy.

As he thought about his mother, the phosphorescent illusion of her appeared again, levitating beside him.

Remember what I taught you about forgiveness, Kathleen's voice whispered in his mind.

Get lost, he replied.

Son, I—

Randy's nostrils flared. "Go away!" he said aloud.

The cerebral specter vanished.

His escorts stared at him as if he'd lost his mind.

"Who the hell are you talking to?" the ponytailed rebel asked.

"Just take me to my father," Randy demanded, seeing red.

The walk continued.

Randy wondered if his mother's consciousness had transferred into him when she died, now living as some kind of entity within his cerebral implant. It sounded far-fetched. Then again, the unforeseen possibilities of the Quilgarian technology were vast. Or maybe he was simply teetering on the edge of insanity.

The rebels marched him past two automatic sliding doors, finally ending his wait. But his arena, a featureless all-white room with a single wall screen, was devoid of Arson.

"What the hell? There's no one here," Randy said.

A holo of Arson took shape, flickering and shifting until it stabilized. "Leave us," Arson commanded his men.

The rebels exited, and the door whisked shut behind them.

Rage burned in Randy's eyes. "You don't even have the courage to face me man-to-man."

"No, that's not it," Arson replied matter-of-factly. "I'm just not interested in fisticuffs with my only son. Last time we met in person, you tried to maim me with a plasma saber. This way, no one gets hurt."

Randy grunted.

Arson said, "Hear me out. Kathleen's death was an accident. A-1 Defense Solutions was my op. My intel said the building would be vacant that night and—"

"Well, your intel was wrong!" Randy lashed out, venting the anger that had been festering inside him for months.

Arson's chin touched his chest, and he pressed a hand to his forehead. The impact of Randy's words had hit hard. "Yes, it was. And I take full responsibility for what happened that night. I constantly think about what I could've done differently, to prevent Kathleen's death." Repentance was written all over his face. "I ask myself, 'Was there any way to reconfirm the floors were clear before detonating the explosives? Should I have called Kathleen to make sure she wasn't at work?'

"My wife's death has traumatized me. I have nightmares about that night. Hell, I was the one who thumbed the detonator." The anguish in his voice rose. "In *no way* has this been easy for me. So spare me your vitriol. I'm not some heartless monster. If it weren't for Sariah, I don't know if I would've been able to go on living."

Bastard. Hurt and indignation compounded, launching Randy into an emotional tirade. "You shouldn't have left! I had to be there for Mom because you weren't! You neglected *your* responsibility as a father and husband—as a man! Who abandons his wife and son to go off and join some terrorist outfit?"

Arson shook his head. "One man's terrorist is another man's revolutionary." As the shuttle bumped against turbulence, the holographic transmission blinked and sizzled.

Randy looked at Arson with an expression that seemed to ask "Are you serious?"

Randy said, "So that's what you think you are, a revolutionary?"

Arson adopted a defensive tone. "It's the *truth*. This is a war the central government caused, after all."

Condemnation enveloped Randy's face. "Your mind's been so deluded by the Coalition's doctrine that you can't think straight."

"Maybe it's your mind that's been indoctrinated and institutionalized to where *you* can't think straight. You've seen the despicable housing conditions and eroding infrastructure. You've witnessed the degradation of people under martial law. The Independent Movement is a revolution.

"Initially, colony selectees, including my parents and me, were thrilled to finally leave a desecrated Earth. We accepted the temporary living arrangements built in the colonies, as subpar as they were. It was understandable. Intergalactic colonization wasn't going to be all rose petals and rainbows, but people believed something better was on the horizon, or so they thought.

"Colony development ramped up with help from the other Union planets, and then it slowed. Colonists watched Eden flourish while their own conditions remained unchanged. The disparities between Eden and Satellite One only grew.

"In my early manhood, I was complacent, working in the quarry pits for decent wages. Then I met your mother while she was on assignment, and she got pregnant.

"I wanted to make something of myself and create a stable life for my family. I wanted you both to have a better life than the one I had growing up. So seven years after obtaining Eden citizenship and working as a manager for JMD Intergalactic, I enlisted in the CDF and fought in the Phazharian and Bhalkran wars.

"When the RUC formed and declared independence, I became angry. I had fought to keep the colonies safe from our enemies, and then the governors of colonies One, Four, and Six, with majority public support, disavowed our Constitution. They *knew* declaring independence would lead to civil war.

"But though I was angry, I understood why people wanted independence. They'd been suffering and ignored for far too long.

"And I could relate to them, not only because I was once a colony citizen, but also because I faced unfair treatment in the CDF from comrades who thought an immigrant had no place as a Guardian. They believed AEGIS had chosen only *them* to be the Commonwealth's protectors. I proved them wrong, though.

"Despite my own experiences and the colonies' hardships, I kept telling myself there had to be another way to achieve equality than disavowing our Constitution. So I fought to reclaim the renegade colonies in the Three-Week War. After that, my superiors assigned me to command Charlie Battalion's Lima Company to help restore law and order.

"Under martial law, I watched people's rights get stripped away —the right to bear arms, to question authority, to even listen to someone like Arman Reza if they chose to. People were being mistreated and oppressed.

"It was like the freedoms I'd sworn to protect were being torn away from my own people by my own government. I felt like I had betrayed my friends, my relatives, my community." Arson paused, working to contain his fury. "Randy, this martial law flagrantly violates human rights!" he shouted, the firestorm inside him becoming more turbulent.

He calmed. "I felt terrible. I asked myself, 'What would my family think of me? What would you, my son, think of me after I betrayed my people?' But what could I do? As a Guardian, I was duty-bound to enforce the government's will.

"Then I met Arman Reza, the catalyst of the Independent Movement." Arson struggled to articulate his admiration of Reza. "His words penetrate your soul and enlighten your mind. He's a messenger of an extraordinary kind.

"Reza made me realize there's no shame in fighting the government. He showed me that I wouldn't be disgracing myself by joining the Coalition. In fact, I'd be honoring the very promises and freedoms this intergalactic republic was supposed to stand for.

"It's like a man once said, 'A great revolution is never the fault of the people, but of the government.'"

Randy chastised Arson for admiring Reza, saying, "Reza's idealistic crusade is the reason that the fanatic who tried to assassinate Gould got those intergalactic visitors killed."

"Reza isn't responsible for every lunatic who misuses, misinterprets, or radicalizes his teachings," Arson countered. "After meeting him, I knew I had to rectify the wrong that I had played a small part in creating. How could I live with myself if I did otherwise? I have family here, living in the nightmare created by the central government stalling development and imposing martial law. I *had* to do something. So I joined the Coalition."

"You didn't have to! I know the colonies have problems, but there were other ways to achieve change. Starting this war was wrong! Colonies Two, Three, and Five didn't result to violence! Instead, they—"

"Haven't done shit!" Arson growled. "The Coalition is the answer to bettering life in the colonies. We give hope to disillusioned people."

In a moment of uncertainty, Randy began second-guessing himself. Had he misjudged his father?

Arson said, "I would've explained to you and Kathleen my

reason for leaving, but who knows what tabs the CDF might've been keeping on you guys to get to me."

Under Commonwealth law, any communication—intentional or not—with war criminals had to be reported to the Defense Department. Failure to do so meant arrest on conspiracy charges. Arson didn't want to put his family at risk. He had communicated with Conlan, but even with the utmost precautions, he couldn't entirely eliminate the possibility of endangering him.

Feelings of betrayal roared within Randy. "You shouldn't have left. Mom suffered because of your decision."

Arson looked mournful, caught in guilt's viselike grip. He had never meant to cause his wife any pain. "I thought Kathleen's family, especially Merriam, would help her cope and—"

Randy would hear no more. "Save your excuses, Father. You need to pay for hurting Mom, dishonoring our family's generations of service, and your dereliction of duty."

A wave of repulsion permeated Arson's voice. "No, it's the politicians who need to pay for *their* dereliction of duty."

"What the hell's that mean?"

A crash of thunder punctuated the moment.

Arson said, "At first, the Coalition's goal was to wear down the government and the CDF until we got what we wanted: an action plan to modernize the colonies or autonomy. But we've concluded that we must overthrow and rebuild the entire government, regardless of whether they give in to our demands. The Coalition's new goal is to end the government as it stands."

The Coalition's new goal gave Randy pause. "So the Coalition is planning a *complete takeover*?" He emphasized "complete takeover" as if the Coalition had crossed a moral line, switching from liberators to would-be dictators.

"What we're planning," Arson said, "is to overhaul this broken system for the betterment and dignity of the *entire* Commonwealth, not just the amelioration of the colonies. What began as a war for colony liberation has become a war to free the Commonwealth from corruption, so it can become the virtuous republic it was always meant to be."

Curiosity got the best of Randy. Arson had piqued his interest. He reeled in his animosity, for now, but it simmered beneath the surface.

He adjusted his tone to sound a little more polite. "Go on." Wrestling with the discomfort of having a civil conversation with his father, he briefly wrenched his gaze from the holo.

"The Coalition has gotten some people within the government to defect," Arson said. "Those inside informants, and a few anonymous whistleblowers sympathetic to the colonies, provided us with some very damning information about several members of the Parliament and lower-level officials."

"Alright, humor me," Randy said. Arson was apparently beginning to break through his son's intransigence.

The screen in front of Randy flickered to life, showing a bracket displaying headshots of Parliament members. At the top of the bracket was Cornelius Gould. The screen zoomed in on him.

"This man is dangerous," Arson said. "Especially in the position he holds. Many people believe he'll run for CE in the next election. If he wins, he'll be even more dangerous.

"What the public doesn't know is that most of the funding for his campaign as a Chairman of the Parliament came from the CEOs of these corporations." Logos of various corporations populated the screen, which included Zenith Combat Technologies and A-1 Defense Solutions.

Randy said, "So, what you're saying is that Gould is indebted to those CEOs. Sure, politics is a dirty game, but what you're describing isn't illegal. A CEO can make a personal donation. He just can't use corporate funds to do it. And yeah, maybe Gould's giving kickbacks for those donations, but that's how the game is played. Not saying I'm okay with it."

"Well, there's more," Arson replied, not done yet. "These corporations are owned by one of the Eight Elite, the Spencer family."

Randy's brow creased. What did Stacie's family have to do with any of this?

"Patrick and Darlene Spencer gave each of these CEOs the maximum number of G-credits allowed for individuals to donate to political campaigns," Arson explained. "All of those credits went to Gould's. The Spencers bypassed the law capping a registered donor's credit limit by illegally funneling donations through their CEOs.

"And we have undeniable proof that it *was* the Spencers' money, not the CEOs', that funded Gould's campaign. Those CEOs were just smokescreens, obedient yes-men used to launder money and cheat the donor tracking system—put in place to cap the wealthy's influence in elections. In exchange for their . . . 'generosity,' Gould awarded the Spencers' corporations lucrative contracts to supply the CDF with tech and weapons.

"So, if a defense contractor isn't part of the Spencers' network, it stands little chance of getting CDF contracts. In essence, Gould is stuffing the Spencers' coffers in return for their support."

Randy said, "What the Spencers and Gould are doing is definitely illegal. But beyond Gould agreeing to award contracts to the Spencers' companies, how much influence do you really think they have over him? He doesn't strike me as someone who'd let himself be anyone's puppet."

"Maybe not," Arson conceded, "but the Spencers have real clout in the government, possibly more than the constituents who elected our officials. And with whatever influence they have over Gould, the planetary partners they want, for expanding their intergalactic enterprise, will be some of the first on his list for Union approval if he becomes Chief. The Spencers could easily become 'first-serve.'

"Think about it. If Gould wins the election, that means one of the Eight Elite would have some influence over the Commonwealth's leader. I'm betting Gould would offer government positions to any of the Spencers' sycophants that they want in his administration, as a favor.

"And Gould isn't the only government official, chairman or lower, being influenced by one of the Eight." The screen flashed, and the bracket of chairpersons reappeared. One frame glowed red. "This is Parliament Chairman Markum Weiss. He's taking bribes from the North family."

Another frame lit up. "Jason Wen, Marshal of Commonwealth Law Enforcement. He's making it harder for our police to take down a specific trafficking operation that's selling our women and children to intergalactic slave networks. That operation belongs to the Prosser family, another of the Eight Elite. Wen's on their payroll, doing what he can to keep the police off their trail."

Arson briefly stopped talking, letting Randy digest what he'd heard so far, then continued. "The Eight are nothing more than a consortium of criminal entrepreneurs, and their crimes go all the way back to Earth Era. Our intel shows many government officials are being corrupted by criminal organizations, but the Eight Elite are by far the most powerful of them.

"We believe other Elite families may also be backing CE candidates. They could all be vying for influence over the highest seat in the government. But we don't think they're at odds with each other, at least not in any serious way. It's more like a friendly game of one-upmanship between them."

A chirp from Randy's wristcom stole a second of his attention.

Arson said, "I've forwarded some of the intel from our inside sources to your wristcom. There's a lot there. Take your time, Son. This shit will blow your mind. And if you're thinking about contacting your company with your wristcom, don't bother. The signal's blocked aboard the shuttle."

Randy's sense of justice had been stirred, but his scholarly mindset kept him from making premature decisions. He'd study the info thoroughly before deciding what to do. "I'll review everything with an open mind."

"Good." Arson sounded glad. "Not every government official is corrupt, but the ones who are need to be incarcerated. The whole system needs to be overhauled, for the colonies' survival and the good of the central government. If no one takes a stand, this corruption will never end. I don't know about you, but I signed up to fight for our republic, not the Eight Elite and a bunch of dirty politicians."

Randy, though still upset with his father for leaving and inadvertently partaking in Kathleen's murder, found the corruption revealed today disturbing. "Let's not pretend. Even without this evidence, the Coalition still would've tried to overthrow the government, because all your efforts haven't amounted to much, and victory is starting to seem inconceivable. This corruption was just the smoking gun needed to make government overthrow more justified."

After a beat of contemplation, Arson said, "Maybe."

"So, what's the plan for this . . . Eden invasion?"

Arson found the phrase "Eden invasion" abhorrent. "It's called Operation Hammer Fall. And the first move is exposing the corruption to the public. But we need a distribution channel with enough range and bandwidth to disseminate the info across Eden and all the colonies simultaneously. It has to bypass net restrictions and stay online long enough for everyone to access it."

"So the Coalition needs to take possession of the Parliament Building to gain control of its broadcast center," Randy deduced. Before tech had advanced, the Chief Executive would use the broadcast center to vidcast all their addresses to the entire Commonwealth, and still used it occasionally. "From there, net restrictions can be lifted, and this info can reach everyone on Satellite One and Eden."

Arson nodded. "Correct. But we're not just taking the Parliament Building. For strategic purposes, we'll also be seizing the Chief's Manor and the Academy."

"How does the Coalition's assault force plan to enter Eden airspace without detection?"

"We've got a starship being fitted with cloaking technology."

Well, that's impressive, Randy thought.

He wondered what race of beings had given the Coalition tech advanced enough to cloak an entire ship. Shells couldn't stay cloaked for long without suffering a massive power drain. Cloaking an entire ship, long enough to breach Eden airspace and reach the Parliament Building, was a feat the CDF hadn't even pulled off yet.

"Tell me, after the Coalition topples the government, then what?" Randy asked. "You guys just establish an illegitimate oligarchy?"

The mere thought of setting up an autocracy turned Arson's stomach. "No, we're not dictators, but yes, we do intend to have input. We plan to collaborate with the honest officials and the public to reform the government and achieve equal footing between Eden and the colonies. We'll let democracy take its course.

The people will decide who replaces the corrupt, and due process will decide their fate."

"So who's spearheading this mission? Who's directing the Coalition's moves and procedures?" Randy asked.

Arson stood silently.

Randy pressed, voicing a suspicion held by many but never proven. "Is it Reza? Is Reza the Coalition's head honcho?"

Arson went ahead with the truth. "Yes, he's the overall decision maker for all the factions."

"What's the makeup of this assault force?"

"It'll consist of three elements composed of armored and unarmored troops, totaling a few hundred. The Reldaldri built the mechsuits you saw some of us wearing at my base, and they're essential for Operation Hammer Fall. My faction's final shipment of suits was en route before your people attacked.

"The shipment was rerouted to my Bravo Force's camp, the second and only other unit of my faction. Those suits are crucial to give us the firepower we need to succeed. We're headed to Bravo Force's camp now to receive the shipment and recuperate."

Never one to be indirect, Randy demanded more info. "So, what's the *full* plan for Hammer Fall?" He wanted the breakdown, the ins and outs.

"The three elements of the assault force—Red, Blue, and Gold —will airdrop onto their respective targets and take them over. Then shield generators will be set up at each site. It's that simple."

Randy considered the plan weak. It certainly didn't inspire any confidence in him. "So it's gonna be a cakewalk, huh?" he said doubtfully. The Academy taught him that piss-poor plans produced piss-poor results.

Arson understood why Randy would be concerned about the odds of success, but it was the best plan the Coalition had for ending the war. "Well, it's a surprise attack. No one could possibly anticipate what we're about to attempt. But we are expecting an intense battle. After all, we both know how fast the CDF's Rapid Response Teams can deploy to reinforce the Quad's security forces.

"So, best-case scenario: we deal with the security forces and Rapid Response Teams, with minimal to no loss of Guardian lives, and get the shield generators in place before hundreds more activated Guardians converge on the Quad to overpower us. Worst-case scenario: we end up battling a massive number of Guardians, and a firefight like no other erupts on Eden soil. We're hoping for the former. We don't want too many Guardian lives put in danger. None, actually.

"Reza has entrusted me with overseeing Hammer Fall's entire contingent. He's also appointed me leader of Red Force, which is tasked with taking over the Manor. Blue will take the Academy. Gold will take the Parliament Building.

"Once activated, the shields will buy us, I'd say, at least seven hours before the CDF figures out how to neutralize them. That's plenty of time to cast the info over the net, let people process it, and allow Reza and the uncorrupted Parliament members to negotiate a peace deal.

"The info will undoubtedly turn the Commonwealth's citizens and the CDF against the central government. I can't imagine anyone wanting a bunch of scumbags to remain in office."

Randy wasn't sold. "Plan sounds kind of iffy to me. Needs more refinement."

This wasn't Arson's first war. As a captain in the CDF, he'd learned that you didn't always have the resources, troops, or time to perfect a plan. And the longer you waited to strike, the more ground the enemy gained. "Nothing's foolproof, Randy. Things don't always go a hundred percent as planned, but we're ready to adapt and modify as needed.

"I want you to join me. Join this revolution. Reza's dream is to create a Commonwealth free of corruption and a CDF that doesn't blow away its own Guardians just for having a heart or difference of opinion, a CDF with true checks and balances. You'll see that the Coalition, if you choose to join, doesn't retaliate against its own, treat opposition forces or Edenites with cruelty, or take prisoners just to torture and beat."

Randy thought about Lars assaulting Kesley. He also thought about the civilian he had saved from an unnecessary beating by two Guardians.

Arson said, "Reza doesn't condone any of that nonsense, and he truly wants all the Commonwealth's peoples to coexist peacefully. And I get it: Just because corruption exists doesn't mean you go join a rebel outfit and betray the oath you took as a Guardian. You're probably thinking there are other ways to oust corruption and ensure the colonies achieve equality. You have to decide for yourself who the good guys and bad guys are."

Randy thought about what Conlan had said: *There are two sides to this war. We . . . we choose the side we believe has the moral high ground. The side embodying our values the most.*

"Maybe I shouldn't have left you and Kathleen. Maybe I should've let others fight the war for colony equality," Arson said. "If that's so, I'm sorry. But you have to understand, it was my honor and dedication to what the Commonwealth stands for that drove me to fight for the Coalition. To me, joining them was no different from leaving you and Kathleen for a long-term deployment."

Deployments are mandatory. You leaving wasn't. And families know where their loved ones are being deployed to. Just more excuses for abandoning us, Randy thought. "What if I don't want to be a part of this?" he asked.

"Then we release you somewhere safe, and you can return to your duty station. Like I said, we don't have a use for prisoners, and we don't interrogate, torture, or do any of that garbage. But please, Son, give joining us some genuine thought."

Locks clacked, freeing the room's door to open. The two escorts came in.

Arson said, "They'll be taking you back to your cell. Sorry we don't have better accommodations, but we'll be landing in a little over an hour. So you won't be in there long."

The ponytailed rebel took Randy's arm. "Come on."

As Randy was being steered away by the men, Arson said, "I really hope you join us."

Almost at the door, Randy stopped. "Tell me, has there been any collusion between you and Conlan?"

"I relayed to him my reasoning for joining the Coalition, and I expressed my grief after Kathleen's death, but no, there was never any collusion. His loyalty to the CDF is without question."

Randy let the two rebels take him out of the room. The holo faded into a blurry haze and vanished.

While Randy was being escorted back to his cell, his thoughts wandered. He was actually starting to believe the Coalition had the moral high ground. After yesterday's eye-opening trip with Kesley, and the damning information his father provided today, he was questioning his military indoctrination.

As he neared the brig, he thought about Stacie. He wondered if she was keeping secrets, if she was involved in her family's illegal dealings. His heart sank at the possibility.

After being taken back to the brig, Randy sat on his cell's bench and powered on his wristcom, accessing the recent download. A holographic folder-selection menu appeared above his wrist. He touched the tag labeled GOULD, and a dozen virtual files materialized.

Using a fingertip, he dragged three files to the right and three to the left. He touched them one by one, opening each in its own window. Suspended in midair were emails, soft-copy documents, G-credit transaction data, graphs, account numbers, and other evidence confirming his father's accusations about the Spencers.

Randy devoured the information, processing every detail.

He accessed the folder on the Prosser family and their trafficking operation, poring over trade-route schematics, expenditures between the family and their field handlers, and even pictures of abducted young women. There was also data confirming Wen's assistance.

Thirty minutes in, Randy still wasn't done. The corruption was real. Gazing at the thirty-plus windows open around him, he had a heart-to-heart with himself. Something had to be done.

Although his rancor toward his father remained, he was able to put it aside for now. He still believed Arson shouldn't have left, triggering Kathleen's moments of mental and emotional collapse, but Arson wasn't the terrible person he'd thought he was. Arson truly believed his reason for fighting with the Coalition was valid.

Randy wouldn't have left to fight in a rebellion at his family's expense if he were in Arson's shoes, but that was him. He and Arson had two opposing schools of thought.

As Randy delved deeper into the information, he considered the unthinkable: He might join the Coalition himself. But he wasn't sure if Reza was truly what he claimed to be—a savior—or just a ruse, a wolf in sheep's clothing, a manipulator seeking power. Randy was determined to find out, and the truth about Reza might ultimately decide where he placed his allegiance. In the meantime, he hoped to avoid any confrontation with the CDF.

"We are now landing," the shuttle's pilot reported over the

intercom.

Time had seemed to pass quickly while Randy studied the files.

The shuttle closed in on Bravo Force's camp, isolated from any sign of civilization.

Randy looked out the barred window. The shuttle was banking downward, seemingly on a collision course with a cliff. He jerked back. *What the hell is—?* The cliff warped, rippled, and fractured as the shuttle phased through it. *Stupid me,* Randy thought, his heart rate slowing to normal. A holographic mirage.

The CDF wouldn't search a no-man's-land for Coalition hideouts without concrete evidence they were operating there, especially since all hot zones were concentrated in Colony Four's urban districts. Still, the mirage added an extra layer of protection for Bravo Force's open camp, just in case.

Once the shuttle was stationary, Randy's cell door slid open.

Sariah Manard walked in. Two lime-green smart jackets hung from her right forearm. She extended her free hand to Randy. "It's a pleasure to meet you, Randal. Arson's always spoken fondly of you." Her voice had a warm, dulcet resonance. It was deep and soothing. Quite a lovely sound.

Randy took her hand and shook it. "Thank you." Though he was still uncomfortable with his father getting involved with another woman, he had no ill feelings toward Sariah.

"Come on, let's get outside," Sariah said. "And put that on. The rain's not coming down heavy anymore, but it's still drizzling."

Randy slid into the jacket and zipped it up.

They left the cell and followed a corridor.

"So, what's the story between you and my father?" Randy asked as two rebels passed them.

"I was a nurse at a medical clinic in Halfin. Like many, I got sick of the injustice, so I joined the Coalition. I learned how to fight. Learned battle tactics. Became a leader. Your father and I fought together often. During his grief, I was there for him, and we fell in love.

"After Kathleen's death, he wasn't sure if he could love again, wasn't sure if he should *allow* himself to.

"But even though we're together, I still see the love he has for Kathleen in his eyes. Your father's a good man. And I don't think Kathleen would want you two at odds."

Randy's features compressed into something close to irritation. He wouldn't be warming up to his father anytime soon.

He and Sariah exited the shuttle into an old dig site, which was steeped in the pitch-blackness of night. Only four spotlights lit up the tarp shelters, portable housing modules, and freight containers converted into domiciles.

They raised their jacket hoods as a light rain fell. Wind whooshed, flinging warm droplets into Randy's face.

He and Sariah swiped the left sleeves of their jackets. The water-repellent material glowed neon green.

Ahead, a handful of rebels ran toward a saucer-shaped spacecraft, their boots squelching in the soggy earth. They wore glow-in-the-dark jackets similar to Randy and Sariah's, the glow lighting their way through the camp. They also used wrist lights.

By the spacecraft, Randy saw rebels speaking with a lavender-skinned, roughly humanoid race. Their robe-like garments, which had numerous pouches, were utilitarian rather than fashionable. A black cloth wrap covered their hairless scalps, and they wore eccentric goggles over their frog-like eyes.

Randy figured they were the Reldaldri and that the craft was the rerouted ship carrying the suits Arson's faction was supposed to receive before the CDF attacked his base.

The cargo hold door groaned open to reveal containers packed with the suits.

Some of the Reldaldri spoke in their native tongue, loudly and harshly. They were clearly irate about the course diversion.

One of them held out a device. A rebel pressed his palm against it. The device beeped. Some sort of signature confirmation of receipt, Randy guessed.

"So, where's Arson?" he asked Sariah.

"Doing damage control," she replied. "Alpha Force was decimated. He owes the chain of command a sitrep."

"Chain of command? You mean Reza?"

"Yes."

A man walked up to them. "Sariah, I'm glad you and Arson made it safely."

Randy estimated him to be in his early forties.

"Randy," Sariah said, "this is David Larkin, leader of Arson's Bravo Force. Larkin, this is Randal Scott, Arson's son."

"Nice to meet you, Randy," David said in a welcoming tone. "I wish I had time to chat, but I have to supervise the offload. Take care." He took off jogging toward the delivery ship.

Sariah walked forward, mud caking the soles of her boots. "Come, Randy, I'll take you to your tent."

"Wait," Randy said. Sariah stopped mid-stride. "A friend of mine infiltrated the shuttle in a rescue attempt. His name is—"

"Jarius Ford. I know. He's fine. No one's going to harm him. But because he can't be trusted, he'll remain detained for now."

Randy couldn't shake his worry for his friend. "I want to see him."

"Tomorrow, you can see both your friend and your father. For now, I'll take you to your tent so you can get some rest. And I'll bring you something to eat."

Inside his tent, Randy sat in a dented metal folding chair. He forked some meat into his mouth from the tray on the makeshift table in front of him. It was a reasonably sized tent, offering enough room to stand comfortably. At his feet, a cell-powered glow-lamp buzzed softly.

He searched the rest of the Gould files for anything that might implicate Stacie—a breadcrumb, a message, some form of proof connecting her to her family's criminal activities. More covert communications and deep-pocket dealings between Gould and the Spencers appeared.

Realization dawned on him. He was fooling himself. He wouldn't find any evidence showing Stacie was directly involved in her parents' schemes. She'd joined the CDF to distance herself from their operations. But that didn't necessarily mean she hadn't known about them. And if she didn't, what would she think when he told her?

Randy shut off his wristcom and eased himself into the hammock strung between four worn wooden poles. Rain tapped the tarp above, a steady, restless patter. He closed his eyes. In all the bombardment of information, he had forgotten the emergency summit was tomorrow. And if the Commonwealth got booted from the Union, chaos would ensue. Tomorrow was going to be a hell of a day.

The roar of a distant liftoff was the last sound he heard before his consciousness receded into sleep.

First Squad of Fourth Platoon was conducting reconnaissance atop a precipice overlooking the camp. Jason's reticle zeroed in on the outbound Reldaldri ship thundering into the drizzly sky, its undercarriage lit by multicolored lights.

He tightened the zoom on his reticle and snapped some

pictures. *Who are you, and what were you doing at that camp?* Rain tinkled off his armor as he ran the pics through his CPU's spacecraft index, hoping for identification. The query came back as UNIDENTIFIABLE, as he'd expected. *Wonder who the Coalition is in cahoots with.*

"Any new developments?" Stacie asked, approaching Jason in her Shell, her helmet racked at her hip. The soft, wet ground made sucking noises as each mechboot sank into it.

Jason shook his head. "Nah, not much movement besides that ship finally leaving. I got some clear pics, but no ID."

The rain stopped, and a shroud of fog crept over the ridge.

Time seemed to drag for Stacie. "So when's the cavalry getting here?" The angst in her chest wouldn't subside.

"The company has just finished securing Arson's hideout and mining its databases. They've got to get back to HQ to recharge their Shells and reequip. We took a lot of casualties, and hell, some Shells aren't even mission capable. I'm operating at seventy percent functionality myself. And the company needs rest. Plus, Commander Seymour wants more intel, so we don't go in blind. It's going to be a while."

"Damn it." Stacie kicked pebbles and wet earth. "Shit!"

"Hey, calm the fuck down, Specialist. I know you're worried about Randy, but I think he'll be okay. Besides, us going down there blind won't do a damn thing to help him. Which is why we need to conduct recon. Hell, we don't know what was off-loaded from that alien ship. Better to go in as prepared as we can be than half-cocked and get our asses handed to us."

Stacie exhaled a frustrated sigh. "Yeah, you're right."

"I'm sending a recon drone down there. You should try to rest up. I know the BUS isn't exactly the best of accommodations, but out here, it's better than the dirt."

"Roger, Sergeant." Stacie started toward the BUS.

"Hey," Jason called out, stopping her.

Stacie turned halfway. "Yeah?"

"After seeing all that carnage back there—and given how worried you are about your boy toy—are you in the right headspace for the fight that's coming? Because when we storm that camp, it's gonna get real—fast. I can't afford any liabilities."

"And you won't have one," Stacie said firmly. "When it's go-time, my head will be exactly where it needs to be."

"It'd better be," Jason warned. If he thought her mind wasn't clear enough for combat, he'd bench her. And to make sure she stayed put, he'd command override her Shell to lock her out of it.

Stacie went into the BUS without another word.

A globe-shaped microdrone deployed from Jason's suit. He activated its stealth cloak and guided it down into the camp. He'd have to be careful. If the rebels spotted the drone, they'd evacuate, ruining the CDF's chance of capturing or killing Arson Scott.

CHAPTER FIVE

Outside the Chief Executive's Manor, a media frenzy was in full swing. Union leaders were arriving for the emergency summit, and the press was there to capture every moment.

News networks provided wall-to-wall coverage, with commentary and recaps detailing how this day came about. Orange-and-black-striped barricades blocked off streets, air traffic near the Manor was restricted, and additional Executive Protection Agents (EPAs) were stationed at the gates.

A hover ferry sailed toward the Manor, flanked by an entourage of battlecruisers. The first of the Union leaders had arrived, Queen Pappalonie of planet Taramassia.

The ferry carried the young queen and her driver, while her sentries rode the battlecruisers in powered exoskeletons, fully prepared to neutralize any threat to her safety.

The antigrav vehicles whisked to a stop. Cameras flashed, and reporters jabbered excitedly into their mics.

The vehicles settled onto the ground.

The ferry's overhead energy dome powered down, blinking and

crackling. The lift descended, bringing Her Majesty down to the phyocrete.

The crowd greeted her with oohs and aahs, as if she were a luminary.

Cameras clicked in a frenzy.

The Taramassians had dark teal skin, outstretched fox-like ears, and tendrils in place of hair, each adorned with gold rings. The yellow sclera of their eyes contrasted with their midnight-blue irises. Four round silver markings decorated their foreheads, matching the color of their eyebrows.

Their planet's ecosphere was a fusion of jungle and technology, as they held nature in high regard.

The queen wore a gold top and skirt made of a sheeny metallic fabric. On her feet were sandals with straps crisscrossing up her stout little calves. On her forehead gleamed a magnificent jeweled tiara, the sign of her position as Taramassia's leader.

As she strolled gracefully toward the Manor's gate with her sentries, her jewelry jingled. She was only five feet tall, so her towering protectors looked like titans beside her.

A wiry reporter rushed forward to snap photos, too close for one sentry's comfort. The sentry growled a warning. The reporter quickly backed up, stumbling and falling onto his backside.

EPAs kept the media at bay as the queen and her guards passed. The media would only be allowed onto the lawn once the Chief was ready to announce the results of the summit.

In the distance, a spectacle of antigrav vehicles hovered toward the Manor, more Union leaders arriving.

In the Chief Executive's office, an overwhelmed Jared Kerner sat behind his polished, commanding desk. Deputy Chief Angela

Norton occupied the brown armchair in front of him.

The space resembled a typical high-ranking executive's: a wall monitor, large windows, tasteful art, and plush, high-end carpeting.

Jared gazed down at a holographic picture of his young Asian wife and seven-year-old daughter, suspended above his wristcom. His careworn expression was a telling sign he was coming apart at the seams.

His eyes were bloodshot, and his appearance was unkempt, hair disheveled, stubble speckling his jaw, suit coat rumpled. Angela, by contrast, was the picture of composure. She was dressed in a well-pressed beige pantsuit that complemented her caramel skin, and her indigo curls were perfectly styled.

Jared shifted his woeful eyes toward Angela, silently pleading for some kind of reassurance that he was still fit to lead humanity's intergalactic republic. "Where did it all go downhill?" he asked ruefully. "After the Three-Week War, stabilization operations were supposed to be simple: send in the CDF, impose martial law for a few weeks, round up the last of the rebels, and restore order.

"But things . . . didn't go that way." He thumbed the slider on the side of his chair, reclining the backrest. Then he gripped his head with both hands. "And now there are uprisings even on Eden, and our incorporated status hangs by a thread."

"Nothing is ever simple," Angela said calmly.

Jared shut off the picture. It flickered, jittered side to side, and then vanished.

He adjusted his rimless square glasses. "Was I too quick to let Gould talk me into going to war with the RUC? Should I have tried alternative solutions? Sent the Ambassador Corps instead? What would my father have done?"

"We can't unmake the past, Jared," Angela said curtly.

It still irked her that Jared had overtaken her in the primaries, riding on the coattails of his father's popularity. He'd been thirty during the election, with far less time in politics than her. She was a decade older and far more qualified to be Chief Executive.

Somehow, youth, vigor, and charisma had triumphed over wisdom and experience. But now Jared's inadequacies, once masked by hype, were coming to light. People increasingly saw him as a figurehead, assuming his advisory committee and trusted consultants like Cornelius were the true masterminds behind the government's ongoing success.

At first, Angela had questioned whether she should accept the nomination for Deputy Chief and serve in what she viewed as a mismanaged Jared Kerner administration. But ultimately, she decided it was a smart move. Having Deputy Chief on her resume would only strengthen her candidacy when the time came to run again.

Jared thumbed the slider forward, elevating the backrest of his chair, and removed his glasses, setting them on the desk. He buried his face in his hands, anxiety overtaking him. "Maybe I shouldn't have let Gould pressure me into going to war so quickly. Then again, he served under my father, and my father always trusted his judgment in military matters."

Such an insecure weakling. So easy to manipulate, Angela thought with disdain. "Well," she said aloud, "our Constitution clearly states that declaring independence is an act of treason. You took Gould's advice and exercised your authority to declare a State of Emergency, authorizing the deployment of troops to squash the insurrection, after giving the renegade colonies a generous five days to cease and desist.

"Parliament had thirty days to vote on vetoing the State of Emergency and withdrawing the troops. They took no such vote, fully aware that treason violated the Constitution.

"Though the Parliament could've intervened and didn't, you could've terminated the State of Emergency and didn't. As CE, you're the Commonwealth's point man; it's ultimately up to you to decide what's best. As for Gould, he's a military hard-liner whose mindset has been shaped by war. He acted the only way he knows how: by going on the offensive.

"If your intuition told you to explore other solutions before deploying troops, then perhaps you should have."

"Well, like you said, we can't undo what's been done. Now we're in a bind: Either we can concede defeat—making the Three-Week War pointless—or keep fighting the Coalition and risk losing our incorporated status, which might happen today anyway."

"I pray to Allah it doesn't." Angela sincerely meant that.

Jared's wristcom chirped. He answered the call. Light and pixels swirled and merged into a chiseled face with a dimpled chin. "Sir," the dark-haired man said, "the Union leaders have all arrived and are being escorted to the master stateroom now."

"On my way." Jared ended the call, and the holo dispersed. He put his glasses back on, pushed his rolling chair away from the desk, and stood. "Come on, let's get this dog and pony show over with."

Jared and Angela traversed the Manor's West Wing, where a red carpet stretched beneath golden chandeliers, and animated wall displays depicted key moments in human history. They passed door after brown door before entering the master stateroom.

In cushioned armchairs, the six other Union leaders sat around the room's rectangular table. Each wore an earpiece that would translate every spoken language into their native tongue.

Jared and Angela sat side by side at the table and put on their earpieces.

The Union leaders noticed Jared's tired, dry eyes. They could see the weight of managing the Commonwealth's chaos was wearing him down.

"My fellow planetary leaders, I welcome you all to Eden. Let the summit now be in session," Jared said.

Following custom, each leader introduced themselves.

"I, Durgraso T'Horbelis of planet Ghanrax, am present," declared a male leader clad in animal skins and fur.

The Ghanrax were a semi-aquatic race. Though they primarily lived on land, they often traveled and hunted underwater. Leathery yellowish skin covered their faces and torsos, while bluish scales coated the rest of their bodies. Small spines bristled along their shoulders, and their webbed fingers and slightly protruding eyes added to their amphibian look.

They were known as a methodical, quick-tempered race.

"I, Ziltilda Ca'Rúshe of planet Dhalgratt, am present," said a female leader. Her muted brown eyes and long, silky black hair made her stand out. She was one of only two female planetary leaders in attendance, the other being Queen Pappalonie, the Eminence of Taramassia.

The Dhalgratt's appearance was defined by their lean, stout builds, sand-colored skin, and the subtle ridges of their low foreheads. Notably, intricate dark markings embellished their backs and broad shoulders. The clothing they wore reflected their need for comfort in their world's hot climate.

"I, Orphazel Khaphadelis of planet Varsh'Ru, am present."

The Varsh'Ru had white skin and lithe bodies with elongated, flexible limbs. Their faces featured slitted nostrils, lipless mouths, and black opaque eyes.

Traditional dress for their planetary leader and top officials consisted of snug purple garments overlaid with gold chain mail.

"I, Baraphelis Da'Nophzar of planet Zirkran, am present."

Zirkrans, known for their high intellect, usually stood between seven and eight feet tall. They were further distinguished by their orange-red skin, a short chin tendril, and deep-set dark eyes beneath sloping, hairless brows.

Baraphelis sat poised in the robe-like garment and decorative shoulder sash customary to his position.

"I, ZorKeld Levatorg of planet Rumanoah, am present."

Broad cheekbones, high foreheads, wide noses, and long, untamed hair were typical of the Rumanoahan people. Their coarse yellowish-gray skin was a natural armor, notoriously hard to penetrate.

ZorKeld, dressed in dark sleeveless attire, sported silver studs in his earlobes and a ring through his nostrils. Already not considered the most attractive fellow by his people's standards, ZorKeld bore a disfigurement from the arena combat sports he regularly engaged in, and dominated.

"I, Pappalonie Valasirus Cetreon of Taramassia, am present."

"I, Chief Executive Jared Kerner of the Commonwealth, am present, accompanied by Deputy Chief Angela Norton," Jared announced.

Durgraso fixed a reproving glare on Jared. "We have assembled here today to discuss the instability and dysfunction of the Union member known as the Commonwealth," he said in a guttural timbre, pointing a finger at Jared. "Represented by its leader, Chief Executive Kerner." From his nostrils came a loud snort of contempt, and the gill-like slits on his neck hissed.

ZorKeld rested his forearms on the table and steepled his fingers. His eyes grew cold as he thought about the two Rumanoahans killed during the assassination attempt on Gould, deaths he considered the result of an avoidable war instigated by the Commonwealth Government.

Animosity laced his voice, directed squarely at Jared. "The Commonwealth has been embroiled in internal conflict for some time. Article II of the Union Charter clearly states that all planetary members agree to abstain from acts of violence, aggression, or any form of belligerence against each other and their own peoples. As stewards of peace and goodwill, we have pledged to leave such barbarism in the bygone eras of our civilizations.

"Article II's Exception to Force Clause does permit the use of force against one's own population for planetary policing or quelling hostile uprisings."

"Correct," Jared quickly interjected. "Three of the Commonwealth's six colonies—One, Four, and Six—revolted against humanity's main governing body. Therefore, we enacted the Exception to Force Clause and launched an offensive to reclaim those renegade settlements."

ZorKeld responded coolly. "Yes, but we have been evaluating the Commonwealth's justification for use of force, Mr. Kerner. During this process, we reviewed the monthly reports your governors were required to send you. Those reports revealed your colonies in a state of immiseration. Your governors attempted to cooperate with you and proposed corrective actions to resolve the situation. You failed to act on any of those proposals."

"We didn't have the resources to implement them," Jared said.

ZorKeld refuted him. "That is debatable."

Jared's expression tightened in protest.

"Now," ZorKeld continued, "our investigative team has been touring your colonies to examine the conditions that the separatist colonies claim led them to seek independence. The team also interviewed the imprisoned governors in person. After much discernment, our consensus is this: The central government's use of force was not justified."

Jared's face paled. Angela's brows twitched with anger. Pappalonie fidgeted, grappling with feelings of regret; she had reluctantly come to the same conclusion as the other leaders.

ZorKeld clarified their reasoning. "Article II defines an uprising as 'the use of violence by an armed group to overthrow a sovereign government.' We do not consider the breakaway colonies' attempt to abandon your star nation *(more than one planet inhabited by a race)* an 'uprising.' We deem it a peaceful retaliatory response to your dereliction of duty.

"Therefore, you, Chief Executive Kerner, are the one who has committed treason, not against your nation, but against the Union Charter. As outlined in Article VI, every planetary leader must guarantee the welfare, well-being, and livelihood of their citizens. They must provide the essentials for survival and must not show prejudice or indifference toward any individual.

"Yes, it is a tall order, but it is the standard required of all Union members. We hold ourselves to high moral expectations. Our shared integrity is what attracts trade and visitors. These expectations are precisely why we conduct thorough investigations of every prospective trading partner."

Jared aimed a thumb at himself. "So, wait, you're saying I'm the bad guy here?"

ZorKeld replied, "You did not act with malicious intent. But you failed to respond to your people's suffering and resorted to force to prevent them from leaving your star nation, which they felt they had to do in order to survive.

"Do you understand what I am saying?" His voice became grittier. "Your people were crying out for a better life, and you failed to provide it."

"Wait, so the formation of the RUC was a *justified* uprising?" Jared's voice rose in astonishment. "Justified treason?" It climbed a tad higher. "Is that it?"

Ziltilda entered the fray, casting her eyes on Jared. "Chief Executive Kerner, as ZorKeld said, we have chosen not to categorize the formation of the RUC as an uprising at all. They did not fire the first shots or attempt a violent overthrow of your government."

To Jared, and to opponents of the Independent Movement, abandoning the Commonwealth *was* the first shot.

Ziltilda said, "You are ignoring your own failings, which incited what we deem to be an understandable act of retaliation."

So these fools think the RUC declaring sovereignty is no different from picketing or sit-ins, Jared grumbled inwardly.

ZorKeld, not yet finished, continued. "The case of the Three-Week War has been an onerous one to review. We initially assumed an uprising had occurred, which would have made your military response permissible. We gave you the benefit of the doubt, as we would any of ourselves when faced with a potential coup or violent disruption.

"But as we examined the findings of our investigative team, we could not endorse your actions. Instead, we came to support the actions of the RUC, which had no intent to commit aggression. They were merely trying to escape what we view as oppression, and oppression has no place in the Union."

Jared's lips pressed into a firm line. So many articles of the Charter were unambiguous. Others, though, were the exact opposite—vague, open to interpretation and debate. Depending on a person's indignation, leanings, or the sway of their heart, they could bend those articles to serve almost any perspective.

Orphazel now spoke. "Our understanding is that after the CDF defeated the RUC's paramilitaries, the remnants of those forces organized into several unified factions known as the

Coalition of Rebel Factions, or simply, the Coalition. Additional pockets of resistance, independent of the Coalition, later emerged. I believe you categorize all these resistance groups as 'terrorists.'

"We questioned whether we could classify these other resistance groups as hostile anti-government aggressors, or, in other words, 'uprisers.' But after much deliberation, we concluded it ultimately did not matter. Your poor leadership was the genesis of your star nation's meltdown."

Jared's mounting frustration made it hard to maintain his professional poise. "So this is all my fault?"

Durgraso snarled. "There is cause and effect, Chief Executive Kerner. The rebellion resulted from your inadequate leadership. We know your laws say a colony declaring sovereignty is treason, thus warranting a forceful response. However, the Union does not view standing up to oppression as treason."

Orphazel reentered the conversation. "What concerns me is that an end to this rampant disorder is nowhere in sight."

"Not so," Jared said. "Just yesterday, we dismantled a major Coalition faction, and we've increased our manpower in the colonies under martial law. The CDF is conducting a large-scale operation to flush out and defeat the insurrectionists who started this mess."

Angela backed Jared up, saying, "Also, rebuilding an entire civilization is a gradual process, and we've incurred massive debts and fought external wars that drained our resources.

"We're doing the best we can and are developing a plan to improve conditions in the colonies. The insurrectionists should have understood that. Instead, they tried to break away from the Commonwealth, recklessly endangering the rest of humanity, because the colonies' resources are vital to our shared survival."

Ziltilda said, "Still, the current state of your colonies is the best you can manage after all these years? *Unacceptable*."

Durgraso drummed his webbed fingers on the table. "I had extreme reservations about allowing you Earthlings into the Union," he growled. The gills on his neck hissed. "I did not want a race that nearly wiped itself out to bring its belligerence here. The Union was meant to be a place of peace. But I voted to accept you Earthlings. As I feared, perhaps I voted wrong.

"Your war has now cost the lives of Varsh'Ru, Rumanoahans, and others outside the Union. Those outside races are furious, and they are demanding reparations from the Union, reparations we are passing on to you. The Union's reputation as a haven of peace, comfort, and safety has been tarnished."

"We're sorry for those losses," Jared said sincerely, "and we understand we must compensate those worlds with reparations, and we will."

ZorKeld, his features set in a brooding expression, made eye contact with each of his colleagues. "We have spoken enough. It is time to get to the point," he said darkly.

Pappalonie shifted uncomfortably in her chair, her pointy ears twitching and jewelry jangling. She dropped her chin in disapproval of the verdict about to be delivered.

ZorKeld said, "Chief Executive Kerner, by a five-to-one vote, it is at our behest that you resign as the Commonwealth's leading official."

Jared jerked, jaw falling. A Chief Executive had just been impeached—not by the people of the Commonwealth, but by an outside body of adjudicators. Perhaps his father had been right in trying to withdraw from the Union.

ZorKeld said, "According to your laws, Deputy Chief Norton now assumes leadership. Norton, you have five days to end this domestic crisis. After five days, we will reconvene to decide the next course of action and whether to impose additional penalties. If you fail to end the conflict within five days, disciplinary measures will begin, including the potential rescinding of the Commonwealth's incorporated status."

Durgraso added, "And during these five days, all tourism must cease."

Pappalonie objected to the five-day deadline—just like she had objected to impeaching Jared. "While I agree that halting tourism is necessary to prevent more innocent lives from being lost to crossfire, five days is insufficient for the new Chief to resolve the conflict. By the authority vested in me as a planetary leader, I cast a vote to extend the time frame by an additional five days."

Ziltilda said, "By a show of hands, shall we extend the time frame?" Only Pappalonie and Baraphelis raised their hands. "It is decided. The time frame for Chief Executive Norton to resolve the Commonwealth's war shall remain five days."

Jared and Pappalonie's eyes met. Unspoken doubt passed between the two leaders.

"We are done here," ZorKeld said.

As everyone filed out, an icy silence lingered.

Pappalonie paused beside Jared. "If there is anything I can do to help the human race, let me know."

"Thank you, Your Eminence. You've always been the most compassionate of the Union leaders."

"I wish you the best, Jared Kerner." Pappalonie walked out.

"I'm sorry, Jared," Angela said with faux sympathy. She was glad to be in charge.

"Thank you." Jared sighed. "Let's not keep the media circus and the public waiting."

They left the room and proceeded down the hall, headed to the outdoor stage on the lawn, where the press awaited.

Jared said, "No matter what, don't let word get out that the Union leaders sided with the rebels. Who knows what the fallout would be. Personally, I don't want to find out." Such controversy could breed more Independent Movement supporters, or it could make people angry at the Union.

Jared and Angela exited the Manor through double doors and walked out onto the stage. The press pool waited to be addressed.

Camera drones transmitted signals to the Parliament Building's broadcast center, which relayed the feed to viewing devices on Eden and Satellite One.

Jared stepped up to the lectern, his demeanor hinting that the summit hadn't gone well. Three EPAs in black suits formed up behind him. Angela stood off to his right.

His gaze swept over the well-dressed reporters. He swallowed, still coming to terms with his expulsion from office. "Members of Parliament, Justices, government officials, and citizens of the Commonwealth, the Union leaders have mandated that I resign from office," he announced, voice dull. The crowd gasped. "They've determined that my leadership no longer meets Union standards. Some of you may agree. Some of you may not. But the decision is final. Deputy Chief Norton will now assume the role of Chief Executive."

Stepping aside, the deposed Chief shook Angela's hand, passing a torch he no longer had the right to carry.

She went up to the lectern confidently. "Citizens of the Commonwealth, the Union leaders have given me five days to end the Coalition's war. First, do not panic—"

BOOM! The stage erupted in a plasma explosion, shattering into a cloud of lethal shrapnel.

Nearby reporters were flung into the air.

The explosion's shock wave disfigured faces beyond recognition, melting features into grotesque smears.

A female reporter's shriek tore through the aftermath.

One EPA writhed, his left arm flayed to the muscle.

A shudder crawled down a reporter's spine as he caught sight of a woman who was little more than a roasted corpse. He screamed into his mic, "The CE and DC have just been killed! Everyone near the stage has suffered injuries!"

Inside the Manor, alarms blared, launching EPAs into action. They flooded the halls, locking down every access point.

In the Executive Bedroom, Jared's wife, Mei Ling Kerner, sat on the canopied bed, holding their terrified daughter. She prayed the commotion in the halls was just a drill or a false alarm.

An EPA burst into the room. "Your husband's been assassinated," he said. Mei Ling gasped. "I'm taking you to the bunker."

EPAs rushed the Union leaders into the reinforced underground bunker. A shadow of confusion and concern fell over the Union leaders' faces.

Outside the Manor, Cornelius sat comfortably in the back of his limo. Through the tinted window, he smiled triumphantly at the raging fire consuming the stage. His sinister plan had gone off without a hitch.

He spoke to Gillian over his wristcom. "It's done. The CE and DC are dead. Time for phase two of Operation New Wave."

Ambulance flyers landed to evacuate the wounded, while fire crews battled the blaze, shooting jets of foam from their vehicles' cannons.

Cornelius' limo rolled off. Now, he would be the incoming Chief Executive.

• • •

Jason and his squad were still atop the cliff overlooking Bravo Camp. They had spent the night conducting recon in shifts, taking turns operating the camera drone. Their nourishment came from meal cubes and nutrient bars.

At some point, they tuned in to the multiplanet simulcast through their Shells, witnessing the first political assassination in Commonwealth history.

As Jason began his next recon shift, he monitored the camp, the camera drone feeding a steady stream of footage to his HUD. He continuously updated Lars, who, in turn, kept Commander Seymour updated while the company rested, regrouped, and rearmed after the assault on Arson's base.

"So, when's backup getting here?" asked Specialist Eli Manson. "We can't let Arson get away. He's one of the Commonwealth's most-wanted terrorists. This could be our only shot."

Jason looked back at the young mocha-skinned man behind him. "Reinforcements should be here in sixty mikes."

"So, what effects do you think the assassination will have on the Commonwealth?"

Jason exhaled. "Gould's already blaming the Coalition. That's going to rile up Independent Movement opponents even more.

"Independent Movement supporters are already crying foul. They're saying Gould orchestrated the whole thing so he could take power and push a hard-line military agenda, one that doesn't just tighten control over the occupied colonies, but expands it to the unoccupied ones. Who knows what new extremes anti-government groups will resort to. They fear this guy."

"Do you think he was behind the assassination?"

Jason shrugged. "Anything's possible."

In her Shell, Stacie leaned against the BUS, anxious to go rescue Randy. She thought of him, and her cerebral implant responded by projecting memories across her HUD as stills: a stroll in a park after their return to Eden from BCT, a shared laugh, a kiss.

Stacie cleared her mind, and the stills disappeared. *Fifty-five mikes until backup gets here. Just fifty-five mikes.*

• • •

Inside his tent, Randy, dressed in some old clothes provided to him, had watched the assassination on a tablet. He then watched Gould swear in and address the public. The new Chief Executive claimed the fiends behind Jared's death were none other than the Coalition. An obvious lie. The Coalition was becoming a scapegoat for everything that went wrong in the Commonwealth.

Randy suspected Gould would exploit the crisis to push the Parliament into expanding Defense Department authority. As he stated in his interview days ago, he wanted special provisions, like surveillance and audits of colony governments that hadn't been indicted for aiding rebel groups.

Randy knew the Commonwealth was about to change, and the Spencers might've known about the assassination, maybe even played a part in it.

The tent flaps rustled. Sariah pulled them aside and poked her head in. "Good morning, Randy. I brought your friend." She and Jarius stepped into the tent's roomy interior. She unlocked the cuffs around his wrists. "Please don't run or do anything foolish." Jarius nodded silently, striving to suppress his growing exasperation. "Randy, I'll be back in thirty minutes with your father."

As Sariah exited, Jarius moved further inside. "I've been worried about you, man. And what the hell is going on? Why are they giving you the royal treatment? Roaming free, private tent—feels like you've got VIP status."

"I'll explain in a bit. There's something I want you to see."

Randy pulled up some of the corruption files, windows of data projecting from his wristcom.

Over the next several minutes, Randy showed Jarius irrefutable evidence that many government officials were corrupt. He also shared details of his revelatory sightseeing trip with Kesley and talked about his conflicting feelings regarding which side, if any, to fight for.

Jarius ran a hand through his hair. "I've been kinda feeling the same way after seeing how messed up things are here in Colony Four. I get why people rebelled. They don't see a better future unless they take drastic steps. But . . . fighting for the Coalition?" He shook his head. "I don't know. We took an oath. And like you said, we don't know if this Reza guy's legit or just another sleazeball trying to acquire power. Could be another Ritter."

"Yeah," Randy agreed. "But I'm gonna stick with the Coalition a little longer and see what I can learn. Trust me, they'll let you go unharmed if that's what you want. They've got no use for prisoners. But I'd like you to stay and check things out for yourself before making that call."

Sariah parted the tent flaps and peered inside. "Randy, your father's outside." She stepped in, holding Jarius' cuffs in her left hand.

"Are those still necessary?" Randy asked, irritated.

"Only until we find the right time to let him go. Maybe tomorrow."

Randy said to Jarius, "I guess you've got until then to decide if you want to stay or head back to the company."

"Who's to say Arson would trust him enough to let him stay?" Sariah said. "Just because he trusts you without supervision doesn't mean he'll have the same confidence in your friend."

"I'd take full responsibility for Jarius," Randy said.

Jarius held out his wrists without protest. Sariah locked the cuffs around them and marched him out of the tent.

Randy exited and found Arson waiting for him. The pain was still there, but it no longer consumed Randy. It didn't control him. That didn't mean he and Arson would suddenly become close. But at least they could exist in the same space without Randy wanting to put a bullet in Arson's skull. A renewed father-son relationship would take time, if it could happen at all.

"Everything's changed," Arson said grimly, holding a tin cup of hot java. "We have to expedite Hammer Fall. Reza knows that militant madman Gould is bad news. With him in power, martial law will get worse, and the hunt for us will only intensify. We have to stop him."

He took a sip from his cup and then continued. "Reza's making an announcement from his stronghold tonight, broadcasting to all Coalition factions via holovid. He's setting a new timetable for Hammer Fall. The good news is that last night's shipment of suits made it safely to his stronghold, just like he wanted.

"That's where the rest of the Reldaldri mechsuits are, and it's where the main assault force will deploy from. He wants me and what's left of my faction there ASAP. I'm guessing that means he's planning to launch the op soon. We're leaving to go there in a few hours."

"So where exactly is Reza's stronghold?" Randy asked.

Arson's eyes flicked away. He hesitated. Randy hadn't chosen a side yet, and that made him a liability. Arson had to tread carefully. After a long pause, he answered. "Colony Five. With no suspected rebel activity there, it's outside the CDF's area of concern."

Randy had been half-expecting that exact answer. "So all the speculation is true. Governess Hayley is supporting the Coalition."

"Yes. She wants the Coalition to win. The only problem is that eighty percent of Colony Five's population feels neutral about the war. They don't want to fight the central government or break away from the Commonwealth, unlike the people in colonies One, Four, and Six. Sure, they want change, but they're fine with pursuing it using political pressure.

"Despite their neutrality, Hayley's been quietly helping the Coalition, offering Reza a safe haven. She's careful, though. She limits how much freedom we have in Colony Five. She doesn't want her people, or the central government, catching on to her support." Arson placed a hand on Randy's shoulder. "I meant for us to catch up, but given recent events, that'll have to wait."

Randy twisted away, escaping Arson's grasp. "I wasn't in the mood anyway," he said with a bite. The resentment over his father's abandonment still lingered, though he understood why he left. They simply had different concepts of right and wrong. "It can wait."

Arson accepted that rebuilding trust would take time. "Okay." He started to leave with Sariah and Jarius, then paused after a few steps. "Have you decided whether to join us yet?" he asked Randy.

"Still thinking."

"Take all the time you need." Arson pointed to a row of improvised shelters. "Chow tent's that way. Get some food. I'll see you later."

Randy walked in the opposite direction from Arson, Sariah, and Jarius.

Kathleen's metaphysical imitation appeared, floating beside him. *Your father's not the insensitive man you thought he was, is he?*

Randy replied, *Maybe not, but that doesn't mean he made the right choice, leaving you and me.*

He made a choice I didn't like, but your father did what he had to do. Knowing his people were suffering was eating at his soul. He wouldn't have been the father or husband he needed to be with that kind of weight on his mind. That's just . . . the man I married. Let go of your bitterness, Son.

Randy scoffed at himself for having a conversation with someone who didn't exist. She was an amalgamation of thoughts, emotions, and memories molded into a lifelike personality he could confide in—an impersonation brought to life by his implant. *Enough of this nonsense.*

Kathleen faded from view.

Randy proceeded to the chow tent, passing weary souls wearing old, tattered clothes. Rebels recovering from injuries moved slowly; some wore slings or bandages, while others were missing limbs. The war had clearly taken its toll on them.

• • •

On the cliff above Bravo Camp, the rest of Fourth Platoon had arrived with Second and Third, while First Platoon remained at the annex.

Captain Seymour himself had come to oversee the crucial op. "Alright, everyone, let's not squander this." His voice conveyed the authority of someone who had braved countless battles and had insurmountable combat knowledge. "Command wants Arson brought in alive. If that's not possible, his corpse is the next best thing.

"And remember, two of our own are down there being held captive. Specialist Scott and Specialist Ford. If you find them, get them out. Now let's go into stealth mode and burn that damn place to kingdom come." *You betrayed us, old friend. Now you pay.*

Before the Guardians advanced, they activated their stealth cloaks, the holographic skins mimicking the surrounding terrain.

• • •

Randy walked back from the chow tent, thoughts still muddled.

He came to a training ground.

A man lay prone beside a woman, coaching her through marksmanship training. "Nose to the charging handle," he instructed. She followed his lead. "Now adjust your aim."

The woman lined up her energy rifle's sights with a large flat rock, slowed her breathing, and pulled the trigger. A pulse of energy vaporized the rock into dust. "Yes!" she cheered.

Nearby, one rebel showed another how to deconstruct a rifle for maintenance. Off to the right, two men sparred in hand-to-hand combat, their chatter suggesting they were enjoying the friendly match. All around Randy was purposeful activity.

He saw good people conscripted into war by desperation, people with heart and a genuine drive to improve colony life. The Coalition wasn't some terrorist outfit bent on seizing control of the Commonwealth. These people were fighting to make it better. And every one of them had treated him with generosity.

Five young rebels stood around a sinewy brown-skinned woman with close-cropped blond hair. She wore black stretch pants, an olive-green tank top, and boots.

She was briefing the five newcomers on the Coalition's ethos.

"First and foremost, we carry out our attacks with the intention of causing little to no casualties," she said. "We are not tyrants or vengeful murderers, no matter what the central government or media say."

She believed in the ethos, and her voice carried a bone-deep commitment to uphold it and instill it in the newcomers. "Edenite or colonist, we want what's best for all," she said, gesturing inclusively with her hands. "Not just what benefits the colonies. We want the original vision of the Commonwealth to be recognized."

His dreadlocks swaying, a swarthy young man raised a hand. "Excuse me, Ms. Lovelace, Why not just take over the central government and treat Edenites the way they've treated us? Like crap. An eye for an eye, you know?"

"Because that's not our way, Malachi. And many Edenites are simply misguided. Their poor opinion of colonists comes from a perception of us as ungrateful grumblers who should accept the status quo. Most are unaware of the inhospitable conditions we endure because the net filters suppress the truth. Let us be the ones who enlighten the New Humanity."

What Randy heard charmed his soul. He understood what his father had meant. The Coalition wasn't like the CDF. Respect for everyone, even the enemy, was the foundation of its ethos. This was the culture Randy had expected the CDF to have.

These rebels were good people guided by moral precepts.

Suddenly, guilt twisted in Randy's chest as he thought about the rebels he had killed at Arson's base. *I'm sorry.*

Emotion clogged his throat.

He swallowed and continued walking as Lovelace kept speaking. He passed an elderly Earth Era war veteran wearing an eyepatch, venting to a younger man with facial scars *(Earth Era war vets were utilized as trainers)*.

The vet said, "I fought wars on Earth, and AEGIS classifies me as nothing more than a manual laborer, like I got nothing to offer society. That damn computer disqualified my wife's sister from Eden citizenship because she's supposedly predisposed to cancer. Hell, people infected by those alien biochem weapons *(during Armageddon)* didn't make the cut either. What happened to them wasn't their fault."

"What a buncha bullshit," the younger man said.

Bullshit indeed, Randy thought.

A young fair-skinned woman pranced up beside him, wearing a white shirt and brown leather pants. Her blond hair was arranged in a long braid. "So, you're Arson's son?" she asked politely, her French accent easily noticeable.

Miffed, Randy let out a breath. Though not in the mood, he stopped to entertain a conversation. "I am." He gently shook the woman's hand.

"I'm Mandy Bardot. Welcome to the Coalition. If there's anything I can help you with, just—" Loud, thudding explosions drowned out the rest of her words, and fear pulled her delicate features taut.

A stray blast punctured her back and tore open her midsection. The blood spray was immense.

Randy's face took on an expression of terror. He stepped back as Mandy's body went limp.

Energy blasts hammered the camp.

A rebel felt his gut lurch from anxiety. "We're under attack!"

An explosion wiped out a section of tents.

Cloaked Guardians atop high slopes opened fire. Their Shells' holographic skins dissolved on command.

"Move! Move!" a rebel barked. He and four others dashed past Randy, jumping into the fight.

Boom after *boom* threw the camp into chaos.

A group of Guardians skated down the slopes, traction skids engaged. They uncloaked and unleashed a hail of energy blasts.

A rebel's chest erupted in a geyser of blood.

Randy's heart began beating rapidly.

When a blast cratered the ground in front of him, rock and dirt peppered his body. *Shit!*

Yelling and swearing reached a fever pitch.

Explosions pulverizing the camp startled napping animals, sending them scurrying into burrows and crevices.

Guardians and rebels peeked out from behind berms, stones,

rock formations, and the camp's makeshift shelters, discharging shots before ducking back under cover.

Randy's implant pinged, tethering to Stacie's. *She's out here somewhere.*

To avoid being an easy target, he sprinted for cover. He came upon the decapitated body of a rebel woman and stopped, cringing. Realizing he might have to defend himself, he leaned down and snatched the energy gun lying next to the headless corpse.

Randy stared at the weapon, hoping he wouldn't have to use it. He dreaded the thought of opening fire on his fellow Guardians. And if he did have to defend any of the rebels, that would imply to the CDF that he had officially joined the Coalition.

"Randy!" a woman's voice cried out.

Randy turned and tucked the handgun between his belt and pants. "Stacie!"

She had followed the signal of their Link.

Her faceplate slid up. Randy was a sight for sore eyes. "Thank goodness you're okay." She exhaled in reprieve and took hold of his wrist. "Let's get you away from here and—"

Randy yanked his arm free. "I can't go. I'm sorry."

Stacie's joy withered. "What do you mean?" Her brows quirked in confusion.

From afar, a boom roared.

"It's hard to explain," Randy said. "Let's just say the Coalition is planning something big, and I want to investigate more."

"You mean play turncoat to go undercover or something?"

Randy brought up a holo-menu from his wristcom. "Quickly, sync with my wristcom. We don't have much time."

"Okay, but can you fill me in?" Stacie asked, perplexed. Her faceplate dropped into place. SYNC COMPLETED displayed on her HUD.

"The info I'm about to send will explain everything." Randy entered a series of numbers and letters on the menu. The wristcom chirped. "There's a video message from me appended." He forwarded the data and the message. Stacie permitted her CPU to accept it. A chime from Randy's wristcom confirmed the transfer. "You may not understand my reasoning for what I'm doing. I hope you will."

Stacie's faceplate rose again, her expression shifting from confusion to worry. "Randy, you're not making sense. What exactly do you intend to—?" He pressed a see-you-soon kiss to her cheek.

"I've gotta go," he said, running away to find Arson.

Hollering, explosions, and the sound of energy blasts merged into a single cacophony.

Frustrated, Stacie threw her hands up. "Randy, what the heck?" Blasts whisked past her, chewing up the ground near her feet and disintegrating rocks. She tossed her head back, zeroing in on where the shots came from. Two rebel men were targeting her from atop an incline. "Shit!" She backpedaled to dodge the next wave of blasts.

Her Oracle instantly lowered her faceplate. More blasts followed. She retaliated with a rapid burst of counterfire from her wrist gun.

Randy glanced back. "Stacie!" His pulse became a frantic rhythm that thrummed in his very throat. He tried to shelve his worry and keep moving. Stacie was in a Shell; she'd be okay, he thought. But his emotional connection to her wouldn't let him leave.

One of the rebels hurled a plasma grenade at Stacie.

Caught off guard, she froze.

Her Oracle made the save, summoning her barrier shield. Energy crackled, ballooning into a protective dome.

The grenade landed in front of Stacie and detonated against the shield. Competing plasma energies ignited a concussive backlash that tore at her legs. "Shit!"

The world around Stacie exploded in a brilliant flash. A blue torrent of destruction with the force of a hurricane yanked her off her feet and cartwheeled her through the air. The overwhelming surge of energy knocked out her visual sensors, plunging her into darkness as she went barrel-rolling across the harsh landscape.

Outside the blast radius, Randy threw a forearm over his eyes to block the blinding light.

Stacie tumbled side to side and bounced against the rocky surface. Her armor clanked and clacked with each impact.

In the explosion's wake, a deep, smoldering crater had formed. Zigzagging fissures spiderwebbed the ground and surrounding rock formations.

The force unleashed provided a demonstration of just how dangerous plasma energy could be.

Damn it, Randy thought. He ran back to Stacie, over fractured earth, and squatted beside her. Heat from the crater radiated against his back. "Stace, you okay?" He touched her hot armor. Mistake. His face pinched, and he jerked his hand away. "Stacie, are you okay?" She didn't respond, incapacitated.

The two rebels sped down the incline to off their target. "Move, Randy," one of them demanded, closing in fast and brandishing his weapon.

"Enough, there's no need to kill her."

"Blowing away a woman doesn't feel right to us," the rebel said. He leveled the barrel of his gun at Stacie. "But in this case, we've got no choice. She's with the people trying to kill us right now. We can't risk her waking up and taking our lives or those of our friends."

Randy rose to his feet unflinchingly, arms outstretched. "You'll have to kill me before I let you touch her."

The two rebels stalked closer.

"You're the boss's son. Just whose side are you on?" the other rebel asked.

"Right now, the side of human life," Randy responded. It sounded heroically corny, but hell, it was the best he could come up with.

"We don't have time for this nonsense," the rebel said, shoving Randy to the ground as he and his comrade moved forward.

Stacie's Oracle rebooted. A slot on her armored thigh popped open, and mini autoguns jutted forth.

Shock paralyzed the rebels. In execution style, a horrific bombardment of bullets riddled their defenseless bodies. Bits and pieces of them littered the ground, soaked in their blood.

Randy, sitting on the dirt, shut his eyes, sickened by the grotesque sight.

The gentle hum of an approaching hover vehicle made him open his eyes. It was a combat sled, a roofless two-seater equipped with blasters on each side and a gun turret at the rear. The sole occupant was a woman at the controls, dressed in a short-sleeved black shirt, loose-fitting pants, and a dark balaclava.

The sled hissed to a stop in front of Randy and the still-unconscious Stacie.

Randy got to his feet, ready to protect his lover.

The driver peeled off her balaclava.

Randy blinked, unable to believe his eyes. The driver was Kesley Whittaker. Fate and circumstance, it seemed, had intertwined their lives once again.

Wind ruffled Kesley's unruly red hair. "Well, don't just fucking stand there, get in."

So she is a rebel. "I can't leave—"

Stacie stirred.

At that moment, Randy made his choice. He jumped into the seat beside Kesley and strapped in. She stamped the acceleration pedal, and the sled zoomed away, dust billowing behind.

Stacie groaned as lucidity returned. Equilibrium off-kilter, she staggered to her feet. Structural damage hampered her every movement.

Her HUD displayed a message moving from left to right: MOBILITY RESPONSIVENESS 30% DECLINE.

She watched Randy speed away with Kesley. *Randy, I hope you know what you're doing.*

Against the bedlam of explosions and gunfire, Arson bellowed instructions, his face guard retracted. He had already issued the order to abandon camp.

"Scott!" a voice called out.

Arson pivoted. Gravel crunched underfoot. "Arnold."

The two former comrades faced each other.

They had endured BCT together, fought wars together, and conquered Officer Candidate School together. But now they were adversaries, fighting on opposite sides of the war.

"Arson, if you come along quietly, I won't harm you," Seymour said.

"You know me too well to think I'd ever surrender without a fight."

"Why, Arson? Why? Why'd you choose the Coalition over the CDF? Why disgrace yourself like this? You spat on the oath you swore to uphold."

In the distance, a high-pitched boom reverberated, followed by a terrible scream. The battle was growing fiercer.

"Quite the contrary," Arson replied, eyes locked on his old friend. "I was dishonoring myself by enforcing a system of oppression that should never have existed. You've seen how colonists live."

"The government was working to improve life for *everyone* in the Commonwealth. Just because you didn't like the pace doesn't mean you get to force it to accelerate by blowing up contractors, attacking military bases, and killing Guardians."

"Change doesn't happen by sitting around and doing nothing. Now enough. I won't surrender, and I refuse to let you berate me and question the love I have for the Defense Force, an institution I still credit for shaping me into the man I am today." With that, Arson activated his face guard.

"Then you've chosen the hard way."

Fléchette explosives dispersed from Seymour's shoulder cannon. They detonated against Arson's chest plate, staggering him backward and shaving away fractions of armor. Exposed structural components crackled.

Arson exhaled through clenched teeth as his armor sparked. Seymour fired energy blasts from his handgun. To make his former XO work for a direct hit, Arson engaged his vernier jets, flying above him.

Seymour elevated his aim, firing wildly in an upward arc.

Arson came down fast, his armored knee striking Seymour's faceplate.

Seymour's teeth rattled on impact. Disoriented, he toppled backward, then got up.

Arson landed, momentum sending him into a forward skid.

Before Seymour could fully recover, Arson spun around. Four spider-leg-like appendages sprouted from the back of his Reldaldri mechsuit. They were blasters.

The gleaming nozzles lit up and discharged energy beams. Two struck Seymour in the chest. Another two tagged his leg panels. He fell down on all fours, smoke rising from the damaged armor.

A warning lit up Seymour's HUD: UPPER TORSO DAMAGE 20% / LEG DAMAGE 15%.

Arson rushed forward and delivered a brutal kick to Seymour's helmet, knocking him flat. Then Arson ignited his vernier jets and blasted into the sky. *So long, Arnold. I hope our paths don't have to cross again.*

Seymour got to his feet, knee actuators creaking. *Damn you, Arson. You won't keep getting away. Your luck will run out.*

The sounds of battle dwindled into sporadic pops and zaps. The firefight at the camp had ended, with the CDF scoring a critical victory.

Miles away, Randy and Kesley's combat sled sat parked beneath the ridge of a plateau, surrounded by barren desert.

Smoke trails coming from the camp snaked into the sky.

Something resembling a purple one-eyed donkey galloped by, hooves trampling parched earth.

Kesley pressed a button on the dashboard to comm Arson. "This is Kesley to Commander Scott. Your son is with me, unscathed."

Arson's reply came instantaneously. "Thank you, Kess. I'm with Sariah and two of my men. We're safe as well. I've confirmed thirty others made it out of that fight too."

"What now?"

"We head to Colony Five, as Reza requested. We'll rendezvous at the abandoned depot. There's a shuttle stashed there."

"Roger." Shifting toward Randy, Kesley hooked her arm over the back of her seat's headrest. "So, you mad I didn't tell you?"

"No," Randy said casually, "I get why you couldn't. I probably would've arrested you on the spot."

"You could've gone back with your company just now. Why didn't you? You on our side now?"

Randy leaned back and cupped his hands behind his head, sinking into the seat's worn cushion. He gazed up at the sky. "I've . . . kind of had a change of heart."

"Kind of? What the fuck does that mean?"

Absentmindedly watching black winged mammals traverse the skies, Randy put his thoughts in order. "Arson showed me how corrupt the central government is. I don't want to fight for them, and I sure as hell don't want to fight for Gould. And after everything you showed me, I get it now: Not nearly enough is being done to help the colonies' people.

"Still, I'm not convinced rebellion was the only way to change things. But I understand why the people of colonies One, Four, and Six became disillusioned with the government. At the same time, it's hard for me to betray the oath I swore to uphold. And I'm not totally sold on Reza." *I might not want to fight for him, either.*

Agitated, Kesley flung her palms skyward. "So are you gonna fight with us or not?" she asked demandingly, tired of Randy's oscillating loyalties.

"For now, I'm neutral in this," Randy replied. Well, it was a start for Kesley. "I'm not committing to anyone's side right now. Hell, maybe I'll just go home and watch everything play out from the sidelines."

Kesley's lips stretched into a teasing grin. "If you do end up joining us: Like father, like son, huh?"

Mortified, Randy snapped upright and twisted toward her. His brow furrowed with scorn. "Even if I joined you guys, I don't have a wife and child," he shot back hotly. "If I did, I wouldn't have ghosted them to join someone's goddamn rebellion."

Kesley gave him a "C'mon, really!" kind of look. "You're a grown-ass man, Randy." She giggled, ticking him off even more. "It's not like he left you when you were some wee li'l boy."

"He caused my mother depression! Don't lecture me! How would you feel if your dad just up and vanished without a word?" Kesley fell silent, no comeback in sight. Point made. "That's what I thought. Now drive . . . to wherever the hell we're headed. It's likely my company has already sent out search teams to hunt down any rebel survivors." He crossed his arms and let out a contemptuous "humph."

The engine cranked, and the sled whizzed over the arid terrain, passing a family of taloned bipeds pecking insects off the ground with their yellow beaks.

The sled entered the mouth of a canyon.

Five minutes of mundane sightseeing helped diffuse most of Randy's tension. "So, relief-aid worker by day, rebel by night," he said, tone tinged with some residual hostility. "How'd you get hooked up with the Coalition?"

Kesley swerved around an outcrop. "Well, I was working for Dynamic Relief Provisions before the Three-Week War, and we were doing a lot of good. Then the war started. After it ended, I saw people getting disrespected even more under martial law.

"Dynamic Relief Provisions wasn't enough for me anymore. I wasn't content. I wanted to empower myself against the central government. I caught wind of a secret Coalition meetup, and I joined. Now here I am, doing good on two fronts—one as a relief-aid worker, the other as a rebel fighter."

"And what were you doing at the comms tower?" Randy asked.

"Arson wanted it rigged so we could try tapping into CDF comms transmissions. I haven't had a chance to go back and finish up." Energy blasts went off behind them. "Shit!"

A CDF hover vehicle glided out of a valley and stayed on their tail. The cannon on its prow fired again.

Kesley recoiled. "A search team found us! Hang on!"

She yanked a lever on the dashboard. Plasma energy lit up the aft boosters, and the sled kicked into high velocity, wind howling. She executed evasive maneuvers, zigzagging to dodge incoming fire.

Blasts struck the canyon walls.

A chip of rock smacked Randy's forehead. "Damn it!"

Kesley veered left and right, avoiding collisions with large craggy formations.

A blast grazed her side of the sled, scorching its surface. Another blast hit the stern, and the sled lurched into a tailspin.

Kesley was unable to regain control. "Fuck!"

The sled ricocheted off the canyon wall, then skidded across the ground, smashing a cluster of furry mammals. It slammed into a jagged outcrop with a metallic crunch, coming to a full stop.

Steam and smoke rose from blown gaskets. The engine sputtered under the crumpled hood.

The CDF vehicle whooshed to a halt beside the wrecked sled.

The Guardian at the controls killed the engine, and he and his battle-buddy disembarked.

Their faceplates retracted and locked into place. One of the men was dark brown with rugged features. His name tag said CLAY. The other was fair-skinned and had a tank-like build. His name tag said BLAIR. Both were privates.

"Alright, get out," Clay demanded, pointing his rifle at Randy and Kesley.

The sled's scrunched-up doors groaned as Randy and Kesley pried them open. They got out with their hands up.

Blair recognized Randy from his prisoner profile. "Hey, that's one of the captives, Randal Scott," he said to Clay.

"You okay, Specialist?" Clay asked.

Randy realized they didn't know he was with Kesley willingly. "Uh, yeah." He lowered his hands and stepped away from her. "Thanks for saving me from these guys," he said, playing along. He wondered how the hell they were going to get out of this mess.

Kesley whipped her energy gun from its holster and pulled the trigger. The muzzle flashed, but the rushed shot missed its intended target, Blair.

"Rebel bitch!" Blair charged, mechboots hammering the ground. Desperate, unfocused shots blazed past him. One blast struck his side, leaving a smoking burn. With a running shoulder attack, he knocked Kesley off her feet. The gun flew from her grip, and her head hit a stone. Blunt force trauma blotted out all consciousness.

Blair undressed her with his eyes, wondering about her dimensions. Her perfect hourglass figure drove him into a state of wild lust. *Damn, she's fucking stacked.* His Shell's rear paneling hissed open, and he took a few steps backward, exiting the suit. It stood idle while he knelt beside Kesley's defenseless body. *To the victor go the spoils of war.*

"Hey, what are you doing?" Randy asked, his voice as sharp as a blade.

Predatory amusement stretched across Blair's square-jawed face. "Chill out." He tossed a toothy grin Randy's way. "I'm just gonna have a little fun with this riffraff before I slit her throat."

Clay exited his Shell. "I'm next."

Randy's hands curled into fists, knuckles turning white. He was about to go berserk on these two depraved Guardians.

Blair straddled Kesley and pulled a knife from the green sheath on his belt, eager to slice open her shirt.

Just then, Kesley's eyes popped open, widening in panic.

Recalling stories from women she knew who had survived assaults by Guardians, she imagined the horror of becoming a victim herself. "Keep your filthy paws off me!" She thrashed against Blair, bucking her hips to try to throw him off.

"Oh, I love it when they fight back," Blair sneered, his voice full of arousal. He fixated on Kesley's writhing body. "Fucking hell, you're hot."

Randy screamed internally.

Kesley knocked the knife from Blair's grip. He responded by backhanding her with brute force, the slap resounding like a gunshot. Her head violently snapped to the side, and she tasted the metallic tang of blood in her mouth. Refusing to give in, she pushed through the pain, her instincts driving her to fight.

A thunderous expression strained the muscles of Randy's face. "Stop it!"

Blair was beyond stopping, beyond listening. He leaned down and dragged his tongue up the side of Kesley's neck.

She raked her nails across his face, gouging his flesh.

He yowled, the wounds searing. "You bitch!" He grabbed her wrists and forced them to the ground. "Be a good girl and stay still!"

Kesley spat in his face, her saliva hitting him square in the eye. "Fuck you, motherfucker!"

Infuriated, he shoved a hand under her shirt, his violating fingers trailing along her rib cage.

Kesley jerked a knee up to fend him off but failed to hit him. Her hips shifted as she fought to free herself. "Get the hell off me!"

"Stop moving!" Blair slid his hands from her midriff to her pants and unbuttoned them.

Randy refused to be a witness of a sexual assault. "Enough!" In a swift motion, he drew his gun and fired a precise shot into Blair's back. Blood splattered, seeping into the fine-grained sand.

Blair's eyes bulged, his mouth hung open in shock, and he collapsed on top of Kesley. She grunted, muscling his body off to the side, struggling to draw breath.

For a second, Clay stood frozen, surprise etched on his face. "Damn you, Specialist!" He punched Randy in the jaw, knocking him flat on his back. "Traitor!"

"It's Guardian misconduct to rape a woman," Randy said, getting up. "He was defacing the Defense Force's good name!"

An energy blast struck Clay in the leg, and he fell down, screaming in agony. Kesley was on her feet, rubbing the back of her head with one hand while her other held her handgun.

Blair's blood had stained her already-dirty clothes.

Perspiring, she walked over to Clay and leveled her gun at him, ready to finish the job.

Randy clutched her shoulder. "That's enough."

"Enough? We should kill the son of a bitch!" The memory of Blair's grimy tongue on her neck made her shudder.

"No, no more killing." Randy's eyes met hers. "The scumbag who tried to violate you is dead. This guy didn't do anything."

"Yeah, he didn't do *anything* to stop his buddy."

"Let's just take their vehicle and go, Kess!" Randy wasn't in the mood to argue.

"*Fine.*" Kesley gave Blair's dead body a parting kick to the ribs. *Bitch-ass motherfucking sicko.* She spat on him.

Clay, in pain, contacted the company with his comm-set. "This is Private Clay. I'm down. Private Blair is dead. The captive, Randal

Scott, has switched sides."

The CDF was now under the impression that Randy had defected. Whether he wanted to join the Coalition or not no longer mattered. The decision had been made for him. His life had descended further into limbo. *Oh, well,* he thought. He knew killing Blair would cause Clay to believe he had joined the Coalition, but he had no other choice.

A gust of wind swirled grit and sand into the air.

Kesley holstered her gun. "Told you we should've killed the bastard."

"Let's just get moving before it's too late!" Randy hollered. "All the noise is bound to attract more search teams! It's probably only a matter of minutes before they're on our asses!"

They jumped into the CDF vehicle and shot off toward their destination.

• • •

At the ravaged camp, Captain Seymour waited for updates from the search parties.

Stacie had heard Clay's APB for Randy over the comms. Confusion and worry squeezed her heart. *Okay, babe, what's going on with you?* She brought up Randy's video message on her HUD, suspense gripping her.

In the recording, Randy explained the same things he had told Kesley: that learning about the government's corruption and witnessing the colonists' suffering had changed his perspective. He still wasn't convinced rebellion was the answer, but he couldn't stomach fighting for a corrupt government.

He had conflicting feelings about the war. He was weighing everything, trying to figure out which side to fight for, if any. But before making a decision, he needed to know more about the Coalition. He needed to understand their grand plan.

The very possibility of Randy joining the Coalition felt surreal to Stacie.

In the last thirty seconds of the message, he gave her the hard truth, telling her the biggest criminal factor in government corruption today was the Eight Elite, including her family.

She tensed.

He told her to check out the folder on Gould. Then the message ended, dissolving into static waves.

She opened Gould's folder with haste. Her eyes widened at the illegal financing of his campaign, all traced back to her parents. *No,* she thought. "Fuck, fuck, fuck," she let loose, just above a whisper.

As she dug deeper, she uncovered more financial kickbacks, not only between her parents and Gould but also between her parents and other politicians. Then she accessed files on the rest of the Eight Elite. What she found shook her to the core: scandals, human trafficking, money laundering. What exactly were her parents involved in, a crime syndicate? Was everything they gave her, everything they owned, bought with dirty money?

Her blood boiled. She needed answers. She needed to know the extent of her parents' criminal activities. What else didn't she know? Were her parents just as malevolent as some of the other Eight families?

When she was a child, she often saw family heads and politicians visit her parents. Her father frequently attended gatherings he vaguely described as "important business meetings." She was unaware of the details of these meetings or how her parents had accumulated their wealth.

She didn't bother asking many questions, as she wasn't particularly interested in her parents' business dealings. Whenever she did inquire about them, the responses she got were always along the lines of "You'll know when it's time." Well, there was no more time to remain ignorant and naive about Spencer Enterprises. "The time" had arrived.

• • •

Randy and Kesley's vehicle exited the canyon and glided over sand dunes of varying sizes.

Randy sat in silence, unpacking everything that had transpired. If he ended up deciding not to fight for the Coalition, what would he do? Could he go back to the CDF, smooth things over, and salvage his military career? As he struggled to envision his future, he cursed himself for getting embroiled in this quandary.

The hover vehicle's boosters powered it up a steep elevation, and then it cruised down the other side.

His strength wilting, Randy was ready to board the shuttle and just snooze for a while, letting sleep's peace sanitize his mind of his unfortunate circumstances.

Though quiet, Kesley was still horrified by how close someone had come to violating her.

They arrived at the rally point, a dark and dreary disused facility.

"This is it," Kesley said somberly. She unclipped a comm-set from her belt and held it against her ear. "This is Kesley to Commander Scott. Your son and I are outside."

Arson replied, "Sariah, myself, and twenty of my men are inside. Open the loading-dock door and get in here. We'll take off as soon as my other ten survivors arrive."

"You heard the man, let's move," Randy said.

Exhausted, they went to the dock door. Kesley slapped the big blue button on a control box, and the roll-up door slowly screeched upward, revealing a shuttle from yesteryear.

They walked into the musty-scented dock. Cobwebs hung from the corners. Old inert machinery, long out of service, sat covered in rust.

Randy studied the craft's makeup. "This thing's an antique." A spooked gray critter resembling a mouse scampered by his foot. "Must be one of the first models developed."

Arson came down the shuttle's stair-ramp, plain-clothed. "Randy, Kesley, glad you made it," he said as he approached them.

Tolerating Arson's closeness brought a look of discomfort to Randy's face, but after a moment, his features settled.

Explosions, muffled by distance, thundered across the desert.

"Commander Scott," a woman said over the comm-set on Arson's belt, "this is Lovelace. The enemy has caught up to us. We're outnumbered and—" After another explosion, the comms channel went dead.

"She's gone," Arson said grimly. "Along with the other nine."

A small weeping sound escaped Kesley. She had obviously known the woman.

Overwhelmed by raw emotion, she clenched her fists, ready to strike something—a wall, a crate, anything.

Randy delicately framed her face in his hands, his touch warm. Sadness glossed her eyes, and rivulets of tears ran down her cheeks. "Hey, I'm sorry," Randy said.

Arson gestured sharply. "Quickly, inside the shuttle."

Arson, Randy, and Kesley hastened up the stair-ramp.

Randy spotted Jarius. "You stuck around, huh?"

Jarius replied, "I talked to your dad. I told him we were collegemates and that I wanted to follow your lead and continue checking things out. He was okay with it."

"Glad you're here."

"I figured someone's gotta keep you outta trouble."

At the controls, the pilot cranked the old engine. It sputtered, cronked, and then died. "Damn it! Come on!"

Now, everyone aboard was on edge.

Holy fucking shit, Randy thought, nervous. *Some escape craft.*

The pilot tapped buttons on the control panel, trying to get the shuttle to behave. The engine coughed and died again. Grimacing, the pilot kept troubleshooting. Finally, the resuscitated engine growled to life.

A collective cheer broke out among everyone.

The landing wheels rolled the craft outdoors, just as three CDF hover vehicles pulled up. Gunners perched at the rear turrets unleashed flurries of bullets.

The shuttle lifted into the sky, sunlight winking off its scarred metal surface. The landing gear retracted, and the old plasma thrusters flared.

The gunners kept firing until the shuttle soared out of range, speeding toward safer territory.

"Damn it," a sergeant in one of the vehicles blurted. He swore again and commed Commander Seymour. "This is Sergeant Downey. Arson's gotten away."

Commander Seymour replied, his voice steady, "Roger, Sergeant. Return to the campsite."

Though Arson had escaped, the day was still a success. The second—and remaining—body of the Scott Faction had been squashed.

Everyone in the escape shuttle was now at ease, out of harm's clutches.

Randy sat next to Kesley. The growing ache in her heart from Lovelace's death washed a sorrowful expression over her features.

Sympathy emanated from Randy. "You two were tight, huh?"

A sob caught in Kesley's throat. "Lovelace was my guide when I first joined the Coalition. She taught me a lot. We became besties, almost like sisters."

Randy wrapped an arm around her and drew her close.

"Thanks." Burnt out and heartbroken, Kesley leaned her head on his shoulder and shut her eyes. A tear slid down her cheek, and he wiped it away for her. "Thanks again," she said, her voice faint.

"No problem." Randy continued holding her.

Kesley felt comforted by his presence. And he had saved her from a horrible fate today. She was in his debt.

Despite her tendency to irritate him, Randy appreciated Kesley. The broadening of his perspectives and evolving view of the war had started with her.

If he were honest with himself, he had developed a crush on her.

Both of them dozed off as the shuttle made its way toward Colony Five.

CHAPTER SIX

The survivors of the attack on Bravo Camp walked from the outlying landing spot for aircraft toward a small, unassuming prefab. They were in a jungle in Colony Five, moving through a makeshift compound. The prefab was Reza's sanctuary.

Governess Samantha Hayley had cordoned off the jungle and declared it a prohibited zone, shielding Reza and his assault force from discovery. Severe fines for trespassing discouraged citizens from even thinking about venturing into the area.

When rebels went to nearby towns for R&R, they had to keep a low profile, and recruiting was absolutely forbidden. The last thing Samantha wanted was to attract the CDF's attention. Any whisper of rebel activity in Colony Five would draw them there. Her people had no desire to get dragged into the war, and Samantha was going to ensure they weren't, all while assisting the Coalition however she could.

Arson and Sariah led the way. Randy and Kesley trailed behind the group, keeping each other company.

"I'm assuming that building is Reza's lair," Randy said to Kesley, his eyes examining the plain, windowless square structure. Once again, Kesley served as his guide through the unfamiliar.

"Yep, Governess Hayley had it constructed for him," she replied. The group went by a waterfall that flowed into a stream. "It's pretty basic. The main room functions as a communications hub, and the other room is Reza's study."

Randy swatted at a swarm of buzzing insects. He saw a massive open-air hangar beside the building. Inside it, Hammer Fall's assault ship—a base-class vessel equipped with sleeping stations—sat grounded. "Where'd you guys get the ship?"

"The Falgoah got it for us."

That surprised Randy. "The Falgoah are helping you guys?"

"Yeah, we formed an alliance with them. They've supplied us with weapons and other resources. They've even volunteered for the assault force. All they ask in return is for Reza to reinstate them to their land."

Randy had studied the conflict between the Falgoah and Chalderat clans thoroughly. Reinstatement of the Falgoah to their land would reignite the blood feud. He knew that letting the two clans continue to duke it out wouldn't be smart. He was sure Reza knew that as well. There needed to be a plan for reconciliation. Randy hoped Reza had one that was solid.

The group passed mobile showers and rows of large waterproof canvases stretched between poles. Beneath the canvases, up to twenty-five rebels slept in sleeping bags or on cots.

"So why aren't you guys using the ship for housing?" Randy asked Kesley.

"It just arrived two days ago," she replied. "The technicians are still installing the stealth-cloak emitters. Reza doesn't want anyone aboard until they're finished."

"How long has the assault force been here?"

Kesley took a few seconds to think before answering. "About two months now. They've been training with the Reldaldri mechsuits and other weapons."

The group stopped. Ahead of them, rebels inside improvised shelters rested. Arson gave instructions to his men, and they tapered off, some going left and some going right.

"Wait here," Kesley said to Randy. She went up to Arson and Sariah to talk to them about something.

While waiting for her, Randy scanned the jungle. He saw a small earth-colored quadruped masticating a fallen bough with its elongated teeth.

Kesley returned to Randy as Arson and Sariah walked off together, holding hands.

"So what's up?" Randy asked.

"C'mon, follow me." Kesley motioned for him to come with her. "You'll be staying with me in my field hut. Built it myself."

Reluctant, Randy squinted. "I'm staying with you?"

"Either that or you can crash with several others under one of the outdoor shelters. But I figured you'd want a little more privacy." In an overly chirpy tone, Kesley said, "Besides, my company's priceless, and *youuuu knowwwww* you enjoy it. Don't play." She winked.

Randy preferred the privacy of Kesley's hut, but he wasn't keen on dealing with her cheeky and occasionally pushy demeanor. He sighed in resignation. "Alright, fine. Let's go."

They stepped inside a log-wood hut with a thatched roof. The interior was sparse, just a bed, table, washbasin, and shower spigot.

"Get some shut-eye," Kesley told Randy. "In about three hours, Reza's going to update everyone on the new timeline for Hammer Fall. I'll be back by then. Got a few things to take care of." She paused at the door, remembering something. "Oh, Arson wanted me to let you know that Sariah will be giving you and Jarius a crash course on operating the Reldaldri mechsuit tomorrow, since you two are joining the assault force."

"Got it. Thanks."

Kesley left Randy to his own devices, going out the door.

Randy lay on the bed, his mind replaying the events that had turned his life upside down. The fact that he was now a Coalition rebel seemed crazy. His thoughts drifted to Stacie. He wondered how she was handling the revelations he'd dropped on her.

Exhaustion overtook him, and he shut his heavy eyelids.

Three hours passed. Night had fallen.

Kesley returned. She'd gotten cleaned up and was dressed in a tank top and shorts. She gently shook Randy awake from his sleep.

His eyes fluttered open. "So, the big moment has arrived, huh?" he asked groggily.

Kesley nodded.

Randy climbed out of bed, and together they went outside into the starlit night. The entire assault force had assembled in front of Reza's sanctuary, large spotlights illuminating the area. Anticipation hung in the air. Everyone was eager to hear from the Coalition leader.

Nocturnal creatures croaked in the background, blending with the indistinct murmur of the crowd.

Kesley spotted Arson and Sariah. She took Randy's hand, and her long strides dragged him forward.

Randy kept a comfortable distance from his father, avoiding eye contact and saying nothing. He crossed his arms over his chest, his eyes fixed on the doors of Reza's sanctuary.

Near Jarius, two Falgoah women were conversing. Like their male counterparts, they had taupe skin, ebony hair, slanted eyes, and a single set of scales extending from their forehead to their nose. Both wore something resembling black jumpsuits. Noting their uncanny resemblance, Jarius assumed they were sisters.

Randy became impatient. *So how long are you going to make us wait, Reza?*

Speak of the devil. The double doors of the sanctuary parted, and Reza emerged, his masked face cloaked in shadow underneath his cowl. He wore a black leathery ensemble with cybernetic strength-augmenting braces coiled around his arms and legs like armor. He set forth at a controlled pace, and three armed men followed behind him in perfect formation.

As he advanced, the crowd fell into hushed reverence. Voices died. Movements stilled. All eyes focused on him. He passed between two tall, flickering torches, their light dancing over the metal of his augmentations.

The holo transmitter at his feet, a disk mounted to a four-foot pole, cast pale light onto his figure. It captured and projected his image across the Coalition intranet, transmitting him in real-time to every faction's base.

He pressed a button on his mask. His voice, amplified and altered by the vocoder, thundered over the assembly. "My fellow freedom fighters, human and Falgoah alike, we stand here bound by a single truth: The Commonwealth Government must fall. And I am honored to stand here tonight among the ones who will bring it to its knees."

Enough grandstanding. Get on with it, Randy thought.

"Your valor will bring equality to Satellite One and return the exiled to their rightful planet. The Falgoah were wrongfully banished from Zelaforia. During the ceasefire, a militia secretly armed by the Chalderat attacked them. It was an underhanded tactic to continue exterminating the Falgoah. In light of that, the Falgoah had every right to break the ceasefire.

"They will be returned to their homeworld, and we will have equality. But Operation Hammer Fall must happen sooner than planned, because a madman now holds the Commonwealth's highest office, Cornelius Gould." The wind bent the flames of the torches. "We have proof that, backed by one of the Eight Elite, he orchestrated the assassination of Jared Kerner. And that's not all. Our insiders confirm Gould has built a secret arms-development facility. This darksite is manufacturing deadly new weapons the CDF will use to snuff us out.

"Jared Kerner was a reserved man; Gould is unpredictable, a wildcard. As Chief, he'll worsen our oppression. He'll impose harsher restrictions on the occupied colonies. He'll even initiate unwarranted surveillance on the unoccupied colonies, something he admitted in his debate with Chairwoman Amaechi.

"This is why our timeline must change. Instead of striking in seven days, we strike in three."

As Randy glared at Reza, a wave of worried susurrations swept through the crowd, too quiet to make out, but clearly laced with concern. The shortened window of preparation understandably unsettled some rebels.

"I know this is burdensome," Reza admitted. "Those training to master the Reldaldri suits will now have to push harder, and newcomers will need to learn faster. But I believe in all of you."

One rebel clapped, breaking the tension. Others joined in. A few cheered. The applause loudened, washing away hesitation as renewed confidence invigorated everyone.

"Governess Hayley has arranged a grand feast for us tonight," Reza added. "So enjoy it."

To Randy, it was clear: Delivering a good meal was Reza's way to pacify nervousness and boost morale.

After a final glance at the crowd, Reza disappeared into his sanctuary, his cowl snapping in the wind.

Randy's face pinched. The inciter of the Independent Movement didn't impress him. He wondered if Reza was the savior people claimed he was or just a false messiah chasing power. Driven by a need to uncover the truth, Randy broke into a sprint. He was done speculating. He would confront Reza face-to-face.

Arson shouted, "Randy, wait!"

Reza's three armed guards trained their rifles on Randy.

Arson raced toward the standoff, with Kesley flanking him.

Jarius crossed his arms and shook his head. *There you go again, Randy, rushing headlong into trouble. That's how you got into this mess . . . and somehow dragged my ass along for the ride.*

"Stand down!" Arson ordered the guards. As Reza's top commander, his authority held weight. The guards complied, lowering their weapons to the low-ready position.

Kesley parked herself beside Randy. "What the devil were you thinking?"

Arson scowled at his son, and a note of reprimand edged his voice. "Reza doesn't have an open-door policy, Randy. You can't just waltz into his domain and expect to get social time with him whenever you feel like it, just like you can't barge into your commander's office anytime you want."

"Is he afraid to talk to us 'underlings'?" Randy asked forwardly. "Does he think he's superior to us, his obedient pawns?"

Overhearing the commotion, Reza stepped back outside. "Randal Scott, I assure you I'm no elitist."

"Sorry, sir," Arson said. "My son's . . . been skeptical of the Coalition . . . and you." He shot Randy a sharp sidelong glare. "But I *think* he's coming around."

"It's alright," Reza said coolly. "Perhaps I can ease his skepticism. If your son wants an audience with me, he shall have one. I'll answer whatever questions he has, within reason."

"Thanks," Randy said.

He, Arson, and Kesley moved forward.

They entered Reza's sanctuary and walked into the central room, where comms equipment chirped and trilled.

Reza said, "Kess, Arson, remain here. I will speak to Randal alone in my study."

"Sure," Arson replied.

Randy and Reza went through the door ahead.

Reza settled into one of the chairs at the wooden table. Randy took the chair opposite him, more than ready to kick off the Q&A session.

Reza twined his fingers together on the table. "Alright, Randal, speak your mind."

"I want to know who you were before you became this . . . great influencer? What turned you into a revolutionary?"

Reza gathered his thoughts. "I was a Guardian, a private. My company was deployed to Zelaforia. Our mission was to assist the High Council in ending the civil conflict between the Falgoah and Chalderat clans. One day, my squad was ordered to open fire on a group of Falgoah warriors who had already surrendered. I refused to take part in the distasteful act." His voice quaked with rage. "They were defeated. There was no need to kill them. But Secretary of Defense Cornelius Gould had enacted a kill order. We were to take no prisoners.

"After my insubordination, I was reassigned from active duty to the Reserves. My new company was later activated to suppress the miners' strike in Colony Four. During that mission, I witnessed another cruel, senseless act. My squad was ordered to open fire on unarmed miners. Just like on Zelaforia, I refused. Consumed by rage, I attacked my squad leader. That was the final straw for CDF

Command. They gave me a dishonorable discharge, for refusing to become a heartless killer."

Again, Randy recalled his drill sergeant saying every enemy was to be dealt with ruthlessly. Even the slightest hint of compassion could mean execution on the spot for a Guardian. "Seems like the CDF adopted a culture of brutality," he said.

"Yes, CDF Command believed that culture was necessary for the survival of the New Humanity. They thought the CDF had to be as merciless as possible to protect humanity in its vulnerable state. A species will go to great lengths to protect itself."

Randy voiced the thoughts churning in his mind. "The RUC was seen as an enemy to the New Humanity, because they were threatening to take away resources from the Commonwealth as a whole. So that ruthless brutality was unleashed on them, even though we're all human beings."

"Yes, but compassion is a strength, not a weakness. I believe it's time for the CDF to evolve its culture and for the central government to be purged of corruption. It's time for a fair and just Commonwealth."

"So what happened after you were discharged?"

"I embarked on a journey of introspection, wandering the colonies as a drifter. I survived off the credits I had and took on odd jobs here and there. As a lottery beneficiary, I considered the colonies home. Not wanting to live a life of insignificance, I contemplated my place in society. During this journey, I saw people suffering from the poor living conditions the government seemed to be doing little to improve. Instead, they were busy profiting from planetary-impact missions on protectorates.

"Driven by the realization that the central government was a source of both good and significant wrongdoing, I understood the necessity for change. I donned this disguise, used the net to speak out against gross injustice, and urged others to resist. My goal was to ignite awareness, and the Independent Movement was born, a result far beyond my wildest hopes."

"So how'd you become the Coalition's leader?"

"To my dismay, the CDF crushed the RUC. The remaining resistance formed the Coalition of Rebel Factions. But they lacked direction. Needing a leader, I stepped in to take command, and they immediately accepted me, since I was the driving force behind the Independent Movement. Now, we're poised to end the central government's malign ways for good, which, I must stress, is affecting civilizations throughout the entire galaxy, not just the Commonwealth."

Reza keyed his electronic bracer, and a holo bloomed to life. He tapped a planet, enlarging the projection. "This is Uandorais," he said. "The Cogrull government has accepted Commonwealth protectorate status. The CDF is helping that government destroy the rebel forces threatening to overtake it. But the CDF has no right to interfere in those rebels' righteous stand."

"How do you know it's righteous?"

"Like colonists, they're merely demanding better of the established order. They despise the Commonwealth for derailing their revolution. People in other protectorates share the same feelings. It could be only a matter of time before Commonwealth antagonists, opposed to our planetary-impact missions, strike Eden soil or the colonies.

"Thom Kerner and Cornelius Gould set our republic on a path that must be reversed. Parliament members have become complacent with the Commonwealth's wrongful planetary-impact missions, because the government profits from them.

"With too few politicians willing to redirect the Commonwealth's course, our mission is crucial. I wish it could have waited until after the results of the election. Perhaps Oviereya will win. If she does, I know she would work tirelessly to turn things around. However, the extent of the change she could achieve is uncertain. She would face resistance from obstinate Parliament members determined to undermine her efforts. Many of them are corrupt and have made deals with the Eight Elite.

"Even if Oviereya could bring about considerable change, the colonies can't wait a year, especially with Gould as Chief. Something needs to be done now."

Randy, a stickler for detail, asked, "So what if everything backfires? What if the uncorrupt Parliament members don't want to cooperate with you in creating a new government? Though they may not have ties to criminals, most of them still believe in adhering to AEGIS's stratification of humanity. Have you thought about all that? Do you have a contingency plan?"

No one could easily pressure Reza into answering questions he didn't want to answer. Sidestepping the questions, he said, "You'll receive more information when the time comes." He stood. "You should go enjoy tonight's meal."

Randy followed Reza to the door and exited the study.

"Get your questions answered, Randy?" Arson asked.

"More or less." Randy remained skeptical of Reza.

Arson, Kesley, and Randy left the building.

Reza went through the rear door of his study to the wooden outdoor deck and rested his arms on the balustrade. His talk with Randy about his past sent his mind down memory lane . . .

Atop the roof of his temporary duty station, Ahmed Hawsawi —the man who would become Arman Reza—nursed a cigarette between his lips.

The sky was aglow with shades of orange and red as the last rays of sunlight pierced the clouds.

The roof-access door shrieked open. Ahmed glanced over his shoulder. His best friend, Lance Grisham, emerged.

"Thought I'd find you here," Lance said. The curly-haired blond plucked a cigarette from his front pocket. "Mind if I join you?"

"Not at all." Ahmed returned his gaze to the city's geometric architecture, structures of edges and angles.

Lance walked up to the parapet, taking up a spot beside his friend. "What's on your mind?"

Ahmed sighed his frustration, uncertainty muddling his thoughts. "Just wondering what the *hell* we're doing here."

Lance chuckled. "You know why we're here. The Noshkanu province is a protectorate. The deal is that the Commonwealth provides the High Council with military assistance to squash the Falgoah uprising in exchange for bitrium and other minerals."

Ahmed replied in a voice of disapproval. "So the CDF is a bunch of contract mercenaries, is that it? Just fucking guns for hire?"

Lance laughed. As long as he wasn't doing anything pro bono, he'd execute all orders without question. "Basically. The government likes to call us peacekeepers, equalizers, or interventionists. We restore harmony to civilizations, reduce crime when governments can't, and defend worlds when they're unable to protect themselves. You know, all that righteous drivel. But it's all for a price, though.

"We've earned a reputation for this heroes-for-hire stuff throughout the galaxy, and the central government is using that rep to benefit the Commonwealth." He tossed his cigarette onto the rooftop and scuffed it out with his boot. "Anyway, we swore to obey the orders of the Chief Executive. We don't get to choose what missions we like or dislike. We don't get to decide what's right or wrong. The only thing we get to do is execute orders, my friend. And we get paid to do it, so I really don't give a fuck."

Ahmed exhaled a stream of cigarette smoke, grimacing. "Well, *I* am a thinking man." He aimed a thumb at himself. "And I'm not sure the CDF should be meddling in disputes over territorial rights. Our being here feels wrong." His conscience troubled him. This mission felt morally dubious for a man of honor like him.

Lance drew his lips into a smirk. "Careful, if Sergeant Bartel heard you talk like that, she'd probably blow a hole into your 'thinking man's' cranium." He shaped his fingers into the form of a gun and pretended to fire a shot. "*Pa-chow.*" Ahmed frowned. "After all, the—"

"I know, damn it," Ahmed interrupted. "It's just like Senior Instructor Wells said: 'The Commonwealth is always righteous.' Maybe that's just cliché bullshit. No government is always righteous." He puffed his cigarette. Then he expelled his next thought, saying, "Fuck, how come the Union cheerleads our efforts to play savior across all these worlds?"

Lance replied, "It's all about presentation. If the central government shows how a planetary-impact mission aligns with the Union's goal of promoting its benevolence and attracting universal allies, they consent to it *(unaware there might be details omitted or ulterior motives)*. Lucky for the Commonwealth, right? 'Cause we got debts to pay, and these missions are helping us pay 'em off.

"But I *do* have to admit, the Union seems to be getting a little concerned about our campaigns of 'good deeds' on other worlds. Eyebrows are being raised." He checked the time on his wristcom. "Hey, we need to head inside to get shelled for tonight's op."

Ahmed dropped his cigarette onto the rooftop and crushed the butt under his heel . . .

As Reza stood on the deck outside his study, his mind recapped the aftermath of that op . . .

Amid their razed campground, eighteen Falgoah clansmen—some just teenagers—held their hands aloft in surrender. The eviscerated bodies of their comrades, who had fought to the death, littered the ground, lying in their own viscera and entrails.

A squad of Guardians in M-X01s trained their rifles on the survivors, red tagging lasers marking them for execution.

A shudder racked Ahmed's limbs. He was horrified. In a firefight, even if it didn't always sit right with him, he'd had no choice but to shoot back. In those do-or-die moments, it was easy to forget the humanity of those trying to kill him. He was a soldier, and so were they, all warriors on a battlefield. His instinct had always been to make it home alive, to help his comrades do the same. But this was different. These people had put down their weapons. They had surrendered. They were no longer a threat.

"C'mon, they've given up! They're unarmed!" Ahmed shouted.

The squad leader, Sergeant DaSalvo, nonchalantly said, "The CDF's orders from Gould are to take no prisoners."

Ahmed's face flushed red from anger. "But this isn't right! Some are just kids! What fucking sense does this make?"

"We don't decide what's right or wrong, Private. We just follow orders."

Hoping to get some support, Ahmed glanced over at Lance.

Lance ignored Ahmed's help-me-out look. He was in full compliance. *Ahmed, this is no time to be a Falgoah sympathizer.*

The hands of some Guardians quivered with unease.

"Fire!" DaSalvo ordered.

Triggers clicked. Crackling gunfire swallowed the frenetic

screams of the dying clansmen. Mowed down, they lay massacred en masse.

Ahmed, the only one who hadn't fired, couldn't desensitize himself to the slaughter. Disgust hardened his features.

DaSalvo marched up to him. He retracted his faceplate, showing his enraged countenance to Ahmed. "Private Hawsawi, you were ordered to fire!" A throbbing vein bulged from his forehead.

Ahmed's faceplate unsealed. He scowled. "Fuck your orders, and fuck Gould."

"Your insubordination will be reported up the chain of command, you understand, Guardian?"

"Whatever."

DaSalvo's faceplate clamped back down. Life scans detected nothing. Mission accomplished. "We destroyed the camp, and all the clansmen here are dead. The cleanup crew will begin body disposal." That meant the cleanup crew would cremate the bodies via flamethrower or dump them into the ocean. "Let's go."

Ahmed stared at the shot-up bodies, silent. These people wouldn't even get a proper burial.

"Ahmed, let's go," Lance said as mechboots thumped away. Ahmed didn't move. "Ahmed, come on!"

Chin down, Ahmed waved Lance off. "Go, Lance, I'll catch up."

"Don't ruminate on this shit too long. It's done. End of story." Lance left with the others.

Ahmed walked past huts fire had gutted, searching for a sign of life. His heart sank to the pit of his belly. He felt appalled. How could anyone numb their soul to what happened here?

The crackle and pop of crisping flesh and bone made his stomach heave.

He coughed hard, smoke strangling his lungs. His mind reeled, reflecting on what had truly transpired here. Under the Commonwealth Government's auspices, he had participated in the Chalderat's systematic cleansing of the Falgoah.

There were Guardians in his platoon who, like him, hadn't wanted to be part of this slaughter. They had remorseful souls, as he did. But they were bound by duty and couldn't risk a reprimand for refusing to obey orders or voicing their disapproval. But was obeying orders worth weltering your soul in the blood of people who had done you no harm? Not all planetary-impact missions were like this, though. The CDF had helped defend worlds against some of the universe's most vile wrongdoers.

Flying predators circled above, hunting for carrion.

While passing the blackened bodies of small children, Ahmed heard shallow breathing coming from a woman.

His searching eyes found her. She was injured but alive. Trying to flee from him, she crawled past the charred bones of friends, nails clawing grooves into the dirt.

Ahmed went to her. She stared at him, eyes wide and terror-stricken, her lungs fighting for oxygen.

He crouched beside her. "I'm not going to hurt you," he said gently. His helmet's external sound port relayed his words in the Falgoah's language.

The woman's heart skipped when she saw a syringe pop out from Ahmed's wrist.

He injected a healing accelerant and pain suppressant into her wounded leg. Then he straightened to full height.

He racked his helmet and commanded his Shell to release him. Couplings unlatched. He unsnapped his harness and exited the Shell to appear as nonthreatening as possible.

The stench of burning flesh hung in the air.

Ahmed mentally instructed the CPU of his standing war machine to continue translating his words in the Falgoah's language through the external sound port.

With the pain of her wound dulled, the woman managed to stand and hobble around. She pinned a hawkish glare on Ahmed and quickly snatched up a plank of wood.

She swung at him.

He dodged. "I don't want to fight!" His Shell translated and echoed his words.

She swung again, the plank slamming into his gut.

He fell onto his back. "I'm sorry!" His Shell translated.

The woman raised the plank, ready to bash in his skull.

With no choice, Ahmed drew his sidearm and fired a fatal shot into her chest.

She crashed to the ground, a geyser of dark orange blood spurting from the bullet hole.

Ahmed got to his feet and holstered his pistol. *No.* He lowered his chin, staring at the woman's lifeless body. *The way she reacted to me . . . I've become a monster to these people.*

A weary Ahmed sat at a metal table in a barren, windowless room, the audible buzz of a lone light bulb overhead adding to the weight in his chest. In front of him sat his platoon sergeant, Sergeant First Class Alicia Bartel.

"You're a lucky man, Private Hawsawi," Alicia said. "For your insubordination, you're being kicked off active duty and reassigned to the Reserves. No more full-time benefits. No steady pay. But it's a far cry from being cashiered."

Ahmed exhaled a shaky breath. "Fine," he said quietly. "Okay."

Alicia slid a datapad across the scarred surface between them.

"Just need your print to make it official."

Ahmed placed his thumb on the signature box of the v-doc. He stood, chair scraping softly behind him, and exited.

Outside the door, Lance was waiting. His eyes studied Ahmed's dejected expression. "So was the consequence of not pulling that trigger worth it? Was it worth it being a Falgoah sympathizer?"

Ahmed paused. That word—sympathizer—carried so much venom. It was how the CDF silenced compassion, how it defamed Guardians who expressed sympathy for the enemy. "Recusing myself from mass murder was every bit worth it."

"And what did you gain? You just threw away a full-time military career, something we worked our asses off for."

Ahmed turned his head just enough to glance over his shoulder. "What I gained was my soul." He walked away.

Twenty-eight miners on strike in Colony Four, protesting the Commonwealth Government, stood outside their work facility. Their voices roared, fists pumping handmade signs.

A squad of Reservists in M-X01s confronted them.

The sergeant in charge stepped forward. His Shell's external sound port megaphoned his voice. "YOU ARE RESOURCE HARVESTERS IN THE EMPLOY OF THE CENTRAL GOVERNMENT. RETURN TO WORK IMMEDIATELY! THIS IS YOUR FINAL WARNING!"

"Screw you!" a man shouted from the front. He hurled a stone that bonged off the sergeant's faceplate.

The miners burst into cheers. More stones followed, pelting the Guardians' Shells.

The sergeant C-commed his squad. *<<Alpha Squad, crowd has turned hostile. Kill parameters are relaxed. Turn selector switch to lethal*

and open fire on my command.>>

Safeties disengaged, rifles locked and loaded.

Ahmed's face contorted with reproach. He opened a private C-comm channel to the cutthroat sergeant. *<<Wait, why are we using lethal rounds?>>*

<<Gould's given us authorization to go lethal when we see fit, and I see fit right now, Hawsawi.>>

Ahmed was on the verge of snapping at the mention of that name—Gould, the Secretary of Defense. He spoke to a woman among the miners through their Link. *<Priscilla, get out of here.>*

<Why?> she asked.

The sergeant said, "Alright, prepare to—"

Ahmed tackled him to the ground, armor banging against armor. "This is madness! I didn't sign up to be a murderer!"

"Off me!" The sergeant whammed his armored knuckles against Ahmed's faceplate, knocking him aside and spiderwebbing cracks across his visor.

Priscilla gasped.

The sergeant stood up. "Open fire, goddammit!"

Staccato gunfire erupted. Miners scattered in a panicked frenzy, desperately fleeing the onslaught.

"No!" Ahmed screamed, watching a spray of crimson squirt from Priscilla. Her body jerked grotesquely, reacting to every bullet shot through it.

Being Linked with Priscilla made the execution a shared nightmare for Ahmed. Dizziness and nausea bum-rushed him. Bile rose in his throat. His body absorbed the keen pain of every bullet. Fighting to stay upright, he was on the precipice of blacking out.

After the gunfire ceased, six bodies lay sprawled in the dirt, Priscilla among them. Their blood soaked the ground in dark glistening pools. Message sent.

The sergeant in charge said, "Let that be a lesson to all you peons: Don't bite the hand that feeds you."

Ahmed's legs gave out. He plummeted to his knees beside Priscilla's body. His heart thrummed in his ears, and his lower lip trembled.

Blood gushed from the holes in Priscilla's chest and from her mouth, a macabre reminder of the brutal cost of defiance.

She brought a quivering hand to the side of Ahmed's face, tears of farewell flowing from her entrancing azure eyes. < *Goodbye, love, I* —> She smiled wanly, and her weak hand hit the ground. As her thick-lashed lids closed, she wheezed. Then her lungs failed.

Ahmed cradled her body in his arms. The world around him blurred, colors bleeding into each other. Then, as the mental aftershocks of experiencing something akin to death overwhelmed him, he slipped into unconsciousness.

Ahmed barged into the visiting Secretary of Defense's office. "You killed her!" he shouted belligerently.

Cornelius jumped from the chair behind his desk. "Security, escort this man out of my office!"

Two men rushed in and seized Ahmed by the arms.

He writhed and thrashed against his subduers' grip, hands clawing for Cornelius' throat.

"How the hell did he get in here?" asked the bearded security officer.

"He forged a level-three pass somehow," his colleague replied. "Tricky bastard."

"Don't worry, Sir, we'll get him outta your sight." The bearded officer yanked on Ahmed's arm. "C'mon, asshole."

Cornelius gestured for them to halt. "Wait a moment." He

moved around his desk with deliberate slowness, hands clasped behind his back. He clutched Ahmed's jaw, fingers digging into bone. "What have I done to . . . unhinge you, Guardian, hmm?"

Ahmed's eyes were bloodshot from tears of rage. "One of the people killed today during the miners' strike was my lover. Her name was Priscilla Kitzron. And it was *you* who killed her! You and your damned permission to use lethal force whenever! Everything falls back on you, you heartless son of a bitch!"

There wasn't a trace of remorse in Cornelius' icy eyes. "No, she got herself killed by revolting with her fellow miners," he said, his tone offensively cavalier.

"She wasn't a miner! She was a missionary from Eden taking a stand with people who'd become her friends!"

Cornelius let go of his Ahmed's jaw. "Whatever." He shrugged dismissively. His indifference was a slap in the face. "Either way, her death was her fault."

Ahmed screamed a primal, heart-wrenching sound.

Cornelius said to his security officers, "Go ahead, remove this vermin from my sight."

The officers hauled Ahmed out of the office.

He received a dishonorable discharge after that act of defiance, and he had no regrets . . .

Wanting to take down the Commonwealth Government, Reza saw the Coalition as a godsend. It was exactly what he had prayed for: his own army.

He had declared that his army would be different from the CDF. It wouldn't employ the cutthroat tactics Gould had sanctioned. It would only kill when absolutely necessary. The torture of prisoners or the rape of women would be severely punished. The Coalition would be a fighting force guided by high moral standards.

Reza initially told his troops the plan for Hammer Fall was to expose the government's corruption by seizing the Parliament Building's broadcast center. Then he'd work with the people and righteous politicians to create a new, equitable government. But months ago, his vision shifted. He concluded: *He* knew what was best, *he* knew the direction the Commonwealth should take, *he* had the solutions for helping the colonies.

He didn't want to risk a new government enacting an agenda that diverged from his. He didn't want to deal with disagreements or red tape. To ensure his vision prevailed, he decided his leadership was all the Commonwealth needed for the foreseeable future. He didn't care if people labeled him a dictator.

After releasing the information indicting the corrupt politicians, Reza knew the people of Eden wouldn't feel a shred of sympathy for them, or for the Eight Elite. But he also knew they wouldn't want him to become the overall ruler of the Commonwealth. They'd demand new leadership chosen through a democratic process. Well, too bad for them, he thought. There was no room for error. This wasn't a time to take chances.

A collaborative effort to build a new government meant the introduction of too many ideas, the clash of differing viewpoints. Reza already had the blueprint. And his blueprint was the only one that mattered, the only one that needed to be enacted.

He also decided the corrupt needed to face true justice. Leaving their fate to the judiciary system, especially Cornelius', was out of the question. He'd be the sword of justice, the overall juror of the wicked. And his sentence for them would be death. The executions would definitely include Cornelius and the Eight families.

He wrestled with this decision. He still wanted his soldiers to believe in the ethos he had established, the ideals that made them better than the CDF. But as a man's positions and conclusions evolved, so did he.

Doubt crept into his conscience as he continued gazing out over the deck. Was this new direction, this compromise in his belief system, truly the right way to go?

The familiar warmth of a gentle hand graced his shoulder. A warmth that could only belong to . . . her. But he knew that warmth was an illusion manifested by his cerebral implant. The Quilgarian tech was using his mental transcript of Priscilla's distinct touch to recreate past sensory experiences.

Priscilla's disembodied serene voice said, *Know that you are doing the right thing, my beloved.* Her likeness materialized, glowing softly. She wore the white dress from their first date.

But—

She pressed a finger against Reza's lips. The touch felt astonishingly real. *Shhhh, you know Gould must be killed,* she said. *And you can't risk letting anyone else build a new government except for you. Don't let what I fought for be in vain.*

A lump formed in Reza's throat. *No, never.*

Then do what must be done. Priscilla faded back into his mental diary, along with her comforting presence.

Reza blinked back tears. It felt good being consoled by her, even if she was only a hallucination. And no, there was no going back to the original plan. He realized what he had to do to usher in the next chapter of the New Humanity.

• • •

Randy had gone back to the hut. He'd already showered and changed clothes before Kesley entered. Sitting on the bed, he reflected on his conversation with Reza, the upcoming operation, the government corruption, and the CDF's misuse of military power and lack of accountability.

When he completed BCT and MOS training, his outlook on the war was simple: The Coalition was the enemy, the CDF was the galaxy's righteous warriors, and his father was a murderer and traitor that needed to be taken out. But now he'd been enlightened.

Basic Training conditioned Guardians to believe that the Coalition and anyone who opposed the Commonwealth Government were the enemy. But Randy learned the Coalition's intentions were noble, and he found out Arson wasn't the villain he had once thought him to be. And though he disagreed with Arson's decision to leave his family and fight for the Coalition, he realized it wasn't right to assassinate the man's character.

The Coalition wasn't the enemy. The CDF wasn't the enemy. Arson wasn't the enemy. The true enemies were Gould, corrupt politicians, and the Eight Elite, along with widespread ignorance and a system that discriminated against colonists. The Coalition was the force dedicated to defeating them. But there was something about Reza Randy wasn't on board with.

Kesley was leaning against a wall, arms folded. "You haven't said much since we left Reza's sanctuary," she commented.

"Not much to say," Randy replied tersely.

"Well, what do you think of Reza? You satisfied since you got a chance to talk to him mano a mano?"

Randy squared his jaw, distrust registering across his face. "Right now, I find it hard to trust many people. We'll see what happens after Operation Hammer Fall."

Kesley laughed. "Such a tight-ass."

Randy got up from the bed, brows knitted. "*Excuse me* for being skeptical. We're bringing this war for colony equality to Eden soil. We could very well kick-start humanity's next holocaust if things go wrong. I think I have a good reason to be a little antsy, don't you think?" Stacie suddenly entered his thoughts, and he began pacing in a circle.

"Would you sit down and take it easy," Kesley said.

"I'm just thinking about a . . . friend of mine, a Guardian."

"The woman you mentioned? Stacie? The one who was out cold when I picked you up at Bravo Force's camp?"

"Yeah, I hope she's okay. And . . . to be honest, I'm still not sure if I'm doing the right thing here."

Kesley sighed and sashayed up to Randy, hips swaying and lips smiling. She slapped her hands onto his shoulders, making him wince. "Stop pacing and sulking, Mr. Worrywart." She chuckled. Randy frowned in response. "Relax, we're about to change the *entire* Commonwealth for the better."

Randy raised an eyebrow—a silent "screw-you" gesture. "Relax? You want me to relax at a time like this? I don't think—"

Kesley fused her lips to his, silencing him.

Blindsided again by an uninvited—but not unwelcome—kiss, Randy gently pried her off him. Color rose in his cheeks. "Um, I'm sorry. I can't—" His mind flashed back to Kesley slipping off her shirt at her home, and to the kiss she planted on him that day. Suddenly, temptation ensnared him.

Kesley egged him on, necking him and sucking face, coming on stronger by the microsecond.

Randy's curious hands made an exploratory excursion over her voluptuous body, traveling the arc of her hips and groping her everywhere within reach. Losing self-control, he captured her well-fleshed backside in a vicious squeeze that made her loins rumble. His restraint was fading fast. Sex drive overtaking him, he ached to divest Kesley of her clothing.

Thinking of Stacie, Randy rejected Kesley's advances, pulling himself away. "This can't happen, Kess. We should—"

Kesley put a finger to his lips, shushing him. "Lighten up, soldier boy. You need to forget about the CDF and all that other past crap. That's over. You're one of *us* now, a Coalition freedom fighter, and it's time to celebrate." Unwilling to cede, she pasted her lips to his again, melting away his protest.

Randy's mind and body urged him to give in and go for it. *No, that's enough,* he told himself, but kept touching Kesley through her clothes, imagining how it'd feel to touch her in the buff. He tried to force himself to desist to no avail, his desperation for sex growing worse.

Kesley backed him against a wall and crashed her lips into his like she owned him. Her kiss was a goddamn assault—wet, sloppy, and unrelenting. She drew back just enough to smirk, their shared spit glistening her lips.

"Knock it off, Kess. I mean it," Randy said mildly but sternly, trying to let her down easy.

Kesley molded her breasts to his chest and brought her mouth to his ear. "And if I say no?" Challenge laced her voice.

Before he could answer, she jammed her tongue into his mouth. She bit his bottom lip and then sucked it gently. Again, she kissed him, while brushing her fingers against the bulge in his pants.

Randy tried to muster some semblance of resistance. He wanted to stop this—he should stop this—but hell, it was hard to.

Thoughts of Stacie reentered his mind, and he tore his lips away from Kesley's. He clenched her biceps and spun her, trading places and pinning her against the wall to restrain her.

Kesley said playfully, "Right where you want me, huh?"

Randy let go of her arms and stepped back. "Enough. We're done." His expression told Kesley he was serious.

"Come on, let me properly reward you for saving me from that creep." Kesley dragged her shirt overhead, and her plump breasts spilled out from underneath.

Randy's eyes were drawn to her beautiful nipples and areolas.

Kesley took his wrist and flattened his hand against her right breast. "Go on, have your way with me." Torn between loyalty to Stacie and his undeniable attraction to this chesty redhead, Randy cupped a generous handful of the soft, supple mound, squeezing it possessively. Its shape felt good in his palm.

Kesley reached down, grabbed Randy's ass, and yanked him closer, plastering him against her salient proportions. She whispered, "I know you're angry, agitated, and stressed. Let me provide some relief. Make love to me. You know you want to."

Thoughts of Stacie prevented Randy from giving in. He craned his head away from Kesley. "I'm sorry, I can't. I—"

"What's wrong?" Kesley furrowed her brows. "Am I not fuckable enough for you?" Silence followed.

Randy glanced at her bare chest before diverting his eyes. He was stressed to the max, and Kesley was offering herself up to him as an outlet. His conscience and libido began playing tug-of-war.

Kesley's eyes narrowed into slits, and her lips pursed. "Fine, forget it." Feeling undesired and embarrassed, she turned to leave. "Maybe you just ain't man enough to handle an older woman," she muttered out of spite. "Maybe you're just a fucking kid who still has daddy issues. You can just—"

Randy's hand shot out, snatching Kesley's wrist. He pushed her down in front of him, the sound of her kneecaps hitting the floor audible. His fingers fumbled with his belt buckle, then nearly tore off his zipper.

As he shoved his pants and boxers halfway down, his aroused, rigid cock sprang free from confinement. Kesley was impressed with the length his pants had concealed.

In less than a beat, Randy had his cock stuffed in Kesley's mouth. His hand fisted a hunk of her hair, controlling her head as he jerked his hips back and forth. A part of him had longed to shut her sassy mouth in this manner.

She licked the underside of his member and swirled her tongue around its head, taunting the sensitive skin. She then opened her mouth wide and took in all his girth, slurping noisily.

With her lips tightly sealed around him, she pulled back in an extra-slow suck, only to devour him whole again.

Randy's conscience screamed at him, reminding him he had a girlfriend. He hated how much he wanted this, how horny he was right now. As he spontaneously sped his pace, Kesley's hands found purchase on his thighs. He drove his cock past her uvula, lodging it in her throat, and ejaculated.

After a strangled, gurgling sound left Kesley, she gulped. Then she released him. Cum and saliva drizzled down her chin.

Still horny, Randy fed his cock to her again. A thrill arose when her nose smacked his pelvis. Gripping her skull, he forced her head to move in sync with his rhythm. Her mouth wasn't the orifice he truly wanted, but it would have to suffice—a compromise between his sexual desires and his commitment to Stacie.

Kesley took him like a pro, her lips, tongue, and teeth working together to ravish him.

Randy had to admit that the sight of her slavishly sucking his cock while sitting on her heels topless was a huge turn-on.

But as he continued deep-throating her, a small voice in the back of his mind told him wrong was still wrong. The clarity hit, and he mustered the discipline to withdraw from her mouth.

Guilt and shame washed over him. Enough was enough. It was time to leave and get his head together.

Before he could zip up, Kesley stood and wrapped her hand

around his still-hard dick, stroking it. "Are we gonna fuck or not?"

Randy said, "I can't—" Just then, Kesley fondled him demandingly. His resolve was now hanging by a thread.

He clutched Kesley's wrist to halt her advances, but he failed to actually remove her hand, her caress so damn soothing.

Kesley said, "Look me in the eye and tell me you don't wanna get it on tonight, don't *need* to." She stroked faster, pushing Randy closer to capitulation. She literally had him by the dick.

Succumbing to seduction, Randy latched onto her hair, pulled her head back, and clamped his mouth over hers. Kissing a path down her body, he suckled the hardened peaks of her breasts. As he indulged, his erection burgeoned even more.

Kesley's body was thick, fleshy, and curvy. It was a succulent, gorgeous shape, and he couldn't resist this opportunity to feel and taste it. Right now, he was dying to get her panties off.

Kesley helped him out of his shirt, fingers skimming his taut muscles. In turn, he worked her shorts down her legs. Then he stripped himself naked in a frenzy.

Randy hoisted Kesley up by her shapely thighs and dumped her onto the bed. Tresses tumbled over her forehead in a sexy disarray.

Like a vulture on carrion, Randy clawed her panties' waistband and tugged. The fabric slid down her broad hips with a whisper of resistance, electrifying him. He yanked more aggressively this time, and the stubborn material surrendered, emitting a sharp, exhilarating *rip* that made his pulse race. He wanted her goddamn panties gone. One final, determined pull tore them clean off, turning them into refuse. Almost instinctively, he crushed them in his fists before hurling them across the room.

Randy sank his knees into the mattress on each side of Kesley, an animalistic thirst in his eyes. Her naked body lay sprawled out before him; it would take a superhuman effort not to fuck her.

Kesley said, "Hey, I can't conceive children, so don't be afraid to go all out, if you know what I mean."

Adrenaline and testosterone building, Randy was more than ready for the coup de grâce. He reached below and wedged his stiff member into Kesley inch by inch, savoring every second. As he plugged himself all the way into her cleft, a wheeze of elation escaped her lungs, and her back arched, breasts jutting upward. After pulling out almost entirely, he plunged back inside her.

Thoughts of his jeopardized career as a Guardian, his strained relationship with his father, and the ceaseless stresses of war consumed Randy's mind. These frustrations fueled every punch of his cock into Kesley's willing body.

"Harder," she gasped. "Don't hold back. Let it all out." She was begging him to harness the anger inside him to amplify her own pleasure, anger he'd been harboring since his mother's death. It was a mutual exchange, a balance of needs—his release for her satisfaction. She was into being dominated and manhandled in the bedroom, something all her partners found stimulating.

Randy was happy to grant her request. He clamped his hands around her ankles and forced her legs to fold back until her joints cricked. He now had her knees smashed against her shoulders, so he could drill deeper into her. His grip intensified as he fucked her into the mattress, cock dunking into her at a downward angle.

Randy accelerated, his tempo feral—savage. He hammered into Kesley with the untamed, primal energy of a man pushed to his limits by life. His future in limbo, he was desperate to unload all the tension roiling inside him. Every sobering thrust into Kesley seemed like catharsis.

It wasn't long before she was a trembling wreck. She relished being fucked as roughly as possible—nothing compared to it.

She struggled to breathe as an orgasm slammed into her. She

came so hard she saw stars, and couldn't even think.

Still holding her ankles down, Randy stretched her legs wider, more harshly than intended. Her submissive body squirmed in ecstasy, every inch of him impaling her nonstop.

"K-keep going," she panted. *Show me what your dick can do.*

Randy's cock became a battering ram, its head pounding her cervix with each vigorous stroke. *This is what you wanted, Kess,* he thought. She'd given him permission to go no-holds-barred, to fuck her senseless. So he kept spearing her relentlessly.

After pulling out, Randy turned Kesley belly-down and yanked her hips into the air. The sight of her bent over—face down, ass up—rocketed tingles up his spine. He ran his eyes over the fullness of both cheeks, then slapped his hands onto them. A resounding *whack* reverberated through the room. He kneaded *all* her ass meat with total abandon, feeling it mash against his fingers.

Not wasting another second, he buried himself to the hilt inside her. The recoil of her ass flogged him as his hips worked.

Soon, a cacophony of clapping noises filled the room, flesh striking flesh without pause.

Believing he'd gotten his fill, Randy reached down to extract himself. Kesley's rear cheeks quivered as he snapped his hips back, a wet *plop* punctuating his exit. Thick, gooey strands of neohuman cum sagged between the head of his shaft and her entrance.

As she tried to push herself up, Randy clutched the back of her neck, keeping her facedown. "No, not yet," he commanded gently. He hadn't gotten his fix after all. He rammed into her again, his thrusts rocking her forward and rubbing her face against the mattress.

Every bed-shaking thud of his hips rippled Kesley's ass. While clinging to the sheets, she bit down on them, muffling a choked whimper that was half protest, half desperate plea for more.

Randy entwined her arms behind her back in a tight crisscross and threshed her cheeks with the full brunt of his loins.

Kesley was in absolute submission, letting him do as he pleased. It had him pumped up. There were no parameters given to him. Anything and everything was welcomed by her—as long as it wasn't harmful and was consensual.

He pulled out and flipped her onto her back. His cock was still thick and throbbing. He grabbed her thighs and spread-eagled them. Then he lined himself up and embedded his cock in her. The impact nearly made her eyes protrude from their sockets.

While Kesley cried out in ecstasy, Randy's mind became a battlefield, the image of his mother's death flashing behind his eyes. He saw the explosion, the flames, the fucking nothingness that was left. Kesley had volunteered to be his outlet, and he had promised himself he'd "hold nothing back," as she requested.

The bed frame shuddered and groaned, screws threatening to pop loose, but he didn't give a damn. Let the bed break.

Kesley took Randy's wrists and maneuvered his hands to her throat. "C'mon, get a little rougher, a little freaky," she demanded, her voice low and seductive. *Don't disappoint me, soldier boy.*

Randy pressed his thumbs against her windpipe, not hard enough to completely restrict her breathing, just enough to stifle a groan. And the masochist in her loved it. He smothered her mouth with his to mute the next groan—a kiss that was more bite than lips.

He then moved his hands from her neck to her shoulders, his full weight pinning her down. His thrusts were a steady force that wouldn't let up—an overwhelming force.

"Harder," Kesley begged. "Give me the roughest you've got."

Her demand was a balm on the angry fire engulfing every cell in Randy's body, music to his ears. His cock pistoned in and out of her dripping slit like a machine that couldn't switch off.

Kesley's nipples stiffened into pebbled cylinders, noticeably jutting out for attention. Leaning down, Randy imprisoned one inside his mouth, teeth grazing the morsel just enough to make Kesley mewl. As he suctioned her other nipple, she writhed beneath him, hyperventilating.

One push into her after another, he fell deeper into a trance that made him forget everything but her intoxicating presence.

"Oh, shit," Kesley hissed. A seismic orgasm hit her. Randy continued to fuck her through the convulsions quaking her body, his cock disappearing balls-deep into her over and over.

As if it were a remedy to his bottled-up frustrations, he pummeled the area between her wide-open thighs at an unrestrained pace, satisfying both their needs.

Kesley wound her legs around him, commanding him to bring it—to do his worst. *This is what I want. Fuck me.* Her heels dug into his ass, cramming his cock as far down as it could go.

With a final, ferocious stab—one pleasing to Kesley—he came. His cum filled her to the brim, oozing out of her and pooling on the sheets. He yanked his cock out, done painting her insides white.

Coming down off the adrenaline rush, his entire body seemed to breathe a sigh of relief. Taking a break, he collapsed beside Kesley. His erection remained rock-hard, pointed toward the ceiling and coated in his jizz—and still spurting.

Kesley had heard stories about the unreal prowess of Highborn men in bed. It seemed the rumors were accurate. However, she hadn't anticipated an experience so orgasmic, so incredible.

She closed her eyes. "So, finally worn out, huh?" she huffed with a laugh. Her eyes popped open when she felt Randy's tongue lick a trail of saliva up her thigh. Rest time was over. She didn't even have time to gather herself before Randy was on her again.

Sparing not one bit of Kesley's flesh, he dropped slobbery kisses all over her body and plucked on her erect nipples.

Insatiable, he dragged her closer, sliding her across the sheets. After shoving her legs apart again, he teased her soaked entrance using the head of his cock. Apparently, he wasn't done yet.

In a sudden move, Kesley rolled their bodies. Now on top, she mounted him—impaling herself on his cock.

Delight drove him crazy as she glided up and down his length, clapping her ass against him. She was a woman on a mission to claim him, to fuck him.

The beads of sweat tracing the curves of her body dripped onto his chest as she worked.

With a quick motion of her hand, she flipped back the hair that had cascaded over her shoulder. Then she paused her hips. "So, you done doubting the Coalition?" she asked, breathing raggedly.

Randy said in an irate tone, "Shut it. I'm still not convinced Operation Hammer Fall is the right move, *okay?*"

Kesley scowled. She had shown him the colonies' deplorable conditions, and he'd seen her nearly get raped, yet he was still waffling? Fuck that. An inferno ignited within her. She viciously jerked her hips, riding him with a ferocity that was almost cruel.

"Damn it, Kess," Randy grunted, "ease up."

Kesley was beyond taking it easy. She was sick of his indecision. "No," she said aggressively, nails scratching his pecs. If he insisted on being so obstinate about joining the Coalition, she figured maybe she'd use him for sex and then be done with him.

Randy was fed up with her too—fed up with her pushiness, her taunts. He counter-fucked her, upthrusting into her and dribbling her jiggly ass cheeks between his fingers.

Kesley retaliated and matched his aggression, grinding herself against him. She clenched her walls around his cock, like she was trying to strangle it.

Randy and Kesley were now simply hate-fucking each other. And Randy was determined to win the skirmish.

Irritation from her calling him "soldier boy" and prodding him boiled over. He jackhammered into her punishingly until euphoria had her whimpering, her head snapping back and arms going limp at her sides in defeat. He'd won the skirmish. *So much for her temper tantrum.* He grabbed her waist, burying his cock so deep he swore he could feel her heartbeat against its tip.

He sat up and leaned all the way forward, toppling Kesley backward. As her back met the mattress again, his cock slipped out of her. Barely a tenth of a second went by before he reentered.

He continuously crashed his hips into hers, a fresh dose of adrenaline in his system. There was no lull, no respite—just consecutive, unyielding thrusts. And his tongue raided her mouth with the same dominance. The urge to fuck her was inescapable.

Kesley rocked uncontrollably beneath Randy, her overstimulated body unsure if it wanted more or wanted to escape for a reprieve. Her moans devolved into desperate, incoherent utterances as he drove into her obsessively. She couldn't string together a single word, only gasp for oxygen.

Randy had gotten Kesley buck naked for one reason: to gratify himself. And for all he knew, this could be his last night in bed with a woman. So he was going to maximize it—fuck Kesley until she couldn't take any more.

Losing himself in his desires, he fastened his mouth on her breasts, while squishing his pelvis against hers, and clamped his teeth down on a tight, throbbing nipple.

Kesley broke out in shivers, and she slapped her hands over her face as if she'd reached her breaking point.

But Randy wasn't about to let her tap out—not yet. This was the home stretch. He wrestled her hands away from her face and crushed her wrists to the mattress. His eyes warned her to brace herself for the finale—and she expected him to deliver.

Since Kesley derived so much pleasure from pain, Randy wrapped his hands around her throat and choked her just enough to blur the line between agony and arousal.

"That all you got?" Kesley panted, continuing to push him.

Randy tightened his fingers, watching her teeter on the brink of unconsciousness. This almost felt criminal—but so good.

Kesley coughed, spewing saliva as her eyes rolled back. Randy didn't let up. She'd agreed to be his plaything tonight, given him certain liberties, and he intended to finish on a high note. He slammed into her without mercy, filling her again and again. His thrusts pulverized her cervix like he was trying to grind it into dust.

He looked for her to give him a sign that he was going too far; she gave none. She craved the edge, the abandon, the moment when control slipped away. It lit something inside her. She wasn't just allowing this; she was urging him on. She was daring him.

He accepted her challenge, keeping up his hyperaggressive pace. She'd probably wake up sore tomorrow.

When he let go of her throat, she gasped desperately for air. Using one hand, he smashed her face sideways into the mattress, and then he pounded so forcefully that cum splashed out around his shaft. After emptying himself inside her, he wiped his cock in his palm and smeared cum over her stomach and breasts—as if branding her as his. But the night wasn't over yet.

CHAPTER SEVEN

Under a gazebo, a spindly pale priest with wizened skin stood on a round platform. He finished Jared Kerner's eulogy, ending with "Amen."

Solemn-faced family members in dark clothing, including Jared's wife and child, rose from the white plastic chairs surrounding the platform. They wept and sniffled.

Cornelius walked up to Mei Ling. "You have my condolences," he said. "Jared was a fine man." He actually managed to sound authentic.

"Thank you," Mei Ling said, strangling a sob. In one arm, she cradled the tricornered Commonwealth flag—a gift customary to the ceremony—that had been given to her. Taking her daughter's small hand, she said, "Come, dear." She wiped at her eyes as she and her daughter made their way to the parking lot. "Thank you again, Chief Gould."

The gazebo emptied, leaving only Cornelius and Thom Kerner behind.

Thom gazed out at the headstones of deceased servicemen,

servicewomen, and dignitaries. Beyond the grand stone markers, a coruscating blue ocean stretched to the horizon.

"Again, I'm sorry about your son, my friend," Cornelius said.

A warm wind brushed their faces.

"I won't pretend my son was some prime example of manhood or set the bar for excellence, but"—Thom sighed—"he didn't deserve to be murdered by these Coalition treasonists."

His son's murderer continued his charade. "Yes, and these treasonists will pay for their cowardly crime."

Thom closed his eyes, reserving a moment of silence for his son. When he reopened them, he said, "Tell me, Cornelius, what of Area 14?"

"Still fully funded and operational. I would never allow our work to be disbanded. I'm actually heading there after I depart from here. Of course, I kept the program a secret from Jared. I had to. He would've terminated it otherwise."

"Yes, he would have," Thom agreed, knowing his son all too well.

"I will move the Commonwealth toward self-sufficiency and cut the Union's leash, just as we planned."

Thom nodded. "Yes, all in due time."

The two old war veterans shook hands and parted ways.

Cornelius' limo and a three-car motorcade sped down a winding solar-paneled street bordered by a mossy green bog.

In the wake of the Union's harsh ultimatum—to end the civil war within five days—and Jared Kerner's assassination, which Cornelius had pinned on the Coalition, fear and apprehension gripped the Parliament. Under pressure, many of Cornelius' critics granted him the authority to proceed as he saw fit to achieve the

Union's desired outcome, which was exactly what he had hoped would happen.

They finally permitted him to initiate surveillance on Governess Hayley, whom the CDF suspected of aiding the Coalition. He also immediately signed an executive order halting the issuance of travel passes, fully quarantining Satellite One's population from the rest of humanity.

Conlan had dispatched an intelligence team to Colony Five. He informed Cornelius they intercepted communications between Hayley and Arman Reza, giving Cornelius all the justification he needed to deploy troops and impose martial law.

"When the occupation force arrives in Colony Five, they'll take Hayley into custody, and we'll get answers," Cornelius said to Gillian, who sat beside him. "Perhaps she'll even lead us to Reza's whereabouts. I will also be expanding our martial-law operations in colonies One, Four, and Six. We'll deploy unmanned aerial drones to monitor sector zones and track movement into and out of private residences, and troop numbers will be raised. The Coalition *will* be flushed out."

Jared Kerner had objected to the idea of omnipresent surveillance. He believed drone use would infringe on citizens' privacy. He thought people should at least have the freedom to move about unmonitored. Patrols were ample enough for him. But Cornelius harbored no such qualms.

"I damn well hope the Commonwealth loses its incorporated status," Cornelius said. "We'd be better off. But it's my colleagues' belief in the Union's usefulness, and their fear of losing them as allies, that pushed them into giving me more authority to deal with the Coalition."

"It's like you taught me: Fear is one of the greatest weapons at your disposal," Gillian commented. She looked out the window at the foggy wetland. The scenery held a beautiful yet eerie ambiance that felt tranquil to her.

Small green arboreal creatures hopped and croaked among the trees, bushes, and bramble.

"How long before we reach Area 14?" Gillian asked.

"Not long."

Cornelius and Gillian were on their way to Area 14, a secret military arms-development site where the next evolution in Defense Force weaponry was being created. Cornelius kept the site's existence hidden from the Parliament and the public because of the unsanctioned weapons in development there.

Only he and Thom Kerner knew it existed. He had even kept it off Jared's radar. The former Chief, whose freewheeling nature was a noted fault, had simply let Cornelius handle all military matters, including arms development, without his personal oversight. Jared never kept himself abreast of where the military's funding went. He trusted Cornelius completely. It was just another responsibility Jared didn't want to be bothered with. If he could shirk a duty and delegate it, he did, and left it at that.

Gillian waited anxiously. Cornelius had promised she would bear witness to groundbreaking feats of military technology no one could yet fathom. He hadn't told her, however, that unsanctioned experiments were in progress.

She couldn't imagine anything surpassing the feats of the plasma-energy weaponry and mechanized combatwear that alien tech had helped develop. The arms in production at Area 14 were the reason Cornelius was confident the Commonwealth could defend itself without Union support.

The bog transitioned into a more eye-pleasing flatland. A short distance later, the limo arrived at a windowless oval facility with a gray exterior. There was a menacing phyocrete wall encircling its perimeter, and there were no signs indicating its purpose.

Cornelius lowered his window. As soon as the guard in the security booth saw the Chief, he punched in a code on his console. Then the security wall's gate slid open.

The limo and motorcade followed an access road leading to the rear of the facility. Gillian's brows quirked when she heard an earth-shaking clang. She wondered what could make such a colossal sound. The limo passed a sign that said WARNING! TESTING GROUND AHEAD! The noise grew louder.

The limo rolled to a slow stop. Gillian's heart lurched at the intimidating sight before her.

A thirty-foot-tall mechanized contraption of neutral grays, with rotary gun-cannons for arms, stomped over the phyocrete grounds. Winged, orb-shaped aerial drones banked downward at the giant metal monstrosity. They fired twin pairs of missiles. Air around the machine vibrated and crackled. An energy shield blossomed, intercepting the projectiles, then shimmered out.

The mech's gun-cannons spun up and ejected a stream of rounds, tearing the drones from the sky.

Through a nearby tower's megaphone, a man said, "Test one complete!"

The mech's cannons whined to a stop, steaming and hissing.

Cornelius exited the limo.

Gillian followed. "Incredible," she said.

Cornelius grinned proudly as he admired Area 14's invention. "Yes, we call it a Juggernaut. Weapons of war like this will enhance our forces' combat capability in the occupied colonies and across all Mission Worlds."

Gillian pointed at a young Guardian standing near the mech. "Wait . . . is he controlling that machine via cerebral interface?"

"Yes," Cornelius confirmed.

Gillian's face hinted at her indignation. This was morally wrong. The only authorized implant modification was for Shell CPU interface. Cerebral implants weren't supposed to control military devices such as flyers, vehicles, or war bots like this. "But it's unlawful to reformat a cerebral implant for that!" she protested.

Cornelius answered mildly. "I plan on getting that changed soon."

Gillian chided him, saying, "Yes, but until then, it's prohibited, and if we're discovered, we'd be—"

"Quiet," Cornelius cut her off. "The Parliament is blind to everything happening here, as is the rest of the Commonwealth. We're not going to be discovered."

Gillian's face betrayed her discomfort.

"Initiating test two!" blared the voice from the tower.

Seven drones converged on the Guardian. With a thought, he malfunctioned two of them, and gravity sent them crashing to the ground. He took control of two others and fired their weapons at the remaining drones, destroying them. He then made the two he had mindjacked crash into each other. Their wrecked metal forms plummeted to the ground.

Gillian watched wordlessly. Implants weren't supposed to be modified to hack electronic systems. *This isn't right.*

"Test two complete," the tower operator announced. "Good job, Private Salcedo."

The private smiled, proud of his performance. But an explosive headache altered his expression into one of horror. He clutched his head and screamed his throat raw, crumbling to the ground.

Two medics in white rushed over. One took a knee and checked Salcedo's vitals using a handheld forensic scanner. The device beeped, flashing a grim notice. Salcedo's life had come to an abrupt end.

Gillian stared in shock. "Wha-?"

"Yes," Cornelius said with regret, "we're still in the beta phase of cerebral-implant modification. We have yet to fully mitigate the strain on the mind when operating a Juggernaut or hacking electronic systems. He lasted longer than the others, though."

Gillian gasped. "Others?"

"Yes, ten fatalities so far. But all for a good cause."

Gillian frowned. *So the end justifies the means?*

Another medic arrived, pushing a rolling capsule gurney.

Gillian said, "Were they aware they could die, being guinea pigs for these . . . experiments?"

The medics placed Salcedo in a white body bag and zipped it up.

"They knew there was risk involved," Cornelius responded emotionlessly.

Gillian, once a Guardian herself, could no longer contain her outrage. Her voice hardened. "What of their families?"

The medics deposited Salcedo into the gurney.

Cornelius said, "Their families were told they were deployed to a colony or were on a tour of service for a protectorate. As far as they will know, their children died nobly in combat."

A lie, Gillian thought. Heat flooded her veins. She had been on board with Jared Kerner's assassination, believing he was a threat to the Commonwealth, but exploiting innocent soldiers, in the name of strengthening the CDF, was extreme.

Cornelius, not one to listen to diatribes for too long, stepped off and motioned for Gillian to follow. "Come, let us go inside. There are more marvels for you to witness."

Part of Gillian didn't want to know what other illegal machinations were being concocted in this clandestine program.

They crossed the width of the testing ground and entered a

metal back door set into the phyocrete wall of the building.

Trailing behind Cornelius down a quiet nondescript hall, Gillian wrestled with her thoughts. *This isn't okay,* she kept telling herself silently, but she was trying to convince herself otherwise. She had placed too much faith in her mentor's leadership to abandon it now.

They turned into another hall.

Ahead, two double doors parted as they neared, revealing a laboratory. Inside, men and women in white lab coats spoke scientific jargon.

On a bed, a Guardian in battledress sat upright.

A gray-bearded scientist studied the data displayed on the beside monitor. "How are you feeling?" he asked the Guardian.

"Just a little woozy," he replied.

"So what's going on here?" Gillian asked Cornelius, unenthused.

"More implant modification. This lab compiles data from all the Nerve Centers on Eden, Satellite One, and every Mission World. After thorough case evaluations, I determined that, despite the CDF's mental conditioning, one major issue is that some Guardians begin to feel empathy for our enemies, such as the Falgoah or the Coalition."

Cornelius tapped a sequence of buttons on a computer panel. Case files of "enemy sympathizing" involving Guardians flashed by on a screen, including Ahmed Hawsawi's.

"The implant updates being made here include empathy dampening, only while Guardians are in their Shells," Cornelius said. "It's for the best. Empathy is an Achilles' heel. Guardians must perform at their peak when engaged in combat. These . . . feelings simply get in the way. The modifications will lead to a more focused, sharper soldier, one unburdened by emotions that might compromise their fighting ability."

Gillian grunted. What Cornelius was proposing was altering the human psyche, creating Guardians stripped of sensitivity and mercy while in combat. To her, sensitivity and mercy, tempered by proper judgment, were virtues.

Cornelius believed he was acting in Guardians' best interests, but to Gillian, these implant modifications didn't seem congruent with his intentions.

Seeing Gillian's discomfort, Cornelius gripped her shoulders delicately and softened his tone—a rare show of compassion from such a blackhearted man. "Gillian, listen. I can see you're uneasy about what I've shown you. But I need you to have faith in me, as you always have. I know what's best for the Commonwealth and the CDF."

Speaking ever so persuasively, Cornelius continued his bid for Gillian's trust. "For goodness' sake, I was a soldier too. It's not my intention to extinguish a Guardian's life if it can be avoided. What's being done here is for the betterment of all Guardians. They need this technology. It will lead to a stronger, more efficient fighting force and a reduction in Guardian casualties. This is what's best for the CDF."

Coaxed into acceptance, Gillian said wistfully, "Fine."

"Come, let's leave and get a meal. You've seen enough."

They left Area 14.

• • •

Knuckles rapped against the door of Randy and Kesley's hut.

"Hey, Randy, you up yet, man?" came Jarius' voice from behind the door. "Training starts in a couple of minutes."

Randy stirred awake. "I'll be right out," he muttered sleepily, rubbing his eyes.

He and Kesley lay tangled together naked atop the rumpled,

cum-stained bedsheets, their body sweat commingling.

Sleeping quietly without a stitch of clothing on, Kesley was an eyeful for Randy to wake up to.

Randy's implant piped sensations from last night into his body, causing a thrill to run down his spine. In a reflexive response, he splayed a hand across Kesley's rear end, caressing its pronounced shape.

He'd experienced the most carnal sex of his life, climaxing more times than he could remember. Kesley had consented to things other women never had—like letting him tie her arms to the headboard while he acted out his fantasies, even rousing her from sleep by thrusting into her whenever he craved more sex. He couldn't get enough; it was as if he'd been possessed. He'd never been with a woman so uninhibited, so kinky.

Already, he was getting hard again. But then he thought about Stacie. Flashbacks rushed through his mind: them enduring BCT together, him sitting by her bedside when she battled infection, dancing at the graduation banquet, and other moments of significance. Guilt seeped in. He had broken their covenant to stay exclusive and be in a committed relationship.

Last night, he fucked the heck out of a woman nine years older than him, had given her the best she ever had. For a young man fresh out of college and the Academy, it should have been a notch on his belt. In the heat of the moment, it was thrilling, but now he felt stupid for jeopardizing his relationship with Stacie all for the short-term satisfaction of a one-night stand.

Randy peeled himself away from Kesley and scooted out of bed.

After washing off under the shower spigot, he walked to the clothing rack and got dressed in a khaki T-shirt and dark green trousers.

While he laced his boots, dread gnawed at him. What would happen when Stacie found out he had sex with another woman? He could try to keep last night firewalled from her, but she'd know something was up. And he didn't want to lie to her.

He'd just made his life more complicated. *Way to go, Randal.* He glanced back at Kesley, who was still asleep. *Last night was a mistake, a dumb mistake. What came over me?*

He valued the positive influence both Stacie and Kesley had on his life, and he found them both attractive. He even had a crush on Kesley. But his heart was with Stacie. She was the woman he truly loved and wanted to build a future with. He knew he had majorly screwed up. He should've left the hut to distance himself from the temptation of getting into bed with Kesley.

Randy finished tying his boots, gripped the door handle, and pulled slowly. Hinges squeaked.

He quietly stepped outside, where Jarius and Sariah were waiting for him.

Jarius wore a black T-shirt and a pair of beige camo-pattern trousers. Sariah was already in her Reldaldri mechsuit, now being referred to as a Hardsuit.

"Let's get going," Randy said in a serious tone.

Sariah strode forward. "Alright, boys, follow me."

The trio trekked down a steep grassy hill, Sariah leading the way.

"So," Jarius said to Sariah, "are we gonna get the chance to try on those fancy Hardsuits and do some hands-on training?"

"Of course," she replied. "You're not just getting a demo. Two men will meet us at the training site with your suits."

"Awesome." Jarius then pinged Randy's implant.

"Yeah, right," Randy whispered, "we're cool, but not that cool."

"C'mon, man, just for a few minutes. Don't want her to hear

what I have to say."

"Alright, fine, just for a few minutes." Randy accepted Jarius' Link request.

Jarius' lips spread into an intrusive smile. *<So, how was it banging an older woman? The babe's got almost a decade on you, right? >*

Randy had a beleaguered look plastered across his face. He had kept his intimate night with Kesley mentally shielded from any snooping. *<What are you talking about?>* he asked, faking cluelessness, but he was doing a poor job of it, judging by his blushing face.

Jarius chuckled. *<I ain't no idiot, dude. You don't sleep with a smoking-hot man-trap like that and not smash her. Besides, I happened to walk by and couldn't help but eavesdrop a little. I heard more than socializing going on, if you know what I mean.>*

<Is my personal business all you wanted to bug me about?>

Jarius shook his head. *<I've been wondering if this is worth it. I'm convinced these rebels are good people, but do you really think we can go up against the CDF and pull this invasion crap off without a hitch?>*

<Don't know about 'without a hitch,' but I think our odds are . . . fifty-fifty.>

With arched brows, Jarius said, *<And that's enough for you?>*

Randy shrugged. *<It's gonna have to be, because there's no going back to the company. Not for me, anyway. You can still opt out of this and go back, though. Is that what you want?>*

Jarius pondered. *<Nah, guess I'm in this for the long haul with you, bro.>*

Waterfalls, green trees, and unusual plant life made the walk quite scenic.

Randy knew he or Arson might well die in the battle ahead. Was it time to stop being standoffish and try to mend fences with his father?

Go ahead, do it, Kathleen's melodious voice echoed inside Randy's mind. *What would it hurt?*

No, Mom. N-O, no. His reply sounded resolute.

This battle might be the last time you see each other. Either of you could be killed, Randy. For the last twenty-four hours, you've been thinking about Linking with your father. That would allow him to feel and understand your pain. It would allow you to feel the love he has for me, and the love he has for you. Are you afraid that exposure will soften your heart? Are you afraid that love will dissolve your anger and remind you why you once revered your father?

The trio arrived at a grassy clearing surrounded by trees. There was an immense lake in the middle of it. "This is it," Sariah said. "This is where we'll train."

His thoughts interrupted, Kathleen's voice left Randy's mind.

Sariah stood facing her trainees, ready to prime them for combat. "Hardsuits operate both similarly to and differently from a Shell. They're similar in that they're thought-operated," she began. She pointed to the tech around her head. "We don't have implants. This neural-sensor headset allows cerebral interfacing by scanning brain activity and transmitting our thought-commands to the CPU." The headset, created with alien technology far too complex for her to understand, was something she avoided going into detail about.

"A Shell's CPU is inside the helmet." She turned around. "The Hardsuit's CPU is located inside the diamond-shaped protrusion midway down the back." She pivoted to face forward again. "A regenerative alloy makes up parts of this suit's armor," she explained. "From what little I understand, it's basically a composite of artificial, robotic cell-like organisms. When the suit takes damage, these nanites self-replicate to repair it."

"Do these suits have an AI Combat Assistant like Shells?" Randy asked.

"Negative," Sariah replied.

Randy wondered who had the superior hardware. Shells might've had a helpful, invaluable AI assistant, but they couldn't self-repair, meaning they couldn't absorb as much damage as the rebels' Hardsuits. And from what little Randy had seen, Hardsuits might even have a slight edge when it came to energy-based firepower.

During the attack on Arson's base, he'd seen a single energy sphere splatter a shelled Guardian all over the bay, like what happened to Emilia. And according to his father, Hardsuits could sustain the use of plasma energy longer than Shells. They could also fly.

Sariah continued her instruction, covering the weapons cache and how to generate energy spheres using their hands.

Thirty minutes in, two Falgoah men on a hover skid brought Hardsuits for Randy and Jarius. It was time for some hands-on training.

• • •

Not particularly wanting to, but left with no choice, Stacie exercised her privileges as a daughter of the Eight. High-ranking military officials on Eden, well aware of who she was, granted her temporary leave from duty, much to Lars' displeasure.

She stood outside the gate of a CDF launch port, dressed in a semiformal chic red blazer, a black flexwear jumpsuit, and red zippered heels.

Clifton arrived in a luxury-class flyer to chauffeur her.

Stacie tapped her foot and clucked her tongue, patience waning. The second the flyer touched the ground, she picked up the black gear bag containing her clothes and scurried up to it.

The canopy hissed upward, and the rear cargo compartment clicked open.

Stacie slung her bag into the rear compartment, slammed the hood down, and plopped into the front passenger seat.

The canopy lowered and snapped shut.

Clifton took the flyer aloft, into moderate air traffic.

"Where are Mother and Father?" Stacie asked with an edge, disgusted by her parents' devious secrets. "I've been trying to call them since I got to the station," she added, tapping her wristcom.

"They're on Babylon Island with the other family heads for a recreational convocation and business assembly."

Stacie had been to the man-made island once, when she was seven. Faint preconscious memories, awakened by her cerebral implant, fast-forwarded through that day: women with fancy hairstyles in flashy regalia, men in pricey suits, hovering valet golems toting Highborns' luggage and shopping carryalls. The memory ended with her looking out the window of her father's limo at a beach packed with partying young adults drinking and laughing.

"Take me there. Now," she demanded.

Clifton winced at her pushy, assertive attitude. "You can't just disrupt a conclave whenever you—"

"The hell I can," Stacie snapped. She wasn't in the mood for any opposition whatsoever. "So take us there. That's an order."

The CDF launch port disappeared into the distance as the flyer sped past gleaming obelisk-shaped office towers.

An irritated expression crossed Clifton's face, deepening the grooves of his forehead. He thought Stacie needed to be verbally disciplined, but alas, he was merely a servant. After sighing away his protest, he said, "Just as bullheaded as your mother, I see."

"Then you can thank her for my stubbornness."

And your vicious tongue as well. Clifton veered into the left air lane, adjusting the flyer's trajectory to go to Babylon Island. "From your tone, I assume something is troubling you."

"Damn right." Stacie brought up a holo-menu from her wristcom and opened four files detailing her family's corrupt dealings, each in its own window. "Did you know about this?"

Clifton activated the flyer's autopilot. "Madam Spencer, your parents have amassed great wealth, and no, not all of it was earned by virtuous means. But that's how the game is played. The Eight families are profiteers. When they see an opportunity to profit—even at the expense of others—they take it.

"Their methods for generating wealth may not align with your moral tenets, but those methods allowed the Eight to become the alpha of humanity and live a lifestyle most people can't even comprehend.

"It was the Eight families' unfathomable wealth that protected them during the destruction of Earth Era, when pillagers, murderers, rapists, and scavengers ran amok in lawless streets devastated by Armageddon . . . when billions died from the aftereffects of alien biochem weapons unleashed by warmongering fools . . . when global environmental destruction caused by those same weapons ravaged the planet."

Clifton would never forget the downfall of Earth Era, every memory a grim reminder of humanity's darkest days. "Chronic drought. Food-supply shortages. Caustic rain eating the flesh of children. All before your time, girl. Perhaps had you witnessed such horrors, you would be more grateful for what the Eight have built for themselves." He smiled and added, "And as a plus, I get paid handsomely thanks to your family's wealth."

Stacie's expression hardened. "The Eight's criminal ways are unacceptable. *Period.*"

Clifton sighed and retook the controls.

Thirty minutes later, Babylon Island came into view. A single causeway connected it to the mainland.

Stacie gazed down at a six-story spiraling white structure at the center of the island. It was the building where the family heads had assembled.

The Eight Elite funded and created the artificial island strictly for themselves. It was off-limits to the public, the authorities, the military, and even the politicians who ran the Commonwealth, unless invited. No one but the Eight and their guests knew what happened on Babylon. And what happened there stayed there. If it didn't, all tattletales ended up on a missing-persons report.

A golden aerial yacht cruised overhead, carrying super-rich young men and women in swimwear who were dancing to a pulsating beat.

Suddenly, the flyer's comm system crackled to life. "This is Babylon Transit Authority. State your identity and purpose," a man's voice demanded.

"I am Elias Clifton II, dutiful servant of the Spencer family. I have Madam Stacie Lynette Spencer aboard. She requests permission to land."

"Stand by." After a brief pause, the control operator came back on the comms line. "I'm afraid Madam Stacie Spencer isn't on the guest registry. I'll have to—"

Stacie leaned forward, planting her palms on the dash. She lowered her mouth close to the mic and said, "Dispense with the nonsense, mongrel, and permit us entry." Definitely like her mother, Clifton thought. "Or my parents will have manacles strapped to your ankles and throw you into the ocean." She definitely wasn't in the mood for opposition today.

"Permission granted," the control operator said hastily.

Clifton dropped the flyer's altitude and touched down on the island's landing port, where other fancy flyers were parked. From there, he led Stacie to a deck full of land vehicles available for guests.

A spotless dark blue car that had a sunroof caught Stacie's eye. Clifton opened the right rear door for her. She settled into the back seat while he placed her bag in the trunk. Then he slid behind the wheel and powered on the car.

As Stacie got comfortable, the intelligent seating system adjusted to her frame.

The car left the landing port, rolling down a solar-paneled throughway. Stacie watched sandy beaches and tropical plants go by.

On one beach, a bare-chested fat man wearing sunglasses and a wide-brimmed hat lounged on a chair. His personally selected servant of the day—a young woman with slate-gray skin, striking yellow eyes, and butterfly-like ears—wore almost nothing below the waist and was naked from the waist up.

She delivered a foamy drink to him, placing it on a nearby table.

Exerting control over his "party favor," he yanked the chain attached to the choker around her neck, pulling her onto his lap.

All along the beach, other young outer-species women wore little to nothing, with bonds of servitude around their necks. Some bore visible welts from whippings. They were nothing more than merchandise to their handlers.

Stacie cast her angry eyes on Clifton. "Those women are obviously not here of their own accord."

"Babylon Island provides exotic luxuries to the Elite's guests and patrons, who are connoisseurs of . . . eclectic extravagances forbidden elsewhere in the Commonwealth." Nothing but sinister men and women with dark, twisted desires.

Drunken Highborn lay on the beach atop blankets and danced to loud music. Two topless women wearing bikini bottoms, both strikingly attractive, flirted with two ripped men. Stacie had long since grown sick of the senseless, decadent party lifestyle.

The car continued into the island's micropolis, leaving the beaches and boardwalks behind for a mishmash of stores, bars, nightclubs, and shady establishments.

An electronic banner outside a Pleasure Station scrolled text from left to right: WELCOME TO GOODTIMES UNIVERSAL: A TREASURE TROVE OF OUTERWORLD PLEASURES BEYOND YOUR WILDEST IMAGINATION.

Hyperrealistic holos of nude alien women flickered outside the entryway, rendered in provocative poses.

Revulsion prickled Stacie's skin. Everything about the island felt sleazy.

The car pulled up to the tall, imposing spiral structure where the family heads had gathered, slowing to a stop at the roundabout.

"The family heads should be in the fifth-floor dining suite," Clifton informed Stacie. "I will wait for you here." He hoped everything would remain civil. A heated Stacie and her mother in the same room were a surefire recipe for catastrophe.

Stacie got out, stiff-faced, and proceeded down a cobblestone walkway. At the large front door, a concierge awaited. He opened it as she approached, and she entered a vestibule replete with tall white pillars, spraying fountains, chandeliers, lounge couches grouped around coffee tables, and mosaic art. There was also a bar and a restaurant.

To her right sat a small, compact attendant at the reception desk. She had pink pigtail buns and wore a teal one-piece skirt that rode high on her thighs.

The attendant put down the e-zine she was reading on her tablet and focused her attention on Stacie. "Greetings, ma'am. Can I assist you with anything?" she asked while adjusting her round wire-rim glasses. Her kind green eyes and peppy voice made her the perfect greeter.

Stacie looked at the unending spiral staircase that rose to the topmost floor. Definitely a no. "Where are the elevators?" she asked curtly.

The attendant aimed a manicured red nail toward a hallway. "Down that way, ma'am."

Stacie's eyes followed the direction of the attendant's finger. Without another word, she passed two well-dressed staff members.

Midway down the hall, a cleaning golem whizzed around, vacuuming.

Stacie approached a set of five elevators. She entered the one in the middle and pressed 5.

The elevator doors clicked shut, and the car hissed up the translucent shaft. It ascended to the fifth floor and stopped. *Ding.* The doors parted.

Stacie walked down a lengthy carpeted catwalk to a pair of mahogany-colored doors with gilded framing. Behind them: the clinking of utensils and dishes, hearty conversation, and mouthwatering aromas.

Nervous and discouraged, Stacie gnawed her lower lip while gripping one of the door handles, and sweat rolled down her face. Was barging in on the Eight's gathering a smart move? Was anger overriding sound judgment? Chin held high, she plowed on and opened the door, making her grand ingress into the rotunda-shaped dining suite.

Fashionably dressed in the finest clothing G-credits could buy, the eight family heads sat around a circular table, a gourmet feast of unique delicacies spread before them. All were avaricious men and women whose thirst for wealth and power had driven them to obtain it using the darkest of means if necessary.

Stacie fixed her smoldering blue eyes on her parents. Darlene wore colorful makeup and a sequined turquoise dress. Patrick was clad in a posh three-piece black suit. "*Mother, Father,*" Stacie called out loudly, sucking the energy out of the room.

The conversation stopped. All eyes stared at her.

Darlene flicked her hand in a dismissive gesture. "Stacie, wait outside. We'll be with you shortly."

"No, Mother, right *now,*" Stacie demanded.

Darlene's jaw tightened, her daughter's disrespectful tone infuriating her.

The family heads at the table snickered and uttered severe remarks in hushed tones.

From beneath bushy brown eyebrows, a heavyset man—whose prominent features included a large mustache and bulbous nose— eyed Patrick and Darlene with amusement. "It's been a while since I've seen Stacie." He chuckled at their daughter's impudence. "She's blossomed into a beautiful young woman but clearly lacks the grace and manners expected of a lady of refinement."

Gales of laughter from the family heads irritated Patrick and Darlene.

Darlene clapped a palm to her forehead, embarrassed. *Damn child.*

Patrick shook his head. His daughter's indiscretion incensed him.

Darlene sprang up from her chair and skirted around the table to Stacie. She gripped her daughter's arm by the bicep. "Come," she hissed.

The door snapped shut as Darlene dragged Stacie out of the

room.

Stacie tore her arm loose. "What are the Eight Elite, Mother, a bunch of crime lords? What are you and Father a part of? I know about the corrupt dealings. I know about your illegal transactions with Chief Gould."

"Power isn't acquired by playing by the rule book, Stacie."

"It's wrong, all of it. The slave trade, money laundering, bribery —"

Darlene jabbed a finger at Stacie. "What's wrong is you barging in here and disgracing the Spencer name."

I was foolish to come here. What did I think was going to happen? "No, what's wrong is you constantly berating me, treating me like some child, like a piece of clay to be molded into your warped idea of perfection. I've had enough! You and Father can both go to hell for all I care!" Stacie spun and stormed off.

Darlene's fury coalesced, her face flushing red. She dashed up behind Stacie, grabbed a fistful of her hair, and yanked hard, wrenching her head back. Glaring into her daughter's eyes, she said, "I'm sick of your tantrums. I will no longer tolerate your defiance, you ungrateful little brat." She yanked harder. "You will respect me. Do you understand?"

"Let go! You're hurting me, Mother!" Stacie screamed, stifling the urge to strike Darlene—something she had been forced to do many times before.

Darlene clutched Stacie's hair tighter. "With you being such a . . . *nymphomaniac*, you're lucky you haven't—"

Stacie twirled and slapped her mother across the face.

Darlene staggered backward and tumbled to the floor. She arched her brows in disbelief, lip bloodied.

Chest heaving, adrenaline pumping, Stacie stood tall. She felt lighter, as if a boulder had been lifted from her shoulders. Striking her mother to expel years of pent-up rage was like therapy.

Darlene got up and seized Stacie's shoulders. "You dare hit me, you classless little degenerate?"

Mother and daughter scuffled, shoving each other into the catwalk's guardrails. Beads broke off Darlene's sequined dress.

Hearing the commotion, Patrick burst out of the dining suite. He saw the catfight escalating out of control. "Stop! What the hell is going on out here?" His eyebrows came together. "The family heads are inside thinking you've both gone insane! We are all intelligent adults, for goodness' sake!"

Darlene and Stacie separated.

The baroness cleared her throat and straightened her dress, trying to recover her dignity.

Patrick hurried to her side and gently dabbed the blood from her lip with a handkerchief. "What the hell has gotten into you, Stacie?"

Stacie scoffed and pointed at Darlene. "Ask your wife." Patrick trembled, visibly pissed off. "You want access to your daughter's mind again, Mother? Well, here!" She pinged Darlene's implant. Darlene accepted the request, restoring her maternal Link. "Here it is, Mother! All of my pain! All the anger from your abuse! All of my *fucking* hate!" Stacie pushed years of unspoken anguish into Darlene's mind.

Three family heads stood in the doorway, wondering what was going on.

A deluge of intolerable pangs wracked Darlene's brain. She gasped, queasy, squeezing her eyes shut.

Every physical and emotional wound she had ever inflicted on Stacie overloaded her nervous system, bringing her to her knees. She shuddered, heart vibrating, mind unraveling.

"What's wrong? Can't take it, Mother?" Stacie said coldly,

determined to make her suffer to the highest extent possible.

Darlene wheezed raggedly, struggling to hold herself together. Explosive migraines detonated in her skull, driving her into the depths of psychic agony. Tears streamed down her face. Unable to focus long enough to deLink, she screamed, "Stop it!"

Patrick intervened, saying, "Enough of this!"

Stacie severed the Link, for her mother's sake. Her head throbbed from the psychic backlash. She exhaled a long, quivering breath. She didn't know how she had just weaponized her emotions. It had been instinctive. The Quilgarian nanotech had a plethora of enigmas to be unlocked and understood, some good, some bad.

Patrick helped Darlene to her feet. With her mind marred and body swaying with vertigo, her knees buckled, but he caught her and held her upright.

Darlene said nothing. Her body spasmed, shivering uncontrollably.

Blood dripped from her nose, staining the carpet. She had never known pain like this.

For the first time in Stacie's life, she saw something unfamiliar in Darlene's expression: guilt. Real human guilt. She had been humbled. Mission accomplished.

A growl rumbled in Patrick's throat. He activated his wristcom. "You want to be a self-made woman, Stacie? Fine. But don't think you can spit in our faces while living off the fortune we built." He stabbed several holokeys with his finger. Then came a confirmatory chime. "I have reduced your account from two hundred million credits to fifty thousand."

He tapped his wristcom's centerpiece, dissolving the holographic interface. "The villa we bought you is now in your name. You're on your own. Talk to us when you come to your senses." He glared disappointedly at Stacie. "You have until sundown to stay on Babylon. Then you're no longer welcome."

Stacie's heart jumped. She had gone from princess to pauper. But keeping a firm voice, she said, "Fine, wouldn't want it any other way." She strode down the catwalk, heading to the elevators.

• • •

Samantha Hayley, Colony Five's governess, was a lottery beneficiary who had returned to Satellite One to improve the lives of her people. But she believed that declaring sovereignty from the Commonwealth and provoking the wrath of the central government was foolhardy. So did most of her constituents, according to the "illegal" exodus polls. Her daughter, however, had disagreed.

Living in Colony Four, Samantha's daughter had fought for colony independence during the Three-Week War, and paid the ultimate price.

Determined to ensure her daughter's sacrifice hadn't been pointless, Samantha began secretly supporting the Coalition of Rebel Factions, unknown to her people but suspected by the Defense Department. She had assisted with arms acquisition and had provided a safe haven for Reza and Hammer Fall's assault force. That was the extent of her willingness to help. But Conlan's intelligence team had blown her cover.

She sat at a shabby wooden desk in her bare-walled office, wearing a white blouse and charcoal-gray pencil skirt. A single framed picture sat on the desktop, a photo of her daughter at nineteen, the age she was killed in action.

Transmitting from his study, Reza appeared on Samantha's computer screen.

"Something is amiss," she said, sipping from a mug of warm liquid. "Several CDF starships landed at our port, without prior notice from the Defense Department."

"Of course not," Reza replied. "That's not Gould's MO. He prefers the element of surprise, especially when he's up to something nefarious."

"Well, when air-traffic control requested their purpose, the response was vague—just that they had orders from the Defense Department and couldn't disclose more. BUSs, combat flyers, and armored assault vehicles deployed from those ships, which worries me." Samantha's professional posture cracked a little.

"This is clearly a military occupation of Colony Five."

Samantha steepled her fingers. "But on what grounds? There's no evidence linking me to the Coalition." She wasn't careless. She had made sure no trail led back to her. Or so she thought.

"Gould isn't Jared Kerner," Reza said. "He's a shrewd madman, one who bucks the system or manipulates government leaders into supporting his schemes. Be careful, Sam. If—"

Samantha's assistant's voice came from behind her office doors. "You assholes can't just barge in here!"

Sounds of a scuffle ensued.

Samantha's brows lifted, and her heart skipped a beat. She glanced at the doors, then back to her screen. "Arman, something's going on. We'll have to continue this later," she said quickly. She mashed a button on her keyboard, and the screen went dark.

The office doors swung open. Three Guardians in black combat gear forced their way past Samantha's assistant, who was trying to block their entry. Two of the intruders were privates; the third wore a captain's chevrons.

The gangly pale-faced officer stepped forward as his two burly subordinates wrestled with the assistant. "Governess, I'm Captain Felix Moss," he said. "I'm here to initiate martial law in Colony Five."

Samantha responded in her businesswoman voice. "What for, Captain? There are no opposition forces here."

Felix sneered. "There's nothing I hate more than a liar. Privates Ashcroft and Taggart, restrain her."

Samantha's jaw set. "Don't any of you dare touch me."

Felix's men shoved the assistant aside and advanced.

Not backing down, the young man marched up to Felix and grabbed his shoulder. "Call off your goons, or—"

A gunshot cracked.

Samantha let out an "eek" and said, "Ritz!"

Ritz crumbled to the floor with a guttural cry, clutching his thigh where Felix had shot him. He groaned, cursing under his breath.

Felix smirked. "That's what you get for putting a hand on a captain of the Defense Force." He lifted his boot and stomped down on the wound, causing Ritz to scream. "Dumb little pipsqueak." He shot two rounds into Ritz's skull.

Samantha recoiled in horror. Then Ashcroft and Taggart seized her arms. "Release me!" she demanded, twisting and writhing.

Taggart clamped a hand around the back of her neck and slammed her upper body onto the desk, knocking over the picture of her daughter.

"Stop struggling, Governess," Felix said. He set a cube-shaped instrument near her face. The device hummed to life, its circuitry glowing with kaleidoscopic light—an Area-14 invention.

Samantha doused her fear with courage and stayed resilient. "What is that thing?" The privates' hands pressed harder, keeping her folded over the desk. Now the first throbs of an excruciating headache hammered at her skull.

It was easy to see that Felix relished her discomfort. "It's called a Mind Sweeper. It's bypassing all the safeguards in your cerebral implant. Once done, it'll Link your implant to mine, letting me probe your mind for your communications with the Coalition."

Fighting to maintain her firewalls against the waves of nausea and delirium attacking her, Samantha rasped, "Bastards . . . you have no right to . . . trespass into my mind." Her breathing grew erratic. "This violates . . . consent law."

Felix scoffed. "Desperate times call for desperate measures, Governess. Chief Gould has authorized us to do everything within our power to prevent the Commonwealth from losing its incorporated status." His implant pinged, connecting to hers. Success. Time for the test. <*Hello, Governess, nice to*—>

Face slick with perspiration, Samantha screamed fiercely and pushed the interloper out.

She writhed, but the privates' hands didn't budge. Tremors overtook her body as she remained pinned flat.

Felix reared back, impressed by her willpower. "You're headstrong, Governess. I'll give you that." He gripped a fistful of her short honey-brown hair and lifted her head. "But you *will* break," he guaranteed in a cold timbre, then let go of her hair.

Felix breached her mental defenses and ravaged her thoughts, foraging through layers of memory.

Samantha's vision clouded and cleared in rapid succession. Her insides squirmed, the liquid contents of her cup threatening to resurface.

A stream of her most cherished memories flowed into Felix's mind: her wedding day, her husband's funeral, her daughter at sixteen in a white T-shirt and yellow beach shorts, laughing as she spun a hula hoop around her hips on the beach.

<*Pretty kid you had. Too bad the little whelp's dead,*> Felix said.

Samantha tried to muscle herself up, painful twinges in her arms, but the privates had her overpowered.

At last, Felix found Samantha's communications with Reza.

He disconnected the Link. "Well, now we've proven you're the treacherous conspirator bitch we thought you were."

The privates released Samantha. She pushed herself up, but her equilibrium was so impaired by the throbbing aftershocks of the mind rape that the room tilted and swayed, and she collapsed to the floor.

A fuzzy haze clouded her vision as she gasped between breaths. She said to Felix, "I hope you suffer the most horrific death, you lowlife piece of filth." A storm of emotions raged beneath the surface—violent ones.

Felix laughed. "So, the prohibited zone is just cover, to keep people from stumbling across your rebel friends." He tapped his wristcom. "This is Captain Moss to Yankee and Zulu battalion commanders. I'm sending you coordinates. Reza and his rebels are there. All other forces continue martial-law operations." He eyed Samantha. "Take her to a BUS and detain her," he ordered Ashcroft and Taggart.

Samantha's vision slowly swam into focus. She glared at her tormentor, the message in her eyes clear: She wanted him dead.

Ashcroft and Taggart picked her up from the floor and locked cuffs around her wrists. Knowing resistance was futile, she offered no struggle and silently allowed them to take her into CDF custody.

• • •

Randy and Jarius had completed their training for the day. Along with Kesley, they were traveling to a nearby town in a rickety zipsled—a roofless utility hover vehicle—to celebrate at a tavern.

The sled was outdated and simple: a flat platform with two seats in the front, a long bench in the back, and two wings with can-shaped plasma boosters mounted underneath. Coalition mechanics had also installed a pair of cheap, low-powered laser cutters to provide basic offensive capability.

They passed rows of large rectangular shipping containers that had been converted into single-person living units.

"I've been inside one of those," Kesley said from the back seat. "They're nicer than you would expect."

The sled left Container Row and entered a part of town with modest buildings and residential homes, nothing near Eden quality, but far more upscale than anything in Colony Four.

Two blocks from the tavern, Randy parked the sled on a lay-by. The trio got out to walk the rest of the way. Passersby regarded them with suspicion.

"So why are these people giving us dirty looks?" Jarius asked, eyes darting left and right.

Kesley replied, "It's a small town. Locals know we're not from here. They probably think we're from an occupied colony, which means we could be rebels. These people don't want the central government breathing down their necks. They think challenging the central government is downright crazy and unnecessary."

"So, not all colony folk welcome each other with open arms."

"Nope."

Once inside the tavern, Randy, Jarius, and Kesley ordered drinks and took a window-side booth. Their voices competed with the din of loud conversation, merry guffaws, and clinking glasses. Both young and old patrons were having a good time.

Thirty minutes in, Kesley excused herself to the ladies' room, leaving Randy and Jarius sitting side by side at the table.

Jarius thought about how the establishment, though not bad, didn't measure up to Eden standards: no server golems, no pictographic holo-menus, and a plain, drab interior. *We live like gods compared to these people,* he thought. He took a sip of his drink and asked Randy, "So, you having any second thoughts about this operation?"

"Right now, it feels like the right move. Do I trust Reza completely? No. But I guess we'll find out if he's a wolf in sheep's clothing."

"What if he does turn out to be just a power-hungry dictator?"

"Then . . . he'll be stopped." How? Randy didn't know. "What about you? Any doubts?"

"I think I'm sticking with this rebel thing for now."

"Your choice. It's not too late to bail." Randy raised his glass mug to his lips and chugged his beer. At the bar, he saw a father and his eighteen-year-old son sitting on high stools. A dusky-skinned barmaid with long, curly raven hair, wearing a red dress and an oblong shawl, poured ale into their mugs from a glass decanter. They toasted, then quaffed their drinks together.

Watching them revived pleasant memories for Randy, memories of him and his father. He remembered when Arson took him for his first drink when he was eighteen.

"Thinking about your old man?" Jarius asked.

"Yeah, just a good memory." Randy gritted his teeth, and his brow furrowed. "Before he betrayed Mom and me."

"What went down was hella fucked up, but it was an accident. Your dad's not a bad guy. If you're gonna proceed with joining this mission, I think you should make some kind of peace with him. There's no guarantee one of you ain't gonna be six feet under when this is over.

"I'm glad I made peace with my biological dad after my mom remarried. The man died a year later in a freak vehicle crash, and if I hadn't forgiven him, I would've carried that regret forever."

Randy took a swig of beer. "If I'm dead, making peace with him won't matter."

"It will to him," Jarius countered.

"Well, tough for him. And if *he* dies . . . well, don't worry, I think I can live with myself. He's been dead to me for quite some time anyway." Randy kicked back more of his drink.

"Enough of the tough-guy act, dude. Be real with yourself. You ain't fooling me."

"Just drop it, man."

"Okay, fine." Jarius took a gander at the ladies' room to see if Kesley was coming out, then grinned. "So, who's better in bed, Kess or Stacie?"

Randy slammed his mug down after taking a gulp. "*Drop it.*"

Jarius said, "You got the hots for her, don't you?" Randy returned to his drink, annoyance showing in his body language. Jarius continued teasing him. "You like those jugs of hers. That wit."

Randy's mind played back a memory from last night . . .

Following their rest break, Randy bent Kesley's torso over the side of the bed. She demanded a hard slap on the rear, so he obliged with a smack that stung her perfect, round cheek. She told him to do it again. The next smack left a red mark.

Getting down to business, he nudged his foot against hers to widen her stance. With his cock stretched to the limit, he gripped her wrists and drew her arms back while propelling his loins forward. The drumbeat of flesh slapping flesh once again filled the room.

It wasn't long before he was thrusting into his own cum, droplets of it leaking out from between Kesley's thighs. At a brutal tempo, he pounded her sinfully attractive ass.

Randy blinked out of the memory. "Listen, what happened between us was just . . . a fleeting moment. It was a one-nighter, no strings attached. Kess was simply . . . a temporary fuck buddy, and she's cool with that. She wanted to have some fun, that's all. But what happened last night was a stupid mistake. It *wasn't* right. I . . . got caught up. And let's be clear: Stacie is the *only* woman I want."

"Well, Stacie's gonna be furious when she finds out what went on between you and Kess."

"No fucking kidding. I'll deal with it when the time comes."

"Good luck with that."

Just then, they heard Kesley chatting with a patron. She made her way back to the table—her braless breasts bobbing—and sat down in the seat facing them. She lifted her glass, holding it high. "A toast to equality, fellas," she said merrily.

Jarius raised his own glass. "Sounds good to me."

Randy's expression stayed neutral. *I don't think we should shout out things like "equality" here.*

The rims of all three glasses clinked.

The comm-set on Randy's belt chirped. He put his mug down, placed the device against his ear, and pressed the talk button. "Scott here. What's up?"

Arson answered from the other end. "Reza wants everyone back pronto. He believes our location has been compromised. We're leaving for Eden ASAP. As soon as you get back, head to the ship."

The comm-set beeped and went silent.

Randy clipped it back to his belt. "That was my father," he said in a hushed tone. "We need to head back now. Our location may no longer be safe. We're leaving for Eden today."

"Sounds like our operation might happen sooner than planned," Jarius whispered.

Suddenly, Felix appeared on the tavern's wall screens. "People of

Colony Five, I am Captain Felix Moss. I am responsible for establishing martial law and am your duly appointed viceroy for the foreseeable future. We have removed Governess Hayley from her position and placed her in our custody."

Heads faced the screens. Randy, Jarius, and Kesley looked at each other in alarm.

Felix said, "She was aiding Coalition forces in their attempt to ruin our great republic. To neutralize this cancer, the CDF will conduct patrols and search homes. I do not wish to complicate your lives and will make every day as trouble-free as possible."

Grumbles erupted among the tavern patrons.

A red-bearded, chubby man whammed his table with a fist. "They think they can just barge into our homes? That's fucking home invasion!"

Another man at a table stomped the floor. "This is the rebels' fault. Why can't they just give up?"

Felix said, "Please do not worry; your privacy and dignity are at the forefront of our concern."

Yeah, right, Randy thought.

"When we root out the cancer, life in Colony Five will go back to normal," Felix assured everyone watching. "I am ordering all citizens to return to their homes for the rest of the day. You may resume daily activities starting at oh-eight-hundred tomorrow, but you must adhere to your new seventeen-hundred curfew and all established moratoriums."

"That's bullshit!" a man shouted, making a displeased gesture.

"Hush," warned a thickset busty blond woman. "If Guardians hear you say things like that, you might end up in front of a firing squad."

BUSs pulled up outside the tavern, chuffing and rumbling. Shelled troops clogged the streets.

Kesley's body tensed.

Jarius got up from the table. "Come on, guys, let's hightail it outta here."

"You don't have to tell me twice," Kesley said, rising to her feet.

The trio strolled out the door casually, remaining low-key.

"You think Hayley ratted us out?" Jarius asked quietly, scanning streets overcrowded with Guardians directing civilian foot traffic.

"Not by choice. The CDF has ways to loosen lips," Kelsey replied, well aware of the CDF's harsh interrogation methods, like injecting pain analeptics into prisoners.

More patrons filed out of the tavern, gabbling.

Guardians' external sound ports megaphoned their instructions to citizens as they coordinated the evacuation. People swore and uttered complaints. BUSs growled to a halt, and more shelled Guardians poured into the area, armor clacking.

"Everyone, go home!" shouted a Guardian who was possibly three blocks away.

Citizens spewed invectives and epithets.

Already, a few overly disruptive men and women were being rounded up.

Funny how these people stayed submissive until they got shitcanned, Kesley thought.

A man in his sixties yelled above the clamor. "The Coalition was right: You guys are just a bunch of no-good brutish thugs!"

A Guardian triggered his rifle. A loud *blam* made people shudder. The slug the Guardian had fired punched into the man's sternum, then exploded out his back.

A brilliant spray of blood splattered across the ground.

Bystanders gasped. A mother shielded her toddler's eyes. A husband pulled his wife close. Several women swooned and collapsed.

"Let that old geezer serve as an example," the Guardian announced. "We declare any dumbfuck who insults the central government or the Defense Force an enemy of the Commonwealth, and we will execute them on the spot."

Kesley grunted. "Son of a bitch didn't have to do that. That old guy was no threat. Was he afraid he was gonna damage his state-of-the-art combatwear with sticks and stones or something?"

Randy gripped her shoulder. "Hey, Kess, keep your voice down. We need to maintain cool heads and get the hell out of town."

The trio quickened their pace, separating themselves from the rest of the crowd.

Shells' Oracles conducted facial recognition scans to identify rebels.

Kesley entered a Guardian's field of vision.

"Identity confirmed: rebel Kesley Whittaker," the Guardian's Oracle said. A red pop-up displayed the data that profilers had logged:

Name: Kesley Michelle Whittaker
Age: 31 / **Ethnicity:** Caucasian / **Gender:** Female
Occupation: courier for Dynamic Relief Provisions
Rebel affiliation: the Coalition of Rebel Factions/Colony Four
Comments: last seen fleeing a rebel camp in Colony Four

The Guardian centered Randy in his reticle. Kesley's data vanished, replaced by a new pop-up. "Identity confirmed: rebel Randal Scott," his Oracle warned.

Name: Randal Eugene Scott (turncoat)
Age: 22 / **Ethnicity:** Caucasian / **Gender:** Male
Military Occupational Specialty/Rank: Land Combatant/SPC

Rebel affiliation: the Coalition of Rebel Factions

Comments: last seen fleeing a rebel camp in Colony Four with rebel Kesley Whittaker

The Guardian aimed his visored gaze at Jarius and consulted his Oracle for an ID:

Name: Jarius Don Ford

Age: 22 / **Ethnicity:** Black / **Gender:** Male

Military Occupational Specialty/Rank: Land Combatant/SPC

Jarius had no rebel ties logged. *Damn, another convert,* the Guardian deduced. He shouldered evacuees aside as he advanced toward the trio. "You three—Randal Scott, Kesley Whittaker, Jarius Ford—halt!" he barked as he stalked forward.

Jarius said, "Run like hell."

The trio broke into a mad dash for their zipsled.

"Stop those three!" The Guardian's eyes tracked them.

Gunfire thundered.

Men and women screamed, and children squealed.

The orderly evacuation had unraveled into chaos.

"Are they fucking crazy, firing while civilians are still evacuating?" Kesley said. Her leg muscles burned as she kicked up her pace.

The trio reached the sled and leapt in, Randy at the controls, Jarius in the passenger seat, and Kesley in the back.

Randy flipped a switch to ON, and the sled's start-up sequence activated.

Bullets whizzed past.

Jarius' nerves were on a razor's edge. "Come on! Come on!"

"Calm down and stop screaming in my ear!" Randy snapped.

"This thing's an antique! It takes time to power up! You know that!"

Behind them, three shelled Guardians sprinted toward the sled.

Kesley reached into a gray cloth satchel and pulled out a plasma grenade. "I'll take care of them." Randy and Jarius looked back at her. "Never leave home without one."

Randy raised a hand. "Wait, Kess. The engine's almost ready. That thing is deadly. They may have families. If we can avoid—"

"I ain't waiting to get killed, Randy." Kesley thumbed the detonator stub and lobbed the grenade. It clunked to the phyocrete and exploded.

Plasma force warped, twisted, and charred the Shells, and it injured the Guardians inside.

Damn it, Randy thought, hating that the Guardians had been badly hurt, maybe even suffered life-threatening injuries.

The yellow ENGINE READY light blinked on, and the laser-cutter indicators flashed green. Antigrav lifters pushed the sled off the ground, and Randy fired up the plasma boosters.

Dust swirled.

The sled started off slow, then accelerated. More Guardians shot at the vehicle, but it was already out of range.

<<*Let 'em go,*>> the sergeant in charge said to all Guardians. <<*We know where they're headed, straight for the jungle compound. Battalions are already en route there, so they'll get what's comin' to 'em. Let's not waste ammo and time goin' after 'em. Let's focus on clearing this area as ordered.*>>

• • •

The zipsled finished a stretch of barren road, entering the jungle to the crackling of gunfire and the sight of dancing flames.

Randy, Jarius, and Kesley had seen the smoke from a distance, confirming their fears: The CDF had made their incursion into the rebels' hideout.

Upon reaching the no-entry point, the trio spotted a breach in the security fence.

Gunned-down rebel bodies lay sprawled across blood-soaked grass. The CDF had destroyed the first line of defense.

Wordless, Randy surveyed the carnage as the sled crept forward at low speed.

Fire crawled, burning the camp's shelters. More gunfire crackled.

I hope the CDF hasn't gotten to our ship yet, Randy thought. He pressed the accelerator. The sled picked up speed as it passed a trail of devastation.

The hiss of energy weapons and the thunder of automatics grew louder. The trio was getting closer to the heart of the battle.

The zipsled sluggishly climbed a steep incline, its engine groaning. At the top, the trio reached level ground and found themselves front and center of a gun battle, Guardians and rebels exchanging shots.

A mini launcher rose from a Guardian's shoulder panel. A scattershot of rocket pods ejected. The marble-sized plasma bombs erupted in a rebel's face, tearing away skin and muscle. He screamed and fell to the ground, cradling what was left of his face.

A bronze-skinned rebel woman with dark ropes of hair hoisted a blaster cannon over her shoulder. She fired an energy blast that blew a Guardian's arm clean off.

A rebel man had a wounded woman in a fireman's carry, hauling her to safety.

Jarius said, "Damn it, where are our armored troops?"

Randy swerved around a tree. "Aboard the ship, preparing to get the hell out of here."

"So these guys are just—"

"Volunteer sacrificial lambs," Randy finished. They were brave souls who'd volunteered to forfeit their lives so their comrades could escape and end the war. He remembered a truism that a drill sergeant had said: *In war, you don't get to save everybody.*

Rebels manned bipod-mounted blasters, launching booming shots of spherical energy.

A heavy thudding sound echoed from deep within the trees, quaking the ground. Frightened rebels turned toward the source.

Branches crunched. Something massive was coming.

A Juggernaut stomped out of the trees, its motorized joints whining. Weapons lockers opened. Slugs, energy blasts, and missiles spat out in a barrage as its torso rotated ninety degrees.

A panicked rebel woman fired wildly at the giant walking arsenal. Unfazed by her small-arms fire, the Juggernaut brought its enormous foot down on her, squashing her into a bloody smear.

"What the hell's that thing?" Jarius yelled.

"It's gotta be a Juggernaut," Kesley replied.

"How do you know what it is?" Randy asked.

"You heard Reza back at the sanctuary. Our intel said Gould's developing advanced weaponry at some secret military test farm. One of them is a Juggernaut, a high-tech robot that's completely thought-controlled."

"No way," Randy said. "That type of implant modification isn't legal."

Kesley scoffed. "Tell that to Gould."

What the Commonwealth would become under Gould's leadership frightened Randy. The madman was going too far.

Three more Juggernauts emerged from the trees' concealment, each cerebrally piloted from control-free cockpits. An energy beam from one Juggernaut sawed a rebel in half, bisecting her.

Randy mashed the acceleration pedal to the floor.

Air slapped the trio's faces as the sled whooshed past bloodshed and burning jungle, scraping against outstretched tree limbs as it neared the hangar.

At the hangar, Randy braked and cut the engine.

Rebels were double-timing it through the rear bay door of the ship.

Randy snatched the comm-set from his belt and contacted Arson. "Dad, we're here."

Arson replied, "Hurry the hell up and get inside the ship. Our troops can't hold the CDF back much longer."

"Let's skedaddle," Kesley said. She hopped out of the sled.

Sariah ushered rebels inside. "Come on, move it!"

Randy, Jarius, and Kesley rushed into the ship. Sariah slipped in with the last trickle of rebels.

The ship rolled out of the hangar and climbed into the sky.

Weapons fell silent.

A Guardian watched the ship vanish into the atmosphere. *Damn, bet Reza's aboard.*

The CDF had come close to taking out the Coalition leader. Close, but no cigar.

• • •

Felix Moss barged into the BUS where Samantha Hayley was being detained. He stomped past buzzing electronics, weapons racks, and storage lockers.

He slid back the cell door's grille cover and peered in at Samantha sitting on a metal bench. His scowl made his foul mood obvious. "Reza has escaped. Where is he going?"

"Like I'd tell you," Samantha snapped, eyes full of loathing.

Felix gave a wicked smile that stretched from ear to ear. "Perhaps I missed some vital information the first time I probed your mind." He rubbed his hands together. "Let's do it again, shall we, Governess?"

Terror reflected in Samantha's eyes. She didn't want to face that agony a second time.

Felix opened the flap of the black bag hanging on his shoulder, pulled out the Mind Sweeper, and powered it on. The latticework of circuitry gleamed ominously.

Pain stabbed Samantha's head as the device tore into her memories. A headache flared instantly. She couldn't take it. "No! Alright, I'll tell you!"

Felix shut off the Mind Sweeper. "I'm all ears."

• • •

On Babylon Island, Stacie strolled the marble-block promenade of Kirkstone Park, marshaling her thoughts and processing her societal demotion. It felt strange no longer being "modern-day royalty," no longer being the princess of the Spencer family. And though her parents had caused her pain, it felt odd to be completely out of touch with them.

On a pavilion, musicians played instruments. Around them, onlookers sipped drinks, laughing and enjoying themselves. A leggy female jogger, wearing purple gel leggings, dashed past Stacie, her white tank top darkened by patches of sweat.

Stacie crossed a footbridge and sat under a tree beside a pond. She needed to reflect and clear her mind.

A woman in a sundress sauntered by, hand in hand with her boyfriend.

Stacie pondered. If she hadn't interrupted the family heads' get-together and caused a scene, if she had just kept her cool, maybe she could've stayed in the Eight and dismantled it from within. Maybe she could've even convinced her parents to turn over a new leaf. *Damn, if I had just played it smarter.*

And yes, she would miss the chauffeuring, the extraneous

spending, the ability to have anything she wanted. She just didn't want to be totally defined by her ascribed status. That was why she had joined the CDF. And she didn't want dirty money involved in sustaining her lifestyle. Anyway, now her identity was solely wrapped around being a Guardian. Apparently, that was all she had left—that and Randy.

Her wristcom beeped a warning notice. She pressed the center disc, and a holo-message hovered above her wrist. It said that all Guardians on Eden, whether they were on active duty or on leave, were being called to action under a declared State of Emergency. They were to report to Defense Force HQ immediately.

Once there, she'd be temporarily assigned to a unit on Eden.

She knew something major was about to go down. Her duty was all she had now. There was no more time to continue dwelling on how she could've confronted her parents differently.

• • •

The Coalition assault ship had exited Hyperspace Leap and was en route to Eden at a speed that afforded the rebels aboard five hours of rest.

Rebels had claimed the foldout wall-berths in no particular order, bedding down for their brief respite.

Randy slept fitfully, tossing and turning. In his dream, he again wrestled with his conscience. He and Kathleen stood in a void of darkness, a pillar of light shining down on them.

This battle may be the end of either of you. Don't miss this opportunity, Kathleen pled. *Link with your father and begin restoring your bond.*

Again, no! Randy said.

Kathleen rested a hand on his shoulder. *Do it, Randy, for yourself . . . and me.*

Randy jolted awake, his mother's words still in his head. He rubbed his palms over his face. *Okay, Mom, fine. Have it your way. You always knew what was best.* He swung his feet onto the floor and pulled on his boots. With soft footsteps, he left the sleeping station, careful not to disturb the napping rebels.

The ship was quiet, save for the low rumble of its engines.

Randy rounded a corner, stepping into a ribbed gyre-shaped corridor, and saw Reza gazing into space through a long window.

Reza prayed everything would go according to his will.

Wishing Priscilla were there to comfort him, Reza felt a warm, loving ambiance swarm around him. Then the apparition bearing her uncanny resemblance appeared once more.

Don't worry, everything will go well, my love, Priscilla said.

"Thank you. I will always be grateful for the serenity you brought to my life."

Who is he talking to? Randy wondered.

With just that brief exchange of words, Priscilla disappeared.

Randy approached Reza. "Who were you talking to?"

Reza spun toward Randy, his boots squeaking against the smooth floor. "Randal, you heard?"

Randy nodded.

Reza said, "Well, a woman was killed during the miners' strike. She was my lover. We were Linked at the time of her brutal death. My mind was tormented as she was executed. It was as if I experienced death with her. Since then, my implant seems to draw on my memories of her—her voice, personality, the clothes she wore—to conjure a lifelike hallucination whenever my heart cries out for her." He turned back toward the window. "Then again, maybe it's the trauma. Maybe I'm losing my mind."

Randy edged closer. "It's the same with me," he shared. "I see my mom sometimes. It's so real."

Reza craned his head sideways, looking at Randy. "So, I'm not the only one."

"No, you're not." Randy stepped beside him, gazing out the window at a drifting asteroid belt. "What do you think it would take to get rid of these . . . phantasms? An implant cleanse? A full implant replacement?"

"Perhaps reconciliation with—or elimination of—whatever caused the pain." For Reza, that meant killing Gould.

Getting back on track, Randy said, "Do you know where my dad might be?"

"The stockroom, I believe. Take a left at the second junction and keep going. You'll see it."

"Thanks."

Reza extended an open palm. "A pleasure talking to you, Randal Scott. And I appreciate you lending your talents and abilities to this fight."

Randy hesitated a moment, as if he might be shaking the hand of someone up to no good. Out of common courtesy, he grasped Reza's hand and shook it. Then he headed to the stockroom as Reza walked in the opposite direction.

In the stockroom, Arson was inventorying armaments and Hardsuits.

The circular hatch's lock mechanism cycled open.

Randy appeared in the hatchway. "Dad," he said, voice low, mind unsettled. He was unsure if this bonding attempt was a good idea. Linking with his father, the man he had once wished dead, still felt bizarre.

Arson clipped his datapad to his utility belt. "Yeah, Randy, what's up?" He sounded unenthused, tired of his son's repeated criticisms, yet he understood the pain behind them. Even so, the back-and-forths had become exhausting.

Randy came down the metal ramp below the hatchway. He

started the conversation casually. "I saw some crazy stuff out there, things that shouldn't even exist."

Arson said, "You mean the Juggernauts?" Randy nodded. "Well, that's just one more reason we need to stop that madman. Word from our insiders is he's developing some kind of implant modification that dulls Guardians' empathy during combat."

Randy's brows rose. "Totally insane."

"Yeah, I know. But I have a feeling you didn't come here just to chat about that. What's on your mind, Son?"

Randy shed his reluctance. "Since we're headed into the fight of our lives, I wanted to kinda bury the hatchet."

"Kinda?"

"I'm not going to pretend I suddenly agree with your decision to leave Mom and me. I'm not going to be fake and phony."

Arson boosted himself up into a sitting position on a container and crossed his arms. "Alright, Son, I'm all ears."

"I've seen the conditions the people of my birth-colony have had to endure. I've seen decent people get mistreated by the CDF. I understand that your heart told you to do something, to take a stand. I still wouldn't have left my family. But knowing Mom, I don't think she'd want me to hate you. I don't think she'd want us to be at odds. I can't say everything's going to be the same, though."

Silence settled between them.

"Anything else, Randy?" Arson asked.

"Yeah, I . . . want us to Link. I think it'll help me understand you, and you understand me. And maybe that'll start some kind of healing process . . . for me."

For a moment, Arson was at a loss for words. He hadn't believed his son would ever want to Link with him again. "Okay, Randy, let's do this." He slid off the container.

Randy bobbed his chin. "Be prepared. Mom and I were Linked

when she died. You're going to feel all of that pain, understand?"

"Son, I've endured incredible physical and mental ordeals."

"None like this," Randy guaranteed. "Ready?"

"Yes," Arson replied confidently.

Randy forwarded the Link request. Arson's implant pinged.

Nervousness rose in Arson, but he held his composure. He accepted the request, and the interchange of emotions, thoughts, and times passed proceeded.

Arson revisited the moment Kathleen was killed, diving into Randy's anguish. Head swimming, tension permeating every limb, he dropped to his knees. He clutched his skull and was unable to form a coherent word. Suddenly, a whirlwind of agony swallowed him.

Randy journeyed into Arson's thoughts that night. He heard his father's voice cry out, *"Wait, someone's still in there! Intel said the building would be vacant tonight!"* Then the explosion replayed. Arson's undeniable love for Kathleen, his guilt . . . *all* of his emotions crashed into Randy like a tidal wave, overloading his mind.

A fog of self-condemnation hanging over him, Arson sat sobbing in the corner of his flyer that night, a broken man. He grieved for days.

Randy then encountered another memory . . .

Arson was in his quarters. Wracked with guilt, he had wallowed in self-loathing and battled suicidal thoughts for days, reduced to a shell of the man he once was.

He held a pistol to his head, staring at a photograph on the table—a picture of him and Kathleen on their wedding day. He whispered a prayer to God, asking forgiveness for his sin, seeking peace with his maker. Only death, he thought, could free him from his pain.

Just as he was about to pull the trigger, Sariah walked in, startling him. "Sariah, what are you—?"

She gasped, rushed to him, and slapped the gun from his hand. It clattered to the floor.

"Killing yourself is not the answer! Get off your guilt trip, Commander!" Sariah threw her arms around Arson. "Kathleen wouldn't want you to end your life. You have too much to live for. Too much to do. The Coalition needs you. Your son needs you. *I* need you."

Arson hugged her, weeping . . .

The memory faded. A lump formed in Randy's throat, and a tear rolled down his cheek. This moment marked a turning point in his estranged relationship with his father.

Arson sat on the floor with his back against the container. He settled his chin against his chest. Now he fully understood the mental trauma Randy had suffered, being Linked with Kathleen during the explosion that killed her—and nearly ripped his soul out. He understood why Randy had rejected his pleas for forgiveness for so long, and maybe, he thought, Randy shouldn't forgive him. Guilt, shame, and humiliation—all his personal demons—resurfaced, dragging him back into the abyss of self-disgust.

Randy extended a hand. Arson stared at the gesture, uncertain why his son would ever forgive him.

"Come on, Dad, get up," Randy said kindly.

Arson took his hand.

Randy helped lift him to his feet.

Kathleen's death had shattered them both. Each had lost the woman he cherished more than life itself.

They stood there, facing each other. Neither of them was sure what to say.

Tears streamed down Randy's face, not for Kathleen, but for Arson. With their minds Linked, he had experienced a man's grief for his wife and the crushing guilt of having caused her death.

Randy felt empathy for Arson, the kind that only Linking—a radical concept made reality—could unearth, as it had been foreseen.

Arson broke the silence, voice cracking. "You should go rest up for the operation."

Randy swallowed and cleared his throat. "Yeah, I think I should." He hugged his father with love and forgiveness. Then he left through the hatchway.

Arson closed his eyes. His son had forgiven him. His son loved him.

He returned to work, fighting off tears of relief.

CHAPTER EIGHT

The Defense Department raised Eden's threat level to red—the highest level. Cornelius had broadcasted an emergency address to the citizens of Eden, informing them that the CDF had detained and interrogated Governess Hayley for collaborating with the enemy. He said she had confessed that the Coalition planned to invade Eden, though she didn't know the exact day or time.

The fight was now coming to humanity's motherworld.

Pandemonium ensued. To secure the streets, the government mobilized the entire CDF and ordered all citizens to remain indoors under a full lockdown until further notice.

Stacie, in battledress, was en route to Defense Force HQ in an air-cab. Below, in Cornerstone City's Terence Plaza, authorities and Guardians were overseeing a large-scale evacuation. Tiny figures and vehicles bustled across the plaza's colorful tiles.

The cab soared past Cornerstone's aerial shopping center, a floating globular structure with wrap-around windows. For the first time, it was a ghost town.

All throughout Eden, it felt like doomsday was approaching,

and Stacie had that eerie calm-before-the-storm feeling, the kind that comes right before all hell breaks loose.

Thoughts of her lover surfaced. She was worried. Randy's message said he was scoping out the other side, the Coalition. He wouldn't actually join them, would he? No, she knew him better than that. Whatever phase of confusion or doubt he was dealing with, he'd come back to the CDF.

The Coalition couldn't possibly poison his mind against her. He held the CDF's values dear and had sworn to protect the Commonwealth from all enemies, foreign and domestic. His personal standards and morals were too strong to be corrupted by Coalition tricks, propaganda, or doctrine.

Boy, she wished he were with her right now. He was like no other man she had met. He knew just what to say to console her. He knew how to work her body in ways that left her breathless and yearning for more. For him, it was virtually a cinch.

She closed her eyes and accessed the feeling of his powerful, tender touch from her cerebral implant's sensory archive. The sensations suffused her body and mind with a dopamine rush. *Randy, I miss you. I need you.*

Elation coursed through her like wildfire. Her breathing changed, the rise and fall of her chest quickening. Deriving pleasure from her lover by using stored recollection data was the next best thing in lieu of actual intercourse with him.

Focusing her thoughts on the mission, she logged out of her sensory archive. *Keep your head in the game, Stacie. Keep your head in the game.*

Stacie's cab landed outside the gate of Defense Force HQ's base. After she got out, the craft ascended into roaming mode and vanished into the sky.

A male guard emerged from a small outbuilding, the security

control center. Stacie identified herself as a Guardian. The guard scanned her retina, confirmed her enlistment, and granted her access to the base.

A comm pedestal was located a few feet beyond the gate. Stacie flipped up the plastic cover and pressed the large red button to request transportation. Five minutes later, a white self-driving commuter van slowed to a stop beside her, its engine barely audible.

She stepped aboard. Inside were five other Guardians in battledress.

"Next stop: Ferrington Gate," said the van's computer.

The side doors sealed, and the van accelerated smoothly.

A screen mounted to the ceiling displayed a newscast. Every headline focused on the looming rebel invasion.

After the van delivered the other Guardians to their destinations, it delivered Stacie to hers.

She stepped down from the van. The doors closed. Electronics chirped, and the van drove off.

Outside, CDF HQ buzzed with frenzied activity. Outbound convoys rolled from motor pools, officers barked orders, NCOs shouted, and Guardians hastened here and there. A sense of urgency electrified the air.

Stacie entered the towering white building. To get directions, she tried to flag down the Guardian jogging in her direction. "Excuse me, Private, could you tell me where—?"

He made a beeline right past her for the exit. "Sorry, no time, toots."

She frowned. *Toots? Damn misogynist.*

More Guardians ran past her, boots clacking against the floor.

Stacie located a directory module, used it to find her temporary company commander's office, and proceeded.

As she neared the office's door, sensors detected her presence, and it slid into the wall. A man in battledress with a captain's rank sat behind a wooden desk. A computer faced him; a polished award placard faced outward.

Stacie rapped on the doorframe three times and recited the procedural spiel. "Specialist Spencer requesting permission to enter, Sir."

"Enter," the captain said.

Stacie went into the office. The door closed automatically behind her.

Standing at regulation distance, she locked her heels together, rested her arms firmly at her sides, and then saluted. "Specialist Spencer reporting for duty, Sir."

"I'm Captain Samuel McBride. At ease." He opened a drawer and placed a datapad on the desk. "I just need your biometric signature to finalize your temporary unit transfer."

"Yes, Sir." Stacie stepped forward, rested her palms on the desk, and studied the detail of her service sketch. She raised her chin, her eyes fixed on McBride in confusion. "Excuse me, Sir, this v-doc has my rank listed as sergeant. I'm—"

"Not anymore," McBride said. "A Staff Sergeant Jason Mansford submitted your name for promotion." Stacie flinched, caught off guard. "He included a service critique citing above-average performance and noted that you've shown strong leadership aptitude as a sub-lead."

Stacie thought that "high leadership aptitude" was laying it on a little thick.

McBride said, "All documentation was approved. Unless, of course, you'd rather stay a specialist."

"Uh, no, Sir," Stacie replied.

Though she had helped take down the Scott Faction, she knew

she hadn't served long enough, hadn't done enough, to truly deserve a promotion. But Jason had a soft spot for her. He saw something in her, which was why he handpicked her as Alpha Team's sub-lead. And hell, she wasn't about to turn down a promotion, earned or not.

She pressed her thumb to the v-doc's signature box. Her temporary unit transfer was now official.

"Excellent," McBride said. "Area B-4 is Delta Company's AO. Your platoon sergeant will get you squared away. Now go, get out of my sight."

"Yes, Sir." Stacie did an about-face and exited. Her promotion stroked her ego. *Now "Sergeant Spencer." Yaassss!*

She went to Area B-4, linked up with her platoon sergeant, got assigned to a squad, and hit the company armory to get shelled. Not long after, her platoon boarded BUSs and headed for the Parliament Building's yard. There, they joined the largest assembly of Guardians they had ever seen.

On the yard, prefabs had been set up as chow facilities and perhaps even barracks.

Bound by the Oath and a sense of duty, the Guardians were ready to give their lives to protect Eden soil. The sheer audacity of the Coalition in bringing the war to their turf ignited a fervor.

No one knew when the invaders would arrive. Until then, the Guardians would remain alert and stay ready.

Though Stacie felt prepared to face whatever the Coalition threw at her, she didn't like being this exposed. Out here, she felt like a sitting duck waiting to be picked off. But there was nothing she could do about it.

• • •

At the rear parking deck of the Parliament Building, a motorcade of limousines and CDF armored vehicles rolled in. The chairmen and chairwomen of the Parliament sat inside the limousines. Armed Guardians in light body armor opened their doors for them and began escorting them inside.

While walking toward the entrance, Chairman Jeff Hutchinson glanced at Oviereya, who was right beside him. "Is this really the safest place for us?"

"Is there any place safer?" Oviereya replied, her sleek dark braids swaying as she strode forward.

With no better ideas, Jeff changed the subject. "These rebels are biting off more than they can chew. Do they really think they can beat the Commonwealth Defense Force? We've spent years and billions transforming the CDF into the most fearsome fighting force of the Interplanetary Union."

Oviereya knew not to underestimate the Coalition. "Threat assessments suggest the Coalition has acquired advanced wearable armaments that may rival or surpass our Shells. They've also enlisted the Falgoah. We don't know their numbers, and we can't predict the full extent of their firepower. But this day didn't have to happen.

"We let systemic oppression fester far too long. This attack on Eden is the result of our neglect."

"The colony citizens are lucky to have what they have," Jeff snapped. "They should be grateful."

More limos arrived. Doors clicked open.

Oviereya's strong features hardened in visible offense at her colleague's lack of compassion. "Nonsense. Edenites became comfortable being the New Humanity's ruling class. They expected colonists to remain their proles. Their unspoken motto was, 'Someone has to do the dirty work, but not me.' For years, colonists were treated like lower lifeforms, and colony advancement got thrown by the wayside."

"Eden had to come first, and must evolve further, if our republic is to become the intergalactic superpower needed to protect humanity," Jeff replied. "Both Edenites and colonists have roles to play. Those roles have different responsibilities, yes, but are equally important. The colony proletariat's role will only grow in value as we expand to trading-partner and Mission Worlds for resource harvesting.

"Face it, Amaechi, AEGIS put the right gears in the right places. We risk stalling humanity's progress if we deviate from the socioeconomic structure it laid out."

Oviereya said pointedly, "The way we live is starkly different from the way they live. Ensuring basic human dignity is no deviation. It's a moral obligation."

"We'll improve life in the colonies eventually. Just not now."

"That mindset is why we've arrived at this unfortunate climax."

Jeff grunted in irritation, signaling the end of the exchange, as the security detail escorted them through twin tinted glass doors into the building's atrium.

• • •

The assault ship's cloaking field had worked like a charm. The ship had made unauthorized planetfall without detection.

Hardsuit on and headgear racked to his side, Randy strode down the corridor that led to the troop hold. He'd be joining Gold Force in the occupation of the Parliament Building, along with Jarius and Kesley.

He saw Kesley staring out of a window. Not part of the Hardsuit element, she wore a royal-blue getup cut close to the body, overlaid with armor attachments—unpowered combatwear provided by the Falgoah. It was being referred to as "protective combat uniform (PCU)," and served as the underlayer for the Hardsuit, like a sleeve.

306

Randy took up a spot beside her.

"This is paradise," Kesley exclaimed. The splendor of the land and the sprawling metropolises were unlike anything she had ever seen.

"Yeah," Randy said, "sorry you had to see Eden for the first time under these circumstances." He placed a hand on her back. "After things settle, I promise I'll take you for a joyride in my sports cruiser."

Kesley spun to him with a thankful smile. "'Kay, sounds good. Thanks." On the spur of the moment, she grabbed the back of his head, threading her fingers through his wavy hair, and claimed his mouth in a fiery good-luck kiss.

Randy quickly pulled away, thoughts turning to Stacie.

"Something wrong?" Kesley asked.

"I just . . . have to get going. It's almost time for the big shebang," he said, moving on. "Stay safe out there, Kess."

"You too, Randy."

As he neared the entry hatch to the troop hold, Randy saw Sariah up ahead. "Hey, Sariah, wait up."

She paused and faced Randy. "What's up?"

He edged closer. "I Linked with my father."

"Yes, he told me."

"Well, I wanted to say thank you. Thank you for stopping him from taking his life."

"I was just doing what a friend would do. Now let's get on with this mission."

Inside the troop hold, armored rebels stood, gripping the wall railings' handholds.

On the eve of change, precombat stress shook the rebels' limbs.

The pressure was on.

"We are now in position over the target areas," the helmsman said over the intercom.

"Alright, all forces, we'll be airdropping into hot water," Arson said. "As you know, the element of surprise has gone to shit. We've got a huge welcoming committee waiting for us down there. After we neutralize them, we'll deploy the shield generators. Avoid taking any lives if possible. These soldiers are just doing their jobs." *So many Guardian lives are about to be put at risk. What a screwed-up situation.*

"Let's do this!" a man shouted energetically, boosting morale.

"Yeah!" came a woman's voice.

Arson commed the helm. "This is Arson. Open the drop doors."

The whirring sound of the floor splitting open signaled the start of what would be the Coalition's most important battle.

The ship hovered above the Quad, cloaked from the naked eye.

Randy swallowed. This would be his first time fighting in the Hardsuit. His cram session with Sariah had gone well, but he still wasn't used to the suit. It felt strange going into battle without heightened awareness or an AI Combat Assistant—like being back in Basic Training, using the outdated M-X01 Shell. The Hardsuit was superior to the M-X02 in some ways, inferior in others. Maybe they were about even.

His heart beat faster as he waited for his father's command. Bringing war to Eden was nerve-wracking, but necessary. He and the others aboard this ship carried the promise of a new Commonwealth in their hands. Ridding his mind of worry, he composed himself for the fight to come.

"Gold Force, you're up first," Arson said.

Tasked with taking the Parliament Building, Gold Force let go of the handholds and leapt out. They ignited their vernier jets to control their free fall.

Wind howled against their armor.

On the Parliament Building's yard, shelled Guardians looked skyward. "Holy shit, it's them!" one shouted.

"Take the fuckers out!" an NCO bellowed.

Guardians' Gatling guns, their primary weapon, vibrated to life and hosed the sky with slugs.

"Come get some!" a Guardian roared.

A CDF armored land vehicle launched a missile.

One rebel, unable to dodge in time, stared wide-eyed as the missile closed in. "Holy Shi-!" An explosion flashed.

Rebels opened fire mid-fall, their energy blasts strafing the ground. Fountains of dirt, grass, and phyocrete splashed upward.

A blast from above blew a fist-sized hole in a Guardian's solar plexus. His feet backpedaled, and he fell sideways.

The Rebels' air-to-ground fire didn't let up. Guardians cursed, shooting upward.

A blaster lowered from the assault ship's underside and accumulated plasma energy. It released an enfilade, forcing Guardians to spread out.

Four robo-cannons rose from their underground compartments. Autoloaders chinked and clanked, chambering explosive rounds. Dual launch chutes fired, sending the projectiles streaking toward the assault ship.

Rebels in the sky intercepted the incoming projectiles with energy blasts, detonating them midair.

Hardsuits made landfall, dropping onto the battlefield.

A horde of Falgoah dispersed from the ship in needle-shaped, triangular-winged fighter bombers. The craft swooped down, unleashing a blitzkrieg on the Guardians below. As explosions flung Guardians like rag dolls, the Falgoah pilots shouted their war cry and pumped their fists.

More armored rebels landed.

Randy jetted into the air. He conjured an energy sphere with his hands and hurled it at one of the robo-cannons. The resulting explosion tore it apart, spraying metal fragments across the yard as flames consumed what remained.

Randy landed just as a blur of bullets zipped past him.

Boom! Shrapnel rained from above. The pace of the battle was accelerating.

This is maddening, Jarius thought. There was no cover, no concealment. There was no way to be strategic. This was an open, all-out gunfight to the last man and woman.

A Guardian's shoulder blasters struck down two Hardsuits. Jarius had the Guardian in his visor's crosshairs. He hesitated to pull his rifle's trigger. This wasn't easy on the soul. He couldn't balk now, though. He had chosen his side.

He pulled the trigger, and a blast of energy shot from his rifle. The Guardian slumped to the ground, a steaming hole in his torso plating. *Damn, this just feels wrong.* He fired two more blasts, striking down another Guardian. *Man, I really don't like firing on my own compadres.*

His shots drew the attention of two Guardians. They turned their weapons on him, firing.

Pulses of energy streaked past him. "Shit!"

He didn't know if the Guardians he'd taken down were dead, but he had no time for guilt. It was fight or die.

He ignited his vernier jets and soared above the melee. The two Guardians still targeting him adjusted their aim, but he took care of them with well-placed blasts before they could fire again.

He landed. *The faster this ends, the better.*

Kesley manned the top-mounted laser turret of a combat hover vehicle.

The rebel at the controls swerved the vehicle alongside one of the robo-cannons.

Now, Kesley thought. Her gloved hands tightened around the twin grips of the gun as she thumbed the firing studs. Twin flashes of energy burst forth, and the cannon became a heap of burning wreckage.

"Hold on!" the driver yelled. "Incoming!" He veered to the left, barely dodging a missile. It slammed into the ground behind them, the explosion juddering the vehicle's frame.

Close one, Kesley thought.

A Guardian lunged at Randy with a plasma saber. Randy sidestepped, grabbed the Guardian's arm, and threw him over his shoulder. While the Guardian lay dazed on his back, Randy drove a plasma-charged punch into his faceplate. The concussive blow knocked him out cold.

Randy was doing his best to disable Shells without killing, but deep down, he knew he wouldn't make it through this battle without taking one single life.

Around him, the brutality of war escalated. Rebels and Guardians gunned each other down.

Suddenly, Randy's implant pinged and buzzed. *Stacie. She's near.*

Weapons roared from all directions.

Stacie, engaged in close-quarters combat, buried her plasma saber into a Hardsuit, melting armor and filament. She summoned more power to the blade, and it grew—flickering wildly. *Ciao, baby.* Her implant gave her notice of Randy's presence. *Randy?* She jerked her arm back, ripping the blade free. Then the rebel crumpled.

Purple sparks scattered as Stacie shut off the saber. Her

implant, like a compass, guided her to Randy. His signal grew stronger the closer she got to him. As her eyes skimmed the grisly battlefield, her implant directed her to the Hardsuit straight ahead.

<Randy, what are you doing?> she asked.

Randy pivoted. <Stace!> He retracted his face guard.

Stacie edged closer. <So, you did join them!> Her voice carried a mix of shock and betrayal.

"You saw the files," Randy said. "Something needs to be done."

Stacie raised her faceplate. Her eyes mirrored her disappointment at Randy's decision. "Yeah, there's a lot of corruption in the government," she said, voice low. "And . . . my mother and father are part of it." Her brows knitted. "But that *doesn't* mean you join a bunch of terrorists. Corruption can be fought another way. We took an oath to defend the Commonwealth."

A shot-up Falgoah bomber plummeted from the sky, air whistling, and crashed into the ground in a puff of fire.

"You say there's another way," Randy replied, "but what is it?"

"I don't have an answer," Stacie admitted. "And it's not our job to have one, anyway. But I know turning your back on your duty is . . . is just plain wrong. The CDF Code of Military Justice makes that clear."

A rogue missile struck the ground nearby. *Boom!* Randy and Stacie's hearts pounded. Chunks of earth flung up and rained back down. That was a close call.

Relieved, Randy resumed the conversation. "This mission isn't just about the corruption. You've seen how colonists are treated, how they're forced to live. Before we went to Colony Four, everything we believed was just an assumption. We could only imagine what life was like for colonists, but imagination couldn't truly grasp the inhumanity of their reality.

"Now we've seen how horrible they have to live. I've even witnessed Guardians brutalize innocent people without cause. Edenites hear those stories and just brush them off as rubbish, just 'Coalition propaganda.' They tell themselves, 'Things can't be *that* bad.' But they are.

"Stace, the government needs to change. The CDF needs to change. And the institutional injustice inflicted on the colonies must end."

"So Reza's going to usher in a new era of equality and not seek any payback on Edenites? And after this magical new era begins, we'll all sing Kumbaya around bonfires together, right?" Stacie scoffed and shook her head. "Give me a fucking break."

Displeasure settled on Randy's face. "You're making a mockery of the genuine hope I, and so many colonists, have."

"No, I'm making a mockery of your stupid fairy-tale thinking, to drill some sense into your head, because I need the Randal Scott I know to wake up." Chopping the air, Stacie's hands punctuated her tirade.

Randy stood firm in the face of her criticisms. "I've been awoken alright, awoken by the reality of what needs to happen."

Stacie wished he'd come back to his senses. "Randy, are you for real right now? You help put in place an oligarchy, then what?"

"No, Reza's not putting himself in power. He plans to work with politicians who aren't in the Eight Elite's pocket, and with the citizens of the Commonwealth, to build a new government that serves everyone." Trying to win his war of words with Stacie, he left out, *I hope.*

Stacie threw up her arms. "My God, do you hear yourself? Take the blinders off, Randy!" This was so uncharacteristic of the Randal Scott she knew.

In the distance, the maelstrom of thudding explosions, zaps, and gunfire went on endlessly.

Randy sighed. "Stace, I know you never thought you'd hear me say stuff like this, but I need you to trust what I'm saying."

<What's gotten into you?> Stacie began probing his mind to unearth what had driven him to stray from the Oath. She found his travels with Kesley, his talks with Arson, and . . .

Randy tried to prevent her from digging further, saying, *< Stace, there's no need to—>*

Stacie's lips parted. A lost expression blanketed her face. She trembled, Shell rattling.

Her mindscan had uncovered Randy's night of enthralling sex with Kesley. She absorbed his sensations. She absorbed the thrill of every touch, every kiss.

She summed up her feelings in just a few words. *<You motherfucking son of a bitch!>* Her infuriated expression disappeared behind her faceplate. Hot plasma crackled from her armguard, and her saber materialized.

She swung the energy blade at Randy, screaming a curse.

He re-formed his face guard and dodged to the side, but not fast enough to avoid receiving a gash in his shoulder plating, which regenerated in seconds. "That night was a mistake. A big mistake."

"Enough!" Stacie kicked Randy, jamming her foot into his gut.

He "oomphed."

Stacie's face was red-hot. "Not only have you joined the enemy, but you sleep with them too!" Her voice was the harshest Randy had ever heard it. "You betrayed your duty, but you also betrayed *me*! *Me*, Randy, the woman who dragged you out of your emotional withdrawal from society! The woman who broke you out of . . . being a loner! The woman who made you smile time after time since your mother's death by the very people you now ally yourself with!" All true, Stacie had been his lifeline—a lifeline out of sorrow

—and had helped him rebound from all the hurt, breathing life back into his soul.

"We had a covenant, Randal Eugene Scott! We agreed to only you and me! We agreed for us to be exclusive! But you betrayed me for some . . . some rebel bimbo."

It was strange for Randy to hear the words "You betrayed me." That was exactly how he had felt about his father. "Stace, I don't want to fight you!"

She wasn't listening. A launcher sprang up from her shoulder. It fired two missiles in quick succession.

Randy thrust his plasma-charged hands forward, generating an energy screen. The missiles hit, erupting into fiery bursts.

The shield dissipated on his command. He shot back using his palm blaster. Stacie instinctively crossed her forearms. The energy blasts struck her, breaking off shards of armor.

"Stacie, no more! Let's end this!" Randy begged.

The memory of Randy's night with Kesley still burned fresh in Stacie's mind, stoking her rage. She had felt Kesley's lips and body overpowering Randy's resolve to respect their relationship.

She vaulted high into the air, letting out a roar of outrage, and slashed downward in a vertical arc toward Randy.

He rolled over his shoulder just in time. The blade sizzled past him and burrowed into the ground. Damn, her reflexes were lightning-fast, he thought, and she was showing no leniency. Hell hath no fury like a woman scorned, he figured.

Locked in their own skirmish, the ex-couple ignored the larger battle raging around them.

Not wanting to hurt his former lover, Randy dove at her, wrapping his arms around her waist. They clunked to the ground, with him on top.

Randy held down Stacie's wrists, the servos of his arms

groaning.

Her Shell's joints hissed as she struggled to break free.

Unyielding, Randy asserted more pressure. "Stop fighting, Stace," he pled. Any other time, he would've enjoyed being on top of her, but not today.

She was now vulnerable. He could've disabled her Shell right then. But tied to her by emotion, he held back.

Capitalizing on Randy's moment of weakness, Stacie drove a knee up and knocked him off.

Turning the tables, she shut off her saber, power-leapt into the air, and crashed a knee into his torso as she came down.

Randy winced. That blow packed a hell of a wallop.

Trapping him between her thighs, Stacie began clobbering his helmet with wild, furious blows. *Fucking traitor.* The teasers and naysayers had hurt her. Her parents had hurt her. And now her lover had hurt her. Her heart cut open, the fury, sadness, and pain bubbled to the surface, making her cry. *Fuck you!*

Disoriented by the barrage, Randy thought, *Gotta get her off.* He fired a close-range shot from his palm blaster, sending her flying. A blast at that distance was dangerous, but he'd held back enough power to damage only the Shell, not the woman inside.

Lying on her back, suit smoking and crackling, Stacie mentally kicked herself. *Sloppy of me. Damn sloppy. I should've been watching his hands.* Her anger had blinded her.

As she rose, Randy quickly launched a taser coil from his bracer. It clamped onto her Shell, and a plasma charge surged through the cable.

Pain smashed into Stacie. On her HUD, CONDITION 8 flashed, code for "not good." Then: SYSTEM OVERLOADING. The charge shorted out circuits and severed her implant-to-CPU connection. Feeling vanished from her arms and legs. All coherent thought and her consciousness receded.

She collapsed onto her back and would be comatose for a while.

Randy deactivated his face guard. Exhausted, he inhaled deeply and exhaled. *Sorry, Stace.* Hurting her tore at him.

He leaned in, removed Stacie's helmet, and tossed it aside. Then he rolled her facedown and palmed the Shell's manual release.

The armor expanded from her body, sliding panels unsealing with a series of chinks.

Randy reached in, gripped her under the arms, and wrestled her free from the suit. He hefted her onto his shoulder, carried her a few paces, and gently propped her against the side of the Parliament Building.

He gazed out at the bodies of Guardians and rebels lying on the yard and cringed. Being both a Guardian and a rebel, watching lives being lost on both sides weighed heavily on his soul. *I sure hope you're wrong, Stace, dead wrong. I hope this turns out alright.*

Spasmodic gunfire echoed. Falgoah bombers landed, and their pilots jumped out, firearms in hand.

Rebels began filing into the Parliament Building. They had suffered fewer casualties than projected. Their Hardsuits' plasma-based firepower had compensated for their lack of numbers.

• • •

Standing on the assault ship's bridge, Reza observed the battle sites below on a battery of screens. His forces were mopping up the last of the Guardians protecting the targets, doing their best not to kill.

Over the ship's comm, Reza heard Arson report, "Reza, I've gotten word that we've taken the Parliament Building." The Coalition had also taken the Academy, which had been evacuated. "I'm now infiltrating the Chief Executive's Manor, and shield generators are being put in place for each building."

"Excellent. A job well done," Reza replied proudly. "When you have Gould, bring him to *me*, in the broadcast center of the Parliament Building."

"Roger, sir."

Reza's mind recapped Priscilla's death. The moment he'd dreamt of for so long had finally come to fruition. It was time for Gould to die, by his hands.

Another set of screens off to the right showed blipping icons representing CDF vehicles. Waves of Guardian forces were being redistributed from the streets of Cornerstone to the Quad.

"Lower the ship into the shield generators' range," Reza ordered his helmsman, who sat at the primary control station.

"Yes, sir." Navigational instruments chirped.

The craft descended, then held a fixed altitude above the Parliament Building.

• • •

Inside the Chief's Manor, Arson and Sariah, encased in their Hardsuits, surveyed the bodies of unarmored Guardians they'd had no choice but to hurt. The four rebels in PCUs who were with them stood watch, their faces grim as they worried about the wounded.

A Guardian in battledress groaned, his side gashed.

Arson estimated the young man to be between eighteen and twenty-two. He deactivated his face guard and knelt beside him. "Here, let me help," he said gently. A syringe extended from his wrist. He plunged it into the Guardian's side, medicating the wound. "That should numb the pain and help you recover."

The Guardian murmured, "Why—" He coughed. "Why . . . are you helping me, *Arson Scott?*"

"Because I don't want you to die. I don't want *anyone* to die. You're just a man doing his duty."

The Guardian managed more words, the pain and bleeding slurring his speech. "If you don't want . . . anyone to . . . die, then wh-why the . . . invasion?" He coughed again.

"This operation had to happen, son. The central government is corrupt, and—"

Sariah cut Arson off, knowing now wasn't the time for talk. "Love, we have no time for this. We have to keep moving."

"You're right." Arson straightened and reactivated his face guard. "Stay alert and stay alive, everyone. Let's move." To the young Guardian, he said, "You'll be fine."

A rebel named Saul said, "I'll take point, Commander Scott." Holding an energy gun with a two-handed grip, he rounded a corner and ran straight into four unarmored Guardians. "Oh, shit!" He immediately retreated around the corner as bursts of machine-gun fire roared.

While in a crouch, he snatched his last stun grenade from his bandoleer and rolled it toward the Guardians.

It exploded in a bright blue flash, unleashing a paralyzing shock wave that knocked the Guardians unconscious.

"Clear!" Saul rose from his crouch.

Sariah said, "According to the building schematics, the next hallway leads to the Chief's office. Let's move."

Unshaken and unworried, Cornelius sat calmly at his desk with his fingers twined. His deadpan face showed no stress or concern. In contrast, Gillian, standing beside him, wore a look of helplessness.

Her worried eyes darted between the door and her mentor. In a low, uncertain voice, she simply said, "Sir?"

"We surrender and remain calm," Cornelius replied inexpressively. "Don't show them any fear."

Gillian nodded. "Yes, Sir." *How does he remain so dauntless in a situation like this?*

"Reinforcements will arrive soon, Juggernauts and more weaponry from Area 14. The CDF will eventually overpower the Coalition's invasion force."

The office doors blew inward. A veil of smoke drifted into the room. Arson, Sariah, and the four rebel fighters stormed inside, bringing their weapons to bear.

Cornelius got up from his chair, composed and unintimidated. He and Gillian lifted their hands in surrender.

Arson commed the assault ship as his men kept the two at gunpoint. "This is Scott to Reza. We have Gould."

Arson's headgear comm squawked. Reza replied, "Excellent. You know where to bring him."

"Yes, sir." Arson opened his face guard and pointed to two of his men. "Kaiden and Mateo, detain the woman with the surrenderees. Tend to their needs as best you can. If they need water or anything, take care of it."

"Right," Kaiden replied. He and Mateo each took one of Gillian's arms and led her out of the room.

Arson grimaced at Cornelius, disgust twisting his features. "See? We're not like you."

Cornelius chuckled. "Obviously. I don't start wars against my own people."

Arson spun on his heel. "Saul, Otto, bring him."

Saul strode up and jabbed the muzzle of his rifle against Cornelius' spine. "C'mon, dirtbag. Move."

"Sariah," Arson said, "I'm headed to the Parliament Building. I need you to stay here and take command."

"Roger that," she replied.

They exited the office.

•••

Inside the now-occupied Parliament Building, rebel fighters were unwinding. The energy dome produced by the shield generators outside had secured the perimeter, for now.

Stacie, in her sleeve, sat against a wall. Her hands were cuffed behind her back, and her eyes were closed. Randy sat beside her in his PCU. He also had his eyes closed.

Across from them, Jarius sat against the opposite wall, now out of his Hardsuit. He watched a newscast on his wristcom. The footage showed Juggernauts and more shelled Guardians surrounding the energy dome outside. The crawl at the bottom of the newscast said COALITION FORCES WIN FIRST ROUND: PARLIAMENT, ACADEMY, AND CHIEF EXECUTIVE'S MANOR OCCUPIED.

The camera drones of another newscast showed clandestine armed groups loyal to the Coalition's mission obstructing Guardians attempting to leave Eden's streets and reach the Parliament Building. These groups had long awaited this day, the day the Commonwealth Government would fall. Reza had counted on them to show, counted on them to be inspired and rise up.

Kesley came over to Jarius. Randy and Stacie's stillness gave her pause. "They asleep or something?"

Jarius shook his head. "Naw, suspended animation. They're just having a little heart-to-heart in a dreamscape, a reality generated by a cerebral implant."

"You Highborns and your fancy brain chips." Kesley plopped down beside Jarius. "Randy mentioned a Stacie. That her?"

"Yeah." Jarius cut off the newscast.

"So, what's their deal?"

"They're lovers deeply bonded by a Link."

Kesley raised an eyebrow. "He never said they were sweethearts, but I kinda suspected. Were things working out between them?"

"Yeah, they were, at least as far as I know. But now they're on opposite sides of the war. And to make matters worse, there's you. If you and Randy hadn't shacked up, I could've easily seen them continuing where they left off, if this war ends in some sorta consensus. But now, with you in the picture, their relationship is *really* on the fritz."

"Hey, I didn't make him do anything he didn't wanna do, and like I said, he never told me he was serious with anyone."

"Would you have still come on to him if you had known?"

A hesitant silence followed. "Like I said, I didn't make him do anything he didn't wanna do."

"Fair enough." Jarius glanced over at Randy and Stacie. *I wonder how things are going. Maybe they can patch things up. Then again, maybe they were two incompatible souls from the start.*

In the dreamscape, Randy and Stacie stood in an expanse of sand, under a magnificent sky of dreamy colors. Blue ocean waves crashed against the shoreline. The beach was a place they were both fond of. Randy had chosen the ideal backdrop for an attempted kiss-and-makeup session.

Stacie wore a greenish-blue one-piece swimsuit and a sheer sarong. Randy wore a white T-shirt and red beach shorts.

As the drama between him and Stacie unfolded, Randy said, "I'd do anything for you, Stacie. You *know* that. *Anything.* Even take a bullet. As for what happened with Kesley, I was frustrated, tired, angry, confused. You name it. I needed an escape. I needed to take my mind off everything. She's attractive, a temptation. My judgment was impaired, and . . . well . . . it just happened. I'm sorry I hurt you. It's not like I'm head over heels for her or anything." He hoped he could repair his damaged relationship with Stacie.

Stacie's emotions were feverish, to say the least.

Her eyes glowed. The air hummed, loud and shrill. Fragments of the dreamscape tore away, shattering into splinters. The rupture revealed a window into Randy's memory of his night with Kesley.

Kesley's high-pitched whimpers reverberated through the air, Randy thrusting into her.

"That looks like willful abandon to me," Stacie said.

Randy refiled the memory, and the dreamscape mended itself. Shamefaced, he bowed his head. "I'll do anything to make it up to you. You're the one I—"

"No. No more bullshit!" Stacie's volatile emotions quaked the dreamscape. "You want her? Fine. You want to be a rebel? Fine. I don't give a fuck." The world around them wobbled and shimmied. The beautiful beach scenery eroded into nothingness as the ethereal construct Randy had created deteriorated.

"Stacie, listen. I know I fucked up, but—"

"Enough!"

Darkness smothered them both.

Randy and Stacie opened their eyes, returning to the hall. Jarius and Kesley rose from the floor.

"You okay, Randy?" Jarius asked.

Randy said nothing. His expression gave the answer: no. Could he ever redeem himself in Stacie's eyes? He got to his feet and walked off. "I'll be back. Just need some breathing room." It was clear he'd get no forgiveness from his former lover.

Stacie shot a furious glare at Kesley. *Rebel bitch,* she thought, biting her lip.

"I'm gonna check on some of the others," Kesley said to Jarius, then walked away.

Now it was just Jarius and Stacie.

"Stace, you alright?" Jarius asked, concerned for his former sub-lead.

"What do you think?" Stacie's body ached from combat, her lover had been with another woman, and she was being held captive.

"Yeah, dumb question. Sorry."

"How, Jarius? How could you join them?"

Jarius took a breath. "I know it seems wrong, and I had doubts. But I think joining the Coalition for this operation is the right move. Believe me, I'm not happy about fighting Guardians."

"If you're so uncomfortable with fighting your own comrades, then why'd you join the Coalition and betray the Oath?"

Jarius leaned his back against the wall and crossed his arms. "Because . . . the shit we were taught wasn't right," he said thoughtfully. "The colonies need help. But that's not all. I was viewing some articles the central government didn't approve of, and the Nerve Center warned me to stop, like I don't have the right to view whatever the hell I want.

"Also, I'm pretty sure Lars was gonna blow me away just because I wondered if there was some legitimacy behind the CFP protesters' actions. You get that, Stace? I was gonna get blown away by my superior. Apparently, being a freethinker is a career killer in the CDF, *literally.*

"Now the Coalition's discovered that Gould has empathy-dampening modifications in the works for our implants, meant to keep us from feeling any regret for the people we kill. That's some scary shit, if you ask me. And that's not the future I want for the CDF. Hell no. Something had to be done, Stace, and the Coalition seemed like the answer. That's all I've got to say."

Stacie closed her eyes and withdrew into her thoughts, still unconvinced the Coalition's invasion was a good thing. She wondered how this standoff was going to end.

• • •

In the broadcast center, located on the top floor, Reza waited for Cornelius to be brought to him. From here, he could have the net filters overridden to release the corruption files and take over all vidcast transmissions, delivering his message to the entire Commonwealth.

A set of metal steps led to the upper-level deck of the room, where one of Reza's technicians sat at the operations console. He was ready to upload the corruption files upon Reza's command.

Patience wearing thin, Reza thought about Priscilla's death, bullets tearing into her body. He remembered reaching for Cornelius' throat, only to be held back by his cronies.

The reinforced metal door slid open. Two rebels in tactical gear escorted Cornelius in at gunpoint.

At last, the moment Reza had been waiting for had arrived. "So, we meet again, Cornelius."

The Chief's posture remained calm and composed. He had survived countless wars and battles; no masked man or barrel aimed at his back could shake his fortitude. "So, I assume we've met, before you decided to hide your face," he said dryly.

"Yes, we have," Reza replied.

"Who are you?" Even in captivity, Cornelius spoke demandingly.

"You'll know soon enough. But first, the Commonwealth must hear the truth about you and your corrupt colleagues."

Cornelius drew his eyebrows together. "What the devil are you talking about?"

Reza said nothing more. He stepped onto the cylindrical pedestal protruding from the floor and signaled the technician to begin the vidcast.

The eighteen-year-old keyed a command on the console.

Above, a dome-shaped installation bathed Reza in a pillar of light. The Commonwealth's net orbiters in space broadcasted his image and voice to every watchable device on Eden and Satellite One.

The technician gave a thumbs-up. "Uplink is green. You're live, sir."

"Citizens of the Commonwealth, I am Arman Reza, leader of the Coalition of Rebel Factions." Reza gave another hand signal. The technician pressed the yellow "send" button. "On the net, you'll now find evidence revealing the true nature of many of your elected leaders. Some members of the Parliament are good men and women; others are among the most vile people to ever hold office. They have forged insidious deals with Eden's wealthiest class, the Eight Elite.

"The Eight are more than just businesspeople expanding their enterprises throughout the cosmos. They're a criminal syndicate. That's why we, the Coalition, have taken control of key government buildings: to oust the scum who degrade our republic and keep colony citizens under the thumb of oppression. Go online. Access the files. See the truth for yourself.

"I encourage all Guardians who abhor these corrupt politicians to lay down their arms and allow a new government to rise."

All across the Commonwealth, people were accessing the leaked files.

Reza continued. "I will take the reins of government to enact the change we so desperately need. As for the unfit, their time is over. Judgment begins now, with Cornelius Gould." He gestured to the two rebels flanking the Chief.

"Move," one of them ordered, shoving Cornelius forward.

Cornelius' frown deepened. The two rebels forced him up onto the pedestal and into the transmission beam, both of them training their weapons on him.

Reza slowly reached for the pistol holstered at his side and brought it to the back of Cornelius' head. "Do you feel fear, like Priscilla Kitzron did?" he asked, voice colder than death.

Cornelius said, "I have no idea what the hell you're talking about."

"Years ago, in Colony Four, there was a miners' strike. Guardians shot and killed a woman. Her name was Priscilla Kitzron. She was my lover. And I was the Guardian who barged into your office that day."

Reza had jogged Cornelius' memory. "You? You're Arman Reza?"

"Yes, *me*." His anger compounding, Reza pressed the gun harder against Cornelius' skull. "And you weren't contrite in the least. Even now, you show no remorse. You're truly a soulless human being.

"People like you should be erased from existence. You're responsible for Priscilla's death. And you allowed defenseless Falgoah to be slain in cold blood for no reason. No reason at all!"

Reza's mind resurrected images of the destroyed Falgoah village. Then a montage of treasured times with Priscilla blinked through his thoughts. With her death about to be avenged, he wondered if she was smiling down on him from Heaven right now.

He heard her voice whisper, *Finish it, my love.*

The gun barked once. Cornelius' body thunked to the floor, his blood sprinkling everywhere. Reza fired three more rounds into the corpse, his own scream transforming into a ragged sob.

Shell casings tinkled across the floor.

Reza dropped to his hands and knees, the gun slipping from his grasp. He dragged air into his lungs and exhaled. *It's done, Priscilla.*

Priscilla's ghostly, translucent incarnation materialized in front of him. *You did it, my love. Let your mind be at peace now.* She faded away, blowing a kiss.

The technician's heart flew into his throat. *Public executions? This isn't right.*

"Sir, are you okay?" one of Reza's men asked him.

Reza's voice regained its strength. "I'm fine." He stepped back onto the pedestal, standing beneath the transmission beam. "Citizens of the Commonwealth, I am your new leader for the foreseeable future. I will be the one to shape this republic into what it was always meant to be." He kicked Cornelius' dead body. "Not this piece of trash. And the other corrupt officials, now in custody here in the Parliament Building, will be next to face justice."

A disturbed expression crossed the technician's face. This wasn't the plan. The Coalition was supposed to hand power over to a transitional government and let the judiciary system try the corrupt officials fairly. Reza had promised to collaborate with the new government and the Commonwealth's people to achieve a win-win for both worlds. Instead, he had just declared a dictatorship.

• • •

Arson had met up with Randy, Kesley, and Jarius in the hallway. The four of them were watching the livecast on the tablet Arson held.

Arson scowled and flung the tablet against the wall. Reza was supposed to help usher in a new government, not take control. There weren't supposed to be any public executions. Judgment was supposed to come from the courts, not the barrel of a gun. And now, Reza had made himself judge, jury, and executioner. Tyranny wasn't what the Coalition stood for. It wasn't what Arson Scott stood for.

So much for the Coalition's idolization of Reza, Randy thought. "I knew it," he said bitterly. "I knew there was something shady about him. He's just another hypocrite, another authoritarian hiding behind a cause."

Stacie, still sitting restrained, pinned a scalding glare on Randy. "Well, Randal, how does it feel putting this autocrat into power?"

"Enough, Stace. I don't have time for a verbal sparring match. We need to figure out how to fix this mess."

"Oh, *whoop-de-do*, now you have to clean up the shitstorm *you* rebels created."

Randy frowned. "You're acting like a child again."

"*Again*? What the hell are you talking about?"

"Yeah, *again*, like when you—"

"Hey, you two," Jarius cut in, "save the melodrama for later. We've got bigger problems."

Kesley chimed in. "Well, I can't say I'm not glad that lunatic is dead." She shrugged, palms up. "And if those corrupt Parliament scum, who kept us colonists in the gutter, end up in front of a firing squad, so be it. Suits me just fucking fine."

Randy chided her, saying, "No, Kess. That kind of senseless brutality is exactly what the Coalition was fighting against. And I didn't join the Coalition just to put another nutcase in power."

Jarius, hearing Reza's voice continue, grabbed the tablet from the floor. Its screen was cracked but still working.

Reza said, "Even as I speak, my knights are infiltrating the estates of the Eight's family heads, bringing the sword of justice to them as well."

Stacie gasped. "My parents!" She looked up at Randy hard-eyed. "And you—who I let touch me, make love to me—helped put this murdering piece of garbage in power, who just sent his bozos to my family's doorstep to murder them. Damn you, Randal Scott."

Kesley showed no sympathy for Stacie. "Yeah, well, maybe your mommy and daddy shouldn't have been a couple of crooks."

"Cut it out, Kess!" Randy shouted. "I know you've suffered under the government, but what Cornelius is doing is wrong."

"Randy's right," Arson said, his voice stern. He had known nothing about the kill squads. Reza had made plans in secret, behind his back and the backs of all the Coalition's commanders. So much for transparency and trust. "Reza's changed. At some point, his heart darkened. This isn't the man I believed in."

Chin lowered and lips sealed, Kesley felt regretful and embarrassed.

Stacie sat in silence, tears beading down her cheeks. Her relationship with her parents had never been perfect, but she had never wanted them dead, not even after all of her mother's parental cruelty, or their illegal dealings.

Good memories surfaced: her mother cradling her as a child, fun outings during her teenage years, warm family dinners where life lessons were passed down with sincerity and care.

Randy's heart ached for Stacie. This wasn't how things were supposed to turn out. He reached out to her cerebrally, only to find she'd terminated their Link. Undeterred, he sent a new Link request, hoping to reestablish their rapport. She rejected it, slamming the door on their relationship. It was far too early for any reconciliation, if there could be any at all. The hurt was still raw, too deep-seated inside her.

No, Randal, you don't get to have access to me, Stacie thought. *You can keep your rebel playmate.*

Arson opened a door to a conference room and gestured. "Randy, Jarius, Kesley, in here, now."

Randy spoke to Stacie softly. "Hey, don't go anywhere."

Stacie refused to make eye contact with him. "Not like I could leave without getting caught." It was true.

Randy followed Arson, Jarius, and Kesley into the room.

As they entered, motion sensors activated the overhead lights. A square crystalline table, surrounded by ten chairs, dominated the modest space.

"So what are you thinking?" Jarius asked Arson. He rested his nervous hands on the back of a chair.

"I didn't join the Coalition to put some tyrant in power." Arson felt duped. "I respected Reza and his vision. But somewhere along the line, he let power get to his head. He's not trying to work with the people or the uncorrupt officials to build a new Commonwealth. He wants to impose his own order. He's become just like Gould and Ritter, and men like that are dangerous."

"So, what, we become the Four Mutineers and take him out?" Kesley asked.

"*Yes*," Arson replied definitively. "If we don't, the fighting's only going to continue, and more young men and women are going to die. Reza was supposed to release the files and call for peace, to end this homicidal insanity. I don't want to see *anyone* else lose their life: Guardian, rebel, Highborn, colony-born . . . *no one*."

Jarius scoffed. "After we take him out, then what? The battle ain't gonna stop just because he's dead, and it's only a matter of time before the CDF figures out a way to knock out the shields. Both the CDF and the Coalition are gonna fight for their respective sides until the bitter end. The bloodshed is only gonna continue, right here on Eden soil, unless—"

"Unless we get what we want, *reformation*," Arson finished for him. "An armistice needs to be agreed upon."

Randy joined the conversation. "So once Gould's dead, who's next in line for the Chief Executive seat?"

Arson replied, "That would be the chairperson with the next highest ranking position to the Secretary of Defense, the

Chancellor of the Supreme Judiciary, Oviereya Amaechi. And we've got her here, being held with the other Parliament members in their meeting chamber."

"Okay," Jarius said, "Oviereya, as Chief, would represent the Commonwealth, but who'd represent the Coalition in this truce negotiation?"

For Arson, that was an easy answer. "Me." He was Reza's top commander, unquestionably the number-two man of the entire Coalition.

Randy thought, *In other words, the right people on both sides finally get into power.* And both were originally colony citizens.

Arson said, "Alright, we've got a plan. Let's put it into motion. Randy, come with me. We're going to get Oviereya and bring her back here to this room."

Randy was more than ready to end the war. "Let's do it."

Arson and Randy left the room, stepping back into the hallway.

When Randy heard Stacie whimpering, he paused. Tears streamed down her face.

Concerned, Randy said, "Hey, wha-?" He saw the tablet Jarius had left beside her. Onscreen, Reza was broadcasting images of the slain family heads, proof of execution sent by his kill squads. Among the dead were Patrick and Darlene Spencer. "I . . . I'm sorry, Stacie. If there's—"

"Just leave me alone," she choked out, sniffling and sobbing, mucus dripping from her nose.

"I—"

"Son, come on," Arson said sharply. "She needs space. Let her grieve."

Damn it, Randy thought. *How'd I let things get this messed up between us?* He turned away as Stacie cried loud and hard.

Side by side, rifles slung, Arson and Randy moved down the

hall and came to a single guard posted at the chamber doors.

"I need Oviereya," Arson said insistently.

"Yes, sir." The guard opened the door. All too easy.

Arson and Randy went into the spacious meeting room. The guard held the door open behind them.

The chairpersons sat around a glass-topped round table.

Despair was thick in the air.

Staying in character, Arson leveled his rifle at Oviereya. "Chairwoman Amaechi, get up and come with us."

A burly chairman at the far end of the table frowned. "Arson Scott. The infamous deserter comes home to—"

"Quiet!" Arson snapped. His eyes didn't leave Oviereya. "Chairwoman Amaechi, I need you to comply."

Without a word, Oviereya rose from her swivel chair and rounded the circumference of the table toward the father-son duo.

Arson grabbed her arm roughly, pulling her forward. She trailed behind him, stumbling to keep pace. "Move it." As they exited the room, he said to the guard, "Thanks. Keep up the good work."

Arson's compliment made the guard proud. "Yes, sir."

Walking back toward the conference room, Arson stayed behind Oviereya, rifle trained on her back. Randy walked beside her, rifle at the low ready.

In the hall, rebels exchanged quiet thoughts about Reza's new course of action, some agreeing with it, others not.

"Executing people isn't right," a man said.

A woman with rainbow-colored hair replied, "Who the hell cares? Those officials are scum. Reza's just cleaning house."

Divisions were already forming within the Coalition.

Oviereya whispered to Randy, "You're Randal Scott, Stacie Spencer's boyfriend and son of Arson Scott, yes?" She gave him a sidelong glance. "I understand why you joined the Coalition. A lot of young men and women defect after seeing how colonists live." Randy marched forward in silence. "I'm sorry the war has reached this point," Oviereya continued. "My fear is that it's spiraling toward a senseless, all-out massacre. Perhaps there's still a way to prevent that from happening, to finally—"

"Agreed," Randy said. "Believe it or not, my father and I are on the same wavelength as you."

What does he mean? "Where are you taking me?"

"To a conference room where you and my father can work something out in private to end this war. You're both now the de facto leaders of the opposing forces."

Oviereya looked flummoxed. "But Reza is still alive, isn't he?"

"Not for long," Randy replied bluntly.

They reached the conference room door.

Stacie still sat on the floor, her eyes full of grief. Jarius stood near her. The second she saw Oviereya, her heart brightened—during what was otherwise a dark time. "Oviereya!"

Oviereya met her gaze compassionately. "Stacie, I saw the vidcast. I'm sorry. I know you and your parents were often at odds, but I also know you valued the wisdom they passed on, and the ways they tried—however flawed—to shape your life. I'm grateful Darlene allowed me to be her midwife. And I'm honored your parents trusted me as your caretaker. I—"

Arson interrupted. "There'll be time to catch up later." He opened the conference room door. "Chairwoman, Randy, inside."

Before going into the room, Oviereya reached out to Stacie through their long-established Link. *<Stay strong.>*

<I will,> she replied.

Arson, Randy, and Oviereya entered the room.

"Please sit," Arson said amicably to Oviereya.

Oviereya pulled out a chair and sat down at the table. Arson and Randy took their places opposite her.

Arson kicked things off. "You already know who I am. Reza's changed, and not for the better. We never wanted a dictatorship. My son and I are going to stop him. But once that's done, the fighting won't just magically end. I'm proposing a ceasefire so we can work out an action plan. All the Coalition wants, Chairwoman Amaechi, is equality."

Oviereya gave a solemn nod. "Arson Scott, you have my word. Once Reza is dead, we'll make a plan for colony progression."

Randy said, "And what about the other chairpersons, the ones not tied to corruption? Are they going to back this plan? Most of them still cling to AEGIS's blueprint for humanity. Honestly, they're a bunch of spineless conformists."

Arson replied, "Anyone in Parliament who's hesitant to restructure the oppressive systems born from that damn computer will have to make a choice: peace or more war. And I *guaran-damn-tee* that if any of them resist, the Coalition will keep fighting. I'll lead that fight myself if I have to. But we're trying to give peace a real shot. After Hammer Fall, the Parliament should be smart enough not to blow this opportunity.

"Chairwoman, once we've dealt with Reza, we'll take you to the broadcast center. Together, you and I will call for a ceasefire."

Oviereya longed for the war to end. "Agreed."

Arson left the chair. "Alright then. Randal, let's go. Chairwoman, please stay here."

Randy and Arson exited the room into the hall.

"Things on track?" Jarius asked.

"Yeah," Randy confirmed.

"Where are you two headed now?"

"To take care of Reza," Arson answered.

Stacie said nothing.

Arson and Randy took an elevator to the top floor.

"Any idea of how we're going to pull this off?" Randy asked.

Arson held up his rifle. "Yeah, we blast him."

Randy, always the planner, said, "What if we're outnumbered by a security detail?"

"There's no time to account for every variable. We'll just have to adapt to whatever situation we encounter."

The elevator hissed to a stop, and the doors slid apart.

They approached the broadcast center. The building was secure, but Reza had expected potential dissent from rebels unhappy with his new direction, so he ordered that three guards be posted at the door.

"We're here to see Reza," Arson said.

"Hand over your rifles," the lead guard ordered. "No weapons are allowed inside."

Shit, Arson thought. *There goes option one.*

He and Randy surrendered their rifles. The other two guards patted them down thoroughly. One pulled a small blade from a hidden sheath in Arson's boot and stared at him incredulously, waiting for an explanation. There went option number two.

Arson said, "Sorry, oversight. I forgot I had that."

"Alright, you're clear, Commander Scott," the lead guard said.

The guards stepped aside, and Arson and Randy entered.

Reza sat at a metal desk, which had been brought from another room. "Arson, Randal, what brings you here?"

Randy said to Arson, *<Other than Reza, there's one guy on the control deck. Not sure if he's armed. What now?>*

Arson's eyes locked on the pistol holstered at Reza's side. *<I'm going for his gun. Just back me up.>*

<Gotcha.> Randy glanced at the big red square on the wall

panel, the emergency lock for the room. Once activated, no one could open the door from the outside without the passcode. *<I'll trigger the lock when it's time. That'll keep the guards out.>*

Arson stepped up to Reza. Randy stayed by the door.

"What's going on, Arman?" Arson asked. "The Coalition's ethos is based on the principles of life, respect, and proper conduct. Not death and domination. What you're doing—taking control, choosing who lives and dies, building a government without public input—is wrong."

Reza rose from his desk and placed a hand on Arson's shoulder. "You're a noble man, my friend. I understand your discomfort. But trusting Satellite One's future with others is too risky. I have to be the one to forge the new republic."

"This will only divide the Coalition. It already is."

"If—"

Now, Arson thought. He reached for the pistol, but Reza was faster. He captured Arson's wrist in an ironclad grip.

"So you chose to betray me," Reza said, mask hiding a disappointed expression. His grip tightened in anger.

Reza, strength enhanced by the cybernetic implements he wore over his arms, lifted Arson with both hands and hurled him into a metal rack. The equipment on its shelves scattered.

"Damn it!" Randy palmed the big red square button on the wall panel, locking the door.

"What's going on in there?" one of the guards shouted from the other side.

The technician wondered whom he should back. His conscience began to tilt toward Arson and Randy.

Randy lunged at Reza, tackling him. They hit the floor, wrestling furiously. Randy ended up on top of Reza, hands clamped around his throat.

"Get off me, fool!" Reza slammed an elbow into Randy's face and knocked him off.

As soon as Reza got to his feet, Arson lunged at him from behind. They tumbled across the floor.

From the control deck, the technician made a split-second decision. He tossed his energy gun down to Randy. "Heads up!"

Randy glanced up and snatched the weapon from the air with a one-handed grab, a feat of hand-eye coordination only an enhanced human could pull off.

Arson and Reza scrambled back to their feet, still trading blows.

Randy took aim. "Dad, move!"

Arson dove out of the line of fire, and Randy pulled the trigger. An energy blast roared from the gun's muzzle, blowing a simmering gap into Reza's chest.

His blood showered the floor as his body fell.

Randy breathed raggedly. *It's over.*

Arson said to the technician, "Thank you. What's your name, son?"

"Arwen. Arwen Dukes," he replied.

"Arwen, you made the right call today."

"Yeah, I didn't become a freedom fighter to help a dictator take over the Commonwealth."

• • •

Inside the broadcast center, Oviereya and Arson stood shoulder to shoulder on the pedestal, under the beam of the relay transmitter above.

Oviereya began the address. "Guardians of the Defense Force, Chief Gould is dead. Though I would've preferred he face trial, I do not mourn him. With his death, I now serve as your new Chief Executive. I am ordering you to stand down."

Arson then spoke. "Coalition rebels, Reza betrayed us. He no longer represented our ideals. My son and I did what had to be done. The war is over. Oviereya and I, as respective leaders of our combat forces, have agreed to a ceasefire."

The rebels and Guardians outside stood down. The energy shields around the Parliament Building, Academy, and Chief Executive's Manor flickered off.

This day marked the advent of a new dawn for the Commonwealth.

CHAPTER NINE

DAYS AFTER HAMMER FALL

In the Chief Executive's Manor, Chief Executive Amaechi sat at the table of the master stateroom with the other Union leaders. Each wore a translator earpiece.

ZorKeld said, "We have reviewed your summary of recent events and reached a decision. The Commonwealth may keep its incorporated status. We have high hopes for you, Chief Amaechi."

Days of worry lifted from Oviereya's shoulders. "Thank you," she replied. "The Commonwealth will live up to the mandates of the Union Charter, ensuring equality for all its people and no more bloodshed."

From Durgraso came a skeptical snort. "It had better."

Ziltilda, clad in a garment of crisscrossing brown leather straps and a spiked choker, spoke. "I believe there is nothing more to discuss." All the Union leaders rose. "Good luck, Chief Amaechi, we will be watching the Commonwealth's progression closely." With an ice-cold edge to her tone, she added, "Very, *very* closely."

As the others departed, Queen Pappalonie, looking glamorous in her jewel-studded bodysuit, approached Oviereya. Her bracelets and anklets jangled. She wrapped her arms around the new Chief. "Let me know how Taramassia may help, if needed."

Oviereya nodded silently.

After everyone had left, she sat at the table, pondering. There was a long road ahead. Healing the divides would take time.

Many Edenites questioned why the central government was being subservient to "terrorists." They resented the idea of letting the rebel fighters walk away scot-free. In their eyes, the rebels deserved punishment for starting an "unnecessary war" and bringing violence to Eden soil. They also didn't like that a colony-born Chief had taken power, fearing she might act against their interests.

On the flip side of Oviereya's dilemma, there were colonists who had unrealistic expectations of the central government.

She'd have to calm the irrational fears of Edenites and earn their trust. At the same time, she would need to show resolve to her own people, some of whom believed that, with a colony-born Chief in power, all their demands would be granted swiftly. Even with all troops recalled from the formerly occupied colonies, tension remained high. If progress took too long, another wave of unrest could follow.

Yes, Oviereya loved her people, but she wouldn't bow to every demand, especially those that were currently beyond the realm of possibility right now.

Besides the pressure of having to remain neutral and satisfy both colonists and Edenites, Oviereya also faced anxiety from not knowing how the upcoming elections would turn out.

Judges would try the corrupt politicians, and special elections would determine their replacements. However, Oviereya predicted that most of the open seats would likely be won by candidates with the same mindset as their predecessors, due to Edenites fearing a colony-born Chief and colonists being outnumbered at the polls.

As for next year's election for her own seat, she knew her opponents would use the deaths of Guardians and Edenites' fears about a colony-born Chief as talking points and political attacks. She had no illusions that her victory was guaranteed.

No one had ever said that leading a post-civil-war Commonwealth would be easy, but she was determined to rise to the challenge.

She sighed and left the room. It was time to travel to Zelaforia for a meeting with the Noshkanu High Council regarding the return of the Falgoah to their land.

•••

Stacie swam through the huge outdoor pool behind her villa, which was nestled in lake country and enclosed by a white picket fence.

In the tranquility beneath the water, her mind quieted, finding relief from the pain of her parents' death. But unease and confusion continued to gnaw at her. She had killed rebels, rebels who may not have been the villains she believed them to be. Yet weren't they responsible for the war, and all the bloodshed that came with it? She had only followed orders. But whose orders? A corrupt government, no more virtuous than the insurgents it condemned? The constant need to justify the war and the lives she had taken was tormenting.

She longed to leave the past behind and move forward with her life. Thankfully, the CDF provided excellent mental health therapists for Guardians struggling with the psychological aftermath of the war. If she needed their services, she'd go.

At the alert dong of her front-door sensors, she bobbed to the surface of the pool. Then she swam to the edge and pulled herself onto the deck.

The sunlight made the water on her naked body glisten, accentuating every muscle and curve.

Her wet feet slapped against the dry walkway as she headed to the back door. Suddenly, her waterproof wristcom vibrated. It was her estranged lover, trying once again to rekindle what they had. She brushed aside the damp blond strands clinging to her forehead, looked down at her wristcom without emotion, and pressed the "dismiss" button. *Give it up, Randal. You're in my rearview mirror now.*

Inside her home, she slipped into a velvet robe, left open down to her navel and closed at the waist with a cloth belt tied in a knot. The skin-pleasing diaphanous material showcased the attractive silhouette beneath.

Wearing slippers, Stacie crossed the hardwood floor of her living room and opened the front door. Her unannounced visitor was a man dressed in a navy-blue suit and black top hat, his grizzled beard framing his wrinkled face.

"My name is Gerald Remington," the man said in a British-sounding accent. "I was your parents' financial custodian."

Stacie leaned against the doorframe, arms folded. "And?" she said impatiently. She was ready to get to the point of Mr. Remington's visit so she could return to her leisure.

"Your parents' will bequeaths their entire fortune and all of their assets and possessions to you, Madam Spencer."

It took a moment for Stacie to register Gerald's words. "Me?"

"Yes, their millions of G-credits, their homes, vehicles—*everything*." He held out a datapad. "I just need your signature." Without hesitation, Stacie pressed her thumb to the device. "That's it. The transfer is complete."

"Um . . . thank you."

"If you need my services, Clifton knows how to reach me. Have a good day." Gerald descended the short set of phyocrete steps.

Stacie went back to her living room. She sat on a sofa and crossed her legs. "Coffee," she said to her housekeeping golem. The ovoid-shaped hover bot brought her a foam cup of her favorite brew, made from Satellite One's best beans. She took the cup from its pincers. "Go complete the rest of your chore log." The golem burbled in response and floated away.

Stacie raised the cup to her lips. Had her parents meant to leave everything to her, or had they simply been killed before removing her from the will? Nonetheless, she had claimed her birthright. She'd gone from princess to pauper to queen, queen of the Spencer fortune. Irony.

As she sipped her coffee, she made a decision: She'd buy herself out of her contractual obligation to the CDF and use her wealth to help others, as wealth should be used. She was sure the other seven families' heirs would take control of their parents' criminal empires and continue their corrupt legacies. She had no intention of letting that happen.

An idea had come to her days ago, to assemble her own private combat team to thwart the other seven families. Now, with her parents' fortune, she finally had the means to turn her idea into reality.

She already had potential recruits in mind, Guardians she'd served with, including Jason Mansford. If they were willing, she'd buy out their contracts from the CDF so they could join her mission.

She took another sip of coffee and smiled. She'd be the start of a new era for the Spencer family name.

• • •

Randy and Arson were at Kathleen's grave.

Arson stooped and set down a bouquet of colorful flowers, then rose to his feet. Moisture welled in his eyes. "I love you, my dear. I'm sorry for what I did. I love you with all my heart."

Randy placed a comforting hand on his father's back. "She knows."

Arson wiped away a tear. "So, how are you holding up?"

Randy's inner turmoil was reflected in his face and voice. "I . . . I've been having disturbing dreams about the battle. They wake me at night. Killing Guardians who were just upholding the Oath hurts, no matter how few. It doesn't matter if it was five hundred or five. And just when you think the pain is gone, it boomerangs right back. It . . . lingers in your mind."

Some of the casualties might've been bigoted thugs, like the Guardian who tried to rape Kesley, and Randy felt no sympathy for them. But there had been no way to tell them apart from well-intentioned Guardians who were simply miseducated—raised in a system that told them they were superior to colonists—and had their biases reinforced by CDF doctrine.

Just like Randy, grief hung over Arson like a storm cloud. "Well, all I can say is we did our best to preserve as many lives as we could.

"I know it won't make the pain go away, but the central government was responsible for the war, just like the Union leaders said. The blood is on *their* hands. They're the ones who oppressed the colonies, attacked the RUC, and declared martial law. If you try to beat someone to a pulp, they're going to fight back. The *government* was the reason armed dissidence happened."

"Yeah, true," Randy said in a melancholic tone.

"How is Jarius holding up?"

"We're all grappling with psychological scars from the war, but Jarius is strong. He'll overcome this, just like the rest of us who endured the fight."

Arson nodded. "Too often, the collateral damage of war is the soldier's mind." Getting emotional, he paused to compose himself, then changed the subject. "So, what's next for you, Son?"

Randy sighed, clearly worn out. "I'm taking a break from military life." He needed a respite from bloodshed. "I promised Kesley I'd show her around, take her for a ride in my sports cruiser. Maybe we'll go on a road trip."

"And Stacie?"

"I've tried calling. She won't answer. I guess our relationship is really over. If I could fix it, I would. But who knows, maybe a miracle will happen and she'll give me another chance. We'll see."

"They say time heals all wounds."

"What about you? Where are you off to now?"

"I'm going back to Colony Four to help my people in any way I can."

"Sounds good."

Arson held out his hand. "It's been great working with you, Son."

Randy grasped his hand, shook, and then pulled him into a heartfelt embrace. "I love you, Dad. Take care of yourself."

They released each other.

Arson said, "I'm proud of the man you've become, Randy. Your mother would be too." He began walking down a gray stone-block path, unaware of the unseen threat that had him in the crosshairs of a rifle.

As Randy watched his father leave, he said, *<Aunt Wells, I know you're there. Come out and put the rifle down.>*

Merriam stepped out from behind a tree, a sniper rifle slung over her shoulder. *<He needs to die, Randy. He needs to pay for my sister's death.>*

Randy saw everything he had been in Merriam's grimace. He saw pure hatred for his father. <*No. My mother—your sister—wouldn't want him to die. Her death was an accident.*>

Merriam's blood ran hot.

Randy said, <*Let go of your hate. Conquer the rage, like I had to. Stop being selfish and think about what Kathleen would want. Besides, Chief Amaechi exonerated all Coalition fighters of any war crimes. If you pull that trigger, you're murdering an innocent man. Is that something you want on your conscience?*>

Merriam's teeth chattered. <*Damn it.*> She stomped off, thoughts swirling. *These traitors cannot just go free. Someone needs to set things right.* She wondered whether she should challenge Oviereya in the coming election.

Randy went to his sports cruiser, climbed in, and started the engine. The vehicle hovered into the air and glided away from the cemetery.

At last, he felt relief now that the war was over.

End

About the Author

Michael J. Brooks holds a BA in Art and an MFA. He is a member of the Independent Book Publishing Professionals Group (IBPPG), and his first novel, *Exodus Conflict*, was a finalist of the 2013 Next Generation Indie Book Awards, in the sci-fi/fantasy category; earned honorable mention from the 2013 London Book Festival, in the science fiction category; and received five stars from *Readers' Favorite*.

As he currently tries to balance his busy life in Washington, DC, he seeks to write fiction novels which are not meant to be only entertainment but to address some of the most crucial issues of our time and explore the trials of being human. He hopes to create characters that people can relate to and stories that will have an impact on them long after they are finished reading one of his novels.

Contact Michael J. Brooks at: authormbrooks@gmail.com

Follow Michael J. Brooks on Twitter at: @AuthorMBrooks

www.authormbrooks.com

REPUBLIC UNDER SIEGE

Threat from Within

By Michael J. Brooks

Wars of the New Humanity

Book Two

About this Book

Content Warning

Republic Under Siege: Threat from Within is an action-filled science fiction book that contains violence, strong language, and detailed scenes of lovers making love.

Content Meter

Medium

Low   **High**

2025 Edition

You are reading the 2025 edition of *Republic Under Siege: Threat from Within*.

2025 edition

Praise for
Republic Under Siege:
Threat from Within

"The second book in the sci-fi series Wars of the New Humanity combines elements of thriller, social inspection, and sci-fi to produce a riveting, refreshingly original story . . . packed with moment-by-moment reactions to pain, surprising twists and turns, and journeys towards healing and revised destinies. Libraries seeking solid sci-fi replete with social and psychological inspections that move from the aftermath of world-changing war into the motives and experiences of young people who would forge new lives and worlds will find the social inspections in *Republic Under Siege: Threat from Within* compelling. It will attract a wide age range, from young adult to adult readers. Ideally, book clubs will also consider *Republic Under Siege: Threat from Within* for its many enlightening moments about the kernels of social change as individuals experience healing, transformation, loss, and novel opportunities."
—D. Donovan, Senior Reviewer, *Midwest Book Review*

"Memorable characters, passionate prose, riveting action, graphic combat scenes, and steamy romance make this technothriller a standout read for new adult audiences. Brooks deftly explores social justice themes related to misogyny, racism, classism, and the balance between revolutionary ideals and maintaining functioning governmental systems while keeping his audience thoroughly entertained with the characters' intertwined conflicts, romantic liaisons, and destinies."
—Kate Robinson, *The US Review of Books*

"Brooks's prose serves the story well, with action scenes powerfully resonating on the page. Interesting questions as to what makes actions that bring about change morally right or wrong are delved into, adding an interesting twist to this sci-fi dystopian tale."
—*The BookLife Prize, 2022*

"**Thoroughly captivating, ingenious, and full of heart-pounding tension.** Brooks has created a richly imagined world . . . The riveting storyline, plus plenty of jaw-dropping action scenes, keep readers on the edge of their seats. Solid and addictive; a SF thriller done right."
—*The Prairies Book Review*

"Michael J. Brooks is a show and tell writer, which I could see right from the beginning of the story, as the scenes were so vivid. Through this story, Michael J. Brooks reminds us that there are consequences to the choices we make and that we can fit in somewhere, no matter who we are or where we come from."
—*LitPick*

"The writer [Michael J. Brooks] excels in describing the resilience of the oppressed. *Republic Under Siege: Threat from Within* is one of the best sci-thrillers that I have read. It is a well-written and awesome book full of action and unpredictability. I recommend others to buy a copy."
—*LitPick*

"It [the book] was an action-packed entertainer till the end."
—**Fangirling Over Frappes, a *Reedsy Discovery* reviewer**

Glossary

(nonalphabetic order)

Earth Era: the era of humanity before intergalactic migration from Earth

Commonwealth: humanity's star nation consisting of four planets—Eden and satellites One, Two, and Three

Eden: humanity's utopian motherworld inhabited by three-fifths of the human population

Satellite One: humanity's dystopian secondary world inhabited by two-fifths of the human population

Advanced Exascale Global Information-collection System (AEGIS): the AI computer system created during Earth Era to divide humanity between Eden and Satellite One

Satellites Two and Three: vacant worlds belonging to the Commonwealth, used for military training exercises and mineral excavation

Edenite/Eden citizen (synonymous terms): human beings living on Eden, whether born on the planet or during Earth Era

Highborn: a moniker referring specifically to human beings born on Eden

Colonist/colony citizen (synonymous terms)**:** human beings living in the colonies of Satellite One, whether born on the planet or during Earth Era

Commonwealth Defense Force (CDF)/Defense Force (synonymous terms)**:** the Commonwealth's military force

Guardian: a soldier in the Commonwealth Defense Force

Cadet: a Guardian in training

Shell: a mechanized, armored combat suit used by Guardians

Commonwealth Government/central government (synonymous terms)**:** the governing body of the entire Commonwealth, which includes the Parliament and Chief Executive's Office

Republic of Unified Colonies (RUC): the republic formed by colonies One, Four, and Six after they declared sovereignty from the Commonwealth

The Three-Week War: the war initiated and won by the Commonwealth Government to reclaim colonies One, Four, and Six after they declared sovereignty from the Commonwealth

The Coalition of Rebel Factions/the Coalition (synonymous terms)**:** a coalition of rebel factions formed by the remnant fighters of the RUC to continue combating the Commonwealth Government

The Quad: the Chief Executive's Manor, Parliament Building, Supreme Judiciary, and Defense Force Academy, on Eden, which are situated in a Quadrangle in the middle of Eden's capital, Cornerstone City

Operation Hammer Fall: the Coalition's operation to invade the Quad, commandeer the Parliament Building and use its broadcast center to cast files exposing government corruption across the net

The Battle of the Quad: the historic battle between the Coalition rebels and CDF Guardians during Operation Hammer Fall

The Interplanetary Union: the intergalactic alliance consisting of the Commonwealth and planets Ghanrax, Dhalgratt, Varsh'Ru, Zirkran, Rumanoah, and Taramassia

****The [   ] symbol represents translation from a character's native language****

Author's Note

In *Republic Falling: Advent of a New Dawn* (Wars of the New Humanity, book 1), humanity is divided between two worlds. The first is Eden, a utopian paradise and the motherworld of the New Humanity's intergalactic republic, the Commonwealth. The second is Satellite One, a dystopian world that serves as the Commonwealth's resource hub. The colonists of Satellite One exist primarily as resource harvesters, essentially government laborers. They live in colonies with subpar conditions and are denied the technological luxuries available to Eden's citizens. By design, they occupy the bottom rung of the Commonwealth's socioeconomic hierarchy.

However, the Commonwealth's immigration lottery system offers colonists a chance to escape their circumstances and live on Eden. Those selected become "immigrants"—ironically labeled, considering they are already citizens of the Commonwealth.

For *Republic Under Siege: Threat from Within* (Wars of the New Humanity, book 2), I asked myself, What happens when someone is transplanted on Eden with hopes and dreams, only to face continued marginalization under a class system? That question gave rise to the character of Akane Sugimori, a nineteen-year-old immigrant introduced in the book's prologue.

To tell Akane's compelling backstory while advancing the present-day adventure, which picks up where book one left off, I structured the narrative with chapter interludes. These interludes transport readers back to Akane's immigration journey, chronicling how she arrived at where she is presently. The story follows a rhythm of present-day chapter, then interlude, and so on.

While Akane is essential to the plot, I was careful to ensure she didn't overshadow our main hero, Randal Scott. At the same time, I continued to advance the arc of Stacie Spencer, who is now Randy's ex.

In the previous book, Randy left the Commonwealth Defense Force (CDF) to side with the colonies' Coalition of Rebel Factions, an alliance he initially saw as nothing more than treasonous insurrectionists. After the Coalition executed their trump card, Operation Hammer Fall, they succeeded in opening the door for colony and immigrant equality.

Now, with no Coalition fighters being prosecuted for war crimes, Randy returns to the CDF branded a pariah, and it seems Akane is one of the few Guardians he can trust. Or can she be trusted?

Akane tries to recruit Randy, one of the colonies' liberators, into what appears to be a social-activist organization fighting for immigrant equality. Thanks to the chapter interludes, readers get to witness how Akane herself was recruited, as she leads Randy through a parallel experience. But there may be far more to this organization than meets the eye.

In many ways, Akane became the linchpin holding the story together, and I hope readers will enjoy following her journey as much as I enjoyed writing it.

Republic Under Siege delivers the same thrilling gunfights and mechsuit battles featured in *Republic Falling*, though the setting has shifted. The last book unfolded during a brutal war; this one takes place in the war's aftermath. It's more of a techno-thriller than a war story, but it continues to explore the themes of rebellion, classism, discrimination, and more. Enjoy!

Intro

"I've been marginalized by an oppressive government system, by a system designed to keep people like me down. But I decided to fight back. You may not approve of my methods, but I really don't give a damn."
—*Akane Sugimori*

PROLOGUE

BEFORE THE THREE-WEEK WAR

Planet: Satellite One
Colony Three
Immigrant Departure Station
(Receiving Area)

Lucky, *damn* lucky. That's what eighteen-year-old Akane Sugimori was. There were colonists who'd kill to be in her shoes. She'd scored the opportunity to untether her future from a destiny of grueling labor—an opportunity to rise beyond a dour life of second-class citizenship. To no longer be lumped with the "lesser" of humanity was a privilege, one that was nearly unattainable.

Eden, the utopia of humanity's intergalactic republic, the Commonwealth, awaited her. So why the fuck was she down in the dumps? This was a dream coveted by nearly every denizen of Colony Three.

Clad in denim shorts, fashionably ripped fishnet stockings, and a black crop top, she sat Eden-bound on the frontmost bench in the receiving area of Colony Three's immigrant departure station, mood somber.

Arms clenched around herself, she tapped the heel of her sneaker boot against the floor in a nervous staccato. She loathed every second that ticked by, waiting for her citizen registration number (CRN) to be announced over the intercom. Soon, her undesired voyage to Eden would begin.

She dreaded being torn away from friends and family. Who would she laugh, dine, and share the pain and pleasures of life with? As inferior to the motherworld as it was, Satellite One would *always* be home in her heart.

To her left, Dad. To her right, Mom. Benjiro and Akari Sugimori were loving parents who'd made substantial sacrifices for her well-being. She wouldn't *dare* ask more of them. They had worked tooth and nail to give her the best upbringing possible. Toiling in the caverns and agricultural fields of Colony Three as government-employed resource harvesters—or, to some, government serfs—was no easy job.

Akane had caused her parents' blood pressure to skyrocket more than once, secretly working the black-market commerce system at age sixteen to ease their burdens. Peddling hard-to-get luxuries to residents of Sector 07 had come with serious risk.

Migrants from former Japan populated the sector, earning it the name NeoJapan. They had preserved their language, culture, art, and history in the era of the New Humanity, during a time when colony selectees had banded together for survival and community, resulting in the emergence of assimilated cultures.

Due to her devil-may-care attitude, Akane had to admit she deserved the scoldings she got from her parents. But, especially now that she'd graduated into adulthood, the obstinate youth refused to let anyone, even Mom and Dad, police her individuality.

Her attitude, mouth, and parent-disapproved fashion choice, right down to the pierced navel, were staying put.

As Akari and Benjiro each anchored an arm around her to console her, she couldn't help but wonder: Was she swapping one hell for another? She knew how to survive in this hell. The new one? Not so much.

She'd heard stories of colony immigrants, lottery beneficiaries like herself, having their once-bright dreams crushed by the harsh realities of life on Eden. The Commonwealth Government had proclaimed the planet a haven of peace, comfort, and prosperity, but Eden's high society, it seemed, wasn't receptive to certain groups of people. Immigrants were issued ten thousand living credits and expected to survive with minimal support or transitional assistance. Even so, for many colonists, Eden citizenship was the prize of a lifetime.

Two staff members walked by. One had blue hair, and the other had brown.

The blue-haired one said, "I betcha some colonies are gonna declare independence soon."

"And ignite a war with the Commonwealth Government? Doubt it. That'd be a stupid move."

After overhearing the two men, Akane glanced at each of her parents. "[Do you guys believe the rumors? Do you think some colonies might actually declare independence and form their own republic? If a civil war starts, you could be at risk. What if—?]"

Benjiro said, "[Don't worry about us or what's happening in the colonies. Your future is on Eden.]"

"[And what if I end up like so many others?]"

"[You won't,]" Benjiro replied confidently. He had faith in his daughter.

As the two staff members headed for the exit, the brown-haired one said, "Can't wait to get back to Eden. I'm tired of this shithole colony already."

The blue-haired one replied, "The immigration lottery's only once a year. Someone's gotta do these temp assignments."

"Yeah, hopefully it's not us next year."

"Registrant C-Nine-Eight-Eight-Seven, proceed to Decon to prep for boarding," a young woman said over the intercom. "I repeat, proceed to Decon."

Scrolling across the wall's massive info display: C-9887 REPORT TO DECON.

Akane ran a fidgeting hand through her short, unruly black hair. *That's me.* Depressed about separating from her parents, she was on the verge of tears.

Two men in their early twenties and a woman Akane's age sat four benches behind the Sugimori family. They were dreamers, anticipating a wondrous life on Eden.

The young man with short auburn hair wore a sleeveless white hoodie and blue jeans. The other had neck-length jet-black hair and was dressed in a T-shirt and cargo pants. As a devoted Mercedes Gardner fan, the woman wore the pop star's T-shirt paired with magenta palazzo pants. She had even styled her platinum-blond hair in pigtails, just like Mercedes often did.

Waiting to be called to Decon, the trio regaled each other with friendly banter and stories of their childhood. The woman was the bubbly one—always smiling, animated gesticulations, laughing often, voice bursting with optimism.

The Sugimoris stood. Akane's chin tilted downward, and her shoulders sagged. She was *so* not feeling this moment.

Akari tenderly framed her daughter's melancholy face with small hands calloused from intensive labor. "[We'll miss you, Akane. But this is your day, a special day. Be joyful.]"

Be joyful? Inside, Akane was crumbling to pieces. *Easy for her to say.*

Benjiro placed a soft, comforting hand on Akane's shoulder. Like her mother, he'd often worried about where and with whom Akane spent her spare time. Much of it had been consumed by socializing with youth outside NeoJapan. She'd adopted non-native behaviors and a non-native patois from her social excursions.

Rebellious since childhood, she only grew more defiant of all authority—parental or otherwise—over time. Tell her not to do something and she'd do the opposite. But because of her rebellious nature, she had become a strong, resilient young lady.

Benjiro was beyond happy for her, and it showed in his wide-set eyes. "[We are proud of you, Akane,]" he said. "[A new life awaits you on Eden, a *better* life. There will be hardships to overcome, of course, but you will persevere.]" Street-smart, resourceful, and armed with exceptional survival skills, Akane knew how to weather tough times, how to roll with life's punches. "[As soon as we're permitted travel passes, we'll come see you.]"

Memories of parental love and affection bum-rushed Akane. "[Thanks, I love you guys.]" She sniffled and bit her lower lip. "[And thanks for putting up with all my harebrained mischief.]"

Peeved, the woman on the intercom repeated herself. "Registrant C-Nine-Eight-Eight-Seven, report to Decon *at once*. What the hell are you doing?"

Akari kissed her daughter's tear-slick cheek. "[We love you too. Now off you go.]"

Akane wiped her glassy eyes with the back of her hand. She snatched her hot-pink backpack from the floor, the cartoony skull on the back fading with age, and slung it over her shoulders. Her main luggage had already been loaded onto the shuttle.

She took off running toward the lone terminal before the

intercom lady could get even more livid. Looking back, she caught one last glimpse of her parents. Who knew when she'd see them again? She waved a tearful see-you-later.

Vision poor from laboring in health-hazardous subterranean caverns, Akari watched her baby girl fade into a blur. A lump of sadness swelled in her throat. *May good fortune smile upon you wherever you go, my daughter.*

The next traveler was summoned over the intercom. "Registrant C-Six-Five-Five-One, report to Decon. I repeat, report to Decon."

"That's me!" the woman with pigtails exclaimed. Überexcited, she bolted from the bench.

Midway down the terminal, Akane encountered a towering, bulbous woman clad in an all-white uniform.

The woman's pudgy, pockmarked face twisted into a scowl of pure detest.

I guess she would be the boarding proctor, Akane thought. *Why the hell couldn't her lazy keister come escort us?*

The proctor wasn't going to fetch the beneficiaries from the receiving area herself. No way. She was an Edenite, on duty; "nadir" had to come to her.

"Call me Ella," the huge woman said in an inhospitable tone. She glowered at the petite eighteen-year-old in front of her. "I'll be your boarding proctor, *pissant.* Do everything I say, and keep your *stinking* mouth shut unless spoken to." Her thick lips expanded into a wry grin. "And don't do anything that might *tick* me off, unless you'd like your Eden citizenship registration revoked. Which, honestly, would make my day."

Geesh, what bug crawled up this fucking asshole's pants? Akane's brows drew together. She subdued the impulse to cuss out Ella.

Ella's forehead creased. Her demeanor radiated the irrepressible enmity harbored in her soul. She despised that yet another "nadir" had been granted access to the upper echelon of the New Humanity. In her eyes, "nadir" belonged here on Satellite One, the New Humanity's resource hub, as nothing more than resource harvesters.

In a belittling timbre, Ella said, "Please acknowledge understanding, registrant C-Nine-Eight-Eight-Seven." She didn't even deign to use Akane's actual name. To her, Akane was nothing more than a CRN.

"Yeah, I gotcha." Akane stayed cool, even though she wanted to go the fuck off. "You won't get *annnyyyy* trouble from me." She was eager to get away from this doofus and get the joyride to Eden underway.

The bubbly blond woman moseyed up, her stride carefree.

Ella's saggy features twitched, and her lips pursed. "Hey, Ms. *Lah-di-dah*, quit dragging your feet!" Startled, the woman tensed up and froze. "Move! Put some pep in your step!"

A flutter of nervousness eclipsed the woman's sunny disposition. "Uh . . . coming right away, ma'am!" She kicked her pace up to a jog and brought herself to a halt in front of Ella.

Ella studied the info displayed on her tablet. Then she swung her hard gaze back up at the blond. "Registrant C-Six-Five-Five-One, Skylar Grace. Correct?"

The woman nodded quickly. "Yes, ma'am," she replied, her usual pep gone. She was more reserved in the proctor's menacing presence.

The two young men who had sat with Skylar in the receiving area rushed up.

Ella checked her tablet again. "Registrant C-One-Seven-Nine-Two, Jacobi Johnston."

"Here," the auburn-haired man replied.

Next, Ella read, "Registrant C-Zero-Eight-Nine-One,

Desmond Castillo."

"That's me," the black-haired dusky-skinned man said, loud and proud.

Ella clipped the tablet to her oversized belt. "Alright, follow me," she ordered. "I'm taking you to Decon so you can disinfect. Don't want you nadir contaminating the motherworld."

Jacobi frowned at the slur. *Nadir? Butt-ugly snob.*

The proctor and her group of beneficiaries veered left into another corridor. Like this entire government facility, it was flawless, squeaky-clean, and sterile, unlike the outdated, lackluster structures common on Satellite One.

Jacobi wandered closer to Akane, encroaching on her personal space. "*Psst*, hey, what's your name?"

His proximity made Akane cringe. "Why?" she replied flippantly. Coping with the pain of leaving behind her friends, family, and everything familiar, she wasn't in the mood for conversation.

Jacobi offered a polite shrug. "We might as well get acquainted. We're all on the same journey, right?"

"All mouths are to remain closed, Mr. Johnston," Ella snapped, shepherding the group forward with a slow, lumbering gait. That was Jacobi's warning shot. Next time, she might not be so merciful.

Jacobi went silent. *What a bitch.*

One-third of the way down the corridor, there was a set of doors to the left and another set to the right.

Ella barked instruction. "Gents, that way." She pointed left. "Ladies, that way." She pointed right. "Once inside, you'll receive further guidance. *Make sure you follow it to a tee.*"

Why do we have to get "decontaminated" like we're infectious, diseased rodents or something? Akane wondered. Well, she had no choice but to comply.

Akane and Skylar stepped into the ladies' Decon. Twelve compact examination pods, connected to a series of pipes, were built into the spheroid wall of the white nondescript space.

The doors whooshed shut behind them, and a disembodied artificial voice said, "Welcome to Decon. Extract all apparel and place it in deposit bins for sterilization." Two rectangular bins ejected from wall lockers. "After discarding apparel, proceed to the sterilization pod of your choosing."

Akane dropped her backpack on the bench in front of the bins, and she and Skylar began unlacing their footwear.

After tugging off her high-tops, Skylar turned to her new traveling companion, sporting a sweet smile. Time to bond. "So, what's your name?"

"Akane." The drab way she answered sent a clear message: She wasn't happy and didn't give a crap about schmoozing right now.

Skylar jerked her shirt overhead and dumped it into deposit bin zero-one, uncovering a silky pink bra.

Squeamish about undressing in front of strangers, Akane blushed and shyly eased her shirt up over her head.

"Why so glum?" Skylar inquired. "We're headed to Eden. We're headed to *paradise*." She spread her arms wide on "paradise." "I hear it's a lot like Earth." Born after Earth Era in Colony Five, she'd never laid eyes on humanity's lost homeworld. She had only seen imagery of its former glory, from a time before Armageddon devastated its environment.

Akane discarded her shirt in deposit bin zero-two, along with her backpack. "I'm just . . . not sure how things are gonna shake out. I mean, what are the odds of us immigrants actually . . . you know, prospering on Eden?"

Skylar threw a monkey wrench in Akane's skepticism, spieling some truth. "Oviereya Amaechi became a Chairwoman of the

Parliament and Chancellor of the Supreme Judiciary. Arson Scott became one of the Commonwealth's most revered war heroes. He earned the pinnacle of military commendations. Arson and Oviereya were able to adapt to Eden culture, overcome hurdles, and shatter barriers.

"Anything's possible, Akane." With bravado, Skylar pumped her fist. "*Motherfucking* anything." She flicked a hand dismissively, as if fanning away the doubt percolating in Akane's mind. "Come on, girlfriend!"

Akane had a tendency to expect the worst. It was her way of shielding herself from disappointment. But that reminder, the reminder that colonists such as herself had risen to prominence in the Commonwealth, elicited a small hopeful smile from her. Albeit small, it was still a smile—a sign she wasn't all doom and gloom.

"I guess there is hope for us, huh?" Akane said thoughtfully.

Skylar punched a fist upward. "Yep!" she chirped. Her animated body language practically screamed "now that's the spirit!"

While the two finished undressing, they shot the breeze, and Akane gradually loosened up. Fully unclothed, they approached the pods, bare feet quietly slapping the spotless floor.

Akane, following closely behind Skylar, cast a quick glance down at her own slender frame, then up at Skylar. Her cheeks burned with envy and admiration as she noted how Skylar's hips jutted out from her narrow waist.

Akane thought Skylar looked like a supermodel. Her fine bone structure, cute heart-shaped bottom, and ample breasts made her a jaw-dropper. And all of it was one hundred percent natural. No black-market body mods.

Self-conscious about her own straight-figured frame, Akane couldn't help but compare. *Why is her bod so fucking perfect?*

Everything about Skylar's body made Akane retreat inward, from the radiance of her skin to the subtle bounce of her curves, both front and back. Not to mention those magnificent legs, which seemed to go on forever. She was a work of art come to life.

The two entered neighboring decontamination pods, ending Akane's bout with her insecurities.

"Initiating sterilization sequence," the automated guide notified them.

A cylindrical vat in the room gurgled to life, releasing a cool chemical mist into the pods through the spinning applicator mounted to their ceiling.

Skylar pivoted toward Akane's pod, pressing her hands against the glass. She was so excited about going to Eden that her sapphire eyes gleamed. "So, whaddya think having our brains modded with a cerebral implant is gonna be like?" She raised her peppy voice over the loud hissing mist gusting against her skin.

Akane pursed her lips, eager to get out of this glass chamber thing and not in the mood for "shower talk" with a hyperactive woman who couldn't stop running her mouth for one second. Not how she thought preboarding would go. Life was so unpredictable.

She replied, "You're able to . . . do some mental Bluetooth thing. Link, that's what they call it, right? Sync your mind with someone else's. Hear their thoughts. See their memories. Experience their emotions. Become one with someone and all that jazz." Her muscles coiled as she imagined Linking minds with someone. "*Souunnnddds* kinda fucking creepy, if you ask me."

"*Nuh-uh*," Skylar said. "Linking is supposed to be a gateway to deepening relationships. It's a way to bond, to form closer ties and expand your cognitive awareness of another person's innermost feelings." In a sultry "Oh, I can't wait!" kind of tone, she added, "A way to manifest an extraordinary sex life too."

Akane's shoulders gave Skylar a "meh."

Skylar sighed. They were talking about one of humanity's greatest technological breakthroughs, and all Akane could offer was a lukewarm reaction?

The unending mist continued to swirl around them, cleansing away foreign bacteria, microbes, and parasites.

Skylar kept the conversation going. "So, what's your goal in life, Akane?"

Akane blinked slowly, as if she were confused. "Huh?"

"You know, the thing that motivates you. That gives you a sense of purpose. That gives you the will to wake up and deal with the muck of life day after day. The thing *you* feel is your reason for breathing."

My ikigai? Akane thought, then replied, "Right now I'm just focused on keeping my head above water and steering clear of trouble on my soon-to-be new homeworld."

"You've gotta aim high, Akane. If you don't know your purpose yet, find it. Me? I'm destined for *stardom*. I'm gonna be a famous singer, like Mercedes Gardner!"

Mercedes was famous alright. The entrancing sound of the pop star's vocals had captivated audiences across Eden and Satellite One. She had also performed on Mission Worlds to boost the morale of Guardians deployed on planetary-impact missions. And her vids usually racked up millions of views.

Akane lifted her eyebrows mockingly, finding it hard to believe that Edenites would embrace an immigrant superstar. *Yeah, right.*

Skylar's expression hardened. She was sick of Akane's pessimism.

Her tone shifted to something not so friendly, a departure from her usual bubbly self. "I know what you're thinking. You're thinking that's a lofty goal for an immigrant, right?" The rising aggression in her voice warned Akane that her bleak outlook had struck a nerve. "You think I should take a step back and conform to reality, isn't that right?"

Akane kept her mouth closed, listening quietly. She didn't want to further piss off her traveling companion.

Skylar's face tightened more. "Friends have told me the same stupid thing. They think I'm some zany airhead, a fucking birdbrain, or ditsy. But it's the conformists who stay content being doormats for the Commonwealth Government. Prosperity seekers like *yours truly* become trailblazers."

Akane heard her mother's words of encouragement echo in her mind: *"Remember, Akane, even the most herculean feats can be conquered."* Her parents had raised her to never cast a shadow on anyone's dreams.

"You're right. I'm sorry," Akane said.

Skylar's features instantly unkinked, softening. "No prob, girlfriend. We're good."

The mist finally stopped. Next, a gelatinous decon chemical lathered them from head to toe. Thirty seconds later, a shower of water rinsed it away. Then the drying cycle activated. After that, the pods' three metal rings spun, emitting purple X-ray beams. A chirp from the medical sensors declared them healthy for travel.

Decon completed, Akane and Skylar retrieved their clothes from the deposit bins and dressed.

Exiting the doors, they saw Ella, Jacobi, and Desmond waiting for them. Ella proceeded to lead the group to the ship hangar, where a single passenger carrier was docked.

The beneficiaries hurried up the boarding ramp, relieved to at last part from their crude, mean-spirited chaperon.

A bulkhead separated the cockpit from the passenger compartment, giving the group privacy. There was seating for up to twenty-five people, so the cabin felt spacious for just four.

The pilot, a woman wearing the standard orange jumpsuit, wrapped up her launch checks and spoke over the intercom, sounding cheerful. "Alright, ladies and gents, this is Deloris, your pilot speaking. We are a go. Sit back and enjoy the ride."

The roll-up hangar door reeled open, and the shuttle rolled out onto the tarmac. Its propulsion system powered up. Engine cycling from a low purr to a high-pitched whine, the shuttle climbed into the sky, giving the group a sweeping overhead view of the colony.

Jacobi stared through a porthole, an aggrieved look in his eyes. A hodgepodge of stacked tenements, small living pods, dilapidated MHUs, and rusting girders of long-unfinished structures— promised to be completed years ago—shrank into specks as the surface grew distant.

A montage of childhood memories flooded his mind. He remembered his parents talking about sitting in auditoriums of resettlement centers as children, government hubs designed to assimilate colonists into the New Humanity's socioeconomic framework, a framework crafted by the Advanced Exascale Global Information-collection System—AEGIS.

The centers' "indoctrination" programs prepared colonists for their roles in society. They were told being resource harvesters was an honor and that the New Humanity rested on their shoulders. The programs conditioned their minds to accept second-class citizenship, an attempt at social engineering. Megascreens displayed images of the lush metropolises to come; Satellite One was supposed to replicate Eden eventually. The Commonwealth Government filled colonists' minds with hope.

After the Phazharian and Bhalkran wars, the Commonwealth Government led the colonists to believe the financial toll from those wars was why the vision promised hadn't come to fruition yet. It was the reason they had to tolerate years of insalubrious living conditions. In actuality, colonists were victims of systemic degradation.

Jacobi turned red just thinking about the squalor of impoverished zones in his sector, colonists' cries for equality discredited by the government and the media. The government seemed to always control the narrative.

The colony labor force was keeping the Commonwealth afloat. They harvested invaluable resources that ensured humanity's star nation remained a thriving republic. *We're the lifeblood of the New Humanity,* Jacobi thought. *But we're treated like spokes on a wheel. We're told our purpose is to be manual laborers for the government and megacorporations.* This was his chance to stick it to the system designed to keep colonists at the bottom of the socioeconomic ladder. This was his opportunity to be the maker of his own fate and honor his mother.

The fatal infection his mother had contracted from the toxins in the mines she had worked in doomed her to a premature death. He watched his emaciated, bedridden mother wilt away, intubated to a shabby life-support system in an underfunded intensive care ward. Mrs. Johnston had wanted her only child to live a life of abundance. Obtaining Eden citizenship was Jacobi's chance to make that life a reality.

As the shuttle emerged into space, its hull juddered.

Skylar sat by a window, stargazing in amazement. *Holy fuck, outer space!*

Akane lounged back in her recliner, her hands resting behind her head. She pondered what trials awaited her on Eden. Knowing a lot of suck was in store for everyone aboard, she'd suggested that

Skylar temper her excitement, but nothing seemed to dampen the jolly optimist's enthusiasm.

Jacobi walked over to Akane's seat, hands tucked into his hoodie's pockets. "Hey, Akane, what's the first thing you're gonna do when we get to Eden?" He was obviously trying to lure her into a social chat.

"Dunno," Akane replied in a barely audible, flat tone.

As someone who'd envied lottery beneficiaries, Jacobi was angered by Akane's apparent lack of appreciation for this golden opportunity. She should've forfeited her lottery win and let a more grateful entrant take her spot, he thought. Scads of admittance factors, some as minuscule as physical and mental disabilities, disqualified colony selectees from Eden citizenship. Some selectees simply didn't meet the IQ requirements. To maximize the human race's survival probability, only the best of it was meant to inhabit Eden. Yet Akane, one of the privileged few who had secured Eden citizenship, was acting all petulant.

"Well, you don't seem all that thankful for this fortunate position we've lucked into," Jacobi said. "This is our chance to no longer be pigeonholed to a lifetime of marginalization. What gives?"

Akane sat upright and went on the defensive, facial expression intense. "Listen, pal, my parents prayed for me to win Eden citizenship, and I intend to honor them. But I'm a realist. That's all. I'd rather serve myself a dose of reality now than psych myself up for major disappointment.

"So, yeah, just because I'm not jumping through the roof right now doesn't mean I don't value this opportunity. I'm just a down-to-earth type of girl. Now stick a fork in it. Beat it."

"I see." Jacobi backed off and took a seat beside Desmond across the aisle.

"So what's up with her?" Desmond aimed a thumb in Akane's direction. "Why is she such a grinch?"

"Hey, I heard that, you jerk!" Akane shouted.

"Sorry!" Desmond bellowed. He then lowered his voice to a whisper. "Why is she so moody?" he asked Jacobi.

Jacobi dropped his volume to "covert level" as well. "She's just trying to stay level-headed. And I get it. Things will probably get worse for us before they get better."

"Hey, you guys talkin' about me?" Akane yelled over at them, suspicious.

"Uh, no, not at all," Jacobi replied. *Geesh.*

Desmond shifted the conversation. "So, what's your dream, man?"

"Knowledge excites me. I want to enroll in one of the universities. I want to study abroad on other planets and commingle with different races, then take that knowledge and do some good." Wanderlust and enthusiasm held Jacobi in their thrall.

"You're the scholarly type, huh?"

Jacobi shrugged. "I guess so. What's your dream?"

"I'm gonna join the Commonwealth Defense Force, enlist in the Land Combatant Corps."

"A friend of mine, a lottery beneficiary, told me the physical challenges at BCT are supertough, as one can expect. But then immigrants like us have to deal with bigoted drill sergeants on top of that. You ready?"

Desmond's overconfident smirk suggested he was beyond ready. "All fine by me, brother. I live for a good physical challenge. It gets me thrilled. And I play all sorts of contact sports in my sector. A buncha prick drill sergeants aren't gonna intimidate me." Desmond liked to get rowdy, roughhouse, and loved weapons. Knowing their son well, his mother and father supported his decision to join the CDF. They thought it was a good career choice for him. "Yup, the military's where I belong, bud."

"Well, you've certainly got the drive. I'll say that much. I'm sure you'll do well."

"Thanks." Desmond's eyes glanced to where Skylar was sitting, behind Akane. Usually extroverted and energetic, she'd finally run out of juice and was now sound asleep. And Desmond found the sight of a peacefully sleeping Skylar adorable. "Hey, just so you know, I got dibs on Skylar."

Jacobi laughed. "You can have at her all you want. I'm not auditioning for 'boyfriend' for either of those two."

"Is that why you keep prowling around that Oriental chick?"

A flush crept into Jacobi's complexion. "It's not what you think. My interest is *strictly* platonic."

Desmond's internal lie detector went off. "Yeah, right, sure it is," he said archly. "Tell me you're not jockeying to get into her underpants."

Jacobi tried to hide the fact that Akane's presence quickened his pulse and set butterflies loose in his stomach. "I'm not in pursuit of anything beyond cordial relations, my friend."

"Uh-huh. Liar."

Her body overtaken by lassitude, Akane closed her heavy eyelids. Thoughts of her parents and the looming possibility of civil war swirled in her mind. Then sleep finally claimed her.

The hull vibrated, and shifting patterns of multicolored light gleamed outside the windows as the shuttle transitioned into Hyperspace Leap.

"Akane, wake up! Wake up, Akane!" Skylar hollered.

Akane groaned tiredly as a pair of hands rocked her from her slumber. She awoke to the sight of Skylar leaning over her.

Akane's mouth turned downward, and her features pinched at Skylar's annoyingly chipper smile. She was on the brink of shoving Skylar to the floor. "What is it, damn it?" She sounded pouty.

Exuberantly, Skylar replied, "We're close now! It's almost time!"

Akane rubbed the grogginess from her eyes. "Really!" Her heartbeat raced.

Skylar retook her seat, her whole body on edge. This was it, the day she'd been waiting for. At last, she was going to see Eden.

"Eden inbound," the pilot reported over the intercom. The planet's single green-and-brown continental landmass grew closer on her viewport screens. A countdown blinked on the console. "Atmospheric entry in three . . . two . . . one."

Piercing Eden's atmosphere, the shuttle rattled and began its descent. It soared above sublime towering feats of architecture, while surfing the turbulence stirred by headwinds.

Conical, pyramidal, and domed edifices with shining windows blurred past, along with other structures alien to a colonist.

Akane leaned into the starboard window, plastering her palms against the glass.

She watched colorful flyers dart over the solar-paneled roadways, amid masterworks of engineering constructed of glass, metal, and phyocrete. "*Holllyyyy* fucking shit!"

The clean-swept surface below teemed with activity. Tiny figures of pedestrians strolled across or rode slideways. They entered and exited a mélange of shops and restaurants.

In awe, Akane trembled. *This is incredible!*

Exclamations broke out from the group. Fingers pointed at this and that.

The shuttle streaked past golden spires spearing the sky. After five more minutes of flight, it decelerated, banked downward, and leveled off smoothly. Its undercarriage repulsors fired as it began a steady vertical descent, touching down on the outdoor landing deck of the immigrant reception station just outside Myrtle City.

The engines gave a final gasp before falling silent. Cooling metal creaked in the hush that followed.

The pilot pressed the intercom button. "Ladies and gents, your trip has come to an end." A panel of blinking instruments dimmed, and the viewport screens showing the outside went dark. "You may now disembark."

The fuselage's door unsealed, and the boarding ramp extended onto the airstrip to let everyone off the shuttle.

The beneficiaries walked down the ramp into the brilliance of a cloudless sky and vivid sun.

A burly, fully bearded porter was unloading their luggage bags from the storage hold—four duffle bags that could be worn on the back or carried using their straps. "Hurry up. Come get your stuff so we can get moving," he barked.

The beneficiaries collected their luggage and followed the porter to a white commuter van.

"My name's Finnegan, by the way," he said as he climbed into the driver's seat. "I'll be dropping you off at Central Square. You can find lodging there and just about anything else you need."

Skylar slid into a window seat. Akane claimed the spot beside her. Across from them, Jacobi and Desmond settled into the same row.

Finnegan input the destination into the van's onboard navigation system, letting autodrive take the wheel.

As the autonomous van made its way to Central Square, throngs of men and women bustled through the city. There were no dirt roads, compact row homes, living pods, and stacked tenements here. The contrast between Satellite One and Eden was stark, like night and day, heaven and hell. On Satellite One, there were no aerial vehicles, and colonists didn't have any of the technological boons that Edenites took for granted.

The van purred to a stop at a red light in the entertainment district. Skylar's starstruck eyes stared at the giant hologram of Mercedes Gardner projecting from a skyscraper's roof. The superstar's ginger hair cascaded past her hips.

That's gonna be me. I know it! Skylar thought.

Skylar pictured scores of fans screaming her name as the concert's MC introduced her: *"Without further ado, the one you've all been waiting for, Skylarrrr Graaccceeee!"*

The van jerked into motion, giving the beneficiaries a rolling view of a strip mall.

High-end storefronts of haute couture infected Skylar with the shopping bug. One sign said OUT-OF-THIS-WORLD GLAM CENTRAL. Another said SO-FINE GALAXY APPAREL. The stores' window displays exhibited extraterrestrial fashion.

Skylar's intrigued eyes twinkled. "Tomorrow, you and I *have* to come back here, Akane."

"*Uh*, shouldn't we be preserving our *credits*?" Akane's brow furrowed.

"Aw, come on, don't be a spoilsport. We've got like four to six months' worth of living credits. And this isn't some backwater world. This is Eden! It won't take us long to get on our feet, not in the land of milk and honey. Live a little, Akane."

"Well—" Akane was close to caving.

Skylar playfully nudged Akane's shoulder with her knuckles. "Oh, don't be a party pooper!"

Akane finally relented to peer pressure. "Okay, fine, but let's not go overboard tomorrow."

"Cool! A girls' day out tomorrow! Yaasss!"

Akane shook her head derisively.

It took only seconds for Skylar to dive back into conversation. "So, have you given it more thought: your purpose, your life mission?"

"My people often refer to it as ikigai. And no, I haven't. I'm focused on staying off the street and making sure I don't go hungry. I'll worry about my *purpose* later."

Skylar offered some unwanted encouragement, ignoring Akane's nonverbal cues, which clearly expressed her irritation with the subject—the facial tics, mashing of her lips together, and grinding of her teeth. "Don't worry, you'll find it," Skylar said.

Akane grunted. She wasn't concerned about finding "it" right now.

The van hissed to a halt at the beneficiaries' destination, Central Square. "This is the drop-off point. Good luck to ya," Finnegan said.

The van's doors unlocked and slid apart to release the beneficiaries into the hustle and bustle. Once everyone had gathered their luggage and exited, the van hummed away.

The city's pristine condition amazed the beneficiaries.

Myrtle City, like other metropolises on Eden, boasted high air quality, spotless streets, and first-rate housing. Not even one building was run-down. The city provided idyllic living.

Skylar watched sanitation golems sweep, scrub, and sterilize streets, slideways, and building windows. "Cool, robots!"

She darted toward a storefront display, drawn in by the flashy apparel. Her foot stepped onto a sensor panel beneath the window, and a colorful cyclone of eye-catching pop-up holos burst to life around her—a swirling three-dimensional showcase of skirts, pants, blouses, and lingerie.

Her eyes glittered with fascination as they flitted left and right. *Superfucking cool.* She tapped the advertisement graphic in one of the floating frames. Instantly, the dress in the advertisement shot out and wrapped itself over her body in a projection of light. She was wearing the hologram over her clothes. "Holy shit."

The holowords BUY NOW circled her head.

Jacobi stared, stunned. It was unlike anything he'd ever seen.

Skylar stepped off the sensor panel, and the entire holographic brochure dissolved, along with the outfit she'd been "wearing."

Desmond canted his head skyward. Above the eateries, boutiques, and corner stores were glass-walled balconies of ultramodern living complexes, and there were tiers of open-air walkways connecting towering retail centers.

Citizens were in high spirits. They seemed carefree, laid-back, and easygoing, unencumbered by the hardships colonists faced. And suicides caused by depression were virtually nonexistent.

Akane had never been gullible enough to view Eden through rose-colored glasses, and now the city's glitz and glamour were wearing thin. The honeymoon was over. Reality had reared its ugly head—exposure therapy. She and her new friends had been transplanted into a world of technology and culture they knew nothing about. They had to fend for themselves and claw their way up the broken rungs of the ladder of immigrant success.

Young Highborn fashionistas, clad in garish smartwear, strutted past Akane. They spoke in unfamiliar jargon while operating wristcoms, playing sim games on gamecom pads, and using other gizmos Akane couldn't even name.

A suffocating feeling welled up in her chest. She felt like an Earth Era relic, light-years behind the curve on mankind's technological evolution, and she felt so uncultured.

Anxiety tightened her muscles, and the pit of her gut churned.

Her fear response was to flee back to Colony Three to cower inside its refuge. But the daughter of Benjiro and Akari Sugimori was no wimp. She steeled her composure and drowned out the voice of weakness in her head.

Eden was her home now, and she'd confront her discomfort and fears head-on. She was going to honor her hardworking parents, who wanted nothing more than to see her flourish on the New Humanity's motherworld.

Curious eyes scrutinized the beneficiaries. Some people stared with repulsion.

Though the beneficiaries were part of the Union's human community too, they were foreigners on this world, and they stood out like a sore thumb—the way they moved and dressed was telling.

Two women walked past Akane, hand in hand. They wore matching attire: light-up miniskirts, short tops that exposed their flat midriffs, and ankle boots. Floating helper golems followed the couple, lugging their overstuffed handbags.

To Akane, this world felt surreal, like a dream.

Questions arose in the back of her mind. What would she and her new friends do for employment? How long would their credit vouchers last before they hit rock bottom? How could they connect with other lottery beneficiaries?

Blithely unconcerned about the severity of their situation, Jacobi, Skylar, and Desmond stood amid a tide of humanity, frissons of excitement prickling their flesh. They saw intergalactic tourists and day-trippers, wearing language translators around their necks, commingling with humans. While the sight was commonplace for Edenites, it was alien to colonists.

People chatted beneath pedestrian shelters, waiting for air-cabs. Teenagers riding hover scooters laughed. Land vehicles honked. Flyers roared overhead. Roads and air lanes buzzed with moving traffic. So many sounds. So much activity.

As her friends soaked in the city's energetic atmosphere, Akane thought, *This is where life kicks you in the ass and gives you a major wake-up call.*

CHAPTER ONE

PRESENT DAY

Star Palace (space station)
Specialist Randal Scott's Cabin

The warm, soothing mix of pristine water and chemical relaxant sluiced from the shower jets, soaking Randy's golden-brown hair and cascading down his well-built frame. He exhaled, relief washing over him as his melancholic mood began to subside. Pressing his palms against the sleek tiled wall, he leaned into the spray, letting it pound his shoulders and back.

He expected to get chewed out by his task force leader, Lieutenant Breckenridge, for the physical altercation he'd started with his teammate last night. To Randy, the mouthy dumb prick deserved a beating.

Randy had returned to the CDF after a three-month hiatus, granted by the few top-ranking allies who still supported him.

Most had turned their backs on him after his "treason." But he had no regrets about switching sides and fighting for the colonies. The civil war's aftermath brought the imprisonment of corrupt government officials, the rise of an interim Chief Executive with morals, and promises of colony reform.

Upon returning to the CDF after his short vacation, he had two career trajectories to choose from: join one of the ongoing planetary-impact missions or be assigned to the CDF's Expedition Task Forces (ETF).

The ETF appeared to be the best choice. Gallivanting across the universe to dispatch human and intergalactic bandits, marauders, traffickers, and ruiners of lives sounded like a good change-up from being stationed dirtside in a combat zone. Been there, done that. But whichever path he chose, one thing was certain: He'd need to get reacclimated to the CDF—a post-civil-war CDF—and get reacclimated to being "Randal Scott."

Before Operation Hammer Fall, he was the young Guardian full of piss and vinegar hellbent on restoring honor to his family's revered name by killing the man who'd tainted it, his father, Arson Scott.

Back then, many lower and upper-ranking Guardians sympathized with Randy and respected him. His sphere of supporters had included brass in the CDF and law enforcement. Favors he requested got approved without hesitation. Now—post-war, post "treason"—the privileges, respect, and reverence attached to his family name were gone. Not that he gave a damn, though; he was still the same man, with or without such prerogatives.

Fellow Guardians now kept their distance. When near, they gave him the silent treatment and condescending side-glances, like he was some contagious vermin, not their brother-in-arms. To them, he was just a traitor, a bastard who'd forsaken the Oath and sided with insurrectionists that brought their campaign of terror to Eden soil.

Now he and other defectors who'd rejoined the CDF were getting the same disrespectful outsider treatment that immigrant Guardians had been enduring for years. These immigrants hadn't committed treason to warrant such treatment; it was because AEGIS had deemed them unfit for Eden citizenship. They were "nadir" meant to be resource harvesters only and were "contaminating" the prestige of the Defense Force.

The disrespect hit a new low when civil war erupted between the Commonwealth Government and seceding colonies, a war that finally ended, after months, with the Battle of the Quad.

Since the war's conclusion, with no Coalition fighters being tried for war crimes, there'd been an upsurge in the mistreatment of immigrants within the CDF: mysterious hangings, rank delays, bullying, harassment. Rigged investigations were doing little to apprehend the culprits. They were protected by a culture of immunity.

Mistreatment of immigrant Guardians and citizens had reached unprecedented levels. Anger was being taken out on Eden's immigrant population because it was their people, those living on Satellite One, who had ignited the New Humanity's first civil war.

The war's end seemed to bring out the worst in the worst of human beings. And in truth, it felt like a civil war was still being waged, a discreet, weaponless one—a war of ideologies and beliefs being fought in the political arena, between compatriots, and among Guardians.

This was supposed to be peacetime, but Randy knew that peace was fragile—brittle. It'd only take a spark to set the Commonwealth ablaze.

He'd hate to be the Chief right now. On one side of the dilemma, immigrant activists were demanding a crackdown on hate crimes. On the other, disgruntled and bereaved nonimmigrants—the majority of Eden's population—were rioting for retribution over the service members killed by the Coalition. Mysterious fringe groups had even posted names and faces of former Coalition fighters on the net, spurring lone wolves to travel to Satellite One and go on a witch hunt.

Times were tumultuous. Chief Executive wasn't a job Randy would ever want. All things considered, Oviereya was holding the Commonwealth together quite well.

Still thinking about the mistreatment of immigrant Guardians, he found the division within the CDF insane, and it was only growing worse. Guardians were supposed to be brothers and sisters. Now, more than ever, that ideal felt like a lie.

Upon his voice command, the shower disengaged and the drying cycle activated, blower vents whistling. Once dry, Randy stepped up to the mirror and wiped away the condensation obscuring his reflection. He examined the shiner around his left eye, a receipt from the brawl he'd started.

Emotions compounded. "Damn it!" he blurted.

He'd just given his task force commander, Captain Valentina Narvaez, a reason to write up a negative counseling statement in his service sketch. And now higher-ups had even more ammunition to screw with his rank promotion, one he was sure was already being blocked by some big-shot officer way above his pay grade. No doubt because he was a "treasonist."

Like all Coalition fighters, including CDF defectors, Randy had been absolved of war crimes by Chief Executive Amaechi. So in a perfect world, his comrades and society wouldn't shun him. The Union leaders themselves had declared the Coalition's rebellion justified. But this wasn't a perfect world, was it? The exoneration of Coalition fighters had only poured fuel on the fire, stoking the anger of many Guardians and Eden citizens.

Passing his fingers over the bruised flesh encircling his eye, Randy cursed the asshole who'd pushed his emotional triggers to the brink of violence, Paul Shaffer.

Randy had thick skin. He knew how to stay cool and ignore petty bullshit. But Paul's cryptic verbal jabs and vexatious teasing had gotten on his last nerve. Enough was enough. He'd tried to deck the prick but missed. That sparked the brawl. Paul took his shot and nailed Randy in the eye. Luckily, Captain Narvaez had stumbled onto the scene and broken up the fight, because Randy was sure he would've kicked Paul's ass into next week.

Paul was definitely someone he'd have to be on his p's and q's around. Not only did the irritant hate so-called traitors, he hated that immigrants were allowed to enlist in the CDF.

Randy stared into the mirror for a long time, the wheels in his head turning. He mulled over who he could actually trust on the nine-man task force he'd been assigned to, Vanguard Alpha.

Lieutenant Carl Breckenridge, the team's field-combat leader, seemed trustworthy. Randy was still feeling him out, but Carl didn't seem to subscribe to the same invidious behavior that Paul did, at least not while in uniform. Maybe he was just putting professionalism before personal bias. Sergeant Jenny Pines seemed cool so far too.

Of the remaining six teammates, Paul and his two buddies, Sergeant Mark MaCallum and Corporal Dan Maddox, were the ones who'd earned permanent spots on Randy's watch list. He'd have to be a fool to trust any of them. Hell, he didn't even want to count on them in a firefight. And that was a crying shame.

Still getting to know the other three—Sergeant Sam Guthrie,

Specialist Jamie (Jay) Lister, and Private Akane Sugimori—Randy felt confident only about Akane. After all, she was an immigrant, from Colony Three *(which had the highest population of Asiatic migrants)*. She understood what it was like being hated.

Akane had welcomed him with generosity from day one of this new mission assignment. And even though she wasn't his usual type—white, blond, athletic build with decent curves—he had to admit that the tomboy wasn't hard on the eyes. She was cute. And reading between the lines, she was a little smitten with him. Infatuated, even. Understandably so. They'd developed good chemistry and vibed naturally. They forced nothing. Their interactions flowed organically.

Given the emotional strain he was under from being ostracized, Akane's presence was a relief. He was fond of her and gravitated toward her upbeat, chill demeanor. Her lively energy was a breath of fresh air. But he had to be careful. At just nineteen, she was young and impressionable. The last thing he wanted was to mislead her into thinking their friendly dynamic was a prelude to romance.

Nope, no romance was brewing. Not now, not ever. It didn't matter how cute he found Akane to be. Getting emotionally entangled with another woman wasn't in the cards. His relationship with Stacie Spencer, virtually the woman of his dreams, had gone up in flames because of him. He'd made the mistake of his life, a mistake he owned.

Because he'd been Linked with Stacie, getting over her wasn't easy. Shared memories, emotions, and sensations from their time together remained ingrained in his cerebral implant. Just thinking about her now, he could practically feel her all over him—her touch, her lips, the soft, creamy press of her naked body as they cuddled. The phantom sensations were so palpable that his spine tingled.

31

Strengthening intimacy through Linking was always an intrinsic risk. If a long-term relationship crashed and burned, romantic partners could experience a short-term case of relationship withdrawal referred to as Cerebral-attachment Syndrome, a constant recycling of feelings, emotions, memories, and sensations. Even recurring dreams of their ex-lover occurred. Thanks to the mnemonic power of a cerebral implant, Cerebral-attachment Syndrome could last from weeks to months.

Trying to move forward with his life, and get past the syndrome, he had tested the waters with Kesley Whittaker. The sex was off the chain, but fantastic sex wasn't enough to sustain a long-term intimate relationship. She just wasn't the woman he wanted to cocreate a lifelong partnership with, so their fling fizzled out. But they remained on good terms. They'd be friends for life, after everything they'd survived together.

Randy shoved thoughts of Stacie out of his head, left the bathroom, and headed for his closet. His cabin wasn't anything to write home about: a fold-out wall bed, an armoire, and a table. Still, it was roomier than the cabins aboard Vanguard Alpha's ship, the *Nightingale*.

From the wardrobe of CDF uniforms and civvies inside the closet, he took out a sleeve and stepped into it. Pulling the thin flex material over the defined muscles of his body, he slid his stout arms into the armholes. Then he yanked up the zipper, drawing the single-piece suit snug over his chest.

Movement for today's op was slated for zero-eight-hundred hours. That gave him a little over an hour until showtime. It was a direct-action mission. Vanguard Alpha had been tasked with raiding the compound of a human-trafficking racket that had abducted several of the Commonwealth's women, along with women from planets outside the Union, adding to an emerging intergalactic diaspora of rescued victims.

The traffickers were also dealing guns, mechsuits, weaponized vehicles, and anything else that would fetch a profit on the black markets of the universe. Human criminals had been lining their pockets off the burgeoning intergalactic trafficking industry since Earth Era and showed no signs of slowing down.

First order of the morning for Randy was chow, as usual.

The two halves of the motion-activated door split as he approached, and he exited his quarters. Crossing the corridor, he ran into Mark MaCallum and Dan Maddox, Paul Shaffer's cohort. The two were having an animated discussion, peppered with profanity.

Mark gestured wildly as he spoke to Dan. "Can you believe this soft-ass Chief? Ethics investigations into CDF culture? Suspending planetary-impact missions *she's* not cool with? This is her idea of . . . reformation." He scoffed.

"Yeah," Dan replied, "she should focus on solving the Commonwealth's debt crisis and leave the CDF out of her reformist warpath."

They heard the sound of boots coming in their direction.

Mark caught Randy in the corner of his eye. He twisted around, a sneering smile playing on his lips. "Well, well, if it isn't Randal Scott—Warrior Extraordinaire, son of the infamous war hero Arson Scott, and most of all, a *traitor*."

"Excuse me," Randy said casually. He made a detour around them.

Dan chuckled. "How's that black eye?" he asked, taking a dig at Randy to waylay him. "Maybe next time, learn how to throw a punch"—he mimicked how to throw a "correct" punch—"before taking a cheap shot at Shaffer."

Jaw clenched, eyes forward, Randy distanced himself from the troublemakers.

"What's wrong? Not in a talkative mood?" Dan said. Randy surged ahead with a relaxed stride, disregarding them, acting unbothered. "Look at you, pretending to be all calm and collected, but deep down, you're just a testy little punk kid, aren't you? Not to mention, you're also a *murderer*." Dan was doing his best to bait Randy into a fight. He was itching to beat down the ex-Coalition fighter, the "traitor."

Randy paused. Miffed, he curled his hands into fists.

Pushing the boundaries of Randy's self-restraint, Dan said, "If you don't like what I'm saying, do something about it. Your move, or are you just a pushover?"

Randy kept his emotions in check. He unclenched his fists and moved on, resisting the urge to kick off another fistfight. No need to give Lieutenant Breckenridge another reason to bust his chops. "I don't have time for your childish antics."

"All bark and no bite," Mark said. He and Dan went back to chatting.

Randy rode an elevator pod down to the mezzanine ring of the Star Palace, the CDF's way station in the X-Quadrant. It consisted of three annular tiers, each lined with wraparound windows.

The mezzanine's concourse was alive with restaurants, entertainment venues, rec areas, and commercial vendors. Many nonhuman merchants had set up shop at the Star Palace, with permission from the Commonwealth Government.

The mezzanine ring functioned like a microcity. The lower ring housed the shipyard. Quarters and a few lounges occupied the upper ring.

These space stations served as rest stops for some task forces and as one-to-three-month lodging for those carrying out multiple missions within their assigned quadrant. Vanguard Alpha had been at the Star Palace three days now, prepping for their op. It would be a short stay. After they rescued the abductees, they would set course back to Eden.

Randy strolled through the busy concourse.

The aroma of exotic cuisines pervaded the air. Guardians ate and bantered with noisy exuberance.

Randy's ears caught snippets of underhanded barbs from Guardians who recognized him as they walked past, some in casual wear, others suited up in sleeves. "There's the traitor . . . Rebel scum . . . Murderer . . . Coalition filth . . . He should be in the grave, not those Guardians . . ."

Randy's watchful eyes scanned his surroundings. He was half-expecting someone to stab him in the back at any moment. Paranoia had him walking on pins and needles. *Is this what it's boiled down to?* he asked himself. *Sizing up my fellow Guardians like they're rabid dogs just waiting to tear into me?*

With the majority of the CDF made up of nonimmigrant Edenites who opposed the colonies' rebellion, Randy felt like a pariah among what was supposed to be his military family.

Up ahead, he spotted Akane sitting with Jay and Sam. The three were feasting on bowls of something flavorful.

They were suited up in their sleeves for the mission. Sam, always upholding an Earth Era soldier's clean-cut image, was freshly shaven and had his hairline high and tight as usual. Randy could tell they were a close-knit trio, bonded by battle.

"Hey, Randy, over here!" Akane called out, voice bright and lively, eyes of adoration glued to him. She jumped from her chair, a mop of straggly bangs tumbling over her forehead. Waving her hand, she flagged him down. "Come join us!"

Randy couldn't help but smile at his admirer's warm invitation. After considering her offer to sit and break bread, he joined his teammates at the dining table. He settled into a chair—Jay to his left, Akane in front of him, and Sam to his right.

From the neighboring tables came laughter, casual chatter, and the clattering of trays and utensils.

Within seconds, a server golem on four wheels rolled up to Randy to take his order. The bot had a cube-like body and a domed head.

Randy chose whatever everyone else at the table was having, and the golem buzzed away.

"Randal Scott, the man who helped liberate the colonies from oppression!" Jay said in a jovial tone.

Randy looked toward the young swarthy man with long dreadlocks. Funny how things turned out, he thought; he was a hero to some Guardians, albeit a few, and apparently a bastard to others. And not being a spotlighter, the "hero" stuff meant nothing to him. He didn't think of himself as some war legend or crave any tribute.

In truth, the Battle of the Quad wasn't a simple tale of "good guys" versus "bad guys." Certainly, there were scumbags in the CDF—a lot of scumbags—but not every Guardian was one.

To Randy, the real villains were the corrupt politicians and the avaricious Eight Elite. The Coalition fighters and Guardians who fought the Battle of the Quad were just soldiers following orders on that abominable day. There were heroes on both sides. In his eyes, the Battle of the Quad had simply been one big, unavoidable catastrophe.

"How was it? What was it like fighting in the Battle of the Quad?" Jay asked. He lounged back in his chair, laced his fingers behind his head, and crossed his ankles.

Flashbacks of Guardians going down pulled Randy's mind back to the horror of the battle. He'd done his best to preserve life but hadn't been able to avoid killing some Guardians. It was war, after all. Composing himself, he replied pointedly, "Hellish." That was the best word for it. "Definitely not table talk for me, know what I mean?" No sense in being retraumatized.

Jay uncrossed his ankles and sat upright. "Gotcha," he said, his levity gone. "I know how damaging combat can be to the psyche. Believe me, I've seen a lot of gruesome violence in the hell zones I've been deployed to." His own mind hadn't come out unscathed; planetary-impact missions were rarely pleasant. "Sorry," he added, apologizing for not being more mindful.

"It's okay."

The server golem returned to the table, carrying Randy's entree and a tumbler of fizzing blueberry peppermint chiller on a tray. After setting the tray on the table, it left to take more orders.

"So, where are you and Sam from, colony or Eden?" Randy asked Jay, making casual conversation—and gathering info to assess who he could trust. Sure, Akane trusted Sam and Jay, and he trusted Akane, but he made his own calls. For now, he'd stay guarded.

"I'm from Colony Six. So is Sam," Jay replied.

Knowing they were colony immigrants put Randy at ease. All immigrants respected the Coalition rebels, which meant Jay's admiration was genuine, not pretend or just an icebreaker.

On a screen in the concourse, an anchorman in his late fifties—with silver hair and a dimpled chin—said, "All votes have been counted. Ron Burchardt, a pro-reform dark horse, has defeated the anti-reform candidate Todd Sieger."

This was the third of several special elections being held to choose successors for the Parliament members jailed after the Coalition exposed their corruption. "Pro-reform" had become the media term for candidates committed to accelerating colony development and addressing the surge in immigrant mistreatment. "Anti-reform" referred to those who favored the current gradualist approach to improving colony life and were reluctant to address the challenges immigrants continued to face.

Boos reigned throughout the concourse, most Guardians there being anti-reform. The applause for Ron Burchardt was tepid at best.

The anchorman said, "It seems like a completely illogical victory, based on pre-election polls. Sieger has demanded a recount, and authorities say they'll be investigating suspected voter fraud."

Guardians angry at the election results grumbled.

The anchorman continued. "Now here is our interview with Damien Sykes, who announced his candidacy for Chief Executive three days ago. If elected, he would become the second youngest Chief in history, at thirty-two."

A handsome golden-tan man with slicked-back dark blond hair appeared onscreen. The Sykes family was one of the Seven Elite, formerly Eight, until Stacie Spencer withdrew from the conglomerate. Like the children of the other slain family heads, Damien had inherited the reins of his parents' criminal empire.

The Seven's bylaws forbade family heads from holding political office, as doing so would undermine the conglomerate's balance of power. But Damien was the odd man out. Now in control of his parents' enterprise, he intended to do whatever he damn well pleased.

Randy and his comrades watched the screen. The interview drew the attention of other Guardians as well.

Damien was regarded as a major front-runner for the Chief Executive seat in next year's election. He was gaining traction, and as a staunch proponent of the current socioeconomic status quo, he had become the poster boy for Eden's anti-reform base. Election analysts predicted he would overtake Oviereya and any other candidates who jumped into the race.

The interviewer, a brunette woman in a pantsuit, asked, "What is your message to the people of the Commonwealth, Mr. Sykes?"

Damien, with a snicker and a sly grin, radiated villainous energy. "Simple. We need justice. A bunch of colony insurrectionists started a civil war and invaded our soil, killing Guardians. Not since the Bhalkran War has there been an attack on Eden. Families are grieving. They deserve to see their loved ones' murderers incarcerated, or better yet, executed.

"A lot of people say the Coalition coming to Eden and removing corrupt politicians was a *good* thing. Okay, hear me out. If I went above the law and killed some psychopathic wife beater, would people be pissed off about it? Of course not. But does that mean I just get to walk away scot-free? No, it doesn't.

"So if someone who goes all vigilante is subject to the consequences of the law, then how the hell do a bunch of treasonists get to skate free?" His bronze eyes glared into the camera. "Tell us that, Amaechi. *Huh?* Tell the emotionally devastated widows and parentless children why their loved ones' killers are loose. It makes no fucking sense.

"Eden's people deserve better. And I understand their anguish; my parents, far from perfect, were murdered by the Coalition. Let's face it, these treasonists could've employed other strategies for accomplishing their colony-equality objective. Instead, they ignited a civil war and invaded humanity's motherworld."

"Well, in the Chief Executive's defense, the Union declared the colony rebellion justified, and she has the authority to exonerate anyone she chooses, just like any other Chief," the interviewer said, unknowingly about to set off a tirade.

39

Damien's brows quirked. The controversial public figure went off. "Exonerate? No, this is different! So don't give me that nonsense! As for the Union playing Big Brother, to hell with their . . . so-called ruling. We need to unseat Amaechi. She's a peace-loving Coalition panderer who needs to be kicked outta office!"

Memories of the Battle of the Quad, refusing to lie dormant, besieged Randy's mind with vivid flashes of combat casualties. His features pinched. Guilt and remorse, for the few lives he'd taken, etched themselves into his face. Then his chin touched his chest.

Jay's green-dyed eyes flicked over at him. "You letting that slimeball get in your head?"

"I'm fine," Randy said flatly, playing down the pain. He sipped his drink, his guilty expression remaining unchanged.

Again, images of the Battle of the Quad slipped into his mind, but he fought them away.

Damien's aggressive tongue continued putting Oviereya on blast. "She's even been promoting the idea of giving the colonies unfettered access to trading partners. You know why that's a dumb idea? Easy, it means Eden would be competing for resources with its own colonies. *Duh*.

"There's a reason things are the way they are. There's a reason we didn't—and shouldn't—deviate from the blueprint AEGIS fashioned for the New Humanity. The system's creators—Doctors Cyrus Kline, Jagr Vlcek, and Atticus Hancroft—knew what they were doing. Oviereya is dismantling our society in a very, very bad way."

After finishing her pink bubbling beverage, Akane slammed her cup on the table and expelled a sigh of disgust. "Damien Sykes, just another fucking Gould."

"Worse," Sam opined. "Gould was well-spoken. He was a

skillful politician. And he was low-key compared to this loudmouth. Sykes is more flamboyant—more of a hothead, more outspoken. He's a demagogue who doesn't give a shit about censoring himself to appeal to the less-extreme or just to save face. Gould articulated himself with finesse. This guy? Not so much. Sykes doesn't play it safe at all, and unfortunately, people are flocking to him."

The thought of Damien becoming Chief put a foul taste in Akane's mouth. "You don't think he'd actually win the election, do you? He's the son of one of the Eight, and the Coalition exposed the family heads for what they were when they published those files on the net. They proved the Eight were just a buncha crime moguls."

Sam said, "Yeah, but Damien's been proven guilty of *nothing*. He's playing dumb, and he's promised to disband all criminal activity. An obvious lie, but in this new era of colonist hate, he's the savior a lot of Edenites are clamoring for. They're energized by this loose cannon, so they overlook what's staring them right in the damn face: the possibility that he's no different from his parents.

"The crazy thing is that I think he has a real shot at unseating the incumbent Chief next year, according to polls.

"Oviereya is soft. This guy's a bloodthirsty, rampaging bull; she's a dove." He sipped his drink. "Oviereya needs to go on the offensive, not just play defense. You try to be passive in a fistfight, your face eventually gets mauled. You've gotta get aggressive in politics, *really* aggressive. Maybe that's not her style, but like on the battlefield, if you don't adapt to your enemy's offense, you're dead."

Listening to Sam, Randy got the impression that he was not only the oldest of everyone at the table but the most insightful and combat-seasoned.

Jay contributed to the convo, saying, "Yeah, but I just can't see some Purist sicko like Sykes becoming the Commonwealth's head honcho." A reproving scowl flickered across Sam's face when Jay said the word "Purist," as if it were forbidden. "We know he's one of 'em," Jay continued, having not noticed Sam's fleeting expression. "He's gotta be. There're even rumors floating around about it now."

Randy raised a brow. "Excuse me, a what?"

"You don't know?" Jay seemed surprised.

"Is there a reason I should?" Randy retorted.

"I guess not. People who *do* hear about Purists usually think they're just fiction, some conspiracy theory cooked up by groupies on the net. Since you were a Coalition rebel, I figured maybe you'd heard about them and that—"

"Sorry, I've never heard of these . . . Purists."

Akane chimed in. "Yeah, understandable. Almost no one knows about them."

"So who are they?"

Akane replied, "They're followers of an extremist movement dedicated to colonist and immigrant oppression. Like Jay said, most people who hear about them think they're just made up. But that's exactly what they want."

Randy listened intently to Akane.

She rested her forearms on the table. "Purists stay incognito. They don't give away who they are. You're not gonna see membership ads on the net or recruitment posters posted around town.

"These people are rotten to the core, the worst of discriminators. Gould was a fucking saint compared to them. These hive-minded, cult-like idealists are *die-hard* believers in AEGIS's social stratification of humanity, like the damn thing was God. They think Eden selectees were 'the ordained' or something.

"Their mission is to preserve the status quo and keep colonists and immigrants down. They've got their slimy tentacles in politics, the government, and even the CDF."

Randy took in everything Akane was saying, but the idea of a clandestine brotherhood of extremists infiltrating all of society's institutions was a lot to accept. Sure, he knew there were extremists out there, but on this scale? He wanted to call bullshit. Maybe Sam, Jay, and Akane thought this . . . hate group was way bigger than it actually was.

Akane said, "All they wanna do is acquire power and gin up fear." Anger flashed in her eyes. "We think Purists within the CDF are behind most of the rank delays, hangings, and harassment of immigrant Guardians. Their keep-the-hate-alive movement is catching fire, attracting followers."

The edge in her voice sharpened. "*Purists* are the ones who used the net to broadcast the identities of Coalition fighters to the public, calling for wackos to hunt them down. Our hunch is that even Sergeant Shaffer's one of—"

Sam craned his head toward Akane, brows knitted. She fell silent, cutting herself off.

Randy, observant and incisive, tried to decipher the enigmatic message on Sam's face. He wasn't quite sure what it meant. It came off as a reprimand, a signal to shut up, as if Akane might be disclosing too much.

"Akane, I think Randy's heard enough," Sam said in a reproachful tone. "Some of this may be a lot to digest. We don't want him thinking we're nuts or something, now do we?"

Everyone became quiet.

Randy's eyes swept over the frozen faces at the table. Not one mouth moved. To diffuse the awkward atmosphere, which was dragging on, he said, "The meal was delicious." He got up. "I'm going to head to the *Nightingale*. I'll see you guys there." He walked away.

Slapping her hands down on the table, Akane pushed herself up from her chair. "Let me talk to him. He might even be able to convince Arson Scott himself to lend us a hand." To emphasize such significance, she added, "War hero. Coalition icon. Reza's *top* commander. *Hell-oh*."

"You think we can trust him fully?" Jay asked, turning his head from Sam to Akane with a skeptical look. "He killed Reza, after all. The Purists had Gould to believe in, we had Reza. And he and his dad took Reza from us."

Sam twined his fingers. He spoke thoughtfully, relaying his opinion. "Jay, Reza was my hero too. And I think he had the right idea, eliminating the Eight family heads and the corrupt officials. Some call it murder; I call it justice. But the fact of the matter is that Reza's change in course was going to end in defeat.

"Him doing a one-eighty and crowning himself sovereign ruler of the Commonwealth would've caused the Coalition's assault force to implode, those for the change and those opposed to it fighting each other. Then the CDF would've taken advantage of the infighting and crushed the assault force entirely. Even if the rebels had stayed united, there was *absolutely* no way they could've overpowered the CDF.

"Hammer Fall was supposed to be a quick op: take over the Quad, release the corruption files to the public, and call for peace. With Reza's new plan, the Coalition would've eventually lost the Battle of the Quad, unless he had some secret ace up his sleeve.

"And don't think Guardians or Eden citizens were going to praise Reza as a savior just because he exposed government corruption and the mistreatment of colonists. Bullshit."

Jay shifted uncomfortably, absorbing Sam's words.

Sam said, "Yeah, it's a tough fucking pill to swallow, but the Scotts made the right call, killing Reza and paving the way for Amaechi to become Chief Executive.

"Don't get the wrong idea, though. I listen to Reza's orations nearly every day. I teach my kids about him, so they'll know the revolutionary he was, not the tyrant most of Eden portrays him to be. But Reza let power poison his head. You take over things internally, not always by force. You infiltrate sectors of the government and military. You game the system. You mete out justice not by public executions but in the most discreet way possible—a way that doesn't draw attention to yourself, a way that leaves no footprints. Plausible deniability. Reza's downfall was himself, Jay."

Jay leaned into the backrest of his chair and took a moment of silence, coming to terms with the truth. "But do you think Randal Scott would cede to our ideals, our way of doing things?"

A driven woman, Akane remained persistent. "Just let me talk to him. I can persuade him to join us." She fixed her eyes on Sam, seeking approval. "Yea or nay, Guthrie?" Her irritation rose as she alternated her thumb between thumbs-up and thumbs-down. "C'mon."

Sam's pale-blue eyes stared at Akane. He could see she was passionate about enlisting Randy's help for their mission. "Alright, he's your assigned prospect now. Feed him info in small doses. No need to overdo it. Use sound judgment."

Akane nodded in understanding and raced off after Randy, a smile tugging on the corners of her mouth.

Jay said to Sam, "Akane's drooling over Randal Scott a little too much. She's getting way too attached. I respect the guy for airdropping onto the Quad and risking life and limb to emancipate the colonies from systematic oppression, but he's not part of our trusted circle yet. It's too early for Akane to be getting *that* cozy."

"Honestly, Jaime, I don't care who Akane gushes over. As long as she's deadass sure where Scott's mindset is at before letting him through our door, she can get starry-eyed over him all she wants."

While navigating the jam-packed concourse of D-Block to catch up to Randy, Akane hollered, "Hey, Randy, wait up!" She jostled shoulder after shoulder. "Excuse me . . . Sorry . . . Pardon me . . . Comin' through."

"Hey, watch where you're goin'," a man snapped as Akane shoved past him.

"Randy!" Akane called out.

Randy paused and wheeled around. "Akane, what's up?"

Akane caught her breath. "We still got some time before the strategy brief. Stroll with me, 'kay?"

I wonder what her aim is. Curious where the conversation might lead, Randy accepted her offer. "Sure, okay. Why not? Like you said, we've got some time, and I'd like to get better acquainted with my teammates."

"Awesome." Eardrums pestered by raucous idle chatter, Akane scanned for a quieter venue. Taking notice of the environmental recreation-domes, she said, "How about a park sim?"

"Yeah, that'll work."

They approached one of the silver dome-shaped constructs. The doors chirped and hissed open. Inside was a hydroponic biosphere simulating a park, complete with fancy white benches, misting fountains, and walk bridges arched over artificial ponds.

The sky was a hyperrealistic holo, bright and blue with puffy white clouds. Piped-in sound effects mimicked birdsong. The plant life, like the colorful flower beds, was organic, grown synthetically.

Good replica, Randy thought as he and Akane began their nature walk. The simulation definitely felt real.

His cerebral implant pinged. Akane had forwarded a Link request. "Yeah, right." He rejected it, shutting down her hopes for a deeper connection—one of the most intimate connections of all.

Akane hadn't expected him to accept a Link request this early in their budding relationship, but it was worth a try. "C'mon, I want you to trust me, Randy. We're already friends, right? So what's the big deal?"

Whoever said we were friends? "Let's cross one bridge at a time. Besides, why the heck would you want to be inside my head?"

Akane gaped. "You're fucking kidding me, right? You participated in one of the greatest acts of heroism in Commonwealth history! The liberators who airdropped onto the Quad that day are rock stars to immigrants like me, especially you and your dad!"

Randy furrowed his brow. Was that why she wanted to Link? To get closer to a so-called "colony hero"? To learn from him? To get an orgasmic thrill from being psychically connected to someone she had a major crush on? The last thing he needed right now was a one-girl fan club.

As they sauntered under a trellis threaded with green vines, Akane said, "Thanks to you and your dad, the ceasefire happened. It's because of you two that Amaechi became Chief and started the Colony Restoration Initiative." While they strolled, holos of Earth Era animals materialized: rabbits, tortoises, squirrels, and others. "Who the fuck *wouldn't* wanna Link with you, man?"

This kid's head was in the clouds, Randy thought, and it was time to bring her back down to reality. He paused their walk right at the trellis' exit and censured her. "Believe me, there's a lot up here"—he pointed to his temple—"that you *don't* want to see. That you don't want to experience. You can't comprehend the chronic trauma the Battle of the Quad cursed me with, faceless dead forever memorialized in my mind.

"You haven't encountered true pain, Akane, *my* pain—the pain of killing fellow Guardians, combined with the pain of killing Coalition fighters I believed were the enemy before I joined them. The mental anguish never fully goes away. You can't outfight it. Its echo always returns to torment me. The strife I live with, Akane . . . you don't want to know.

"And sure, I could've refused to participate in Hammer Fall. I could've just gone back to Eden and sat on the sidelines, joined neither the CDF nor the Coalition, to protect my conscience." He sighed. "But I don't regret participating in Hammer Fall. I can't pull a time machine out of my ass and rewrite history, anyway.

"But because of that battle—because of the sacrifice I made—I can't even live out my own fucking military career in peace. I'm always having to keep my head on a swivel, fearing a Guardian will knife me in the back for revenge. Best you protect the sanctity of your mind from any spillage of my unpleasant misfortune."

In an offended tone, Akane struck back. "Hey, *wiseass*, save the roasting for some newbie fresh out of Basic. I already know something about living with pain." The headstones of Skylar Grace and Desmond Castillo flashed in her mind, along with the headstone of a woman dear to her. Akane Sugimori wasn't a newcomer to pain and suffering.

"Do you?" Randy questioned her.

"Yeah, and I know what it's like to live with paranoia too. I'm an immigrant, a target for Purists inside and outside the CDF. And you're a target as well, because they hate every rebel who fought for Satellite One, us immigrants' homeworld."

Randy rolled his eyes. "Here we go with this 'Purist' psychobabble again."

An outrush of emotion burst from Akane's mouth. "They're a real threat, *goddammit*, to people like *you* and *me!*"

She grabbed Randy's sleeve at the chest, twisting the fabric in her fist. "Those lowlifes took someone special from me, so don't ever *fucking* lecture me about pain." The acrimony in her voice, the fire in her eyes—Randy had never seen her in such an incensed state. "I don't wanna see you, one of our heroes, found hacked into a million pieces by these shitbags. You get me, Randy?"

Though he wished she'd drop the "hero" stuff, her passionate outburst firmed Randy's features. He now regarded the youngster more seriously.

Akane said, "Purist groups all across Eden are plotting to dominate central and region state government, law enforcement, and the CDF. Cliques of these people exist in all our institutions, but you wouldn't recognize them, not blatantly. Remember, these people aren't just stuck-up Eden citizens with a high-and-mighty attitude. These people are *dangerous*."

"So, these Purists are like a . . . shadow society or something, operating under everyone's noses."

Akane uncurled her fist, letting go of Randy's sleeve. "Bingo. A lot of Purist groups are independent, but they're all acting in solidarity toward a common goal: to keep Eden free of immigrant integration, continue exploiting colonists as servile resource harvesters, and ensure the current immigrant population remains at the bottom of society.

"They inspire leaderless resistance, lone actors committing acts of violence in the name of their warped manifesto. Our republic is under siege by Purist groups. But they've got opposition, people working to counter them."

So, some sort of shadow warfare's going on? Randy thought.

"The opposition espouses Reza's ideals but rebukes his late methods of executing those ideals," Akane said. This talk of warring sides gave Randy déjà vu. "It's a game of chess, an arcane war between two diametrical mentalities that—"

Okay, enough with the crumbs. It's time for real answers, Randy thought, fed up with Akane's cryptic behavior. "Just how do you know all this, Akane, *huh?*" he pressed, interrupting her.

Akane's wristcom chirped. "Aw, man! It's almost showtime. I can get into the nitty-gritty later. Right now, we gotta haul ass if we don't wanna be late for the mission brief. And trust me, we don't wanna piss off Breckenridge." She jetted out of the dome, ending the conversation on a cliffhanger.

"To be continued, then," Randy muttered to himself. *Who are you, Private Sugimori?*

Akane wasn't a quick study. There seemed to be a lot more to her than met the eye.

INTERLUDE ONE

FIVE DAYS INTO THE THREE-WEEK WAR

Planet Eden

Akane strolled through an empty construction zone, dressed in embellished jeans and a black T-shirt. Around her were substructures, half-finished buildings, and idle construction equipment.

Rejected again! she thought. *I can't even land a fucking assembly-line gig at some golem factory. Because my citizen registration number flags me as an immigrant. Because AEGIS decided I should be just a lowly resource harvester chucking dirt somewhere. It's clear the corporate execs who control the private sector here don't want an immigrant like me "stinking up their joint."*

I'm sick of this asinine bullshit. I thought coming here was supposed to turn my life around, Mom and Dad. I thought coming here was supposed to be my big break.

Homesick, she longed for Sector 07, NeoJapan: grimy alleyways, ramshackle living units stacked one atop the other, no modern tech, none of Eden's scenic beauty. A colonist might think she had a few screws loose for wanting to return to that place.

The lottery's just a sham. Caught in a fever of anger, she kicked over a trash receptacle. "I fucking knew it!" Her ears might as well be steaming.

The receptacle tumbled across the phyocrete, flinging litter.

A roving police golem on three wheels sped toward her. Its antenna bulb, round eyes, and rectangular voice slot flashed as it admonished her. "Warning, warning!" it said, waving its tubular arms. "There is a one hundred credit fine for vandalizing public—"

"Shut up!" Akane kicked the four-foot blocky robot onto its side and let out an exasperated huff.

A policeman had witnessed the misdemeanor while sitting nearby in his interceptor, a black-and-white hover vehicle. He pressed the accelerator and glided over to Akane, parking beside her. His coarse, throaty voice tore through the air. "Hey, you! Stupid girl!"

Akane recoiled, panic taking hold of her. She knew she was in deep trouble.

The policeman climbed out. His thin lips, set beneath a dark mustache, compressed into a grim line. "It's illegal to vandalize public property and assault a policing golem." Behind dark shades, his eyes radiated antipathy for miscreants.

Perspiration slickened Akane's brow. "Yeah . . . I, uh—" Head bowed, she hooked both thumbs between her belt and pants. Like a child who'd just been scolded by an adult, she toed the dusty ground.

"You want to go to jail?" The policeman thrust a finger at her. "What the heck's wrong with you, kid?"

Akane raised her head, gathered her courage, and spoke her mind. "It's just that lottery beneficiaries like me have it tough. We're given a measly ten thousand credits to make ends meet and told, 'Go make a life for yourself. Shoot for the stars.'

"This planet's supposed to be the Zion of humanity. But immigrants like me are treated as if we're inferior to everyone else. Why do people wanna make us feel like we don't belong?"

The policeman's eyebrows came together, his features contorting.

What are you frowning about, dickwad? Akane thought.

"So, you're one of them, one of those ungrateful immigrant degenerates," the policeman said. "Just a wannabe Highborn from some ghetto, cesspool colony who's got a chip on their shoulder. Even if you were handed the world, you'd still find something to bitch about. 'I don't get this. I don't get that. I don't get what the Highborn get.' All that woe-is-me crap. Figures why you think you can just vandalize property and get away with it. Hands behind your back, missy."

Akane cocked a brow. "Really?" she said with a dry laugh. "I kicked over a fucking trash can and a mindless automaton."

The policeman wasn't going to engage in a back-and-forth. "Turn around and put your hands behind your back. *Now.*"

Akane's heart skipped a beat. "But—"

The policeman's frown deepened. "Turn around, you little brat, and put your damn hands behind your back! I'm not gonna say it again!"

Fear stiffened Akane's shoulders. Shaking, she complied.

Cold metal clamped around her wrists, locking her arms in place.

"Hey, that's a little *too* tight," she said, teeth clenched so hard her jaw hurt. The policeman jammed the muzzle of his firearm against her spine. "What the—?"

"Quiet, nadir." The policeman glanced around conspiratorially. The coast was clear. Absolutely no one else was around. "There are enough immigrants on Eden. We don't need any more of you obnoxious pissants here."

Aghast, Akane became a bundle of nerves.

The policeman thought, *Whiners like you are the reason brave men and women are being gunned down in some idiotic civil war.*

Just as his finger slipped into the trigger well, a vicious roundhouse kick slammed into the back of his skull. He lost his grip on the pistol, and it clattered to the ground along with his shades.

His feet floundered, fighting to recover balance. As he massaged the back of his throbbing head, he turned around—red-faced. "Who the hell—?"

Standing before him was a woman in her late twenties who had an ocher complexion, complemented by a long braid of caramel blond-streaked hair. Ready to beat him down if necessary, she shot him a stare that screamed: Back the fuck away from Akane, or else.

The broad-shouldered amazon of a woman towered over the dirty cop, who was a head shorter. Her running shorts exposed a pair of athlete's legs, and her sports bra showed off her sculpted abs and solid arms. It was glaringly obvious she kept herself in tip-top shape.

The policeman's head still ached as he closed in on Akane's fearless rescuer. "Lady, I'm gonna make you regret messin' with me."

His threat was meant to intimidate the woman. It didn't. Not by a long shot. She stood firm—an immovable object—and didn't even bat an eyelid. She knew she could take the asshole, not out of hubris, but out of *skill*.

Just as the policeman was about to throw a punch her way, she swiveled her hips and spun into a second roundhouse. The kick autographed his forehead with a nasty red gash and dropped him before he could make his move, putting him to sleep.

Akane was impressed. This woman was fast. She was powerful. She hit with explosive force. She was lightning and thunder, and her physique was something fierce, stout and strong. And it was appealing to the eye, feminine curves blatantly noticeable. Who the hell was this good Samaritan?

That takes care of him, the woman thought.

Relief washed away the tension in Akane's muscles. "Th-thank you." Her voice strained for strength.

The woman knelt and searched the policeman's pocket for the cuffs' key fob. *Got it.* She touched the fob to the cuffs' transceiver.

Metal clacked to the ground. Akane was free.

The woman then tossed the fob aside. "Are you okay, girl?"

"Um, yeah, thanks to you." Akane rubbed and flexed her sore wrists. Her gaze dropped to the policeman's crumpled form. "You throw a helluva kick." She tilted her head back up at her tall, athletically built rescuer. "My name's Akane, by the way."

An eccentric face of blended ethnicity gave Akane a kindhearted smile. "I'm Simone Conyers. Sergeant Simone Conyers."

"Sergeant? Are you a policewoman?"

"No, CDF. Luckily, I frequent this construction zone on my jogging route."

"Thank goodness."

"Is there anything I can do? Maybe take you home?" Simone glared at the unconscious policeman. She had nothing but disdain for him. "After I make sure this disgrace of a human being gets locked away, of course."

Akane stood in embarrassed silence. "I, um, don't have a home," she admitted. "I've just been lodging at different places for weeks or months at a time while trying to get on my feet. No luck yet." Moisture welled in her eyes. "I don't know what I'm gonna do. My credits won't last forever, and—"

Simone gently settled a hand on Akane's shoulder. "I'm an immigrant too. It was difficult for me at first. You can stay with me."

Akane stared at Simone as if she couldn't believe what she had heard. "Re-really?" she stuttered.

"Of course." Simone took Akane into her muscled arms and held her.

"Thank you, Simone," Akane squeaked out. She was glad to have a permanent home on Eden.

The warmth and safety of Simone's embrace instantly neutralized all the fear, anxiety, and uncertainty that had been eclipsing Akane's hope and morale day by day.

Simone unfolded her arms. "It's no problem. You're a fellow immigrant. Now I'm going to contact the authorities. When they get here, I'll give my witness statement, and they'll lock up this piece of garbage. Why don't you sit down until they arrive?"

Akane nodded. "Yeah, sounds good." She walked over to a stack of phyocrete blocks and sat down, taking a load off.

Simone knelt beside the policeman and peeled back the cuff of his left sleeve, uncovering a distinct tattoo of a winged skull and crossbones. Her expression grew rigid, fury burning in her oak-brown eyes. *A Purist. I knew it.*

• • •

WEEKS LATER

Inside Simone's penthouse residence, Akane—dressed in jeans and a dark blue top—sat browsing social media on the holographic interface of her wristcom. She was waiting for Simone to return from a shopping trip so they could go out for dinner.

The wristcom chirped. MESSAGE FROM SKYLAR flashed across the interface. Akane jumped from the sofa, smiling. She was relieved to finally hear from her friend. She knew Skylar had been having a rough time. That's why she'd been ghosting her, Jacobi, and Desmond for the past three days, ignoring all their calls and texts, making them worry.

Akane eagerly opened the message.

Skylar: Akane, I wanted to say farewell.

Despair ripped the smile off Akane's face, and heartache accumulated in her chest. *What?*

Skylar: You were right all along. This world doesn't take kindly to us immigrants. It'll never accept us. I tried. I really tried. But I can't go on anymore.

Akane: What are you talking about?

Skylar: I can't live like this.

Akane's trembling fingers dialed Skylar's number. The wristcom rang. *Come on, Skylar, answer.* Akane's body quivered, her chest tightened, and tears filled her eyes. Skylar refused to pick up.

Skylar: Goodbye, girlfriend. And thank you. Love you a bunch.

Akane: Skylar, what are you saying? Where are you?

No answer. A sick feeling swelled up inside Akane.

Akane: Skylar?

Thunder roared, lightning flashed, and the gray sky unleashed a flood, sheets of rain beating the windowpanes.

For five minutes, Akane paced back and forth, gnawed her nails intermittently, and kept trying to reach Skylar. The iciness spreading through her veins served as a warning that something terrible had happened.

In today's cyber-enhanced world, news traveled fast. It didn't take long for the headlines to go viral: YOUNG WOMAN LEAPS OFF ROOF OF APARTMENT COMPLEX.

The headlines wrecked Akane. Bereft, she collapsed to her knees. The neighbors could most likely hear the heart-wrenching shriek that came from her throat. Sobbing and wailing, she hammered the floor until her knuckles were red.

Just as Akane had salvaged herself, standing to her feet, the front door opened, and Simone entered. She was clad in a yellow water-repellent trench coat and a black bell-bottom jumpsuit. Worry registered on her face. "Akane, what's wrong?" She dropped her shopping carryalls, and purchases of clothes and cosmetics tumbled out from them.

Akane kicked over the coffee table. "I hate this world! I *fucking* hate it!"

Simone peeled off her coat. She then hurried to Akane and gripped her biceps. "Akane, what's going on?"

Akane squirmed. "Let me go!"

Simone shook her dramatically. "Akane, stop it! Tell me what happened!"

"Get away from me!" Akane tore herself from Simone and sat against the wall, tucking her knees to her chest.

Simone sat down next to her. "Akane, please tell me what's wrong."

"What isn't?" Every muscle in Akane's face convulsed. Anger, disgust, and grief shaped her expression. "Skylar managed to grind her way to an okay life. She got a secretary gig. In her spare time, she was working on her singing career and dabbling in modeling.

"She was trying to make things happen, but a couple of stupid bitch-ass Highborn kept harassing her at the office *just* because she was an immigrant. When she sent her demos to promoters and studio owners, they were impressed. They said 'I love your voice.' But when they found out she was an immigrant, they sent her packing." Akane hugged her knees.

As Skylar's hopes and dreams were being obliterated, Akane had watched her joy wither over time, until she became a shell of her former self. The glimmer her eyes once held had faded.

Akane said, "She sent me a goodbye message today. Said I was right all along." She whimpered, tears soaking into the front of her shirt. Constant harassment, relentless cyberbullying, and rejection from society had pushed Skylar over the edge. "Saw it on the news. She leapt off her six-story apartment complex."

Akane remembered Skylar's relentless optimism. She had always been a motivational person, a true morale booster. She had dreams of becoming a star, and now she was just a mess of shattered bones, her beauty splattered across some street.

"I'm sorry," was all Simone could manage. Sorrow clenched her heart.

Akane broke out in sobs. "As for me, I got another rejection. That's the fourth university I applied to." She wiped her eyes with her forearm. "The truth is that I'm being blackballed, aren't I? And it's because I'm an immigrant." Emotions spiraling, she cried out, "Skylar was shunned for what? Being a human being who had no say where she was born? How could any sane person believe that's fair?"

Simone said, "It's not. But too many people believe in AEGIS's blueprint for humanity and want to ostracize immigrants from society. They're intent on preserving the Commonwealth's current social structure." *We can thank AEGIS's creators—Cyrus Kline, Jagr Vlcek, and Atticus Hancroft—for the oppression we immigrants have to deal with.*

Akane's brow creased in anger. "There are too few of us in these major circles of influence, government and whatnot." She shook her head. "We're told we, too, can make it, just like any other Edenite, but that's a buncha crap. We've been sold a pipe dream.

In reality, we immigrants don't have a snowball's chance in hell of achieving real prosperity."

Simone smiled. "We *do* have a chance. Oviereya Amaechi is one of us, a colony immigrant, and look at her: She's a chairwoman and the Chancellor of the Supreme Judiciary. Then there's Arson Scott, who became a beloved war hero, respected captain, and recipient of the Commonwealth Meritorious Service Medal."

Akane scoffed. "Yeah, I keep hearing that, and it's getting old." She was tired of such redundant platitudes. "So two people made it big. Great. That's cool and all, but what about the rest of us? Are we all just gonna forever be desk jockeys and hirelings at golem factories?" Wryly, she added, "Hooray, next-level slavehood. A step up from being a resource harvester."

"It's true we're underrepresented. It's true we're being denied economic opportunities, merely because AEGIS didn't select us for Eden citizenship. You and I aren't supposed to be even breathing the same air as the 'upper echelon' of the New Humanity. But a lot of us immigrants are fighting to upset the balance of power.

"I was determined to make sergeant, no matter the pushback, so I could do my part in diversifying the CDF's leadership.

"You see, we can either embrace the spirit of subservience or the spirit of rebellion. I choose the latter. From within the military and political system, I play my part in transforming this biased society. I won't allow my lineage to be disgraced, or my future bloodline to be trapped in an endless cycle of disrespect and marginalization."

Akane said, "You keep mentioning you volunteer for some group trying to turn things around. So, is it like a nonprofit or something? Can I join? And what exactly do you guys do? If it's not totally on the up-and-up, don't worry. I used to do a lotta black-market dealing back in Sector 07."

Simone replied, "We're involved in a lot of social-impact initiatives, but that's not something you need to be concerned about right now." *Who knows, maybe she has what it takes to be an asset to us.*

"Well, I've been thinking about something," Akane said, changing the subject. "Since my aspirations for attending a university keep getting flushed down the toilet, I wanna join the CDF."

Surprised, Simone was wordless for a moment. "Really?"

"Yeah, I wanna do what you do. I wanna be a Guardian in the ETF and go after the Commonwealth's 'most wanted.' And I wanna be on *your* team. What's it called again? Vanguard Alpha?"

"Joining the CDF isn't a bad move, but I don't have the influence to guarantee your assignment, Akane."

"C'mon, you don't have *any* connections?"

Simone curled a finger around her chin, contemplating names in her mind. "Well, I just *might* be able to pull a few strings."

"Awesome, so when are we going to the enlistment station?"

Night had fallen. The rain had lessened to a drizzle, pitter-pattering against the windows.

Simone sat at the desk in her living room. The lights were off, and she was dressed for bed in a filmy backless nightie.

The faint glow from her laptop's net browser cast a soft light over the pronounced exoticism of her features.

After taking a sip of warm tea, she darted her fingers across the keypad. The text that came onscreen said ENTER ENCRYPTION KEY.

She typed a numerical code.

The screen flashed:

Resist oppression
Initiate change
Stop violence against immigrants
Engage in activism

An icon appeared—a raised fist bordered by a circle. Inside the lower half of the circle was a single word: **R I S E**.

She was now logged into the encrypted portal.

BEGIN CHAT WITH SAM GUTHRIE blinked onto the screen. She dragged the cursor to ACCEPT and clicked the touchpad.

> Chat Stream <

SAM: Report.

SIMONE: I like her. *Smiley Emoji*

SAM: Where's the kid now?

SIMONE: Asleep in her room. I want to bring her in. Reminds me of myself. And she's whip-smart.

SAM: That's nice, but does she have what it takes to champion the cause and be an agent of disruption?

SIMONE: She's still a work in progress, but she's been on-planet long enough to taste the bitter struggle immigrants face. Actually, she never deluded herself with romanticized illusions of Eden or the central government's promises. Real down-to-earth girl.

SAM: Being down-to-earth doesn't qualify her to join us.

SIMONE: She was facing hard times when I found her. Her friend committed suicide today. She's been hit with discrimination at every turn. She's full of anger, ready to act. Her blood is boiling. She's been emboldened to fight for equality. Immigrants who've been pushed to the edge like her are ripe. She fits the profile. And she's enlisting tomorrow. We need more recruits with military training.

SAM: Not convinced yet. *Thumbs-down Emoji* If her heart is soft, she won't be mentally equipped to handle everything we might ask of her. Let's revisit this conversation after she gets back from BCT, if she survives it.

SIMONE: Roger.

Simone drank more tea. *She'll survive it.*

"Hey, what are you up to?" Akane asked, jarring Simone out of her thoughts. She edged closer, in yellow-polka-dot white pajamas and flip-flops.

Simone's mouth froze in a partial gape, and her heart thudded.

She slapped the laptop shut and spun around in her swivel chair. Nervously, she brushed stray strands of hair back into place and clamped a hand over her pounding heart. "Akane, you startled me. I didn't even hear you walk up." Had Akane seen the screen?

"Yeah, so what are you working on at this time of night?" Akane took a veggie chip from her snack bag and munched on it.

No, Akane hadn't seen the private chat log. Simone was sure of it. Close call. Regaining her composure, she said, "Just . . . nothing important, really."

"Oh, okay." Akane stuck another chip into her mouth. "Well, I can't get back to sleep," she said, chewing. "I'm gonna watch some TV for a while, if that's cool with you."

"Yeah, that's fine. Knock yourself out." Simone stood, tugging down the hem of her rucked-up nightie. She scooped up her laptop, tucking it under her arm, and headed to her room. "Good night, Akane."

Akane raised two fingers, forming the peace symbol in response.

Simone disappeared from Akane's view. *You've got what it takes to be one of us, Sugimori. I'm right about you. I know it in my gut. We'll show you how to turn all that pain into power, into transformative action. You'll become a weapon for the cause, like me.*

Akane sat on the sofa, channel surfing. She saw a commercial for a Mercedes Gardner concert at Starlight Colosseum and couldn't help but think of Skylar.

The impulse to cry arose, and Akane rubbed her eyes.

She missed her friend's buoyant nature, her unwavering positive attitude. *Life fucking sucks sometimes.*

CHAPTER TWO

Star Palace
Shipyard

The *Nightingale*, a class-A space vessel, had crew cabins and a galley to support in-ship living for when Vanguard Alpha was assigned a long-distance mission. And it had a state-of-the-art weapons package that allowed it to hold its own in battle.

Vanguard Alpha had assembled in the *Nightingale's* conference room. The war table they stood around projected a 3-D topographical map that provided them a detailed lay of the land. Graphs suspended above the display presented data on regional climate, land elevation, wildlife species, and more.

A goateed black man had the floor. He was Lieutenant Carl Breckenridge, Vanguard Alpha's field leader.

Akane sauntered up to Randy's side, stood on her tiptoes, and whispered into his ear, "Remember, watch out for Shaffer." She scowled at the douchebag. "Chances are he's even a ringleader."

Randy silently bobbed his chin. Whether or not Paul was a Purist, he had intended to keep his defenses up when around him.

Carl jabbed his pointing stick at the red cubical vector graphic in the middle of the display. He spoke with an air of command, going over the avenue of approach. "We'll land twenty-three miles from the compound, where they're holding the slaves." Which was on planet Randarex. "Three weeks ago, Defense Force Intelligence intercepted one of these traffickers' ships and rescued thirteen abductees.

"Three of the women were from Eden; the others were from undocumented worlds. Intel can't guarantee whether the compound we're about to raid has Commonwealth abductees or not, but there's a very good chance. Even if there are no human abductees, the women from those outer worlds still need to be rescued from these dirtbags and returned safely to their families."

Bridging the linguistic barriers of outerworld slaves and locating their unmapped homeworlds was a difficult undertaking. Situations like this often resulted in displaced young women. Queen Pappalonie had been granting rescued slaves from outer worlds asylum on Taramassia until the Commonwealth could identify and locate where they came from.

Carl said, "Once the *Nightingale* lands, we'll make our approach on hoverbikes, staying inside the compound's surveillance blind spot. After a quick recon, we'll cloak and enter the rear access."

Sergeant Jenny Pines, an albino woman of European descent in her early thirties, raised her alabaster hand. "Question: What kinda heat are they packing?" she asked, voice noticeably accented.

"Unknown," Carl replied. "We'll find out when we get there. Any more questions, people?"

He got nothing but silence.

Nope, Akane thought. *Basically: go in; bang, bang, bang; rescue captives; head back to Eden; and then relax until we get our next marching orders.*

Carl continued, after giving everyone ample time to speak up. "Alright, no questions, then." He tapped a glyph on the war table's touchpad with his finger. The holographic map dissolved into pixels and dissipated. "Ten mikes prior to landing dirtside, you're to be shelled and locked n' loaded. Clear?"

"Yes, Sir," Vanguard Alpha replied in unison.

"Good. You're all dismissed." Everyone turned to head out. "Except you, Specialist Scott. I need a word with you."

Paul snickered as he left.

Randy grunted.

He marched up to Carl. *Okay, here comes the scolding.*

The door hissed shut.

Carl's brow furrowed. "Specialist Scott, what in the world were you thinking, starting a damn slugfest with a noncom (noncommissioned officer)?"

Fuming, Randy disregarded deference. "You're barking up the wrong tree! Shaffer's the one who provoked *me!*" he made clear, jerking a thumb at himself. "So put him in your hot seat!"

"You were the one who tried to sucker punch him, Scott, throwing the first blow." According to witnesses.

"This is absurd. I have a mission to prep for." Randy pivoted and began stomping away.

"I didn't dismiss you yet, Specialist."

Randy stopped, but he kept his back to Carl. The last thing he needed right now was a write-up for being recalcitrant.

He was seething, his lips pressed tightly together. Why'd he have to get a bad rep because of some immigrant-hating asshole?

He gave Carl more backtalk. "I have nothing else to say, Sir. Now I need to go prep for the mission. You can chew me out more after it's over. Sound good?"

"I'm not your enemy, Scott. I fought alongside your father."

Why am I not surprised.

"I'm actually rooting for you, my friend's son, to go far in the CDF. We need good soldiers like you. I just don't want to see you self-sabotage your career, so keep that temper of yours in check. If someone's messing with you, report it to me. There's no need to play the tough guy and take matters into your own hands like you did last night." That incident had gotten Carl a chewing-out session of his own from Narvaez. "Understood?"

"Understood, Sir."

"Look, I've got mad respect for you. Fighting in the Battle of the Quad wasn't nothing. Just don't go getting into scrapes with any more Guardians. You feel me, Specialist?"

"No guarantees," Randy said defiantly and walked out.

Carl shook his head and exhaled an irate breath.

The anchors securing the *Nightingale* disengaged. The shipyard door yawned open, splitting apart along a horizontal seam. A runway with marker lights extended into the starry wilderness of space.

"Vanguard Alpha, you are clear for takeoff," said a man over the shipyard's speaker system.

With pre-liftoff checks complete, the *Nightingale's* helmsman engaged the engine. Plasma thrusters flared as the ship rolled across the runway and glided into space.

Accelerating, it headed outsystem.

• • •

Planet Randarex

Stacie Spencer—now one of the richest women in the Commonwealth since becoming the sole proprietor of her parents' enterprise—had gone on a PR campaign across the interview circuit. She needed to reassure her parents' noncriminal business clientele that she had no knowledge of their web of illegal commerce. She vowed to end all unlawful domestic and intergalactic ventures. And she promised herself she would use her family's fortune for just causes, not merely for profligate spending.

But Stacie refused to stand by while the other family heads continued their parents' criminal legacies. To thwart them, she assembled a four-person tactical combat team.

The team was officially registered as a bona fide bounty-hunting entity. Bounty chasers supplemented the CDF's task forces in apprehending malefactors, both intergalactic and human, who disrupted the Commonwealth's peace and safety. But the registration was a front, a clever smokescreen. As bounty chasers, Stacie's team could legally purchase arms and remain off Defense Force Intelligence's radar.

In truth, Stacie's mission was one of vigilantism. So if caught red-handed, the team would face serious consequences. But they were willing to take the risk.

Her dedicated crew included both familiar and new faces. Jason Mansford, who had led First Squad of Lima Company's Fourth Platoon, served as the team's second-in-command. Eli Manson, another former comrade, brought expertise in hacking and demolitions. Ryoko Nahara, the third ex-Guardian on the team, had also fought alongside First Squad. Lastly, there was DeShaun Watkis, a young friend of Jason's with four planetary-impact missions under his belt.

Stacie and her team were on Randarex because her intel had confirmed that the trafficking operation, the same one the CDF was tracking, was the work of Damien Sykes.

Since chasers weren't allowed to have mechsuits, she equipped her team with the best threat-reduction body armor and combat smartgear money could buy.

Their featureless helmets' visor was capable of visual magnification, infrared vision, heat-signature tracing, and a slew of other functions. The rest of their gear had more nifty features, including an emitter on their belts that could generate a holographic camouflage field.

Stacie dropped to one knee, lowering herself into the concealment of overgrown weeds and thick foliage. She punched a black-gloved fist skyward, commanding her team to follow suit. They quickly complied, kneeling in unison.

As a former Guardian who'd worked her butt off to earn the mantle of Warrior Extraordinaire, Stacie got a thrill out of being back in the field. When she wasn't wining and dining, hitting her personal gym, shopping, or indulging in leisure activities, this was where she preferred to be—with her team going after bad guys, not stuck in boardrooms or business meetings. It was exhausting having to playact the sophistication and savoir faire expected of an entrepreneur of her supposed stature. She was "modern-day royalty," after all.

"Businesswoman" just wasn't her forte, at least not yet. She didn't possess her parents' entrepreneurial acumen, and being thrust into the driver's seat of a financial empire was no cakewalk. She was learning on the job, so to speak. But this job, here on Randarex, she knew how to do well.

Stacie aimed her visored gaze at the traffickers' secluded compound, which consisted of a large, dull, windowless building and a scattering of small prefabs.

She magnified her optics by blinking three times. As she meticulously scanned for defense systems, she caught sight of a man with a rifle slung over his shoulder. He was dressed in dirty pants and a muscle shirt.

The man was taking a frightened young human woman—wearing jeans, a tank top, and boots—to the corroding entrance door of the main facility.

"Move faster!" he barked, giving her a one-handed shove.

The captive's feet scrambled for stability.

At the door, the man punched in a code on the access panel. Bolts and latches clacked. The door screeched open.

A stoutly built figure in tactical pants and a black tank top stood in the doorway. Stacie blinked twice, triggering her visor to freeze-frame a close-up of the hairless man's rugged mug. If eyes were indeed the window into the soul, his were the eyes of a stone-cold killer, a killer whose rap sheet included just about every criminal offense imaginable.

That has to be the lieutenant of this operation, Jacob Kilbourne, Stacie concluded. Her intel had given her the lowdown on him. He was every bit a scumbag.

Her helmet's sensor scans detected combat mods inside his body for strength, healing, and speed. And there were endoskeletal plates inside his chest, to repel bullets.

"She the last of the merchandise?" Jacob asked his henchman.

"Yeah. All the broads have been off-loaded."

The captive sobbed.

"Let's toss her in the pen with the rest and get some chow," Jacob said. He snared the woman's wrist in an ironclad grip and dragged her into the building. "C'mon, get in here."

The door lowered as the two traffickers and the captive disappeared from Stacie's vision.

Abject disgust filled Stacie's face. *Women uprooted from their homelands and treated like animals in a menagerie. If we find proof this operation belongs to Sykes, that smarmy bastard's toast; he'll never get the chance to run for CE.*

71

There were plenty of words Stacie could use to describe Damien: narcissist, prick, playboy, delusional, cunning, hotheaded, arrogant. She preferred "run-of-the-mill asshole."

He deserves to be in jail. Better yet, he deserves to be six feet under for what he did to Cassie. Outrage sizzled within Stacie.

She recalled the bruises on Cassie McCanns' face that awful night. Yep, Damien was a run-of-the-mill asshole, and that was putting it mildly.

She shook her head, forcing away the bitter memories.

Oddly enough, Cassie had just returned to Eden after completing an offworld assignment for her employer. She'd left without telling Stacie, and hadn't let her know she was back, either. It had been two years since they'd last seen each other. Two whole years!

Stacie figured Cassie never mentioned her assignment because she'd been furious, and still was. After all, she was the one who'd introduced Cassie to Damien.

Well, she intended to make it up to Cassie by putting Damien Sykes where he belonged—behind bars. She just needed evidence to connect him to this trafficking racket.

"Okay, people," she said, "we're going in. This should be an easy op. Just ten hostiles with energy weapons. No powered combatwear or any heavy artillery. We need to take one of these creeps alive, though." *Unfortunately.*

Jason took up a position right next to her. "Hey," he said in a hushed tone.

Stacie flipped her visor up so that it rested atop her helmet. "Yeah? *Question?*" she whispered back, clearly exasperated and not eager to delay the team's advance.

Jason lifted his own visor. "You sure your informant's reliable? We don't want to go in biting off more than we can chew because of faulty intel."

"Beltasia Corbezeus isn't exactly an angel, but she's an information broker who takes pride in her rep. She's got high standards. She wants to maintain her clientele and keep her revenue stream flowing. That doesn't happen by being a slouch."

"How'd you find this Narphaisian info broker?"

"I found out she did some sleuthing for my parents. She got them intel on rival interstellar operations. I got in touch with her to do some sleuthing for me, *okay?*" Stacie's "gee whiz" expression told Jason he should drop this conversation.

But Jason wasn't done. "So she works both sides of the fence, good or bad, and has no real morals?"

Stacie shrugged, palms up. "Yeah, well, sometimes you've gotta make uncomfortable alliances to get things done."

Jason didn't trust easily, particularly when it came to shady businesspeople. "Let me get this straight." He had a challenge on the tip of his tongue.

OMG, Stacie thought. Couldn't he just roll with the plan?

"We're supposed to wager our lives on the intel of some . . . freelance mercenary info collector?"

Jason's protests were irritating Stacie. Still, she knew his caution came from experience. As a former CDF squad leader, he understood that when soldiers' lives were on the line, the wrong decision could lead straight to the morgue.

"*Someone* has to rescue those slaves," Stacie said.

"You could've just informed the CDF and let them handle it."

"And have Defense Force Intelligence breathing down my neck, wondering why I'm *illegally* waging a personal war on intergalactic crime instead of chasing bounties like we're supposed to?" Stacie shook her head. "No thanks. I'd rather not end up staring out the bars of an orbital prison. Besides, the only person I trust to take down the Seven Elite is *me*. Who knows who they've bought? Anyone could be in their back pocket."

Preparing to move out, she flipped her visor back down.

Jason sighed in resignation and lowered his visor. "Okay, fine, let's get this over with." In his command voice, he said, "Chameleon mode, people."

Each team member tapped their belt, activating a cloaking field. The camo protocols adapted to the green-and-earthy tones of the forest.

Everyone rose from their crouched positions.

"As planned, we're going in from the rear," Stacie said. "First, we take out the back-door security cam."

She removed the microdrone attached to her belt and set it on the ground. She guided it into the air using the control keys on her bracer. Times like this, she wished she were in a Shell, utilizing neural-control interface. With her resources, connections, and credits, she could've had her own mechanized combatwear built. But the Commonwealth Government didn't allow any private entity to rival the CDF's power.

The drone's video feed appeared in Stacie's optics. She aligned the crosshairs of her targeting reticle on the security camera mounted above the back door. Target locked, she triggered the drone's microblaster. A narrow beam of energy shot out, scrapping the camera.

Stacie recalled the drone and reattached it to her belt. "Okay, let's move."

The team hustled down a hill. Underbrush crunched beneath their boots as they circled to the rear of the building.

Inside the traffickers' main facility, a man with a red mohawk sat at a control console. He told Jacob, "The back-door camera feed just died. I'll go check—"

Jacob cut him off. "No, no need." He grinned sharply. "Our visitors have likely arrived." His voice rose as he said, "Everyone, pause what you're doing! Let's get ready to welcome our guests! You know what to do!"

Around him, bodies moved in a hurry.

Eli connected three color-coded cables from his bracer to the back door's interface ports. He went through the rigmarole of code-hacking to bypass the security lock. After two tense minutes, he heard the satisfying click he'd been waiting for. "Eureka."

Moving as one, the team advanced down a wide, dark, grungy corridor.

They cleared an empty room to the left, then another to the right. A few paces ahead, the hallway opened into a large square space packed with cages, some containing women from the Commonwealth, others filled with women from multiple worlds. Most appeared between eighteen and twenty-five, the traffickers' ideal age range. Some bore bruises and contusions. All were visibly distraught.

Stacie spotted the woman she had seen outside.

The team spread out into the slave hold, their footsteps cautious and measured.

The lights mounted to their rifles sliced the darkness.

From the cages came desperate pleas for help.

Relief overcame a human woman when she saw the team. "Please, get us out of here." Tears clustered in her hazel eyes.

Eli pressed a finger to his lips. "*Shhh*. We're going to get all of you out. But first, we need to take care of your abductors, okay?"

The woman nodded.

A single door in the center of the far wall led to the facility's main room. Eli, acting as breach man, placed a charge on it. He stepped back and tapped his bracer's touchpad, triggering the detonation.

The blast blew the door outward. Rifles at the ready, the chasers fanned out into a cavernous, warehouse-like enclosure housing shipping containers of munitions and a few combat vehicles, items that would fetch a high price from planetary warlords, despots, and tyrants.

"Nobody move!" Stacie shouted.

Jacob clapped in mock applause, one henchman standing to his right and one to his left, all three clad in protective gear.

Each of Jacob's men had an arm around the neck of a captive, using them as human shields.

The gagged women mumbled.

"The jig's up!" Jacob had a lupine smile on his face. "Welcome to our humble abode!" He was completely unruffled.

A subtle tremor ran up Jason's spine. *They were expecting us. Not good.*

Loud footfalls thudded across the metal grate-floor of the catwalk connecting two upper-level platforms.

The team angled their heads upward.

Two traffickers in exoframes stood on the catwalk. They aimed their wrist-mounted guns down at the team. One of the mechanical chassis, painted crimson, had a white number one on its shoulder; the other, painted blue, had a number two. Exo-One and Exo-Two.

Stacie and her crew were in a hairy situation.

Jason didn't like the odds the team was up against. *Damn, funneled right into a deathtrap. And so much for these guys not having any powered combatwear. And I count over ten of them.* His HUD tallied twenty hostiles, and there could be more. *Fucking faulty intel.*

A lime-green woman with reptilian eyes emerged from behind Jacob, cackling wickedly—the wily Beltasia Corbezeus.

She wore a purple legless getup, which exposed the dark green dalmatian-like spots on her arms and legs. Her thigh-high boots had numerous buckled straps and a scabbard each, sheathing knives. The leathery brown belt fastened around her waist holstered an energy gun.

Stacie yearned to tear Beltasia apart. *Double-crossing bitch sold us out.*

The hands-free translator around Beltasia's neck echoed her words in the humans' language. "Don't be so angry. I'm an information broker." After getting Stacie the intel she needed, Beltasia sold Jacob the details he needed to foil today's foray—the date and time. A devious grin widened her green cheeks. "Couldn't resist the opportunity to get double paid."

Two-timing charlatan. Stacie trained her rifle on the deceiver. "Any special words for your obituary?"

Jacob leveled a handgun at Stacie. "Whoa now, let's not get trigger-happy here!"

Stacie ignored his warning, her hands shaking as she kept her aim locked on Beltasia.

Jason directed a chastising frown at Stacie and slapped her rifle's muzzle downward. "We're in no position to resist. They'd pick us off before we can even blink."

"Listen to your friend," Beltasia said smugly. She faced Jacob. "Now, Mr. Kilbourne, all I need is my compensation and I'll be on my merry way. Nice doing business with you."

"Of course."

Jacob's handgun flashed. Beltasia went down, a geyser of blue pulp exploding from her chest. That was her compensation, for ratting the traffickers out in the first place.

Jacob realigned his weapon, making it clear to Stacie and her team that they'd be next if they resisted. "Hands up!"

Jason's eyes, still fixed on Stacie, narrowed further. He couldn't understand what she was hesitating about. Surrender was the only option that would keep the team alive, at least for a while. "We've got no choice. Those exoframes have the high ground. One move and we're dead."

"Ten seconds is all you got!" Jacob shouted. "We already have one cadaver to clean up." He glanced down at Beltasia's body. "Spare us the trouble of having five more." He began counting.

"Your call, boss lady," Eli said to Stacie. "I say we take 'em."

Jacob counted to five.

Stacie froze. Surrendering was the last thing she wanted. And if they did surrender, wouldn't they be as good as dead anyway? *We could make a run for it. No, what am I thinking? We'd get knocked off in a heartbeat.*

"Three seconds left!" Jacob held up three fingers.

Sweat slid down Jason's face. He gritted his teeth and muttered angrily, "Stacie, give the fucking order to surrender."

"One!" Jacob shouted.

Stacie threw her arms up. "Okay, fine! We give up!" *This way, maybe we can pull off an escape. Maybe.*

"Hang 'em up!" Jacob ordered his men.

Ryoko spun and made a break for the exit. *Outta here.*

One of the exoframes above unleashed a devastating energy blast that tore open her back. Red splotches and bits of flesh violently splattered over the walls and floor. Her body lay, the massive hole burned into it still smoldering.

Jason shook his head. *Stupid.*

The traffickers moved in and took the chasers into captivity.

Outside, Vanguard Alpha stood on a nearby hilltop under a dense canopy of green-leafed branches. From their vantage point, they had a clear view of the compound.

Carl had deployed an aerial microdrone and sent it into the building. His AI Combat Assistant—the Oracle—handled the flight path, weaving the drone between lanes of shipping containers, crates, and parked vehicles. "Stand by, people. I'm sharing my visuals . . . now."

The ACCEPT FEED prompt flashed on everyone's HUD. They accepted.

The drone's visual relay showed Stacie and her team, their arms held aloft by chains.

"Who are they?" Carl wondered aloud.

Randy flinched. Eyes agape, he looked nonplussed. "Stacie?" he blurted. *What the heck are you doing here?*

"You know her?" Akane asked. Recognition clicked. Since taking over her parents' enterprise, Stacie had been in the limelight more than ever. "Wait, isn't that Stacie Spencer? Who's she to you?"

The evocative sight of Stacie's face conjured up a wave of memories for Randy: a kiss, a nature walk, laughter and joy. "We served together. And she's my ex." The reminiscence of their naked bodies making tactile confessions of love zinged from his implant to every nerve ending inside him.

"Your ex? What happened? What'd she do?"

"More like *what did I do.*"

Randy recalled Stacie's fury when she discovered his coupling with Kesley Whittaker: *"Not only have you joined the enemy, but you sleep with them too! You betrayed your duty, but you also betrayed **me**! **Me**, Randy, the woman who dragged you out of your emotional withdrawal from society! The woman who broke you out of . . . being a loner! The woman who made you smile time after time since your mother's death by the very people you now ally yourself with!"*

Then he remembered how Stacie had censured him after her parents' execution by Reza's kill squads: *"And you—who I let touch me, make love to me—helped put this murdering piece of garbage in power, who just sent his bozos to my family's doorstep to murder them. Damn you, Randal Scott."*

Shaking off the memories that were keeping him from staying focused, Randy said to Akane, "But this isn't story time. Eyes on the mission."

Paul queried his CPU for an ID on Stacie:

Name: Stacie Lynette Spencer
Chaser agency registration: 5-EL0519
Position: Lead Chaser

"She's the leader of a bounty-hunter agency," Paul notified everyone. "But she's trespassing. Chasers aren't cleared to be in X-Quadrant. It's all ETF-campaign jurisdiction. She and her team are facing fines and potential imprisonment." *What a dumbass. The lady's got a net worth in the millions but wants to play space cowgirl and flirt with danger.* He shook his head in ridicule.

Randy rushed to Stacie's defense. "Maybe she and her team were just pursuing a bounty and had to pass through," he suggested.

Paul said, "If that were the case, she should've requested transit authorization. Permission isn't optional, Scott."

Carl's baritone voice ended the chatter. "Okay, it's time to get moving. Forget the back entrance. New plan of attack. We're blowing a doorway into the west wall. And with no abductees in the line of fire, we can cut loose."

"No abductees in the line of fire?" Randy spat. "Don't those chasers count?"

Carl replied, "Yeah, try not to hit the chasers with friendly fire. That's a no-brainer. I was more worried about innocent women being in the line of fire than a bunch of chasers who just made themselves felons by breaking the law. Now let's stop wasting time.

"Randy, Akane, Paul, and Sam, you're with me. Jenny, Mark, Dan, and Jay, sweep those outbuildings and get any captives you find to the *Nightingale*.

"To be on the safe side, we'll maintain radio silence and communicate using C-comms only. Activate stealth mode."

The Shells cloaked.

Carl said Vanguard Alpha's motto. "Let's bring the thunder."

The team split off.

Inside the main facility, Stacie and her crew were lined up in a row, hands suspended above their heads by chains that hung from the ceiling. Their body armor and smartgear had been stripped from their uniforms.

Jacob grabbed Stacie's jaw, his fingers digging into bone. "Alright, just who the hell are you guys? You're definitely not CDF."

"Oh, we're just tourists," Stacie quipped. "I love a good safari, you know?"

Jacob answered Stacie's witticism with a vicious slap.

On the catwalk overlooking the ground floor, the two exoframe operators, now dismounted from their machines, watched the scene unfold. They laughed and took swigs of alcohol from metal flasks.

Jason, who was next to Stacie, glared at Jacob. He wanted to tear the creep's head off.

Stacie stayed tough. She refused to show Jacob even the slightest hint of pain. She wouldn't give him the satisfaction.

"Again, who are you people?" Jacob demanded.

"We're just a bunch of sightseers," Stacie replied, her slapped cheek still throbbing.

You think you're funny, don'tcha? Jacob slammed a punch into Stacie's gut, knocking the air from her lungs. She wheezed and coughed. "Don't toy with me, bitch."

Jason struggled to contain his anger, but it finally burst forth in a loud shout. "Hey, leave her alone, asshole!"

"Shut the fuck up!" Jacob fired back. "You'll get your beating soon enough."

An earsplitting explosion announced Vanguard Alpha's arrival, blasting a hole in the left wall and slinging debris everywhere.

Jacob tensed. "What in the name of—?" He didn't wait to find out who or what was coming. He hightailed it behind a container and unslung his energy rifle.

His men scattered for cover too, weapons in hand.

Vanguard Alpha appeared in the opening, their black-and-gunmetal forms exuding an air of dominance.

They dodged an onslaught of blasts from traffickers who'd taken up defensive positions behind crates, containers, vehicles—anything that could serve as cover.

On the catwalk, the exoframe operators wore panic on their faces. They were about to go up against Shells, arguably the most lethal mechanized combatwear in the Interplanetary Union—

wearable armaments of immense killing power.

They scrambled back into their exoframes' cradles, inserting their arms and legs into the interior armature's control brackets. Securing mechanisms clacked, locking them in. Metal parts clinked. The machines came alive with electronic whirs. Pistons hissed.

Sensory scans mapped their muscular signals, translating them into movements for the exoframes' modular limbs.

The operators fired their wrist weapons at Vanguard Alpha, autobursts vibrating the metal chassis.

Noisy shooting filled the air.

Bullets from Vanguard Alpha's rifles pierced containers. Traffickers' energy blasts ruptured metal drums, coating the floor in a yellow-green chemical ooze.

Now that the CDF had come to the rescue, Jason's jittery nerves stilled. Then he remembered that he'd just broken the law. But he and the rest of the team had known what they were getting into when they hung up their BDUs to fight Stacie's personal war. And they were getting paid handsomely to do so. *Well, better to be detained by the CDF than these maniacs,* he thought. Hopefully, the CDF would go easy on the team—though it didn't have a track record of leniency—or maybe Stacie had an ace up her sleeve.

"Stacie, hang on!" Randy shouted over the weapons fire.

Stacie frowned. *Randal.*

<<*Randy, Akane, Paul, take the exos,*>> Carl ordered over the C-comm. His rifle shot a conflux of bullets. <<*Sam and I will deal with these thugs.*>>

<<*Gotcha,*>> Randy said. A blast struck his shoulder, jolting him back a step. *Damn it.* He located the shooter and fired a three-round burst. The enemy snapped backward against a wall in a spray of blood, then slid down its surface, smearing it with red streaks.

That takes care of him.

Randy turned his attention to the threat above. He docked his rifle, summoned his plasma saber, and power-leapt, exploding into the air. Exo-One fired energy blasts from its shoulder mounts. Missed shots blew holes in the ceiling. Debris rained down. One lucky blast caught Randy in the chest midair, and he plummeted to the floor.

His HUD blacked out, then rebooted.

A diagnostic check reported negligible damage. All vital components were fully operational.

Even though his Shell's shock inhibitors absorbed the brunt of the fall, he got a good taste of the impact. His body ached because of it.

Akane craned her head in his direction. "Randy!"

A plasma beam belched from the barrel protruding from Exo-Two's front panel, aimed at Akane.

Her Oracle triggered her barrier shield just in time.

The vortex of energy swirling around Akane ballooned outward into a protective dome, blocking Exo-Two's high-powered beam. Then the shield shrank until it vanished.

"Hey, keep your head in the game, dollface!" Paul shouted as he reached back for his rifle. "Let's not worry about Scott right now!"

A missile deployed from Exo-Two, homing in on Akane. Quick to react, she vaulted onto an elevator platform docked at the second level. But the missile adjusted course, tracking her.

Frantic warnings lit up her HUD. *Shit. Smart missile.* Threat-detection systems highlighted the projectile in a glowing yellow circle.

The Shell's CPU fed her real-time data on its speed and estimated time to impact.

Her Oracle responded to the incoming threat. "Countermeasure applied." The AI triggered the Shell's EMP defense.

The missile reversed course and smashed into Exo-Two, detonating in a red-orange explosion that tore away chunks of metal and killed the operator inside.

The wrecked exoframe tumbled over the guardrail, bounced off metal containers, and crashed to the floor. Damaged electronics fizzed and crackled.

One goon down, Akane thought.

Gun compartments on Exo-One sprang open. A rapid-fire volley of bullets hammered Paul's Shell. The Kryoplaste held strong, remaining unbreached.

Enough of this shit. Time to put the peashooter away. Paul locked his rifle to his back. A recess on his thigh opened, delivering his handgun. He removed it from the securing clips and returned fire, muzzle disgorging sizzling energy blasts.

Akane dropped beside Paul in a crouch, one hand slapping the floor. Just being near the suspected Purist, and being called dollface, made her cringe. Still, she unholstered her handgun and fired alongside him.

A frontal force field generated by the exo repelled their blasts.

Paul fumed. *Oh, great, a defensive shield.*

Suddenly, Randy descended from above. He landed behind Exo-One and activated his right-wrist plasma saber.

Alerts went off on the operator's HUD. He whirled around to face Randy, blasts from the energy guns below still lancing toward him.

<<*Cease fire. I got him,*>> Randy said to Akane and Paul.

He raised his arm for an overhead slash, but as he brought the blade down, the operator captured his wrist in the exoframe's skeletal metal fingers.

"Not today," the operator snarled.

The exoframe's arm shrieked under the strain of holding back Randy's blade.

Struggling to counter the Shell's strength, the operator sweated profusely. "Damn it."

At the speed of thought, a second saber flared from Randy's opposite wrist. He drew back his fist and drove the blade straight through the exoframe's chest plating, into the man inside.

Sparks erupted.

The operator howled as the blade burrowed into him. His exoframe had now become his coffin.

Randy powered down both sabers.

The exoframe teetered.

Randy hopped back as it thunked onto the catwalk floor.

The power gauge on Randy's readout showed that using both plasma sabers had drained an entire unit of energy. He, like all Guardians, hoped that the development of the M-X03 would solve plasma weaponry's excessive power consumption, a problem that made good old-fashioned lead still necessary.

The M-X03 was set to incorporate technology from the Reldaldri mechsuits now in CDF possession, so it would definitely have flight capability. Randy couldn't wait to test the new model.

Jacob had been detained by Carl and Sam. The rest of the traffickers lay dead or mortally wounded.

One barely-alive trafficker coughed, choking on his own blood.

Sam went up to him and finished him off with a kill shot to the head. *No mercy for the wicked,* he thought. Blood pooled around the corpse.

Randy hopped down from the catwalk, landing near Akane and Paul.

"You alright, Randy?" Akane asked. She sealed away her handgun. "That fall you took must've been a doozy."

"I'm fine. Now come on, let's free those chasers." He had Stacie on his brain and was eager to make sure she was okay.

Paul held out an arm to stop him. "Just hold up one friggin' minute, Specialist Scott. These chasers violated Commonwealth law, *remember*? Let's leave them hanging until we're ready to detain them."

"Yeah, mellow out," Akane said to Randy. "We've got a bunch of slaves that need our help. The chasers can sit tight for now."

"Right," he muttered in reluctant agreement.

Carl walked over to Stacie. His faceplate slid away. "Stacie Lynette Spencer, you and your team are now in CDF custody for contravening Commonwealth law. Do you understand?"

Blah, blah, blah, Stacie thought. "Uh-huh," she said to Carl, sounding completely unworried.

She seemed nonchalant, Jason observed. Maybe Stacie *did* have connections that could get them out of this mess. He hoped she did, anyway.

<<*Breckenridge to Pines, status report,*>> Carl transmitted.

<<*We've recovered ten captives and are bringing them to the Nightingale for aid,*>> Jenny replied.

<<*Good work.*>> "Randy, Akane, Paul, sweep this place for captives," Carl ordered aloud.

"There *are* captives here," Jason said. He tilted his head toward the slave hold. "They're down that way."

Carl glanced at the blown-in door. "You heard the man. Move it."

Akane, Randy, and Paul took off.

"Thanks," Carl said to Jason.

"Hey, I was a Guardian too. We're all on the same side here."

"Maybe so, but you don't break the law. Righteousness is what a Guardian stands for. You should've remembered that."

"We were just trying to help the slaves, that's all." Jason's face grew somber at the thought of Ryoko. "Hey, one of our teammates was killed. Her body needs to—"

"We got it," Carl interrupted. "We'll find out where they took her body and get it cryofrozen for transport back to Eden."

"Thank you."

Carl walked off, shaking his head. *Sloppy-ass chasers.* He made his way over to Sam, who had Jacob on his knees with his wrists pinioned behind his back.

Jacob watched Carl approach. He contemplated when to make his move.

"Alright, on your feet," Sam said. "You're being taken into CDF custody."

Jacob hadn't planned on going anywhere. *Now!* he told himself. The strength-enhancing mods in his arms broke the cuffs. In a flash, he leapt up, pulled a disc-shaped mine from his belt, and clamped it to Sam's chest. Then he bolted.

Sam recoiled. "What the—?" An explosion detonated in front of his face, blasting him to the floor.

Stacie and her crew looked stunned, hearts pounding.

Jacob thought the distraction would be enough for him to get away. He made a beeline for the hole Vanguard Alpha had blown in the wall.

Carl aimed his wrist gun and fired an energy blast. "Oh, no you don't."

Jacob's blood spurted like red liquid projectiles.

He was finished.

Sam pushed himself up. A lattice of damaged circuitry flickered beneath the jagged metal of his semidemolished chest plate. His

HUD read: DAMAGE SEVERE.

"Are you injured?" Carl asked.

Sam removed his helmet. "I'm fine. But my Shell's going to need serious repairs."

"That can be arranged. We can even get you another Shell. We can't get you another life."

Sam smiled.

Randy stepped out of the slave hold. "Everything okay in here? We heard the explosion."

"Everything's fine, Scott," Carl replied. "How are the captives?"

"They're okay."

"Good, let's hurry and get them to the ship."

• • •

Randy, Akane, and Jenny were docking their Shells in the *Nightingale's* arms vault.

Randy shut the glass door of his Shell's recharging pod.

Akane appeared at his side and clapped him on the back. "Hey, mission complete, and the captives are gonna be A-okay." Physically, anyway. "C'mon, kick it with me in the galley for some R&R."

Randy held her optimistic gaze. "Not now," he said, declining her offer. His expression was serious, and his voice was stern, mind on Stacie. He peeled his eyes away from Akane. "I'm going to go view the chasers' interrogation."

Akane cocked her head. "'Kay. Catch you later, then."

Randy watched her leave out the vault hatch. *We'll definitely talk soon, Akane. I want those answers you owe me, after all.* He'd have plenty of time to get those answers, since Vanguard Alpha was on downtime for the next two weeks per duty rotation.

"Scott," Jenny said, her accent thick, an accent which had hints of Scottish, Finnish, or maybe even Australian origins. It was clearly a blended accent from one of the New Humanity's assimilated cultures.

Randy spun to her as she came closer.

She had her sleeve unzipped a few inches past her clavicles to cool off, exposing a strip of skin. "You like her, eh?" she asked.

Randy's brows lifted. "Akane? Yeah, she's cool, but I'm not champing at the bit to get her into the bedroom, if *that's* what you're implying."

Jenny undid her hair ribbon. Whorls of reddish-brown tresses tumbled free, framing her face. "So yer interest is strictly professional, huh?"

"And personal, I guess. But in the platonic sense."

Jenny clicked her tongue. Then she shook her head skeptically. "She's a beaut, and you two seem to be getting close. But alright, if you say so.

"By the way, you seem tense lately. I'm guessing it's got something to do with Guardians giving you hell because you fought for the Coalition. Am I right?"

"Well, yeah. Safe to say, my military career hasn't been so great since the Battle of the Quad."

"Just pay me a visit anytime you wanna blow off some steam," Jenny said flirtatiously. She winked before turning to leave.

Her sleeve—snug against her curves—explicitly highlighted the contours of her shapely backside, stoking Randy's libido.

Unlike the militaries of Earth Era, the CDF allowed Guardians to engage in sexual activity while on active duty. And Jenny had just given Randy the green light for a sleepover.

At the hatchway, she looked back at him, those pretty aquamarine-blue eyes of hers sparkling. "I hope you take me up on my offer." She walked out, deliberately swaying her hips in an exaggerated fashion.

The hatch closed, taking Jenny's lovely posterior out of view, much to Randy's disappointment. Her invitation was tempting, especially since most Highborn women gave him the cold shoulder, treating it like blasphemy to sleep with a so-called traitor.

Being an ex-Coalition fighter came with so many downsides: ridicule from fellow Guardians, judgment from society, and women ignoring him, even though they wouldn't have before.

Still, none of that mattered right now. What did matter was Stacie's future, and at the moment, it seemed pretty damn bleak.

• • •

Paul had brought Stacie to the *Nightingale's* interrogation room. She was the chasers' leader, so it made sense to start with her.

Frowning, he said, "Fess up."

Stacie sat in a chair behind a metal table, wrists shackled, her hair loose and disheveled from its bun. She remained unfazed by Paul's imposing, musclebound presence. "I told you, those traffickers captured us while we were en route to—"

Paul slammed a fist into the table. Her defiance was shredding what little patience he had left. "Maybe you're suffering from rich-twit syndrome and think you can weasel your way out of this, but I *guarantee* you that's not gonna happen. Now tell me the truth, or that photogenic face of yours is gonna need surgery to fix all the—"

Stacie interrupted him. "Sergeant, I guarantee you my *photogenic* face will remain untouched." She angled her head at the surveillance camera in the upper corner of the room, a subtle reminder that they were being recorded. Brimming with confidence, she added, "And so will every limb on my photogenic body, assuming you want to keep your job with the CDF." She kicked her heels up on the table.

Arrogant bitch. Paul swiped her feet off the table. "Enough posturing!" He swore that if Carl weren't watching outside, he'd give her face a makeover. "No connections you've got are gonna insulate you from this blunder."

"How do you know that? You got my personal-friends list or something?"

Stacie's chutzpah was unraveling Paul's composure. He was about to blow a gasket. "Shut up!"

In the corridor outside the door, Randy and Carl were watching the interrogation on a wall screen.

"He's not making any progress," Randy said, stating the obvious. Stacie was a hard nut to crack, trained by the CDF itself to resist interrogation. "Let me try. We served together. She might talk to a familiar face."

"It's worth a shot, I guess."

"One request, though."

"What?"

"Cut the camera." Which meant both video and audio.

"I can't do that."

"Then just the audio. It'll help me gain her trust."

Carl silently evaluated Randy's request. The regs said both the audio and video had to be on for all interrogations, but he conceded. "Alright, Scott, I'll cut the audio." He pressed the intercom button on the wall panel. "Shaffer, I need you for a sec."

Paul glowered at Stacie. "Saved by the bell. Lucky you."

She casually plopped her boots back on the table. *Sorry, no dice, baby.* "Toodles," she said in a chirpy, over-the-top pitch, waving one of her shackled hands.

Paul growled and keyed the door's release code. *You're a tough one, Spencer, but everyone breaks eventually.*

Once outside, he grumbled to Carl, "She's such a fucking irritant." Frustrated, he ran a hand over his silver-blond flattop.

Carl said, "Let Scott give it a shot. He's got a rapport with her, might get something out of her."

Paul glared at Randy, his eyes hard. "Go ahead, have at her, Mr. Big-Shot Hero."

Feelings for Stacie, engendered by thoughts of the past, crept up on Randy. He entered the interrogation room, and the door sealed behind him.

Carl got in Paul's face. "'Dollface?'" he snapped, referencing the sexist slur Paul had called Akane. She'd reported the unprofessional conduct to him. "'Mr. Big-shot Hero?' You need to watch your mouth and act like the professional you're supposed to be. I know all that training didn't leak out of your fucking brain. So straighten up, you feel me? Or *I'll* straighten you up. And if I have to, I *guaran-damn-tee* you won't like it." Carl had zero tolerance for boorish behavior.

"I gotcha, boss," Paul replied, but he didn't sound sincere.

Carl knew Paul wasn't really sorry. "I hope so."

Paul pivoted and walked away. "Hopefully Scott has better luck with her." *I'd prefer to work that dumbass dishwater-blond over till she begs me to stop. Maybe even inject some pain analeptics into her vessels. That'd loosen her lips.*

Inside the interrogation room, Randy stood across from Stacie. Her sculpted features and piercing cobalt eyes intoxicated his mind, evoking old lovey-dovey feelings. "It's been a while, Stace," he said gently.

Amused, Stacie arched an eyebrow. She slid her boots off the table. "Really? They sent you?" She tut-tutted, entertained by the absurdity of him thinking she'd ever divulge anything to him.

Randy kept his poker face and tuned out the rising emotions. As he pulled back the chair in front of the table, the fixture on the underside of its seat slid along the floor track.

93

He sat down and scooted the chair forward. "The audio's off. They can't hear. It's just you and me. You already know you're neck-deep in trouble because you traveled into territory off-limits to chasers."

"Whoops."

"This isn't the time for jokes. You need to talk. What are you doing in X-Quadrant?"

Hurt hearts didn't mend quickly, and the proof was on Stacie's face. "Go fuck your rebel playmate."

Randy couldn't fault her for still being upset. "I apologized for my . . . infidelity. Like I told you, it's not something I planned on happening."

"Apology not accepted," Stacie snapped.

"I tried flowers and candy."

With notorious Spencer cruelty in her tone, Stacie said, "And I *trashed* them with joy."

"You sound like your mother." A woman Randy had never met in person, only spiritually through his and Stacie's Link.

Stacie grunted. To her, that was a big snub. Being likened to her mother was basically calling her a bitch. But the truth was undeniable—she *had* picked up some of her mother's traits. Like mother, like daughter. "Why don't you leave me alone and go stick your dick in that redheaded bimbo of yours."

"Kesley and I aren't together anymore. We never really were." Their relationship turned out to be one of convince, not genuine affection, just a lengthy hookup.

"So was her heart on lease like mine? Did you cheat on her too?"

Randy was losing focus on his task: questioning Stacie. "Damn it, Stace, what do you want me to do? What can I do to make it up to you?"

"Too bad you can't '*make it up*' to my parents. Because they're no longer *alive*," she said, rubbing their murder in his face.

"First you hate your parents, then you don't, then you do again. Make up your mind, Stace."

Stacie's parents, especially her mother, had been overly hard on her, but she'd also experienced many beautiful moments with them. "I wanted them to change. To understand me. To cut ties with whatever illegal crap they were into. I wanted them to leave the Eight. I never wanted them *murdered*."

"Reza killed them, not me," Randy said, defensive. "And it would've happened whether I was involved in Hammer Fall or not. You *know* that."

"That doesn't make it any easier to accept that my boyfriend helped put their murderer in power."

"Reza pulled the wool over the Coalition's eyes. There's a judicial system meant to deal with criminals; he deemed himself above it. But I tried to rectify my part in his government takeover. I'm the one who shot him, remember?"

"You should've done it sooner. Then my parents might still be alive."

Randy opened his mouth to argue, then stopped. "You know what? Enough of this." *I'm totally off track here.* He forced himself to refocus. "What are you doing in X-Quadrant? Maybe I can help you get out of this ditch you dug."

"I don't want your help, Randal."

"Dial back the attitude. This is serious, Stace. You could face jail time."

Stacie shifted in her chair, bringing her cuffed hands behind her head. "Sounds comfy." Having nothing more to say, she stared at Randy in silence, waiting for him to leave.

"Forget this." Randy had had enough of Stacie's irreverent

attitude. He rose from his chair and withdrew from the conversation. He might as well have been talking to a brick wall. As he headed for the door, he said, "I hope you don't get locked away, Stace. I really mean that."

"I won't. I have connections to people in high, *high* places, if you know what I mean."

Randy realized who she was talking about. It had slipped his mind that Oviereya Amaechi, the Chief of the Commonwealth, had helped raise Stacie as a child, something few people knew. He was one of them. Stacie was like a daughter to Oviereya, and Oviereya was like a second mother to Stacie, a mother way more cherished than her biological one.

Randy left.

Stacie remained motionless. Seeing her ex after all these months stirred up ghosts of sweet memories. A fleeting pinprick of Cerebral-Attachment Syndrome pulsed. *No, thanks. No nostalgia for me,* she told her cerebral implant. *I'm not interested in a relapse.*

She quickly banished the memories. She'd considered an implant cleanse once or twice, but the potential neurological side effects were too risky: reduced short-term memory, temporary motor impairments, difficulty Linking. Anyway, being the one hurt, not the one who did the hurting, she had beaten Cerebral-Attachment Syndrome more quickly than Randy had. There was no need to take any drastic measures in her healing process.

She leaned back. All she wanted now was to get home and soak in a long, relaxing bath. She needed it after the enervating day she'd just had.

• • •

In the corridor, Paul and Akane crossed paths, walking toward each other from opposite directions.

As Paul edged closer, Akane's features darkened. Try as she

might, she couldn't hold back the tide of rage rising within her. "You know you're gonna bite the dust for murdering her. If I could, I'd cap your ass right now."

Paul smirked, enjoying her discomfort. He planted a hand on her head and ruffled her scruffy hair like she was some misbehaving mutt. "I don't have a clue what you're talking about, kiddo."

Akane slapped his hand away. "Bug off, creep. Stay outta my orbit."

Paul departed, his unsettling laughter echoing throughout the corridor. The sound of his boots clacking the floor grew fainter as he moved farther away from Akane.

The corners of Akane's mouth twitched. She wanted to gouge out Paul's eyeballs. *Purist filth. You're just a dead man walking, Shaffer. A dead man walking.* She flexed her fingers into the shape of a gun and pretended to fire. *One day, for her.*

INTERLUDE TWO

DURING MARTIAL LAW IN COLONIES
ONE, FOUR, AND SIX

Planet Eden

Akane and Simone stood on the rooftop of Simone's residential complex, admiring the breathtaking view of the city as the sun dipped below the horizon.

Simone's cornrows were tied back into a thick flowing stream. She wore a purple one-piece pretzel swimsuit, while Akane wore a dark blue bikini top with matching shorts.

Around the massive communal pool, men and women in swimwear mingled, chatting and laughing. One at a time, attractive people of all skin colors somersaulted off the diving board.

"Geronimo!" a heavily tattooed man shouted before cannonballing into the water.

Simone leaned forward, resting her forearms on the waist-high safety wall. She gazed out at the awe-inspiring panorama of high-rises and skyscrapers. She loved coming up here; it always helped clear her mind.

Ignoring the slight pang in her head from being chipped with a cerebral implant at the enlistment processing station today, Akane glanced around at the rambunctious activity.

Eden being a judgment-free society, bare-chested women lounged poolside and couples shamelessly made out in the open. No behavior was taboo; nothing was forbidden, unlike in NeoJapan. When troubles were nearly nonexistent and people could overdose on bliss, why would anyone care about the affairs of Satellite One, another planet, regardless of its inhabitants being fellow human beings?

Simone turned from the cityscape and looked at Akane, who was massaging her temples again. "Stop doing that." She laughed. "That won't help."

"Yeah, I know. Just an impulse. My head should stop feeling weird soon, huh?"

"Yes," Simone assured her.

To complete her ascension to neohuman, Akane had undergone not only chipping but genetic metamorphosis at the enlistment processing station. "Well, physically I feel . . . superfantastic."

"I remember my conversion. Now you've got expedited healing, heightened reflexes, boosted immunity and stamina, youth longevity—"

"Wait, so does that mean I'm gonna look eighteen for the next fifteen years or something?"

"The anti-aging spurt kicks in at different ages for different people. For you, maybe around twenty-five."

"Okay. Good to know."

A soothing warm breeze graced their faces.

"You ready for your first day at the Academy tomorrow?"

Simone asked.

Enthusiasm lit Akane's face. "You know it!"

"I'm glad to hear that. And with Desmond starting too, you'll have a friend there to watch your back."

"Definitely a plus."

Simone was delighted to see Akane happy. She had come so far in adapting to life on Eden. When she first arrived, she couldn't even operate a gamecom pad, let alone a wristcom—tech that was entirely foreign to her. But she and her friends had brought themselves up to speed. Akane's indestructible resolve reminded Simone of herself when she first arrived.

After a thoughtful pause, Simone said, "Akane, I want you to join me in mental communion. It's not easy for me to say this, but your company has meant a lot to me. It would be an honor to be your first Link."

Akane instinctively stepped back, palms extended in a reflexive "no thanks" gesture. "Let's hold off on that." Even after the psychological-safety and proper-consent classes, Linking still wasn't something she'd normalized. "I'm not sure I want someone poking around in my head, or if I want to be poking around in someone else's."

"You've got it all wrong, Akane. Human beings share feelings, thoughts, and experiences through words. We build bonds by sharing time, sharing beds, sharing life. Linking is next-level sharing, next-level love."

Simone's disarming smile—the smile of the woman who had saved Akane from a Purist cop, cared for her, and guided her—offered reassurance. It told Akane her mind and memories would be safe, encouraging her to Link.

"Come on, Akane," Simone said. "Don't miss out on this part of the human experience, this part of the New Humanity."

Akane mulled it over in silence. Did she really want to skip out on Linking forever? Her first Link would be a major milestone, and she might as well share it with someone who truly cared about her. "Oh, what the hell. Sure, let's do this."

Simone forwarded the Link request, pinging Akane's implant.

It seemed so simple, Akane observed, almost as easy as saying hello or shaking someone's hand.

She accepted the request. Then the marriage of minds began, thought convergence initiated.

<*Akane, can you hear me?*> came Simone's garbled voice from inside Akane's mind. Then it sharpened, sounding clearer. <*Akane, can you hear me?*>

<*I can,*> Akane responded.

<*You and I are a lot alike, you know? Who we are today was forged by similar hardships. See for yourself.*>

Akane felt her consciousness detach from her body. She found herself standing within a nebulous cerebral construct, an environment Simone had manifested. Its purpose was to help Akane navigate Simone's memories.

All sorts of colorful patterns undulated in the skies of the dreamscape.

In this ethereal space, Akane appeared as a ghost-like figure.

A row of doors materialized, one after another. Each was a portal into a fragment of Simone's past.

<*Go on.*> Simone's disembodied voice reverberated from all directions.

The door farthest to the left glowed.

Akane stepped inside it . . .

In Colony Six, twenty-year-old Simone sloshed through mud.

She raced toward her destination as fast as humanly possible, her yellow raincoat whipping in the wind. *Please still be there.*

She huffed, oxygen rushing in and out of her lungs.

Lightning split the murky sky. Thunder growled. A deluge of rain hammered the ground.

As her foot plunged into a pothole brimming with rainwater, her leg folded. She fell hands-first into the soggy earth. *Damn it.* She scrambled to her feet and pushed forward, half-stumbling, boots caked in mud.

Up ahead, she saw the dull-silver crescent-shaped freight shuttle, beckoning her to come. It was time to leave this life behind. She'd heard so much about Eden. She had dreamt of this day.

A large-chested man in his forties with a Bandholz beard stood outside the shuttle. "You're late, woman! Come on! Everyone's waiting on your keister so we can take off!" Rain drizzled off his shaved scalp.

She'd made it. Thank goodness they hadn't left. "Th-thank you for waiting. Dax, right?"

"Yeah, that's me." Getting straight to the point, Dax said, "Got your ID?"

Simone could hardly catch her breath. "Yeah," she panted.

"Well, don't just stand there, show me."

Thunder boomed.

Simone reached into the inner pocket of her raincoat. Her shaky hand pulled out a plastic card, almost dropping it.

Dax snatched the bootleg registration card and examined it. "Kasim's definitely a pro Counterfeiter. This looks legit." He glanced at the ID again: C-ZERO-THREE-THREE-EIGHT. The "C" stood for "colony," marking Simone as an immigrant, a lottery beneficiary. "Kasim couldn't make you a nonimmigrant

ID?"

Simone shrugged. "He said it'd raise more red flags in a background scan."

Dax gave the forged ID back to her. "Okay." His feet left big shoeprints in the mud as he went to the cargo-hold door. Gripping the manual crank, he began to twist.

The door spooled upward. Inside the hold were three men and one woman with black-market IDs. They sat among unmarked crates and containers, on a metal floor coated with motes of dust and debris from countless cargo runs.

"Get in," Dax told Simone. He was smuggling them all to Eden.

Simone climbed inside.

A gust of wind whooshed into the hold, carrying droplets of rain. Thunder crackled.

Grunting, Dax twisted the crank again, and the cargo-hold door unspooled, sealing the travelers inside.

The faint red glow from the overhead lights bathed the dark interior.

Simone settled next to the woman, who wore a red hijab and a decorative dress. She had olive skin and long, curly raven hair, and she was in her twenties.

Simone turned to her. "Hi, I'm Simone."

The woman smiled. "Khadija."

They shook hands.

Sitting against the rear wall, the three men chatted, speaking in a Slavic language. They sounded excited and full of hope.

As the engines growled to full power, the cargo hold rattled.

Simone toppled sideways. "*Omph!*" She righted herself and rubbed her elbow, which had struck the floor.

Khadija rested a hand on Simone's back. "Are you okay?" Her

words were slightly stilted, English being her second language.

"I'm good."

The shuttle ascended into the howling tempest, rain crashing against its metal body. Then it left Satellite One, rocketing into space.

"So, which province do you intend to live in?" Khadija asked, her words deliberately spaced for proper enunciation.

"I'm not really sure. I don't exactly have a plan."

Khadija retrieved a handheld device from the pouch on her belt. "Here, let me show you some viable options for us immigrants." She pressed a button, and the four-by-four screen displayed a two-dimensional map. Eden's continent was divided into region states, and those were further divided into provinces, collections of cities and towns.

She tapped a region state, magnifying it. "This is Region State Six." She tapped it again. "And this is Province Eight of Region State Six. People say it's one of Eden's most immigrant-friendly provinces. But that's because many of the First live there."

The First were the earliest colony immigrants transported to Eden. In the early years of humanity's reset, before the lottery's inception, the central government had needed laborers to accelerate Eden's development. Therefore, the Parliament and the Chief Executive imported several million colonists to do the work. These individuals were thoroughly vetted, deemed the best of an "inferior crop."

In addition to monetary compensation, the government promised them Eden citizenship at the conclusion of their service, a move that sparked controversy among original Edenites. It was the first time AEGIS's blueprint for humanity had been compromised.

Although they were living better than on Satellite One, these first immigrants found themselves relegated to the bottom of Eden's labor market, and the government withheld their genetic upgrade. Financial constraints and other excuses were provided as reasons. In truth, the government didn't want immigrants to prosper on par with original Edenites. Not to mention, government officials wanted to stay in favor with their voter base.

Even though they were at the bottom of Eden's socioeconomic ladder, the First still enjoyed a life better than what they had on Satellite One. Some of them even amassed considerable wealth and used it to support loved ones back home.

A number of wealthy First established relief nonprofits to aid colonists. Others, less fortunate, turned to the criminal underworld, engaging in intergalactic trafficking and other illicit activity.

"Do you know if there's a way to link up with them?" Simone asked. "The First."

"I don't, but I'm sure we can find one. However, not all immigrants—First or lottery beneficiaries—will help us."

"What do you mean? Aren't we all in this together?"

Khadija shook her head regretfully. "Some immigrants are snooty. They think they're on the same level as original Edenites, the people chosen by AEGIS to reign dominion over Eden. They believe they've risen to greatness and avoid associating with new immigrants.

"They fear compromising their success, their societal status. They want to stay in the upper echelon's good graces and are afraid that associating with new immigrants might jeopardize that. These *social climbers* have forgotten where they came from. It's shameful."

The two young women continued getting to know each other.

Simone, as a newly minted Guardian, had often found herself sitting alone at mess-hall tables. When she was deployed on planetary-impact missions, feelings of isolation and loneliness often gripped her. She had few true friends in her platoon. Most of her comrades were nonimmigrants and kept their distance, holding fast to the wrongful beliefs instilled in them by AEGIS—that they were the superior breed of human and the CDF was their domain.

After transferring to the ETF, Simone met Sam Guthrie and Jamie Lister, two people who became real friends.

Akane approached another door in the dreamscape. A shield of light blocked her from entering. When she turned left, more shields blinked over other doors. These memories were being firewalled, blocked from her cerebral implant. They were things Simone didn't want her to see yet, or that she had to earn the right to access.

Akane opened her eyes and left the dreamscape, returning her consciousness to the physical plane. She batted her thin-lashed eyelids, blinking sparkles from her vision.

Simone opened her eyes too.

Linking turned out to be not so weird for Akane after all. "Cool."

Simone fake-punched her shoulder. "See? That wasn't so bad."

A group of attractive guys walked past, heading for the rooftop exit. They directed a flurry of wolf whistles and catcalls at Akane and Simone.

"Did you see the phat ass on that tall brown chick?" one of them said, referring to Simone.

"Yeah," another responded. "Fucking amazing."

The thong tucked between Simone's thick, meaty ass cheeks

left nothing to the imagination.

Simone laughed at the men's compliments.

"I can't blame 'em for wilding out over you," Akane said, pointing at her. "That's a bodacious figure you've got there. Total badassery."

Simone definitely had a body that warranted stares—every muscle chiseled, every curve perfectly shaped.

"I think some of those eyes were on you, Akane."

Akane's brows shot up in mock hilarity. "Nah, I don't think so."

"Why's that?"

"Because 'killer bod with curves' trumps 'petite Japanese chick.'" Simone exemplified power and allure, not her.

Simone said earnestly, "*Ridiculous*, Akane." She gently took her friend's chin between her thumb and forefinger. "You're a gorgeous young woman. Don't believe otherwise."

Akane's face warmed. "Uh, well, thanks. I appreciate the—"

And then the unexpected happened.

Unspoken feelings and pent-up impulses, intensified by Linking, bubbled up inside Simone. She gripped Akane's shoulders, leaned in, and pressed her lips to hers.

Simone's hands slid to Akane's waist as she drove the kiss deeper.

Flabbergasted, Akane lurched back, unsticking her lips from Simone's.

An awkward pause stretched between them. Neither woman knew what to say.

Simone scratched the back of her head and stuttered, "I . . . I'm sorry. Was that not okay?"

Akane, just as nervous, toyed with her bangs. "Oh, no, it's okay. That just . . . caught me off guard. Kinda sudden, you know?"

She swallowed. "Anyway, I did like it. I mean, I'm into guys and gals, so—" She trailed off, unsure where the conversation was going.

"Akane!" someone shouted, breaking the tension.

Akane jumped at the sound of the familiar voice. "Jacobi!" Desmond stood beside him. "Des!"

Desmond went up to Akane, cool-guy shades on. "Simone invited us over to celebrate your first day at BCT tomorrow. Mine too."

He opened his arms for a hug, and Akane launched herself into his embrace.

They held each other for a long, sentimental eight seconds before letting go.

Jacobi edged closer. "It's been a while, Akane." His face flushed—he still had a crush on her.

"Good to see you too, J. Good to see both of you guys," Akane replied warmly.

"It's a shame about Skylar. I wish she were here with us." Jacobi's chin hung, and his shoulders slumped.

Desmond stepped between them and flung an arm over each of their shoulders. "Yeah, it's a bummer that Skylar isn't here anymore, but she wouldn't want us sulking day in and day out, right? Now come on, let's get wet!"

Akane punched a fist skyward. "Hell yeah!"

"You guys have fun," Simone said. "I'll head down and get supper ready." She walked toward the rooftop exit, silently chastising herself. *What was I thinking, lip-locking with Akane? Stupid me.*

Akane shimmied out of her shorts, revealing a high-waisted bikini bottom. "Des, Jacobi, come on!" she called out, running to the pool.

Jacobi momentarily lost his train of thought, distracted by Akane's beauty: pretty eyes, angular cheekbones, and a lean figure. Despite the amount of near-naked women around, his eyes were only on her.

Desmond elbowed him. "Still in love, huh?"

"Oh, just shut up, man. I'm dating someone, anyway. And it's going well."

"She's probably some plain Jane you ain't even into. Stop being a wimp and work up the courage to tell Akane you like her."

"Des—"

"Come on!" Akane hollered from the poolside, interrupting Jacobi. She dove into the water.

"Let's go, man," Desmond said. He and Jacobi dashed to the pool.

As the last glimmers of daylight faded, night crept over the city.

Simone lay awake in bed. Outside her window, the night sky glittered with stars.

Tomorrow, Akane would start her first day at the Academy. Simone would miss her. Not having Akane's presence for three months would leave a void in her life. She'd grown used to her company, *needed* it.

Simone rolled onto her side, restless.

She loved Akane a lot. Akane had become her best friend, and she wanted to protect her. And one day, she wanted Akane to know the part of her life that she'd kept firewalled from her in the dreamscape, the part of her life that was RISE.

A soft knock tapped twice on the door.

"It's open."

Akane stepped in, dressed in a spaghetti-strap camisole and a pair of skimpy panties.

Simone's eyes followed her as she approached the bed. "Akane, what is it? Are you having jitters about your first day at BCT? It's only natural to—" Akane crawled onto the bed. One strap of her camisole slipped precariously down her shoulder. Simone's heart rate went up. "Akane, what—?"

<Simone, I'm great. Chill the fuck out.> Akane's eyes made her intent unmistakable. She wanted to show her appreciation for Simone's love and support through physical intimacy. *<Like I said earlier, I'm down with what happened between us.>* Her lips moved closer to Simone's, a hairbreadth away from a kiss. *<And I'd like more.>*

Before long, their nightclothes and underthings were on the floor.

The electrifying sensations flowing between their Linked minds, as they consummated their friendship, amplified every touch and kiss. Euphoria slammed into Akane as Simone's lips explored her body, titillating her in the most intimate of places.

Naked flesh pressed against naked flesh, and the desperate whimpers of the women morphed into fervent moans.

The feeling that overwhelmed Akane was indescribable. Bones trembling, lungs expelling shallow gasps, she reached her first climax of the night—one of many to come.

• • •

FIVE WEEKS INTO BASIC COMBAT TRAINING

Satellite Two
Boot Camp

Cadets stood at parade rest in the torrid heat, lined up outside their company HQ in tight formation—sleep-deprived, muscles sore from rigorous training. Their battledress clung to them, soaked with sweat.

Bleak and barren, the obsidian landscape surrounding them offered little to admire, save for the mesas and volcanic mountains in the distance.

A drill sergeant stood in front of the formation, stern-faced. "Colony insurrectionists are the *sole* cause of this war that's killing our comrades. Fueled by Independent Movement ideology and Arman Reza's liberation philosophy, these dissidents seek to subvert authority and establish a republic independent of the Commonwealth. Which is treason! Their aim is to sow chaos and defy the rule of law."

Cadet Desmond Castillo, bold to a fault, spoke up. "You're wrong!"

The drill sergeant locked his eyes on him. "What did you just say, boy?"

"*Des,*" Akane hissed. She yanked his shoulder. "Calm down, or you'll end up in remedial re-education."

Akane had backbone; she wasn't one to silence herself. But Simone had warned her to never challenge the drill sergeants, no matter how crass or offensive their remarks. Speaking up might feel righteous, but it could brand her as an Independent Movement sympathizer—and get her killed.

"I can't ignore this guy's bullshit any longer, Akane," Desmond said. Hard-nosed, he continued to challenge the drill sergeant. "Yeah, it's technically treason for a colony to separate from the Commonwealth. But the government pushed the citizens of colonies One, Four, and Six into rebellion. Armed dissidence, ya know? I realize peace has to be restored, but that won't happen if we keep painting the Coalition as bad guys. We need to—"

111

Quickly and fluidly, the sergeant drew his pistol.

A shot rang out.

The bullet struck Desmond square in the forehead. He collapsed instantly, blood spraying the reddish-brown earth.

Akane gasped, and her heart froze inside her chest.

Cadets chilled to the core quivered. Color drained from faces scared witless.

The sergeant holstered his weapon. "Independent Movement sympathizing is a behavioral sign of an insider threat, so Cadet Castillo had to be put down. I suggest the rest of you think twice before following in his footsteps, unless you want to be removed from service as well."

Akane could hardly believe her eyes. *A Guardian killing a comrade for exercising free speech? Insane.* She hadn't expected even the most anti-immigrant drill sergeants to be *this* brazen.

What none of the cadets could see was the drill sergeant's skull-and-crossbones tattoo, the mark of the Purists. *It's our job to purge the CDF's ranks of these deficiencies, these unchosen. Gotta keep the military pure,* the sergeant thought.

• • •

MONTHS AFTER BCT

Planet Kendaldras

Simone said over the C-comm, <<*Alright, Private Sugimori, it's game time. This is only your third field mission as a member of Vanguard Alpha. Don't screw up your shining record now.*>>

<<*Relax, Sarge, I got this,*>> Akane replied.

<<*You'd better not botch it, Private.*>>

Yada yada, Akane thought.

Simone was Akane's friend, but out in the field, she was still her superior.

The enemy would be on high alert. Over the past few days, CDF task forces had hit five of their bases in a coordinated offensive. The final six were going down tonight. Vanguard Alpha's mission in this joint operation was to destroy this base deep in the forests of Kendaldras.

A pang of sadness rippled through Akane. *I wish Desmond could see me in action.* Shaking off the emotion, she activated her Shell's stealth cloak. *Time to get to work.* Her jumper struts launched her into the air, catapulting her over a fence of laser bands.

She landed in a crouch and then stood to full height. *Easy.* She jogged toward the east side of the building. Though she was in stealth-cloak mode, she'd still have to be tactful in her approach. Stealth cloaks did a good job of camouflaging a Guardian but didn't make them a hundred percent invisible, and there was the telltale rustling of grass with each step of a mechboot.

<<*This is Shaffer. Charge set,*>> Paul transmitted over the C-comm.

<<*Same here,*>> said Simone. <<*Akane?*>>

Akane replied, <<*I'm just about—*>> Energy blasts streaked past her, one zipping over her shoulder. "Fuck!" The hairs on the back of her neck rose. <<*Enemy engagement! I'm taking fire!*>>

Two Kendaldrak charged straight at her, their forearms locked into cylindrical energy blasters. They wore thick, scaly armor with high collars. Skintight hoods concealed their hairless heads, and glowing goggles covered their eyes.

Akane unholstered the rifle from her back and returned fire. *How in the universe can they see me while I'm cloaked? It has to be those bizarre goggles. Must be made of some gnarly tech.* A blast struck her shoulder, chipping away fragments of Kryoplaste. *Sonuva—!* She gritted her teeth and emptied three rounds into the attacker who hit her, taking him out. Then she gunned down the second Kendaldrak. *Ha, eat lead!*

Pumped full of bullets, he lay on the ground, convulsing and gurgling on the green blood upwelling from his mouth.

A strobe light coming from the guard tower scoured the darkness, sweeping for intruders. Voices shouted in a language unintelligible to the human ear. The firefight had drawn more hostiles.

Akane's Shell auto-translated the voices that were getting nearer. "Find and kill all intruders," one said.

More Kendaldrak were closing in on her position.

Moving fast, she docked her rifle and slapped a charge onto the building. <<*Charge set,*>> she let the team know. She spun around and made tracks, augmented strides carrying her away from danger.

A foot chase ensued, hostiles racing after her. Spears of energy flew by. *Damn, that was close.*

Flanked by gunfire, she swung her arm sideways while running, wrist gun spitting plasma blasts. The agile figures behind her dodged and discharged blue-white bolts from their arm cannons.

Akane jumped back over the laser fence and took off. Missed shots from her pursuers sliced the air, their glare lighting up her armored frame. <<*Akane here. I'm clear! Blow the sucker!*>> She maxed her run speed, kicking up a rooster tail of grass and dirt.

More shots came her way, and then a grandiose mushroom cloud of smoke and fire thundered into the starlit sky.

Akane skidded to a stop and whirled around, chest heaving. The enemy base was now a smoldering wreck. *Fuck yeah!* She smiled triumphantly as embers snowed like scorched confetti.

A fort of steel prefabs had been set up as a forward operating base for the task forces assembled for the operation. With all eleven enemy bases taken out, the Guardians of the joint force celebrated. They were in their sleeves, enjoying the moment.

"We secured five thousand weapons," Sam said to Simone. "You know the drill. Cook the books and make sure De'Angelo smuggles at least a thousand to the Coalition."

"Roger," Simone replied. After taking a moment to give it some thought, she said, "You know, I think it's time we bring Akane in."

"I know she's your bestie, and she handles herself well in the field, but that doesn't mean she'll cut the mustard."

"Let's find out."

Sam paused, considering. "Okay, do it. But feed her info in small doses. Bring her in slowly. No need to overdo it."

Simone bobbed her head. *Welcome to RISE, Akane.*

At a nearby table, Paul, Mark, and Dan chatted, nonalcoholic drinks in hand.

Mark glared at Akane, who was holding a cup and talking to another female Guardian. "Ugh, another damn immigrant." He downed a third of his drink. "These pissants don't belong in the CDF with us, AEGIS's chosen. They think they're as good as us, but they ain't. You can put sugar on shit, but it's still shit." *And that's exactly what these insolent immigrants are,* he thought. Hatred wrinkled his brow.

Paul smirked wickedly. "Well, by the end of tonight, there'll be one less of these *curs* in Vanguard Alpha."

"You about to pull something?" Dan asked.

Paul nodded. "Damn right. We've gotta do our duty, don't we?"

The three men laughed.

115

Mark raised his drink. "Amen to that, brother."

"For the purity of the republic," Paul said.

Mark and Dan repeated the Purist motto in unison: "For the purity of the republic."

Akane was with Simone, inventorying confiscated firearms stacked on pallets inside the trailer of a BUS.

Akane said, "That's it for me." She clipped a datapad to her belt.

"Good," Simone replied. She then segued into the long-awaited talk she wanted to have. "By the way, you mentioned wanting to know more about the activist group I'm part of. You even asked if you could join."

"Yeah, I remember."

"Jay and Sam are members too. We've all been watching you grow into the woman you are today, and we think you'd make a great addition to the group. We're called RISE. Our goal is to get more immigrants into those power circles you and I always talk about. We're a secret group, though. No one outside of us knows we exist. That's to protect our members.

"I'd like to bring you in, but there's a vetting process. It's nothing you can't handle. So . . . are you interested?"

"You fucking bet I am!" Akane said without hesitation. "Anything you're a part of, I wanna be too!"

"The final call isn't mine to make," Simone let her know. "But you're a high-speed Guardian. I'm confident you'll ace the initiation process."

"So what's next? What do I have to do?"

"I'll fill you in once I wrap up here. It'll be a quick talk. Should only take about thirty minutes."

"Okay."

"Great, I won't be much longer." Hands on Akane's shoulders, Simone leaned in and planted a kiss on her lips.

Akane and Simone weren't lovers, but they were friends with benefits, which made for an unorthodox mentor-mentee relationship when out in the field. Simone had once suggested they stop being physically intimate, but Akane wanted to keep it going. To her, there was nothing wrong with fooling around every now and then, especially when she was feeling horny.

Simone pulled her lips away. "We'll meet by the riverside. Sound good?"

"Sounds good to me, Sarge." Akane's voice turned sultry. "And I think we should celebrate tonight's victory . . . if you know what I mean."

Simone matched her tone. "Sure."

They'd have to be more careful this time. During another joint mission on Planet Bazular, they had decided to engage in a little leisure-time sex in their tent, and their naked silhouettes had put on an unintended show for a few Guardians. They were embarrassed, even though the CDF permitted sexual activity on active duty.

Before Akane left the BUS, Simone gave her a friendly pat on the rear. *She'll make it,* she thought as Akane walked out of sight.

She finished logging her batch of weapons after twenty minutes and stepped out into the tranquil stillness of the night. Turning left, she walked along the lengthy trailer of the BUS.

The sinister eyes of a man crouched in the bushes tracked Simone. When he saw his opportunity, he snuck up behind her.

Just as Simone was about to clear the trailer's concealment, a gloved hand clamped over her mouth.

She let out muffled cries, eyes wide with fright.

The attacker clicked the knife hilt he held. An energy blade flared to life, and he drove it into Simone's back, cutting through flesh, muscle, and bone.

When he pulled the blade out of her, she collapsed, a charred, smoking hole in her chest. As she gasped for breath, he leaned down and said, "Enjoy the afterlife, immigrant bitch. Your plucky little gal pal is next."

Simone recognized the man's voice. "Sh-Shaffer." Her eyes closed, and Paul dashed off into the night.

Akane had become concerned. Simone hadn't shown up at their meeting spot, and their Link was unresponsive. A mounting sense of dread frazzling her nerves, she returned to the BUS, worry blanketing her face. When she saw her friend lying deathly still, a knot twisted in her gut, and her knees buckled. The bloodcurdling scream she released jolted Guardians from their sleep.

All the Guardians were now awake and alert. Search teams had been dispatched to comb the forested terrain for Simone's killer.

Sam sat at one of the bench-tables with Jay. "No one saw who did it," Sam said. "The commander thinks one of the Kendaldrak must've come for some payback. He figures that maybe some were outside the explosion's radius, but we both know that theory's bullshit."

"Yeah," Jay agreed. "My guess is it was a Purist. Could've been someone from our team or one of the other task forces. They were probably watching Simone, just waiting for the right moment." He looked over at Akane, who sat two tables away, crying into her palms. "What about her?"

"Simone wanted her to join us. We should honor that." Sam stood and gestured for Jay to follow. "It's the least we can do."

They went to Akane's table and sat across from her on the opposite bench.

"Hey," Sam said gently, "we know you're hurting, but did Simone ever mention what she, Jay, and I are involved in?"

Akane sniffled and lifted her head, meeting their eyes. Grief jammed her throat, and she could hardly see through the sheen of tears. "Yeah. She said you're part of some activist group called RISE."

"That's right," Jay replied. "We can't prove anything yet, but we don't think it was a Kendaldrak who killed Simone. Our hunch is it was a Purist."

Sam elaborated. "Basically, a member of an immigrant-hating extremist group. Just like RISE, they're a secret; no one knows they exist. They're infiltrating the highest levels of government, the CDF, and law enforcement. Their sole objective is to ensure immigrants remain powerless and to keep colonists a bunch of labor slaves. The group we're a part of counteracts them."

Akane made a vow to her heart: The Purist who murdered Simone would suffer a fate worse than death. "I want in. I wanna find the butcher who murdered my friend. I want revenge." Her voice dropped to a low and gritty timbre. "I'm gonna kill this creep, whoever they are." Her expression was a foretoken of what awaited Simone's killer, and it was going to be painful, bloody, and messy.

The same yearning for vengeance stirred within Sam. "We want justice too. And we *will* find that bastard."

"We'll fill you in more tomorrow," Jay said. "When we get back to Eden, you'll meet the rest of the group."

CHAPTER THREE

ONE DAY AFTER VANGUARD ALPHA'S RETURN TO EDEN

Planet Eden
Chief Executive's Manor

Chief Amaechi stood facing the window behind her desk, hands clasped behind her back. She wore a purple pencil skirt that had gold decorative accents. A matching suit jacket with padded shoulders and dark heels completed the executive ensemble.

She stared at the mob of vindictive protesters corralled outside the manor's gate. They were shouting for retribution, demanding that Coalition fighters be held accountable for crimes against the Commonwealth. Hand-written signs said "Death to the Chief," and that wasn't even the worst of them.

The aftershocks of the Battle of the Quad had injected a fresh dose of venom into the New Humanity.

Oviereya wondered, Was this continuum of hate incurable? Could people not rise beyond it? Was peaceful coexistence a

Sisyphean task? As mankind transcended into the New Humanity, it had apparently dragged along Earth Era's deficiencies.

Outside, the cries and curses of protesters filled the air. A cordon of EPAs in riot gear stood stationed at the gate, ready to subdue any aggressors.

Oviereya asked herself "Am I good enough? Can I do this?"

A male EPA in a dark suit came into the office. "Madam Chief, your guest has arrived."

"Send her in." Oviereya's voice mirrored her morose mood.

The EPA left. After five seconds, Stacie entered, dressed in a crisp turquoise blouse tucked into khaki pants. As she walked forward, the carpet muted her heels.

Oviereya remained at the window, gazing at the protesters. "Hello, Stacie," she said, greeting the young woman who was like a daughter to her, and whom she had just saved from being locked away in an orbital prison.

Stacie moved further into the office and paused. "It's been a while since we've talked." She attempted to access their Link. There was no response from Oviereya's implant. "I see you've terminated our Link." She'd expected as much, but it still stung—just a touch.

"Of course. I'm Chief Executive now. Even with my implant's firewalls, I can't risk the *slightest* leak of the confidential information I'm entrusted with." As long as Oviereya was Chief Executive, she had to end all Linked interpersonal connections, nuptial Links excepted. It pained her to relinquish such a crucial aspect of life.

Stacie went up to the executive desk. "So, what's it like at the top? Must be incredible, making history as the first immigrant to become Chief Executive, even if it happened by default."

Oviereya felt her heart fall. "Honestly? It's cold at the top. I wanted to be a changemaker. I wanted to pave the way for unity and equality among all the Commonwealth's peoples—original Edenites, colonists, and immigrants. But now—"—her voice dimmed, as though all hope had been drained from her spirit —"immigrants are protesting all over Eden, outraged by the surge in hate crimes. Meanwhile, nonimmigrant Edenites are furious. They want every Coalition fighter punished. Some of those vengeful souls are gathered outside my window right now.

"I've spent many sleepless nights trying to find a way forward. But I've realized this problem can't be solved by me alone. It cuts across cultural and ideological lines. I can't wave a magic wand and make the hate go away. Only society, united, can end this us-versus-them mentality. Yet the Chief is always held responsible for the Commonwealth's unresolved issues."

"I'm worried about you," Stacie said. "I don't need a Link to see how stressed out you are."

Oviereya's face, still turned toward the window, betrayed her exhaustion. "It comes with the territory, I guess. But enough about me. Let's talk about you. What were you doing in X-Quadrant? Why are you putting your future at risk?"

"I'm dismantling the Seven's operations." The need to take down the Seven Elite vibrated in Stacie's chest.

"And why are you doing that?"

"I don't know the full extent of my parents' wrongdoings." Stacie wondered why they had resorted to such despicable actions. "Maybe they were only involved in the lesser offenses—bribery, racketeering, money laundering, extortion—instead of the more heinous ones like human trafficking, murder, or drug smuggling. But I can't say for sure. I'm still combing through databases, trying to uncover the truth—and root the evil out of Spencer Enterprises.

"What I *do* know is my parents never protested the crimes the other families were involved in. Of course they didn't. The Eight were all one big happy criminal conglomerate. Going after the Seven is my way of making amends for my parents' sins. Okay?"

"If you want to make amends," Oviereya said, "don't break the law. Donate to charitable causes or try philanthropy."

"I'm already doing all that. *And* I'm taking down the Seven."

Oviereya spun around, her long ebony locs whipping the air. Her strong features steeled.

By the pointed look on Oviereya's face, Stacie knew she was about to be scolded, albeit out of nothing but love.

"Let me make one thing clear: The Seven is not your concern." Oviereya wished Stacie weren't so stubborn. "Word is your recklessness even led to a young woman being killed."

Stacie bit her lower lip, Ryoko's death tugging at her soul. "I feel for her family. But that wasn't on me. She ignored orders."

A muscle in Oviereya's jaw twitched. "I beg to differ. And if you execute another unlawful mission, don't expect me to save you. As much as I love you, I'm not your get-out-of-jail-free card. I despise when the powerful or wealthy escape consequences because of their connections. It goes against my principles. I refuse to partake in such injustice. So this was a onetime deal."

"I know," Stacie said humbly. "I'm grateful you helped me out. But the seven family heads have kept their parents' criminal empires alive. So what am I supposed to do? Leave everything to the CDF and law enforcement? They've failed for *years* to bring them down. Someone has to do something. And I believe the trafficking outfit the CDF recently busted is tied to Damien Sykes, *your* opponent in next year's election."

Oviereya narrowed her eyes. "Do you have proof?"

Stacie was a little embarrassed, to say the least. She wasn't the type to talk a big game and not back it up. "Well, it's nothing concrete, but—"

"Just turn over what you know to the CDF, Stacie, and let them handle it from here," Oviereya interrupted. "I've already ensured that you and your team won't face any charges. But if you keep going after Damien and the rest of the Seven and get caught again, don't expect me to bail you out. I won't be your crutch. I'm not willing to risk my reputation as Chief Executive, not even for you." The Office was bigger than their relationship.

Stacie intended to go after Damien until he was dead or behind bars, for Cassie. "I can get to Damien in ways the CDF can't, and —"

"Damien is already being investigated by Defense Force Intelligence," Oviereya revealed. "But not for trafficking. Still, whatever you have, even if it seems insubstantial, could help DFI build a case."

"Okay, so what *is* he being investigated for, then, if not trafficking?" Stacie asked, genuinely curious.

"He may be involved in a domestic extremist group. Whether he's a financial backer or a figure of authority is still unclear, but there's strong evidence tying him to them."

Stacie pushed for additional information. "Tell me more about this group Damien's involved with."

"The group launched a virulent movement aimed at keeping Eden free from colonist integration, preserving the Commonwealth's class system, and halting progress for immigrants. None of that is illegal, but they may be violating laws in the process. Damien could be connected to those violations.

"The members of the group call themselves Purists. Since its inception, other Purist groups have formed, but the one Damien is involved with is the original and the largest. That's all I can tell you. The rest is need-to-know."

"I can get close to Damien, *really* close," Stacie insisted. "I can get him to confess his involvement in this . . . cult, or whatever it is. I can find out what they're up to. And maybe I can even tie Damien to the trafficking operation."

"Why are you so adamant about taking down Sykes? It's more than just because he's one of the Seven, isn't it? Does this have anything to do with Cassie McCanns?"

Memories of Cassie's bruised body unsettled Stacie's mind. She blinked them away. "Yes. She *never* would've gotten hurt if I hadn't introduced them to each other."

Stacie and Damien had once been casually involved, until her mother caught wind of their relationship. The rules were clear: No two children of the Eight were allowed to be in an intimate relationship of any kind. Intermarriage and the merging of family empires were strictly forbidden. Forced to end their relationship, Stacie moved on to other lovers. But, being the headstrong and rebellious woman she was, she continued seeing Damien in secret from time to time.

Eventually, she introduced him to a friend, Cassie McCanns. The two hit it off, but Cassie soon discovered Damien had other girlfriends. He'd told Cassie she was his one and only—his paramour, as he liked to say. It was a lie.

The night Cassie found out about Damien's other bedfellows, a heated argument erupted between them. Though she claimed she was done with him, Damien's charm kept luring her back to him. Then the abuse began. At first, he claimed it was an accident, a single slap. But he turned out to be a serial abuser. He manipulated Cassie into a cycle of psychological and physical torment.

Cassie had encountered a side of Damien that Stacie hadn't, but had inklings of. A controlling, possessive, and dangerous side. Stacie ultimately convinced Cassie he'd never change and urged her to press charges. But the charges never stuck. Damien had bought off the jury. He was a son of the Eight, after all, virtually impervious to the justice system. In the aftermath, Cassie's physical wounds healed, but the mental scars lingered.

"I can use his attraction to me to my advantage," Stacie said.

"Realistically, how close do you think he'd actually let you get?" Oviereya asked. "After you accused him of abuse and helped take him to trial, don't you think he'll be suspicious if you suddenly try to rekindle your relationship with him?"

"I know him. It won't be hard to make him believe I'm eager to crawl back into his arms. He thinks his power, wealth, and new political spotlight can rope in any woman, no matter how much of a self-absorbed jerk he is. That megalomaniac would love to get his grubby mitts back on me. He's *never* stopped trying."

Even after the rigged trial that cleared his name, Damien continued to sporadically message her over the years.

Stacie said, "All I have to do is give him the impression I've come around, that I'm drawn to his new status. He'll think his efforts finally paid off, that I've come to my senses now that he's in the public eye. People like him, Madam Chief, are obsessive control freaks. They think they can hurt a woman and then win her back with their mind games, fake charm, and manipulation tactics. I know his type all too well.

"And I'm sorry to be blunt, but he thinks with his dick way too much to let a woman he's desperate to reclaim slip through his fingers. I've got that narcissist pegged.

"So here's what I'm proposing: Let me go undercover for the CDF as a confidential informant. You know how much taking down Damien means to me."

Stacie remembered the digital tabloids Damien had paid to smear Cassie after the trial: COUNTRYSIDE BUMPKIN

FAKES ABUSE TO STEAL MONEY FROM THE SYKES FAMILY.

Stacie imagined how humiliated Cassie must have felt. It was no surprise Cassie had cut off all contact with her. Stacie was certain Cassie blamed her for introducing her to a monster.

Oviereya sighed, taking in Stacie's fiery expression. "Stacie, I don't know." She didn't want to put Stacie in harm's way.

"Come on, this wouldn't be the first time a chaser worked with the CDF on a contract basis." The CDF had a history of outsourcing high-risk, cloak-and-dagger missions to chasers when they needed to deny involvement and sweep things under the rug.

Oviereya thought over the proposition for a long moment. "General Conlan, Chief of Defense Force Intelligence, will be in touch," she said at last. "I'll defer to his judgment. So your involvement in this investigation isn't guaranteed. If Conlan approves, you do exactly what he says. Understood?" Her tone left no room for debate.

Stacie tipped her chin. "Gotcha. Conlan gets full carte blanche."

"Go now."

Three steps from the door, Stacie paused and turned around. "Oviereya, please take it easy. Don't burn yourself out."

"Thank you, Stacie. I'll be fine."

"Hey, do you ever miss Mom and Dad?"

"I do."

"It's crazy, isn't it? After all the wrong they did, after all the pain Mom caused me, I still get choked up when I think about them."

"Well, they loved you," Oviereya said softly. "And I know she was hard on you, but your mother absolutely *adored* you, her little baby girl. She was an imperfect mother, no doubt, but she wanted what she thought was best for you—to be the family's successor. A successful one."

Tears rose in Stacie's eyes, and she swallowed. "Now look what you've done, got me all teary-eyed."

"We simply love those who loved us, even if their love was flawed."

Flawed love, huh? Stacie thought. That sounded like her mother's kind of love. "Yeah, we do," she said. Just as she was almost out the door, she paused again. "Hey, Oviereya, don't worry, you're doing an outstanding job. You're not some pseudo-Chief. You're the real deal."

"What makes you think I need a pep talk, young lady?"

"You might be older and wiser than me, but we shared a Link for *years*. You can't fake it with me. All that doubt is just antiquated second-class programming still running in the back of your mind. You're a kick-ass Chief. Don't let anyone tell you otherwise. You hear me?"

Oviereya's spirits lifted, and her self-doubt dissolved, snuffed out by a wave of confidence. "You know me too well. Thank you, Stacie."

"What are friends for?" Stacie exited the office.

Oviereya faced the window, gazing pensively at the protesters. The crowd had grown. The Commonwealth was a mixed bag of ideologies. Not all nonimmigrant Edenites were dead set against colony advancement. Not all anti-reformists were Purists. Some held biases; others were simply misinformed, but they weren't Purists. Also, not all colonists and immigrants were saints. There were dangerous extremists among them.

She wondered what she could do to bring the Commonwealth's fractured society together. How was she supposed to win the upcoming election?

Conspiracy theories claimed she had colluded with the Coalition to steal the Chief Executive seat. Others claimed that, if elected next year, she'd alter Eden's demographics to a fifty-fifty split by replacing half of all nonimmigrants with colonists. Misinformation campaigns were feeding Eden citizens lies, such as that she planned to phase out all planetary-impact missions.

Oviereya supported the CDF being an interventionist force, but not contract mercenaries. The power to save lives and make the universe a better place should be used responsibly. She was only canceling the shady missions, the ones launched for government profit—for blood money. They were missions that had the CDF backing the wrong side or supporting genocide, leaving behind war-shattered communities. Such missions wouldn't bode well with the Union if they found out about them.

An EPA burst into the office without knocking. "Madam Chief, there's been a bomb threat from one of the protesters. We're taking you to the bunker."

"Let's go." Oviereya left with the agent.

• • •

On the heels of a successful rescue mission, Randy, Akane, Sam, and Jay went to a club for a nighttime celebration.

Randy, Sam, and Jay sat around a table with drinks. Akane was on the dance floor, gyrating to the pulsing techno beat. Her sexy party-girl outfit included a tube top, a miniskirt that barely reached her thighs, and sheer thigh-high stockings clipped to garter belts. She never missed a chance to make a fashion statement.

Sam said to Randy and Jay, "According to the report, all the women from the Commonwealth that trafficking ring abducted were colonists."

There was no shortage of disgust in Jay's expression. "Maybe that operation belonged to some Purist fat cat."

129

"It wouldn't be the first," Sam replied. "There's no way to tell for sure. Sometimes these trafficking rings target colonists because Eden's defenses are tougher to bypass, though not impossible if you've got the right criminal infrastructure."

Randy didn't seem to be listening. His mind was on Akane as his eyes followed her across the dance floor, through a sea of partying nightlifers.

She had painted her face white like a Geisha's, red winged eyeliner framed her eyes, and she had written Japanese characters on her arms in V-ink.

A woman danced near Akane, her appearance snagging Randy's attention. The excessive piercings decorating her face, the glimmer bracelets hanging from her wrists, and the colorful bead-lights festooned on her skirt made her stand out. To Randy, she looked like a dancing ornament. He didn't quite understand this neo-dress-up club culture that had emerged within the past couple of years. Outfits ranged from tame to utterly outrageous.

As his eyes stayed locked on Akane, who was lost in the rhythm, Randy found himself wondering about her. He wanted to know more about her past. She seemed to be growing on him by the day.

Sam took a swig of his drink and laughed at Randy's entranced look. "She's quite the dancer, huh?"

"Seems so." Randy watched her twerk. She was a quintessential hipster, always on top of contemporary fashion. And apparently, she followed all the latest club trends.

Jay said, "Don't let her size and easygoing demeanor fool you. She'll go full beast mode if you mess with her or her friends."

Akane moved under the florescent light show of colorful circles and blinking lasers that illuminated the dance floor. A young fair-skinned man posted up in a corner was checking her out. He was attractive, about five-eight, and in his early twenties. The aura of mystery Akane exuded—her face painted white and eyelids tipped with vivid red wings—held his gaze. It was now or never. He asked her to dance. She accepted.

"It's nice to see her happy," Sam said.

He closed his eyes, remembering the emotional toll Simone's death had taken on Akane. Depression and sadness had nearly swallowed her mind and soul, fitful night-long laments making it hard for her to sleep sometimes.

A heartfelt smile for Akane appeared on Sam's face. "It's taken her a long time to rebound from the funk she was in, a lot of fortitude to arrive at this place of happiness. It wasn't easy for her to get past the hurt, the hurt that crushed her." *A big thanks to the entire RISE organization too,* he thought.

Randy said, "Akane mentioned these Purists you guys keep talking about murdered someone close to her. Is that what you mean by 'getting past the hurt'?"

Sam nodded. "Yeah."

Reflexively, Randy winced in sympathy. *I know that kind of pain.* It was a pain that never truly stayed buried. He thought about the tragic accident that claimed his mother's life and made his father a widower. "Was she Linked with this person when they were killed?"

"No. Not to my knowledge."

Thank goodness for that. "So, what exactly happened?"

"That'd be her story to tell."

Randy changed the subject. "She mentioned some kind of shadow war going on between these Purist groups and an opposition force. Are you guys and Akane part of that force? And what exactly is it you do?"

"Answer to question one: yes. The answer to question two is . . .

complicated."

"I'm listening." Randy's brows furrowed. "And *no* dodging." His irritation with cryptic bullshit had reached its peak.

"We're basically a small, privately funded organization of social activists, Scott. That's all. Even with Oviereya as Chief, there need to be people on the ground fighting for colony and immigrant equality. She's not the supreme authority of the Commonwealth. Anti-reformist Parliament members do everything they can to obstruct her efforts."

"You activists got a name?"

"We're called RISE. We engage in political and social activism. We provide forums and safe spaces for marginalized immigrants to speak their minds, to express their pain. We help immigrants find employment and fight discrimination. We use media channels to debunk superstitions about colonists and push back against bigotry. We spread awareness about political candidates who actually intend to make a difference, and we hold them accountable. We also lobby for causes that support colonists. Purists basically do the exact opposite."

"Who started Purism?" Randy asked.

Sam replied, "The twisted mind behind Purism goes by the name Quinn. No one's ever seen his face. No one's even heard his real voice. He only appears in vids as a shadow, speaking through voice-anonymizing software.

"His identity remains a mystery. Quinn probably isn't even his real name. Sometime after Reza started calling for colony equality and preaching his liberation philosophy, Quinn emerged and started a counter-movement. He became a figure just as enigmatic and influential as Reza, except on the opposite side of the ideological battle.

"Quinn began releasing his vids over the dark net, urging

people to 'not let the republic be contaminated by Independent Movement sympathizers and reformists.' He called his devout followers Purists, claiming they were knights fighting to uphold AEGIS's design for humanity. He warned that dismantling that design would bring suffering to families. Fearful, paranoid sycophants bought into his manipulation.

"Quinn founded the first and largest Purist organization, the Brotherhood for Humanity's Salvation.

"Many extremists rallied around the Purist cause and formed their own groups. The White Knights of the Republic, the Black Wolves, and the Justice Society are just three of many. But they all revere the man who started it all, Quinn. Anything the Brotherhood or Quinn puts out, they follow.

"Through coercion, Purists have deterred immigrants in multiple communities from voting. Progressionist politicians, under duress from Purists, have rescinded their support for reform legislation after their families were threatened. And honestly, I can't blame them for backing out. When your loved ones' lives are on the line, what the hell do you do?

"RISE existed long before the Brotherhood for Humanity's Salvation, and I can tell you, we've never seen a more dangerous group of colony and immigrant haters than this. It was the Brotherhood who recently published the identities of Coalition fighters on the net, marking them for death. That was a directive from Quinn.

"And we believe Damien Sykes, a man who could become the Commonwealth's next Chief, is involved with the Brotherhood."

"These Purists sound like a dangerous bunch," Randy said. "But I have to say, I'm not too worried about ex-Coalition fighters. They all live on Satellite One, except maybe CDF defectors like me. What are the odds of Purists, or lone wolves under their influence, or any extremist, getting to Satellite One? Traveling to the planet isn't exactly like catching an air-cab to your local supermarket."

"Well, don't underestimate the ambitious mind of a determined fanatic. Some of these people can be pretty resourceful, and you never know what connections they have." Sam took a sip of his drink. "I know you're skeptical about RISE. We all were at first—me, Jay, and Akane—when we got approached. That's why I've given Akane permission to take you to our sanctuary tomorrow, so you can see what we're about firsthand."

Randy flicked up a brow. "Permitted?"

"I'm one of RISE's leaders," Sam revealed. "We're cautious about who we let into our house, just like you wouldn't let just anyone walk through your front door or be around your family. We want immigrants to feel safe, and stay safe, under our umbrella. Purists would love for some sellout to reveal our location. We can't afford weak links in the chain. You know what I mean?

"But you seem okay, Scott. You seem trustworthy. Go with Akane tomorrow. At the very least, you'll know of a place to escape to if you ever need to get away from all the crap you've been catching, just for doing the right thing. Just for liberating the colonies."

"I'm not promising you anything, like I'll join or something," Randy warned, dispelling any preconceived notions or clandestine motives.

Going head-to-head with Randy's assertiveness, Sam shot back, a subtle edge in his tone. "I didn't ask you for any commitments, now did I?"

Randy mulled over Sam's offer. A place to escape to sounded good to him, but he'd keep his guard up. "Okay, I'll go check you guys out tomorrow with Akane. It couldn't hurt."

"Good."

Randy got up from the table. "Gotta take a leak." He walked away, following the mens' restroom icon on the wall.

"Is this wise?" Jay asked Sam.

"It's just the first step, Jay. This doesn't mean he's got my endorsement yet. But Scott *is* good people."

"That doesn't mean he's *good* for us."

"It's not like we're taking him deep." Sam took another swallow of his drink. "Akane thinks he's a suitable candidate, and he trusts her. So let's see where things go." *Right now, he feels alone, isolated. People have turned against him. If there was ever a time Randal Scott would be open to joining RISE, it's now.*

As Randy left the club to head home—while Sam, Jay, and Akane kept partying—he heard someone shout, "Hey, you!"

He twisted around. Three men were stalking toward him. The one who'd shouted had arms covered in tattoos and wore his long dark hair in a ponytail.

"Yeah, what?" Randy said with a bite, defenses up.

"I know you. You're Randal Scott." The tattooed man sounded like he had an axe to grind with Randy.

"So what's it to you?"

"You Coalition filth killed my brother during the Battle of the Quad."

Randy extended an open palm, gesturing for the man and his friends to maintain their distance. "I'm not happy about Guardians being killed. The Coalition didn't want anyone to die. But it was a war, a truly senseless war, and in war, people die. There was never any fairy-tale scenario where equality was going to happen without bloodshed. I'm sorry for your loss, I really am."

"Your 'sorry' doesn't mean a damn thing!" The tattooed man

swung a fist at Randy, but he sidestepped the attack.

"I don't want to fight you. And fighting me won't bring your brother back." Sympathy was killing Randy on the inside.

The tattooed man stared daggers at him. "Maybe not, but beating the tar out of one of you Coalition punks will make me feel a hell of a lot better!"

The three men spread out around Randy like predators circling prey, cutting off his path to his flyer. With no choice but to fight, he squared off, sizing them up. In front, the tattooed man who had a score to settle. To the left, a guy with a spiky green hairdo. To the right, the tallest and most jacked of the three, a man practically built like a tank.

The guy with the green hair came at Randy, fist raised. Randy kicked him in the back of the knee, collapsing a joint and sending him falling face-first to the phyocrete.

The tattooed man lunged next. Randy ducked under his punch and shot upward, driving the heel of his palm into the underside of the man's jaw.

Three against one, Randy's attackers overpowered him.

The shredded guy caught Randy in a choke hold from behind.

Randy planted an elbow into the man's ribs. The brute recoiled, his square-jawed face contorting from the impact. But then he cinched the hold tighter, crushing Randy's throat. He was a freak of nature, insanely strong.

Shit, Randy thought.

The tattooed guy drove a fist of vengeance into Randy's gut, causing air to explode from his lungs.

A follow-up punch cracked Randy in the jaw.

Just then, Jay, Sam, and Akane exited the club, laughing and talking, until they spotted Randy being assaulted.

"Hey!" Sam shouted. "I'm Sergeant Sam Guthrie of the

Commonwealth Defense Force! Leave that Guardian alone, or I'm calling the authorities!"

The green-haired guy said, "Hey, no need to go down for this piece of trash. We roughed him up good, though."

The tattooed man clenched Randy's jaw. "You're lucky. I don't see how scum like you can look yourself in the mirror." He spat in Randy's face. "Come on, let's get out of here."

The muscleman who had Randy in a choke hold released him.

Randy dropped, knees and hands smacking the phyocrete.

His three attackers walked off.

Akane ran to Randy and crouched beside him. "Hey, are you okay?"

He groaned and forced himself upright, body aching, a thin rivulet of blood trickling from his mouth.

Akane rose with him.

"No need to worry. I'll be fine, Akane." Randy felt like he'd just been hit by a freight ship.

"Maybe you should get checked out by a doctor."

Randy spat blood onto the ground. "No. I said I'm fine."

Jay said, "Hey, if you need anything, champ, let us know."

Randy rubbed his throbbing jaw. "Yeah, thanks, but I'll be okay. I've taken worse." He squared his shoulders, kept his head high, and set off for his sports cruiser, one arm clutching his ribs. Even breathing proved to be a challenge, much less walking.

Akane followed. "Randy, I can come with you if—"

What he wanted right now was to be alone. "I don't need a babysitter, Akane. I'm a big boy. What part of 'I'll be okay' don't you get?"

Akane refused to back off. "You might be okay physically, but it just helps to have someone to talk to, you know?" Randy made a face, reiterating his wish to be alone. "Just 'cause I'm nineteen doesn't mean I'm inept at comforting somebody when they're down in the dumps," Akane stated, dismissing any idea that her age made her incapable of consoling him, if that was what he thought.

I never said you were. The frustration on Randy's face slackened. Akane was just trying to be a good friend, that's all. He pulled her into a side hug and rid his tone of irritation. "Thanks, but I'm good." There was no need to be mad at her. "I'll see you tomorrow for our trip."

He climbed into his sports cruiser, revved the engine, and lifted off for home.

The departing flyer kicked up a gust that sent Akane's wavy hair fluttering. She was disappointed that Randy had rejected her offer. She could relate. She understood what it was like to feel alone. To feel shunned. To feel like an outcast. Didn't he see that?

She'd bounced back from plenty of hard knocks in life, perhaps tougher tribulations than the ones he'd faced. He was born in a colony but raised on Eden, after all. He was essentially a Highborn, and it's not like he had a world of life experience on her. He was twenty-two years old, just three years older than her.

See you tomorrow, Randy. She cared about him, more than he knew. All she wanted was to be there for him.

Jay wrapped an arm around her shoulder. "I know you're worried about him. The guy'll be okay. He's Randal Scott. Let's head home and get some rest."

Akane, Jay, and Sam walked to the flyer they had carpooled in.

• • •

Randy had activated the autopilot.

He sat hunched forward, elbows on his thighs, fingers laced. His beating outside the club haunted him. *Is this my life for the foreseeable future?*

He thought about Paul's offhand insults, the whispered slights from Guardians who loathed him, and the delaying of his rank promotion, the screwing of his career. What was next? Another beatdown tomorrow? Was it only a matter of time before someone tried to put a bullet in his head? Would he have to spend every waking hour watching his back?

It felt like him against the world. And even someone as strong-willed as he could only take so much. The emotional toll of being branded a traitor by comrades and society was wearing him down.

He knew being a Coalition fighter would come with burdens after the war. But his expectation was that change would accompany them. One would think the animosity toward colonists would've subsided now that net filters were no longer suppressing the truth. Streamers, bloggers, and citizen reporters of Satellite One were free to expose their suffering. But Edenites seemed to cling to the same redundant responses:

> "What did you expect? We're still recovering from two wars, a financial meltdown, and an ongoing debt crisis. You don't start a civil war and kill people. You wait until things get better, until the government can offer more aid. You colony folks need to calm down."

> "The Commonwealth was trying to help you people, until you rebelled. Maybe the colonies would've seen more progress if you hadn't gone off the rails and started a war. *Duh.*"

> "Come on, you're not starving. Sure, the colonies aren't like Eden, but there aren't enough resources right now to make both planets paradise. Hard

decisions had to be made, and AEGIS made them. If you just hang in there, things will improve."

When would society finally recognize that colonists, as well as immigrants, deserved true prosperity?

Emotionally drained, Randy needed to confide in someone. Minutes ago, he thought solitude was what he needed, but he was wrong. He didn't need to be an island right now.

He tapped a few numbers on the control console, and the comms signal, routed through outer-space net orbiters, reached Satellite One.

The head and shoulders of Sariah Manard projected across the flyer's windshield. She sat in a modest bedroom, wearing a nightgown. "Whoa, Randy, what happened to you?" She could easily tell from his face he'd been beaten.

Randy managed a weak smile, the resonance of Sariah's lovely, sonorous voice taking the edge off. It felt good to see her.

At first, he'd been uncomfortable with his father getting involved with someone new, but, if anyone, Sariah was a good choice. She actually reminded him of his mom in some ways. Like Kathleen, she was a strong woman who had a kind soul.

"I got my ass kicked, that's what happened," he replied.

"No kidding. By who?"

Randy bypassed the details and got straight to the reason for his call. "I just need to speak to my father real quick. Is he around?"

Sariah nodded. "Arson, your son's on comms," she called, moving off-screen.

Arson's manly face, beard neatly trimmed, slid into view.

Shirtless, he sat down in a chair and rubbed his tired eyes. "Son, it's late, what—?" He paused as the injuries on Randy's face registered. "What happened? *Who did this?*"

"I got ganged up on, Dad, by some Coalition haters. But that's not even the worst of it. Feels like every Guardian's against me just because I sided with the Coalition."

Arson reached over and grabbed a shirt, pulling it over his hairy chest. "I figured things would be rough for you in the CDF," he said, buttoning up the shirt. "I can relate, to some extent." He was a veteran of war and of society's prejudice. "When I enlisted, it seemed every one of my comrades was against me because I was an immigrant, because only those chosen by AEGIS to inhabit Eden belonged in the 'prestigious' CDF. They kept snubbing me, talking trash behind my back. But I was able to win them over, earn their respect and gain acceptance.

"I ignored disparaging insults, stayed the course, and proved my critics wrong. I became someone Guardians admired, original Edenite and immigrant alike. But that was a different time. Believe it or not, a less hostile time. Once the RUC formed and the Three-Week War started, the discrimination toward immigrants spiked. It went from a one to a five. Hell, I imagine it's at a ten nowadays."

Randy said, "I didn't think everything would be all hunky-dory after the Battle of the Quad, but—"

"I know," Arson cut in, years of hard-earned wisdom at play. "You thought Eden's people would finally understand why young Guardians like you defected, why they joined the Coalition, now that the colonies' full calamity has been exposed. You thought things would start to get better. But they haven't. Not yet. And truth is, they might get worse before they do.

"Edenites are furious that Guardians died at the Coalition's hands. They don't see the whole picture. It's not like we had a choice. The Coalition had an ethos. It had *morals*. We ran first, fought last, and only killed if our backs were against the wall. And colonists didn't cause the New Humanity's civil war. The

Commonwealth Government's failure to address their suffering was the impetus.

"The natural response to inequality is to take a stand against it, even if that means taking up arms. It's been that way since Earth Era, since time immemorial."

Arson gave a grim look and continued. "The Coalition won, but the war isn't over. A civil war is still being waged, a war of hearts and minds, of ideologies. You'd think by now people would understand the circumstances that pushed colonies One, Four, and Six to rebel."

"So what the heck do we do?" Randy asked.

"I wish I knew. Edenites aren't going to unlearn years of an indoctrinated supremacist mindset in just two or three months. I don't have an answer, Son.

"By the way, how are you holding up? Still having nightmares?"

"Yeah," Randy sighed. "The lives I took, of both Coalition rebels and Guardians, still weigh on me. Trauma's a beast."

"You know, there are support groups you can go to. I've started one here in my zone for former Coalition fighters. You could—"

"I'll think about it, Dad."

"Okay, you're a grown man, Randy. I won't tell you what to do. I just wanted to put that out there. Is there anything you need from me? Is there *anything* I can do?"

"I'll be fine, Dad, and I appreciate the talk."

"Are you sure?"

"Positive."

"Well, if you ever do need anything, don't hesitate to reach out. I'm always here to talk, no matter the time."

"Thanks, Dad. By the way, have you ever heard of an immigrant activist group called RISE?"

"Doesn't ring a bell. During the civil war, many anti-government resistance groups formed, some ultraextreme, like the People's Revolutionary Party of Colony Four. Most of them have dissolved. Maybe RISE is one of the few still in operation. Do you think they're dangerous or something?"

"I don't know. I want to learn more about them. Secret organizations usually have secrets to hide, and if RISE has any, I'd like to know what they are."

"Tell you what, I'll check with some of my old Coalition buddies and see what turns up."

"I appreciate that."

"Okay, I'll keep you updated."

"Awesome. Oh, Lieutenant Carl Breckenridge says hello."

A memory made Arson brighten. "Tell him I said hello back."

"Will do. Good night, Dad."

"Same."

The video transmission ended.

The air lane Randy was traveling brought him to the Quad, reawakening the horror once again: explosions cratering the Parliament Building's yard, a storm of energy blasts and bullets hitting Coalition rebels and Guardians.

Randy shook his head, trying to fight away the uncomfortable memories.

Akane had been right. Talking to his dad had helped, but it would help even more to have someone *physically* with him tonight. He needed someone to drink with, confide in, laugh with. He used to depend on Stacie to realign his emotional compass when it was off-kilter. She knew how to pry him out of his reticence. She was someone he could lean on, talk about his feelings to without judgment, and cuddle with at night during disconcerting moments like this.

He needed companionship right now. There was no point in

pretending otherwise. But who could he turn to?

He thought about it and figured, Why not? He set a new course, and the flyer shifted air lanes.

• • •

After five knocks, Jenny Pines opened the door of her apartment. She wore a slinky red nightie that was so short it revealed a smidgen of her backside. "Randy! You look a mess!"

Randy stood with his hands in his pockets. As much as he tried to front, he couldn't hide how low he felt. "It's just a few bruises. They'll heal by morning."

"Well, even looking like a train wreck, you're still a handsome bloke, Randal Scott."

That actually drew a laugh from him, his first in a while. And it felt good. He couldn't remember the last time he had laughed. "Thanks. You said you were going to visit family up north during our off-duty weeks. I took a gamble and hoped you hadn't left yet. I just . . . need some company right now. You mind if I—?"

"Nah, not at all," Jenny said coolly. "What're teammates for? Make yerself at home, luv. I'll pour us some drinks."

"Thanks, Sergeant Pines, I'd like that."

"Hey, none of that 'sergeant' stuff. Call me Jenny, or Jen, whichever you prefer."

"Thanks, Jen."

"Do you like whiskey?"

"To tell you the truth, anything sounds good right about now." Randy stepped inside.

Randy and Jenny quickly dispensed with the formalities, shedding all their clothes in the bedroom.

Jenny lay on her back as Randy leaned over her, admiring her smooth pale skin and full, round breasts.

His lips brushed her neck, sucked on her standing nipples, and continued their journey downward, dropping delicate kisses along her naked body.

Dying to satiate his urges, Randy opened her legs wide and rubbed the length of his shaft against her clit, warming her up. Heat seared her cheeks, and her mind spun with anticipation.

Randy pushed a full thrust into the crease between her lovely, thick thighs, stuffing every inch of his cock into her.

She gasped as she felt him stretching her, filling her completely.

Randy's head snapped back as he savored the feeling of her walls sheathing him.

Struck by euphoria, Jenny tensed up and shut her eyes, gripping the bedsheets. The sibilant sound rushing from her lips morphed into a breathy moan.

Randy began moving at a leisurely pace, taking his time. Then, in a burst of adrenaline, he sped up, repeatedly slamming his loins against hers.

His steely erection speared her again, again, and again—tirelessly, ferociously. Each palliative thrust brought him some temporary relief from his frustrations. Sex was the best remedy he could ask for tonight.

Taking a break, they lay next to each other.

Randy stared out the window to his right, moonlight casting its glow on him and the beautiful woman beside him.

Jenny turned to him, nuzzling his neck. "What are you thinking about, Scott?"

Randy's personal crisis bedeviled his mind. "This unending cycle of animosity. Am I going to be fending off haters for the rest of my life?"

Jenny snuggled in closer, her body warm against his side.

Randy's heart pounded.

Jenny swept a hand through his hair. "Listen to me, Scott." Her whisper-soft voice sent a tingle prickling over Randy's flesh. "This animosity won't last forever. *Nothing* does. I don't know when, I don't know how, but humanity *will* pull it together. And don't let yer detractors get to you. Don't let 'em break you down.

"You're Arson Scott's son. You're the guy who took out Arman Reza and ended his menace, with your pop's help, of course. You're the reason Chief Amaechi, the first colony-born Chief, is leading the Commonwealth. And yer legacy ain't done being written yet.

"And don't think all Guardians hate you. I was born n' bred right here on Eden. I'm Highborn."

Randy laid a thank-you kiss on her cheek. "Thanks, Jen. I needed to hear that." He sat up. "I should probably get going. I have to meet Akane tomorrow to—"

Jenny pulled him back down onto the bed. "You're not going anywhere, Specialist. That was just a warm-up. I ain't done fuckin' you." This dishy young man had shown up at her doorstep, later stripping naked in her bedroom and putting his gym-goer's bod on full display. He had enticed her with his faultless physique and impressive dangling man-parts. He wasn't about to leave so easily.

"I just assumed—"

Before Randy could finish, Jenny shifted on top of him, straddling his gorgeous sculpted torso. She pressed her hands flat against his firm chest. "You're staying the whole night, and that's not a request; that's an order, Specialist."

Randy's body thrummed with desire.

His hands traced the small of Jenny's back before sliding down to cup the globes of her ass. He squeezed them ravenously, his fingers sinking into her creamy porcelain flesh.

Jenny rose slightly, escaping his grasp, and then descended onto his upstanding erection. She jerked her hips back and forth with wild abandon, gripping the headboard for leverage.

The faster she moved, the more the bed shook and creaked. "If I'm too much for you, just say 'Mayday.'" She locked her thighs around his hips and kept fucking herself on him. Her walls clenched his girth, and her clit rubbed against his pubic bone with every downward grind. Sliding up and down his cock, she impaled herself repeatedly. He was as hard and straight as a rod of Kryoplaste—much to her satisfaction.

Randy clung to her waist and rammed himself into her, matching her pace. As he bucked his hips, his eyes stayed fixed on her luscious breasts jiggling above him.

For a moment, his mind wandered to tomorrow's meeting with Akane. What was in store for him at RISE's base? Suddenly, Jenny tightened her walls around his cock, and all thoughts of tomorrow vanished in a haze of lust. Right now, his sole focus was on one thing: pleasure. Which was exactly what he needed tonight.

INTERLUDE THREE

Planet Eden

Sam, Jay, and Akane were in a ground car, cruising down a scenic roadway.

From the back seat, a restless Akane said, "Are we almost there yet?"

"Almost," Sam replied from behind the wheel. Jay sat in the passenger seat beside him.

Through her earbuds, Akane listened to one of her favorite jams—a catchy neo-flow techno-pop tune—as she watched trees, green plains, mountain ranges, and colorful flowers go by. She wore a pink top, jean shorts that had suspenders, and white sneakers. *There's nothing out here . . . but I guess that's the point.*

The car turned onto a narrow access road and pulled up to a gate. Sam held out a remote control, pressed a button, and the gate slid open, granting the car entry to the road beyond.

RISE HQ sat in a remote clearing, surrounded by forest. Sam slowed the car to a stop in the outdoor parking lot of the expansive two-story building. Several other vehicles were parked there too.

Akane examined the building. *This is a pretty big place.*

Sam turned off the car's engine. "Welcome to RISE HQ."

Everyone got out of the car.

Akane shut off her music and tucked her earbuds into her pocket.

The trio entered the building's ground floor. Inside, there were cubicles, communal rec areas, and shared workspaces. The place looked makeshift but had a homey feel to it.

People milled about, chatting and laughing.

Akane swept her gaze across the numerous computer stations in the room. "What's all this?"

"Our operations center," Sam replied. "It's come a long way since we first got it off the ground."

Machines hummed, their algorithms scanning the net for electronic communications from Purists and other extremists who posed threats to the immigrant community.

"What exactly does it do?" Akane asked.

Sam explained, "It searches the net for traffic from anti-immigrant extremist groups, especially Purists, allowing us to thwart their schemes. It also helps us identify government officials who want to undermine equality. Sometimes we're even able to seize financial assets from wealthy businessmen who support immigrant oppression, redirecting them to benefit RISE or the Coalition.

"We've stopped plots by Purist groups to bomb immigrant homes or gun immigrants down in cold blood. These are coordinated attacks happening right under the authorities' noses, because protecting immigrants isn't their priority, especially now that there's a civil war raging on our homeworld. Someone has to keep our people safe. That someone is us, RISE."

"Cool." Akane was A-okay with that.

Sam addressed the room. "Hey, everyone, this is Akane! She'll be joining us!"

Handshakes and hugs bombarded Akane.

"Welcome!" exclaimed a young woman.

"Wassup?" said an umber-skinned man in a gray hoodie, seated at a nearby workstation. "Name's Zeke," he added.

"Nice to meet you," Akane said.

The generous greetings continued, hands waving, voices offering hellos.

Akane felt good—felt wanted, felt like she belonged.

Sam made a hand gesture. "Akane, let me show you around."

Akane finished her conversation with a woman and followed Sam. He brought her to the legal aid office, the community hub where immigrants came to socialize, and the upstairs rooms that provided homeless immigrants shelter until RISE could help them get on their feet. Then he took her outside.

Akane saw men and women engaged in marksmanship drills, laser lights from practice guns shooting holographic targets. Several other RISE members sparred in hand-to-hand combat exercises.

A feeling of unease gathered in Akane's chest as she wondered what was going on out here. "So, what's this, a . . . paramilitary or something?"

"It's protection. We're at war, and sometimes we have to defend ourselves." Sam patted Akane's back. "Don't worry, we're not some insane militia trying to take over Eden."

Now that Akane's concerns had been put to rest, the unease in her chest went away. "Well, that's a relief."

"Now, I'm not going to front," Sam said. "Sometimes we have to put people down, because the law can't, or won't. But they're always bad people. *Like Simone's killer.* Like the Purists I mentioned, the ones who want to bomb innocent immigrants' homes. Do you have a problem with that, Akane?"

Akane's thoughts spiraled back to the miserable night she saw Simone's lifeless body. A sense of duty stiffened her spine.

Not only did she feel guiltless about killing bigots who subjugated her people like chattel, she felt it was her duty to remove such people from society, by death if necessary. Yeah, she preferred death for them, actually. To hell with prison. "Nah, I don't have a problem with that. If you guys are putting down savages like Simone's killer, it's all fine n' dandy with me. It's no different from taking out bad guys as Guardians of the ETF, right?"

Sam nodded. "Glad to hear it. We need more people with military experience. We were thinking you could help train recruits, maybe start with basic self-defense for newcomers."

"Sounds superb. I wanna help however I can. I wanna fight for equality, like Simone did. I'm all in." *This is it, Skylar—my ikigai.* With a drive born from a need to help others, Akane had worked the black markets of her home colony, and now she was here, joining RISE. She should've realized it sooner: Her ikigai was to protect, to liberate, to fight for equality. A humdrum life wasn't for her, not with her restless, rebellious spirit.

"There's one more thing I want to show you," Sam said.

He led her down into an underground phyocrete bunker.

The overhead lights clicked on.

Seven Shells stood in docking pods: six M-X02s—four male models, two female—and a lone M-X01.

Akane's eyes lit up. "Whoa, Shells?" she exclaimed. "How the fuck did RISE get ahold of CDF property?"

"We fudged some inventory numbers and altered a few shipping logs. Seven was all we could get. Any more would've raised alarms.

"We've overridden credentialed authentication, so anyone can access these Shells. We also disabled signature tracing to prevent any Nerve Center from tracking them. That means no C-comms, audio transmit/receive functionality, or Nerve Center software updates. However, the weapons package is fully installed and operational."

To address any moral qualms Akane might have, he added, "Now, you might think that's stealing, but believe me, the Defense Department has more than enough funding to manufacture war machines. They can replace seven Shells. We just need to be ready in case Purists or any other anti-immigrant group decides to come for us. These Shells are strictly for protection."

Akane released a dry chuckle. "Well, stealing a little from our oppressive government is no biggie to me. I've been bucking their system since I was sixteen, dealing in the black markets of my home colony."

"You're truly RISE material, Akane. Simone would be proud. Come on, let's head inside and grab some chow. There's more I want to talk to you about."

CHAPTER FOUR

ornerstone Park: Elysian fields of colorful flowers, well-manicured grass, and turquoise trees.

Stacie Spencer stood atop a footbridge spanning a lake, her wide-brimmed sun hat shielding her from the sun's rays. The strappy yellow dress she wore flowed freely around the arcs of her hips, its pleated hem riding high on her thighs, drawing attention to her attractive legs. The outfit was custom-forged by her personal stylist. She hadn't dressed up *just* for Damien, though. Stacie often wore her sexuality on her sleeve, and she made no apologies for it.

"Has your prince arrived yet?" Jason asked over her wristcom.

"No, but he'll show. Even on short notice, he wouldn't pass up seeing me. He's probably just running a little late."

General Conlan, initially reluctant, had ultimately approved Stacie's plan to assist Defense Force Intelligence as an undercover informant. He also signed off on her request to let her team run point on the operation. They'd gather intel and evidence, reporting directly to him.

Having a chaser go undercover had its perks. If the plan backfired and Stacie was caught meddling in Damien's affairs, the

CDF could plausibly deny any involvement, not that framing a chaser appealed to Conlan; Stacie was simply DFI's "in." And if at any point he thought she was in real jeopardy, he'd pull the plug on the operation.

Stacie watched a flashy limo roll into the distant parking lot. *Yep, that's him,* she thought. She told Jason, "He's here. Maintain radio silence until you hear from me."

"Okay, be careful, and if you need anything, just comm me."

"I'll be fine, Jason."

She adjusted her dress, making sure the hidden wireless microphone was secure.

From the back of the limo, Damien appraised Stacie's appearance. Drop-dead gorgeous, she was definitely something to gawk at. *She must have to beat them off with a stick. It's a wonder she's gone unclaimed for this long.* He said to his driver, Jasmine, with zest, "There she is. More stunning than ever."

Jasmine replied, "Don't you find it odd that she's entertaining face time with you after ignoring you for years?"

"Attention addicts like her run at the beck and call of the limelight. They crave the alpha male, he who elevates their status. That would be *me*, the man who's going to win next year's election. Power lures women like honey attracts bees."

"Bees, sir?"

"Brush up on your Earth Era Insecta," Damien said in a berating manner, as if Jasmine were a complete dullard. That was his usual modus operandi, making people feel small, weak, or stupid whenever he got the chance.

"Will do, sir," Jasmine said obediently. All she cared about was her pay.

Damien straightened his tie.

Jasmine asked, "What is it you see in Ms. Spencer, besides her physical attributes?"

"The bylaws and prehistoric traditions of the Eight, which our parents created, expect us, their children, to conform and uphold the institution's sanctity. Stacie Spencer is like me, restless and uncontrollable. She has a contumacious spirit.

"It was that spirit that led to our surreptitious romance, one unapproved by our organization's bylaws. That same spirit drove her to do something no other child of the Eight has done, enlist in the Defense Force. And my spirit has called me to defy the bylaws and throw my hat in for the Chief Executiveship. I am a lion, and she is a lioness. In Stacie Spencer, I see my counterpart. We're cut from the same cloth.

"There is no shortage of contenders for my attention. Not at all. But they're just pets—ephemera. Good for bed, but not much else. The flavor of the week, you might say. They don't intrigue me like Stacie Spencer does, and I seek a queen. Dare I tarnish my family name by letting the inadequate take a permanent seat at my side, especially if they're to be the First Lady of the Commonwealth. That answer your question, Jazzy?"

"It does, sir. I imagine a rebellious woman like Stacie Spencer might be a tad difficult to deal with."

"And that is the challenge, the thrill of the pursuit," Damien said, invigoration inundating every word. "It takes an apex predator like me to tame an exotic creature."

He got out of the limo and shut the door. Checking his reflection in the window, he straightened his white blazer and smoothed back his slick hair with a practiced sweep of his hand. Satisfied, he made his way toward the bridge, where his princess awaited.

Stacie watched him saunter down the cobblestone walkway. He had an arrogant stride and a charming but smarmy expression on his face. And he radiated an aura of untouchability. He acted like he owned the universe. A high IQ, sharp business acumen, natural charisma, and looks that had helped him finesse the pants off countless women ensured his confidence was always sky-high.

Triumph consumed his features as he closed the distance between him and his erstwhile lover. In his mind, he'd finally won her back. She'd come to her senses, realized he was innocent of Cassie's accusations. The anger had finally blown over. She was no longer the silly girl who'd once walked out of his life. Victory.

Nerves kicked in for Stacie. *Here we go.*

Damien's hungry gaze roved over her. A woman like Stacie was his Achilles' heel—flawless skin, sculpted legs, a slim waistline, and curves to boot.

Stacie waved dramatically. "Damien!" she said in a bubbly, high-pitched tone, her delivery just a tad over the top. She was playacting like her former self, which put knots in her stomach.

Damien joined her on the bridge. "Stacie, long time, no see." He edged closer.

Stacie kept hamming it up, pretending to be ecstatic about seeing him. "Indeed! I've been a busy girl."

"So I hear—protecting the Commonwealth, fighting in the Battle of the Quad against Coalition invaders." He leaned in, took Stacie's hand, and kissed it. Then he straightened his six-foot-two frame. "It's good to see you, my dear. I've missed you."

"I've missed you as well, Damien." Stacie was cringing inside.

"Oh, pardon my manners." Damien caressed her jaw, then wound threads of her hair between his fingers. "I was so captivated by your succulent beauty that I forgot to ask, How have you been since those Coalition *bastards* murdered our parents?"

Stacie pretended a sigh. "It's . . . been a challenge."

"Yes, of course." Damien thought about his father. "It has been a challenge for me as well, losing the man who taught me everything I know, the man who made me strong. The news of Amaechi letting the Coalition off the hook enraged me, just like it enraged the other children of the Eight. Someone needs to set things right, and that person will be me. And if you ever need a shoulder to lean on, I'm here for you."

"Thank you, Damien. I appreciate that." *I don't need anything from you, you deranged sociopath.*

Damien braced his forearms against the bridge's balustrade. "Crazy, isn't it? Our parents' empires now belonging to us. We knew we'd eventually take the reins, but not this soon, and not like this."

"No, definitely not like this." Stacie sounded genuine, thinking of her parents.

"No, but we mustn't let what they built for us—" Damien's wristcom chirped. "Excuse me for a moment." He walked a few feet away and spoke into his wristcom.

Stacie couldn't hear the man on the other end.

"You mean now?" Damien shouted furiously, drawing the eyes of passersby.

There it was, Stacie thought. That uncontrollable anger, the Damien that could emerge at the flip of a switch.

A voice babbled urgently from the other end of Damien's wristcom.

"Alright, fine!" Damien snapped. He headed back over to Stacie, mumbling.

"Bad news?" Stacie asked.

"My deepest apologies. I have matters that require hands-on attention."

"No worries." Stacie manufactured a smile. "Shall we resume tonight?" she asked eagerly, giving the impression that she was yearning for more quality time.

Damien returned the smile. "You read my mind. I'm actually hosting a fundraiser at one of my estates tonight. You know the deal: mix and mingle, solidify support, rub elbows." His wanton hands slid around Stacie's waist and dragged her closer. "It would be an absolute pleasure if you accompanied me."

His palms sank into the fabric of her dress, indulging in the feel of her comely figure, which had been refined by CDF training and power workouts since he'd last slept with her. As he recalled, she used to love it when he touched her, when he took her into his arms.

"Of course. It sounds like fun." Skin crawling, Stacie wanted to kick Damien in the teeth.

He kissed her jaw. "I'll have a driver swing by your place to escort you."

"Until then." *Now take your hands off me, you filthy creep.*

Damien released Stacie and made his way back to the limo.

Once he was out of view, Stacie exhaled. She felt like she was going to barf. *What the hell was wrong with me, getting involved with someone like him?* Old, naive Stacie had definitely left the building. Her taste in men had evolved. It was different back then, before she matured—before Randal Scott, a caliber of man she hadn't experienced prior to meeting him.

Stacie said into her wristcom, "The meeting got cut short."

"What happened?" From the sound of his noisy surroundings, Jason was around a bunch of people.

"He had some kind of business emergency to tend to. Running a financial empire, unexpected stuff happens all the time, believe me. But he invited me to some shindig tonight. I'm going. I need to butter him up more, then see if I can get a confession out of him, to connect him to the trafficking and show all the people he's no different from his parents." *And to finally get justice for Cassie.*

"Be careful."

"Always. I'll keep you posted."

• • •

Akane was at the wheel of her spiffy yellow convertible, with Randy sitting beside her. They were headed to RISE HQ.

"Curious," Randy began, wind ruffling his short, wavy hair, "what are the qualifications for joining RISE, besides being an immigrant?"

"Everyone's screened and vetted before they're allowed to become a member," Akane answered, not giving a direct answer.

"Screened and vetted how?"

"Dude, you ask *too* many questions. That's not even something you need to be concerned about right now."

More evasiveness, Randy thought.

Akane pulled into RISE HQ's parking lot. "We're here." She was excited for Randy. "C'mon."

They got out, and Akane led the way forward.

Birds perched in treetops chirped.

"How many members does RISE have?" Randy asked.

"*Mmm,* 'bout seventy-three of us live here; others live off-base, and we've got an extensive network of supporters."

They went into the building.

A man with thick facial hair in his early forties looked at Akane like he'd just seen a ghost. He was practically brawn stacked on brawn and wore a blue denim vest, red shirt, and jeans. "Well, well, if it isn't Akane Sugimori! Haven't seen you in a while! What's the deal? You don't love us no more?"

Akane shrugged. "Yeah, well, y'know, apprehending evildoers throughout the cosmos doesn't always leave your favorite girl here with a lotta time to make house visits."

The man approached her and gave her a hearty pat on the back. "Yeah, I know. I'm just messin' with you. Good to see you. Damn good."

"Ditto."

Zeke waved. "Akane, wassup?"

"Nothing beyond the usual," she replied.

"It seems like you're quite popular here," Randy commented.

Akane knew there was nothing preferential about her treatment. "Nah, we're just all family."

Randy observed his surroundings. Busy men and women sat at workstations, fingers dancing across keyboards. Others stood in pairs, holding touchscreen tablets and discussing subjects of importance. "There's a lot of activity going on." Randy's mind kicked into analytical mode.

"Yeah, of course. Election day's near. We're social activists."

All of this equipment gave Randy the impression that more than just election-day business was happening in this room.

A blur of multiple voices said, " . . . Canvassers deployed . . . Donations up by ten percent . . . New ads posted . . . Caught some Purist chatter on the dark net . . ."

A man in his mid-twenties with blue hair, buzzed short on one side and long on the other, walked up to Akane and her guest. "Who do we have here, a newcomer?" It didn't take long for him to recognize who the "newcomer" was. "Oh, shit, you're Randal Scott!" He craned his head sideways. "Everyone, it's Randal frickin' Scott, Arson's son!"

RISE members greeted Randy.

A bum-rush of handshakes wore out his arm.

Akane recalled her first time coming to RISE HQ, a heartwarming experience. Watching Randy receive the same reception made her happy inside.

A mocha-skinned woman in a tawny button-down shirt and jeans—black-and-brown hair arranged in a braided faux-hawk—hurried down a set of metal stairs to the ground floor. "Hey, close your mouths!" she commanded. Everyone fell quiet. The woman now owned the room. "Quinn's broadcasting on the dark net! Bring up the audio feed now!"

Randy assumed she held a leadership role.

A short-haired brunette woman struck several keys on her computer console.

The loudspeakers blasted Quinn's altered, artificial-sounding voice. "To all my Purist brothers and sisters, the next special election is two days away. During the last one, Ron Burchardt, a reformist, won, but only because of interference from RISE. For the purity of the republic, we cannot afford any more electoral losses in this war. Every immigrant that votes could tip the scale.

"Next election day, ensure as many as possible do not cast a ballot."

The transmission ended.

Anger flooded Akane's veins. *Damn, first Quinn's directive to hunt down ex-Coalition fighters and now a directive to stop immigrants from voting.* Fire burned beneath her skin.

The woman with the faux-hawk anchored her hands on her hips, her rigid stance exuding authority. "You heard that, everyone. The Brotherhood is serious. We're now on heightened alert for predominantly immigrant communities. Expect spikes in violence. We have to ensure immigrants exercise their right to vote without incident. I know we can't cover all communities, but we can cover some. I'll need volunteers for voting-station guards, patrolmen, and vehicular escorts."

Akane and several others raised their hands courageously.

"Good," the woman said. "Khalid, Umer, Wes, make sure all

volunteers get an assignment."

The three men responded in unison: "Yes, ma'am."

Everyone returned to business as usual.

The woman strode up to Randy and Akane. "Akane, it's nice to see you around. ETF treating you well?"

"Can't complain," she replied.

"Good. I really appreciate what you, Sam, and Jay do. You guys help hold it down in the CDF for us immigrants, calling out mistreatment, guiding new immigrant Guardians when you can." The woman turned to Randy. "Randal Scott, it's great to meet you. I was told you'd be here today." She clasped his hand. Her grip was strong and confident, just like her voice and even the gaze in her chestnut eyes. "Janice LaCroix, head of RISE operations."

By Randy's estimation, she was in her early thirties. He shook her hand and then glanced around. "So this equipment lets you guys monitor the net for Purist traffic, I assume."

"It does, and it serves other functions."

Sam approached. "I'm glad you made it, Scott. I wasn't sure if you'd change your mind and decide not to come."

"Well, I'm here."

Jay walked up next. "Randy, good to see you, champ."

Being so close to Jay's family, Janice spoke to Jay in a way that wasn't just friendly but familial. She might as well be a blood relative. "Jamie, it's been a while. How's the wife and child?"

"Nicole and Zola are doing well," he replied. "And Zola's loving fifth grade."

"Good to hear that. Tell them both I said hello."

Randy felt a genuine sense of togetherness here. These people truly cared about each other. They acted like kin.

"Most of us are heading to the mess hall," Sam said. "Randy, Jay, Akane, why don't we go too?"

Randy's stomach rumbled. He could use a bite. "Sounds good."

"It's this way," Akane said cheerfully. "Just follow me." Randy trailed behind her.

Well, she's certainly happy he's here, Sam thought. *Let's see if he disappoints or eventually joins.*

Randy and Akane crossed a hallway.

Janice leaned into Sam's ear and whispered, "In forty-five minutes, Code Red meeting."

Sam's eyes widened. Code Red meant something major was about to go down. "Does this have anything to do with the Coalition fighters' identities being publicized online or Quinn's announcement just now?"

Janice shook her head. No, this meeting was about something else. Something big. "You'll find out in forty-five minutes. Go eat." She offered no further details and walked away.

The discontented expression on Sam's face made it obvious that he didn't like being kept in the dark.

Randy and Akane sat at a far-off dining nook in the mess hall.

"So, do you still see that apparition of your mom?" Akane asked.

Randy sipped his tangy citrine-colored drink. "No, not since I made amends with Dad."

"I don't know. It seems kinda nice keeping a piece of a loved one's essence with you after they're gone."

"That's kind of what Linking does anyway, without the ghosts," Randy said, thinking of Stacie.

"Well, you've got a point there." Akane's own experiences with Simone were forever diarized within her cerebral implant.

Randy hesitated. Then, haltingly, he asked, "So, who was the person special to you who was killed?" He hoped he wasn't sticking his nose where it didn't belong.

"She was a Guardian—a sergeant—in Vanguard Alpha, and a member of RISE too. Her name was Simone Conyers. She saved my life from a Purist prig, a cop actually, who was gonna shoot me just because I'm an immigrant. After that, she took me in, let me stay with her.

"Her dream of diversifying CDF leadership inspired me to enlist. I loved her. She was a true-blue friend. And she's no longer alive because a gutless Purist coward murdered her, knifing her in the back. We believe it was Paul Shaffer. He might even be a member of the Brotherhood."

"Shaffer? Do you have proof he killed Simone?"

Akane's countenance changed to something darker, something murderous. "Enough to convince *me*." She didn't have the slightest doubt. But it wasn't a hundred percent confirmed that Simone's killer was Paul, which was why Sam wouldn't let Akane kill him, *yet*. However, she believed Paul was guilty. "We think he and his posse, Dan and Mark, are making careers as Guardians while advancing Purist causes as civilians."

A man urgently said, "Hey, yo, turn that up!"

The crawl at the bottom of a live newscast on a wall screen read: BREAKING NEWS: ACTIVE SHOOTER GUNS DOWN THREE EX-COALITION FIGHTERS INSIDE COLONY ONE.

Behind the serving counter, a chef grabbed a remote and increased the volume.

Onscreen were a male and female anchor, both dressed in professional attire.

The man said, "Our own Gisele Lockhart was in Colony One covering the Colony Restoration Initiative's progress when murder and mayhem erupted in Zone 12 of Sector 05, just ten minutes ago."

"Gisele, take it from here," said the female anchor.

Gisele's live feed streamed grainy at first, net orbiters across the Commonwealth adjusting to stabilize resolution. White noise faded. Distortion lessened. Behind Gisele, three dead men lay riddled with bullets as colony authorities, reinstated following the end of martial law, sectioned off the grisly crime scene with yellow caution tape.

A stunned crowd had gathered around the massacre.

Gisele said, "Just moments ago, my camera crew and I heard gunfire coming from this area." Her two-person crew operated twin hovercams using remotes. "According to eyewitnesses, a van pulled up, and a man dressed in black stepped out and opened fire on the crowd using a high-powered automatic weapon.

"Although other civilians were injured, it appears the gunman specifically targeted the three men who are now deceased." First responders zipped the bodies into black bags. "We've been told the victims were former Coalition fighters.

"We have a witness to this brutal massacre here with me now." The hovercams shifted to a teen with a ruddy complexion. She had pink pigtail braids and wore a white shirt, hoodie, and slim-fit jeans. "Tiffany, can you tell us exactly what you saw?"

"It . . . it was just like you said," the sixteen-year-old stated. "This van came barreling through really, really fast. It nearly ran everyone over." She made frantic gestures, swinging her arms. "Then this guy dressed in black jumped out and started shooting at the three guys. The shooter yelled something . . . something like 'For the purity of the republic,' I think."

Akane punched her right palm. "It's just as we feared. Purists, or lone-wolf extremists influenced by their preposterous ideology, have finally gotten to Satellite One. They're acting on the Brotherhood's . . . on Quinn's directive to get payback for Operation Hammer Fall. You can bet there'll be copycats, like it's open season on ex-Coalition fighters. *Motherfuckers.*"

"Terrible," a man in the serving line said solemnly.

Concern clouded Randy's eyes. His father was arguably the most notable of all former Coalition fighters. That put a bull's-eye on his back. Having been attacked outside the club, Randy had already gotten a taste of the violence against ex-Coalition fighters. Would he or his father be the next target for some group of gun-toting maniacs?

Inside Akane, a storm of hate, revulsion, and rage brewed. She wished she could vent her spleen by tearing the balls off those fucking murderers. "No doubt, come election day, crazies are gonna act on Quinn's other directive too: stopping the immigrant vote. Like Janice said, we can expect an uptick in violence in immigrant communities."

A muscle tensing in his jaw, Sam approached Randy and Akane's table as the newscast continued. A young man followed close behind. "Randy, I'm sorry, but your visit's going to have to be cut short," Sam said. Forty-five minutes had passed. It was time for Janice's meeting.

"Why? What's up?" Akane asked. Sam leaned over and whispered "Code Red" into her ear. Her brows perked. "Oh, shit," she blurted, bolting to her feet.

What's with all the secret whispering? Randy wondered.

Sam jerked a thumb over his shoulder at the young man behind him. "Randy, Jeshua here is going to take you back home. Sorry."

Randy wasn't going to budge so easily. "Care to fill me in?"

"Some of us have an emergency meeting, and the operational tempo around here is about to kick into high gear."

"Are Purists about to pull something you guys know about?" Randy asked, trying to sleuth out the truth.

"I'm afraid I can't tell you what's going on. But no visitors are allowed right now."

Randy stood and shot Sam a hard-eyed glare, a reminder that he wasn't sold on RISE just yet.

Randy and Jeshua set off for the exit.

Sam rounded up eleven other RISE members from the mess hall. They knew what this was about. Janice had summoned them. Leaving their interrupted meals behind, they rose and left with Sam.

In the strategy room, twenty-seven men and women joined Sam, Akane, and Jay. These were RISE's solutioners, an ad hoc kill team.

Janice LaCroix, head of operations, was the founding council's organizational overseer. By day, she worked as an assistant office manager at a golem manufacturing company.

She said, "First of all, I want to thank every one of you for volunteering to be part of RISE's Strike Team. Solutioners aren't deployed often. Killing is messy, and we don't want to get on the radar of DFI or the authorities. We're not trying to go public, but tonight, you're being called to action.

"Damien Sykes is throwing a soirée tonight, and you're crashing it. The council has designated him a critical threat, and we have the chance to rid the Commonwealth of him."

Sam shook his head in disapproval, eyes fierce. He had a protest on the tip of his tongue but held it.

Janice said, "Sykes winning the Chief Executiveship would be a disaster for both colonists and immigrants. Our hackers accessed his guest registry and conducted a data pull. At least ten of his guests are confirmed Purists. The rest likely support colonist and immigrant oppression, but we can't confirm that, or if they're Purists.

"The confirmed Purists are to be eliminated. But Damien Sykes is the priority target. Once he's eliminated, you exfil. And you will use nonlethal force on all security personnel and anyone else who isn't a Purist. Understood?"

"Understood," everyone replied together.

"Good. Be geared up and ready to roll out by nineteen-hundred hours."

The solutioners filed out.

Sam went up to Janice. "I need a quick word with you." This mission wasn't sitting well with him.

While leaving, Jay said to Akane, "This double life is gonna wear me out. You would think we'd be able to get some rest before we're rotated in for our next ETF assignment. *Sheesh.*"

"There's plenty of time for beauty sleep." Akane was ready for action. "This is big. This is our chance to knock off Damien Sykes."

The sliding door shut. Sam and Janice were now alone.

Sam spoke in an even, measured tone. "I don't like this, not one bit. Pulling risky stunts like this attracts investigations from the authorities and Defense Force Intelligence. That's why we don't do drive-bys like that hit squad today. We stay off the radar as much as possible.

"Shoot, we'll rig elections, even resort to blackmail to keep Purists and immigrant haters out of power, but this? There's just too many ways this op could go awry. What was the council thinking?"

Janice boosted herself into a sitting position on the desk, fingers clasping the edge. "The council deemed Sykes a critical threat, Sam."

"Yeah, you said that already."

"And that's why you solutioners are being deployed."

"So we're acting irrationally out of fear? There are other ways to keep Sykes from winning the election. This is reckless."

"We've assassinated people before," Janice said matter-of-factly, stating a simple truth.

"And I don't mourn those assholes, but those ops were more discreet—poisonings, car bombs, arranged accidents. And those targets were small fry compared to Damien Sykes.

"Think about it, if we take out a big fish like him in an open assault on one of his estates, anti-reformists won't hesitate to weaponize it. They'll spin it as an attack by an immigrant or colony extremist group. That could ignite a level of colonist/immigrant hatred we haven't seen before, full-blown chaos in the streets."

Janice replied, "I know this is drastic. I know we risk exposure. Yeah, it could all go sideways, and killing Sykes might be the spark that lights an inferno. But I'm just the messenger."

"The council's on Satellite One. You're their eyes and ears on the ground. You're leading the charge here on Eden. You've got clout. Maybe they'll listen to—"

"I already tried, Sam," Janice interrupted. "They're not listening to me."

Sam mumbled something angry under his breath.

"We're at war. Our enemies murdered Coalition heroes today. Eliminating Sykes would serve as payback. It'll show the Purists that we can get to them too."

"This is a fucking terrible idea."

"You're in command of the Strike Team, Sam. We've only got one shot at this, so make sure it goes smoothly."

Sam sighed. "Yes, ma'am." He left.

• • •

A long limousine pulled up to Damien's mansion, one of several mansions he owned.

Damien waited outside in a wrinkle-free white suit. On his finger gleamed a gold ring engraved with the Sykes-family signet: a palm holding the world.

One of the limo's doors opened. Stacie exited, dressed to the nines in a strapless sequined halter dress that hugged her in all the right places.

Shiny gemstones adorned her neck and wrists. Turquoise eye shadow that matched her dress highlighted her eyes. And just to keep up appearances, she wore a ring bearing her family signet.

Her wispy blond hair bounced on her bare shoulders as she strutted toward Damien.

Even from a distance, her infectious aura seemed to envelop him. *Well, well, the belle of the evening has arrived.* Self-satisfaction entered his eyes. He knew that if he held out, she would come back to him. Most women always did.

Stacie saw that the fenced-off perimeter was well-guarded. The place was crawling with security, men in suits patrolling every edge of the property.

"Be careful," Jason's voice said from her earrings. Stacie had insisted her team sit this one out, but Jason had talked her into letting them tag along. They stayed close to the mansion in a van, just in case she needed backup. "If you need us, we're here."

"I'll be fine." Stacie flounced up to Damien and twirled, showing off the dazzling scintillating dress. "You like?" she asked with exaggerated cheer.

"Yes, quite the fetching outfit." Chivalrous, he invited her to take his arm. "Come, my dear."

She hooked her arm around his.

A doorman opened one of the tall gilded double doors, and they went inside, into the tasteful decor.

People of status sat at circular tables draped in white linen, laughing and chatting. At the wine bar, a server in formal wear mixed drinks for a small group, while white-shirted chefs wheeled carts filled with exquisite dishes.

"Damien," someone called out.

A commanding older man, wearing a dapper black suit and a ruffled cravat, approached Damien and Stacie. Stacie recognized the face but couldn't place it. She assumed she'd seen the man on the Academy's wall of distinguished service members.

"I just wanted to say that you are *exactly* the kind of Chief the Commonwealth needs right now." The man raised his champagne glass in honor of Damien.

Recognition dawned on Stacie. He was Malcolm Horowitz, a retired CDF colonel and a U.S. serviceman during Earth Era.

"What this Chief has permitted turns my stomach, allowing treasonists to go unpunished. *Despicable*," Malcolm said. "She's even fighting to strip NCOs and officers of the authority to execute insider threats on judgment alone." He scoffed. "This woman's menace needs to be stopped."

Damien intended to do exactly that, defeat Oviereya in the coming election. "Thank you. I trust I have your support."

"Indeed, you do. Well, enough of my rambling. It'd be rude of me to keep you from this fine lady." He stepped off to leave Damien and Stacie to themselves. "May you win the election."

Damien asked Stacie, "Shall I get us drinks?"

"Yes, please do."

Damien went to the wine bar.

As Stacie waited for him to come back, guests greeted her. She recognized CDF service members, politicians, scions of immense wealth, and industry leaders from fields ranging from science to engineering. But there was an air of entitlement and superiority about them that sent a cringey feeling worming its way through her, a feeling reminiscent of the one she'd gotten at many Eight Elite gatherings and Highborn parties, except worse. These people reeked of arrogance.

Damien returned with two glasses of wine.

Okay, time to get down to business, Stacie thought.

Damien handed one of the glasses to her.

She held it high for a toast, pretending to be Team Sykes. "To your victory next year." The rims of their glasses clinked, and they drank. Now it was time for her to get some answers. "Damien, dear, have you ever heard of Purism or Purists?"

Caught off guard mid-sip, Damien coughed and cleared his throat. "What's it to you?" Caution underscored his tone.

"Is that a 'yes'?"

"You answer first," he replied, words clipped.

Stacie downed more of her wine. She followed the script she'd rehearsed a thousand times in her mind. "Running my parents' empire, I've heard whispers about . . . some radical cult. I think some of my parents' business clients might be involved with these weirdos."

Damien lifted a quizzical brow. "And you thought to ask me because—?"

Stacie knew Damien was no fool and that she had to be careful. She replied smoothly, "Because I have no one else to ask. Ever since leaving the Eight to spread my wings, I'm not exactly popular with the other family heads."

"And I'm trying to keep the authorities out of my hair. If I've got carryover clientele from my parents involved in some psycho cult, I need to know." She hoped he was buying it. "You're a smart guy," she added, flattering him, "and you seem to know a lot." Then she hit him with the thought of losing her, like he had just screwed up. "But if you're going to be up in arms over me asking a simple fucking question, I can just go home." She slammed her glass onto the table. It tipped over, spilling red wine across the white linen.

She spun around, to leave Damien without a date.

He grabbed her wrist. "No need to storm off, my dear." He set his glass down and curled an arm around her waist. "Stay. It'd be a shame for you to have gotten all dressed up for nothing."

"Then give me a fucking answer, or I'm out of here," Stacie said demandingly.

"Quite the negotiator, aren't you?"

"Got it from Mom." Stacie tapped her foot and crossed her arms, sending Damien a look that said "go on, start talking."

"You drive a hard bargain." Damien decided to provide Stacie an answer. "Purism isn't a cult. It's a religion. And its followers aren't weirdos. Christians believe in Christ. Muslims in Allah. Purists believe in the science and technology that birthed the New Humanity, the work of Cyrus Kline, Jagr Vlcek, and Atticus Hancroft.

"AEGIS purged the New Humanity of deficiencies and qualified us, Eden's chosen caretakers, to be the helmsmen of the Union's human community. This jewel we call home wasn't big enough for all of mankind, and we were selected to be here." Selected based on social ranking, health, life expectancy, IQ, education, and more unfair determinants. "How would you feel if someone were just *handed* the title of Warrior Extraordinaire, when you clearly *earned* it? We, Eden's chosen, went through a process too."

So these Purist dweebs are a bunch of stuck-up, sanctimonious pro-

caste separatists, Stacie thought.

Damien said, "The purity of AEGIS's grand design for a better mankind has been jeopardized by reformist initiatives and legislative tokenism like the immigration lottery. At its core, Purist activism is about preserving AEGIS's framework. Tampering with or defiling that framework will only lead humanity to repeat its own destruction. I, for one, don't want to see that happen.

"It is the misguided—Coalition and Independent Movement sympathizers—who have continued to defile the system. Such foolish mooks plunged the Commonwealth into civil war, proving AEGIS right, that they are not fit to be among us here on Eden.

"These low-level thinkers have shown they belong where they are, as resource harvesters. And that's not a bad thing. But can you imagine people like that, people who simply cannot grasp why the system must remain as it is, gaining influence in Eden's government or military? They are not on par with us, as determined by their value coefficients."

Stacie was quailing on the inside.

Damien said, "Purists are fighting, nonviolently, to keep Eden's bloodline from contamination by the impurities of the inferior class. If Chief Amaechi prevails, the Commonwealth will be doomed.

"Nadir, those who didn't cut the mustard to be here, do have a place in our society, as resource harvesters. That is where they are best suited to contribute to humanity. No one wants to see them perish, be killed, or live unsuccessful lives. These unfortunate people just don't know what's best for them. Purism is about protecting them from themselves just as much as it is about protecting us Edenites." *Even if violence is necessary to prove a point.*

It was exactly the kind of snobbish blather Stacie had expected to hear from Damien. "I see, and who started this so-called religion?"

"That, my dear, no one knows. A mysterious figure calling himself Quinn began preaching the truisms of Purist ideology over the net. Call him a counterpart to Arman Reza, if you will.

"Purism caught fire after the Three-Week War. Chat forums and virtual networks clung to Quinn's doctrine. Then Purist groups formed, unaffiliated, yet aligned. All peers. You won't see them making public statements, though, especially with Amaechi in office. But they're harmless. In our society, you're free to believe what you want, right?"

Stacie was well aware that this was a free republic, but she was also aware that sometimes people used their beliefs to justify harming others. "True. And are you a *follower* of this religion? You seem to know an awful lot about it."

Damien threw his head back, letting out a duplicitous laugh. "I'm simply an academic."

Stacie didn't believe him one bit.

"Mr. Sykes," came a male voice unmistakable to Stacie. The man emerged from a huddle of guests.

Stacie's pulse quickened. *Paul Shaffer?* Why was he here?

"Stacie," Damien said, "meet Sergeant Paul Shaffer."

"Oh, we've met before," she replied. She remembered how infuriated Paul was when she refused to tell him anything about her business in X-Quadrant.

"Then I'm assuming you two know each other from the CDF. From a mission, perhaps?"

"You could say that."

"Well, Sergeant Shaffer is one of *many* Guardians supporting me and has been an asset to my campaign." Damien sounded proud of the number of service members backing him.

Paul recalled Stacie's obnoxious attitude during the

interrogation. *Bitch.* Irritation crawled over him, but he maintained his poise. "I wish you were in office now, Mr. Sykes, and not that soft reformist, Amaechi."

Stacie grimaced. That "soft reformist" was her friend—and a mother figure.

"I wish I were too, Sergeant," Damien said. "But by next year, I will be. You can bank on that."

Paul gave a subtle nod and then gestured with his chin, signaling that he and Damien needed to speak privately.

Damien turned to Stacie. "I need to speak with the sergeant for a moment. Business stuff."

Stacie was glad to get a break from these two creeps. "Sure. I'll be at the wine bar." She kissed Damien on the cheek, then walked off, flashing Paul a smirk. *Loser.*

Once Stacie was out of earshot, Paul said, "First, I just wanna say if I had known that trafficking operation was your outfit, boss, I would've—"

Damien flicked his wrist, dismissing the matter. "Don't worry about it, Sergeant. You weren't supposed to know. None of those traffickers knew I was behind the operation either. And even if you *had* known, you'd have had no choice but to comply with your orders. Everything's fine. The CDF has nothing that traces back to me."

"Thanks. By the way, that dame's one of the chasers who tried to compromise your operation. It can't be a coincidence that she's here, worming her way into your good graces."

"Thank you for letting me know, Sergeant. I appreciate your concern. You're one of my finest lieutenants and a prime role model for our young Purist neophytes. But Stacie Spencer is completely oblivious to my involvement in the trafficking industry. Don't worry about her."

"If you say so, boss."

"Go enjoy yourself, Sergeant." Damien nudged Paul's shoulder with a chummy fist bump.

Paul wandered off. One thing he enjoyed about working for Damien was how well he treated his subordinates. He took good care of them.

A young man spoke into a handheld mic. "Ladies and gentlemen, may I have your attention?" He stood atop the landing of a red-carpeted staircase, looking sharp in pressed pants, a dress shirt, bow tie, and waistcoat.

Conversations stopped. A few people murmured. What was this about?

The man said, "Please give a warm welcome to Mr. Sykes' special keynote speaker—" There was a long pause. Everyone waited anxiously. "—Doctor Atticus Hancroft!"

Gasps and reverent whispers of shock and excitement filled the room.

At the wine bar, Stacie recoiled. *Atticus Hancroft?* **The** *Atticus Hancroft?* He was the last living creator of AEGIS, and one of Eden's first-ark settlers. At his age, the man rarely made public appearances.

In a sumptuous black suit, Atticus emerged from a door behind the announcer. Wrinkles and crow's feet lined his timeworn face, deep grooves furrowed his forehead, and his hair was thinning and gray. Though elderly, he appeared to be in good health. He didn't seem weak or fragile.

Damien was confident that if any guests tonight had lingering doubts about supporting him, and were considering throwing their weight behind other candidates, having Atticus in his corner would change their minds. Independent Movement antagonists and people outraged by Coalition fighters being let off the hook respected Atticus.

Atticus took the mic from the announcer. "Distinguished ladies and gentlemen," he began, "I am proud to say I've known Damien Sykes for quite some time. He is an extraordinary businessman, a brilliant thinker, and a natural leader.

"I know he will make an outstanding Chief Executive. Like me, he understands our republic is being endangered by reformists and extremists who seek to compromise the balance—the harmony —that keeps our society thriving.

"Humanity had brought itself to the brink of extinction but survived and forged the Commonwealth, with the help of the Union and other worlds beyond the Union's borders.

"AEGIS laid the foundation for the New Humanity. But the state of our republic is in jeopardy. Independent Movement proponents. Terrorists like the Coalition. Pro-reform politicians. Radicals. These people have one agenda: to destroy our republic. We now have a de facto Chief, a woman who openly champions their destructive ideals. She cannot win next year's election.

"I call on you to vote for Damien Sykes. A vote for Sykes is a vote for the right path. It is a vote to keep Eden free from those unfit to be here, those better suited to the role they currently occupy. Save our republic." He delivered his endorsement masterfully.

The audience gave him a standing ovation.

Stacie, however, was creeped out by the mad genius's speech. Sure, she loved attention and had lived a rarefied life, but never had she believed that any segment of humanity was inferior, defective, or undeserving of a shot at prosperity.

She understood that Eden's real estate wasn't big enough for all of humanity. Tough choices had to be made. Still, she wanted the government's promise to the colonists honored, the promise that their world would be an "Eden" too. And yes, when she was a Guardian, she had believed the colony rebellion was unjustified, like most Edenites did.

Damien greeted his VIP with a perfunctory half bow. *<Thank you for coming. You have my sincerest gratitude,>* he said to Atticus, their Link transmitting his voice.

<Think nothing of it, Damien. You've always been my prize disciple.> Atticus placed a hand on the wildcard's shoulder. *<You are on the cusp of fulfilling what I believe is your destiny. Someone must step up to maintain the taxonomy of humanity.>* He glanced over at Stacie. *<That's the late Patrick and Darlene Spencer's daughter, isn't it?>*

<She is.>

<Careful, Damien, don't let your penchant for pretty women distract you from your campaign.>

<Don't worry, it won't.>

<Very well. I must go now.>

<Thank you again, sir.>

With pride, Atticus said the Purist motto. *<For the purity of the republic.>*

<Yes, for the purity of the republic.>

While Atticus was on his way out, several guests stopped him for handshakes and comments on his speech.

Outside, Atticus got into his limo and departed.

As the vehicle sped away from the mansion, five armored cargo vans raced past in the opposite direction, their fronts retrofitted with heavy battering rams. The grooves on Atticus's forehead deepened. His intuition told him those vans, heading straight for Damien's estate, spelled trouble.

179

Sam, Akane, Jay, and five other solutioners, dressed in dark fatigues, sat on two benches inside the rear hold of one of the vans. In just a few minutes, they'd don their balaclavas and crash Damien's fundraiser.

Jay held up a double-barreled handgun, which was the primary weapon for the mission. He executed a quick functions check. "Sweet," he said, admiring the craftsmanship.

The gun was programmed to go lethal only for the Purists logged into its CPU, a measure to help the Strike Team avoid dispatching the wrong people. One of the barrels dispersed nonlethal taser rounds; the other, lethal rounds. But even with that safety feature, the team needed to be careful.

Akane examined the weapon, its smart-grip auto-customizing to the size of her fingers. *I wonder how Janice scored these Tarzekian weapons.*

Jay shifted his head toward Sam. The Strike Team's leader was a reserved man, but this was quiet even for him. "You haven't said a word. Something bothering you?"

Sam exhaled a hiss of air from his nose. "It's just that . . . this could turn into a clusterfuck really fast."

"We got this. Don't worry."

On edge, Sam didn't share Jay's optimism.

Damien's wristcom buzzed. Its message-notification light blinked. He tapped the device's centerpiece, and a message from Atticus swelled into view in a text bubble, warning him of the approaching threat. His face tightened into a scowl. *Damn it.* It had to be RISE.

Stacie glided over from the bar, her third glass of wine in hand. "How did you get Atticus Hancroft to back you?"

"I met him at one of his seminars and have been under his tutelage."

"Tutelage for what?"

Damien knew they needed to leave the mansion fast. "Right now, we should—"

Gunfire crackled outside.

Pandemonium broke out in the mansion.

Damien brought his wristcom to his mouth. "Wallace, report. What the hell's going on?"

His Chief Watch Officer replied, gunfire thundering in the background, "Perimeter breach. A coupla vans just crashed the gate. It has to be RISE, sir."

"Shit." *Solutioners, RISE's hit men.* Damien knew solutioners weren't deployed often. RISE usually kept a low profile. Did they fear his candidacy that much? He considered this attack a badge of honor.

More gunfire roared, closer to the mansion this time.

The front doors exploded inward. Solutioners rushed forward. Interior security drew firearms from the shoulder holsters beneath their suit jackets and fired.

Damien overturned a table and ducked, dragging Stacie down beside him. He reached into his jacket and produced a collapsible handgun. Extendable and flip-out components clacked. Then he was wielding a full-length weapon.

"Stay down," he told Stacie. He sprang up, squeezed the trigger three times, and stooped back down. "When we get the chance, we need to make a break for the stairwell and get to the car park on the roof. Follow my lead."

A barrage of rounds from solutioners and security pounded the room.

Guests screamed and fled in all directions.

A solutioner spotted Damien out of the corner of his eye. "Primary target acquired!" He fired at Damien, gun bucking in his hand. Bullets chipped splinters off the table Damien and Stacie were using as cover.

A stray bullet caught a guest in the side. The once-elegant function had become a shooting gallery.

Paul sheltered himself behind a pillar. He leaned around the tall white fluted column and leveled Damien's attacker with three shots, protecting his and his cohort's ticket to promised central-government positions.

Akane saw Paul. *Shaffer's here? He wasn't on the guest list.* The death of Simone plagued her mind again. *This is my chance to kill him.* Thoughts of revenge were inescapable.

She didn't care that Paul hadn't been officially confirmed as Simone's killer. In her heart, she knew it was him. He was going to pay tonight.

She switched to lethal rounds and exploded into motion, charging toward Paul while shooting wildly.

Amid the chaos, ornaments, glassware, and expensive things shattered.

A bullet from Akane's gun struck Paul's pillar. *Shit,* he thought, flinching. His eyes flitted sideways, to the petite angry woman coming for his life. He pointed his weapon at her and cut loose, firing off a rapid succession of shots.

Akane twisted out of Paul's line of fire, dove, and rolled over her shoulder, coming up in a crouch behind a long buffet credenza. Paul didn't let up, still determined to take her out.

Akane popped up and tapped the device on her wrist. An energy buckler crackled to life. It flickered as Paul's bullets crashed into it. With her shooting hand, Akane returned fire.

Paul sprayed more bullets in her direction.

She started to move closer, but a bullet out of nowhere wounded her shoulder, derailing her momentum. Her face contorted behind her mask from the pain. She found the shooter and blasted a taser round at him. The paralyzing shock incapacitated him instantly.

Akane looked back to where Paul had been, but he was gone. She scanned the storm of gunfire. *Shit. Where the hell did he go?* He wouldn't just abandon Damien. He had to still be out there, fighting.

Stacie and Damien, still taking cover behind the overturned table, waited for the right moment to escape to the stairwell.

Stacie's heart thundered in her chest. "I don't suppose you have another gun?"

"Afraid not," Damien said. They had to get to the stairwell. It was now or never. "Let's go!" He jumped up and ran, Stacie staying close behind him.

As they made their getaway, he triggered his gun, shooting bullets across the room. His shoulder rammed the stairwell door's push bar, and they retreated inside.

The door fell shut behind them, muffling the firefight.

Stacie struggled to keep pace with Damien, her heels hindering her climb up the staircase.

A solutioner shoved open the swinging doors of the second-floor landing. He reached for the gun holstered on his hip, but before he could draw, Damien sent three rounds into his bullet-resistant vest. The impact pitched the solutioner backward through the doors he'd just entered from.

They've infiltrated upper floors too, Damien thought. *They're trying to cut off all exits.* He hoped they hadn't reached the car park yet.

Damien and Stacie ascended the zigzagging flight of stairs. Footsteps clattered behind them, nearing rapidly. Solutioners were in hot pursuit.

Damien and Stacie reached the rooftop. A dozen luxury flyers sat on the landing terrace, their glossy hulls gleaming under floodlights.

Damien grabbed Stacie's arm and guided her to a sleek mauve two-seater. "Come on." He keyed his wristcom, and the flip-up canopy clicked open. "Ladies first. Get in."

He didn't have to tell Stacie twice. Chest burning from labored breaths, she leapt into the passenger seat.

The rooftop door whooshed open. Sam Guthrie stormed through, Jay at his side.

"Damien Sykes!" Sam shouted, raising his weapon.

Damien fired first.

One bullet caught Jay in the leg. He collapsed, clutching the wound. "Damn it!" he cried out.

Sam retaliated, firing back.

Damien quickly tossed his gun into the flyer and jumped behind the controls. A bullet grazed his shoulder, staining his suit with blood. He hit a button on the dashboard. The canopy snapped shut, and a light flashed from red to green.

Sam's bullets pinged off the armored flyer as it lifted into the night sky.

In the distance, sirens wailed. Blue-to-red strobes from approaching police flyers flashed in the night. Someone had called the authorities.

Not good, Sam thought.

Over his wristcom, a solutioner said, "Time to vamoose, Sam. Authorities inbound."

"Roger." Sam knelt, dragged Jay's arm over his shoulder, and helped him to his feet. "Let's get that wound taken care of and get you back to Nicole and Zola."

Jay grunted in pain as he limped, step by step, to the exit with Sam.

Inside the flyer, Stacie said, "Damien, are you okay?" She would've preferred the bullet had hit him in the head.

"The wound's superficial. Nothing to worry about. I'll be fine," he replied, sounding frustrated. He was livid that his fundraiser had ended in chaos.

He retrieved the gun from the floor, collapsed it, and slid it into a compartment underneath the dashboard.

"I heard your security guy mention RISE," Stacie said. "Who the heck are they?"

"They're a pro-reform extremist group. A violent one. They obviously attacked me because they fear my candidacy." Damien couldn't wait to burn RISE to the ground. He just needed to find their base.

Stacie wanted to press him for more information. She knew he was holding back. But there was no need to push. Not yet. Pressuring him now might arouse suspicion and jeopardize her mission, or even get her killed. It was better to take things slow.

The flyer decelerated as it approached the three-floor house sitting on one of Damien's ultraexpensive properties.

The property's defense system cleared the flyer to land inside the gate, on the lawn.

"I'm sure the authorities will want to question me and others who survived the attack," Damien said. "They'll probably pay me a visit tomorrow. I'm sorry the night had to end in such disarray."

"Hey, at least we're alive. And despite dodging bullets, I had a good time." Not really. Not by a long shot. In fact, the longer she spent with Damien, the more she felt like puking.

"I enjoyed your company as well, as I always have." He leaned in, his mouth finding hers. Then his lips trailed down to her clavicle.

Stacie fought to keep the disgust off her face and twisted away. *Yuck.* "Sorry, I'm just not in the mood tonight. I'm a little exhausted after all the, you know, shooting."

"Of course, I understand. Shall we reconvene tomorrow, perhaps? Lunch?"

"I'll clear my schedule."

"Excellent. Take one of my flyers home. I have quite the selection in—"

"I'll just take an air-cab. I'll be fine." Stace didn't want to use anything that belonged to her friend's abuser. The thought of doing so was abhorrent.

"As you wish."

They stepped out. Damien pressed a button on his wristcom to open the gate for Stacie, then went inside his house.

Stacie called an air-cab using her wristcom. The moment it landed, she hurriedly climbed in and headed home.

Damien removed his suit jacket and shirt, tossing them on the floor. After he spoke a voice command, one of his medical-service golems approached and initiated treatment for his wound. Microbots deployed from the interior storage of the golem's midsection and got to work, applying medical unguent to the nicked skin before suturing it.

Once the microbots finished, the golem called them back.

Damien made his way to his Feng Shui-inspired study, impeccably decorated with opulent white furnishings. Bone-tired, he slumped into an armchair.

He brought up his wristcom's interface and dialed a number.

A hologram of Atticus's face materialized. "Damien, are you alright? The attack on your estate is all over the news."

"I'm fine, sir."

"RISE, I assume."

"Yes, the ever-present thorn in our side."

"Be careful. This assassination attempt means they fear you. They're becoming more brazen."

"It appears so, but I'm not surprised. My chances of winning the election keep improving. I owe that to you and your teachings. They've guided me, transformed me. Being chosen to Link with you—the *founder* of Purism—and absorb your knowledge and mindset is an honor."

Atticus was the mystery instigator, the anomaly known as Quinn, the leader of the Brotherhood for Humanity's Salvation. To him, influence was the ultimate power. And as Quinn, he had clearly influenced many Edenites.

"Think nothing of it," Atticus said. "I simply recognized your potential and sought to elevate it. Now rest. The authorities will be knocking at your door tomorrow."

"Yes, and I am prepared."

"Well, I bid you a good night, friend." The video transmission ended.

For Damien, being called a friend by the founder of Purism was awesome.

The mind's eye of Atticus Hancroft had awakened him to the "perceived" dangers facing the New Humanity. Atticus's teachings had edified his life and given it purpose. He had become infused with a desire to change society. The interpolation of immigrants would end with him, and he'd continue to implement AEGIS's blueprint for humanity. He'd ensure the unworthy never gained power.

Like Stacie, he had sought a higher calling. She had joined the CDF to escape her gilded cage, desperate to be more than just the "princess" of the Spencer family. Speaking of . . .

He tapped his wristcom. Images of Stacie floated above it. Microdrones had captured them during the fundraiser without her knowledge.

Damien glued his gaze to her, tracing her curves. He wetted his lips with his tongue, eager to possess her. To him, she was the epitome of physical excellence—solid, statuesque, and well-developed. This woman had hit some genetic jackpot, he thought. He was mentally gushing over her perfection.

He unzipped and reached inside his pants.

The memory of the first time he'd made love to Stacie rushed back. He had thrust into her until she nearly came undone, her fingers knotted in his hair, her hips arching against him. He ached for the feel of her bare skin. It was like warm satin stretched over sinewy muscle.

The more he reminisced, the more his erection strained against his palm. He kept stroking himself, his grip tightening. Before long, he was spilling cum into his clenched fist.

His father had instilled in him the belief that anything could be his. He simply had to take it. And he had declared that Stacie Lynette Spencer would be his.

• • •

Rain pummeled the awning of the restaurant's outdoor seating area. A chestnut-blond woman sat with Stacie at a table for two. She was Cassie McCanns: young, demure, and susceptible to manipulation. Damien Sykes had taken advantage of her easily.

"Enough," Stacie said. An angry wave of her hand sliced the air. Even with the makeup, the bruising on Cassie's face was still evident.

"It ends today."

Cassie replied, "He—"

"Won't change. You know that." Stacie was tired of Cassie glossing over Damien's behavior.

Cassie sat silently, her mind replaying good times: flowers waiting on her doorstep, thoughtful gifts, pampering, surprise visits to her workplace, planet-hopping vacations. Who would want to give all that up?

Damien was a charmer. He knew how to win a woman's heart, how to romance her.

But the arguments, when they happened, were severe. And during them, Cassie paid the price. She made him do it, made him hit her, Damien would say.

"Stacie, I—" Cassie began, her youthful, innocent face reflecting hesitation.

"Come on, let's go after him. We can press charges. I'll foot the bill for everything."

Cassie's chin dropped. "Stacie, you know—"

When Cassie raised her head, Stacie found herself staring at a mirror image of her own face.

Doppelganger Stacie's features contorted, becoming a sinister mask. **"You're right, it's all your fault! You're incompetent! You couldn't see past his facade and delivered me into the hands of a demented monster! You're responsible for these bruises and all of my mental scars!"**

Everything began dissolving into a dark glob.

Stacie, still in the air-cab, gasped, awakening from the bad dream. *It was my fault. I ignored the signs of who . . . what he was.*

She sighed. Tomorrow, she'd debrief with Conlan, and they'd plan their next move. *I'm going to make up for it, Cassie. I'm going to get him, for you.*

• • •

Randy was up watching newscasts on his TV. The firefight at Damien's estate was the top headline and was trending across the net. His gut told him that his shortened visit to RISE HQ, the important meeting Sam had mentioned, and tonight's attack were all connected. But that was just speculation, for now. He'd have to unearth the truth. And he swore he would.

His father had already checked in with some ex-Coalition fighters. He hadn't found out anything about RISE yet but planned to follow up on another lead tomorrow.

Randy wondered, *What really is RISE? Some kind of social-justice vigilante outfit, taking the law into their own hands? What are you involved with, Akane?*

INTERLUDE FOUR

A metal door swung open, slamming against the wall. Akane, Sam, and Jay walked into the compact space.

A disheveled-looking man sat in a lone chair, hands restrained behind his back and mouth gagged.

He mumbled fearfully.

"Wh-what's this?" Akane asked, her voice shaky. She had no idea she was about to carry out an execution.

"Your final test, Akane," Sam said. "Jay, proceed."

Jay screwed a silencer onto the end of a pistol, then extended the weapon to Akane grip-first.

Akane hesitated to accept it. "What's that for?"

"Just take it. It'll be okay," Jay said coaxingly.

Akane's trembling fingers settled into the grip's ridges.

Sam glared at the captive like he wanted to kill him himself. "This man is one of the Highborn who kept harassing Skylar at her job. He's one of the bullies who pushed her over the edge. Now, you might be thinking bullying and harassment aren't punishable by death, but this asshole needs to pay for the way he treated her. Skylar reported him to upper management, and they ignored her complaints because she was an immigrant. That's right, isn't it?"

Akane recalled Skylar's stories of the harassment she endured at work. It was so disgusting. "Yeah, that's what she told me." Her shoulders sagged as she stared solemnly at the floor.

Sam gripped the man's chin. "Because management wasn't going to do a damn thing, you just kept getting bolder and started playing a little game of touch and grab, didn't you?" Sam looked back at Akane. "That's what Skylar said, right?"

"Yeah," she replied, her voice heavy with sadness.

"Go on, Akane, finish him. Make him pay," Jay said.

Working up the nerve to kill the man wasn't easy for Akane. *This shouldn't be so hard, but it is. Why?* "I . . . I just don't—" The pistol rattled in her trembling hand.

Piss saturated the man's pants as he mumbled a plea for mercy he didn't deserve.

Sam could hardly wait for him to die. "Do it, Akane. Erase this son of a bitch from existence." Akane's finger tentatively hovered over the trigger. "I bet you're thinking: He didn't murder anyone, and he's not like Simone's killer. But if we let him go, he'll just find another immigrant woman to harass. He's a waste of air."

Tears streamed down Akane's cheeks. Memories of a joyful Skylar blinked through her mind. She remembered Skylar's enthusiasm: *"Me? I'm destined for **stardom**."*

"Do it!" Jay shouted.

Internally, Sam rooted for Akane to take this last step. "Prove you can do what needs to be done to our enemies."

He'd been in Akane's position before, when he first joined RISE. He'd wondered if a man not formally sentenced should die by his hand. But RISE needed warriors, men and women willing to take justice into their own hands when the system failed. He became what immigrants and colonists needed him to be: both shield and axe—the shield that kept harm at bay and the axe that severed the heads of those who meant them harm. Law be damned.

Akane lowered the pistol. She just couldn't do it.

Sam exhaled, more disappointed than angry. "It's okay," he said understandingly. "This isn't a disqualifier. It just means you're not ready for the harder jobs. I just hope that when we find Simone's killer, you don't balk."

Disgust for those who were prejudiced against immigrants surged within Akane. She yanked the trigger twice. Two muted pops went off, and blood and brain matter slathered the walls and floor. The man's dead body slumped forward.

That's for Skylar. Tears kept flowing from Akane's eyes.

"Good job," Sam said. "Simone would've been proud."

Red rivulets ran down the blood-smeared walls.

"Here, I got it." Jay took the pistol from Akane.

She was grappling with her first illegal kill. Was it justice or murder? Maybe murder was justice sometimes.

Sam knew better than to waste guilt on scum. "Don't second-guess yourself. You did the right thing."

Akane dipped her chin in a resolute nod and fixed her gaze on the lifeless body. *This isn't what we wanna do, but sometimes it's necessary to ensure our safety.*

She had completed the vetting process. She was now a full-fledged member of RISE.

CHAPTER FIVE

Stacie stood in Conlan's office, finishing her debrief about last night. "That's it, Sir. But with the way Damien spoke about these Purists, he has to be involved with them."

"All just conjecture."

"Yeah, I know, no substantial evidence yet. But I'll get some."

"Be careful. Continue to exercise extreme caution. If you ask too many questions too fast, that might tip him off."

"Yes, Sir. Anything on this RISE organization yet?"

"Cyber Intel uncovered some ramblings on chat forums, people claiming they're part of RISE and declaring it the new Coalition." Conlan steepled his fingers, flesh meeting the metal of his cybernetic prosthetic. Then he closed his eyes in contemplation. Purists? RISE? What was going on in the Commonwealth?

"I'm meeting Damien today for an outing. I'll squeeze more info out of him about these Purists and RISE. And I'll eventually get a confession out of him about his trafficking operation."

"Be careful."

"Yes, Sir."

Stacie was about to leave until Conlan said, "Have you talked to Randal lately?"

Annoyance painted Stacie's face. "Why, Sir?"

"I know he misses you. At the graduation banquet, you two seemed like such a wonderful couple. He told me what sparked the breakup, but how long are you going to stay mad at him for one moral folly? Give him a chance to make things right."

"With all due respect, Sir, I'm not interested in talking about Randal Scott. He and I are done. *Finito.*"

"I see. I'm still rooting for you two, though."

"Can I go now?"

Conlan knew when to leave well enough alone and dropped the topic of Randal Scott. "Yes, you're dismissed." He shifted his eyes to his computer screen, and Stacie departed.

• • •

Satellite One
Colony Four

Arson and Sariah drove up outside a tavern in a rickety car. A Coalition buddy of Arson's was supposed to meet him there and share what he knew about RISE. Arson intended to make good on his promise to Randy and uncover what he could about the secretive organization.

Sitting in the front passenger seat, Arson said to Sariah, "I'm going in. Keep an eye on the vehicle behind us." A black van had followed them. Its occupants thought they were unnoticed, but they were wrong. "The moment someone moves, let me know."

"Will do."

Arson kissed Sariah's cheek. "Thanks. I won't be long."

After exiting the car, he approached the tavern, opened a pair of barn-style doors, and entered a room full of raucous, jawing patrons.

195

Men flirted with waitresses. People cheered and booed uproariously while watching a game of field hockey on a big screen. Cue sticks clacked against billiard balls. Bottles were raised to mouths. The scent of smoldering cigarettes and alcohol was potent.

Arson scanned the boisterous crowd for his Coalition friend, Sergei Gurin, former commander of the Gurin Faction.

Sergei, seated at one of the booth-tables, spotted Arson.

Sergei's attire was simple: olive-green shirt, tan cargo pants, black boots, and a wool overcoat. In front of him sat a half-finished mug of amber liquid. He smiled at Arson, a man he greatly respected. Despite becoming a lottery beneficiary and living in Eden's opulence, Arson had never forgotten his roots. He had betrayed the CDF to fight for the Coalition.

Some lottery beneficiaries forgot where they came from after getting a taste of paradise. They had "made it." But Arson Scott still considered Satellite One home. Even now, exonerated of war crimes and allowed to return to Eden, he remained in this outdated colony to support restoration efforts and help people rebuild their lives after months of military rule. Arson Scott wasn't the type to rest on his laurels.

Sergei lifted a hand, waving Arson over.

"Sergei, good to see you," Arson said, approaching the table.

"Come, sit," the Russian replied merrily. Arson settled into the seat across from him. "It's been a while, Arson."

"It has."

Sergei reminisced. "Do you remember that time we were supposed to take out that convoy of Shells and the charges didn't go off?" He shook with laughter. "*Phew*, I thought we were dead for sure."

A sequence of events spiraled through Arson's recollection: crackling gunfire, energy blasts, grenades exploding. "But we gunned our way out of that situation and got the job done, *without* killing a single Guardian," he said proudly. "We might have sent a few to the infirmary, though."

"Yes, I'm lucky to have fought alongside you."

"Same. And the Coalition's efforts paid off, just like we hoped."

"Thanks to Operation Hammer Fall. It must've been a *glorious* day, the Battle of the Quad."

"I wouldn't call it glorious. We just did what had to be done. Unfortunately, there were Guardians we couldn't avoid killing."

"That wasn't our fault." Sergei had not only fought for the Coalition, but for the RUC in the Three-Week War as well. He remembered homes and buildings being carpet-bombed into ash and rubble. "The government started the conflict. We simply fought back. They could've let Colonies One, Four, and Six have their independence. Even the Union leaders concluded those colonies were justified in breaking away from the Commonwealth."

"Yeah, and now with Amaechi in office, things are getting better. Construction's ramping up. Old, beat-to-hell MHUs are being retired. Plans are in the works for the colonies' first university. Finally, steps are being taken to close the chasm between the prosperous and the marginalized."

Sergei took a gulp of his drink. "Sad to say, my friend, but this progress won't last. Amaechi became Chief by default, next in line after that madman Gould's death. She's just a temp, a placeholder until the winner of the upcoming election takes over. And that winner, unfortunately, won't be her.

"We colony citizens and our immigrant brothers and sisters on Eden are the minority. Conformist Edenites, who want to preserve their monopoly on prosperity, will outvote us. Sure, some nonimmigrants who have common sense will vote for Amaechi, but they are few.

"In this new era of colonist and immigrant hate—and anger toward former Coalition fighters—most Edenites are going to vote for someone other than Amaechi. Maybe it'll be that lunatic Damien Sykes, or even a centrist. But it's going to be someone aligned with their values, someone who gives them what they want.

"That candidate, whoever they are, might even annul Amaechi's ruling absolving all Coalition fighters of war crimes." A humorless laugh escaped Sergei. "Just think about that. By this time next year, you and I could be playing holo table-games in some maximum-security orbital prison.

"And not even all colony citizens are on the same page. The people of colonies Two, Three, and Five never joined the RUC, and they opposed the Coalition's formation. They were fine jumping through hoops, negotiating endlessly, and slogging through red tape, enacting change at a snail's pace. They saw the Coalition's rebellion as a setback that worsened relations between the colonies and the central government.

"But those of us who fought with the RUC and the Coalition had sense. We chose to accelerate change. We didn't just stand by hoping for it, or sit around praying for divine intervention. We said 'no more lying down.'" Sergei's voice rose. "We're the ones responsible for the progress happening today!"

Heads turned toward Sergei, his volume far too loud.

Arson made a calming gesture, signaling Sergei to keep it down and be mindful of the other patrons. "I won't say you're wrong. But I'm hopeful. I'm hopeful Amaechi will win next year's election."

Sergei scoffed. "*Bah*, even with the net filters down, even now that we colonists can expose how horribly we've been treated, Edenites still turn their noses up at us, believing themselves superior. I guarantee you, Arson, a storm is on the horizon.

Perhaps another war."

Exhausted from fighting, Arson wanted no more war. "I pray you're wrong, Sergei. It's been good chatting, but I need to get down to business. I can't keep Sariah waiting outside forever."

"Ah, yes, your new . . . lady friend."

"Let's cut to the chase. You said you could tell me about this RISE organization. Who are they?"

"Our best hope."

Arson frowned, growing impatient. His tone stiffened. "I'm going to need more than that."

"We're a pro-reform activist group," Sergei supplied.

A question played across Arson's features. "We?"

"I have been a member since the first year of its inception. You should join too, my friend."

Arson's eyes narrowed. "So, is RISE some product of the Independent Movement, or some entity formed during martial law? And what exactly does RISE do?"

"Firstly, RISE formed well before the Three-Week War. Initially, its mission was to raise awareness about the colonies' deteriorating conditions, advocate for equality, and get more immigrants into the CDF, the government, and positions of power.

"After the Three-Week War ended and martial law was imposed on colonies One, Four, and Six, RISE's mission broadened. It began fighting for increased funding for Assisted Living Centers and supporting the Coalition. In short, we do what needs to be done to make reform a reality. In the election between Ron Burchardt and Todd Sieger, Burchardt won because of RISE."

That news jolted Arson. "What do you mean?"

Sergei replied, "We hacked a voter database here and there,

bribed a couple of people. Sprinkle in some blackmail and a few threats, and then . . . *voilà*: Burchardt wins. Not by much, not by a landslide, but just enough to make it look like a legitimate upset victory. Though, of course, the authorities are investigating."

Arson snarled derisively. Manipulating election results went against his principles.

Sergei said, "Oh, don't be so surprised, Scott. Did you actually think a pro-reform candidate like Ron Burchardt had a real chance in this era of colonist and immigrant hate? Come on. Someone has to even the playing field in these elections."

"We'll never know if Burchardt could've won legitimately, will we? Sometimes miracles happen. Believe in people, Sergei."

Sergei rolled his eyes. "We colonists tried *believing* for years, and where did it get us? Nowhere. That's why the RUC formed."

Arson's disdain for election fraud creased his forehead. "Tampering with elections is wrong, and illegal."

"Amaechi's fairy-tale Chief Executiveship doesn't stand a chance of lasting without RISE." Sergei was convinced that RISE's tactics were necessary. "You should join us, my friend. We've become the new Coalition. But you won't have to worry about guerrilla warfare, *unavoidable* shootouts, or leading hit-and-run attacks on CDF bases and arms contractors. RISE's fight is different. Our tactics aren't like the Coalition's. We're a liberation force working behind the scenes, not fighting on the front lines of a battlefield.

"We're making plans to swing as many of the special elections as we can in our favor. We could use you on our side, the great Arson Scott. We'd benefit from your input, your leadership."

This was a "no" for Arson. He refused to involve himself in anything unethical. If RISE's connection to rigged elections was discovered, it would only further demonize colonists and immigrants, fueling public hatred and almost certainly ensuring Oviereya's defeat in next year's election.

But Arson couldn't keep openly criticizing Sergei and RISE. He needed to play along, to infiltrate the organization and find a way to shut it down. Though he doubted RISE could stay hidden from Defense Force Intelligence and the police forever, the sooner it was dismantled, the better.

Trying not to sound too gung-ho just yet, Arson said, "I . . . I don't know. I mean, you're not totally wrong about our chances in these elections."

"Of course not. And Tristan Gelano is one of the three founders, the shot-callers who are our council, if that means anything to you. And you know Tris is smart. She won't let RISE or its members get exposed, including you, if you join. Assuming that's what you're worried about, you'll be safe."

"Tristan? Our mining colleague?"

Sergei chuckled. "Yes. What other Tristans do we know?"

From inside the car, Sariah saw three men leave the van behind her. They wore masks, dark clothing, and long trench coats.

Sariah brought her handheld comm-set to her mouth. "Arson, movement headed in your direction."

Arson heard Sariah's warning in his earpiece and told her to stay put. Instincts screaming at him to get his weapon out, he reached into his trench coat. "Three guys tailed us," he told Sergei, drawing a handgun. "Whoever they are, they're about to make a move."

Sergei also pulled a handgun from his coat. "I am not a violent man. But as we used to say in the Coalition: When violence comes to you, violence begets violence."

"I suggest everyone take cover!" Arson shouted. "Things are about to get messy!"

The barn doors swung wide as the three men charged in, their automatic weapons spraying bullets all around.

"For the purity of the republic!" one of them shouted.

People screamed in horror.

Arson and Sergei scattered in different directions, slipping between patrons fleeing to the nearest exits. But many didn't get far, cut down by a barrage of wild gunfire.

"Arson Scott, you're a dead man!" one gunman yelled.

These three Purists were after Arson, and killing colonist scum who had caused the civil war was just a bonus.

The bartender reached under the counter and grabbed a shotgun. "Bastards!" The double barrels exploded in a loud blast, but the rounds missed. His targets were still standing.

One of the Purists fired his submachine gun at the bartender. Bullets riddled him, and his blood flecked the counter.

A woman hiding under a table sobbed.

Sergei avenged the bartender by pumping a flurry of bullets into his killer's back.

One of the remaining two Purists turned his weapon on Sergei. The other chased after Arson, who'd sprinted out an exit, hoping to divide the Purists and draw them away from the bar patrons.

A bullet nicked Sergei, flaying skin from his shoulder. "Damn it!" He sprinted for the bar counter as bullets peppered the wall parallel to him.

He jumped behind the counter, feet landing beside the dead bartender, and ducked.

The Purist continued firing madly.

Splinters of wood shot up from the counter and cascaded over Sergei. He sprang to his feet, shot four rounds, and ducked again. *Damn, didn't get him.* He rose and fired a short burst. Still no success. He dropped back into a crouch as more gunfire from his attacker pierced the air.

The Purist's gun finally ran empty; the dry, mechanical clicking of a depleted chamber betrayed his vulnerability. He reached into his coat for a new clip.

Sergei seized the moment. He popped up and triggered a couple of shots.

One bullet punched through the Purist's arm. He howled and lost his grip on his gun. Now unarmed, it was over for him.

Sergei adjusted his aim and squeezed the trigger—once, twice, three times—ending the murderer's rampage.

The smell of spent rounds hung in the air.

Sergei released an unsteady exhalation.

Out back, Arson crouched behind the tavern's dumpster as bullets slammed into it and the brick wall behind him. He peeked over the edge and fired.

His target went down, hot lead drilling holes into him. As soon as the body dropped, Arson sprinted back inside.

"Sergei!" Arson shouted, reentering the tavern.

"Arson, are you alright?"

"Yeah."

Sariah rushed inside, gun in hand. Arson had told her to stay put, but she couldn't sit around in the car any longer, and she'd never been one to stay out of the action anyway.

"Holy shit." Her eyes swept over the crumpled mess of dead patrons.

"I'm assuming you're Sariah," Sergei said.

"I am."

"Good to meet another fellow Coalition fighter."

"Who were these guys?" Sariah asked Sergei.

"Purists. A thorn in the side of immigrants and colonists." Upon checking their bodies, he found Purist tattoos on one's neck and the other's wrist. And one of them had shouted the Purist motto—that was a pretty dead giveaway. "Somehow, they've expanded their movement to Satellite One."

Sariah found the word "Purists" deeply disturbing. "What the fuck are Purists?"

Sergei explained, "They're an extremist group of immigrant haters, driven by the belief that AEGIS declared part of humanity superior. Their toxic ideology, Purism, has influenced government leaders, Guardians, police—you name it. Some Purist groups are methodical and organized; others are just gun-crazy maniacs, like the ones who attacked this tavern."

"Any idea how many groups there are?" Arson asked.

"Over a dozen," Sergei replied. "We suspect Damien Sykes is involved with the biggest one, the original group that spawned all the copycats. It's called the Brotherhood for Humanity's Salvation. Damien might even be its leader. One thing's certain, he *is* a Purist. And if he wins the Chief Executiveship, it'll be the ultimate Purist power grab. That cannot happen."

Sariah said, "I can believe he's one of these *Purists* alright, with the rubbish that comes out of his mouth. So, who founded Purism?"

"A man calling himself Quinn," Sergei replied. "Quinn could be one man or more. Quinn could even be a woman."

Arson's inflamed eyes roamed the devastated tavern. Shot-up men and women lay sprawled across the floor. The Purists had come for him, but they didn't have to involve innocents.

They were acting on Quinn's—Atticus's—call to action: to take out Coalition fighters.

Sergei's heart wept for the dead. "You see, this is why RISE exists—to stop killings like this, to counter the Purists' political power plays, to make equality a reality. Join us, both of you."

Arson's thoughts whirled.

Police sirens grew closer.

• • •

Randy sat at his desk in his condo, videoconferencing with Arson through a laptop.

"I've heard about these Purists," Randy said. "It was the three RISE members who befriended me that filled me in." He hadn't told Arson their names, or that they were Guardians of Vanguard Alpha. Sam, Jay, and Akane were actually good people trying to look after him. It didn't feel right to rat them out.

"Well, Sergei arranged a meeting with this council for me tomorrow," Arson said. "I'm playing along to get closer. As pissed as I am about what happened at the tavern, and about the three ex-Coalition fighters who got gunned down, RISE still isn't good for the Commonwealth. What they've done, interfering in the election process, is illegal.

"Yeah, they've got good intentions. They're not scumbags like Purists are, but wrong is wrong. Both RISE and Purists have to be stopped. They both violate the law to advance their agendas. Purists do it to maintain the unfair status quo. RISE does it to achieve equality."

"So you meet with this council, and then what? Take them out?" Randy asked.

"I wouldn't rule it out entirely. I'll do whatever's necessary to protect the Commonwealth. But it's not my place to decide people's punishment for their wrongs. I'm not Arman Reza.

"What I'm going to do is meet with the council to uncover their plan for compromising the upcoming elections, then contact Conlan so Defense Force Intelligence can take further action. He's the one person we both know would listen to us."

A dear family friend, Conlan was one of the few people within the CDF who still respected Arson. Conlan had respected him even when Arson was fighting for the Coalition, because Conlan understood the civil war wasn't black and white, but gray.

Arson said, "But Conlan won't commit DFI's resources unless we come to him with something solid, not hearsay or theories or some 'this person told me that' nonsense.

"I'm not happy about taking down a well-intentioned activist organization. I even know one of the council members, Tristan. It's a shame RISE couldn't stick to *legal* activism. Apparently, they've decided that going outside the law and resorting to extreme measures is the best way to help immigrants and colonists, the best way to bring about social change. That makes them extremists. That makes them dangerous.

"I want true reformists and Amaechi to hold power, but the legal way. There are no such things as 'good extremist groups' and 'bad extremist groups.' It doesn't matter what their intentions are.

"We need to gather as much info as we can before going to Conlan. We need to know how large RISE really is. It could have multiple bases.

"The council operates things from Satellite One, according to what Sergei told me. We need to know who's leading the charge for them on Eden. Even if DFI took the council into custody, there might be someone on the ground to assume command."

Randy said, "That person could be this woman named Janice LaCroix. She mentioned she was the head of operations. From what I've seen, though, RISE has only one central base here on Eden, the place I was taken to. But you're right; we don't know that for *certain*. They might have several branches. If the Defense Force takes out that one base, there could be others."

"Okay, so do what you can to learn more on your end, and I'll do the same on mine. Just keep letting your three friends believe they can recruit you. Let them keep trying to reel you in."

"'Superspy' isn't part of my skill set," Randy joked. "The Academy didn't cover that."

"Same here, but we'll make do."

"So, I guess we're working together."

"Yep, and just a warning: This RISE member you told me about—the female, whoever she is—could be very dangerous. Extremist groups like RISE take advantage of the hurt and the weak. They catch them at the right time—when they're emotionally vulnerable, when they're down and out—and then offer them a place, a home, a family, a *mission*. That's how they earn their victims' allegiance.

"I'm simply suggesting she might be radicalized to the point where she can't comprehend that RISE, however well-intentioned they are, is detrimental to her, immigrants, and the Commonwealth. I'm not saying it's her fault. Our exclusionary society breeds extremist activist organizations like RISE and makes marginalized immigrants susceptible to radicalization."

Randy stood up for RISE, saying, "Yeah, but all in all, RISE just believes they're doing the right thing, the necessary thing. They don't see themselves as *radicalizing* anyone, just enlisting people who are willing to fight for equality and *want* to."

"No matter how just or right they think they are, *they're not.*"

Arson cautioned his son, adding, "Be careful around this girl."

"Let me worry about her."

"Alright, fine. I'll be in touch, Son." The screen went blank.

Election fraud? Blackmail? All for immigrant and colony equality, huh? Akane was a Guardian moonlighting as a RISE member, and Sam and Jay were partners in crime, was that it? *What have you gotten yourself into, Akane?*

• • •

Damien waited for Stacie at a two-person table shaded by a wide umbrella.

She approached in a red top that clung to her braless breasts, its low neckline drawing attention to her décolletage. Perfectly fitted jeans and red heels completed the outfit.

As she swayed her denim-clad hips, she slipped into character —old Stacie.

Damien questioned her intentions. Was she really interested in him or more so the information he could provide her? He thought about what Paul had said. Was this some sort of subterfuge?

Damien might've been head over heels for her, but he wasn't a dimwit. If Stacie was putting on a charade, who was she working for? The CDF, her former employer?

Every step Stacie took projected confidence and sexual prowess. Reaching the table, she sat down in the chair facing Damien and hooked a leg over a knee. "How's the shoulder?"

"Fine."

"So, tell me more about RISE," Stacie said, sounding enthusiastic.

"Why do you want to know more about RISE?" Damien's voice carried an undercurrent of distrust.

Stacie gave him the answer she had prepared. "I was a sergeant in the CDF. I fought a war to defend our republic from the

Coalition. The Coalition killed my parents. Now Coalition-lite has taken aim at me—*me*, the daughter of Patrick and Darlene Spencer. I need to know as much as I can about these people to defend myself.

"They were after you, you say, but it certainly didn't matter to them that I was in the crossfire, and they may come after me next. I need to protect Spencer Enterprises. I need to make these people pay. It'd be blasphemy for me to let them get away with nearly killing me.

"My mom and dad taught me that no one, and I mean no one, fucks with the Spencer family. They made sure that anyone who did never did again, gave them the scare of their life. So quit playing, Damien. Tell me about RISE. Trust is the foundation for all personal relationships. You want me to trust you, right? How else can we . . . take things further?"

Damien went back and forth with himself, unsure if he should believe her answer. "Well said, my dear. I understand your concern about these people, and as you said, we must trust each other." Maybe she was being sincere, he thought. "What I know is that three people lead RISE: Tristan Gelano, Franco DeFalco, and Julian Hurst. They are RISE's council.

"They're headquartered somewhere in Colony Four, I believe. They do well at keeping their whereabouts undisclosed. I've got people working to pinpoint their location. The gun-toting ruffians who attacked my estate were solutioners, RISE's Strike Team.

"RISE must have a base here on Eden, a place where they run their vigilante operations."

Stacie said, "So this council runs things from Satellite One, and their lackeys on Eden carry out their orders."

"Yes. I will find RISE's Eden base and make them pay for their assault on my estate. You better believe it."

"These Purists, you know more about them than you've been letting on. Spill it. Are you affiliated with them?" Stacie hoped that, at last, she would get some answers, her earrings capturing every word. "I want to trust you, Damien, but you have to let me in."

Damien lounged back in his chair, thinking. "Okay. I'll give you your answers tomorrow tonight. You'll be joining me to watch the election results come in. I'll tell you more then."

"Where are we going?"

"You'll find out tomorrow night. Like you said, trust is the foundation of all relationships. You trust me, don't you?"

"Yes, Damien, I do." *Never in a trillion years.*

"Well, let's just leave it at that for now and enjoy ourselves, shall we?"

"Fine by me." At least she had more information on RISE she could report to Conlan in the meantime. Defense Force Intelligence was a powerful entity. They were better equipped to locate this council than Damien. The CDF had jurisdiction on Satellite One that he didn't have and could go anywhere. They could even lock down entire sectors while searching for this council, this supposed threat to Commonwealth law and order.

Stacie flagged down a server golem to place her order. After it logged her meal and moved on, she asked Damien, "Did the authorities have any luck identifying any of the solutioners?"

"No. All those solutioners hid behind masks, and the event floor was too contaminated to extract DNA from any who might have bled. But the authorities weren't aware of the skirmish on the roof, nor did I inform them about it." He preferred that he and his Purist legion take care of RISE. "My forensics specialist extracted DNA from the blood of the one I shot." The memory of his bullet striking Jay flashed in his mind, and he smirked. "Paul Shaffer has a connection inside law enforcement who will get him a match. Once they do, I'll wring the location of RISE's base out of that solutioner."

"Vengeance is a dish best served cold, they say," Stacie said.

"Indeed."

•••

THE NEXT DAY

Colony Four

Mid-morning, Sergei and Arson were in a two-door flatbed cargo truck, traveling an unpaved, uneven road. Through the truck's windows, they saw Guardians—mobilized by CDF Command due to Conlan's intel from Stacie—questioning pedestrians, shopkeepers, and outdoor vendors.

Sergei struggled to steady the racing thoughts clawing at his focus. The CDF had deployed an army of Guardians to the colony, and word was that they were asking about Tristan Gelano, Franco DeFalco, and Julian Hurst. Somehow the CDF had gotten tipped off about RISE's council, about the *entire* organization. Now they were in hunting mode.

The CDF was committed to eliminating domestic threats to the Commonwealth, and RISE had made the list, after attacking CDF service members, government officials, scientists, and business leaders at Damien's fundraiser.

Throngs of Guardians in black-and-gray camo, swarming the street, gave Sergei flashbacks of military rule. *Damn, who could've told them about the council?*

Perturbed colony citizens watched as Guardians spilled out of BUSs and flooded their zone, reminding them of a time of raids and arrests, reawakening old mental wounds.

Arson hung his head out the open window and glanced at the side mirror, conducting another routine check for tails as the truck rumbled past firebombed buildings—ruins of the Three-Week War. A handful of vehicles traveled the same pitted road.

"Anyone following us?" Sergei asked as the truck went under a crumbling overpass.

"I don't think so." Arson wondered how the CDF had gotten wind of RISE. It was ironic that the CDF and he were trying to track down the council at the same time, but it seemed he'd get to them first.

Deserted shops, now dwellings for squatters, lined a Disaster Area, their signs cracked, windows shattered, and interiors looted by desperate souls. Bomb craters, felled trees, and mounds of rubble filled the strip of land.

As the truck left the Disaster Area, Arson shook his head. *Thank goodness we've got Oviereya in office working on restoration.* Jared Kerner didn't do much of anything.

The drive lasted twenty-five more minutes before Arson and Sergei arrived at an Assistance Living Center.

The council's here? Arson thought.

"Come," Sergei said, getting out of the truck.

A female service worker in a gray tracksuit leaned against a cistern tank, a cigarette dangling from her lips. Early forties. Wild dark orange hair. Cerulean eyes. Willowy frame. Thin face.

"Alexandria!" Sergei called out joyfully.

The woman took the cigarette between two fingers and pulled it from her lips, exhaling a plume of smoke into the air. "Sergei, what're you doin' here?" she asked, her drawl pronounced. "It's not your usual day."

"I know." Big and strong, he wrapped her in a crushing hug and then released her.

"What's with all these dang Guardians trawlin' around our colony?"

"They suspect something. What exactly, I don't know."

"Do you think they found out about RISE?"

"That's my hypothesis. But I have a meeting with the council. And I brought a guest."

Alexandria took a good look at the man with Sergei. "Oh, man, Arson Scott."

Arson shook her hand. "A friend of Sergei's, I assume."

"Yeah, he and I go way back." She flicked the cigarette onto the ground and crushed it under her heel. "Come on in."

All three headed into the center.

"Sergei!" shouted a seven-year-old boy.

Sergei patted him on the head. "Good to see you too, Lynx. Now go play."

The orphaned boy ran outside.

Alexandria said, "Hopefully, these kids will have a proper home and parents again soon."

"Oviereya's going to make that happen," Arson assured her.

"If she's in office long enough," Alexandria added.

Sergei didn't want to waste another second on chitchat. "Follow me, Arson. The council awaits."

They left Alexandria behind.

Sergei led Arson into the center's refectory. They arrived at a set of stairs that descended into a basement storage room filled with wooden crates, well-stocked shelves of supplies and nonperishable food, two dormant emergency power generators, a pegboard of tools, and miscellaneous equipment.

Motion-sensor lights buzzed on as Sergei and Arson reached the bottom of the stairs.

Sergei flipped open the housing of a wall-mounted access panel and yanked a lever downward. A hidden entrance rumbled open. "Beyond here is RISE's Satellite One operations hub."

Arson stepped in behind Sergei. The door shut. How clever of the council to use an Assistance Living Center as a front for their operations hub after martial law was declared. Assistance Living Centers had been designated safety zones, off-limits from Guardian search and seizure unless the CDF had direct evidence of insurgent activity. That had been Jared Kerner's mandate. At least the man had some kind of value system.

Inside the operations hub, machines and computers hummed. Men and women sat at various workstations and in cubicles, staying in contact with RISE's Eden headquarters.

So, this is the council's safe house, Arson thought.

A woman—late forties, asymmetrical haircut, black shirt and tawny corduroy pants—was speaking with a technician, her expression serious. But when she noticed Sergei and Arson, her demeanor shifted. "You've arrived," she said, facing them. Leaving the technician, she walked over, her smile bright. "So good to see you, Arson."

Arson nodded. "You as well, Tristan." They hugged. "I was told there are three of you."

"My colleagues are not here. They're out with family. Those quarries, though . . . *whew* . . . they nearly killed us. I was happy for you when you obtained Eden citizenship and left with Kathleen. I knew you'd become something special."

"Thank you." Arson wished Tristan weren't involved in RISE. She was such a good person. Maybe he could convince her and the rest of the council to change.

"So, Sergei has told you about RISE and the work we do," Tristan said.

"Yeah."

"What do you think? Will you join us, even if just as a consultant? Your expertise would be greatly valued."

"Tristan, I don't know. Interfering in the free election process? I'm sure RISE does a lot of good, but you have to do it clean."

Tristan wasn't fond of breaking the law, but she believed it had to be done. "I wish we could. But reformists have only a slim chance of winning elections. Voters who support the oppressors outnumber colonists and immigrants. Society has conditioned their minds to fear change, and the natural response to change you fear is to fight it, just like the natural response to inequality.

"Outvoted, we'll never get the reform we need in our republic's government by playing fair. That means we have no choice but to play dirty, but we're doing it for the right reasons. RISE will stop tampering with elections once things are made better, made right.

"Purists. Anti-reformist politicians. Spin doctors. Pundits. They are all against us, Arson. We must prevail against overwhelming odds, and we need to use unfavorable methods to do so."

Arson's lips tightened.

A small warning chime sounded.

"What's that? What's going on?" Arson asked, dropping the conversation.

A man at a monitor replied, "Alarms have been triggered. Guardians are in the building."

Sergei stepped onto the operations dais and went to the man's side. He planted his palms on the computer panel and leaned over the soundless, grainy black-and-white feed on the monitor. Cameras showed a dozen Guardians. Alexandria was engaged in a heated exchange with one of them, a female Guardian who appeared to be in charge.

The shouting match between Alexandria and the Guardian in

215

charge (GIC) intensified.

Alexandria made a move for something in her pocket. A weapon? Maybe. The GIC ordered her to keep her hands visible. She didn't comply. A male Guardian reacted, taking no chances. His weapon discharged. Blood doused the floor. Alexandria fell down, alive but bleeding from the leg. In a fit of anger, two service workers jumped the Guardian who shot her. Chaos ensued as a fight broke out between Guardians and service workers.

Bellicose Guardians tased their attackers with shock batons, subduing them and trying to prevent the situation from escalating further. For now, they were holding back from using lethal force.

The GIC fired two shots into the ceiling with her rifle to defuse the situation. Everyone froze. Then she shouted something. A frightened young man raised his arms and mouthed a response. The GIC and two lower-enlisted male Guardians followed him out of the room, while the rest stayed behind to secure the area and tend to Alexandria. The fight was over, with no casualties.

Sergei looked up from the monitor. "I think he's taking them here."

The technician at the computer panel clicked over to another feed, hallway camera four. Onscreen, the young man—held at gunpoint—was leading the three Guardians forward.

"Quickly, initiate deletion protocol," Tristan ordered.

Technicians' fingers flew across keyboards. Numbers, letters, and symbols flickered rapidly on monitors as machinery whirred and beeped.

The hidden entrance door slid open. The three Guardians entered, marching the young man into the room.

His face bore the weight of remorse, and his shoulders slumped in shame. He was disappointed in himself for giving in to fear and leading the Guardians to the council's safe house.

"It's okay, Chris," Tristan said.

"No one move!" the GIC shouted. Everyone raised their hands. "I'm Sergeant First Class Ryleigh MacRae." She recognized Tristan's face from the reference picture that had been provided. "You, identify yourself."

Tristan replied calmly, despite the tension of the moment. "My name is Tristan Gelano."

"You're coming with us for questioning," Ryleigh told her.

Tristan whispered to Arson and Sergei, who stood behind her, "Don't worry. I seriously doubt they have anything incriminating on me, and all evidence of RISE has just been wiped. Once I'm released from CDF custody, I'll contact the rest of the council, and we'll reach out to both of you."

Ryleigh's rifle clacked as she leveled it at Tristan. "Hey, no talking. Get over here, now!"

Tristan moved forward. One of the lower-enlisted Guardians grabbed her bicep and took her away.

Contempt saturated Ryleigh's expression as she confronted Arson. "Arson Scott. It doesn't surprise me you're involved in this somehow. Once a traitor, always a traitor."

"Involved in what? Volunteering at an Assistance Living Center?" Arson said, feigning innocence.

Ryleigh chuckled. "I doubt this secret room full of high-end tech is part of normal center operations. Now all of you, move. And don't try anything stupid."

She and her subordinate marched the group through the hidden entrance, ready to open fire if anyone resisted.

Once upstairs, Ryleigh ordered Tristan to sit on a stool. She obeyed. Ryleigh pulled up a stool of her own and began to browbeat Tristan with pointed questions and accusations, to intimidate her into confessing her involvement in RISE.

At this point, all the CDF had on RISE were the unfounded claims Damien Sykes had shared with Stacie, which was that Tristan Gelano, Franco DeFalco, and Julian Hurst had set up a shadow vigilante organization on Eden and were leading it from Satellite One. That wouldn't be enough to detain Tristan for long.

Ryleigh continued grilling Tristan, but Tristan didn't let the pressure loosen her tongue. She denied any connection to RISE.

Arson stood silently in a corner, waiting for his interrogation to start. The CDF getting this close, despite having no solid evidence, meant Defense Force Intelligence was on their game, he thought. He didn't think he'd have to this soon, but it was time for him to call in backup. He'd bring Conlan into the loop, updating him on what he and Randy had uncovered about RISE.

As Arson waited for Ryleigh to finish with Tristan, he wondered how Randy was doing on his end.

• • •

Randy's thoughts were on his dad as he walked from his parked sports cruiser toward Akane's dome-shaped home. Arson had missed their scheduled check-in, but he was a tough son of a gun, a war hero and former Defense Force captain. Arson could take care of himself.

Randy paused at Akane's door for a long, contemplative moment. He was fed up with the prevarication from her, Sam, and Jay—their half-truths and cryptic answers. He was tired of only getting bits and pieces of information about RISE, only what *they* wanted him to know.

His brow furrowed as he recalled what Sergei had told Arson about RISE's unlawful social-justice tactics.

Randy was supposed to keep playing along, maintain RISE's trust, and gather intel about their plans for the upcoming elections.

But like he'd told his dad, "superspy" wasn't part of Guardian training. He just wanted straight answers. He wanted Akane to be forthcoming with him.

No, he wouldn't bungle the mission; he had more sense than that. But getting deeper into RISE didn't mean he had to be indirect with Akane. Avoidance wasn't his style.

He'd demand real answers from Akane, and then he'd go on temporizing, pretending he was still feeling RISE out. In reality, they never stood a chance of recruiting him.

Randy—steamed—pounded on Akane's door unannounced. Questions about RISE had been nagging him, testing his self-control.

After checking the external viewer, Akane slid the door partially open. She wore an oversized T-shirt, its wide, drooping neckline half-exposing her shoulders. Her freshly shampooed hair was wet and uncombed. She'd just rushed out of the shower. "Randy, what the fuck, man? I thought it was the cops or something."

Astute as usual, Randy eyed the bandage on her shoulder. He was sure that injury was from the attack on Damien's estate. He felt deceived.

"How'd you get that injury?" he accosted Akane, his emotions getting the better of him.

"How'd you get those lousy manners?" Akane slammed the door in his face.

Randy knocked loudly three times. He continued to falter in his choice of words, still coming off way too abrasive. "Akane, open up! I'm serious here!"

Akane cracked the door and poked her head out. "War hero or not, that's not a hall pass to just show up at my doorstep unannounced. My mom taught me that's rude," she said, cranky.

"Yeah, dumb move. I'm sorry," Randy apologized.

The door banged shut again.

He knocked gently. This time he spoke without the pushiness. "Hey, can I come in? I just want to talk."

From behind the door, Akane replied, "*Uhhhh*, well, you're just gonna have to wait outside until I'm dressed."

"How long will that be?"

"You'll have to wait there and see. Oh, well."

Damn it, Randy thought. He needed to calm down and get his emotions in check. He didn't have to be passive while trying to get answers from Akane, but he couldn't be quick to temper either. Nobody wanted to talk to a hothead.

He readjusted his attitude, practicing emotional discipline.

After circling in place for an extended period, he heard the door open. Akane slouched against the frame, her right elbow resting on the paneling, her left hand on her hip. Her hair was still uncombed, but she was fully dressed this time, wearing a different shirt and baggy cargo shorts that sat low on her hips. "Come on in, and don't bring any bad mojo with you."

"Thanks. Sorry for showing up unannounced." Randy stepped into Akane's tidy abode. With the scent of burning incense permeating the air, he immediately felt a sense of zen.

The ultramodern design of the house featured walls made of phyroplastek, some of which had containment alcoves. At the center of the space was a communal area, elevated on a circular step-up dais. Within this area were an Oriental-style love seat, two armchairs, and a coffee table positioned beneath a chandelier. A mini-gym, enclosed by plexiglass, contained weight equipment and a punching bag. In the left corner of the house, next to the arched window, there was a bed that could be lowered into the floor. A standard kitchenette with a four-person dining table completed the setup.

Randy's eyes explored the cozy space. *Nice.*

Akane pointed at the shoe rack. "Leave your kicks at the door."

Randy took off his sneakers and set them down on the rack. "So, what happened to your shoulder?"

"You a detective now?" Akane said, visibly annoyed. "Since you're dying to know: I fell hover-boarding." Randy didn't believe her. "Don't worry, no one's ever died from a minor bruise."

They walked farther inside.

"Incoming stream from parents," the home's virtual assistant alerted Akane.

"Put them on holoscreen." A rectangular holoscreen expanded beside Akane in midair. "[Mom, Dad, how's it going?]" A smile blossomed on her face.

"[We are just calling to check up on you,]" Akari said.

Benjiro followed with, "[Yes, how have you been?]"

"[I'm good, guys,]" Akane replied. "[Just been busy *taking down* bad guys across the universe.]" She struck the air with a punch-kick combo. "[*Hi-yah!*]" Her parents laughed. "[Hey, I promise to call you back. I have company.]"

"[Well, we don't want to interrupt, then,]" Benjiro remarked.

"[See you later. Love you.]"

Akane ordered her virtual assistant to end the stream, and the holoscreen disappeared.

She sat on the love seat and crisscrossed her ankles.

Randy lowered himself beside her. "When's the last time you saw them in person?"

"Since I first left Satellite One. During the Three-Week War, net connectivity and long-range comms got disrupted in my home sector. For the longest time, my parents had to travel outside the sector to get a signal to me. Since Oviereya took office, the communications grid has been fully restored."

"How'd they take you joining the CDF?"

"It scared them at first. Mom especially freaked out. It took her a while to come around, but she did. They both support my decision now, especially with the credits I send home."

Randy heard a meow and tilted his head downward. "A cat?"

"Yeah, genetically engineered to mimic the real deal. Her name's Bubbles."

The cat rubbed against Randy's leg. He leaned over and patted its gray pelt.

Akane said, "Do you ever wonder what happened to all the animal lifeforms we left on Earth during the exodus? Maybe they're all like . . . mutants now or something."

That made Randy laugh, but his expression quickly turned serious. He remembered why he was there: to get answers about RISE.

Akane got up. "Let's move over to the kitchen." They took seats at the dining table. "Sushi? Made it myself."

"Never had it."

"There's a first time for everything."

Randy popped sushi into his mouth. *There's no need to wait. Just get down to it.* After chewing and swallowing, he said, "I'm not going to play games. I'm just gonna get to the point. My dad got in touch with a Coalition buddy of his, who told him what RISE does. He said their tactics aren't always lawful, even though they're for good causes."

This was unexpected for Akane, Randy learning this much about RISE without *her* telling him. But she stayed relaxed. "Does that bother you?" she asked, chewing on sushi.

"It does. I'm a Guardian, and righteousness is what we're supposed to stand for. I need you to come clean with me, Akane.

No half-truths. None of this shifty bullshit. It was RISE who attacked Damien's estate to kill him, wasn't it?"

"Is that what your dad told you?" Akane asked coolly.

"No, that's my hypothesis. Now tell me, Has RISE played judge, jury, and executioner for other people they deem bad guys? What other unethical actions have you guys taken in the name of equality?"

Akane wanted to bring Randy into the fold, like Simone brought her in. She was supposed to ease him into the organization, guide him slowly day by day, like Sam and Jay did for her. She had thought Randal Scott—one of the liberators of the colonies, a former Coalition fighter, the son of Arson Scott— would surely be on board with joining RISE.

Her hopes had been high. She had thought that Randy just needed to learn about all the good RISE was doing for immigrants, for *his* people, and then he'd surely want to be involved in such an impactful social-activist organization.

Maybe she *had* let her affections blind her. The vetting process was supposed to weed out prospects who weren't compatible with RISE. Had Randy failed the test?

Maybe his values were just too uncompromisable for him to be down with RISE's tactics. But then again, maybe he just needed some more persuading for his thinking to be converted to "the RISE mindset."

"Finish your meal," Akane said after a long, thoughtful pause. "Then we're headed out."

Randy's brows quirked. "What? Where are you taking me?"

"Leefside Grove, a town in Precinct Twelve. Before you go casting judgment on RISE's ethics, you need to get the full picture. Plus, I volunteered to be a voter-station watchguard today, at the east Leefside voting station. I could use the company, and

223

depending on how crazy these Purists get, I might need some backup too. So heads up, it's gonna be a long day."

Randy would use the time to talk some sense into her. "Okay, fine." *Whatever it is you're gonna show me, Akane, doesn't mean my mind's gonna change about RISE. Wrong is wrong. Period.*

As Akane shoved down another bite of sushi, Randy took notice of the framed photo atop a table. In the picture, Akane had her arm around another young woman, who was blond, bright-eyed, and full of health and cheer. Both were flashing their pearly whites. Randy could tell they were close. "Who's she? If you don't mind me asking."

Akane washed down the sushi with tea. She squeezed her eyes shut, attempting to ward off grief's clutches. "Her name was Skylar Grace. She was my friend, one of the three lottery beneficiaries I made the journey to Eden with."

She laughed at her old more pessimistic self. "Skylar got on my damn nerves at first, but she grew on me. We became good friends." Her voice cracked, throat constricting. "She was beautiful, inside and out." A lone tear drizzled down her cheek.

Randy bit his lip, staring into her sad eyes, eyes that held a story of pain.

Akane cleared her throat. "She loved Mercedes Gardner and wanted to be a singer just like her. She had big dreams, man, like all of us immigrants." She rubbed her eyes and swallowed, battling the torturous ache in her heart. "But she's dead."

"What happened?"

"Marginalization. Harassment. Bullying. That's what happened. There were even a couple of Highborn at her workplace who kept messing with her. One of them, a man, got too bold. He started physically messing with her. Management didn't do jack. To them, Skylar was just an immigrant bitch overreacting and trying to make trouble, trying to garner sympathy."

Akane's next words came out like broken glass. "She couldn't take all the unfair treatment that society had dumped on her. So she threw herself off a building."

Damn. The sentiment on Randy's face was one of remorse. "I'm . . . sorry, Akane," he bemoaned.

Her harrowing tale went on. "Another of my day ones, Desmond, enlisted the same time I did. We went to BCT together. I made it; he didn't. A drill sergeant was berating the Coalition, berating the colony revolution. Desmond wasn't the type to withhold his opinions. He challenged the drill sergeant. For that, for being an 'Independent Movement sympathizer,' he was dishonorably discharged with a bullet to the head."

Randy cringed, gritting his teeth. *Geez.*

Akane wasn't done. "After that, someone killed my best friend, my kindred spirit, Simone." Admiration for her bestie filled her. "She was the baddest bitch I knew. No doubt her murderer was Paul Shaffer, her own comrade and a Purist bigot. Loss after loss, I had to battle depression. I had up days and down days."

Randy shifted in his chair, his body language hinting at his discomfort with all of Akane's losses.

"Jay and Sam introduced me to RISE." Akane owed the organization more than she could easily express. "There, I found a safe place for immigrants, a place where I didn't have to worry about being degraded or demeaned, and I found family. RISE saved me, Randy. If it weren't for them, I might've given up on life, like Skylar."

Randy rested his chin between his thumb and index finger and quietly processed Akane's life story. He didn't know what to say.

Akane said, "So, when you go accusing RISE of wrongdoing, think about all the good they've done. That includes saving my life and the lives of other immigrants.

"When we get to Leefside, you'll get a good sample of the impact RISE has had on the immigrant community of Eden. Then you can make your judgment." She stood, walked to one of the wall alcoves, and grabbed two pistols. Then she offered one of the pistols to Randy. "Here. These are dangerous times. You might need it."

After the assault outside the club, Randy would've been a fool not to accept the weapon. He got up from the table and took it.

Akane put on some shoes and went to the door. "Shall we?"

Randy retrieved his shoes from the rack. "Let's go."

• • •

In Akane's convertible, Randy and Akane cruised Leefside Grove—a rustic town in every sense.

The car passed supermarkets, shops, clothing outlets, and strip malls.

A sign in front of a building under construction read: EARTH ERA MUSEUM COMING SOON TO LEEFSIDE.

Akane turned onto another street. "As you know, most of the government municipalities of region states are anti-reformist. RISE has played a major role in helping immigrants gain an economic foothold here in Leefside. Many of the establishments you're seeing now are owned by immigrants. The oppressors used to own them, but over the past few years, immigrants have bought them out. You know how that happened? RISE."

"How'd RISE get the funds?" A note of accusation crept into Randy's tone. "Did they steal it from the government?"

"Yeah," Akane admitted. "And RISE also got some endowments and did fundraising too."

They drove into a suburban community where subdivisions sprawled for miles.

Children played joyfully on brilliant green lawns.

Akane said, "This is an immigrant community, and a lot of the First live here."

"First? You're referring to the first immigrants, right?"

"Yeah." Akane pulled over and parked beside a row of nice homes. She opened her door and stepped out. "Come on, we're taking a little walk."

Randy got out and followed.

Akane strolled forward on the sidewalk. "Mr. and Mrs. Feller live in that house over there." She pointed to a single-floor brick home that had a square patio. "They're immigrants."

A seven-year-old boy played in the front yard. Once he saw Akane, he ran onto the sidewalk, beaming. "What are you doing here, Akane?"

Akane stooped and wrapped him in a hug. "Just passing through, Ryan. Go play now." The boy darted back to the lawn. Akane said to Randy, "Funny how AEGIS's 'chosen ones' don't consider immigrant children Highborn." They were often referred to as Lowborn, another slur like "nadir." "Ryan was on the brink of death three months ago. His family couldn't afford the heart mods to save him. You know who paid for them? RISE."

The thought of parents nearly burying their child stirred something deep inside Randy. *So young to be on death's doorstep.*

Akane said, "RISE raised money and redirected some funds from our government oppressors. Better that money help immigrants live than pay for military proliferation or wasteful government programs."

Randy kept his thoughts to himself, disagreeing with RISE's actions but choosing not to dispute Akane.

"There's a family about three blocks from here," Akane went on. "They were attacked by some immigrant-hating Highborn who claimed the beatdown was self-defense.

"RISE covered their legal fees, and the attackers got what they deserved, jail time. Not as much time as an immigrant would've gotten if the roles had been reversed, but still a win." She pointed down the street, at a grayish octagonal building. "That foundry used to be owned by a nonimmigrant. Now it belongs to a young immigrant entrepreneur. RISE helped him buy out the previous owner. Immigrant hiring at that foundry has gone up since then.

"RISE is deeply involved in the prosperity of immigrant communities all over Eden, not just this one. If RISE didn't exist, the immigrants of Leefside, and other towns like it in this province, wouldn't have had all the success they've had.

"If it weren't for us, a child would've died, and assaulters would've gotten away with their crime. RISE even ran voter registration drives to help Amaechi win her seat in the Parliament, back when many immigrants thought voting was useless, thought their vote wouldn't make a difference.

"Do you see now, Randy? Do you see why RISE is necessary?" She hoped for a shift in his perspective.

Randy remained silent, dissecting everything Akane had said and shown him. RISE had done so much good. But at the same time, RISE had committed illegal acts—crimes.

Akane continued advocating for RISE's existence. "There are millions of immigrants on Eden, and I'd say about eighty percent have never received their genetic metamorphosis or a cerebral implant, and not by choice. That's the government barring them from neohuman conversion. And the excuses are always the same: a lack of funding, CDF enlistees come first, a program is in the works to make it happen. *Blah, blah, blah*."

Something happened to Akane's voice—a rush of sympathy entered it. "Immigrants who go underground to get enhancements become vulnerable to fraudulent black-market dealers. A lot of bootleg cerebral mods are hazardous to their health. People end up damaging their brains or getting stuck with mods that offer inadequate Linking capabilities.

"Immigrants just want what's theirs. They want to be part of the New Humanity. Who knows, maybe the discrimination regarding genetic metamorphosis will finally change with Amaechi in office. That'd be thanks to you Coalition fighters."

Randy appeared torn. Akane had exposed him to an uglier side of Eden, a side RISE was fighting to change. Even so, some of the tactics used to achieve that change were still wrong.

"What's on your mind, Randy? What are you thinking right now?" Akane asked after the silence stretched too long.

"To tell you the truth, I don't know what to think at the moment," Randy answered evenly.

"That's fine. No pressure." Akane knew arm-twisting wouldn't get him to join RISE. "Come on, I've gotta get to the voting station. RISE already has two guys there, Hank and Vaughn. I'm joining them. It's just a ten-minute drive from here."

Randy and Akane headed back to the convertible.

The car breezed past more homes on the way to Leefside's east voting station.

On the local net radio, a female broadcaster said, "This just in: A young immigrant man, early twenties, was found bludgeoned in an alleyway. He's being transported to a hospital in critical condition. It's believed he was the victim of what appears to be increasing violence against immigrants on this election day."

"That's exactly why RISE members are out in Leefside today, to keep people safe," Akane commented.

"Keeping people safe is the authorities' responsibility," Randy said as Akane lowered the radio's volume.

229

"Well, from what I just heard, they're not doing a bang-up job. Sounds like they could use a little help."

A black van traveling in the opposite lane honked a hello, and Akane waved.

Randy knew his intuition was right, but he sought confirmation from Akane. "RISE?"

"Yeah. We've got teams patrolling Leefside neighborhoods to protect immigrants, and volunteers like me pulling security at voting stations that need it. Think of us as . . . neighborhood guard dogs today."

There was a burning question on Randy's mind, one he'd been avoiding. He tossed hesitation to the wind and spoke. "Tell me, Akane, have you killed for RISE?"

Akane's silence was all the confirmation Randy needed. She was trying to conceal the truth behind a veneer of stoicism.

"Akane, tell me the truth," Randy pressed. "Don't bullshit me."

Randy had already learned more about RISE than he was supposed to at this stage of vetting. Akane concluded there was no need to tiptoe around the truth. "Yeah," she admitted. "I got even with the uppity Highborn bastard who was sexually harassing Skylar."

Randy's face conveyed everything—he rejected her revenge killing. "Vigilante justice? That's okay with you?"

Akane's features set. "That asshole had been having his merry way with her. Come on, are you gonna feel sorry for a piece of shit?"

Randy, opposed to vigilantism, didn't answer, restraining his anger. Then, after a beat, he said, "Since you suspect Shaffer killed Simone, are you planning to murder him too, like you did Skylar's harasser?" He fought the urge to shout. He was aching to grab Akane and shake some sense into her.

Akane stayed focused on the road, enjoying the feel of the wind ruffling her hair. She replied, "As soon as Sam gives me the green light, you betcha." Her admission was rife with satisfaction. She didn't have a second thought about killing Paul.

Randy suppressed a grunt and shook his head. If Paul was a murderer, and it wouldn't surprise Randy if he was, it was still wrong to kill him. Paul, who'd thrown numerous verbal jabs, was no friend of his. But the law was the law.

Randy understood the soul-searing craving for vengeance, though. Not too long ago, he'd wanted to eliminate his father. However, the law had deemed his father a terrorist at the time.

He had to talk Akane out of killing Paul and get her out of RISE.

Speaking of his father—he still couldn't reach him. Had something happened at the council headquarters, where his friend Sergei had taken him? *Dad, I hope you're alright.*

• • •

Arson Scott sat on the bench of a detention cell inside a BUS parked outside the raided Assistance Living Center. He'd survived a round of intense questioning by Ryleigh MacRae and was waiting to make his one courtesy call, to contact Conlan.

He heard the cell door click open, and Ryleigh stomped in.

She shoved a tablet at him. "Here, make your call."

Arson snatched the tablet from her hand, giving her the same unpleasant attitude. "Thanks."

She jerked her chin up and crossed her arms over her chest.

Arson poked at the tablet's touchscreen, and Conlan's image wobbled into view.

"Arson?" Conlan said.

Surprise registered on Ryleigh's face when she heard Conlan's voice. Arson had a direct line to the Chief of Defense Force

Intelligence?

"Hey, old friend, I'm in a bit of a snag," Arson said. "The CDF's after RISE, I assume. And I'm also assuming, as Chief of Defense Force Intelligence, you know what RISE is *and* know about the raid that just happened."

"How do you know about RISE, and where are you?" Conlan asked.

"I was at the raided safe house of RISE's council. I'm currently being detained inside a cell in a BUS." Arson angled the tablet's front-facing camera so that Conlan could see Ryleigh. "Before we talk any further, just so you know, we've got company."

"Give us thirty minutes alone," Conlan ordered Ryleigh. "When we're done, release him."

She stumbled over her words, flabbergasted. "Y-yes, Sir." She exited the cell, giving them privacy.

Conlan said, "Now that it's just you and me, let's talk."

• • •

Randy and Akane arrived at the voting station, located in another predominantly immigrant community in Leefside, and got out of the car. Simply dressed townspeople trickled in and out.

A light-complexioned woman with chin-length flaxen hair called out Akane's name, delighted to see her. She was thinly built and wore a shirt, blue jeans, a denim vest, and boots.

Akane said to Randy, "This is Johanna Wright. She's a RISE supporter and a friend of mine. She's the voter administrator for this station. It was Simone who introduced us." She winced, haunted again by the mental image of Simone's lifeless body lying in the grass.

"Yeah, Simone was a sweetheart," Johanna said. "Man, the three of us had some good times." She squeezed Akane's shoulder. "I know you miss her, kiddo. I do too."

"You and I aren't the only ones. She touched a lot of lives."

"Yes, she did."

"Hank and Vaughn are inside already, right?" Akane asked, changing the subject.

"Yeah, and I'm glad they're here. They've already chased off two shady characters today." Johanna made a face. "I heard on net radio that a man was bludgeoned in an alleyway. Something's really gotten the crazies riled up today."

Akane knew that was because of Quinn's directive, his call to action. "Don't worry, we'll keep this center safe."

Johanna pressed a hand over her heart in gratitude. "Yes, thank goodness for RISE." She craned her head toward Randy. "It's good to meet you, Randal Scott."

Randy nodded. "Likewise. Are you an immigrant as well?"

"No, I was born right here on Eden." She took both of Randy's hands in hers. "But I'm a woman of faith. God wants all His people to prosper in this star nation He's blessed us with, despite our vices, which led to the annihilation of humanity's birthplace."

Suddenly, the loudening growl of an engine startled them. A customized van, built like a tank and nearly twice the size of a standard van, was on a collision course with *them*. Military-grade armor encased its body, and it had massive steamroller wheels.

In a spasm of panic, Akane drew the handgun tucked between her belt and pants. "What in the ever-loving fuck?" Impulse screamed at her to take out the driver. The gun kicked in her hand as she fired at the windshield. Each bullet struck and ricocheted off the bulletproof glass. With the pedal to the metal, the driver increased the van's speed, intent on running her over.

Fear rendered Akane immobile.

"Akane, what the fuck are you waiting for? Move!" Randy shouted as he darted out of the way.

Akane unfroze and hurled herself out of the van's path, rolling across the ground. Johanna dodged left and ran, the van narrowly missing her.

The driver jerked the steering wheel right and slammed the brakes. The van's wheels screeched as it swerved in a semicircle, the driver coming for Johanna. There was blood rage in his eyes; he was hellbent on turning her into roadkill.

Terrified, Johanna moved her legs faster.

"Johanna!" Akane screamed.

The driver stomped the gas, and the van crushed Johanna, her bones crunching and blood gushing out from underneath the steamroller wheels. She was this maniac's first victim of the day, and he wouldn't stop with her.

Akane shrieked, "No!" Seeing Johanna get mushed numbed her to the core.

The driver veered off in a new direction.

Randy grimaced, uncertain what this lunatic would do next.

Out for immigrant blood, the driver floored the gas pedal, crashing the van through the station's doors.

Voters screamed and scattered.

The driver braked hard, bringing the van to a screeching halt. Then he climbed out, a deadly automatic weapon in his hands.

Akane shakily rose to her feet. Her elbows and forearms were chafed, her shirt had been dirtied, and her eyes were wet with grief. "Johanna!" she cried, still reeling from the death of her friend.

Machine-gun fire roared from inside the station. Sharp pops from handguns followed, Hank and Vaughn shooting back at the attacker. They were in a desperate fight to protect innocent voters —immigrant voters.

Randy snatched his gun from his belt. "I'm going in! You stay put! Wait for the authorities!"

"But those are immigrants in there, my people. I can't—"

"Just stay here, Akane!" Randy knew she was too shaken to be of any help.

He dashed through the opening the van had made. The station's now-twisted metal doors lay on the floor, and rebar protruded from the damaged wall. He sprinted right up next to the van, which appeared almost unscathed due to its military-grade armor.

Damn, he'd entered a gory nightmare—bullet-riddled bodies lying on the floor, human viscera strewn everywhere. The sight was brutal to bear, even for a soldier like him.

Randy spotted two dead men with handguns beside them. They were Hank and Vaughn.

Some survivors had barricaded themselves inside rooms, while others had hidden in utility closets, hoping the attacker would just go away.

Randy tensed as a man in makeshift riot gear, cobbled together from scraps of metal, rounded the corner. It was the attacker, finished with his sweep of the station. He was big and heavyset. And he had a balding scalp and a long, scraggly beard that hung from beneath his metal mask.

Randy raised his gun in a two-handed grip and emptied half a clip, *blam* after *blam*.

The bullets pinged off the attacker's improvised armor system.

I have to stop this guy, Randy thought.

The attacker raked his weapon back and forth as its rotating barrel thundered, filling the air with bullets. He was like a one-man firing squad.

Randy ran to the rear of the van, debris crunching under his feet. "I'm a Guardian! Put the fucking weapon down!"

The gun's barrel whined to a stop, hissing smoke. "Naw, I don't think so!" the attacker yelled back, then unleashed another fusillade, keeping Randy pinned behind the van.

"Why'd you do this?" Randy's voice barely carried over the metallic ping of bullets ricocheting off the van's reinforced exterior.

The attacker released the trigger of his weapon and replied, "These immigrants will put reformists in power. They'll put *Amaechi* back in power. She's working with them, you see. It's all one big conspiracy. Once reelected, she's gonna deport half of us nonimmigrants, trade us out for colonists. I'm not letting that happen to my family! No way, man!"

Randy ground his teeth. *This guy's fucking delusional.* Sweat dripped down his forehead. This was the result of outlandish smear propaganda about Amaechi, propaganda put out by Quinn and the Brotherhood. *I have to take this guy down and save whoever's still alive.*

Randy played his gambit and dove sideways, firing a string of bullets. Two of his shots struck home—one in the unprotected sliver of the attacker's midsection and another in his leg—just as Randy's shoulder hit the floor.

The attacker was now down.

Randy rose, shoulder aching, and walked up to him. "You're finished! The authorities—"

"A White Knight of the Republic never *ever* gives in!"

One of the Purist groups Sam mentioned, Randy thought. *Wait, what the hell's he—?* The White Knight yanked a cord on his belt. A series of beeps warned Randy to get the hell out of there. *Shit, a bomb!*

Just then, a woman and her seven-year-old daughter crept out of a locked room. "Is . . . it safe to come out?" the woman asked.

Randy screamed, "Run! Get out of here, now! There's a bomb!" He took off toward the exit.

The beeping accelerated. The bomb was seconds from blowing.

Randy glanced over his shoulder. The mother and daughter were too far from the exit. They weren't going to make it.

He dashed out of the building. Glancing over his shoulder again, he saw the mother and daughter gasping for breath.

The girl tripped.

Her mother pulled her up. "Come on, sweetie, we need to—"

A plasma explosion devoured the building's interior, sending shock waves in all directions. Windowpanes burst into fragments.

The force of the blast slung Randy off his feet.

Ejecta shot into the air and cascaded down.

"Randy!" Akane cried, shrouded in a cloud of smoke and debris. Her ears rang. Did Randy make it? Or had the blast claimed him? Her pounding heart battered her chest.

The roof, structurally compromised, collapsed. Akane jumped at the harsh, resounding crash.

Slowly, the smoke started to clear, and Akane's ears stopped ringing. She saw Randy rise within the haze, unsteady but alive.

She ran to him and threw herself into his arms. He drew her close, both of them covered in soot and sweat.

"I'm glad you're okay," Akane said with shallow breaths. Her heart relaxed, returning to a normal beat.

"There was a . . . mother and child." Randy had fought in the civil war, so he'd seen plenty of death as a first-year Guardian. But never—*never*—had he been witness to a child's life being extinguished. "That kid couldn't have been older than seven or eight." He could hardly keep his voice working. "I . . . couldn't stop him." His hands curled into fists. He kept seeing the girl's face— her wide, innocent eyes; her freckled cheeks; her cute pug nose. "That son of a bitch had an explosive ordnance on him. I had him down. Maybe if I'd just been quicker, shot him in the throat or something, then—"

"Don't do this to yourself. *Don't* wallow in shame." Akane pulled Randy against her, arms squeezing his clammy back. "What that punk-ass bitch did isn't your fault."

"I can't help but think—" Could he have done something differently? The answer was no.

"It's okay, Randy. It's okay," Akane said softly. "We're not on a battlefield, but this is a war. And unfortunately, we can't save everyone, just like no one could save those three ex-Coalition fighters."

"That doesn't make it any easier." Sorrow laced every one of Randy's words.

"I know. But be at peace with the fact that you did everything you could."

They held each other in a long, tender moment as fire crackled in their ears and sirens approached.

What an election day.

Police land and aerial vehicles arrived at the scene.

Randy said, the sorrow in his voice thickening, "We should go, but I guess we need to give statements to the authorities first."

"Yeah." Akane's tone was equally heavy. *Everyone killed today was an immigrant like me. Why?* Tears threatened to spill from her eyes. "After we leave, I don't wanna be alone."

Randy's next words emerged as a croak. "Me neither."

"Then let's keep each other company, go back to my place and watch the election results come in." Akane fought to suppress the pain born from the deaths of Johanna and a mother and her child. But the dam broke. Tears carved tracks into the ash on her cheeks. "Whaddya say?"

"Yeah, I'd like that." Randy valued Akane's friendship above all else right now.

• • •

Stacie sat in the back of a ground limo beside Damien. She wore white pants and a red top that had one strap resting over her right shoulder.

Because Damien still wasn't ready to trust her with the location of their destination, he had blindfolded her.

"Are we almost there yet?" she asked, for what seemed like the hundredth time to Damien.

"Ten more minutes," he replied.

"You know, not being blindfolded would be nice. It's kind of irritating."

"Sorry, dear. One of many lessons my father taught me was to err on the side of caution. I'm responsible for the safety of others and cannot jeopardize their well-being. You'll understand better once we arrive at our destination."

"You talk about your dad a lot, but I never hear much about your mom. What's the deal?"

A tense silence dragged before Damien answered. "Let's not toy with each other. We both know our parents bypassed the law to amass their fortunes, no matter what we tell the government or the media. The files released by the Coalition barely scratched the surface of what they were involved in. The more my mother learned about my father's dealings, the more uncomfortable she became. So she abandoned us."

"I see."

The news played on a screen lowered from the ceiling.

The anchorman said, "We now have more information about the sadistic attack at a Leefside voting station, where an active shooter gunned down several immigrants and then detonated an explosive. It's being reported that a Guardian was on the scene. He ran into the building to stop the murderer and succeeded in neutralizing him, but couldn't prevent him from triggering the bomb. The Guardian's name is Randal Scott, and he—"

Randy? Stacie thought, tuning out the anchorman. That sounded like him, him and his heart of heroism. He'd always believed he had a moral obligation to help people, to save lives. It was one of the qualities she'd found most attractive about him.

The anchorman said, "Despite the attack, immigrant voters continued to go to the polls. Earlier today, not long after the attack, Chief Executive Amaechi made this statement."

On the replay, Oviereya denounced the terrorist attack. "Tragedy has befallen a community. The attack on the voting station today in Leefside was a despicable, heinous act by a heartless coward. Perhaps not as horrific, but you will hear about other outbreaks of violence against immigrants that also occurred today. These are nothing more than fear tactics from small-minded people who want to disrupt our election process. I urge all immigrants not to be discouraged. Do not let the fearmongers win. Continue to exercise your right to vote." The replay ended.

Stacie stifled her disdain. She couldn't show it, not with Damien, a Purist, right beside her.

"All polls have closed," said the anchorman, "and now the vote count is well underway."

Damien watched the vote count fluctuate.

The screen showed young political newcomer Tim MacGowan, a reformist, neck and neck with anti-reformist Warrick Radaker. Damien needed as many anti-reformists in Parliament as possible so he could implement his and Atticus's agendas with ease.

He hoped tonight would be a victory for anti-reformists, especially after all the work the Brotherhood had put in by hacking voter databases to purge immigrants from them, making immigrants ineligible to vote. Not to mention, Brotherhood street teams had made threatening calls to immigrant homes, warning them not to vote; roughed up immigrants who were on their way to the polls; and blackmailed region state leaders into closing voting stations in immigrant communities so it would be harder for immigrants to exercise their rights.

Stacie felt the vehicle swerve onto another street and jerk to a stop.

An adenoidal male voice said, "Mr. Sykes, good evening, sir."

A security guard, Stacie figured. Her ears continued to paint a visual picture. Clacking noises—had to be locks. A shushing sound and some rattling—that was a gate opening.

After five minutes, the limo stopped again.

"You may remove the blindfold now," Damien said.

Stacie took it off. They had arrived at a windowless gray building surrounded by a phyocrete wall.

"Where are we?" The lenses on Stacie's pupils were recording visuals for documentation, and her stud earrings were capturing audio. DFI really provided the coolest spy tech, she thought.

"We're at the compound of the Brotherhood for Humanity's Salvation. The Brotherhood is the first and largest Purist organization. Quinn started it."

"How are you connected to all this?"

"I was bestowed the honor of being Headmaster by Quinn himself," Damien revealed.

"So that means you know who Quinn is?"

"Yes, but that's not something I can disclose to you. I'm sure you understand."

"And you Purists are just activists upholding AEGIS's grand design for humanity? And you guys do everything in accordance with Commonwealth law?"

"Of course," Damien lied. "Now come, let's go inside."

241

Stacie and Damien approached the dark, intimidating structure.

Stacie was already getting eerie vibes from this place. An utterly cold feeling chilled her veins.

At the double doors, which bore the Purist emblem, two men stood chatting. When they saw Damien, they quickly stiffened and saluted.

"Good to see you, Headmaster," one of them remarked.

"Relax," Damien said.

The other man opened the door for Damien and Stacie, and they went into the building's vestibule.

"We'll be going to my personal suite, where we can watch the election in private," Damien told Stacie, "but I have to check on some of the men first."

Being trapped in a room with Damien was a total no-go for Stacie. *Okay, take it easy. You can finesse your way out of this.*

They moved down a hall and entered a room full of unsavory characters, Purists holding an election watch party.

"It's Headmaster Sykes!" a man said as he saw Damien and Stacie come in. It was Paul Shaffer. "Everyone, hush up!"

The loud, cheerful chatter died. Someone muted the screen's audio.

Every eye homed in on Damien. Postures straightened.

Damien didn't condone the tactics of the rogue White Knight who'd attacked the east Leefside voting station. Crashing through a building with a souped-up van and mowing down a mass of people wasn't his style. To him, that kind of violent barbarism, for the sake of killing a few immigrants, was senseless, and it brought the meddlesome attention of the authorities. Damien preferred to play his cards smarter—more cleverly, more craftily, more subtly. Nevertheless, he wouldn't waste the opportunity to talk up Purists and their cause.

"I won't be long," Damien said. Everyone listened attentively. "Today, a brother—a member of the White Knights—took his own life, fearful of the future state of our republic."

He must be talking about the guy who blew himself up at the voting station, Stacie thought. *So the White Knights are a Purist group.*

Damien carried on with dramatic flair. "I don't condone death by one's own hand. You Purists are far too important to lose. Blame the reformists and Amaechi for our brother's demise today.

"What drives a man to take such violent action? What drives him to sacrifice his life in the name of Purism? The answer: desperation. Desperation to save himself and his family from a daunting fate—being deported to Satellite One if Amaechi were to win the next election. Desperation to preserve our republic as it is, as it was meant to be. Though I don't condone his actions, he died a hero, a hero for our republic."

Hearing Damien dote on a sicko disgusted Stacie. *That murdering piece of filth was no hero.*

Cheers filled the room.

"Please," Damien said, "continue the party."

Someone unmuted the screen. Conversations resumed.

Paul expressed his praise to Damien face-to-face. "That was a good speech, Mr. Sykes."

Damien slid an arm around Stacie. "I understand you and Paul have had a bit of a confrontational encounter."

Paul pretended he was over it. "It's water under the bridge for me."

"I hope the same goes for you," Damien said to Stacie, hinting that her coexisting with Paul wasn't optional.

She clicked her tongue, still pissed. "All in the past."

"Good." Damien unwrapped his arm from around Stacie. "Paul

is actually the Brotherhood's Chief Enforcer, when he's not busy with his duties in the ETF. I'd hate for there to be any ill will between the two of you. You might be seeing more of each other."

Paul stepped closer to Damien. "Boss, I got something I need to talk to you about."

Damien turned to Stacie. "Wait in the hall for me."

She silently left the room and stood just outside the door.

Damien and Paul isolated themselves from the others in a corner. "Sergeant, if this is about Stacie again—"

"Nah, I've got nothing else to say about her, though I still think it's a big mistake letting her get close to you. But you're the boss. What you want, you get."

"So what is it?"

"My contact in law enforcement was able to match the DNA of that solutioner you shot on the roof."

"Don't keep me waiting, Sergeant."

"His name is Jamie Lister. I serve with the guy in Vanguard Alpha. My contact also pulled his address."

A menacing smile hooked the corners of Damien's mouth. "Excellent. Take Mark and Dan and beat RISE's location out of him. But not tonight. Handle it tomorrow. For now, enjoy the party."

"Thanks, Mr. Sykes." Paul returned to his brothers.

Damien rubbed his hands together eagerly. Now, back to Stacie.

Outside the door, Stacie stood with her arms crossed, nerves worsening. She had to finish up and get out of here. She'd already planted a micro audio transmitter in Damien's limo tonight, and she'd planted one in the flyer she and Damien had used to escape the fundraiser. Also, she had pretended to drop her purse to conceal a tracker beneath the limo before getting in and being blindfolded. That tracker would lead Defense Force Intelligence straight here.

She intended to plant one or two more transmitters in Damien's suite before hightailing it home. This place, and these Purists, were making the hair on the back of her neck bristle.

Damien left the room. "Let us continue to my suite, so we may have some privacy."

"About time," Stacie said flirtatiously, pretending to play right into his arms.

They entered an elevator and rode two floors up. After exiting, they walked down a hall and went into Damien's suite.

The room was about eight-hundred square feet and featured expensive carpet, a comfortable L-shaped couch, armchairs, a love seat, wall art, and a Jacuzzi.

Stacie's instincts told her to hurry.

A muted screen, nearly the size of the entire wall, streamed election coverage.

Stacie wandered around the room. "Wow, nice spread." She discreetly slipped her hand under a table and planted one of her listening devices. "So, Damien, I know the Sykes family has utilized the trafficking industry to build their fortune, and I was wondering if you might give me some guidance on how I, too, could break into the industry."

"Is that so? Who told you we were involved in trafficking?"

"Oh, just . . . a few of my company's executives who did business with your parents."

"We can talk business another time."

Darn, she was aiming for a confession. Well, it was worth a try.

Damien loomed over her. "End stream," he commanded the suite's virtual assistant. The megascreen winked off. "I didn't bring you here just to watch the election or talk business. I brought you here so we could be alone and indulge in each other, like old times. If I recall, you loved our physical escapades."

Yes, Stacie remembered the assignations filled with copious drunken sex and endorphin-boosting drugs. The thought sickened her now.

Damien leaned in, nuzzling her neck with his lips. He was eager to satisfy his lust.

Bluh. Stacie chewed the inside of her cheek. "Um, Damien, sweetheart—" She jerked away and unintentionally backed herself against a wall. "I . . . need to leave, I'm afraid. I'm sorry. Business, you know?"

Damien wasn't buying her excuse for needing to leave. "Really?" he said skeptically. "I'm sure it can wait." He pasted his lips to hers and thrust his tongue into her mouth.

Stacie slid sideways along the wall, escaping Damien. "I'd love to stay, but I—"

A vein pulsed in Damien's temple. Feeling toyed with, he lost his patience and punched the wall. "What the fuck is your game, Spencer?"

There it was, Stacie thought, that uncontrollable anger that always emerged when someone deprived him of his wants, defied him, or challenged him. His father had raised him to be a spoiled punk kid.

Damien's gaze bore into her. "You've been asking a ton of questions. And for someone who supposedly wants to pick up where we left off, you seem mighty evasive."

Stacie snickered. "What's my *game? Ha*, I assure you—"

Damien gripped her throat and pushed the back of her head against the wall. He wished he could rip the truth out of her.

Cassie McCanns' bruised face flickered in Stacie's mind.

"Who are you working for?" Damien demanded.

The wrath vibrating in his fingertips suffused Stacie with fear. *Gotta think fast.* Her manufactured straight-faced expression lent no hint of dishonesty. "Working for?" She laughed, rolling her eyes like his accusation was completely ludicrous. "*Puh-leeze.* I do the bidding of no one. Why would I? I'm the queen of Spencer Enterprises. All I do is on my *own* accord, Damien."

Not believing her, Damien let go of her throat and frisked the sides of her midriff. "Are you wearing a listening transceiver?" He dug his hands into the side and rear pockets of her pants, searching for micro devices.

Get your filthy hands off me. "A listening device? What, you think I'm a . . . spy or something?" Stacie said sarcastically.

"I take no chances, woman. I'd have to be a fool. So I guess we'll find out, won't we? And there's only one way to do that." A strip search. "Disrobe, *now.* And that's not a request. It's not like I haven't seen you naked before."

Fuck you to hell. Stacie needed to sedate his hotheadedness and get out of here. She'd hate herself for this, but . . . "Damien, relax, you're getting all spooked for nothing." Framing his face in her hands, she pressed her lips to his, offering up her moist tongue— like she was still into him.

The anger stiffening Damien's features disappeared. He kissed her back with barbaric intensity, his hands splaying across her rear end in a greedy, self-serving way. He was lusting to dominate her.

Stacie broke the kiss. She had permitted enough. "Sweetie, I promise, tomorrow night we'll continue this, and it'll be very rewarding," she said in a playful, seductive timbre. "I'll even wear the red teddy you liked *soooo* much." She sounded too saccharine that time, almost fake. "But I need to go. Now please be a gentleman and escort me out of here."

Damien remained wary. Maybe Paul was right. Maybe her

trying to disrupt his trafficking operation and then suddenly reconnecting with him wasn't a coincidence. "Fine." He'd have someone monitor her. If she were up to something, he'd uncover it. "I'm excited about what tomorrow night will bring. Don't go back on your word and disappoint me."

"I wouldn't dream of it." She'd cancel on the asshole tomorrow.

She and Damien exited the suite. Once outside the building, he blindfolded her again and had one of his men drive her home.

• • •

Three hours into the election-night coverage, Randy sat on the love seat in Akane's home, watching candidates' vote percentages rise and fall, while Akane showered. What a roller coaster of an election. It was impossible to tell who was going to win. Every race was a toss-up.

Randy once again contemplated what he should do about RISE. He was supposed to be working with his father to dig up more dirt on them and whatever interference they might be planning for the next round of special elections.

Technically, RISE was an extremist organization. They'd meddled with the democratic process, stolen government funds, and assassinated people they deemed deserving of death. But those people were men like Damien Sykes, or the deranged bastard who blew up a little girl today. RISE did illegal things for good causes, but still, wrong was wrong. Illegal was illegal. And Randy was a Guardian, sworn to protect the Commonwealth from all enemies, foreign and domestic. That included organizations like RISE and the Brotherhood.

RISE was flouting the law, but they were also advancing social justice for immigrants and colonists. That was where the dilemma came in for Randy.

He hadn't told his dad where RISE's base was. But when the

time came to contact Conlan, as planned, he'd be asked to reveal its location. And if he did, what would happen to Sam and Jay? Both had wives and children. And what would happen to Akane?

She was his friend, someone who had treated him with kindness since he returned to the CDF a pariah. And today, they had grieved together, bearing witness to a cold-blooded act of violence.

Randy wondered: What do you do when someone you care about, someone you love, is on the wrong side of the law? He struggled between his feelings and his duty.

Done with her shower, Akane—wrapped in a pink robe—emerged from the bathroom. "How's the election going?"

Randy tapped the remote control, cutting off the wall-mounted screen. "Truth is, it'll be sometime tomorrow before we know who the victors are." He pushed himself up from the love seat and approached Akane, halting at a measured distance. "Are you going to be okay?"

Memories of Johanna removed Akane from the present. She cast them out of her head and closed the distance between her and Randy some more. "It's not fair. It never is, though."

Randy gazed into her sad eyes, unsure of what to say. He moved closer and settled his hands on her shoulders.

The care and compassion in his touch set Akane's blood ablaze.

Would he . . . *could* he reveal RISE's location to his father and Conlan when the time came? Could he break Akane's heart, destroy what was essentially her family here on Eden? RISE was full of people she knew and loved.

Randy said, "We can't bring the dead back. All we can do is mourn, celebrate their life, and keep them alive in our hearts and minds. They might be gone, but they'll *never* be forgotten." He thought of his mother.

"Yeah, it's tough, though."

"I know." Randy continued holding Akane by the shoulders and leaned in dangerously close, the minuscule space between their lips shrinking. A voracious look flickered in his eyes, impossible to hide.

Damn it, he wasn't trying to get emotionally entangled with another woman right now, he reminded himself. And Akane, still unpersuaded to leave RISE, was a member of what was considered an extremist group. She had committed murder, destroyed private property, and aided in an attempted political assassination. And she intended to kill a Guardian, Paul Shaffer. That was basically premeditated murder. Nevertheless—staring into her pretty eyes, emotions swirling, sex cravings running wild—he just couldn't . . .

Randy continued to fail at keeping a platonic distance. Noses touching, their lips were now just shy of a kiss.

The logical part of Randy's mind urged him to walk away and go home. According to CDF Code of Military Justice 3-12, the consequences for a Guardian who willingly associates with criminals, extremists, and domestic terrorists were dishonorable discharge and prison time. But Akane's lips were right there, daring him to kiss her. And under that robe, she had on nothing but a pair of panties, if anything.

Akane shut her eyes and sighed. "Well . . . I guess you've gotta go." Her tone implied she didn't want him to leave. "Um, maybe I'll see you to-"

Before Akane could finish, Randy grabbed her waist and pulled her flush against him. He fastened his lips to hers, finally breaking the boundary of friendship. Enough bullshit.

A wave of arousal colored Akane's cheeks.

Fueled by adrenaline, Randy kissed her more urgently, sucking on her lower lip, intertwining his tongue with hers.

Down below, he felt himself getting hard.

Akane leaned into the kiss, elation prickling her flesh.

Randy finally detached his lips from hers and withdrew his hands from her waist.

They stared at each other, breaths bated, hearts racing. Their eyes spoke volumes. No words were needed. They both knew where the night was headed.

Their lips met again, hungrier this time, and their tongues danced in each other's mouths.

Randy couldn't fight his desires any longer. He needed to feel Akane's body—skin to skin. There was no way this night ended without both of them naked and his hips between her thighs.

He worked quickly to unknot her cloth belt, thirsting to plug his burgeoning erection into her.

The belt slipped loose, falling to the floor.

Akane shrugged the robe off her shoulders. She stood clad in her silk panties, her small cute breasts and trim waist exposed.

Randy grasped her lean, limber frame and pulled her in once more, his member pressing against her through his pants—a sample of what was to come.

They moved recklessly around the room while kissing, exchanging tongues and sharing saliva.

In their frenzy, they bumped into a table. Something fell off of it and thunked to the floor. Neither cared.

Randy's hands roamed over Akane's body, clutching her hips, sliding up her thighs, cupping her backside. He committed every detail of her to memory.

She wished he would just take his damn clothes off already and get down to business. She wanted to fuck.

Their lips clashed as euphoria electrified Randy's veins. At this point, going home to reconsider getting deeper involved with an

251

"extremist" was utterly impossible.

Akane's implant alerted her to a Link request from Randy, which she accepted. The synchronized drumbeat of their hearts reverberated in their ears and souls. Passion infused every touch and kiss. Their psychically connected minds confirmed their shared desire for one another.

In a psychedelic blur of fevered kisses, touching, and stumbling, Akane ended up seated on one of her tables.

Randy tore her panties down her legs, leaving her completely naked, except for the pinstriped socks on her feet. Then he dropped his pants and boxers in one motion.

Akane got turned on by the sight of his hardness.

Bracing herself for what she'd been yearning for, she clasped the table's edges and parted her legs. Eagerly, Randy tucked the head of his rigid cock into the slit between them. She inhaled sharply, her heart pounding. Holding her by the waist, Randy pushed his hips forward, gradually stretching her folds. Her entrance was a tight fit, and needless to say, he liked it.

She lay back on her elbows, taking him in.

Once he was completely rooted inside her, he paused for a moment, allowing her to adjust to his size. Then he drove into her, his rhythm unyielding.

Her entire body came alive, waves of euphoria bombarding it.

Randy threw all his strength into each thrust, consumed by his desire for this beautiful young woman. He loved her symmetrical facial features, her sylphlike body, and the satisfying tightness between her thighs.

With their minds Linked, they crashed through the intimacy threshold, sensations and emotions merging into an all-encompassing force that stimulated every fiber of their being.

A dizzying wave of ecstasy struck Akane, nearly making her

faint, and Randy felt every pulse of it due to their Link. Invigorated by it, he instinctively accelerated his pace, each spear of his cock into Akane rattling the table.

The smacking of skin against skin filled the air, mingling with Randy's grunts and Akane's whimpers.

Overcome by an insatiable hunger, Randy pulled Akane up from the table to her feet. He cradled her buttocks and hoisted her up. She wrapped her legs around his waist and her arms around his neck, anchoring their bodies together. She was ready for whatever he had in mind.

Pressing her back against the wall, Randy slid into her again.

The friction, the heat, the sound of their bodies colliding—it all exhilarated him. His thrusts became more forceful, more dominating. Each one was a confession of how badly he'd been wanting to fuck Akane.

She silently cursed as she felt his aroused cock expand further and widen even more inside her.

Eventually, Randy set her down, and their lovemaking transitioned to the bed.

Randy held Akane's wrists against the mattress, his gaze traveling slowly over her body. She was slight, a stark contrast to his usual preference, yet he found himself increasingly attracted to her. He lowered his mouth to her skin, trailing savage kisses downward.

Her body arched instantly at the touch of his lips. He continued his intimate exploration, and when his mouth reached the place where Akane wanted him the most, she gasped, her face flushing.

His lips made wet noises. Akane's palms flew to her hair, her fingers tangling in the strands. She didn't know what to do with herself. Randy was *undeniably* talented.

They rolled across the bed, positions shifting. Sometimes their kisses were tender, other times fierce. When Randy moved above Akane again, she reached down and guided his cock to her entrance—both of them wanting the same thing as he entered her once more.

She felt him sliding back and forth inside her, the pleasure almost torturous.

As they continued surrendering to each other, their Link laid bare their feelings—preventing them from hiding, suppressing, or denying them—even as they wrestled with whether, or how, to speak them aloud.

Randy was thankful for Akane's warmhearted welcome on his first day as a member of Vanguard Alpha, appreciative of her warnings about Purists, and grateful for her companionship, which had lessened the loneliness of being branded a "treasonist." Then there was his fear of losing her when the White Knight who had attacked the voting station nearly ran her down.

Akane had been concerned about Randy's well-being, his life, since day one. She refused to let him—one of her heroes and a fellow immigrant—fall victim to some Purist, like Desmond and Simone had. Love had been the root of her constant worry and warnings, and when the voting station exploded, her heart stopped. She was terrified she'd lost him.

A wondrous, spellbinding hurricane of white-hot psychosomatic stimulation engulfed their Linked minds as a naked exchange of feelings and emotions began, the mental amplifying the physical.

Randy sat back on his heels, pulling Akane onto his lap and thrusting upward into her.

Their Link allowed him to experience her trials firsthand: the sorrow of leaving her parents; the devastation of losing Skylar,

Desmond, and Simone; the horror of watching Johanna get run down, powerless to stop it. He wished he could tear away every layer of her pain.

He held her in place, fingertips kneading her back in a silent show of affection. For Akane, his touch was like emotional acupuncture—soothing, centering.

Giving herself to him, body and soul, felt therapeutic. She knew Randy couldn't erase her pain, but he could help numb it. Sex would be her anesthetic.

Bucking atop his lap in time with his thrusts, Akane said, <*Fuck me harder. Give it to me. Rock my fucking world.*>

Committed to doing just that, Randy dipped his face into her chest and kept drilling into her while suckling her stone-stiff nipples, causing her to moan in pure exaltation.

Akane tightened her arms around Randy's solid torso, hands bunching the gorgeous muscles of his back. He jerked her naked body closer, fucking her nonstop.

A cry of ecstasy tore from her throat, spurring him on.

In one smooth movement, he guided her onto her back, never letting their bodies part. He continued burrowing into her without pause, each thrust stealing her breath.

The bed frame groaned and shuddered.

A pressure swelled in Randy's groin, demanding release, but somehow, he held it at bay.

As the stroking of Akane's insides intensified to something beyond feral—beyond words—an overwhelming orgasm threatened to split her in half.

Randy considered the consequences of continuing without protection, but it was a struggle for him to pull out. He was too absorbed in the experience, both emotionally and physically, and didn't want to stop.

Somehow, he slowed his pace, fighting to regain control. But using cerebral communication, Akane assured him that she'd taken a contraceptive capsule before her shower, just in case they were intimate that night.

Freed by that knowledge, he hooked her legs over his shoulders and leaned forward, folding her lithe body in half. Holding back had been killing him.

Abandoning all restraint, he jackhammered into her with a barrage of uncontrollable, wild thrusts. Every carnal instinct, lustful desire, and primal urge to fuck Akane surged forth within him.

Akane's breath hitched, words failing her as she yielded to his onslaught. Her nipples stood erect, rock-hard and hypersensitive.

As she was being fucked out of her wits, she said, <*That's right, let me be your healthy addiction tonight.*>

Randy thought about Code of Military Justice 3-12. Every spear of his cock became a vehement protest against it. Whether or not she was regarded as a dangerous extremist, he wouldn't rue the night he got into bed with this spirited teenager from NeoJapan.

The pressure building in his groin reached its peak. Groaning a guttural sound, he surrendered, his release detonating inside Akane as his entire body trembled from the intensity of it.

Satisfied, relieved, he pulled out and rested beside her.

Akane blew a puff into her bangs and inhaled to regulate her breathing, postcoital tingles dancing across her flesh. After such a dreadful day, fantastic sex was exactly what she needed.

Still hungry for more, she straddled Randy's midriff and plunged into his lasting erection, which was soaked in cum.

She knew he still harbored feelings for his ex, but after she worked her magic tonight, he'd be saying "Stacie who?"

She rocked her hips fervently. Responding in kind, Randy

arched his body. His hands found the curve of her back, then journeyed lower, gripping her ass cheeks as he rose to meet each of her fearsome movements.

Akane massaged her breast, thumb circling the nipple. Eyes half-closed, she gyrated her hips like an exotic dancer, wringing a desperate sound from deep in Randy's throat. Sweat glistening on her skin, body moving sinuously, she looked like a sexy mirage made flesh.

She moved faster now, her muscles working overtime as she set a frantic pace. Randy's fingers struggled to maintain their grip before he finally tightened them, hanging on to her ass. She had a lot to get out of her system, and her sex drive wasn't waning anytime soon.

Arousal coursed through her. "Fuck," she panted, her head falling back.

She bent over and nipped Randy's shoulder, tasting him. He folded his arms around her so intensely—flattening her against him—that she felt them dig into her bones. Shuddering, he climaxed again.

They both came to a stop, Akane lying on top of him, her head pressed against his chest. She savored the feel of his defined body as she regained her breath, the ridges of his hard muscles pleasing to her skin.

<*Thank you,*> she said.

His hands caressed her.

She had had sex with several men and women, but tonight was by far the best she'd ever had. She felt like the luckiest nineteen-year-old woman in the Commonwealth.

Randy could stay like this forever, Akane's warm bare form draped over him. He placed one hand on the small of her back and the other on her backside. Then he claimed her mouth. He wanted her. Her flesh. Her bones. *All* of her.

He eased himself back into her while she remained facedown atop him, his hips now perfectly nestled between her thighs. As her body rose and fell, matching the motion of his loins, she expelled a contented moan that ignited sparks in his core.

In the throes of passion, Randy thrust into her at a tempo that was almost criminal. He couldn't bring himself to stop. Soon, another sobering release from him creamed her insides some more. Every nerve ending in her body screamed, threatening to burst. Then there was a pause, a moment of quiet stillness, a brief respite for them both.

Throughout the night, Randy and Akane explored each other's bodies in a hypnotic indulgence neither would forget.

But even as their lovemaking continued, Randy's mind returned to the question that troubled him: When the time came, could he disclose RISE's location to his father and Conlan, knowing it would break Akane's heart?

FINAL INTERLUDE

AFTER THE BATTLE OF THE QUAD

Planet Eden
Expedition Task Forces Headquarters
(Vanguard Alpha's Area of Operations (AO))

"No fucking way!" Akane said to Sam. "Are you pulling my leg, man?"

"You know me. I don't kid around," he replied.

"So lemme get this straight. Randal Scott, Arson Scott's son, is joining Vanguard Alpha *today*?"

"Yep."

"We've *gotta* convince him to join RISE. Just think about it, one of the liberators of the colonies joining us? He'd be a tremendous asset."

"Whoa, take a step back," Jay said. "We don't recruit prematurely. We have to find out if he's truly a fit for us, colony hero or not."

The doors to Vanguard Alpha's AO slid open as Randy stepped through, dressed in neat, well-pressed battledress.

It was his first day on assignment, his first day as a member of the ETF. He didn't know what to expect from Vanguard Alpha. So far, every Guardian he'd met since returning to the CDF had treated him like crap.

Akane snapped her eyes toward Vanguard Alpha's newest member, staring at him like he was some mythical hero. She skipped over to him excitedly, a warm greeting written on her face. "Welcome to Vanguard Alpha!" She smiled from ear to ear. "I'm Akane."

Randy smiled back at the bright angular face in front of him. "Thanks. You know what? You're the first Guardian to say anything even remotely polite since I returned to the CDF from my leave of absence."

"'Cause you were a rebel, right? Well, I'm an immigrant. I've had my fair share of being ostracized, so I know how you feel."

It's good to be around someone who does, Randy thought.

"But hey, heads-up, we've got some dicks on the team." Paul Shaffer, Dan Maddox, and Mark MaCallum, to be exact.

Randy expected as much. "Not surprised."

Akane hooked her arm around Randy's, and he gave an awkward glance at the overly flirty gesture.

"C'mon," she said, "you need to report to Lieutenant Breckenridge to finish in-processing, right?"

"Uh, yeah, that's right."

"Lemme escort you to his office," she insisted.

"Um, okay. Thanks."

They walked right past Sam and Jay without so much as a hello, Akane clearly wanting Randy all to herself for now.

A pair of doors hissed open to a corridor.

"So, where are you from?" Randy asked, making small talk.

Akane was psyched to be conversing with Randal Scott.

"Colony Three," she replied. "You were born in Colony Four, right? That's where your dad's from."

"Yeah, that's right. But I was a baby when my parents brought me to Eden. I'm an immigrant, I guess, but not really. I grew up among Highborn."

A few chatting Guardians in battledress passed them.

Akane said, "So you were privileged compared to us lottery beneficiaries, but you didn't grow up with a privileged mindset, did you?"

"Well, not every Highborn does. But my dad was an immigrant, a lucky lottery beneficiary like you. Over the years, he told me stories about how people looked down on him because AEGIS didn't choose his bloodline. He became an Edenite by luck of the draw, which still made him a 'nadir.'

"Despite facing bias, he taught me to respect everyone—colonist, immigrant, nonimmigrant. This included people harboring a skewed view of society, people who endorse systemic inequalities. My dad said they weren't always to blame for their beliefs. They were products of their upbringing.

"During my school years, I befriended a lot of Highborn. Many of them didn't even know I was the son of an immigrant. And believe me, I heard plenty of arrogant talk from my so-called friends. Not all of them, but enough.

"I could never understand why anyone would think they were superior to another human being just because of where AEGIS assigned them to live. My dad was an immigrant, after all, and he was one of the most awesome people I knew.

"As I got older, formed my own opinions about society, and studied Earth Era history, I started to think the requisites for Eden citizenship were unfair. But I also understood that some sort of selection process was necessary to divide humanity between its new

261

planetary habitats. I thought maybe the requisites used were just the best option at the time, a time when humanity was on the brink of extinction.

"How else do you divide up Earth's remaining people between two planets, when only one offers the best chance of survival? I certainly didn't have any better ideas. Like everyone else, I believed the government would eventually elevate the colonies, give them what we had on Eden.

"When the Three-Week War started, I thought the insurrectionists were traitors, just like most Edenites did. I saw them as impatient complainers who couldn't wait for the Commonwealth to recover from the Phazharian and Bhalkran wars and obtain the resources to fix the colonies.

"But after the CDF won the Three-Week War and the Coalition formed, I went to Satellite One for the first time, as a new Guardian. I was ready to carry out the oath I had taken to defend the Commonwealth. I even believed my mission to eliminate my father, who'd defected, was just."

Akane said, "And when you got to Satellite One and saw how bad things really were, how people were still suffering after years of empty promises, you realized the truth and joined the right side."

"Yeah," Randy said. "With some help. A rebel named Kesley Whittaker and my father opened my eyes. But switching sides wasn't a straightforward decision. I went back and forth with myself for a while. Eventually, I saw joining the Coalition for Operation Hammer Fall as the right thing to do." Then, in a hero voice that came naturally to Randy—a voice that left Akane thirsty for osculation—he said, "My dad always told me to do what I believe is right. Right in my heart. And I guess that's what I did."

Akane was getting goose bumps just being near this man, the good kind of goose bumps. There was something about the way he carried himself that had her gushing over him. He had an air of valor about him. And then there was that handsome face. He practically exuded virility.

Akane felt the chest-rattling urge to drag him off to a supply closet and conduct her own in-processing procedure, no clothes allowed.

She envisioned them together in the bedroom. Oh, yes, she had made up her mind: Come hell or high water, she was going to engage in Linked copulation with Randal Scott. Sooner or later.

Up ahead were the doors to Lieutenant Breckenridge's office.

"That's it, the lieutenant's office." Akane paused, a little nervous. "Hey, um . . . you wanna grab some chow later? Maybe keep getting to know each other?"

"Yeah, that'd be great, Private Sugimori."

"Cool." Butterflies fluttered in Akane's stomach.

Randy liked Akane so far. She was small in stature but packed with personality. Maybe they'd become good friends.

As Akane was leaving, she stopped. "Hey, Randy?"

"Yeah?"

"I'm glad you joined the Coalition to help free the colonies from oppression. I'm glad you followed your heart. Thank you for doing 'the right thing.'" With that, she walked away.

Randy went toward Breckenridge's office. "Thank you, Akane," he subvocalized.

CHAPTER SIX

Randy, fresh from his morning shower and shirtless in a pair of jeans, sat on Akane's bed. As Akane was finishing up her shower, he stared at the text message he had received from Arson five minutes ago, holowords hovering above his wristcom. It laid out everything that had happened. The CDF had raided the council's safe house while Arson was meeting with Tristan Gelano, and they took him into custody for questioning. He used his one courtesy call to contact Conlan and fill him in on what he and Randy were doing—infiltrating RISE, which they believed to be a threat to the Commonwealth.

Conlan informed Arson that he'd learned about RISE from none other than Randy's ex, Stacie Spencer, who was apparently working with DFI on a covert investigation into Damien Sykes, a Purist. So Stacie, Conlan, and the duo of Randy and Arson were all pursuing the same objective. What a strange twist of fate. The message concluded with the next course of action: The four of them would hold a videoconference in five hours and make a plan to take down both RISE and the Brotherhood.

Randy knew Arson and Conlan would ask him to provide the

location of RISE's base. He pondered what he should do.

Akane emerged from the shower, her lissome figure nude, and walked to the closet to get dressed.

She was barely seventeen when she snuck away from home and had sex with a man for the first time. It was an experience filling to the soul. However, last night had surpassed that and all her other intimate encounters.

Looking over at Randy, she grinned. She had never been a vain woman, but she had to give herself some credit for being the first Asian woman Randal Scott had ever fucked. She wasn't even his usual type, but she had learned that "killer bod with curves" didn't always overshadow "petite Japanese chick." Must be her magnetic personality.

Noticing Randy seemed distant, she asked, "Randy, somethin' up?" She tugged a pair of underwear up her hips. There was no response from Randy. "Randy? *Yoo-hoo*," she said after a pause, fastening the front clasp of her bra.

Randy kept glancing at her, unsure what to say. He opted for, "I'm fine." An obvious lie.

What was he supposed to do, keep the location of RISE's base a secret from Conlan and his father while continuing with business as usual in Vanguard Alpha? Was he supposed to just pretend that Akane wasn't involved in a vigilante social-justice organization?

Ever scrupulous, he rested his elbows on his thighs and interlaced his fingers, deep in thought.

Akane felt fur brush her leg and heard a meow. She leaned over and gave Bubbles a good-morning pat.

Randy remained silent, fidgeting. He stole another glance at Akane. She looked enticing—slim figure with ribs faintly visible beneath smooth skin, exotic eyes, adorable smile. His mind took him back to last night, the two of them lost in a world of pleasure.

It had been beautiful.

Clad in her white cotton lingerie, Akane joined Randy on the bed and sat against the headboard. "Well, you don't seem *fine*." She glided her fingers over his shoulder and pressed a kiss to his cheek. "What's up?"

He stared into her eyes thoughtfully, wondering how he could convince her to leave RISE. Acting on impulse, he answered her kiss with one of his own, pecking her lips.

In an instantaneous reaction, she began necking him.

Randy eased her down onto the mattress, stretched her out, and unsnapped the front clasp of her bra. He gathered her hands above her head, holding her wrists down, and kissed her along her breastbone, neck, and jaw.

He didn't want to attend the four-way conference today. Staying in bed with Akane and having endless sex sounded far better. This whole Brotherhood-versus-RISE secret war was something he'd rather ignore. He was tired of ultraists singing the praises of dead men like Cornelius Gould and Arman Reza, keeping their spirit alive in the name of some imagined "greater good."

The rise and fall of Akane's small bare chest quickened, a thrill traveling down her spine. "Damn. Wanna go again? I'm always down for—"

Randy interrupted her. "Listen, Akane." He kissed her lips. Suppressing his desire for her was challenging, especially since he'd already halfway undressed her. "I need to be honest with you." He combed his fingers through her tousled hair. "In a few hours, my father and Chief of Defense Force Intelligence Michael Conlan are going to ask me where RISE's base is."

Worry tautened Akane's forehead. "Are you gonna snitch on us?"

"No." The word snapped from Randy's mouth, rigid and definitive.

Akane's face took on a distrustful frown. She was unsure whether to believe Randy. "You'd better not." She knew he was a man who often lived and died by his values. Would he go against them to keep RISE's base a secret when the Chief of Defense Force Intelligence and his own father asked for its location?

Cogently, Randy said, "I won't reveal where RISE's base is, Akane."

"Promise me. *Promise* me I have your word." She needed to hear the right answer.

After three heartbeats of silence, and an impatient grunt from Akane, Randy finally replied, "You have my word." He stroked her rib cage in a gesture of devotion.

If there was one thing Akane was sure of, it was Randy's feelings for her. Last night, as they made love, their Link had shown her those feelings were strong. She knew that Randy giving up RISE's location would wound his soul.

"I'm glad you decided to do the right thing." A pause. "Uh, so, are you gonna let me up or finish stripping me naked?"

Slow to leave Akane's side, Randy let his eyes linger on her breasts. Caught in the jaws of arousal, he sucked on Akane's nipples. Right now, he wanted nothing more than to stay.

Because of the intimacy of mental communion, Randy had formed a strong emotional bond with Akane. She was the first lover he'd Linked with since Stacie, once again experiencing the ultimate connection with a woman.

Knowing he needed to go, he stopped just short of removing Akane's panties. One more second and they would've been on the floor. "I'd better get going." He gave Akane's nipples another suck apiece before pulling on a tank top.

Akane sat up and refastened her bra. "Am I gonna see you later tonight?" She hoped he'd say yes.

"Um, I'm not sure. I might be busy tonight."

Akane walked Randy to the door, still unsure of what he would do. His guarantees hadn't been enough to alleviate her concerns.

After Randy left, Akane flopped back onto her bed. Bubbles jumped up and perched beside her.

As she rubbed the cat's soft fur, she thought, *Don't go back on your word, Randy.* She could only hope that his feelings for her, the magic they'd shared last night, the bond their Link had deepened, and his reluctance to disappoint her would be enough to keep him from revealing RISE's location.

● ● ●

At home, Randy had been pacing back and forth in a straight line for the past three minutes, waiting for the four-way powwow to start. Indecision gnawed at him. His thoughts seesawed between giving up RISE's location and keeping it to himself. A choice of this magnitude wasn't easy.

His father's words held his conscience hostage: *"There are no such things as 'good extremist groups' and 'bad extremist groups.'"*

Is there? Randy questioned. *No, what am I saying?* A lawbreaker was a lawbreaker. What to do? Give RISE's location to Conlan? Betray Akane?

Randy's mind drifted back to earlier this morning . . .

The blinds filtered the sun's light as he and Akane awoke from an orgasmic high, the room still thick with the scent of sex. They lay next to each other, stark naked, sharing their innermost thoughts through their Link. Akane whispered seductive things in Japanese, enthralling him. In an endless cycle of kissing and caressing, they continued to unmask their feelings, waves of exhilaration propelling them forward . . .

Randy snapped himself out of the memory. He'd given Akane his word he wouldn't reveal RISE's location, but he still hadn't decided what to do. He was trying to find a middle ground, some way to keep his word without breaking his commitment to the mission. *What's the answer here?* His internal conflict raged on.

He thought about the terror he and Akane had endured at the voting station, how that moment had bonded them. His cerebral implant's inscription of their intimate night rekindled the warmth he'd felt from her naked body draped over his.

Her heartbeat echoed in his mind like an endless rhythm. The thrill of her lips working their magic on him down below, in an act of fellatio that felt surprisingly experienced for a nineteen-year-old, engulfed his senses that instant.

"What do I do?" he said aloud. Should he give up RISE's base?

His home's virtual assistant made an announcement. "Reminder, meeting in one minute."

Randy composed himself. *Okay, Scott, get it together. Just . . . do what's right in your heart.*

He sat at his desk, clicked on his computer, and joined the videoconference.

His screen split into two windows. One showed Arson from the shoulders up; the other showed the same of Conlan.

"It's good to see you, Randy," Conlan said warmly. It had been two months since they last saw each other, following the end of the civil war.

"You as well, General," Randy replied.

A third window appeared as Stacie joined the conference.

269

Wearing a sleeveless white turtleneck blouse beneath a red blazer, she sat in a brown armchair in her home office. The polished filigree brooch on the blazer caught the light in the room, shining brilliantly.

Behind her, a display of trophies and awards from Cadwell Institute of Higher Learning covered the wall: track, swimming, zero-G fencing, and racket puck. Among them was a plaque marking one of her highest honors, Warrior Extraordinaire.

From the outside, Stacie might have seemed like a prissy princess, but she had deliberately taken on rigorous challenges to transcend that image. She had even defied her parents by enlisting in the CDF instead of being groomed to succeed them.

"Hey, everyone," Stacie said.

Seeing his ex brought back old feelings and a wave of nostalgia for Randy.

Conlan kicked off the meeting. "Let's start by piecing together how we got to this point. Before we begin, please note that by participating in this conference, you've agreed to keep everything discussed here strictly confidential. I'll need verbal confirmation from each of you." Everyone gave their assent. "Good," Conlan continued. "Chief Amaechi was the one who recommended Stacie for this assignment. Since Damien Sykes is one of the Seven Elite, Stacie is familiar with him, as her family was once part of the conglomerate."

Stacie interjected, unabashed about her past, "Basically, Damien and I had a thing. Just to clarify."

"Right," Conlan said. "Apparently, Damien is still infatuated with Stacie. That's why I recruited her to go undercover for DFI. I knew she could leverage their past relationship to get close to him and help us investigate his ties to a dangerous extremist movement called Purism. Its followers call themselves Purists, and we've confirmed that Damien is the Headmaster of the first and largest Purist group, the Brotherhood for Humanity's Salvation.

"Stacie gained Damien's trust and worked her way into his good graces. She and her team of chasers have been collecting intel and reporting directly to me. During a fundraiser hosted by Damien, the two of them were attacked by a group of masked, armed assailants. Damien revealed to Stacie that the attackers were members of an organization called RISE. They are another extremist group, one fighting for immigrant and colony equality. But regardless of how righteous their cause may seem, they pose a threat to peace, stability, and the rule of law.

"Stacie's report was the first time I'd heard of RISE, and I immediately tasked my intelligence teams with investigating them. They uncovered very little. Stacie later learned from Damien that RISE is led by a three-person council based in Colony Four.

"With that information, the CDF deployed a force to hunt down the council. A team of Guardians traced them to an Assistance Living Center, where they maintained a hidden safe house. Only one member was present at the time, Tristan Gelano. The Guardians took her in for questioning. With nothing substantial to hold her on, they eventually released her. However, they also took my friend Arson Scott into custody at the center. Arson, maybe you can take it from here for a bit."

Arson said, "Randy is keeping their identities to himself for now, but a few days ago, he was approached by three RISE members. They saw someone society had mistreated for being a former Coalition fighter and tried to recruit him. Randy asked me if I'd ever heard of RISE. I hadn't, so I reached out to an old Coalition buddy to see what I could dig up.

"It turns out he's been a member of RISE for quite some time, since the organization's first year in operation. He told me about

271

Purists and the Brotherhood. He wanted me to join RISE and took me to the council's safe house at the Assistance Living Center so they could try to persuade me and dispel my skepticism.

"Randy and I set out to gather as much concrete evidence as possible so we'd have something solid to bring to Conlan—facts, not just conjecture. Then the CDF could take action to shut down RISE. It was while I was meeting with Tristan Gelano that the CDF raided the Assistance Living Center and took both of us into custody.

"I used my one courtesy call to contact Conlan. I told him everything, and that's when we realized we were all on the same mission: stopping RISE, the Brotherhood, and all Purist groups. None of them have a place in the Commonwealth."

Conlan said, "Stacie, anything you'd like to add?"

Stacie nodded. "Damien took me to the Brotherhood's compound last night. He had me blindfolded, so I didn't see the route we took to get there. But that place made my skin itch. The way these Purists think is insane.

"Fortunately, I planted a tracker on the limo we took to the compound. I also wore a listening device whenever I was around Damien, so DFI's been recording everything. And I planted a few bugs in key locations."

Randy knew that going undercover for DFI was risky, yet Stacie had embraced the danger when she could've simply been enjoying her new fortune. He respected her for that, just as he respected her for enlisting.

His heart ached from the thought of the pain he had caused her.

Stacie said, "During my interactions with Damien, I confirmed that he's the Brotherhood's Headmaster, the guy directly under Quinn."

Arson felt uneasy seeing Stacie again. The only other time they had met was when Randy had detained her in the Parliament Building during Operation Hammer Fall. "How's your cover?" he asked her, worried for her safety.

"Well, Damien has obviously become suspicious. During my jog this morning, I noticed someone following me. The same guy's been lurking outside my place, probably thinking he's gone unnoticed. He's gotta be one of Damien's goons.

"Oh, and Randy, Paul Shaffer was at the compound, a member of your task force."

Figures, Paul's with the Brotherhood, Randy thought.

Conlan took over the conversation. "DFI has reviewed hours of audio surveillance. There's enough evidence to charge the Brotherhood with multiple crimes against immigrants. We even have a recording of Damien admitting to trafficking. The CDF will raid his estates while he's at his rally tomorrow and move to apprehend him afterward. The CDF will also be executing a raid on the Brotherhood's compound.

"Arson says Tristan Gelano will eventually reach out to him. When that happens, he will lead us to the council, and we'll take them into custody." Conlan shifted his attention to Randy's window. "Randy, I understand your three talent scouts brought you to RISE's base here on Eden."

This was it. Randy had to decide. "Yeah."

"Good. We can raid RISE's base and shut down their operation."

Randy thought about all the good RISE had done. He thought about Sam and Jay. He thought about Akane. His expression exposed his ambivalence toward revealing RISE's location. "These people aren't bad. RISE is just trying to make the Commonwealth better. Whatever action we take, we can't harm them."

273

Conlan had a duty to fulfill. To him, no matter how good RISE's intentions were, they had to go. "Randy, RISE interfered with our elections, according to Arson's friend Sergei and Stacie's intel. They also took justice into their own hands when they tried to assassinate Damien Sykes—the target of *my* investigation. Who knows how many other people they've killed?

"And I'm not shedding tears for people like Damien, but the justice system, not vigilantes, decides a person's fate. The Commonwealth doesn't need RISE or the Brotherhood, or any other Purist gang. They're poison to our society. They indoctrinate susceptible minds with their ideology and manipulate people into supporting their cause."

"After I give you the location, then what?" Randy's features became stony. "The CDF sends in the troops?"

"Yes," Conlan replied. "We need to confiscate any data they have, find out how much damage they've done to our election infrastructure, and uncover whether anyone inside the government's institutions is secretly aligned with them. But if they surrender peacefully, no harm will come to them. We're not planning to kick down the door and start shooting everyone, Randy."

Randy's jaw muscles tensed, his hesitation showing.

"Randy," Arson said, "I understand that some of these people have convinced you they're your friends, but—"

"They *are* friends, Dad," Randy shot back.

"You need to find some new friends, then," Stacie said matter-of-factly.

Randy ignored her and went on. "They aren't bad people. That's all I'm trying to say."

"Maybe you're right," Arson said. "But the Coalition fought the Battle of the Quad to give colonists a voice and expose the injustice they've suffered. And, sure, some Edenites have changed their mindset. But let's be real, no one expected an instant paradigm shift after the war. Societal transformation takes time. It's an incremental process. And groups like RISE and the Brotherhood aren't part of the solution; they're roadblocks."

Randy gnashed his teeth.

Conlan's demeanor softened. "Randy, give us the location, son."

Chin down, Randy wondered what to do. He didn't want to betray RISE. He didn't want to betray Akane. She had trusted him —*him*, one of her heroes.

He remembered the smiles and handshakes of the RISE members who had welcomed him.

Stacie noticed the apprehension in Randy's eyes. She could tell he was torn between his duty and his desire to protect people he had, for some reason, come to care about. Randy, though imperfect like anyone, had a heart of gold. That was one of the qualities that had drawn her to him. He always wanted to do right by people, by humanity. And once, he had treated her like the most precious thing in existence.

For the first time since their breakup, Stacie spoke to Randy kindly. "Randy, come on." His eyes clung to her. "I know this decision is tearing you up. I can tell you care about these three RISE members who you've been in touch with. And maybe they aren't bad people, but you swore an oath to protect the Commonwealth from all enemies, foreign and domestic. I know that oath means something to you. So what's it going to be? Are you loyal to your duty, or are you loyal to RISE?"

Stacie's words struck a chord within Randy, evaporating the uncertainty enveloping his mind.

• • •

It was nighttime. Dressed in a long-sleeved moisture-wicking shirt and jogging pants, Jay pulled into his driveway in a ground vehicle. He'd just returned from a run in the park.

He immediately noticed the house's lights were off. Nicole and their daughter, Zola, were usually still awake at this hour.

He got out and inspected the front door for any signs of forced entry. Nothing. But that didn't rule out the possibility that someone had hacked the biometric lock. And he was unable to access his Link with Nicole. Maybe she was just asleep.

He pressed his palm to the biometric reader on the door. It zipped open, and he stepped into the living room, which was steeped in darkness and chillingly quiet.

"Lights on," he said. The house's virtual assistant didn't respond. "Nicole. Zola," he called out. His unseeing eyes scanned the room. The knot of worry in his chest built into an agonizing, heart-stopping pressure.

Suddenly, something metallic clinked to the floor near his feet. A sensory-debilitating gas dispersed into the air, and he sagged into unconsciousness.

Jay groaned awake, eyes squinting against dim light. He sat in a chair, wrists zip-tied behind his back. He was in the basement. In front of him, a blurry figure slowly came into focus. It was Nicole. She, too, was bound to a chair, her wrists pinioned behind her.

Standing beside her was Paul Shaffer, the man responsible for her bloody nose, bruised face, and split lip.

Jay's eyes stung with tears at the unbearable sight of his battered wife. "Nicole!"

Paul unsheathed a dagger from his belt and hovered it near Nicole's vulnerable throat.

From behind Jay, Mark MaCallum and Dan Maddox came down the stairs, entering the basement. All three Brotherhood Purists were in plain clothes.

"Hello, Jamie," Paul said. A crooked smirk hitched the corners of his lips as he pressed the tip of the dagger to Nicole's neck.

"Shaffer, you hurt my wife, and for that, I'll—"

Paul cut him off. "You're not in a position to do anything, Specialist. And we know you're with RISE."

A pop-out microblade extended from the ejector cartridge inside Jay's left sleeve, and he began sawing at the zip tie. He figured the blade would come in handy if some Purist punks got the drop on him. He just needed to stall long enough to free himself.

"Tell us where RISE HQ is, or wifey gets a set of brand-new scars," Paul threatened.

Nicole said to her husband, *<Jamie, don't tell them anything, you hear me?>*

<Where's Zola?>

<With her cousin, at my sister's place, for a sleepover. We need to—>

"Hey!" Paul shouted. "No mind-talk while we're around!"

Jay ignored him. *<I have a knife on me. I'm cutting myself free right now. We just need to keep them yapping until—>*

Paul dragged the dagger across Nicole's neck with just enough pressure to break her skin and put fear in her eyes.

Jay trembled, their Link forcing him to share in her pain.

"I told you, no Linked conversations while we're here!" Paul held the bloodied dagger up to his face. "I suggest you listen, or I'll do to both of you what I did to Sergeant Conyers."

"I knew it was you who killed Simone," Jay said. He continued to work at the zip tie with his microblade.

"Where's RISE HQ, Jamie? I'm not kidding around, as you can

see."

"Listen to him, pissant," Dan said. "Cooperate, or die."

Unadulterated hatred contorted Nicole's visage. "Why don't you just shut the hell up, bigot?"

"Now that wasn't very classy." Paul pressed the dagger's tip into Nicole's shoulder, deep enough to draw blood. "I suggest you watch your mouth, or you'll be needing prosthetic replacements for all your limbs."

Nicole winced as a trickle of blood raced down her brown flesh. Jay clamped his teeth, battling the pain he felt in his shoulder too.

Nicole said to Jay, voice quivering, "Don't tell them a-anything."

Paul grinned. "I think it's time for your facial, *Nicole*." He laid the flat of the dagger's steel against her cheek.

A gamut of emotions raided Jay's mind. "No!" He couldn't watch his wife be tortured any longer. He yielded and gave up the coordinates to RISE's base.

"Smart man," Paul sneered.

Nicole glared at her husband. *<Jay?>*

<I had no choice.>

"Thanks for your help," Mark told Jay. He pulled a handgun from behind his back. "Congratulations, you win a quick death. It's better than the slow option, trust me. Though, I have to admit, the slow option's way more fun."

"No, not yet," Paul ordered. "We keep him alive until we verify those coordinates."

"Right," Mark replied, "that makes sense. We can't take this shit stain's word at face value."

Paul said, "I'll take the others and check out the location. If it's legit, you can finish 'em both off. If Jamie lied? Torture part two begins."

As Paul headed upstairs, Jay frowned. Paul was reneging on his promise to let Nicole go if the coordinates weren't fake.

Moments later, the roar of Paul's flyer taking off reverberated from somewhere nearby.

Mark said to Dan, "Let's see what they've got in the fridge."

"I'd say 'don't go anywhere,' but it's not like you can," Dan teased Jay and Nicole.

Mark and Dan left the basement.

They returned after grabbing a bite.

Dan smiled diabolically. "Alright, Shaffer's confirmed—" Nicole remained restrained, but Jay was nowhere in sight. Dan reached for the pistol on his hip. "Where'd—?" A crowbar slammed into the back of his skull, killing him instantly.

Mark spun around, eyes wide. Jay let out a hair-raising scream and swung the crowbar again, bashing in Mark's head.

After Mark's body dropped, Jay breathed hard. He let go of the blood-stained crowbar, and it clattered to the floor. Then he cut the zip tie binding Nicole's wrists.

As they embraced, Nicole sobbed into his shoulder.

Jay said, "Let's get you fixed up. Then we need to get you to your sister's place. The Brotherhood knows I'm with RISE. We can't stay here."

Jay helped Nicole up the stairs.

• • •

Randy knocked on Akane's door. No answer. He knocked again, louder this time. Only the chirping of nocturnal insects answered. "Come on, Akane, open up."

Lights flicked on inside. The front door slid open. Akane—dressed in a mesh negligee that revealed a tantalizing glimpse of her pretty lingerie—poked her head out. "Randy!" she said, surprised but pleased. "Wasn't expecting a pop-in, but come inside!"

He entered, his steps timorous. He wasn't sure how to break the news. The door hissed shut behind him. "Akane, I—" She kissed him, stealing the words from his mouth. "Akane—" he tried again.

Another enticing kiss smothered the rest of his words. Akane obviously didn't want to talk right now.

Randy gently pushed her away. Under normal circumstances, he wouldn't refuse her advances. He'd love nothing more than to get back in bed with her, but that wasn't why he came. "There's something I need to tell you."

Impulsive and hormonal, Akane gave him another kiss, this one fiercer. "Tell me later, 'kay? Take your fucking clothes off." Clearly a command, not a request. She reached to unfasten his pants.

Temptation was staring Randy in the face, but he stayed firm. He moved Akane's hands away. "No, it's important."

Akane released an impatient sigh. "Fine. What is it?"

"I—"

Randy's hesitation gave Akane pause. "Randy, just tell me."

It took much effort for Randy to get the words out. "I . . . gave RISE's location to DFI."

Akane's mood soured. "Are you fucking bullshitting me right now?"

"I *had* to, Akane," Randy insisted.

Akane tightened her fists until her nails bit into her palms, disappointment swelling in her chest. "I trusted you. And after everything we experienced yesterday . . . and did last night, you turn my family in to DFI?" She felt betrayed, having given Randy access to her mind and body. "Damn you!" She shoved him hard.

He stumbled but caught his balance. "Stop, Akane." He kept

his cool in the face of her aggression.

Memories of last night flooded Akane's mind: Randy's hands cradling her face as they kissed, her breathless gasps, his lips and tongue devouring her between her thighs. "So, that's how it is? Fuck me and then sell us out, huh?" She shoved him again, forcefully. "Was that the plan?" Acid invaded her veins. "*Motherfucker!*" Her fists became hammers as she whaled on his chest. "Traitor!" Angry tears reddened the white of her eyes.

Randy grabbed her wrists, trying to restrain her. "Cut it out, Akane!"

Furious, she fought to break free. "Let me the hell go!" She tried to kick his knee but missed, and her slipper went flying to the other side of the room.

Her implant replayed more memories of last night, their bodies drawn to each other like magnets.

She flung her arms upward, but Randy held on to her wrists. Her mind raced with thoughts of the CDF rounding up all her friends. "*Motherfu–*" Randy attempted to pull her into a comforting embrace, but she resisted, jerking back. "I said—"—she grunted —"let go!"

Akane saw Randy as someone who'd just harmed her family, siccing Defense Force dogs on them.

They collided with a table. Something crashed to the floor. Furniture overturned. Bubbles scurried under the bed, hiding.

Randy lifted Akane over his shoulder. Her legs flailed in the air, and she let loose bilingual curses. He set her down in a supine position on the bed, pinning her wrists to the mattress.

She wiggled and squirmed. "Son of a—!"

"Stop it. *Now.*"

"—bitch!" she finished through clenched teeth.

"Please, Akane, enough," Randy pled, eyes searching hers. He hoped the worst of her fury had passed.

Akane calmed her breathing, perspiration glistening her brow.

"Stop fighting me," Randy urged. "I'm not your enemy."

"Right now, it sure feels like you are."

"I'm sorry, but I had to do it."

"Just get off me," Akane said in a less hostile tone, settling down.

"Fine, but don't attack me again." Randy let go of her and got off the bed, his clothes rumpled and damp.

Akane got off the bed too, strands of hair plastered to her forehead and the hem of her negligee riding up.

Randy knew that, after Johanna's death and the attack at the voting station, Akane was already devastated. He had expected her to get pissed off once he told her he'd given up RISE's base. He thought he could soften the blow by explaining himself in person. Maybe even Link with her to prove his sincerity. He hadn't intended to spark a fight.

Akane straightened her negligee's hem. "So, did you know you were gonna betray me before or after the panties came off?"

"You know I didn't plot to sleep with you and then betray you," Randy replied. "You *know* that's not me."

Akane snarled under her breath.

"The CDF doesn't know you're with RISE," Randy said. "You can still move forward with your career as a Guardian." He tentatively reached for her shoulder, hoping to comfort her and show her everything would be okay.

Akane stepped back, out of reach. "Don't touch me! My mom always said that's a privilege. One you don't have anymore."

"Listen, you can still fight for immigrant equality, the *right* way, the legal way. But RISE is history."

Akane ground her teeth. Sam and Jay had been right all along.

Randal Scott didn't fit the mold of a RISE member. Now the CDF was going to raid RISE HQ because of her. Because she'd convinced Sam to let her bring Randy into the fold. "I can't believe this! Why?" She whipped her arms out wide in anger. "Why'd you betray us? You promised you wouldn't!"

RISE was helping immigrants. Randy hadn't wanted to end the organization. "I'm sorry, Akane. It's not like it was an easy decision. But RISE has broken the law. As a Guardian, I can't just turn a blind eye."

Akane nibbled on her bottom lip. Why couldn't he understand? "Everything we do is to fight this oppressive system."

"So the end justifies the means?"

Akane snorted. "It's not like the CDF has been the universe's do-gooders all the time."

"I'm not here to debate morality."

"Just get the hell outta my home."

Randy needed Akane to listen. "There's still time to warn everyone before—"

Akane's wristcom chirped, receiving a message. *What's this?* Akane accessed the message. It was from Jay. She read it. Her heart skipped, and the color drained from her face.

Randy took a step closer. "What is it?"

"Why do you care, sellout?"

"Just tell me."

"HQ's about to be attacked."

"What? The CDF isn't moving in until—"

"No, not by the CDF. By the Brotherhood."

"How the hell did they find RISE?"

Akane summarized Jay's message. "Long story short, Paul and his bitch boys, Mark and Dan, paid Jay and Nicole a visit." She rushed over to her closet. "They roughed up Nicole and forced Jay to give up RISE's location. Jay took care of Mark and Dan, though. He's on his way to HQ now. He already tried contacting Sam but had no luck. Most people are asleep at this hour."

"I'm coming to help."

Akane scoffed. "*Pfft*, whatever." She shook her head. Forgiveness wasn't on the table right now.

She stripped off the negligee and threw on jeans and a shirt.

Randy reached out to her through their Link, hoping the sincerity of his emotions—the weight of his decision to surrender RISE's location—would curb her outrage. *<Akane, you know I'm serious when I say it wasn't an easy decision, right?>* His thoughts were pleading for understanding.

<Stay outta my mind.> Akane disconnected their Link. She then grabbed a pistol from a wall alcove. "I'm outta here." She ran out the door, shoes still unlaced.

"Wait up!"

Akane hopped into her flyer, parked in the driveway, and took off.

Randy sprinted to the lay-by where his sports cruiser sat and jumped inside. He stabbed the ignition button. The start-up sequence engaged, electronics hummed to life, and the flyer zoomed into the night sky.

Akane was already far ahead.

Randy tried to reach his father over the comms. Nothing. Next, he dialed Conlan's number. Nothing. *Damn it.* He keyed in another contact. Five chirps rang out from the dashboard. *Come on, Stace.*

On the seventh chirp, a holo expanded over the windshield. Stacie, groggy and rubbing sleep from her eyes, appeared in a diaphanous fuchsia-colored chemise. "Randy, it's late. What is it?" she asked, speaking into her wristcom's visual interface. Randy's grave expression sobered her instantly.

"The Brotherhood's attacking RISE HQ," Randy said. Stacie sat upright. "I know it's late, but try to get in touch with Conlan. Call him a *million* times if you have to."

"Wait, where are you going?"

"I'm headed to RISE HQ now."

"To do what?"

"Whatever I can."

"Hey, be careful. The Brotherhood's . . . fucking crazy."

"Thanks, Stace." It felt good, him and Stacie being on the same team. It felt good not arguing about the past. "See if you can get in touch with Conlan."

Stacie nodded. The holo shrank and blinked away.

• • •

An army of Brotherhood Purists, clad in nondescript tactical gear, converged on RISE HQ, led by Paul Shaffer. They stood atop a grassy elevation.

Finally, tonight we rid the Commonwealth of these nuisances. Paul used his binoculars to scope out the perimeter. *No defense system that I can see. Easy.* He hand-signaled one of his soldiers.

The broad-bodied man nodded and set a rocket launcher on his shoulder. He put RISE HQ in his launcher's crosshairs and pulled the trigger. A flaming rocket blew open the eastern side of the building.

Frantic alarms went off inside.

Janice launched herself out of bed. The first theory that came to mind was that the unthinkable had happened: Purists, most likely the Brotherhood, had found RISE HQ. She quickly swapped her nightclothes for pants, a shirt, and a pair of boots.

She hit the intercom button on the wall module. "All bodies, arm yourselves! We are under assault!" She grabbed the handgun on her nightstand.

Trained solutioner or not, everyone was going into battle.

Faint gunfire echoed beyond her walls.

Holding her gun in a two-handed grip, she leaned halfway out her door and scanned the hallway.

Strobe lights flashed from red to blue as the alert siren blared.

An armed Purist in a balaclava left one of the rooms lining the hall, having cleared it. When he saw Janice, he raised his handgun.

She slid back into the room just as he shot two rounds at her.

She leaned back out and returned fire. Her bullets zinged past him. He pointed his gun at her to shoot again, but then four bullets ripped open his back.

The Purist went down, revealing Sam behind him—pistol warm, fury burning in his eyes. "Janice, you okay?" he shouted over the wailing siren.

"Yeah!" She hurried to him. "Thanks for the save."

"I didn't think this would ever happen."

"Well, it has."

Gunfire roared inside the building.

Sam said, "Come on, we need to help hold down the fort."

They rushed toward the operations center, where the heart of the battle was raging. Once they entered, they opened fire on the invaders.

Bullets flew back and forth across the operations center.

On one side of the room, RISE members hunkered behind electronic equipment, pinned down. On the opposite side, a phalanx of Brotherhood Purists guarded the breach they'd blasted in the wall. They were going to ensure that no RISE member would escape.

More Purists, all in tactical gear and balaclavas, poured through the opening, joining the firefight against their hated nemesis.

Sam and Janice had taken cover behind a console. They fired, killing three Purists. Bullets zipped back at them, forcing them to duck.

Gunfire pummeled thousands of credits' worth of machinery and equipment. Showers of sparks erupted. Computer screens shattered into fragments. Damaged electronics popped and sizzled, smoke flowing into the air.

Automatic fire from the Purists' weapons mowed down RISE members, leaving the room draped in gore.

Janice rose from her position behind the console and squeezed off two rounds. One bullet put a hole in a Purist's neck; the other penetrated his heart. Before his body crumbled, Janice had already taken out another Purist.

Bullets whisked in her and Sam's direction, destroying more equipment. One slammed into her chest, and she fell backward.

Her gun hit the floor.

"Janice!" Sam unloaded a few shots, then crouched beside his wounded comrade.

Blood pooled beneath Janice. Her breaths came shallow and weak.

In a faint voice, she said, "This . . . is it for me. Goodbye, Sam."

"No! You can make it! Stay with me!" Sam clamped his hands over the bullet hole, desperate to staunch the bleeding. Janice's white shirt turned crimson under his palms.

A RISE member shouted, "Incoming! Move!"

A grenade exploded.

A cacophony of screaming and cursing filled the air.

Hanging on by a thread, Janice said, "The fight . . . is over . . . for me, my friend." Her eyes shut, and she stilled. She was gone, her final resting place RISE HQ—a sanctuary for immigrants.

Sam's eyes misted over as he stared at his bloodied fingers, but there was no time for tears.

Purists hurled Molotov cocktails, glass shattering across the floor. Flames and smoke consumed the room.

Sam coughed. He choked on his words as he shouted, "Everybody, out!"

The two sides charged, merging like colliding tidal waves.

Sam and the remaining RISE members fought their way past the Purists blocking their escape, clearing a path out of the building.

Six of Sam's bullets hit their marks, dropping six Purists. He found satisfaction in every body that fell. *For Janice.* He dashed past the corpses of fallen friends. *We'll get the Brotherhood for this. All of them.* Smoke clogged his nostrils, making him cough.

He and the surviving RISE members barreled through the thick, acrid smoke, finally bursting out into the night air. But they weren't free, far from it. They stared down the barrels of more guns than they could count.

Paul took his place at the head of the assemblage. "End of the line, RISE!"

Sam's bones quaked at the familiar voice. "Shaffer!"

Paul dragged off his mask, unveiling a devilish grin. "Yep, it's me. The one and only!"

"We always suspected you were a Purist," Sam said, his tone as sharp as a knife. "And it was *you* who killed Simone, wasn't it?"

"Yes, sirree!" Paul admitted proudly. "But knowing that doesn't do much for a dead man."

"I'm not dead yet, Shaffer."

"Oh, that's about to change. Now, I already know Jay's one of your little RISE friends. My boys and I paid him and his pretty wife a visit, tortured your location right out of him."

"What? What did you do? If you've harmed them, I'll—"

"You'll what? Kill me?" Paul laughed darkly. "I gave Mark and Dan permission to get rid of Jay and his wife once I confirmed the coordinates were legit. They would've taken care of their little girl too, if she'd been there."

Sam's eyes twitched.

"Don't worry, you'll be joining them soon," Paul said. "Oh, and by the way, Damien Sykes sends his regards. He wanted to make sure you die knowing it was him who finally took you all down. He really wished he could be here to watch you die, considering how much of a pain in the ass you've been."

"Damien? So he *is* the Brotherhood's leader."

"Yep. And let me guess, Akane's part of RISE too. That's why you, Jay, and she are always so chummy, having your little sidebar powwows."

Sam stayed silent.

The Purists' guns clacked as they took aim.

RISE members held their ground, fingers on their guns' triggers.

A standoff.

Sam couldn't stop thinking about the RISE members who'd already been killed. "What is this all about? It makes no sense! We're *all* human beings!"

Paul replied, "If you still don't get it, you're dumber than I thought. Let me spell it out for you. This is about saving the New Humanity. Saving it from colonist domination. Saving it from politicians who are working to ship half of us nonimmigrants out to make room for your kind. Saving it from ruin."

Sam bared his teeth. *Typical Purist nonsense.*

"Alright, finish 'em off, boys," Paul ordered.

Both sides fired their weapons. Though they took some Purists down with them, the outnumbered RISE members were slain.

• • •

Akane landed her flyer beside the burning remains of RISE HQ. Jay's flyer touched down next to hers.

The canopy of Akane's flyer popped open. She jumped out. Bodies were everywhere. *Oh, no. Is everyone . . . gone?* She swallowed the bile rising in her throat.

Sam, lucky to still be alive, sat against a tree. Blood seeped from the stab wound he had received from Paul during the frantic melee. Paul had wanted him to die a slow, painful death. He wanted Sam to be haunted by the sight of his fallen friends as his life ebbed away.

When Akane saw Sam, she gathered her bearings and raced to him.

Jay trailed right behind her, guilt twisting in his gut. *This is my fault. **I** gave up RISE HQ.*

Akane knelt next to Sam, the orange glow of the fire washing over her face. "Sam, you're gonna be okay, right?" The sound of flames crackled in her ears.

"I don't think so, Akane," he replied weakly. When he saw Jay come up, he thought, *Well, I'll be damned. He's okay.*

Part of RISE HQ's roof caved in. The loud crash startled Akane and Jay, debris tumbling into the inferno.

Sam forced himself to speak. "The Brotherhood ambushed us. Shaffer was here, leading the charge. We were right. It was him who killed Simone."

Of course it was, Akane thought.

Jay looked visibly ill. "This is my fault. I gave them our location. I—"

"No," Akane cut in, "don't blame yourself for this. Shaffer and his dirtbag crew tortured your wife."

Sam struggled to nod. "She's right, Jay." His skin had gone

pale, and sweat drenched his brow. Had he not been neohuman, he might have been dead by now. "Damien Sykes did this. Paul admitted Damien's the Brotherhood's leader. He sent Paul, Mark, and Dan to torture you and Nicole. He sent the Brotherhood here . . . to wipe out RISE. If you want to blame someone, Jay, blame Damien."

Irrevocable anger scorched Akane's veins. "Sykes is gonna pay!" she vowed. "Shaffer too!"

"Right now, Akane, just . . . let it go," Sam said, strength slowly withering. "RISE's fight . . . is over. Forget about this . . . for a while. You can still make a difference, though, in the CDF."

Akane's eyes were ice-cold. "No. Sykes can't get away with this, and he won't. Maybe Reza was right. Maybe a good old-fashioned public execution is what's needed to make a statement." She ran off, fighting back tears.

"Akane, wait up!" Jay called out.

"Jay—"—Sam coughed—"keep her safe. Go."

"What about you?"

"Go, Jay. That's an order, damn it."

The wail of emergency vehicles grew closer, and CDF flyers were approaching fast. Stacie had finally reached Conlan.

Jay peeled his eyes away from Sam, who might be dead by the end of tonight, and ran after Akane. *Hopefully, those emergency responders will get here in time. Hang in there, Sam.*

Randy and Stacie's flyers landed, along with those of the CDF and emergency responders'.

Fire crews disembarked. They grabbed the hoses attached to their vehicles and blasted suppressant foam over the burning building.

Randy left his flyer. His blood froze as he surveyed the mass of dead bodies. When he spotted a medic about to roll Sam away in a capsule gurney, he broke into a sprint. Stacie followed close behind. It was obvious that she had left home in a hurry—she had tied her hair in a messy ponytail, and she wore a T-shirt and sweatpants.

Randy said to the medic, "I'm Guardian Randal Scott. He's stable, right?"

She replied, "Yes, he is."

"Good, I need a quick word with him."

"Sorry, I have to—"

"It's okay," Sam told her.

The medic turned to Randy. "Ten minutes. That's it." She delivered her words with an indignant bite.

After the medic moved away, Randy started speaking to Sam. "Is everyone—"

"Yeah, everyone's gone, Scott," he responded. The life-saving fluids and healing accelerants being siphoned into his veins had him feeling better. "Except those who live offsite. And guess who was leading the assault on RISE HQ? Our buddy, Paul Shaffer."

"Yeah, I learned he was a member of the Brotherhood earlier," Randy said. "Akane beat me here, right? Where is she?"

"She and Jay took off. And Akane's pissed. She's going to kill Damien. He's responsible for this. He's the leader of—"

"Yeah, he's the leader of the Brotherhood, their Headmaster," Stacie interrupted, coming up beside Randy. "We found that out already. But this Akane can't kill him. The CDF's about to raid all his estates and the Brotherhood's compound tomorrow, and they're going to take Damien into custody. He's involved in intergalactic trafficking of weapons and women. DFI needs him alive to tell them more about his operation, to tell them where more innocent victims are being held."

"Not to mention, Michael Conlan would stop at nothing to

find who assassinated the target of a DFI investigation," Randy interjected. "If Akane kills Damien, she'd eventually get locked up in an orbital prison. I can't let that happen. She's my friend."

"Friend?" Stacie said inquisitively.

"Yeah, she, Jay, and Sam here are members of Vanguard Alpha. They're the three RISE members who've been trying to recruit me. I guess you could say we became close." Randy asked Sam, "Do you know where Akane and Jay are?"

Sam thought about Akane's words: *"Maybe Reza was right. Maybe a good old-fashioned public execution is what's needed to make a statement."*

"Nope," Sam said. "But I'm betting they'll crash Damien's rally tomorrow and take him out there."

Stacie scoffed. "The rally's going to be swarming with security. Fat chance anyone gets close enough to Damien to fire even one shot."

"Akane's not going to do this stealthily, sneaking past security and all that bullshit," Sam replied. "She's going to do it publicly and blatantly, with Jay's help. And with a Shell, she can slaughter anyone who gets in her way, which she just might, seeing as how pissed she is right now."

Stacie's eyes went wide. "Where the hell's she getting a Shell from? She can't just check one out of a military installation like a book from an old-school Earth Era library."

"Our bunker," Sam said. "That's where she ran off to. We acquired seven Shells and stored them there. Six are M-X02s—four male type, two female. The other's an M-X01. All security parameters have been deactivated."

"Where's this bunker?" Randy demanded.

"Behind the Sejuela Trees. The access panel's actually built into one of them, the lone one farther off from the rest."

Stacie asked, "How the heck did you guys heist some Shells?"

Right now, that was irrelevant to Randy. "Who cares, Stace?"

The medic returned. "Time's up." She pressed the close-lid command on the gurney's keypad, and the transparent sliding cover hissed shut. Then she took Sam to an ambulance flyer.

Randy said, "Stace, I . . . I need your help to stop Akane. I can't take her and Jay by myself."

"You don't have to take on *anyone*. Let's just inform Conlan. The CDF will put out an APB on both of them, and—"

"No! If Akane's captured, she'll be put away! Right now, no one else knows she's a member of RISE. My dad and Conlan don't even have her name. All they know is that a woman and two men from RISE befriended me. They don't know those three RISE members are Guardians in the ETF. What I want to do is save Akane, save her from herself—from her rage."

"So you're going to deradicalize her? You haven't been able to talk her into leaving RISE so far; what makes you think you can convince her to abort her assassination mission?"

"I have to try."

"This woman means a lot to you, doesn't she?"

"Yeah, she's the first person to treat me like a comrade and a human being since I came back to the CDF from leave. She's my *friend*."

"Did you two Link?"

"Yeah, so?"

"Well, I know you. You're not Linking with someone unless they're pretty special to you. Did you . . . sleep with her?"

A wrinkle appeared between Randy's eyebrows. "Yeah, we had sex, Stace. What's that got to do with anything?"

"I'm saying your judgment might be impaired by your *feelings* for this woman," Stacie said, gesturing emphatically. "If we try to stop her and her friend on our own—with no backup from the CDF or law enforcement—and we screw this the hell up and they kill Damien, it's on *us*, Randy.

"I stomached a lot to help DFI get dirt on Damien. You don't know what it's like forcing yourself to be in the company of someone you despise. I let Damien *touch* me, feel me, kiss me. I did that so he could be brought to justice.

"If the CDF puts out an APB on Akane and her friend, they can scour this *entire* region state to find them. This could end tonight. There's no need to risk fouling DFI's investigation into Damien—fouling all my efforts, everything I tolerated."

Randy was determined to save Akane. There was no talking him out of it. "So let's not screw this up, then."

Stacie shook her head. "Unbelievable."

"Akane has lost everyone she knows and loves. She came to Eden with other immigrants. You know what happened? One of her friends threw herself off a building after prolonged exposure to immigrant discrimination. Another was shot in the head during his and Akane's BCT, just for expressing his *unpopular* opinion on the civil war. Then Paul Shaffer killed her best friend, a Guardian named Simone who took her in. Now her RISE family is dead, and it's all because of *Damien Sykes*.

"Destroying RISE was the last straw for Akane. That's why she's on a rampage. So if we alert DFI and they nab her, convict her, and destroy her career, it'll be because of Damien. Do you really want to let him do that to this young woman, who's already suffered enough? She's just nineteen. You want to let Damien have another win, ruin another life?"

Stacie said nothing, letting Randy's passionate speech marinate in her thoughts.

"Stace, I'm asking you to help me, please. You know I'm right about this. Destroying Akane's career and her life by getting her locked up would be unfair to her and her parents."

Oh, fuck me. Stacie sighed. *I don't know why the hell I'm doing this.* "Okay, Randal, *fine*. I'll help you stop these two. But *if* your friend doesn't listen to reason, she might be a lost cause, and we might have to put her down. Just sayin'."

"We won't have to." Randy knew it might take a fight to get Akane to stand down, but he wouldn't have to take her life.

"So what's our play?"

"Sam said RISE had seven Shells. That means there's five more. We'll need two to stop Akane and Jay."

"So now we're stealing government property?" Stacie didn't want to face theft charges from the government.

"You got a better idea of how to stop two shelled Guardians hellbent on assassinating a Chief Executive candidate? You wanna what, throw sticks and stones at them? Don't worry, we'll ensure the CDF gets its hardware back."

"Alright, we'll do things your way."

"Okay, so we'll come back here in the morning,"—Randy glanced at the Guardians and police combing the area—"when the place isn't swarming with Guardians and law enforcement. I doubt they'll find the bunker. Sounds like it's well hidden. The CDF and the cops aren't searching for access panels built inside trees."

"Okay, so I'll see you back here at . . . noon?"

"The rally starts at fifteen hundred. Are you sure that'll give us enough time to transport the Shells? And where are we going to stage, anyway?"

"I'll take care of transporting the Shells. Noon's plenty of time. Leave the staging ground to me."

"Okay."

Stacie headed to her flyer. "See you tomorrow."

Randy's eyes drifted over the fallen RISE members. Tomorrow, the Brotherhood would be finished. He looked forward to hearing about the raid on their compound, and he hoped every one of those bastards would be killed.

He climbed into his flyer and went home.

• • •

Akane and Jay sat in the attic of a RISE supporter's home, trying to cope. Randy knew where Akane lived, so they couldn't risk going back to her place.

Sullen-faced, they finished their meals. Then they set their ceramic plates on the floor beside them.

Akane drew her knees to her chest. "It's still hard to believe, man. Everyone is gone. Just about." RISE had been her family away from her family, and they were now dead, thanks to the Brotherhood.

Jay placed a hand on her shoulder. "We'll get Sykes tomorrow —for them."

The attic's sliding floor panel creaked open, and an old woman poked her head up. "Are you two okay? Is there anything I can get you?"

"No, we're fine, Ms. Simmons," Akane replied.

"Alright, just let me know if you need anything."

The panel slid shut.

"Come on, let's try to get some sleep," Akane said, curling up under the covers of her makeshift pallet.

Jay lay down in his pallet and shut his eyes, trying to purge the macabre image of slaughtered friends from his mind. He thought about his wife and daughter. To keep them safe, the Brotherhood and every other anti-immigrant extremist group had to be eliminated.

As Jay slept, Akane prepared to go take care of Paul Shaffer. She wore leggings, a shirt, and a hoodie for her mission. *Gotta do this one solo, Jay.*

She remembered the day she discovered Paul might be Simone's killer . . .

Akane stormed up to Sam. "Why didn't you tell me about Shaffer?"

"What are you talking about, Akane?" Sam replied calmly.

"Why didn't you tell me he was the bastard who killed Simone?"

"Who told you that? Was it Jay?"

"Doesn't matter. It's true, though, isn't it?"

"We strongly suspect he's the one who killed Simone."

Akane whirled around. "That's it, I'm gonna—"

Sam snatched her wrist with so much force that she nearly tripped. "You're not doing anything, Akane."

Oh, yes the hell I am. She wiggled her wrist, struggling to escape Sam's grasp—the only thing delaying her from exorcising her bloodlust.

Sam said, "Listen to me. Shaffer might be an immigrant hater and a jerk, but we don't just kill everyone who despises us. I promise you, when we're one hundred percent sure he killed Simone, you'll have your shot. But not before. Understood?"

Akane reluctantly obeyed Sam's orders. He was a leader within RISE, after all. "Yeah, Guthrie, I got you. I won't harm a hair on Shaffer's head until you give me the green light, 'kay?" Her words held the sting of acquiescence. She'd defer vengeance, but patience had an expiration date, and it was approaching fast.

Sam unclasped her wrist. "Good. You have my word, Simone

will not go unavenged." He wanted Simone's killer dead too.

At the destroyed RISE base, just before Akane left, Sam confirmed Paul was Simone's murderer. It was finally time for Akane to unleash hell. Tomorrow, she and Jay would deal with Damien, but tonight would be Paul Shaffer's reckoning. The inferno inside Akane wouldn't die down until she had blood.

• • •

Paul, riding in an air-cab, guzzled the last of the liquor from the bottle in his hand. He'd celebrated tonight's victory with strippers and alcohol. It was a damn good time.

Funny, he couldn't get in touch with Mark or Dan. Maybe they were out partying too. He figured they'd check in by morning.

The cab touched down outside his apartment complex. Paul got out, tossed the empty bottle into a trash receptacle, and headed inside, ready to sleep off the buzz.

He entered an elevator and pressed the button for the sixth floor. Once there, he walked down the hallway to his apartment and pressed his palm to the biometric reader. A chirp confirmed the security scan, and the locks disengaged.

Yawning and stretching, he stepped inside.

The door hissed shut.

Before he could activate the lights, he heard a click from behind him. He spun around. A slender figure holding a plasma knife lunged from the shadows, the red eyes of their mask glowing.

Paul reacted fast. He flung the coffee table at the intruder.

It crashed into her, knocking her off her feet. The knife flew from her grasp, skidding across the wooden floor.

Paul charged. As the intruder scrambled to get up, he seized her throat with one hand, slamming her back against the wall.

"Lights on," Paul commanded.

The room lit up. He saw the intruder was wearing a hockey-style mask that had glowing infrared insets.

He jerked off the mask. "Akane!" He chuckled. "Trying to take me out, huh, pipsqueak? Ballsy, but dumb." His fingers dug into her throat, throttling the life out of her.

The edges of Akane's vision blurred as her lungs begged for oxygen. *Not gonna let this motherfucker do me in.* She drove a knee into Paul's groin.

He howled. "Damn it!" His hand released Akane's throat. "*Fucking* little import!"

Akane sucked in precious air. "That's for all the shitty days of heartache!" She shoved past Paul, diving for her knife.

Doing his best to ignore the throbbing in his groin, Paul tackled Akane from behind, ramming his body into hers.

They both hit the floor hard.

Akane clambered to her feet, body aching. Paul, still on the floor, caught her ankle and yanked, sending her crashing down face-first.

He stood, still holding her ankle.

She kicked free, throwing him off-balance. As he stumbled backward, she sprang upright and scooped up her knife.

She pointed the blade of energy at him, her murderous eyes promising his demise. "This *import's* about to send you to Hell."

Paul rolled his shoulders, joints cricking. Then he cracked his knuckles and assumed a fighting stance. "That so?"

Akane slashed at him, aiming to take off his head. "For Simone!"

He dodged.

With stormy eyes, Akane screamed and raised the knife high. She brought it down fast, as if she intended to cleave Paul in two.

He caught her wrist before the blow could land. "Still crying over that dead bitch," he taunted. "How touching."

They scuffled, fighting for control of the knife. Paul's grip tightened to an unbearable intensity, forcing Akane to drop it. With both arms, he lifted her above his head and tossed her across the room. She slammed into a couch, her flailing foot kicking a vase off the side table.

Paul picked up the knife. "Say hello to Simone for me." He stalked toward Akane to finish her off.

Akane's yearning for revenge wouldn't allow her to be defeated. She rose onto all fours, grabbed the fallen vase, and launched it at Paul. It struck his face, breaking his nose. The excruciating pain fogged his head and wrenched the knife from his fingers.

"You little shit!" he roared. He buried his face in his hands as warm blood flowed from his nostrils.

Moving on pure adrenaline, Akane retrieved the knife. While Paul was still stunned, she blasted herself at him and lodged the energy blade into his chest, making him pay for all the tears she had shed.

Paul wailed in agony.

Yes, suffer, asshole, Akane thought. The heartache from Simone's death flared up, not to ebb until Paul was a corpse.

He crumbled backward, lifeless eyes staring blankly at the ceiling.

Akane leaned over, ripped the blade from his chest, and clicked it off. *I got the son of a bitch, Simone. I finally got him.*

She picked up her mask and drew her hoodie over her messy hair. Body hurting all over, she limped her way out the door.

● ● ●

Jay woke at the creak of the attic's floor panel sliding aside.

Akane hobbled up the stairs with scrapes on her face, a swollen bottom lip, and bruises under her clothes.

Jay propped himself up on an elbow. "Akane, what the—?"

"Yeah, I look like shit, right?" Akane slipped into her pallet.

"What happened?"

Exhausted, Akane curled up and tugged her hoodie low over her head. "I took care of Shaffer."

"Hey, you could've let me come—"

"No, I had to do it alone."

Though Jay would've preferred Akane let him help, he understood. "Well, I'm just glad you're safe." He was also glad Simone's death had been avenged.

"Let's get some sleep. Sykes is next."

Without another word, both closed their eyes.

CHAPTER SEVEN

Satellite One
Colony Four

RISE's council—Tristan Gelano, Franco DeFalco, and Julian Hurst—sat at a table in the room of a run-down building.

Franco stroked his gray beard in consternation. "It's still hard to believe the Brotherhood destroyed everything we built."

Tristan was tough. The enemy's victory wouldn't eclipse her resolve. "It's tragic. But there are countless immigrants on Eden hungry and willing to take up the fight for equality. RISE is an idea, and ideas never die. RISE will be reborn."

A determined expression settled on Julian's weathered face. "Indeed. That's why we're here, to discuss the rebirth of RISE."

Knuckles rapped against the rotting wooden door.

"Our guests have arrived," Tristan said. She stood and opened the door.

Sergei and Arson walked into the dilapidated room.

Tristan hugged Arson. "It's good to see you." She turned and embraced Sergei. "You too."

Sergei felt defeated but refused to let it show. "These are unfortunate times."

"Yes," Franco replied, his hands clasped together on the table. "But when you get knocked down, you get back up. We will rebuild RISE stronger—better."

Julian said, "Arson, Sergei, we appreciate you joining us today."

At the roar of vehicles reverberating outside, Franco jumped to his feet and yanked aside the ragged canvas covering the window. He saw BUSs unloading Guardians. "The Commonwealth Defense Force is here."

Tristan froze in place. "What? How did they find us?"

"No one tailed us; I'm certain," Sergei said.

Julian shot up from his chair. "We need to leave. There's an underground exit—"

Arson whipped his handgun from its holster. "No one's going anywhere."

Sergei pulled his own weapon, aiming it at Arson. "Of all people, I never expected you to betray us."

"RISE is dead, and it's going to stay dead," Arson declared. "There needs to be peace among all the Commonwealth's peoples, but that can't happen while extremist groups are manipulating elections and recruiting the youth into their madness."

Sergei's voice erupted. "I thought you were a changemaker, a revolutionary!"

"I was a revolutionary. The Coalition fought and won the civil war to remove corrupt leaders, free the netscape from censorship, and clean up the central government. It was supposed to be the people who chose their new leaders, through honest, fair elections. But groups like RISE and the Brotherhood are sabotaging that."

Sergei was about to fire.

Arson beat him to the punch, blowing a hole into his arm.

Sergei staggered backward, the pain causing him to relinquish his weapon.

"Nobody else move!" Arson barked. "I don't want to kill anyone, but I will."

Guardians filed into the room, bringing their rifles to bear.

"You're finished," Arson said to Tristan, Julian, and Franco.

The Guardians cuffed the council members and Sergei.

Arson stared at Tristan, his eyes reflecting the anguish of having to apprehend her. "I'm sorry. Know that I support RISE's cause, just not their tactics. If you guys had been open to changing them, maybe this—"

"Save it," Tristan snapped.

A Guardian grabbed her arm and led her away.

The Brotherhood's next, Arson thought. The CDF would raid their compound today, along with Damien's estates. They would also take Damien into custody after his campaign rally.

• • •

Randy and Stacie stood atop a half-finished building overlooking Damien's rally site, a property Stacie now owned. She had secured it as their observation post for today's stakeout. On the rooftop docking platform sat a boxy transport flyer. It contained the Shells they'd gotten from RISE's underground bunker.

Both Randy and Stacie were suited up in the sleeves Randy had obtained for them.

Stacie's team of chasers was stationed at the rally site below, eyes peeled for Akane and Jay, while she and Randy monitored the situation from above.

The area around the stage setup had reached full capacity, packed with clamorous Damien Sykes supporters. The overflow crowd gathered along the barriers lining Damien's limo route, desperate for a glimpse of their champion.

Randy lowered his binoculars. He and Stacie had a clear line of sight over the rally. Whether Jay and Akane were among the mass of people remained to be seen. But they'd presumably attempt to take out Damien in their stolen Shells, not civilian attire.

He'd heard a news report about authorities finding Mark MaCallum and Dan Maddox dead in Jay's basement. Akane told him the Brotherhood forced RISE's location out of Jay by roughing up his wife, so it was clearly self-defense. The report also mentioned that Paul Shaffer had been stabbed in his apartment. Randy didn't need to guess who the culprit was. He had to stop Akane from killing Damien too, from ruining DFI's operation, from staining her hands with more blood.

Beside him, Stacie lit up a cigarette to quell her nerves. She regretted not telling Conlan about Akane and Jay's plan to assassinate Damien, but it was too late now. She and Randy had taken matters into their own hands, for better or worse.

The potent scent of nicotine traveled into Randy's nostrils, and he coughed. "I thought you quit."

Stacie plucked the cigarette from her lips, exhaling smoke in a slow stream. "Still working on it," she snapped.

Randy faced the rally site once more and gathered his thoughts. He wanted to make peace with Stacie, even if they couldn't get back together. He figured he might as well try again. *Here goes nothing.*

He turned to Stacie. "Stace, I don't want to be enemies. I know I hurt you, and for the hundredth time, I'm sorry. The truth is that no other woman has been the right fit for me. Not Kesley. Not anyone. Not even . . . Akane, apparently." He edged closer to her. "I'm not asking you to get back with me, but after everything we've been through together, I don't want to lose you as a friend. I don't want to be on bad terms.

"When I was in a dark place, you brought light to my life."

Stacie listened, her cigarette simmering between her fingers.

Randy said, "Hell, maybe I would've gone insane after my mother's death if it weren't for you. I *need* you, Stace. Just . . . do me a favor. Link with me. *Just* for a minute."

His eyes pled with her. "You'll see I'm serious. You'll feel how sorry I am and how lost I've been without you. This isn't some rehearsed kiss-and-makeup bullshit. I mean every word." He paused. "If we can't get back what we had, fine. But I don't want us at each other's throats. So please . . . Link with me."

Linking, the ultimate empathy bridge, had helped mend things between him and his father. He hoped it could do the same for him and Stacie.

"I just want you to know I'm being sincere," he said.

Stacie remembered how Randy stood by her side when she was bedridden during BCT, how he cheered her on when she wanted to quit, how he motivated her and pushed her to finish. She wouldn't have graduated from BCT without him. It was because of him that she had been a Guardian—major brownie points in her book.

Loud, excited voices from below interrupted her reflections as she considered whether to Link.

She tossed the cigarette away. "Hey, sounds like the program is about to start. We need to watch out for Akane and Jay."

Randy sighed. "Right." He returned to the parapet, without an answer from Stacie. Then he lifted the binoculars up to his eyes and tapped the zoom function. *When are you gonna show, Akane?*

Stacie spoke into her wristcom. "Jason, report."

Jason moved amid the flood of bodies. He had on casual

clothes and dark sunglasses.

Rally-goers, packed shoulder to shoulder, chanted for Damien.

"No sign of our targets yet," Jason said to Stacie. "But Eli, DeShaun, and I are staying on our toes."

"Copy," Stacie replied.

Air-lane traffic had been suspended within a twenty-mile radius, and authorities had blocked every entry point except one to control the flow of people.

A paunchy middle-aged man, sporting a "Vote for Damien" pin on his shirt, nudged Jason's shoulder with his elbow. His eyes gleamed with unsettling fanaticism. "Guy's gonna save the republic, man. He'll stop the immigrants from takin' over and make sure all those Coalition traitors get what they deserve."

"Uh, yeah," Jason mumbled awkwardly, eager to distance himself from the man. He slipped away, eyes scanning the restless crowd for any sign of Jay or Akane.

The air pulsed with venomous chants of "Kill the Coalition filth," "Deport the immigrants," "End the lottery," and "Put Amaechi behind bars."

So much rage. So much hate, Jason thought, unnerved by the sight of hundreds of bitter, angry faces.

Eli and DeShaun, dressed in plain clothes, went up to him.

"Insane. All this animosity, I mean," Eli said to Jason, shaking his head. "And there are some real oddballs here."

"Yeah." Jason tamped down the disquieting feeling that was prickling his skin and refocused on the mission. "Stay alert, you two. We can't let our assassins slip by us. Odds are they'll show up in those stolen Shells, but . . . you never know."

"Right," DeShaun said.

The team split off.

One by one, prominent public figures took the stage. Each

delivered speeches filled with hateful rhetoric—overblown, inflammatory, and utterly turgid.

• • •

Oviereya, sitting at her desk in the Executive Office, watched a live stream of the rally on her laptop. She'd known there would be backlash after she exonerated all Coalition fighters. But it was the right thing to do, given that the rebellion had arisen from years of government neglect. Even the Union leaders had stated that the rebellion wasn't treason but rather a justified reaction to systemic oppression.

After Damien was arrested and exposed as a criminal today, his enraged supporters wouldn't simply disappear. They would still demand that Coalition fighters face trial, and they would fight, protest, and riot to preserve the status quo. And when another anti-reform politician inevitably emerged to take Damien's place, they would flock to him, their next self-proclaimed savior.

The election for the Chief Executiveship remained an uphill battle. Yet, Oviereya held onto a fragile hope. After learning about the government's mistreatment of the colonies and hearing reports about violence against immigrants, some citizens began to reevaluate their perspectives. But the divisions ran deep. The Commonwealth would remain a fractured society for some time, unless some catastrophic event suddenly brought everyone together. Oviereya prayed such a thing would never happen.

• • •

At the rally, the moment everyone had been waiting for arrived.

Flanked on both sides by boisterous supporters pressed against the crowd-control barriers, Damien's limo slowly made its way to the stage.

Fists pumped the air. Hurrahs thundered. Hands clapped.

Damien sipped a martini in the back of his limo and peered out the one-way glass windows. His adoring fans' effusive praise energized him.

His father had taught him to be the best at anything and everything he pursued. Weakness and defeat were unacceptable.

Damien had respected his father, a man of strength, power, and fortitude. Now, he was gone, stolen from him by Arman Reza's death squads—by the Coalition. And Chief Amaechi had just let those insurrectionists walk free.

Damien swore he'd set things right. He'd overturn Amaechi's exoneration of the Coalition fighters and hold them accountable. He would also make proud the second most influential figure in his life, Atticus Hancroft.

Everything was coming together. He was certain he'd win the Chief Executiveship, and it seemed Stacie was back in his life. But was she really? What was this game of cat and mouse she was playing?

He didn't fully trust her yet, and with good reason. That was why he'd kept her blindfolded while they traveled to and from the Brotherhood's compound. That was why he had someone watching her. So far, his operative had reported nothing concerning. That was a good sign, because he'd hate to eliminate her. But he would if necessary.

I wonder how Ms. Evasive is doing. Damien sent Stacie a message on his wristcom.

She accessed the message, frowning. Did she really have to keep playing along? If Damien somehow evaded indictment, she might have to continue helping Defense Force Intelligence. So yes, for now, it was best to play along.

Damien: How are you, my dear?

Stacie: Stellar. I'm at home watching the rally. Quite the fan base you've got.

Damien: Indeed.

Stacie: Rooting for ya! Go get 'em!

Damien: See you tonight afterward?

Stacie: Most definitely.

Stacie rolled her eyes. *I can't wait for this creep to get busted today. I just have to keep those two RISE lackeys from killing him.*

Damien's limo pulled up next to the stage.

The announcer bellowed over the sound system, "Now here he is, the next Chief Executive of the Commonwealth, Mr. Damien Sykes!"

The crowd roared.

Damien got out of the limo in a posh burgundy suit. He ascended the stairs, stepped onto the stage, and strode confidently to the lectern.

Paul Shaffer was supposed to be onstage with the other two bodyguards. Damien had heard about his death on the news, which he assumed was the work of RISE remnants. He hated losing a good soldier, but the show had to go on.

He spoke into the mic. "First, I want to thank every one of you for your support." The crowd burst into cheers and whistles. "Why does a man who has everything—everything he could ever want—run for Chief Executive? The reason is simple: I refuse to sit by and watch our republic sink into the abyss. I refuse to watch men and women who committed the greatest atrocity in Commonwealth history walk free. And yes, I said greatest. I refuse to let our republic be destroyed."

Stacie scowled. *You're running because you're a narcissistic egomaniac.*

Randy noticed the telling look on her face. "What's the deal between you and Sykes? You said you two had a 'thing' going?"

"Yeah. We were involved. My parents found out and put an

end to it. Eight children don't intermingle romantically. But Damien and I kept secretly hooking up. In hindsight, it was a shitty relationship."

Randy sensed there was more to Stacie's ire than just a past relationship she regretted. Her expression right now practically radiated repugnance. "I get the feeling he's wronged you pretty badly in some way."

A muscle in Stacie's cheek twitched. "I introduced Damien to a close friend of mine, Cassie." The memory of Cassie sobbing after the jury's verdict flashed through her mind. "Damien played her, manipulated her into thinking he actually loved her. She was just another trophy to him. Another conquest. A fucking pet. A plaything. Like the rest of his bedfellows." Her voice darkened as she said, "And he slapped her around more than once." The desire to rip Damien's heart out boiled in her veins. "She and I took him to trial. But he got away scot-free."

"What happened to Cassie?"

"She took a job with Galactic Excavation Incorporated, one of the big players in its industry. They've got her traveling to different worlds, studying minerals to gauge their value to the Commonwealth. She just got back to Eden recently."

"Have you talked to her?"

A deep longing for her friend shone in Stacie's eyes. "I haven't spoken to her since the trial. It's obvious she blames me for introducing her to Damien, for everything that happened, for that circus of a trial." She wrapped her arms around herself as a wave of self-reproach crashed down on her.

Stacie's emotions were like a palpable weight descending upon Randy. "Sounds like you're just guessing," he said encouragingly. "You don't know that for sure."

"Oh, I know." Shame flooded Stacie's soul. "The way she

looked at me outside the courthouse, before she got in that air-cab . . . It was silent and as cold as ice. That said everything.

"She ghosted me after the trial, never answered my calls or messages. She didn't even tell me about the new job that would send her into the depths of the galaxy. I heard about that from a mutual acquaintance. So yeah, I'd say she's pissed at me, in my humble opinion."

"Still, you don't know how she feels for sure. And you shouldn't blame yourself for what happened. It was Damien who hurt Cassie, not you."

Stacie, burdened by guilt, felt a heavy feeling in her chest. "I'm the one who introduced them. I ignored the warning signs . . . things about Damien I should never have brushed off."

"Like I said, *he's* the one who hurt your friend, Stace. Not you," Randy said in that hero voice that came naturally to him.

He's always trying to make people feel better or give them hope, Stacie thought. One of Randy's many irritatingly good qualities. "Yeah, well, anyway, he's finally gonna pay." She oriented herself toward the rally. "Normally, I wouldn't care if your friend killed him. But DFI needs him alive to gather information about his trafficking operation and save women who are probably being used as playthings right now. That's why I put myself in risky situations to get close to him."

She thought about the kiss she gave Damien at the Brotherhood's compound to allay his suspicion. "I despised every second of being around him. I didn't suffer through all that bullshit just to let this fall apart. DFI's investigation is more important than your friend's vengeance."

"That much, we agree on," Randy replied.

Switching gears, Stacie asked curiously, "So, how's Jarius?"

Randy smiled a little. "He took my advice, decided to

commission into the Ambassador Corps. He's at Officer Candidate School."

"Good for him."

Randy returned his attention to the rally.

The crowd clung to Damien's every word.

"The pundits call me 'extreme,' a 'loose cannon,' a 'wildcard,'" Damien said. "Well, I'm all that and more!" An applause boomed. "We don't need some coward in office, or a spineless centrist that tries to walk the middle line. We need someone who'll preserve AEGIS's framework for humanity. Someone who won't let Amaechi tear down our military's proud culture. Someone who'll hold Coalition fighters accountable for their untenable actions. I will be that person."

Damien's political bombast made Stacie's head throb. She wished he would just shut the hell up.

Randy lowered his binoculars. "Stace, Akane and Jay will probably make their move soon. We need to get shelled and head down there. We can't stop them from up here."

"Let's suit up, then."

Stacie pulled up her wristcom's holographic interface and pressed an icon on a drop-down menu. The transport's sealed doors swung outward, and a platform extended from the cargo hold, delivering the two standing M-X02 Shells to her and Randy.

She tapped another icon. The platform clicked free from the track it was connected to and hovered into the air. Using the interface's directional controls, she guided the platform down in front of her and Randy.

The rear paneling of her Shell opened, and she entered the rubberized interior. Then she grabbed the helmet from the magnetic catch on her hip and slid it over her head. The faceplate zinged shut. Brackets locked, and the CPU's wetware uplinks synced to her implant. Icons, readings, and diagnostics scrolled across her HUD.

Smart fibers contracted to fit her frame. Telescoping tiles of Kryoplaste shifted, rearranging themselves. The Shell morphed into an extension of her body, every joint optimized for mobility.

After the CPU completed its diagnostic check, Stacie flexed her wrists and arms. Mind/machine integration complete, the CPU's unmatched computational power flooded her implant with information. Her mind instantly registered the approximate headcount of rally attendees, possible enemy approach vectors, and even small details such as the building's exact height. Yet the constant data stream never felt like a neural overload.

With enhanced strength and speed, an arsenal capable of leveling a building, and cerebral access to the entire netscape, Stacie felt like a combat goddess. The Shell's power vibrated her bones. It thrilled her every time she suited up. The mechanized battle suit was a formidable weapon, and now the unthinkable had happened: Two extremists had control of two Shells and were about to use them to carry out a public execution.

Randy's Shell completed its user configuration, tailoring itself to his proportions. He rolled his shoulders and tested the fit, punching the air with a one-two combo. *Fits good.* He flicked his wrist. *Click.* He'd worried the hacked suits wouldn't be fully operational, but they were, aside from comms. They also lacked the latest Nerve Center software updates, but that wasn't a showstopper.

"Stace," Randy said.

"Yeah?"

"We've got no C-comms or audio comms. We should Link."

Stacie's brows soared. "What? No way. I'm—"

"I get it. I know we're not . . . together anymore, and yeah, you're not crazy about the idea. But we need to maintain communication. It's not going to kill you. Come on, just for the mission."

Stacie hesitated, deliberating. Randy was right. "Okay, Randal. Fine."

Silently, Randy concentrated and sent the Link request.

Stacie's implant pinged. The reestablished Link allowed her to feel Randy's love for her, his self-disappointment, and his longing to be with her again.

Randy wasted no time, proceeding with the mission. "Stace, let's get into position."

Staying on task, Stacie brought herself out of Randy's mind, but his feelings continued whispering to her amygdala. "Okay."

They transitioned into stealth mode. The Shells' holographic cloaking skins shimmered, reflecting their surroundings like liquid glass.

Randy hopped down to platform one of the construction scaffolding. Stacie thunked down beside him. Together, they leapt from platform to platform until they reached the ground.

Damien said, "The Coalition dropped onto our soil—*Eden* soil —and launched an invasion that killed service members simply defending their land! Why is it that the Coalition fighters lose nothing for taking those lives? They just get to continue living with no punishment, no repercussions!"

The crowd booed.

A man in the sea of attendees shouted, "That ain't right! That's a buncha bull!"

Damien heard him and seized the moment. "Exactly, my friend. It's time to make them pay! It's time to—"

CRASH!

Something plummeted onto the stage, spiderwebbing cracks

into its wooden surface.

The crowd gasped.

Two camouflaged figures stood in front of Damien. They were Akane and Jay in their Shells.

The two bodyguards behind Damien grabbed pistols from inside their jackets and opened fire.

Bullets hit the Shells, rippling their holographic skins. Of course, no damage was done to the armor.

The crowd screamed and scattered in every direction.

The Shells' cloaks disengaged.

A wrist gun unfolded from the housing on Akane's forearm. She fired tranquilizer darts into the guards' chests, and both collapsed onto the stage instantly.

Akane leveled her arm at Damien. A simple thought switched her wrist gun to plasma-burst mode.

Damien raised his hands in surrender. "Easy there."

"Your fate won't be as merciful as theirs, you murdering bastard," Akane said.

She activated her external sound port, which amplified her voice like a bullhorn. "PEOPLE, I AM FROM COLONY THREE. I'VE BEEN MARGINALIZED BY AN OPPRESSIVE GOVERNMENT SYSTEM, BY A SYSTEM DESIGNED TO KEEP PEOPLE LIKE ME DOWN. BUT I DECIDED TO FIGHT BACK. YOU MAY NOT APPROVE OF MY METHODS, BUT I REALLY DON'T GIVE A DAMN.

"AND I HAVE NO SYMPATHY FOR THIS MAN, DAMIEN SYKES. HE'S A PIECE OF TRASH. HE ORDERED THE MURDER OF MY FRIENDS, GOOD PEOPLE WHO WERE TRYING TO MAKE A DIFFERENCE. FOR THAT, I SENTENCE HIM TO

DEATH."

Rally police shouted to the fleeing masses, "Move! Move! Move!"

Jason, Eli, and DeShaun pushed against the flood of bodies, converging on the stage.

"Hey!" Jason yelled at Akane and Jay, drawing their attention.

The chasers fired their pistols. Bullets ricocheted off the Shells' armor.

Jay aimed his wrist gun at them. "Knock it off!"

Akane pivoted back to Damien. His arms were still up, but he'd taken several steps backward, ready to make a break for it.

From within the stampede of fleeing bodies, Randy and Stacie, Shells cloaked, power-leapt into the air. They landed in front of Damien, blocking Akane and Jay from their target.

The cloaks deactivated on command.

"Enough, Akane," Randy said. "You two don't have to do this."

"Like hell we don't," Jay retorted.

Stacie motioned for her team to fall back. Jason nodded, and they set off at a run.

The crowd was gone, leaving the plaza to be an arena for the inevitable fight.

Police officers still on the scene kept their distance, speaking into radios and monitoring the standoff.

Stacie stepped closer to Akane and Jay. "DFI has evidence linking Damien to the same criminal operations as his parents. He's going to be taken into custody. There's no need for you to kill him."

"What evidence?" Damien asked demandingly.

Randy looked back at him. "You shut up."

Akane shook her head. "There's no jail in the universe that can keep him locked away. He'll just buy his freedom with all the money he's made off his criminal empire. Shit, he's probably got a château in Hell waiting for him—after I send him *there* to make sure he never hurts anyone else."

"We can't let you do this," Stacie said. "DFI needs him alive to interrogate him."

Damien's brows arched as he processed the familiar voice. "Wait a minute. Stacie, is that you?"

Stacie's faceplate slid up, and she spun on her heel. "Yeah, it's me. Surprise."

Damien's face flushed. Stacie had played him. Paul Shaffer had been right. "You *bitch*. I should—"

Stacie blasted a tranquilizer into his shoulder. His body tensed as the drug took hold, and he fell back-first onto the stage. "I've heard enough of you for today." She lowered her faceplate, ready to engage Akane and Jay if she needed to.

The police continued holding their position, watching warily.

Stacie, huh. So Randy's teaming up with his ex-girlfriend, Akane thought. "Move!" she ordered. "I don't wanna hurt you guys, but I will!"

<Stace, get Damien as far away from here as you can,> Randy said.

<That'll leave you here alone with both of them.>

<Yeah, I know. No choice.>

<Okay, just . . . be careful.>

Stacie leaned down, preparing to hoist Damien over her shoulder.

"No you don't!" Akane lifted her arm as her wrist gun powered up, glowing hot. It was seconds from firing.

Stacie paused and contemplated her next move, leaving Damien on the stage's floor.

Randy intercepted Akane before Stacie could. A compartment on his chest clicked open, and a disruptor mine shot out. It

319

clamped onto Akane's Shell and discharged a crippling field of plasma energy that destabilized her implant-to-CPU connection. The feedback slung her backward off the stage, leaving her incapacitated.

That shock should keep her down for a few minutes, Randy thought.

"Akane!" Jay roared. An energy blast from his wrist gun zapped Randy's shoulder. Another blast grazed Randy's side, shaving away bits of Kryoplaste. The damaged areas crackled.

Jay's weapon flared again, but Randy activated his barrier shield just in time. The glowing dome enveloped him, deflecting the next volley of blasts and protecting Stacie and Damien, who were behind him.

Stacie hefted Damien into her arms. *<Randy, you good?>*

Energy blasts splashed against Randy's shield. *<I'm good. Move!>*

<Be careful.>

Stacie slung Damien over her shoulder and power-leapt, clearing twenty feet and landing atop a car. She jumped again and leapfrogged across vehicles.

"You're not getting away!" Jay vaulted into the air to go after Stacie.

Randy dissolved his shield and leapt. Midair, he tackled Jay with a bear hug, and they spiraled downward together, barrel-rolling until they crashed into the ground. Shattered phyocrete exploded upward like a geyser and then rained down, pelting their Shells.

Randy exhaled and rolled onto his back, away from Jay. Staring up at the sky, he saw Akane soaring over him to pursue Stacie. She had already recovered from the disruptor mine's shock. *I have to stop her.* He got his feet beneath him, his Shell sparking from the damage done by the fall.

Jay grunted as he stood, his armor dented and scarred. "You're on the wrong side today, Scott!"

"No, you're the one on the wrong side, Jay!"

Randy fired a succession of shots from his wrist gun. One blast slammed into Jay's torso, but the rest veered off target, striking empty vehicles and blowing chunks out of nearby buildings.

Randy's Shell's public-protection protocol pushed an advisory across his HUD:

Local environment: Urban / Dense civilian population
Property-damage probability: High
Enemy assessment: One hostile / Equivalent offense and defense capabilities
Resolution recommendation: Convert to gladiator mode / Close-quarters engagement only

Randy's Oracle said, "It is strongly recommended the user accept the proposed resolution to minimize public-property damage and reduce civilian risk."

Randy understood that engaging in mechsuit combat within a civilian area was dangerous. "Proceed," he ordered.

"Converting to gladiator mode," the Oracle responded. "Reallocating power to enhance close-quarters abilities. Disabling all long-range offense to prevent unintended discharge."

A diagram of Randy's Shell appeared on his HUD. The fists, knees, and mechboots glowed red, showing that energy had been rerouted from long-range weapons to boost striking power. Mobility indicators flashed, signaling a thirty percent speed increase.

"Gladiator mode activated," the Oracle confirmed.

Jay's Oracle issued the same protocol. His Shell transitioned into gladiator mode as well.

At blurring speed, Randy and Jay exchanged strikes and counter-blows, pushing their Shells to the limit.

The CPU, the AI Combat Assistant called Oracle, and the user all operated as a seamless unit. The CPU analyzed the enemy's movements, predicting their next actions. Those predictions were then transmitted directly to the user, while the Oracle provided real-time offensive and defensive recommendations based on them. The Oracle also served as a safeguard, overriding user control when necessary to execute blocking maneuvers.

Both Jay and Randy thrust plasma-charged fists at one another. They were basically concentrating plasma energy into a single component of their Shells and propelling it outward as a condensed micro-field.

Randy's glowing, powered fist collided with Jay's chest plate dead center, delivering a loud, percussive dong. At the exact same instant, Jay's fist whammed Randy's chest in the same spot. Sparks of energy scattered as both bodies twisted backward from the sheer force of the impact. Knocked off-balance, the two men floundered for stability, their mechboots clacking.

A dark scorch mark and scuffs marred Randy's armor where Jay's strike had landed. He reset his combat stance, exhaling three breaths. "Stop it, Jay."

Jay mirrored the stance. "So you can gang up on Akane with your friend? I don't think so, brother."

They circled each other, fists poised.

Both searched for an opening and watched for the next attack.

Jay said, "No offense, but I knew you weren't cut out for RISE, Scott."

"No offense taken."

"Just to let you know, I don't hate you or anything. I still respect you for what you've done for the colonies. Right now, we're just on opposite sides."

"I appreciate that. And hey, I get it. Your friends are gone, and you want Damien to pay. He will, but not your way."

"Gonna have to disagree there."

Sorry it had to be like this, buddy. Randy made his move. His jumper struts propelled him into a leaping glide, fast enough to look like he was skimming the air, about five inches off the ground. Guardians had coined the trick "air sliding." He rammed his shoulder into Jay, hurling him ten yards away.

Jay's Shell clanked to the ground and skidded to a stop. He sat up. "Deploy short-range defense agents," he ordered his CPU.

Three golf-ball-sized drones ejected from his Shell and levitated above Randy. They zapped him with laser beams, chiseling away at his armor.

Enough. Randy summoned his plasma saber, a flicker of energy extending into a full-length blade. Flustered, he swung at the drones, but they zigzagged and darted here and there while shooting at him from all angles.

Randy's Oracle activated his barrier shield as a countermeasure. The ballooning dome of energy expanded outward, swatting the drones from the air. They tumbled across the ground, sparking and steaming.

"Thanks, Oracle," Randy said.

"User is welcome."

The barrier shield dematerialized.

Jay bolted toward Randy, plasma saber flaring, ready to strike him down if necessary.

A flash-bang shot out from under Randy's wrist. It exploded in a burst of blinding light, stopping Jay mid-charge and stinging his eyes.

"Damn it!" Jay used a forearm to cover his visor.

As the light faded, he lowered his arm, eyes still burning. Randy hadn't moved. He appeared to be standing there, waiting.

Jay said to his Oracle, "Abort civilian-protection protocol for ten seconds and re-enable wrist guns." Override completed, Jay fired. The blast went straight through Randy. It was a decoy, a diversionary holo. "Where—?"

A blast struck Jay from behind. Randy had temporarily deactivated his civilian-protection protocol too.

Jay fell face-first. Randy jumped, and as he came down, he drove a plasma-charged knee into Jay's back plate.

He screamed from the bone-crushing impact.

Randy, with one knee on Jay's back, reached down and ripped the helmet off his head. After tossing the helmet aside, he said, "Lights out, Jay." He dispersed a mist of knockout gas from the micro-sprayers embedded in his fingertips.

"You can't—" Dizziness and nausea overwhelmed Jay as he blacked out. He'd be unconscious for at least three hours.

Randy palmed the Shell's manual release and stood. Then the armor expanded and retracted from Jay's body.

He turned to the policemen keeping their distance and hollered, "My name's Randal Scott. I'm a Guardian. He's down. You can arrest him now."

Radios crackled, and five officers advanced to take Jay into custody.

Now it was time for Randy to find Stacie.

Stacie huffed, catching her breath. She was on the rooftop of a tall building. Damien lay nearby, still unconscious from the tranquilizer. *I hope Randy's okay. Now to—*

Akane leapt onto the rooftop. She landed in a crouch just feet from Stacie. "Gotcha!"

Damn, she tracked me. Stacie was impressed. "I know Damien's the leader of the Brotherhood. I know he sent his goons to kill your friends. I hate him too, maybe more than anyone. He abused a friend of mine, treated her like trash. But I can't let you kill him. I went to great lengths to help DFI gather enough evidence to take him down properly."

"Tough." Akane's plasma saber ignited, casting a purple glow on her armor.

She swung in a wide arc, the energy blade cleaving away a piece of Stacie's shoulder plating.

Stacie jumped back, staying outside the saber's reach.

Her Oracle then said, "Public-protection protocol recommended."

"Negative. I'm on a fucking roof. There aren't any civilians up here."

"It is suggested the user reconsider," the Oracle urged.

"No!"

Akane lunged, swinging wide three times.

Stacie dodged two of Akane's attacks, but the third carved a deep gash down the center of her Shell.

She's not kidding around, Stacie thought.

With lightning-fast reflexes, she ducked under Akane's side-sweeping strike. Then she sprang up and locked her arms around Akane's waist. With a powerful heave, she suplexed Akane onto her back, falling with her.

Akane's teeth chattered from the impact.

Stacie kipped up and drove her mechboot down at Akane's helmeted head. Before Akane could throw up an arm to block,

Stacie's stomp connected, cracking her visor and rattling her brain. Zigzags of static and red error messages flickered on Akane's HUD.

Stacie raised her mechboot for another stomp, this one infused with plasma energy.

Akane rolled, and Stacie's foot smashed into the rooftop, creating a web of cracks.

Lying on her side, Akane aimed her wrist gun at Stacie and fired. As the blast hit Stacie's chest plate, her torso arched backward, but she kept her mechboots grounded.

Akane got up, knee actuators groaning.

Stacie recovered fast. She engaged her jumper struts, catapulting herself into a somersault. The moment she landed behind Akane, she wound her arms around Akane's helmet, trapping her in a headlock.

Akane struggled to break free, growling.

Stacie yanked back on her grappling hold.

In a firm, no-nonsense tone, Stacie said, "Stop it. I'm trying not to hurt you, for Randy."

"That so?"

"Yes. I could snap your neck right now, and I should. You're a criminal. Your whole organization is criminal."

"Criminal? Wasn't it not too long ago that you and your team of chasers were breaking the law by being in X-Quadrant, to go after traffickers not assigned a bounty? My, my, aren't you morally flexible? You're just a damn hypocrite."

"That's right, you're a member of Randy's task force. So you were there, huh?"

"Yep."

"Well, I didn't shoot up a fundraiser like your friends did. They put *noncriminals* in danger. Maybe some were discriminators or dirtbags, but they weren't criminals." Akane clawed at Stacie's arms, but Stacie only tightened her hold. "Damien was the target, and honestly, I probably would've been happy if he had caught a bullet to the skull. But RISE's assault team sure wasn't worried about everyone else in the line of fire, me included. I was there undercover for DFI."

"I was there too, bitch. Guns had a safety mechanism. Stunner rounds only for undesignated targets."

"Do you know what happens when a stunner round hits someone in the eye? Not pretty, kid."

"Just let me go!"

"Request denied," Stacie said. Akane snarled. "Randy shared your tragedies with me. I understand you've been damaged by—"

"Damaged? You're talking like I'm a wrecked car or someone fried my brain. Try marginalized. Oppressed. Bullied. Disadvantaged. Stigmatized. Disempowered. Or simply treated like shit." Akane's mechboots thumped against the roof as she fought to free herself from Stacie's ironclad headlock.

"Okay, terrible choice of words. I'm just trying to say I under-"

"No, you *don't* understand." Akane made every effort to crack Stacie's grip. No success. "What would a richling like you know about what immigrants like me deal with? People like you love to patronize us with your snooty commiseration."

That got Stacie pissed. She wrenched harder on Akane's neck. "What would I know? Oviereya Amaechi, the Commonwealth's Chief, was my mother's midwife, and she's like a mother to me."

Akane blurted, "What?"

"You heard me."

"So let me guess, your parents took pity on her, the poor immigrant, and gave her a job."

"Yeah, something like that. But they never treated her cruelly.

I'm not saying they didn't believe they were her societal superior. We were a family of the Eight, the so-called 'alpha' of all Edenites. To my parents, no one was on our level. But my point is that I grew up with an immigrant as my caretaker, a woman who'll be immortalized as one of the most important figures in Commonwealth history. I don't *patronize* anyone. I don't think I'm superior to any human being. So don't paint me with the same brush that you paint the people who marginalize you."

"Enough! You're in the way of me killing Sykes, the enemy of my people! That's all I know!"

Akane drew on her Shell's augmented strength, bending forward to hurl Stacie over her back.

Stacie crashed onto the rooftop, a metallic clang ringing loudly.

Damien was still lying unconscious. It was an easy kill for Akane. She leveled her wrist gun at him. *Sayonara.* The gun's accumulator hummed to life, collecting plasma energy.

Randy descended behind Akane. Launching himself into an air slide, he rammed his elbow into her back at full speed, throwing off her aim. The blast discharged from her wrist gun zoomed through the air and evaporated before it could hit anything.

Akane rose. "Just because I like you—and the sex was bomb—doesn't mean I'm not gonna hurt you, Randy."

Touché, he thought. "Please, Akane, stop."

"You know, I don't get it. You fought with the Coalition. Why wouldn't you fight with RISE?"

"The Coalition had an ethos. They had honor. They didn't plot assassinations or rig elections. They disrupted supply chains, blew up weapons depots, used digital activism to promote change."

"They had their tactics; we had ours. Move, Randy."

"I can't let you kill Damien. But this isn't about protecting him. I don't give a shit about that asshole. I'm doing this to protect *you.*"

"How touching," Akane said, sarcasm in her voice. "What about protecting RISE, my family? You gave them to DFI."

"I was hoping you could warn everyone before the CDF's raid. Then . . . maybe they could go on living normal lives. And with the council gone, maybe the organization wouldn't start up again." A clash of emotions and principles roiled within Randy. "Despite RISE providing shelter for immigrants, legal aid, and other services, it had to end. But anyway, it was the Brotherhood who got to RISE first. They're responsible for your friends' deaths—not me, not the CDF."

"Which is why I'm killing Damien. Outta the fucking way!" Akane fired both her wrist guns at Randy. The weapons' recoil sent vibrations up her arms.

Randy brought up his barrier shield, blocking the blasts. He had to stop Akane from getting herself imprisoned. There was no way he could let that happen, not after all the kindness she'd shown him.

Suddenly, Akane's HUD displayed a danger advisory: HOSTILE APPROACHING FROM BEHIND.

She stopped firing at Randy and whirled around.

Before Akane could discharge a single blast, Stacie sprinted and slid across the rooftop on her armored knees, sparks trailing behind her. Executing a sweeping kick, she knocked Akane off her feet.

Randy powered down his shield and followed Stacie's attack, a barrage of blasts from his wrist guns hammering Akane's Shell. Her battered armor sparked, crackled, and popped under the assault.

Akane's HUD flashed a warning: MOBILITY REDUCTION 75%. Refusing to give up, she forced herself back to her feet. Limbs sluggish from the damage, she found it hard to move.

Randy watched her sway. *It's over, Akane.*

Akane's Shell was in critical condition, and her body was exhausted, but grit kept her standing.

She was a fighter, a goddamn survivor. And survivors like her didn't go down easy, even as fatigue screamed at her to quit.

Though her jerky, pixelated HUD impaired her sight and she could barely defend herself, she staggered toward Randy, one stiff step at a time—to keep fighting, to get to Damien.

Stacie finished the fight, driving a plasma-charged high kick into Akane's helmet.

Akane felt like her brain was banging against her skull.

As the world around her spun, she thumped to the rooftop, unconscious.

Randy took off his helmet and caught his breath. He glanced down at Akane, then turned to Stacie. "Thanks for your help, Stace. Thanks for not going to Conlan, for not having an APB put out on her. Saving her means a lot to me. I owe you."

Stacie removed her helmet. "You don't owe me anything. My pleasure. What now?"

"Contact Conlan so the CDF can take care of Damien." Randy's eyes shifted back to Akane. "I'll take care of her."

CHAPTER EIGHT

Akane groaned awake. She was in a bed, but where? She squinted, her vision blurry, her mind struggling to think.

"Akane," Randy said. He approached the bedside, hands tucked in his pants' pockets.

"Randy, you—" Akane tried to move. Chains clinked and rattled. Randy had cuffed her wrists and ankles to the rails of the headboard and footboard of the bed. It wasn't his bed, though. "So, what? Are you turning me in to the CDF?"

Randy sat in a chair beside her. "Akane, RISE is gone, and Damien's behind bars, awaiting trial. It's over." His face and voice were stern. "No one knows you killed Paul Shaffer. No one knows it was you in that Shell trying to assassinate Damien, because I covered for you.

"Technically, I'm aiding and abetting a felon." He sighed. "And why am I doing it? Because I care about you. Move on, Akane. Focus on your CDF career. Just . . . go live your life."

"Someone's gotta fight for equality. My ikigai is to—"

"I get it, Akane," Randy cut in. "Colony and immigrant equality can and *will* happen. The Coalition made that possible with Operation Hammer Fall. The net is finally what it was meant to be: a free information system. No filters. The government no longer controls the flow of information. People can speak freely—to the entire Commonwealth—about their welfare, about their grievances.

"Change won't happen overnight. It may take years. But it will happen, piecemeal."

"I'm not gonna lie down like a dead dog and let my friends die for nothing! Someone has to continue RISE's fight! Someone has to stop Purists!" Akane yanked on the restraints. "Now lemme go!" That stubborn fire of hers wasn't going out anytime soon.

"*No*," Randy replied assertively. "And the Purist movement is about to be in shambles. The Brotherhood, the largest Purist group in the Commonwealth, is about to fall. The CDF's hitting their compound soon. The other Purist groups will be walking on eggshells, knowing they could be next."

Akane's brow furrowed. "You can't fucking keep me here, Randy."

"I don't intend to, but here's what you're going to do." Randy's tone implied that he wasn't open to compromise. "You're going to contact Breckenridge and tell him you're taking a leave of absence, effective immediately. Go home to your parents. You told me the last time you saw them in person was before you left for Eden. Pay them a visit."

Akane's eyes watered as she thought about her mother and father.

Randy said, "What would they think if they knew you were running around committing illegal acts, jeopardizing your career as a Guardian? You want to honor them, right? Go home for a while, Akane."

Akane stammered, "Wha-what about Sam and Jay?"

"Emergency responders took Sam away. He's alive. He was probably questioned about what he was doing in the area. Whatever lie he told must've worked. And since the Brotherhood wiped out RISE's base, there's no evidence linking him to the organization anyway. So yeah, he's lucky.

"As for Mark MaCallum and Dan Maddox's bodies in Jay's basement, it was self-defense against intruders. But after our fight, the authorities took Jay into custody. He's in jail now. I don't know how bad his sentence will be. It could be light, since Damien wasn't killed.

"And it's not like I'm happy about Jay getting locked up. I'd rather he got no jail time. I know how hurt he was, seeing all his friends dead. I tried to get both of you to stand down, but it didn't happen, and actions have consequences. Who knows, since we have an immigrant Chief in office, maybe he'll be pardoned.

"You'd be locked up too if I'd turned you in. I'm giving you a second chance. Make your parents proud, by fighting for equality the right way. If you come back to Eden and I find out you've joined another extremist group, or you're still messing with elections or pulling stunts like this, I will drag you straight into Defense Force custody. Don't test me. Understand?" He'd be torn if Akane risked getting arrested again.

Yeah, Akane wanted to honor her parents and make them proud, but she also wanted to honor her friends' sacrifice. "No promises, man."

"Then for now, just go home. Go heal."

Akane closed her eyes as she thought about NeoJapan, her home. "Yeah, I think home is what I need right now."

Her RISE family had been destroyed, but her biological family was still alive, and they were yearning to see her in person—to hug her, to comfort her, to love her.

Randy unfastened the restraints on her wrists and ankles.

Akane sat up and swung her legs over the side of the bed. "Is this your place?"

"No."

"So whose place is it?"

"I brought you to someone who could watch over you while I explained what happened to Conlan and returned the stolen Shells. He's a friend of yours. You told me about him. With CDF resources, it wasn't hard to track him down."

There was a knock at the door.

"You can come in," Randy said.

The door whistled open, sliding aside.

"Hey, Akane," said Jacobi. His friendly smile sent a jolt of warmth to her chest. He wore a white dress shirt and dark slacks.

Akane stood and hugged him, crying. "Jacobi, it's been a while, man."

"Yeah, I know. It's good to see you. Randy told me everything. You gonna be okay?"

Akane sniffled. "Yeah, I'll be fine."

"Good." Jacobi held her closer, leaving no space between them. "You've come a long way. I'm sure your parents are proud of you, and . . . I'm sure Skylar is proud of you too. She's looking down on you from above. I know it."

"Thank you."

"And . . . I know this activist organization you joined is gone, but you can still find other ways to fight for equality, ways that won't get you in trouble." Jacobi kissed Akane's forehead. "I don't wanna lose you, Akane."

"I appreciate you, J. I really do."

Randy exited the room to go take care of some business.

• • •

Brotherhood Compound

The doors to the Brotherhood's headquarters blew open. Guardians in BDUs and body armor stormed into the building's vestibule.

"Hands up!" a sergeant barked.

Lying in wait, the Brotherhood Purists opened fire.

A bloody firefight erupted throughout the building. After the dust settled, the Guardians stood victorious, having suffered not a single casualty. The Brotherhood was finished.

•••

THE NEXT DAY

Chief Executive's Manor

Oviereya was streaming a state-of-the-republic livecast to the citizens of Eden and Satellite One.

She stood on the stage of the Manor's lawn, speaking into the lectern microphone as reporters snapped photos and recorded the address. "People of the Commonwealth, extremist groups have been operating within our republic, attempting to advance destructive agendas. One such group was the Brotherhood for Humanity's Salvation. Its members were Purists, bigots dedicated to oppressing immigrants and colonists. Unfortunately, the Brotherhood is not the only Purist group in existence. There are others. Similarly, there are extremist groups advocating for equality.

"Last night, the CDF conducted a raid on the Brotherhood's compound. They discovered that Damien Sykes, now in custody, was leading the organization under the guidance of the Purist founder, who called himself Quinn. Based on a comprehensive analysis of communications data and the raids on Damien's estates, investigators confirmed that Quinn is actually Atticus Hancroft, the last living creator of AEGIS. He has yet to be apprehended, and intelligence suggests he may have already left the planet.

"Additionally, two suspected members of an immigrant extremist group called RISE are believed to be the assassins who attacked Damien's rally. However, investigators are still working to confirm those details.

"RISE was the largest immigrant extremist group known to us. I say 'was' because it has been dismantled. Sadly, it was the Brotherhood that dismantled it. The CDF intended to offer RISE a peaceful opportunity to surrender, but regardless, they are gone.

"As I mentioned, the Brotherhood is no more, but Purism— the ideology that birthed the Brotherhood, Quinn's ideology— remains. RISE is gone, but the extremist mindset it embodied has not disappeared.

"To all citizens of the Commonwealth living on Eden and Satellite One, do not allow these extremist groups to lure you into their dangerous crusades. I realize that our society is deeply divided. Some of you demand Coalition fighters face trial. Others desire political reform and long to see reformist leaders win elections to drive change. But none of those causes justify supporting or joining extremist movements.

"The Brotherhood and RISE both interfered in our electoral process. In response to their interference, no election results will be certified until investigators determine the full extent of the damage. Once the facts are clear, I will work with the Parliament to decide next steps and implement reforms to fix the vulnerabilities within our election infrastructure.

"Beware: Purists and radical activists have entrenched themselves in our institutions, which include the government, the

CDF, and the police. We will root this cancer out of our society. There must be peace between immigrants, colonists, and native Edenites. Extremist groups, regardless of how righteous they believe themselves to be, are obstacles to peace and equality.

"Our fractured republic faces great unrest, and I understand that healing will take time. Opinions, hearts, and minds cannot change overnight. But together, all of humanity must make steps toward reconciliation.

"We cannot allow extremist groups to continue spreading their toxic ideologies. And you, the people, can help. If anyone tries to recruit you for an extremist group, or if you know of anyone involved in such groups, report them immediately to Defense Force Intelligence or the police.

"Wherever you are, may blessings fill your life."

The livecast ended.

• • •

TWO DAYS LATER

On a balmy day, Stacie sat under the awning of the outdoor seating area of the last restaurant she and Cassie had dined at. She'd reached out to Cassie via text message, inviting her to reconnect over lunch. To Stacie's surprise, Cassie had said yes.

Nervous, Stacie fiddled with a strand of her hair. She then stared down at the table, once again mentally rehearsing what to say. It had been such a long time.

The clicking of heels neared. "Stacie." It was the unmistakable, lovely voice of Cassie McCanns.

Stacie lifted her chin. Cassie wore a vibrant yellow sundress, and her hair was twisted into a long braid. "Oh, wow, you look wonderful, Cassie. Come sit," Stacie said softly.

Cassie sank into the second chair at the table. "Stacie, it's so good to see you." Her warmhearted greeting completely undercut Stacie's assumption that she was furious.

Stacie stilled, searching for the right words. Cassie didn't seem defensive, upset, or angry. Not at all. "Cassie—" She paused. The right words still eluded her.

Cassie's brows quirked in confusion. "Stacie, why are you acting weird? What's going on?"

Stacie bit her lower lip. "Cassie, I want you to know I'm so incredibly sorry for what happened to you. But I got him, Damien Sykes. I helped the CDF put him behind bars. I wanted to make up for putting you in harm's way."

Cassie lowered her eyelids briefly. "Oh, Stacie, I never blamed you for what happened."

"But you left without a word. You never told me about your new job. I figured you were mad. Mad about the way the trial ended. Mad at me for Damien's abuse and the tabloids that called you a liar. It was all my fault, after all." The salty taste of tears reached Stacie's tongue as her cobalt eyes flooded. "I'm really, really sorry, Cassie. Please believe me."

"No, you're not responsible for what that monster did. You don't control him." Cassie's voice quavered. "After the trial, I just needed to heal. Damien smacked me around, but I kept going back to him. Then came that awful trial, which he walked away from unscathed. I felt humiliated, but not because of you.

"I had to get away, to forget the scars, the bruises—all of it. So when Galactic Excavation offered me a spot on their expedition team, I took it. And you weren't the only one I ghosted. I ghosted a lot of friends and family. I retreated into isolation.

"I'm sorry I didn't talk to you after the trial. I just needed to be alone . . . until it was time for me to leave off-planet. But I was never angry at you."

Cassie recalled storming out of the courthouse toward her air-cab after the verdict. Stacie had run after her, and just before getting into the cab, she'd given Stacie a tearful look of disappointment, the one etched in Stacie's memory. "That look on my face wasn't about you," Cassie continued. "I was disappointed in myself for not having the dignity to walk away from Damien. I was young and naive."

Stacie rubbed her teary eyes. "No, you were strong. You were strong enough to walk away in the end."

"With your help, sister. And for that, I'll always be grateful. I'm sorry you've carried that guilt all this time. I owe you an apology."

Stacie muffled a cry. "Thank you, Cassie."

Cassie smiled. "But . . . I *am* glad you helped take down that son of a bitch."

Stacie laughed. "Me too."

Watching a newscast on his wristcom while waiting for his meal, a man at a neighboring table exclaimed, "No way, Sykes is dead?"

Cassie and Stacie shared confused looks.

Stacie brought up a news site on her wristcom. "Let's see what's going on."

The holowords of the article hovered in front of her:

> Yesterday, Defense Force Intelligence, aided by a covert inside informant, took Damien Sykes into custody for his involvement in the domestic extremist group known as the Brotherhood, and to question him about his ties to trafficking. Guards found Sykes dead in his cell an hour ago. There is no known cause of death, no camera footage, and no evidence. The investigation is ongoing.

"Do you think one of the Purist groups did it?" Cassie asked. "Maybe they were afraid he'd squeal to DFI."

Stacie's features pinched. She knew Purists wouldn't take out their *champion*. They'd sit back and hope that he'd win his trial. "No, it wasn't any Purist group that got to him."

"How do you know?"

Stacie's brows drew together. "Because I know the Seven Elite. It's forbidden for any of us . . . *them* to run for Chief Executive. I'm guessing they voted to get rid of Damien, after giving him time to withdraw his candidacy. The right opportunity must've finally presented itself."

"Well, either way, he's gone."

"And *that*, my friend, is something I'll toast to."

They picked up their cocktail glasses from the table and clinked them together.

As Stacie sipped her drink, her mind wandered to the information Damien's confession could've exposed, such as the players involved in his trafficking operation. But her efforts to bring him down hadn't been entirely in vain; the CDF had likely retrieved valuable intel during the raid on his estates.

CHAPTER NINE

Satellite One
Colony Three
(Sector 07)

NeoJapan, cultural pluralism at work. Everywhere, signs of the citizens' Japanese heritage were visible: street art, clothing, jewelry, and more.

Akane walked along an unpaved road, a duffle bag slung over her shoulder. The aroma of skewered meats roasting on food vendors' grills teased her senses.

Merchants flagged down pedestrians. Bicycles zipped through narrow alleyways. Buskers performed for small crowds. Children cavorted in the road. Akane was home, and it felt good to be home.

She reached her parents' housing unit and paused. It'd been so long. *Here goes,* she thought. Haltingly, she went up to the door and knocked.

She almost cried when she heard her mother say, "[It's open.]"

Akane stepped inside.

Voices shouted, "[Surprise!]"

Tears ran down Akane's face as she saw her closest friends gathered for her homecoming, a lovely meal and cake waiting on the table.

"[Akane, oh my gosh!]" her friend Kimiko exclaimed. "[How is Eden? Is it as awesome as they say?]"

Akane sobbed. "[Kimiko!]" she shouted, squeezing her friend in a hug. *Thank you, Randy, for giving me a second chance.*

• • •

Randy lay awake in bed, watching the blue sky outside his window fade into dusk. *Akane, how are you doing out there, my friend?* She'd definitely left her signature on this chapter of his life, and he missed her.

His wristcom chirped, drawing his attention. It was a message from Akane.

Akane: Randy, I'm doing well. Thank you for not turning me in. Thank you for this second chance.

Randy smiled and messaged back.

Randy: No problem. Stay out of trouble.

Akane replied with a two-finger peace emoji.

Randy was right about Akane needing to go home—to heal, to start over. And he was right about something else: Stacie was really the woman for him. He treasured the heartfelt, unforgettable moments he and Akane had shared; however, it seemed they weren't meant to be an item forever. He hoped she would avoid getting involved in any further extremist activities once she returned to Vanguard Alpha.

Thinking about Stacie, he wondered how she was doing, so he sent her a message.

Randy: Hey, Stace, we made a good team out there. How are you doing?

Two minutes passed, and then a response popped up.

Stacie: Yeah, we kicked ass. I'm doing okay. I reconnected with Cassie. It turns out you were right. She didn't blame me for what happened. After the trial, she just needed space. How are you?

Randy: It's been a rough few days. Honestly, I'm feeling kind of lonely right now.

Stacie: Yeah, I feel you. I've been through a lot lately too, from going undercover to trying to run my parents' organization the right way. Can you imagine me running an intergalactic megabusiness like my parents'? Tremendous responsibility! Yikes! I'm only twenty-two and barely know the first thing about their operations. I've got a lot to learn.

Randy: Hey, wanna meet up and continue this chat over dinner?

There was a thirty-second pause, which felt longer to Randy.

Stacie: *Smiley Emoji* Yeah! Sounds good, babe!

Randy: Let bygones be bygones?

Stacie: I think I can do that. Where are we meeting?

Randy: How about your favorite go-to spot, Ultimate-Taste Cuisines?

Stacie: You remembered. I'm down. What time?

Randy: In an hour?

Stacie: I'll see you there.

Randy headed to the door, grateful for second chances.

Acknowledgments

Every author needs a good editor. I would like to thank the editing duo of Xyana and Leilani Dewindt. I didn't realize it at first, but there were moments when my characters' actions or words didn't quite align with who they are. Thankfully, Leilani's sharp eye for developmental editing caught these inconsistencies, leading to rewrites that helped keep my characters true to themselves. She also encouraged me to "show, not just tell."

One example is Skylar's suicide. In the original draft, the scene began with the aftermath of it, Simone entering the apartment to find Akane sitting against the wall, knees drawn to her chest, devastated. Leilani suggested placing the reader directly in the moment, allowing them to experience Skylar's suicide as it unfolded and truly feel Akane's emotional response.

Leilani also pointed out that Akane should show more resistance when Randy asked her to go home. I had originally written her as more compliant, but Leilani reminded me that Akane, being the stubborn woman she is, wouldn't go along so easily. I rewrote the scene to give her the attitude she's known for.

Thank you, Leilani, for helping me stay true to Akane's character. And thank you to both you and Xyana for your thoughtful edits and recommendations. I can't list them all here, but they absolutely helped refine *Republic Under Siege: Threat from Within* and make it a stronger novel.

I would also like to thank Ann for her illustrations of Akane. You captured exactly how I envisioned her. And my cover designer, Ida Jansson, did a phenomenal job as always.

Lastly, I would like to thank every single reader. Your time and support mean everything to me.

Credits

Author

Michael J. Brooks holds a BA in Art and an MFA. He is a member of the Independent Book Publishing Professionals Group (IBPPG), and his debut novel, *Exodus Conflict*, was a finalist of the 2013 Next Generation Indie Book Awards, in the sci-fi/fantasy category; earned honorable mention from the 2013 London Book Festival, in the science fiction category; and received five stars from *Readers' Favorite*. He has been featured on The Authors Show and in the Spring 2022 edition of Review Tales Magazine.

Editors

Xyana and Leilani Dewindt are two creative sisters who graduated from the University of California, San Diego. Xyana has a BS in Cognitive Science with ample experience in academic research and editing journal articles. Additionally, Xyana is specialized in unique product, studio, and lifestyle photography. Leilani has a BA in Literature/Writing and is specialized in editing fiction and non-fiction novels, journal articles, and admission essays. She has been editing such works for the past four years and was an editor for UCSD's literature magazine.

Illustrator

Ann is a Russian freelance artist who provided the illustrations of Akane. She loves to draw and paint. You can find her artwork on Instagram at anygoart.

Cover Designer

Ida Jansson has been working with authors and publishing houses since 2010, designing covers, book interiors, websites, and all sorts of promotional materials. Ida works under the company name Amygdala Design. She also has a background in Biomedical Science and Psychology with special interest in the brain.